ROBINSON CRUSOE

broadview editions
series editor: L.W. Conolly

Frontispiece to the first edition of *Robinson Crusoe* (1719).
By permission of The Huntington Library, San Marino, California.

ROBINSON CRUSOE

Daniel Defoe

edited by Evan R. Davis

broadview editions

Library and Archives Canada Cataloguing in Publication

Defoe, Daniel, 1661?-1731
  Robinson Crusoe / Daniel Defoe ; edited by Evan R. Davis.

(Broadview editions)
Includes bibliographical references.
ISBN 978-1-55111-935-9

  I. Davis, Evan R.   II. Title.   III. Series: Broadview editions

PR3403.A1 2010   823'.5   C2010-901323-9

Broadview Editions
The Broadview Editions series represents the ever-changing canon of literature in English by bringing together texts long regarded as classics with valuable lesser-known works.

Advisory editor for this volume: Michel Pharand

Broadview Press is an independent, international publishing house, incorporated in 1985. Broadview believes in shared ownership, both with its employees and with the general public; since the year 2000 Broadview shares have traded publicly on the Toronto Venture Exchange under the symbol BDP.

We welcome comments and suggestions regarding any aspect of our publications— please feel free to contact us at the addresses below or at broadview@broadviewpress.com.

North America
Post Office Box 1243, Peterborough, Ontario, Canada K9J 7H5
2215 Kenmore Avenue, Buffalo, NY, USA 14207
Tel: (705) 743-8990; Fax: (705) 743-8353
email: customerservice@broadviewpress.com

UK, Europe, Central Asia, Middle East, Africa, India, and Southeast Asia
Eurospan Group, 3 Henrietta St., London WC2E 8LU, United Kingdom
Tel: 44 (0) 1767 604972; Fax: 44 (0) 1767 601640
email: eurospan@turpin-distribution.com

Australia and New Zealand
NewSouth Books
c/o TL Distribution, 15-23 Helles Ave., Moorebank, NSW, Australia 2170
Tel: (02) 8778 9999; Fax: (02) 8778 9944
email: orders@tldistribution.com.au

www.broadviewpress.com

Typesetting and assembly: True to Type Inc., Claremont, Canada.

PRINTED IN CANADA

Contents

Acknowledgements

In preparing this edition I have incurred many debts. To Hampden-Sydney College I am grateful for invaluable summer research funds and sabbatical support. The librarians at the Huntington Library, the Clark Library (especially Scott Jacobs), and the Margaret Herrick Library were unfailingly helpful with the images of Friday's rescue. Colleagues at Hampden-Sydney— Jerry Carney, Caroline Emmons, Earl Fleck, Nicole Greenspan, Ralph Hattox, Ken Lehman, Janice Siegel, and Mike Utzinger— have graciously permitted me to flood their inboxes with questions about footnotes. Cristine Varholy, Sarah Hardy, and Lowell Frye have nudged the project forward at key moments. The introduction and appendices have been enriched by suggestions from Julie Dugger, Nick Frankel, Oscar Kenshur, Chris Nagle, Max Novak, Nick Williams, Clark West, Steve Yandell, and the anonymous reviewers of the initial Broadview proposal. Throughout the project, I have consulted and profited from the work done by previous editors of *Robinson Crusoe*: Thomas Keymer and James Kelly, W.R. Owens, John Richetti, Michael Shinegal, Olaf Simons and Christopher Villmar, and George Starr. I have tried to keep in mind that the target audience for the edition is students, and I am enormously appreciative of those Hampden-Sydney students, especially Matthew Huff, who have read drafts of the book in my classes.

Most importantly, I am grateful to my family, who have been both encouraging and patient. My wife, Mary, has generously balanced the tap tap tap of my editing with the much sweeter sounds of her music. Our children, Benjamin and Ravenel, who will be only too happy to see Crusoe off his island, make everything worthwhile. To them this edition is lovingly dedicated.

Introduction

The outline of Crusoe's story is simple enough: shipwrecked alone on a Caribbean island, Crusoe overcomes his initial terror and settles into a relatively comfortable and industrious routine. Bible reading intermingles with the daily work of milking goats, growing barley, and building his houses, until out of that equanimity he is jolted by a single footprint on the beach, harbinger of his encounters with cannibals and his relationship with Friday. After twenty-eight years he is rescued by pirates and returns to England. But if the bare sketch is both simple and familiar, it also has proven to be astonishingly fertile, and as an inspiration for later works, it is unrivalled in western literature. In poems, novels, and pantomimes, in film and on television, Crusoe's descendents proliferate. They arrive in their solitary spaces by ship, by canoe, by Peugeot, plane, and rocket ship. Some are homesick, others oblivious to home; some are glad to be relieved of their domestic obligations, others eager to recreate a lost domesticity in an island fantasy. They are pragmatic, romantic, religious, secular, desperate, insouciant, insufferable. Many scribble in journals; a few disdain writing, since how can one day on an island differ from every other endless day? From *Swiss Family Robinson* to *Lord of the Flies*, J.M. Coetzee's *Foe* to J.G. Ballard's *Concrete Island*, *Gilligan's Island* to *Lost*, *Cast Away* to *Robinson Crusoe on Mars*, Defoe's novel continues to exert its imaginative force.

Perhaps more than any other novel, *Crusoe* inspires a mindset of "What if ...?" As Walter Scott observed, "there is hardly an elf so devoid of imagination as not to have supposed for himself a solitary island in which he could act *Robinson Crusoe*, were it but in the corner of the nursery."[1] So it is not surprising that besides influencing later fictional narratives, *Crusoe* has also served as a touchstone fable about education, masculinity, economic individualism, Christian redemption, political foundations, and European colonialism. Indeed, if Crusoe treats the island as a blank slate on which to write his own fantasies of himself and the world around him, so too Defoe's novel itself has become a cultural myth that for three hundred years has enabled writers to project their anxieties, fantasies, ideals, and contradictions.

Every retelling of Defoe's novel is necessarily selective, passing

---

1   Walter Scott, quoted in Pat Rogers, *Robinson Crusoe* (London: G. Allen & Unwin, 1979) 78.

over some parts of the narrative as it lingers on others. Most commonly, critical assessments and the imaginative transformations called Robinsonades omit the off-island details. Jean-Jacques Rousseau, for instance, recommended that the novel be purged of all its "rubbish," leaving only the story of Crusoe on the island (362). Readers who are acquainted with the novel mostly through its adaptations might not know that Crusoe is enslaved for two years by Moors or that his shipwreck occurs while he is on an illegal voyage to Africa to buy slaves for his plantation in Brazil. If Friday and the cannibals who bring him seem nearly unforgettable, the same cannot be said of Friday's father, sixteen Spaniards, and a crew of English mutineers who also arrive on the island. The post-island scenes—Crusoe's trek through the Pyrenees, the wolf attack, the episode of Friday taunting a bear and then shooting it point blank—rarely make their way into Robinsonades. Nor do Crusoe's adventures from the often-forgotten second volume, including his return to his island and his subsequent travels through Africa and Asia.

But though *Crusoe* sometimes seems to disappear behind its own fame, no retelling has ever been as popular as the original novel, which in almost three hundred years has never been out of print. The first edition of *The Life and Strange Surprizing Adventures of Robinson Crusoe*, "written by himself," appeared on 25 April 1719. Just two weeks later, it was followed by a hastily printed second edition, then four more distinct printings by August. As Defoe's nemesis Charles Gildon spitefully remarked, "there is not an old Woman that can go to the Price of it, but buys thy Life and Adventures, and leaves it as a Legacy, with the *Pilgrims Progress*, the *Practice of Piety*, and *God's Revenge against Murther*, to her Posterity" (314).[1] Within a year, it had been pirated, abridged, and serialized. Abroad, it was scarcely less popular: in 1720, it was translated into both French and German; in 1721, into Dutch; and in subsequent decades into Italian, Danish, and Swedish. The steady pace of editions in the eighteenth century gave way to a deluge in the nineteenth. According to one tally, "By 1900 there were at least 200 English editions, including abridged texts; 110 translations; 115 revisions and adaptations; and 277 imitations" (Rogers 11). By the twenty-first century, translations had appeared in Sudanese, Turkish, Hebrew, Hindi, Russian, Welsh, Czech, Polish, Ukranian, Inuit, and Telugu.

---

1 John Bunyan's *The Pilgrim's Progress* (1678), Lewis Bayly's *Practice of Piety* (1613), and John Reynolds's *The Triumph of God's Revenge against Murther* (1621-24) were best-selling Puritan works.

Though Defoe could scarcely have imagined the extent of his novel's popularity, he clearly anticipated that its sales would be strong, for the first volume ends with a teasing promise of a sequel that would include a return to the island, a narrative of the men and women who populated it, and further encounters with cannibals: "All these things, with some very surprizing Incidents in some new Adventures of my own, for ten Years more, I may perhaps give a farther Account of hereafter" (304). Readers didn't have to wait long: on 20 August 1719, Defoe's publisher William Taylor began selling *The Farther Adventures of Robinson Crusoe*, which, like the first volume, quickly went into multiple editions, and which, throughout the nineteenth century, was often reprinted together with the first volume. On 6 April 1720, Defoe published a third volume, the *Serious Reflections during the Life and Surprising Adventures of Robinson Crusoe: with his Vision of the Angelick World*. As the title indicates, it is not another narrative but rather a series of essays about solitude, honesty, conversation, religion, and angels, all ostensibly written by Crusoe. This third volume has never been as popular as the first two, and the essays often reflect less of Crusoe than of Defoe himself.[1] But though readers anticipating yet more of Crusoe's adventures would be disappointed, the preface remains an important, if contradictory, statement of Defoe's principles of fiction, and the essay "On Solitude" reconceptualizes a central theme from Crusoe's island.

Most of the hundreds of Robinsonades are now deservedly reduced to footnotes, but whether as a narrative exemplar, a religious allegory, a national stereotype, a colonialist myth, or simply a lasting source of pleasure, *Crusoe* has resonated deeply with more canonical writers. "Was there ever yet anything written by mere man," asked Samuel Johnson, "that was wished longer by its readers, excepting *Don Quixote*,[2] *Robinson Crusoe*, and the *Pilgrim's Progress*?"[3] Walter Scott, who derided Defoe for tossing out incidents "like paving-stones discharged from a cart," still felt moved by the desire "to read every sentence and word upon every leaf."[4] James Joyce, who referred to Defoe's novel as "the English *Ulysses*," asserted that "The whole Anglo-Saxon spirit is in

---

1   See G.A. Starr, introduction, *Serious Reflections During the Life and Surprising Adventures of Robinson Crusoe*, vol. 3, *The Novels of Daniel Defoe*, ed. George Starr (London: Pickering and Chatto, 2007).

2   The novel *Don Quixote* (1605-15) by Miguel de Cervantes.

3   Samuel Johnson, quoted in George Birkbeck Norman Hill, *Johnsonian Miscellanies*, vol. 1 (Oxford: Clarendon P, 1897) 332.

4   Scott, 72, 71.

Crusoe: the manly independence; the unconscious cruelty; the persistence; the slow yet efficient intelligence; the sexual apathy; the practical, well-balanced religiousness; the calculating taciturnity."[1] Virginia Woolf found the novel a "masterpiece," not because it presents compelling natural descriptions or probing psychological insights or reflections on death, but rather because of its plainness and simplicity: "by means of telling the truth undeviatingly as it appears to him—by being a great artist and forgoing this and daring that in order to give effect to his prime quality, a sense of reality—[Defoe] comes in the end to make common actions dignified and common objects beautiful."[2] More recently, *Crusoe* has inspired poems, essays, and novels by major writers including Elizabeth Bishop, Michel Tournier, Derek Walcott, Umberto Eco, and J.M. Coetzee.

Defoe's Life

In 1719 the English novel, as it came to develop, did not yet exist; in the print culture of the eighteenth-century, full of so-called romances, histories, and narratives, the word "novel" was often used interchangeably with "romance" to denote any long work of prose fiction.[3] But if *Crusoe* was to come from anyone's pen, it must have been from Defoe's. By the time he wrote *Robinson Crusoe*, Defoe was already fifty-nine years old, and the novels for which he is now famous—*Moll Flanders, Roxanna, Colonel Jack*—still lay several years in the future. It was as a journalist, a poet, a writer of conduct books and political tracts that Defoe was known. Still, as Max Novak and John Richetti both explain, Defoe's recent writing had prepared him for the imaginative leap he was to make with *Crusoe*. His conduct book *The Family Instructor* (1715), for example, gave Defoe a canvas to explore domestic scenes and to hone his talent for dialogue. In his journalistic narratives such, as the *Minutes of the Negotiation of Monsr. Mesnager* (1717), he learned to fabricate compelling human narrative out of recent political history. His journal *The Review*, in which from 1704 to 1713 he wrote broadly about foreign and

---

1   James Joyce, "Daniel Defoe." Trieste Lecture, trans. Joseph Prescott, *Buffalo Studies* 1 (1964) 25.
2   Virginia Woolf, *The Second Common Reader* (New York: Harcourt, 1960) 57.
3   J. Paul Hunter, *Before Novels: The Cultural Contexts of Eighteenth-Century English Fiction* (New York: Norton, 1990) 25.

domestic affairs, from the war with France to prostitution and filial disobedience, let him sketch characters in miniature, dwelling on narrow episodes and anecdotes. His experience as a journalistic mole in the Tory papers of the 1710s, which entailed writing on all sides of an issue, prepared him to don a novelistic mask and to inhabit the character of Crusoe, who not only sees multiple sides of an issue but who seems constitutionally unable to avoid doing so. And perhaps most importantly of all, the sheer quantity of Defoe's writing over the course of his career meant that by the time he began writing extended prose fictions in the last decade of his life, he had developed a facility for speedy composition matched by few of his peers.

In Charles Gildon's *Life and Strange Surprising Adventures of D— D- F—* (1719), the character Daniel quips to Crusoe, "you are the true Allegorick Image of thy tender Father D—l; I drew thee from the Consideration of my own Mind; I have been all my Life that Rambling, Inconsistent Creature, which I have made thee" (315) Gildon intended the comment as a barb, but Defoe seized on the idea in the preface to the *Serious Reflections*, where he insisted that "there is a Man alive, and well known too, the Actions of whose Life are the just Subject of these Volumes, and to whom all or most Part of the Story most directly alludes, this may be depended upon for Truth, and to this I set my Name" (306). Putting aside Defoe's facetiousness—the name that is affixed to this preface is not "Daniel Defoe" but "Robinson Crusoe"—it would be a mistake to read *Crusoe* as an allegory in any usual sense of the word. Crusoe is not a disguised Defoe, and the various attempts to discern one-to-one correspondences between character and author have led to distortions of the novel, the life, or both. And yet, the novel does present variations on the themes of Defoe's own life. Crusoe's energetic ambivalence toward both money and religion; his essential isolation, even when surrounded by other people; his inability to sit still and his desire to ramble; his urge for control, however contingent—all reflect the Daniel Defoe of 1719.

Daniel Foe was born in the Cripplegate parish of London, probably in the autumn of 1660, the same year that the ascension of Charles II marked the end of the Puritan Commonwealth and the restoration of the Anglican Church. (He would add the *De* to his name only in 1685.) Though Defoe's father was a successful candle merchant and a member and later warden of the Butchers' Company, the Foes' religious commitments meant that Daniel's childhood was marked by exclusion from dominant elements of English public life. In 1662, Parliament passed the Act of Uniformity, which required clergy to use the revised Book of Common Prayer—in effect, to declare their allegiance to the Church of England. The Foes' pastor, Samuel Annesley, refused to conform, and the Foes were soon worshipping as Dissenters. That decision would reverberate throughout Defoe's entire life, making him unable to attend Oxford or Cambridge universities, or, following the first Test Act, to hold public office.

Excluded from the English universities, Defoe was sent by his father to Newington Green Academy, run by Charles Morton, a college specifically for Dissenters, which compensated for its lack in status with an education in many ways superior to that which Defoe would have received elsewhere. New ideas were quickly integrated into the curriculum, classes were taught in English rather than Latin, and in place of the emphasis on classical literature, students received a strong education in modern languages, mathematics, and science. John Locke's *Essay on Human Understanding*, banned at Oxford, was keenly studied at Morton's Academy. Throughout his career, Defoe would be ribbed about his weak command of classical languages, but he had the satisfaction of knowing that his pragmatic education gave him an excellent preparation for modern middle-class life, including a life in business.

The primary purpose of Morton's Academy, though, was to prepare students for the ministry. At home, Defoe had already memorized large parts of the Bible, and he probably assumed when he entered Morton's that he was headed toward a career in the church. At some point in the early 1680s, however, Defoe changed his mind, perhaps realizing that his restless, active personality was better suited for a world of business than for the more contemplative life of a clergyman. "It was my Disaster," he later wrote, "first to be set a-part for, and then to be set a-part from the Honour of that Sacred Employ."[1] Soon, he was set up in trade, where his prospects initially seemed quite promising, not least because of the substantial dowry of £3,700 that Mary Tuffley brought to their marriage in 1684. Defoe was energetic, well-educated, well-capitalized, and well-connected. His business dealings were diverse: an import/export business in woolens, wine, tobacco, timber, and other goods; an investment in maritime insurance; a manufacturing company of brick and tile. Like

---

1 Daniel Defoe, *Defoe's Review*, vol. 8 (New York: Facsimile Text Society by Columbia UP, 1938) 754.

Crusoe, however, Defoe had a knack for over-reaching. Looking back on his decision to sail to Africa to buy slaves for his plantation, Crusoe laments, "I that was born to be my own Destroyer, could no more resist the Offer than I could restrain my first rambling Designs" (79). Defoe must have written from first-hand knowledge, for he frequently became involved in questionable ventures that soon went bad. He was sued repeatedly, including once by his own mother-in-law, whom he defrauded as part of a venture to manufacture perfume from the musk of civet cats, and once by the inventor of a diving machine created to salvage treasure from the ocean floor. In 1692, with over a hundred creditors demanding payment, Defoe went bankrupt for £17,000 and landed briefly in Fleet Prison and King's Bench Prison. But Defoe was always resilient—to his critics, unabashedly so—and despite the humiliation of the episode, it was not long before he was in business once again.

Despite his decision to pursue business rather than the ministry, Defoe wrote often about both religion and economics throughout his career, and both play structural roles in *Robinson Crusoe*. On the one hand, Crusoe has been a favorite of economists, who see in him a pure model of *homo economicus*, allocating his resources, calculating the value of goods and labor, measuring his rate of consumption. When Crusoe considers his blessings and misfortunes, for instance, he tallies them up in the manner of a double entry account book. And as many critics have noted, his interactions with others involve the brusque calculation of an economic transaction. When he learns upon returning to England that his parents are dead, he reflects simply, "my Father was dead, and my Mother, and all the Family extinct ...; and as I had been long ago given over for dead, there had been no Provision made for me; so that in a Word, I found nothing to relieve, or assist me; and that little Money I had, would not do much for me, as to settling in the World" (281).

At the same time, for a Puritan businessman like Defoe, economic success and failure are never distinct from Providence, and Crusoe is always attuned to signs of his own election. The wheat that crops up unexpectedly on his island "was really the Work of Providence" (113). When an earthquake nearly destroys his cave, Crusoe attributes it to "the invisible Power which alone directs such Things" (122). Upon realizing that the cannibals have always gone to the opposite side of the island, he notes the "special Providence that I was cast upon the Side of the Island where the Savages never came" (185). The open question this poses for readers is how seriously we are to take the allusions, prayers, and conversion. For some, the novel is "in a profound sense ... secular."[1] Or as Karl Marx famously claimed, "Of his prayers and the like we take no account, since they are a source of pleasure to him, and he looks upon them as so much recreation" (382). For others, the narrative approaches allegory, conforming to the "familiar Christian pattern of disobedience-punishment-repentance-deliverance."[2] Far from being insignificant, Crusoe's conversion is a key turning point in the narrative. Occurring nine months after the shipwreck, it marks the birth of a new relationship with the island, producing a Crusoe who is not only more content but who is also more adventurous, willing for the first time to fully explore the island. More importantly, Crusoe's constant search for Providence behind daily events enchants the world. If God's will lies behind both nature and the accumulation of wealth, then Crusoe's task is to read the script of the world made legible.

In 1702, Defoe's career took a dramatic and irreversible turn. While pursuing his business projects, he had also written a number of works, including pamphlets in support of a standing army; *An Essay on Projects*, in which he proposed a college for women, a national bank, and the construction of highways; and *The True Born Englishman*, his poetic defense of King William. But little had prepared him for the maelstrom that resulted from his pamphlet *The Shortest Way with Dissenters*. In this satire of High Churchmen such as the famous preacher Henry Sacheverell, Defoe adopted their tone, creating a fanatical spokesperson who concludes with the prayer "that the Posterity of the sons of Error may be rooted out from the Face of this Land for ever."[3] The mimicry cut too close, offending both Dissenters and High Churchmen alike. Soon Defoe found himself charged with seditious libel, incarcerated in Newgate Prison, and sentenced to pay a fine and to stand three times in the pillory. Remarkably, Defoe managed to turn the punishment to his advantage: the mob that would have typically tormented someone in the pillory instead rose to his defense, and he actually arranged to have his poem *A*

---

1 Leopold Damrosch, *God's Plot and Man's Stories: Studies in the Fictional Imagination from Milton to Fielding* (Chicago: U of Chicago P, 1985) 210.

2 J. Paul Hunter, *The Reluctant Pilgrim: Defoe's Emblematic Method and Quest for Form in Robinson Crusoe* (Baltimore: Johns Hopkins UP, 1966) 20.

3 Daniel Defoe, *The Shortest Way with the Dissenters* (London, 1702) 29.

Hymn to the Pillory sold while he was standing there. To be freed from prison, he agreed to act as both author and agent for Robert Harley, then Speaker of the House of Commons. Over the next decade, Defoe would serve as a spy for the government, often traveling through England and Scotland promoting Anglo-Scottish union.

When he left jail, again facing financial ruin, Defoe was a changed man. As his biographer Paula Backscheider observes, "The anger at the injustice and the pain lingered, but like the heroes and heroines of his novels, he refused to brood over the past, became more suave, and started a new life as a writer, not a merchant."[1] Unable to make a good living by trade but pressed to support his wife and seven children, he turned to writing newspapers, conduct books, atlases, government reports, public poems, and secret histories. In politics, Defoe remained generally committed to Whig (i.e., liberal) positions; in religion, he was always a Dissenter, consistently opposed to the Test Act. But his close association with Harley during the Tory years of 1710-14 and his willingness to stretch his allegiances and to write for Tory publications, even if he meant to undermine them, make it hard to overlook his mercurial affiliations. Even so, the unsought training he had received in imitation, mimicry, and projection, was equipping him to write *Robinson Crusoe*.

Despite its popularity, *Crusoe* probably brought Defoe little more than £100, and Defoe continued to look for new sources of income. He had always been attracted to the ideal of the gentleman merchant-farmer, and in 1722 he leased a large tract of land outside of Colchester, securing the timber rights for ninety-nine years. By the middle of the decade, he was trading in various commodities, from metal buttons, leather, and cloth to anchovies, honey, cheeses, and oysters, as well as making plans for another tile factory. At the same time, Defoe was still writing, editing, or contributing to a half dozen newspapers and capitalizing on the success of his fiction. In the five years following *Crusoe*, Defoe wrote his novels of travelers, highwaymen, planters, pirates, pickpockets, and prostitutes: *Captain Singleton* (1720), *Moll Flanders* (1722), *A Journal of the Plague Year* (1722), *Colonel Jack* (1722), and *Roxanna* (1724). After 1724, he turned away from novels, but in his subsequent travel and conduct books, political and economic essays, works about magic and the

---

1 Paula R. Backscheider, *Daniel Defoe: His Life* (Baltimore: Johns Hopkins UP, 1989) 126.

occult, he retained his fondness for fictional vignettes that animate most of his best work.

At the end of the second volume, Crusoe claims that he has "liv'd 72 Years a Life of infinite Variety, and learn'd sufficiently to know the Value of Retirement, and the Blessing of ending our Days in Peace." Like his hero, Defoe had experienced a "Life of infinite Variety" matched by few of his contemporaries. But unlike Crusoe, Defoe continued to face serious financial and familial problems to the very end. In the late 1720s, a debt from his first bankruptcy surfaced, and Defoe, unable to pay the £800, again went into hiding. His businesses at Colchester had crumbled, his health was deteriorating, his favorite daughter Sophia had married after contentious wrangling over the dowry, and his son Benjamin, with a large family, was practically destitute. In the last few months of his life, Defoe moved into a house in Ropemakers' Alley, not far from Grub Street, home to many of the century's hack writers. On 24 April 1731, he died intestate, probably from a stroke, and was soon buried in the famous Dissenting cemetery Bunhill Fields; his wife, Mary, died eighteen months later and was buried alongside him. At the time, the grave was marked with a brass plaque. But nearly a century and a half later, in 1870, a twenty-one foot marble monument was erected on the site, paid for by "the boys and girls of England." It simply reads, "Daniel De-Foe. Born 1661. Died 1731. Author of Robinson Crusoe."

Crusoe among the Castaways

In his 1800 poem "The Castaway," William Cowper describes a boy fallen overboard in the Atlantic, his storm-tossed ship unable to return for him. Initially, the boy seems representative of existential aloneness shared by both the speaker and also the reader: "Misery," Cowper writes, "still delights to trace / Its semblance in another's case." But rather than end with the comfort of this shared solitude, Cowper severs the link: we all perish alone, says the speaker, "But I beneath a rougher sea, / And whelmed in deeper gulfs than he." The speaker, in other words, has trumped the reader and the castaway: we think *we* are alone, but he is even more so.

Solitude in Defoe's world is different. More than other literary periods, the eighteenth century is often described in terms of its sociability: its coffee houses, clubs, and confraternities, its print culture, and its public sphere. As Defoe's contemporary essayist

Joseph Addison famously wrote, "Man is a sociable animal." Writers from Jonathan Swift to Samuel Johnson agreed; solitude as they saw it was productive not of great literature or fresh insight, but of madness, error, and solipsism: the solitary authorship of Cowper and the Romantic period, however fanciful, would have to wait. To use a metaphor from Swift, a solitary author was a spider spinning flimsy and filthy webs from its own gut rather than a social bee creating honey and wax, sweetness and light.

How then, we might wonder, does a novel about an isolated individual become one of the best-selling books of the century? There is no shortage of loners in eighteenth-century fiction, including most of Defoe's protagonists. But whether in prison, on London streets, in country houses or inns, or on colonial plantations, they live in populated worlds. Only Crusoe on his island inhabits a physical solitude equal to his inner condition. A Crusoe without his island solitude would seem scarcely to be a Crusoe at all.

Defoe was a topical writer, whether responding to the hurricane that hit London in 1703, to the negotiations surrounding the Treaty of Utrecht, or to his own experience of being pilloried. An insatiable reader—of travel tales, economic tracts, religious pamphlets, romances, and journalism—he had no shortage of events to draw upon. So where did the tale of island solitude come from? As he decided to write a castaway narrative, Defoe might have thought of a French pirate marooned on the island of Mauritius, who ate nothing but tortoise, went mad, and tore his clothes apart; or a Dutch seaman left on St. Helena, who exhumed his comrade and set himself to sea in the coffin; or a "Fleming named Picman" who lived for eleven months on a rocky island off the coast of Scotland, eating mostly seagulls.[1] Defoe probably would have read about John Segar, stranded on St. Helena for a year and a half, wearing goatskins, "crazed in minde but halfe out of his wits," who died "for lacke of sleepe" eight days after being rescued.[2] He would certainly have known of Robert Knox, captive for nineteen years on the island of Ceylon (now Sri Lanka), where he built houses for himself, captured and bred goats, accumulated property, and regularly read

---

1 These incidents are described in Adam Olearius, *The Voyages and Travels of the Ambassadors ...Whereto are Added the Travels of J. Albert de Mandelso*, tr. John Davies (London, 1662).

2 Richard Hakluyt, *The Principal Navigations,Voyages, Traffiques and Discoveries of the English Nation*, vol. 2 (London, 1599-1600) 108.

his Bible. As he wrote the description of Crusoe naming Friday, perhaps he thought of Captain William Dampier's 1684 rescue of a Moskito Indian from Juan Fernandez Island. Explaining that the Indian had been given the name Will by the English, Dampier observes, "they have no names among themselves; and they take it as a great favour to be named by any of us; and will complain for want of it, if we do not appoint them some name when they are with us: saying of themselves they are poor Men, and have no Name."[1]

Such accounts have often been viewed as potential sources for Defoe's novel. But while there is no doubt that Defoe drew on castaway narratives for details of island life—food, flora, routines, and episodes—at times *Crusoe* can work against their ideologies and narrative structures. One of the best known stories of island solitude was Ibn Ṭufayl's *Hai Ibn Yokdhan*, an Arabic fable of solitary upbringing and education that had been repeatedly translated during Defoe's life.[2] Abandoned as a newborn by a princess or born out of clay, Hai Ibn Yokdhan grows up in complete island isolation where, according to the work's full title, "*by the meer light of nature* [he] attain[s] the knowledge of things Natural and Supernatural, more particularly the Knowledge of God, and the affairs of another Life." The problem for Defoe with such a story was that it seemed to endorse a theory of natural religion; as its title implies, it suggested that individuals could be saved through reason alone, even without scriptural revelation. It is a possibility that Crusoe considers after Friday arrives: "I sometimes was led too far to invade the Soveraignty of *Providence*, and as it were arraign the Justice of so arbitrary a Dis-

---

1 William Dampier, *A New Voyage Round the World*, 5th ed. (London, 1703) 86-87. For other accounts of castaway narratives that may have influenced Defoe, see Arthur Wellesley Secord, *Studies in the Narrative Method of Defoe* (New York: Russell & Russell, 1963); Hunter, *Reluctant Pilgrim*; Maximillian E. Novak, *Defoe and the Nature of Man* (London: Oxford UP, 1963); David Fausett, *The Strange Surprising Sources of Robinson Crusoe* (Atlanta: Rodopi, 1994).

2 It is a sign of the relative fame of *Hai Ebn Yokdhan* that just a few months after *Crusoe* first appeared, Alexander Pope compared one of his friends not to Crusoe but to Hai Ebn Yokdhan ("the self-taught philosopher") and Alexander Selkirk. He wrote to Lord Bathurst, "I believe you are by this time immers'd in your vast Wood; and one may address you as to a very abstracted person, like Alexander Selkirk, or the Self-taught Philosopher." The preferred transliteration from the Arabic is *Hayy ibn Yaqzan*. I am using the name as it appeared in the book Defoe would have read.

position of Things, that should hide that Light from some, and reveal it to others, and yet expect a like Duty from both" (223). But he goes on to reject it, just as Defoe consistently rejected deistic claims that privileged natural over revealed religion. For Crusoe, by reason and judgment alone "every Man may be in time Master of every mechanic Art" (103), but only with the addition of Scripture can he be saved.

By far the best known inspiration for *Crusoe* was a Scotsman, Alexander Selkirk, who survived four years alone on Juan Fernandez Island off the coast of Chile. As the sailing master of an English privateer called the *Cinque Ports*, Selkirk had quarreled with his captain, Thomas Stradling, insisting that their ship was no longer sea-worthy, and when given the chance to stay on the island, he took it. For the next four years, Selkirk lived on goat meat, cabbage, and turnips, dressed in a "Goat's Skin Jacket, Breeches, and Cap, sew'd together with Thongs of the same."[1] Like Crusoe he "said he was a better Christian while in this Solitude than ever he was before, or than, he was afraid, he should ever be again" (326).

Selkirk was well known in the early century, but not until the end of the century did he take on his distinct role as the "real" Robinson Crusoe. By the 1780s, it became something of a (misguided) commonplace that Defoe had merely stolen Crusoe's story from Selkirk. The nineteenth century, which witnessed huge growth in editions and imitations of *Crusoe*, further popularized Selkirk. In 1851, Joseph Xavier Saintine published a book about Selkirk called *The Solitary of Juan Fernandez, or, The Real Robinson Crusoe*, in which he declared that Crusoe and Selkirk are "really the same personage."[2] In 1966, the Chilean government renamed Juan Fernandez as Robinson Crusoe Island, apparently untroubled that Crusoe was shipwrecked in the Caribbean, Selkirk in the Pacific. More recently, the Selkirk industry has again shown signs of growth, with books and articles titled *Selkirk's Island: The True and Strange Adventures of the Real Robinson Crusoe* (2001), *Marooned: The Strange but True Adventures of Alexander Selkirk, the Real Robinson Crusoe* (2005), and "The Real Robinson Crusoe" (2005).[3] But Crusoe's island is richer than

---

1 Edward Cooke, *A Voyage to the South Sea* (London, 1712) 37.
2 M. Xavier. *The Solitary of Juan Fernandez*, trans. Anne T. Wilbur (Boston: Ticknor, Reed, and Fields, 1851) 139.
3 According to one popular anecdote of doubtful veracity, an alderman of Oxford named Tawney was so enamored of *Crusoe* that he "used to read Robinson Crusoe through every year with great delight, and thought every part of it as much matter of fact as his Bible."   (continued)

Selkirk's. His diet is more expansive, his sleep is sounder, his salvaged equipment is more useful, his inner life more visible. Though Crusoe, unlike Selkirk, is condemned to a solitude he did not choose, he makes that solitude abundant, charting out the time of his days as purposefully as he orders the possessions in his cave.

Defoe's literary tendency was to synthesize and transform, not to plagiarize. Consider, for instance, the way that he approaches the thorny problem of Crusoe's trustworthiness. One strong enticement of the castaway narrative as a genre lies in the solitude of the experience: if solitude is the stage for especially stark display of the self, then castaways would seem to be uniquely positioned for this form of self-knowledge. But at the same time, the very condition of solitude renders the experience unverifiable. How do we know, in other words, that the castaway's account is credible, and that the experience of returning to society has not compromised the solitude that is being described? One way to address the tension is to appeal directly to the castaway's actions, as happened in the case of Selkirk. Referring to other castaway narratives, Woodes Rogers writes that "whatever there is in these Stories, this of Mr. *Selkirk* I know to be true; and his Behaviour afterwards gives me reason to believe the Account he gave me how he spent his time, and bore up under such Affliction" (328).

A second approach, one taken by Defoe, was to tell the story twice: once as journal, once as memoir. In less artful hands, the repetitiveness of a journal might simply suggest the monotony of the days. Leendert Hasenbosch, who in 1725 inhabited Ascension Island for six months until his death, is a good example:

The 11th Ditto, I carried all the Wood from my Tent into the Country, and likewise some of my Clothes.
The 12th Ditto, Nothing Remarkable. The 13, 14, 15th, Look'd for Water, but found none. The 16th Ditto, Found some Fowls Eggs, which I brought home and eat; us'd my Water very sparingly. The 17th, Nothing. The 18th, As before.

Upon being told that the story was a fiction based on the story of Alexander Selkirk, he reportedly responded with a sigh, "Your information may be correct, but I had rather you had withheld it, for by thus undeceiving me, you have deprived me of one of the greatest pleasures of my old age." J. Byerley and J.C. Robertson, Vol. 1, *The Percy Anecdotes, Collected and Edited by Reuben and Sholto Percy* (London, 1868) 544.

The 19th, Nothing Remarkable. The 20th, Nothing worthy of Note.[1]

But in Crusoe's hands, the journal will be a record of cognitive and temporal fulfillment:

> I now began to consider seriously my Condition, and the Circumstance I was reduc'd to, and I drew up the State of my Affairs in Writing, not so much to leave them to any that were to come after me, for I was like to have but few Heirs, as to deliver my Thoughts from daily poring upon them, and afflicting my Mind; and as my Reason began now to master my Despondency, I began to comfort my self as well as I could. (101)

Emerging from a tradition of Puritan diary keeping, whereby a journal is the vehicle for reflection on one's own spiritual progress, Crusoe's journal also serves the more secular need to present solitude to an audience. Crusoe worries that the narrative doubling will be tedious, since "in it will be told all these Particulars over again" (105). But it is a risk worth taking: along with his umbrella, his goat-skin cap, his parrot, and the coins he has squirreled away, the journal is one of the few souvenirs Crusoe saves from the island. It is his artifact of solitude. Hasenbosch's editors claim that his journal "*carries all possible Marks of Truth and Sincerity*" (340). If readers have any doubt, "The Original Manuscript from whence this Journal was printed, may be seen at the Publishers" (341). Defoe, who presents Crusoe's tale as a "just History of Fact" (45) cannot put the journal on display at the publisher's, but by presenting parts of the story twice, he can leave it to his readers to recognize its truthfulness.

The journal also illustrates the double nature of Crusoe's solitude. It splits Crusoe in two, between the Crusoe who writes from London for a readerly audience and the Crusoe who writes for himself on the island. On the island, he lives for himself and for God—the individual ostensibly unencumbered by society— but he is also amongst us readers, aware of our narrative needs, putting himself on show. The distinction between public and private language quickly breaks down: despite Crusoe's promise to give us the "exact copy," there are moments when it becomes impossible to know whether we are reading the journal or a later commentary. But that is the point, for in the haziness, Defoe

---

1 Leendert Hasenbosch, *An Authentic Relation ... of a Dutch Sailor* (1728) 20.

effectively socializes solitude. In the *Serious Reflections*, he makes the seemingly counterintuitive claim that all his island confinement "was no solitude," and further that "I enjoy much more solitude in the middle of the greatest collection of mankind in the world, I mean, at London, while I am writing this, than ever I could say I enjoyed in eight and twenty years' confinement to a desolate island" (358). The claim seems less bizarre when we realize that even in his first volume, when solitude seems so thoroughly physical, he is already making solitude portable, a function of mind rather than geography. If such a solitude has a particular coldness to it—"we love, we hate, we covet, we enjoy, all in privacy and solitude," (357) he says—it is worth noting that in reading *Crusoe*, we are all alone together. Coleridge praised Defoe's ability to "make[ ] me sympathize with his presentations with the *whole* of my being."[1] If Crusoe's solitude seems to be extreme, it aims at the same time to be archetypal.

Friday's Imprint

Exactly halfway through the novel, on a day like every other day, Crusoe encounters a single footprint on the beach: "It happen'd one Day about Noon going towards my Boat, I was exceedingly surpriz'd with the Print of a Man's naked Foot on the Shore, which was very plain to be seen in the Sand" (176). Just before this encounter, he has described his life in terms that make him seem like a homeowner who has finally unpacked the boxes: his enclosure, with separate pens for feeding and slaughter, holds nearly fifty goats; the dairy provides him with butter and cheese; his clothes have taken on their famous goatskin look; his "two Plantations"—the fortification on the beach near his "duly cultivated crops" and his "country seat" near the goats and grapes— are fully mature and abundant; he relishes the image of "me and my little family sit[ting] down to dinner" (171). Confident in his use of this solitary colony, he has cultivated an equally confident sense of himself.

The footprint breaks the spell. The island that he has tamed suddenly becomes threatening, and his sense of self is upturned: "after innumerable fluttering Thoughts, like a Man perfectly confus'd and out of my self, I came Home to my Fortification, not feeling, as we say, the Ground I went on, but terrify'd to the last Degree, looking behind me at every two or three Steps, mistak-

---

1 Pat Rogers, *Defoe: the Critical Heritage* (Boston: Routledge and Kegan Paul, 1972) 81.

ing every Bush and Tree, and fancying every Stump at a Distance to be a Man" (176). His "fortification" becomes a "castle" or even a "cell"; he briefly entertains the thought of digging up his barley and tearing down his enclosures; he stops building fires or firing his gun; and his daily prayer becomes a discomposed shadow of its former self. Not least, his discovery of the remains of a cannibal feast disorders his powers of inventions. "[T]he Frights I had been in about these Savage Wretches," he tells us, "and the Concern I had been in for my own Preservation, had taken off the Edge of my Invention for my own Conveniences" (187-88). Invention has not ceased, but it has been redirected. Instead of making beer from his barley as we have come to expect, "my Invention now run quite another Way; for Night and Day, I could think of nothing but how I might destroy some of these Monsters in their cruel bloody Entertainment, and if possible, save the Victim they should bring hither to destroy" (188). Before the footprint, Crusoe has imagined himself to be in control of his inventive mind, but when faced with other humans for the first time, he discovers that his invention is dictating its own course, as if the colonial imagination has its own logic that tugs him along in its wake.

In the final paragraph of his 2001 biography of Defoe, Max Novak observes that *Robinson Crusoe* has recently "become a classic text for postcolonial studies, though it is uncertain whether its protagonist and its author are to be regarded as heroes or villains."[1] That is not to imply any uncertainty about Defoe's enthusiasm for colonialism, which he viewed as a crucial element in the expansion of British trade. Throughout his career, Defoe periodically wrote proposals for the creation of colonies, first in the South Seas, then on the Atlantic coast, including one that appeared in his *Weekly Journal* shortly before the publication of *Robinson Crusoe*:

> We expect, in two or three Days, a most flaming Proposal from the South Sea Company, or from a Body of Merchants who claim kindred of them, for erecting a British Colony on the Foundation of the South-Sea Company's Charter, upon the Terra Firma, or the Northernmost Side of the Mouth of the great River Oroonoko. They propose, as we hear, the establishing a Factory and Settlement

---

1 Maximillian E. Novak, *Daniel Defoe: Master of Fictions* (Oxford: Oxford UP, 2001) 706.

there, which shall cost the Company 500000 pounds Sterling.... This, it seems, is the same country and River discovered by Sir Walter Rawleigh, in former Days, and that
which he miscarried in by several Mistakes, which may
now easily be prevented.[1]

Typically for Defoe, the impetus for the plan was economic, for
despite the reference to his hero Raleigh, Defoe was not primarily interested in military conquest. As Michael Seidel argues,
"He was not by nature a pirate nor a plunderer; he was a trader,
a maker, a manufacturer, a projector, a negotiator."[2]

One critical element of the colonial trade, of course, was
slavery. Scholars have sometimes credited Defoe with criticizing
slavery decades before concerted abolitionist crusades had taken
hold. In his poetic satire *Reformation of Manners* (1702), he
targets English slave traders:

The harmless Natives basely they trepan [cheat],
And barter Baubles for the *Souls of Men*:
The Wretches they to Christian Climes bring o'er,
To serve worse Heathens than they did before. (388)

But although the poem criticizes the mistreatment of slaves, Defoe
never condemned slavery as an institution. He was a shareholder
in the Royal African Company, which supplied slaves to the
English colonies, and he never questioned the right of Europeans
to buy and sell Africans and Amerindians. His tone regarding
slavery is often one of stark moral indifference, for in his economic
works, slaves become necessary elements in a colonial cycle that
begins and ends in trade: "those who know how far our Plantation
Trade is Blended and Interwoven with the Trade to Africa, and that
they can no more be parted than the Child and the Nurse, need
have no time spent to convince them of this; The Case is as plain
as Cause and Consequence: Mark the Climax. No African trade,
no negroes; no negroes no sugars, gingers, indicoes, etc; no sugars
etc no islands; no islands no continent; no continent no trade."[3]

Crusoe's story unfolds within that cycle. In his first voyage to
Africa, he turns a forty-pound investment into "almost 300 l," a

---

1 Daniel Defoe, *Weekly Journal,* 7 Feb 1719.
2 Michael Seidel, *Robinson Crusoe: Island Myths and the Novel* (Boston:
   Twayne, 1991) 41.
3 Defoe, vol. 9, *Defoe's Review,* 89.

seven-fold return that "fill'd me with those aspiring Thoughts which have since so compleated my Ruin" (60). Following another trading voyage, during which he is enslaved for two years by Turkish Moors, Crusoe settles in Brazil, where he establishes himself as a planter of tobacco and sugar cane. As soon as he has cash, he buys a slave, and soon he and the other planters are scheming for him to make a slaving voyage. Luckily for Crusoe, his 28 years on the island don't interrupt the daily functioning of his remarkably profitable plantation. When he returns to England, it is to astonishing wealth.

European colonialism and the slave trade thus draw the map on which Crusoe adventures, but Crusoe himself remains blissfully disinclined to reflect on the human costs of that trade. When he escapes from his enslavement in Morocco, for instance, his experience doesn't prevent him from quickly selling his fellow-escapee Xury to the Portuguese captain who has rescued him. (Eventually he will come to regret his decision, but only because he and his neighbor need Xury's labor as they plant tobacco and sugar cane: "we both wanted Help, and now I found more than before, I had done wrong in parting with my Boy *Xury*" [75].) Nor, as his contemporary Charles Gildon remarked, is he inclined to see his island shipwreck as a sign of divine punishment: "He sets out upon new Adventures, as Supercargo to a Portuguese ship, bound to the coast of Guinea to buy slaves; and tho' he afterwards proves so scrupulous about falling upon the Cannibals or Man-Eaters, yet he neither then nor afterwards found any check of Conscience in that infamous Trade of buying and selling of Men for Slaves; else one would have expected him to have attributed his shipwreck to this very Cause."[1] Rather, Crusoe moves in the economy of the Atlantic slave trade without consciously reflecting on its moral dimensions.

Through Friday, whom Crusoe describes variously as "my savage," "my man," "friend," and "faithful, loving, sincere Servant," Defoe does instantiate his understanding of the master-slave relationship. It is a relationship not without pleasures. After twenty-five years of island isolation, Friday's arrival initiates "the pleasantest Year of all the life I led in this Place.... I had a singular Satisfaction in the Fellow himself; his simple unfeign'd Honesty, appear'd to me more and more every Day, and I began really to love the Creature; and on his Side, I believe he lov'd me

---

1 Charles Gildon, *Robinson Crusoe Examin'd and Criticis'd*, ed. Paul Dottin (New York: J.M. Dent & Sons Ltd, 1923) 14.

more than it was possible for him ever to love any Thing before" (226). In the second volume, when Friday follows Crusoe's command that he speak to a group of armed natives and is killed, Crusoe's lament for "my poor Friday, whom I so entirely loved and valued" is as heartfelt as Crusoe ever musters:[1]

> Poor honest Friday! We buried him with all the decency and solemnity possible, by putting him into a coffin, and throwing him into the sea; and I caused them to fire eleven guns for him. So ended the life of the most grateful, faithful, honest, and most affectionate servant that ever man had.[2]

W.R. Owens argues that given Defoe's own tolerance of slavery, he would feel no compunction in describing Friday as a slave if he intended him to be one: "It seems implausible, to say the least, that Defoe would have felt it necessary to disguise the fact that Friday was Crusoe's slave had he regarded him as such or intended him to be understood as such. Friday is not a 'slave' in any meaningful sense of the term, but is instead Crusoe's faithful servant and friend."[3]

But it is worth considering the shifting language that Defoe uses to describe Friday, for the lines between friend, servant, and slave are often indistinct. Even before Friday is brought to the island as the main course in a cannibal feast, Crusoe has already fantasized his existence. He has imagined slaughtering cannibals and rescuing a slave who gratefully "became my Servant" (214). In both the dream and reality, Crusoe readily distinguishes between the "good savage" (Christian, subservient, foreswearing human flesh) and the "bad savage" (pagan, assertive, cannibalis-

---

1 Not all readers have been impressed with Crusoe's display of emotion at Friday's death. Charles Dickens, who found the second volume of Crusoe to be "perfectly contemptible," wrote to his friend John Forster, "there is not in literature a more surprising instance of an utter want of tenderness and sentiment, than the death of Friday." Charles Dickens, *The Letters of Charles Dickens*, ed. Graham Storey and Kathleen Tillotson, Vol. 8 (Oxford: Clarendon P, 1995) 153. Though it scarcely absolves Crusoe of Dickens's critisicm, one might note in response that the deaths of Crusoe's parents and wife elicit even less tenderness.

2 Daniel Defoe, *The Farther Adventures of Robinson Crusoe* (London, 1719) 211-12.

3 W.R. Owens, introduction, *Robinson Crusoe. The Novels of Daniel Defoe*, ed. W.R. Owens (London: Pickering & Chatto, 2009) 42.

tic), a distinction often captured by the novel's illustrators.[1] (See, for example, p. 412.) Twice after his rescue Friday places Crusoe's foot on his head "in token of swearing to be my Slave for ever" (218). The gesture is confirmed in the language that Crusoe gives to him: "I made him know his Name should be *Friday*, which was the Day I sav'd his Life; I call'd him so for the Memory of the Time; I likewise taught him to say *Master*, and then let him know, that was to be my Name; I likewise taught him to say, YES, and NO" (220). We might expect Crusoe to teach Friday English in order to have conversations, but his purpose instead is purely utilitarian; he values Friday's speech because it enables Friday to "understand the Names of almost every Thing I had occasion to call for, and of every Place I had to send him to" (226). Not surprisingly, Crusoe assigns him the most arduous labor. In a scene that anticipates Defoe's later novel *Colonel Jack*, in which Jack works as an overseer on a Virginia plantation, Crusoe sends Friday and his father to hew a large tree, sending with them the Spaniard "to oversee and direct their work" (255).

As Owens observes, Crusoe never explicitly calls Friday a slave. He does, though, imagine him as a slave before he arrives, accept his gestures as signifying his voluntary enslavement, and require him to work without compensation. That he can also imagine Friday as his "faithful, loving, sincere Servant" is not a repudiation of his enslavement but rather an integral part of its fantastical fulfillment. As a thoroughly reformed cannibal ("The Savage was now a good Christian" [233]), Friday performs the labor of a slave while obviating the anxieties that accompanied the system of slavery.

Despite Crusoe's assertion that Friday has made him "a much better Scholar in the Scripture Knowledge, than I should ever have been by my own private meer Reading" (233), Friday's presence makes Crusoe no less insular than he had been before. As Patrick Brantlinger comments, Crusoe's solipsism "can be read as a parable of all the forms of imperialism and political divisiveness that have divided people through history into masters and servants, the dominant and the dominated."[2] But if Crusoe's relationship to the island, to Friday, and to the natives is steeped in a colonial history of occupation and slavery, his colonialist

---

1 Rebecca Weaver-Hightower, *Empire Islands: Castaways, Cannibals, and Fantasies of Conquest* (Minneapolis: U of Minnesota P, 2007) 97.

2 Pat Brantlinger, *Crusoe's Footprints: Cultural Studies in Britain and America* (New York: Routledge, 1990) 2-3.

enterprise is hardly an unvarnished success. In *The Farther Adventures of Robinson Crusoe,* he returns to his island only to discover that three of the Englishmen he has left there are effectively at war with two others and with the contingent of Spaniards, that houses have been torn down and crops torn up. In his absence, the Spaniards have been hesitant to kill the rebellious English, and cannibals have repeatedly attacked one another and the Europeans on the island. Crusoe, in other words, begins to look more like an absentee landlord than the planter of a successful colony. Moreover, even in the first volume, Crusoe's colonization of the island reveals its fragility. His declarations of mastery are most confident either when he is alone or when he is surrounded by animals: "I had the Lives of all my Subjects at my absolute Command. I could hang, draw, give Liberty, and take it away, and no Rebels among all my Subjects" (171). He insists that everyone from Xury to Friday to the Spaniards to the English swear their allegiance to him, yet that very insistence underscores his anxiety that he appears to lack authority. While displaying its colonial fantasy, *Crusoe* also demonstrates the inherent anxieties that such a fantasy engenders.

The doublings that emerge from Crusoe's colonial project— Crusoe as authoritarian commander and anxious castaway, Friday as friend and as slave, the island itself as "my Reign, or my Captivity, which you please" (163)—have been an integral part of Crusoe's mind from the beginning.[1] When Crusoe responds to his parents, reacts to money, reflects on his island condition, or considers killing cannibals, the words *but, yet,* and *however* scatter the prose like so many U-turn signs. We might expect, for instance, a certain consistency to follow his conversion, when he exclaims, "Now I look'd back upon my past Life with such Horror, and my Sins appear'd so dreadful, that my Soul sought nothing of God, but Deliverance from the Load of Guilt that bore down all my Comfort" (128). But two sentences later, that load of guilt is considerably lighter: "My Condition began now to be, tho' not less miserable as to my Way of living, yet much easier to my Mind; and my Thoughts being directed, by a constant reading the Scripture, and praying to God, to things of a higher Nature: I had a great deal of Comfort within, which till now I

---

1   Michael Seidel considers such doubles, or "island replicates," in "*Robinson Crusoe*: Varieties of Fictional Experience," *The Cambridge Companion to Daniel Defoe,* ed. John Richetti (Cambridge: Cambridge UP, 2008) 190-95.

knew nothing of; also, as my Health and Strength returned, I bestirr'd my self to furnish my self with every thing that I wanted, and make my Way of living as regular as I could" (128). The sentences don't simply signify a change in perspective, for they both present themselves as extended states of mind. As Defoe's early critics noted, it is hard to see how they can coexist.

But they do coexist, and with few apologies for his quick turns of mind. Crusoe regrets his actions and thoughts frequently enough, but rarely in a terribly sustained way. Quickly, he moves on to other tasks. Like his author, he is able to shift from self-inflicted disappointment to new projects with astounding rapidity. In one memorable scene, Crusoe decides to build a canoe big enough to take him off the island. After months of labor, he finishes it, only to realize belatedly that he has no way to move it to the water. "This griev'd me heartily, and now I saw, tho' too late, the Folly of beginning a Work before we count the Cost; and before we judge rightly of our own Strength to go through with it" (154). He knows that he should have known better, and we might wonder whether the canoe has been a means of escape or a convenient excuse to fill monotonous time with meaningful labor. Almost immediately, though, regret for his thoughtlessness is replaced by self-satisfaction as he watches divine and worldly blessings coincide: "I had nothing to covet; for I had all that I was now capable of enjoying: I was Lord of the whole Mannor; or if I pleas'd, I might call my self King, or Emperor over the whole Country which I had Possession of" (155). Soon enough, that feeling too will pass. Some readers find Crusoe's changes in thought, action, and loyalty to be shallow, even hypocritical, just as some of Defoe's critics found his shifting allegiances to be mercurial, even shameless. But for others, Crusoe's self-protective nimbleness, like his remarkable inventiveness, is a reason to return repeatedly to the novel, not because it shows us things as they are or should be, but because it displays so engagingly the human shortcomings and compensations that accompany fantasies of how they *might* be.

Daniel Defoe: A Brief Chronology

1659   [Crusoe lands on island]

1660   Born Daniel Foe to James Foe, a candle manufacturer, and his wife, Alice, in the London parish of St. Giles, Cripplegate

Restoration of Stuart monarchy with coronation of Charles II

1662   Act of Uniformity requires clergy to consent to the revised Book of Common Prayer; the Foes follow their pastor, Samuel Annesley, and begin worshipping as Dissenters

1665   The Plague of London kills more than 70,000 people

1666   Great Fire of London; 90% of London's living accommodations burn; the Foes' rented house survives

1673   First Test Act excludes Catholics and Dissenters from public office

1676-79?   Attends Newington Green Academy, run by Charles Morton, in preparation for the Presbyterian ministry

1681   Decides to pursue trade rather than enter the ministry

1683-92   Establishes himself in Cornhill as a wholesale exporter of woolens; invests in trade of wine, tobacco, timber, and other goods

1684   Marries Mary Tuffley, daughter of a wealthy wine cooper, with dowry of £3,700

Between 1687 and 1701, they have at least five daughters and two sons

1685   Death of Charles II; James II accedes to the throne

Participates in the Duke of Monmouth's unsuccessful rebellion against James II; unlike most of the rebels, Defoe escapes capture and punishment

1686   [Crusoe leaves island]

1688   Following his father, becomes a member of the Butchers' Company

William, Prince of Orange, lands in England; James II flees to France

First publication, *A Letter to a Dissenter from his Friend at the Hague*, in support of Revolution

1689   Accession of William and Mary

1691	Attacks election abuses in *A New Discovery of an Old Intreague*, his first published poem
1692	Declared bankrupt for £17,000; committed briefly to Fleet Prison and King's Bench Prison
1694	Begins brick and tile manufacturing in Essex
1695	Officially adds the prefix *De* to name
	Becomes accountant to one of the commissioners for a newly imposed glass tax
1697-1701	*An Essay on Projects*, Defoe's first published book
	Travels in England and Scotland as agent of William III
1698	Offers a proposal to King William for a settlement on South American coasts
1701	*The True-Born Englishman*, his most popular poem, in support of King William
1702	Death of King William III; Accession of Queen Anne
	The Shortest Way with the Dissenters, a satire on the extremism of High Churchmen such as Henry Sacheverell
	Reformation of Manners
1703	Arrested for writing *The Shortest Way* and sentenced to stand three times in the pillory; sent to Newgate, where he spends five months, during which time his business sours and he again goes bankrupt; released through Robert Harley's influence
	A Hymn to the Pillory
1703-14	Acts as an agent for Harley (except for a period during 1708-10 when Harley is out of power)
1704	*A Hymn to Liberty*, Defoe's tribute to Marlborough's victory at the Battle of Blenheim
1704-13	*The Review*, Defoe's periodical on foreign and domestic affairs, trade, and politics
1706-07	Travels extensively in Scotland, reporting to Harley and writing in support of Union
1706	*Jure Divino*, a twelve-book poem in defense of King William
	Caledonia, a poem in praise of Scotland, designed to elicit support for Anglo-Scottish Union
1707	Act of Union between England and Scotland
1709	*The History of the Union of Great Britain*
	Alexander Selkirk rescued by Woodes Rogers from Juan Fernandez Island

1711	Parliament establishes South Sea Company to fund government debt
1713	Arrested briefly for libel
	South Sea company is granted monopoly on Spanish-American slave trade
1714	Death of Queen Anne; accession of George I, first Hanoverian king
1715	*The Family Instructor*, his first conduct book
1716	Begins writing for *Mercurius Politicus* and other Tory papers
1719	*Robinson Crusoe; The Farther Adventures of Robinson Crusoe*
1720	South Sea Bubble bursts
	Memoirs of a Cavalier; Captain Singleton; Serious Reflections ... of Robinson Crusoe
1722	Purchases land and timber rights for several hundred acres in Essex
	Moll Flanders; Journal of the Plague Year; Colonel Jack
1724	*Roxana; A General History of the Pyrates; A Tour Thro' the Whole Island of Great Britain* (completed 1726)
1725	*The Complete English Tradesman* (Volume II in 1727)
1726	*The Political History of the Devil*
1727	Death of George I; Accession of George II
1728	*A Plan of the English Commerce*
1731	Dies "of lethargy" (probably a stroke) in lodgings in Ropemakers' Alley, London; buried in Bunhill Fields, London
1732	Mary Tuffley dies; buried in Bunhill Fields
1871	Defoe's grave reopened during the construction of a twenty-one-foot monument to "the author of *Robinson Crusoe*," paid for by "Boys and Girls of England"

A Note on the Text

At the end of *The Life and Strange Surprizing Adventures of Robinson Crusoe*, Defoe hints toward a sequel: "All these things, with some very surprizing Incidents in some new Adventures of my own, for ten Years more, I may perhaps give a farther Account hereafter" (304). His expectation that his work would justify a second volume was correct. The first edition was published on 25 April 1719; within two weeks, a second edition appeared, followed by four more by August. Defoe, meanwhile, was hurriedly preparing his sequel, *The Farther Adventures of Robinson Crusoe*, which appeared on 20 August 1719. (Piracies were also rapidly appearing, giving Defoe even more reason to rush *The Farther Adventures* quickly into print.) Assuming print runs of approximately 1,000 copies, this makes *Robinson Crusoe*, if not a bestseller on the level of Jonathan Swift's *Gulliver's Travels* (1726), at least a clear commercial success. The speed of composition and production, however, creates particular challenges for editing Defoe's work.

Defoe's authorized publisher in 1719 was William Taylor, whose name appears on all six initial octavo editions. But Taylor did not print the book himself. For his first edition, he enlisted the services of the printer Henry Parker. In the second edition, which appeared on 9 May, thirteen gatherings were printed by Parker, four by Hugh Meere, and four by William Bower. Then, with the book selling well, third and fourth editions—that is, two new settings of type—appeared on 6 June, both of them bearing the designation *third edition* on their title pages, both also printed by Parker, Meere, and Bower. (Scholars generally refer to these as the "lion" and "phoenix" editions respectively, in reference to the tailpieces on the last pages of text.) On 7 August Taylor published two more editions—properly the fifth and sixth editions—which both bore the label *fourth edition* and were both printed entirely by Parker.

Taken together, these editions exhibit a huge number of textual variations. Some, such as upside down letters or extra letters (e.g., *acccount*), are clearly printers errors; in those cases, I have silently corrected the text. Others are changes in words (e.g., the first edition's "straight *strong* Limbs" becomes "straight *long* Limbs" in the sixth); except where noted, I have retained the text of the first edition. But by far the most frequent variation, which requires a special word, involves punctuation.

To a reader accustomed to twenty-first century grammatical conventions, the first edition of *Robinson Crusoe* can seem hopelessly mispunctuated, replete with fragmented clauses, run-on sentences, capricious commas. And indeed, it appears that Defoe's own readers in 1719 must have shared some of this reaction, since the later printings tend to tidy up the anomalies of the first edition, even as they introduce new ones of their own. For instance, where the first edition reads:

> I consulted several Things in my Situation which I found would be proper for me, 1st. Health, and fresh Water I just now mention'd, 2dly. Shelter from the Heat of the Sun, 3dly. Security from ravenous Creatures, whether Men or Beasts, 4thly. a View to the Sea, that if God sent any Ship in Sight, I might not lose any Advantage for my Deliverance, of which I was not willing to banish all my Expectation yet.

the sixth edition (fourth B) reads:

> I consulted several Things in my Situation which I found would be proper for me, 1st. Health, and fresh Water I just now mention'd. 2ndly, Shelter from the Heat of the Sun. 3rdly, Security from ravenous Creatures, whether Man or Beast. 4thly, a View to the Sea, that if God sent any Ship in Sight, I might not lose any Advantage for my Deliverance, for which I was not willing to banish all my Expectation yet.

Though few readers are likely to find the first edition more readable than the second, it is not merely capricious; rather, it is consistent with the first edition's tendency to separate independent clauses with commas and to follow numerals with periods. Though the later edition conforms more closely to the rules of punctuation as they would come to be codified, the first edition is not completely without its own logic.

The problem of punctuation is exacerbated by our lack of a manuscript. Very few Defoe manuscripts survive. Certainly he could write a polished hand, as he shows in the "Historical Collections" which he gave to his future wife. But the manuscript of *Crusoe* probably more closely resembled that of *The Compleat English Gentleman*, published posthumously. As the editor of that text observes, "Defoe scarcely puts any commas, and only very rarely puts a full stop or other mark" (xix). His use of abbreviations, moreover, is daunting:

Defoe uses a short, thick, horizontal stroke for *and*, only occasionally employing the sign &; a short, thick, oblique stroke from right to left for *that*; a similar one from left to right for *the*; but sometimes the well-known y(t) and y(e). An *o* with a horizontal stroke means either *which* or *what*; if crossed obliquely from right to left, it means *particular*. Two connected *o*'s stand for *good*; a long stroke with an *o*, for *notwithstanding*.[1]

If Defoe wrote *Crusoe* in a similar form, then we can only imagine how much editing must have been left up to the compositor of the first edition. It is probably safe to say that, especially in the matter of accidentals, the text of the first edition must vary substantially from the manuscript Defoe wrote.

Despite the challenges posed by the first edition, however, it remains the best available copytext. There is no indication that Defoe oversaw any of the changes made in the later editions, which have the further disadvantage of being produced by multiple printers, resulting in differently predisposed compositors for different sections of the text. It is not hard to imagine a thoroughly modernized *Crusoe*—there are many such editions available—that smoothes out all the rough spots of Defoe's prose, but what such editions gain in readerly ease they lose in characterisitically Defoevian style. Whether by accident or by art, Defoe created a text that matches its protagonist: neither Strunk nor White, but sprawling, rambling, and discursive.

My approach to the text, therefore, has been conservative. Working from a photocopy of the first edition (held by the British Library ESTC T072264 18th c microfilm reel 6536), I have used the first edition as my copytext, comparing it frequently to the other five Taylor editions of 1719. I have silently accepted the errata listed at the end of the first edition and have changed obvious printers' errors as described above. I have not, however, standardized or modernized the often inconsistent spelling. Most of the words whose spelling seems archaic are nonetheless homophonic with today's spelling (shoar/shore, cargoe/cargo, etc.), and I have indicated potential confusion (e.g., *humane* for *human*) in footnotes. I have generally retained the punctuation of the first edition, except in cases where the meaning of the prose is seriously undermined, in which cases I have relied on the punctuation from later editions. Those cases are enumerated in the list that follows. I have also retained the italics and capitalization of the first edition.

---

1   Karl D. Bülbring, ed. *The Compleat English Gentleman* (London, 1890) xix.

Except for printers' errors and the published errata, the following list enumerates the changes made from the first edition. The first phrase indicates the text as it occurs in this edition; the second indicates the punctuation of the first edition.

p. 51: God knows, on the first] God knows. On the first

p. 51: Waves to rise] Winds to rise

p. 52: *Storm, why*] *Storm why*

p. 54: bitter End] better End

p. 57: *Seafaring Man. Why*] *Seafaring Man,* why

p. 68: waste] wast

p. 70: we got off the Hide] we got of the Hide

p. 78: State of Health] State Health of

p. 80: Partners in the Voyage, I] Partners in the Voyage. I

p. 80: the first of September, 1659, being] the   th of   ,
       being

p. 81: *Guiana*] *Guinea*

p. 89: belonging to the Boat] belong to the Boat

p. 123: in Reach of my Bed;] in Reach of my Bed?

p. 131: own Weight, I took] own Weight. I took

p. 132: render] rend

p. 136: abroad in the Rain, I took Care] abroad in the Rain.
        I took Care

p. 138: Twenty Leagues off.] Twenty Leagues of.

p. 151: That if I] That I if

p. 159: my Ink's being wasted] my Ink's, being wasted

p. 160: shoot] shoor

p. 164: my Boat along] my Boat a long

p. 165: or who have been]or, who have been

p. 165: the other Side, I say] the other Side. I say

p. 167: to get it about; as to the East Side] to get it about as to
        the East Side

p. 173: this, instead] this. Instead

p. 173: *Moletta*-like] *Moletta*, like

p. 174: farther off, being] farther of, being

p. 187: Gun once off] Gun once of

p. 191: Knowledge of me] Knowledge me

p. 197: loose] lose

p. 201: Arms as I was; I perceiv'd] Arms as I was. I
        perceiv'd

p. 223: could not be, but] could not be; but

p. 224: accordingly] according

p. 232: possibly] possible
p. 246: undermost, wisely] undermost wisely
p. 291: when (seeing the Winter] when seeing the Winter
p. 291: of Man) I propos'd] of Man. I propos'd
p. 296: said I to him, *Friday*] said I to him *Friday*

THE
LIFE
AND
STRANGE SURPRIZING
ADVENTURES
OF
ROBINSON CRUSOE,
Of *YORK,* MARINER:

Who lived Eight and Twenty Years,
all alone in an un-inhabited Ifland on the
Coaft of AMERICA, near the Mouth of
the Great River of OROONOQUE;

Having been caft on Shore by Shipwreck, wherein all the Men perifhed but himfelf.

WITH

An Account how he was at laft as ftrangely deliver'd by PYRATES.

Written by Himfelf.

LONDON:

Printed for W. TAYLOR at the *Ship* in *Pater-Nofter-
Row.* MDCCXIX.

Title page of the first edition. By permission of The Huntington
Library, San Marino, California.

Crusoe's island, from *Serious Reflections during the Life and Surprising Adventures of Robinson Crusoe* (1720).
By permission of the William Andrews Clark Memorial Library.

THE PREFACE

If ever the Story of any private Man's Adventures in the World were worth making Publick, and were acceptable when Publish'd, the Editor of this Account thinks this will be so.

The Wonders of this Man's Life exceed all that (he thinks) is to be found extant; the Life of one Man being scarce capable of a greater Variety.

The Story is told with Modesty, with Seriousness, and with a religious Application of Events to the Uses to which wise Men always apply them (viz.[1]) to the Instruction of others by this Example, and to justify and honour the Wisdom of Providence in all the Variety of our Circumstances, let them happen how they will.

The Editor believes the thing to be a just History of Fact; neither is there any Appearance of Fiction in it: And however thinks, because all such things are dispatch'd,[2] that the Improvement of it, as well to the Diversion, as to the Instruction of the Reader, will be the same; and as such, he thinks, without farther Compliment to the World, he does them a great Service in the Publication.

---

1 That is to say, namely. Defoe uses the abbreviation *viz* (short for the Latin *videlicet*) frequently throughout *Crusoe* to introduce an explanation or amplification.

2 To dispose of something quickly, to finish. The implication is that this kind of writing will be read quickly.

THE
LIFE
AND
ADVENTURES
OF
ROBINSON CRUSOE, &c.

I was born in the Year 1632, in the City of *York*, of a good Family, tho' not of that Country, my Father being a Foreigner of *Bremen*, who settled first at *Hull*: He got a good Estate by Merchandise, and leaving off his Trade, lived afterward at *York*, from whence he had married my Mother, whose Relations were named *Robinson*, a very good Family in that Country, and from whom I was called *Robinson Kreutznaer*;[1] but by the usual Corruption of Words in *England*, we are now called, nay we call our selves, and write our Name *Crusoe*, and so my Companions always call'd me.

I had two elder Brothers, one of which was Lieutenant Collonel to an *English* Regiment of Foot in *Flanders*, formerly commanded by the famous Coll. *Lockhart,* and was killed at the Battle near *Dunkirk* against the *Spaniards*:[2] What became of my second Brother I never knew any more than my Father or Mother did know what was become of me.

Being the third Son of the Family, and not bred to any Trade, my Head began to be fill'd very early with rambling Thoughts: My Father, who was very ancient, had given me a competent Share of Learning, as far as House-Education, and a Country Free-School generally goes, and design'd me for the Law; but I would be satisfied with nothing but going to Sea, and my Inclination to this led me so strongly against the Will, nay the Commands of my Father, and against all the Entreaties and Perswasions of my Mother and other Friends, that there seem'd to be something fatal in that Propension of Nature tending directly to the Life of Misery which was to befal me.

My Father, a wise and grave Man, gave me serious and excellent Counsel against what he foresaw was my Design. He call'd

---

1   The German name suggests either "nearer the cross" or "to cruise, to journey" [Ayers, p. 405].

2   In June 1658 Sir William Lockhart (1621-75) was sent by Oliver Cromwell to reinforce French troops against the Spanish in the Battle of the Dunes, leading to the Spanish surrender of Dunkirk. Dunkirk remained an English possession for several years, and the battle was seen as an important victory in the expensive and unpopular Anglo-Spanish war.

me one Morning into his Chamber, where he was confined by the Gout, and expostulated very warmly with me upon this Subject: He ask'd me what Reasons more than a meer wandring Inclination I had for leaving my Father's House and my native Country, where I might be well introduced, and had a Prospect of raising my Fortunes by Application and Industry, with a Life of Ease and Pleasure. He told me it was for Men of desperate Fortunes on one Hand, or of aspiring, superior Fortune on the other, who went abroad upon Adventures, to rise by Enterprize, and make themselves famous in Undertakings of a Nature out of the common Road; that these things were all either too far above me, or too far below me; that mine was the middle State, or what might be called the upper Station of *Low Life*, which he had found by long Experience was the best State in the World, the most suited to human Happiness, not exposed to the Miseries and Hardships, the Labour and Sufferings of the mechanick[1] Part of Mankind, and not embarass'd with the Pride, Luxury, Ambition and Envy of the upper Part of Mankind. He told me, I might judge of the Happiness of this State, by this one thing, *viz.* That this was the State of Life which all other People envied, that Kings have frequently lamented the miserable Consequences of being born to great things, and wish'd they had been placed in the Middle of the two Extremes, between the Mean and the Great; that the wise Man gave his Testimony to this as the just Standard of true Felicity, when he prayed to have neither Poverty or Riches.[2]

He bid me observe it, and I should always find, that the Calamities of Life were shared among the upper and lower Part of Mankind; but that the middle Station had the fewest Disasters, and was not expos'd to so many Vicissitudes as the higher or lower Part of Mankind; nay, they were not subjected to so many Distempers[3] and Uneasinesses either of Body or Mind, as those were who, by vicious Living, Luxury and Extravagancies on one

---

1 Employed in manual labor.
2 Proverbs 30: 8-9: "Remove far from me vanity and lies: give me neither poverty nor riches; feed me with food convenient for me: Lest I be full, and deny thee, and say, Who is the LORD? or lest I be poor, and steal, and take the name of my God in vain." The "wise man" is King Solomon, to whom the Book of Proverbs has been traditionally attributed. (Biblical quotations in the notes come from the King James Version, first published in 1611, the standard translation used in Protestant churches during Defoe's lifetime.)
3 Illnesses, disorders.

Hand, or by hard Labour, Want of Necessaries, and mean or insufficient Diet on the other Hand, bring Distempers upon themselves by the natural Consequences of their Way of Living; *That* the middle Station of Life was calculated for all kind of Vertues and all kinds of Enjoyments; that Peace and Plenty were the Hand-maids of a middle Fortune; that Temperance, Moderation, Quietness, Health, Society, all agreeable Diversions, and all desirable Pleasures, were the Blessings attending the middle Station of Life; that this Way Men went silently and smoothly thro' the World, and comfortably out of it, not embarass'd with[1] the Labours of the Hands or of the Head, not sold to the Life of Slavery for daily Bread, or harrast with perplex'd Circumstances, which rob the Soul of Peace, and the Body of Rest; not enrag'd with the Passion of Envy, or secret burning Lust of Ambition for great things; but in easy Circumstances sliding gently thro' the World, and sensibly tasting the Sweets of living, without the bitter, feeling that they are happy, and learning by every Day's Experience to know it more sensibly.

After this, he press'd me earnestly, and in the most affectionate manner, not to play the young Man, not to precipitate[2] my self into Miseries which Nature and the Station of Life I was born in, seem'd to have provided against; that I was under no Necessity of seeking my Bread; that he would do well for me, and endeavour to enter me fairly into the Station of Life which he had been just recommending to me; and that if I was not very easy and happy in the World, it must be my meer Fate or Fault that must hinder it, and that he should have nothing to answer for, having thus discharg'd his Duty in warning me against Measures which he knew would be to my Hurt: In a word, that as he would do very kind things for me if I would stay and settle at Home as he directed, so he would not have so much Hand in my Misfortunes, as to give me any Encouragement to go away: And to close all, he told me I had my elder Brother for an Example, to whom he had used the same earnest Perswasions to keep him from going into the Low Country Wars, but could not prevail, his young Desires prompting him to run into the Army where he was kill'd; and tho' he said he would not cease to pray for me, yet he would venture to say to me, that if I did take this foolish Step, God would not bless me, and I would have Leisure hereafter to

---

1 Obstructed by, held back by.
2 To throw into an undesirable state.

reflect upon having neglected his Counsel when there might be none to assist in my Recovery.

I observed in this last Part of his Discourse, which was truly Prophetick, tho' I suppose my Father did not know it to be so himself; I say, I observed the Tears run down his Face very plentifully, and especially when he spoke of my Brother who was kill'd; and that when he spoke of my having Leisure to repent, and none to assist me, he was so mov'd, that he broke off the Discourse, and told me, his Heart was so full he could say no more to me.

I was sincerely affected with this Discourse, as indeed who could be otherwise; and I resolv'd not to think of going abroad any more, but to settle at home according to my Father's Desire. But alas! a few Days wore it all off; and in short, to prevent any of my Father's farther Importunities, in a few Weeks after, I resolv'd to run quite away from him. However, I did not act so hastily neither as my first Heat of Resolution prompted, but I took my Mother, at a time when I thought her a little pleasanter than ordinary, and told her, that my Thoughts were so entirely bent upon seeing the World, that I should never settle to any thing with Resolution enough to go through with it, and my Father had better give me his Consent than force me to go without it; that I was now Eighteen Years old, which was too late to go Apprentice to a Trade,[1] or Clerk to an Attorney; that I was sure if I did, I should never serve out my time, and I should certainly run away from my Master before my Time was out, and go to Sea; and if she would speak to my Father to let me go but one Voyage abroad, if I came home again and did not like it, I would go no more, and I would promise by a double Diligence to recover that Time I had lost.

This put my Mother into a great Passion: She told me, she knew it would be to no Purpose to speak to my Father upon any such Subject; that he knew too well what was my Interest to give his Consent to any thing so much for my Hurt, and that she wondered how I could think of any such thing after such a Discourse as I had had with my Father, and such kind and tender Expressions as she knew my Father had us'd to me; and that in short, if I would ruine my self there was no Help for me; but I might depend I should never have their Consent to it: That for her Part she would not have so much Hand in my Destruction; and I should never have it to say, that my Mother was willing when my Father was not.

---

1 Typically, an apprenticeship began at age fourteen.

Tho' my Mother refused to move[1] it to my Father, yet as I have heard afterwards, she reported all the Discourse to him, and that my Father, after shewing a great Concern at it, said to her with a Sigh, That Boy might be happy if he would stay at home, but if he goes abroad he will be the miserablest Wretch that was ever born: I can give no Consent to it.

It was not till almost a Year after this that I broke loose, tho' in the mean time I continued obstinately deaf to all Proposals of settling to Business, and frequently expostulating with my Father and Mother, about their being so positively determin'd against what they knew my Inclinations prompted me to. But being one Day at *Hull*, where I went casually, and without any Purpose of making an Elopement[2] that time; but I say, being there, and one of my Companions being going by Sea to *London*, in his Father's Ship, and prompting me to go with them, with the common Allurement of Seafaring Men, *viz.* That it should cost me nothing for my Passage, I consulted neither Father or Mother any more, nor so much as sent them Word of it; but leaving them to hear of it as they might, without asking God's Blessing, or my Father's, without any Consideration of Circumstances or Consequences, and in an ill Hour, God knows, on the first of *September* 1651 I went on Board a Ship bound for *London*; never any young Adventurer's Misfortunes, I believe, began sooner, or continued longer than mine. The Ship was no sooner gotten out of the *Humber*,[3] but the Wind began to blow, and the Waves to rise in a most frightful manner; and as I had never been at Sea before, I was most inexpressibly sick in Body, and terrify'd in my Mind: I began now seriously to reflect upon what I had done, and how justly I was overtaken by the Judgment of Heaven for my wicked leaving my Father's House, and abandoning my Duty; all the good Counsel of my Parents, my Father's Tears and my Mother's Entreaties came now fresh into my Mind, and my Conscience, which was not yet come to the Pitch of Hardness to which it has been since, reproach'd me with the Contempt of Advice, and the Breach of my Duty to God and my Father.

All this while the Storm encreas'd, and the Sea, which I had never been upon before, went very high, tho' nothing like what I have seen many times since; no, nor like what I saw a few Days after: But it was enough to affect me then, who was but a young

---

1 To propose.
2 Running away.
3 An estuary on the east coast of northern England.

Sailor, and had never known any thing of the matter. I expected every Wave would have swallowed us up, and that every time the Ship fell down, as I thought, in the Trough or Hollow of the Sea, we should never rise more; and in this Agony of Mind, I made many Vows and Resolutions, that if it would please God here to spare my Life this one Voyage, if ever I got once my Foot upon dry Land again, I would go directly home to my Father, and never set it into a Ship again while I liv'd; that I would take his Advice, and never run my self into such Miseries as these any more. Now I saw plainly the Goodness of his Observations about the middle Station of Life, how easy, how comfortably he had liv'd all his Days, and never had been expos'd to Tempests at Sea, or Troubles on Shore; and I resolv'd that I would, like a true repenting Prodigal, go home to my Father.[1]

These wise and sober Thoughts continued all the while the Storm continued, and indeed some time after; but the next Day the Wind was abated and the Sea calmer, and I began to be a little inur'd to it: However I was very grave for all that Day, being also a little Sea sick still; but towards Night the Weather clear'd up, the Wind was quite over, and a charming fine Evening follow'd; the Sun went down perfectly clear and rose so the next Morning; and having little or no Wind and a smooth Sea, the Sun shining upon it, the Sight was, as I thought, the most delightful that ever I saw.

I had slept well in the Night, and was now no more Sea sick but very chearful, looking with Wonder upon the Sea that was so rough and terrible the Day before, and could be so calm and so pleasant in so little time after. And now least[2] my good Resolutions should continue, my Companion, who had indeed entic'd me away, comes to me, *Well* Bob, says he, clapping me on the Shoulder, *How do you do after it? I warrant you were frighted, wa'n't you, last Night, when it blew but a Cap full of Wind? A Cap full d'you call it?* said I, *'twas a terrible Storm: A Storm, you Fool you,* replies he, *do you call that a Storm, why it was nothing at all; give us but a good Ship and Sea Room, and we think nothing of such a Squal of Wind as that; but you're but a fresh Water Sailor,* Bob; *come let us make a Bowl of Punch and we'll forget all that, d'ye see what charm-*

---

1 In Jesus' parable of the prodigal son (Luke 15: 11-32), a younger son asks his father for his inheritance, spends it profligately in a foreign country, and eventually returns home repentant. His father kills the prize calf for him, "For this my son was dead, and is alive again; he was lost, and is found."

2 Lest.

ing Weather 'tis now. To make short this sad Part of my Story, we went the old way of all Sailors, the Punch was made, and I was made drunk with it, and in that one Night's Wickedness I drowned all my Repentance, all my Reflections upon my past Conduct, and all my Resolutions for my future. In a word, as the Sea was returned to its Smoothness of Surface and settled Calmness by the Abatement of that Storm, so the Hurry of my Thoughts being over, my Fears and Apprehensions of being swallow'd up by the Sea being forgotten, and the Current of my former Desires return'd, I entirely forgot the Vows and Promises that I made in my Distress. I found indeed some Intervals of Reflection, and the serious Thoughts did, as it were endeavour to return again sometimes, but I shook them off, and rouz'd my self from them as it were from a Distemper, and applying my self to Drink and Company, soon master'd the Return of those Fits, for so I call'd them, and I had in five or six Days got as compleat a Victory over Conscience as any young Fellow that resolv'd not to be troubled with it, could desire: But I was to have another Trial for it still; and Providence, as in such Cases generally it does, resolv'd to leave me entirely without Excuse. For if I would not take this for a Deliverance, the next was to be such a one as the worst and most harden'd Wretch among us would confess both the Danger and the Mercy.

The sixth Day of our being at Sea we came into *Yarmouth* Roads; the Wind having been contrary, and the Weather calm, we had made but little Way since the Storm. Here we were obliged to come to an Anchor, and here we lay, the Wind continuing contrary, *viz.* at South-west, for seven or eight Days, during which time a great many Ships from *Newcastle* came into the same Roads, as the common Harbour where the Ships might wait for a Wind for the River.

We had not however rid here so long, but should have Tided it up the River, but that the Wind blew too fresh; and after we had lain four or five Days, blew very hard. However, the Roads being reckoned as good as a Harbour, the Anchorage good, and our Ground-Tackle very strong, our Men were unconcerned, and not in the least apprehensive of Danger, but spent the Time in Rest and Mirth, after the manner of the Sea; but the eighth Day in the Morning, the Wind increased, and we had all Hands at Work to strike our Top-Masts,[1] and make every thing snug and close, that

---

1 Even with the furled sails taken down, the bare poles still create significant wind resistance; hence, the crew has taken down the top mast.

two much wind for the ship the Ship might ride as easy as possible. By Noon the Sea went very high indeed, and our Ship rid *Forecastle in*,[1] shipp'd several Seas, and we thought once or twice our Anchor had come home;[2] upon which our Master order'd out the Sheet Anchor;[3] so that we rode with two Anchors a-Head, and the Cables vered out to the bitter End.[4]

By this Time it blew a terrible Storm indeed, and now I began to see Terror and Amazement in the Faces even of the Seamen themselves. The Master, tho' vigilant to the Business of preserving the Ship, yet as he went in and out of his Cabbin by me, I could hear him softly to himself say several times, *Lord be merciful to us, we shall be all lost, we shall be all undone*; and the like. During these first Hurries, I was stupid,[5] lying still in my Cabbin, which was in the Steerage, and cannot describe my Temper: I could ill re-assume the first Penitence, which I had so apparently trampled upon, and harden'd my self against: I thought the Bitterness of Death had been past,[6] and that this would be nothing too like the first. But when the Master himself came by me, as I said just now, and said we should be all lost, I was dreadfully frighted: I got up out of my Cabbin, and look'd out; but such a dismal Sight I never saw: The Sea went Mountains high, and broke upon us every three or four Minutes: When I could look about, I could see nothing but Distress round us: Two Ships that rid near us we found had cut their Masts by the Board,[7] being deep loaden; and our Men cry'd out, that a Ship which rid about a Mile a-Head of us was foundered. Two more Ships being driven from their Anchors, were run out of the Roads to Sea at all Adventures,[8] and that with not a Mast standing. The light Ships fared the best, as not so much labouring in the Sea; but two or

---

1 The bow of the ship is dipping underwater.
2 Become detached from the sea floor.
3 A heavy anchor used in emergencies.
4 Every last bit of anchor cable is extended.
5 Stupefied, stunned into insensibility.
6 1 Samuel 15: 32-33: "Then said Samuel, Bring ye hither to me Agag the king of the Amalekites. And Agag came unto him delicately. And Agag said, Surely the bitterness of death is past. And Samuel said, As thy sword hath made women childless, so shall thy mother be childless among women. And Samuel hewed Agag in pieces before the LORD in Gilgal."
7 The crews have cut down their masts close to the deck in an attempt to stabilize the ship.
8 No matter what the consequences might be.

three of them drove, and came close by us, running away with only their Sprit-sail out before the Wind.

Towards Evening the Mate and Boat-Swain begg'd the Master of our Ship to let them cut away the Foremast, which he was very unwilling to: But the Boat-Swain protesting to him, that if he did not, the Ship would founder, he consented; and when they had cut away the Foremast, the Main-Mast stood so loose, and shook the Ship so much, they were obliged to cut her away also, and make a clear Deck.

Any one may judge what a Condition I must be in at all this, who was but a young Sailor, and who had been in such a Fright before at but a little. But if I can express at this Distance the Thoughts I had about me at that time, I was in tenfold more Horror of Mind upon Account of my former Convictions, and the having returned from them to the Resolutions I had wickedly taken at first, than I was at Death it self; and these added to the Terror of the Storm, put me into such a Condition, that I can by no Words describe it. But the worst was not come yet, the Storm continued with such Fury, that the Seamen themselves acknowledged they had never known a worse. We had a good Ship, but she was deep loaden, and wallowed in the Sea, that the Seamen every now and then cried out, she would founder. It was my Advantage in one respect, that I did not know what they meant by Founder, till I enquir'd. However, the Storm was so violent, that I saw what is not often seen, the Master, the Boat-Swain, and some others more sensible than the rest, at their Prayers, and expecting every Moment when the Ship would go to the Bottom. In the Middle of the Night, and under all the rest of our Distresses, one of the Men that had been down on Purpose to see, cried out we had sprung a Leak; another said there was four Foot Water in the Hold. Then all Hands were called to the Pump. At that very Word my Heart, as I thought, died within me, and I fell backwards upon the Side of my Bed where I sat, into the Cabbin. However, the Men roused me, and told me, that I that was able to do nothing before, was as well able to pump as another; at which I stirr'd up, and went to the Pump and work'd very heartily. While this was doing, the Master seeing some light Colliers,[1] who not able to ride out the Storm, were oblig'd to slip[2] and run away to Sea, and would come near us, ordered to fire a Gun as a Signal of Distress. I who knew nothing what that meant,

---

1 Coal ships.

2 To release the anchor.

was so surprised, that I thought the Ship had broke, or some dreadful thing had happen'd. In a word, I was so surprised, that I fell down in a Swoon. As this was a time when every Body had his own Life to think of, no Body minded me, or what was become of me; but another Man stept up to the Pump, and thrusting me aside with his Foot, let me lye, thinking I had been dead; and it was a great while before I came to my self.

We work'd on, but the Water encreasing in the Hold, it was apparent that the Ship would founder, and tho' the Storm began to abate a little, yet as it was not possible she could swim till we might run into a Port, so the Master continued firing Guns for Help; and a light Ship who had rid it out just a Head of us ventured a Boat out to help us. It was with the utmost Hazard the Boat came near us, but it was impossible for us to get on Board, or for the Boat to lie near the Ship Side, till at last the Men rowing very heartily, and venturing their Lives to save ours, our Men cast them a Rope over the Stern with a Buoy to it, and then vered it out a great Length, which they after great Labour and Hazard took hold of and we hall'd[1] them close under our Stern and got all into their Boat. It was to no Purpose for them or us after we were in the Boat to think of reaching to their own Ship, so all agreed to let her drive and only to pull her in towards Shore as much as we could, and our Master promised them, That if the Boat was stav'd[2] upon Shore he would make it good to their Master, so partly rowing and partly driving our Boat went away to the Norward sloaping towards the Shore almost as far as *Winterton Ness*.

We were not much more than a quarter of an Hour out of our Ship but we saw her sink, and then I understood for the first time what was meant by a Ship foundering in the Sea; I must acknowledge I had hardly Eyes to look up when the Seamen told me she was sinking; for from that Moment they rather put me into the Boat than that I might be said to go in, my Heart was as it were dead within me, partly with Fright, partly with Horror of Mind and the Thoughts of what was yet before me.

While we were in this Condition, the Men yet labouring at the Oar to bring the Boat near the Shore, we could see, when our Boat mounting the Waves, we were able to see the Shore, a great many People running along the Shore to assist us when we should come near, but we made but slow way towards the Shore,

---

1 Hauled.
2 Smashed, broken open.

nor were we able to reach the Shore, till being past the Light-House at *Winterton,* the Shore falls off to the Westward towards *Cromer,* and so the Land broke off a little the Violence of the Wind: Here we got in, and tho' not without much Difficulty got all safe on Shore and walk'd afterwards on Foot to *Yarmouth,* where, as unfortunate Men, we were used with great Humanity as well by the Magistrates of the Town, who assign'd us good Quarters, as by particular Merchants and Owners of Ships, and had Money given us sufficient to carry us either to *London* or back to *Hull,* as we thought fit.

Had I now had the Sense to have gone back to *Hull,* and have gone home, I had been happy, and my Father, an Emblem[1] of our Blessed Saviour's Parable, had even kill'd the fatted Calf for me;[2] for hearing the Ship I went away in was cast away in *Yarmouth* Road, it was a great while before he had any Assurance that I was not drown'd.

But my ill Fate push'd me on now with an Obstinacy that nothing could resist; and tho' I had several times loud Calls from my Reason and my more composed Judgment to go home, yet I had no Power to do it. I know not what to call this, nor will I urge, that it is a secret over ruling Decree that hurries us on to be the Instruments of our own Destruction, even tho' it be before us, and that we rush upon it with our Eyes open. Certainly nothing but some such decreed unavoidable Misery attending, and which it was impossible for me to escape, could have push'd me forward against the calm Reasonings and Perswasions of my most retired Thoughts, and against two such visible Instructions as I had met with in my first Attempt.

My Comrade, who had help'd to harden me before, and who was the Master's Son, was now less forward than I; the first time he spoke to me after we were at *Yarmouth,* which was not till two or three Days, for we were separated in the Town to several Quarters; I say, the first time he saw me, it appear'd his Tone was alter'd, and looking very melancholy and shaking his Head, ask'd me how I did, and telling his Father who I was, and how I had come this Voyage only for a Trial in order to go farther abroad; his Father turning to me with a very grave and concern'd Tone, *Young Man,* says he, *you ought never to go to Sea any more, you ought to take this for a plain and visible Token that you are not to be a Seafaring Man.* Why, Sir, said I, will you go to Sea no more?

---

1 Representation, type.
2 See p. 52, note 1.

That is another Case, said he, *it is my Calling, and therefore my Duty; but as you made this Voyage for a Trial, you see what a Taste Heaven has given you of what you are to expect if you persist; perhaps this is all befallen us on your Account, like* Jonah *in the Ship of* Tarshish.[1] *Pray*, continues he, *what are you? and on what Account did you go to Sea?* Upon that I told him some of my Story; at the End of which he burst out with a strange kind of Passion, What had I done, says he, that such an unhappy Wretch should come into my Ship? I would not set my Foot in the same Ship with thee again for a Thousand Pounds. This indeed was, as I said, an Excursion[2] of his Spirits which were yet agitated by the Sense of his Loss, and was farther than he could have Authority to go. However he afterwards talk'd very gravely to me, exhorted me to go back to my Father, and not tempt Providence to my Ruine; told me I might see a visible Hand of Heaven against me, *And young Man*, said he, *depend upon it, if you do not go back, where-ever you go, you will meet with nothing but Disasters and Disappointments till your Father's Words are fulfilled upon you.*

We parted soon after; for I made him little Answer, and I saw him no more; which way he went, I know not. As for me, having some Money in my Pocket, I travelled to *London* by Land; and there, as well as on the Road, had many Struggles with my self, what Course of Life I should take, and whether I should go Home, or go to Sea.

As to going Home, Shame opposed the best Motions that offered to my Thoughts; and it immediately occurr'd to me how I should be laugh'd at among the Neighbours, and should be asham'd to see, not my Father and Mother only, but even every Body else; from whence I have since often observed, how incongruous and irrational the common Temper of Mankind is, especially of Youth, to that Reason which ought to guide them in such Cases, *viz.* That they are not asham'd to sin, and yet are asham'd to repent; not asham'd of the Action for which they ought justly to be esteemed Fools, but are asham'd of the returning, which only can make them be esteem'd wise Men.

In this State of Life however I remained some time, uncertain what Measures to take, and what Course of Life to lead. An irre-

---

1 In Jonah 1, the prophet Jonah attempts to flee from God by sailing to Tarshish. When the ship nearly breaks apart in a storm, the sailors throw Jonah overboard, saving themselves and leaving Jonah to be swallowed by a fish.

2 An outburst.

sistible Reluctance continu'd to going Home; and as I stay'd a while, the Remembrance of the Distress I had been in wore off; and as that abated, the little Motion I had in my Desires to a Return wore off with it, till at last I quite lay'd aside the Thoughts of it, and lookt out for a Voyage.

That evil Influence which carryed me first away from my Father's House, that hurried me into the wild and indigested[1] Notion of raising my Fortune; and that imprest those Conceits so forcibly upon me, as to make me deaf to all good Advice, and to the Entreaties and even Command of my Father: I say the same Influence, whatever it was, presented the most unfortunate of all Enterprises to my View; and I went on board a Vessel bound to the Coast of *Africa*; or, as our Sailors vulgarly call it, a Voyage to *Guinea*.[2]

It was my great Misfortune that in all these Adventures I did not ship my self as a Sailor; whereby, tho' I might indeed have workt a little harder than ordinary, yet at the same time I had learn'd the Duty and Office of a Fore-mast Man; and in time might have qualified my self for a Mate or Lieutenant, if not for a Master: But as it was always my Fate to choose for the worse, so I did here; for having Money in my Pocket, and good Cloaths upon my Back, I would always go on board in the Habit[3] of a Gentleman; and so I neither had any Business in the Ship, or learn'd to do any.

It was my Lot first of all to fall into pretty good Company in *London*, which does not always happen to such loose and unguided young Fellows as I then was; the Devil generally not omitting to lay some Snare for them very early: But it was not so with me, I first fell acquainted with the Master of a Ship who had been on the Coast of *Guinea*; and who having had very good Success there, was resolved to go again; and who taking a Fancy to my Conversation, which was not at all disagreeable at that time, hearing me say I had a mind to see the World, told me if I wou'd go the Voyage with him I should be at no Expence; I should be his Mess-mate and his Companion, and if I could carry any thing with me, I should have all the Advantage of it that the Trade would admit; and perhaps I might meet with some Encouragement.

---

1 Insufficiently considered.
2 A slaving voyage. See Appendix F, "Defoe on Slavery and the African Trade."
3 Attire.

I embrac'd the Offer, and entring into a strict Friendship with this Captain, who was an honest and plain-dealing Man, I went the Voyage with him, and carried a small Adventure[1] with me, which by the disinterested Honesty of my Friend the Captain, I increased very considerably; for I carried about 40 *l*.[2] in such Toys and Trifles as the Captain directed me to buy. This 40 *l.* I had mustered together by the Assistance of some of my Relations whom I corresponded with, and who, I believe, got my Father, or at least my Mother, to contribute so much as that to my first Adventure.

This was the only Voyage which I may say was successful in all my Adventures, and which I owe to the Integrity and Honesty of my Friend the Captain, under whom also I got a competent Knowledge of the Mathematicks and the Rules of Navigation, learn'd how to keep an Account of the Ship's Course, take an Observation; and in short, to understand some things that were needful to be understood by a Sailor: For, as he took Delight to introduce me, I took Delight to learn; and, in a word, this Voyage made me both a Sailor and a Merchant; for I brought Home *L.* 5. 9 *Ounces* of Gold Dust for my Adventure, which yielded me in *London* at my Return, almost 300 *l.* and this fill'd me with those aspiring Thoughts which have since so compleated my Ruin.

Yet even in this Voyage I had my Misfortunes too; particularly, that I was continually sick, being thrown into a violent Calenture[3] by the excessive Heat of the Climate; our principal Trading being upon the Coast, from the Latitude of 15 Degrees, North even to the Line[4] it self.

I was now set up for a *Guiney* Trader;[5] and my Friend, to my great Misfortune, dying soon after his Arrival, I resolved to go the same Voyage again, and I embark'd in the same Vessel with one who was his Mate in the former Voyage, and had now got the Command of the Ship. This was the unhappiest Voyage that ever Man made; for tho' I did not carry quite 100 *l.* of my new gain'd Wealth, so that I had 200 left, and which I lodg'd with my Friend's Widow, who was very just to me, yet I fell into terrible Misfortunes in this Voyage; and the first was this, *viz.* Our Ship making her Course towards the *Canary* Islands, or rather

---

1 A financial venture, speculation.
2 £40.
3 Tropical fever accompanied by hallucinations.
4 The equator.
5 Someone who trades with the coast of Africa, especially a slave trader.

between those Islands and the *African* Shore, was surprised in the Grey of the Morning, by a *Turkish* Rover of *Sallee*,[1] who gave Chase to us with all the Sail she could make. We crowded also as much Canvass as our Yards would spread, or our Masts carry, to have got clear; but finding the Pirate gain'd upon us, and would certainly come up with us in a few Hours, we prepar'd to fight; our Ship having 12 Guns, and the Rogue 18. About three in the Afternoon he came up with us, and bringing to by Mistake, just athwart our Quarter, instead of athwart our Stern, as he intended, we brought 8 of our Guns to bear on that Side, and pour'd in a Broadside upon him, which made him sheer off again, after returning our Fire, and pouring in also his small Shot from near 200 Men which he had on Board. However, we had not a Man touch'd, all our Men keeping close. He prepar'd to attack us again, and we to defend our selves; but laying us on Board the next time upon our other Quarter, he entred 60 Men upon our Decks, who immediately fell to cutting and hacking the Decks and Rigging. We ply'd them with Small-shot, Half-Pikes, Powder-Chests, and such like, and clear'd our Deck of them twice. However, to cut short this melancholly Part of our Story, our Ship being disabled, and three of our Men kill'd, and eight wounded, we were obliged to yield, and were carry'd all Prisoners into *Sallee*, a Port belonging to the *Moors*.[2]

The Usage I had there was not so dreadful as at first I apprehended, nor was I carried up the Country to the Emperor's Court, as the rest of our Men were, but was kept by the Captain of the Rover, as his proper Prize, and made his Slave, being young and nimble, and fit for his Business. At this surprising Change of my Circumstances from a Merchant to a miserable Slave, I was perfectly overwhelmed; and now I look'd back upon my Father's prophetick Discourse to me, that I should be miserable, and have none to relieve me, which I thought was now so effectually brought to pass, that it could not be worse; that now the Hand of Heaven had overtaken me, and I was undone without Redemption. But alas! this was but a Taste of the Misery I was to go thro', as will appear in the Sequel of this Story.

---

1 From the sixteenth century to the early nineteenth, the Barbary Coast, which stretched from Morocco to Tripoli, was infamous for the looting and kidnappings by pirates ("rovers"). The Moroccan seaport of Salé was a well-known base.

2 Muslim inhabitants of northwestern Africa.

As my new Patron[1] or Master had taken me Home to his House, so I was in hopes that he would take me with him when he went to Sea again, believing that it would some time or other be his Fate to be taken by a *Spanish* or *Portugal* Man of War; and that then I should be set at Liberty. But this Hope of mine was soon taken away; for when he went to Sea, he left me on Shoar to look after his little Garden, and do the common Drudgery of Slaves about his House; and when he came home again from his Cruise, he order'd me to lye in the Cabbin to look after the Ship.

Here I meditated nothing but my Escape; and what Method I might take to effect it, but found no Way that had the least Probability in it: Nothing presented to make the Supposition of it rational; for I had no Body to communicate it to, that would embark with me; no Fellow-Slave, no *Englishman*, *Irishman*, or *Scotsman* there but my self; so that for two Years, tho' I often pleased my self with the Imagination, yet I never had the least encouraging Prospect of putting it in Practice.

After about two Years an odd Circumstance presented it self, which put the old Thought of making some Attempt for my Liberty, again in my Head: My Patron lying at Home longer than usual, without fitting out his Ship, which, as I heard, was for want of Money; he used constantly, once or twice a Week, sometimes oftner, if the Weather was fair, to take the Ship's Pinnace,[2] and go out into the Road a-fishing; and as he always took me and a young *Maresco*[3] with him to row the Boat, we made him very merry, and I prov'd very dexterous in catching Fish; insomuch that sometimes he would send me with a *Moor*, one of his Kinsmen, and the Youth the *Maresco*, as they call'd him, to catch a Dish of Fish for him.

It happen'd one time, that going a fishing in a stark calm Morning, a Fog rose so thick, that tho' we were not half a League[4] from the Shoar we lost Sight of it; and rowing we knew not whither or which way, we labour'd all Day and all the next Night, and when the Morning came we found we had pull'd off to Sea instead of pulling in for the Shoar; and that we were at least two Leagues from the Shoar: However we got well in again, tho' with a great deal of Labour, and some Danger; for the Wind

---

1 Slave owner (frequently in *Crusoe* spelled *patroon*).
2 A light sailing boat often attending a larger ship.
3 Probably a misprint for *Moresco*, a Moor from Spain.
4 Half a league: one and a half miles.

began to blow pretty fresh in the Morning; but particularly we were all very hungry.

But our Patron warn'd by this Disaster, resolved to take more Care of himself for the future; and having lying by him the Long-boat of our *English* Ship we had taken, he resolved he would not go a fishing any more without a Compass and some Provision; so he ordered the Carpenter of his Ship, who also was an *English* Slave, to build a little State-room or Cabin in the middle of the Long Boat, like that of a Barge, with a Place to stand behind it to steer and hale home the Main-sheet; and Room before for a hand or two to stand and work the Sails; she sail'd with that we call a Shoulder of Mutton Sail; and the Boom gib'd over the Top of the Cabbin, which lay very snug and low, and had in it Room for him to lye, with a Slave or two, and a Table to eat on, with some small Lockers to put in some Bottles of such Liquor as he thought fit to drink in; particularly his Bread, Rice and Coffee.

We went frequently out with this Boat a fishing, and as I was most dextrous to catch fish for him, he never went without me: It happen'd that he had appointed to go out in this Boat, either for Pleasure or for Fish, with two or three *Moors* of some Distinction in that Place, and for whom he had provided extraordinarily; and had therefore sent on board the Boat over Night, a larger Store of Provisions than ordinary; and had order'd me to get ready three Fuzees[1] with Powder and Shot, which were on board his Ship; for that[2] they design'd some Sport of Fowling as well as Fishing.

I got all things ready as he had directed, and waited the next Morning with the Boat, washed clean, her Antient and Pendants out, and every thing to accomodate his Guests; when by and by my Patroon came on board alone, and told me his Guests had put off going, upon some Business that fell out, and order'd me with the Man and Boy, as usual, to go out with the Boat and catch them some Fish, for that his Friends were to sup at his House; and commanded that as soon as I had got some Fish I should bring it home to his House; all which I prepar'd to do.

This Moment my former Notions of Deliverance darted into my Thoughts, for now I found I was like to have a little Ship at my Command; and my Master being gone, I prepar'd to furnish my self, not for a fishing Business but for a Voyage; tho' I knew not, neither did I so much as consider whither I should steer; for any where to get out of that Place was my Way.

[handwritten margin note: plans to use boat to escape]

---

1 A light musket.
2 Because.

My first Contrivance was to make a Pretence to speak to this *Moor*, to get something for our Subsistance on board; for I told him we must not presume to eat of our Patroon's Bread, he said that was true; so he brought a large Basket of Rusk or Bisket of their kind, and three Jarrs with fresh Water into the Boat; I knew where my Patroon's Case of Bottles stood, which it was evident by the make were taken out of some *English* Prize; and I convey'd them into the Boat while the *Moor* was on Shoar, as if they had been there before, for our Master: I convey'd also a great Lump of Bees-Wax into the Boat, which weighed above half a Hundred Weight, with a Parcel of Twine or Thread, a Hatchet, a Saw and a Hammer, all which were of great Use to us afterwards; especially the Wax to make Candles. Another Trick I try'd upon him, which he innocently came into also; his Name was *Ismael*, who they call *Muly* or *Moely*, so I call'd to him, *Moely* said I, our Patroon's Guns are on board the Boat, can you not get a little Powder and Shot, it may be we may kill some *Alcamies* (a Fowl like our *Curlieus*) for our selves, for I know he keeps the Gunner's Stores in the Ship? Yes, *says he*, I'll bring some, and accordingly he brought a great Leather Pouch which held about a Pound and half of Powder, or rather more; and another with Shot, that had five or six Pound, with some Bullets; and put all into the Boat: At the same time I had found some Powder of my Master's in the Great Cabbin, with which I fill'd one of the large Bottles in the Case, which was almost empty; pouring what was in it into another: and thus furnished with every thing needful, we sail'd out of the Port to fish: The Castle which is at the Entrance of the Port knew who we were, and took no Notice of us; and we were not above a Mile out of the Port before we hal'd in our Sail, and set us down to fish: The Wind blew from the N.NE. which was contrary to my Desire; for had it blown southerly I had been sure to have made the Coast of *Spain*, and at least reacht to the Bay of *Cadiz*; but my Resolutions were, blow which way it would, I would be gone from that horrid Place where I was, and leave the rest to Fate.

After we had fisht some time and catcht nothing, for when I had Fish on my Hook, I would not pull them up, that he might not see them; I said to the *Moor*, this will not do, our Master will not be thus serv'd, we must stand farther off: He thinking no harm agreed, and being in the head of the Boat set the Sails; and as I had the Helm I run[1] the Boat out near a League farther, and

---

1 An acceptable past tense in lieu of *ran*.

then brought her too as if I would fish; when giving the Boy the Helm, I stept forward to where the *Moor* was, and making as if I stoopt for something behind him, I took him by Surprize with my Arm under his Twist,[1] and tost him clear over-board into the Sea; he rise immediately, for he swam like a Cork, and call'd to me, begg'd to be taken in, told me he would go all over the World with me; he swam so strong after the Boat that he would have reacht me very quickly, there being but little Wind; upon which I stept into the Cabbin and fetching one of the Fowling-pieces, I presented it at him, and told him, I had done him no hurt, and if he would be quiet I would do him none; but said I, you swim well enough to reach to the Shoar, and the Sea is calm, make the best of your Way to Shoar and I will do you no harm, but if you come near the Boat I'll shoot you thro' the Head; for I am resolved to have my Liberty; so he turn'd himself about and swam for the Shoar, and I make no doubt but he reacht it with Ease, for he was an Excellent Swimmer.

I could ha' been content to ha' taken this *Moor* with me, and ha' drown'd the Boy, but there was no venturing to trust him: When he was gone I turn'd to the Boy, who they call'd *Xury*, and said to him, *Xury*, if you will be faithful to me I'll make you a great Man, but if you will not stroak your Face to be true to me, *that is, swear by* Mahomet *and his Father's Beard*, I must throw you into the Sea too; the Boy smil'd in my Face and spoke so innocently that I could not mistrust him; and swore to be faithful to me, and go all over the World with me.

While I was in View of the *Moor* that was swimming, I stood out directly to Sea with the Boat, rather stretching to Windward, that they might think me gone towards the *Straits*-mouth[2] (as indeed any one that had been in their Wits must ha' been supposed to do), for who would ha' suppos'd we were saild on to the southward to the truly *Barbarian* Coast,[3] where whole Nations of Negroes were sure to surround us with their Canoes, and destroy us; where we could ne'er once go on shoar but we should be devour'd by savage Beasts, or more merciless Savages of humane[4] kind.

But as soon as it grew dusk in the Evening, I chang'd my Course, and steer'd directly South and by East, bending my

---

1 Crotch.
2 Straits of Gibraltar.
3 Crusoe here is punning on the Barbary Coast (see p. 61, note 1).
4 In later editions, the spelling is often altered to *human*.

Course a little toward the East, that I might keep in with the Shoar; and having a fair fresh Gale of Wind, and a smooth quiet Sea, I made such Sail that I believe by the next Day at Three a Clock in the Afternoon, when I first made the Land, I could not be less than 150 Miles South of *Sallee*; quite beyond the Emperor of *Morocco's* Dominions, or indeed of any other King thereabouts, for we saw no People.

Yet such was the Fright I had taken at the *Moors*, and the dreadful Apprehensions I had of falling into their Hands, that I would not stop, or go on Shoar, or come to an Anchor; the Wind continuing fair, 'till I had sail'd in that manner five Days: And then the Wind shifting to the southward, I concluded also that if any of our Vessels were in Chase of me, they also would now give over; so I ventur'd to make to the Coast, and came to an Anchor in the Mouth of a little River, I knew not what, or where; neither what Latitude, what Country, what Nations, or what River: I neither saw, or desir'd to see any People, the principal thing I wanted was fresh Water: We came into this Creek in the Evening, resolving to swim on shoar as soon as it was dark, and discover[1] the Country; but as soon as it was quite dark, we heard such dreadful Noises of the Barking, Roaring, and Howling of Wild Creatures, of we knew not what Kinds, that the poor Boy was ready to die with Fear, and beg'd of me not to go on shoar till Day; well *Xury* said I, then I won't, but it may be we may see Men by Day, who will be as bad to us as those Lyons; *then we give them the shoot Gun* says *Xury* laughing, *make them run wey*; such *English Xury* spoke by conversing among us Slaves, however I was glad to see the Boy so cheerful, and I gave him a Dram[2] (out of our Patroon's Case of Bottles) to chear him up: After all, *Xury's* Advice was good, and I took it, we dropt our little Anchor and lay still all Night; I say still, for we slept none! for in two or three Hours we saw vast great Creatures (we knew not what to call them) of many sorts, come down to the Sea-shoar and run into the Water, wallowing and washing themselves for the Pleasure of cooling themselves; and they made such hideous Howlings and Yellings, that I never indeed heard the like.

Xury was dreadfully frighted, and indeed so was I too; but we were both more frighted when we heard one of these mighty Creatures come swimming towards our Boat, we could not see him, but we might hear him by his blowing to be a monstrous,

---

1 Explore.
2 Small draught, usually swallowed in one gulp.

huge and furious Beast; *Xury* said it was a Lyon, and it might be so for ought I know; but poor *Xury* cryed to me to weigh the Anchor and row away; no says I, *Xury*, we can slip our Cable with the Buoy to it and go off to Sea, they cannot follow us far; I had no sooner said so, but I perceiv'd the Creature (whatever it was) within Two Oars Length, which something surprized me; however I immediately stept to the Cabbin-door, and taking up my Gun fir'd at him, upon which he immediately turn'd about and swam towards the Shoar again.

But it is impossible to describe the horrible Noises, and hideous Cryes and Howlings, that were raised as well upon the Edge of the Shoar, as higher within the Country; upon the Noise or Report of the Gun, a Thing I have some Reason to believe those Creatures had never heard before: This Convinc'd me that there was no going on Shoar for us in the Night upon that Coast, and how to venture on Shoar in the Day was another Question too; for to have fallen into the Hands of any of the Savages, had been as bad as to have fallen into the Hands of Lyons and Tygers; at least we were equally apprehensive of the Danger of it.

Be that as it would, we were oblig'd to go on Shoar somewhere or other for Water, for we had not a Pint left in the Boat; when or where to get to it was the Point: *Xury* said, if I would let him go on Shoar with one of the Jarrs, he would find if there was any Water and bring some to me. I ask'd him why he would go? Why I should not go and he stay in the Boat? The Boy answer'd with so much Affection that made me love him ever after. Says he, *If wild Mans come, they eat me, you go wey.* Well, *Xury*, said I, we will both go, and if the wild Man's come we will kill them, they shall Eat neither of us; so I gave *Xury* a piece of Rusk-bread to Eat and a Dram out of our Patroon's Case of Bottles which I mentioned before; and we hal'd the Boat in as near the Shoar as we thought was proper, and so waded on Shoar, carrying nothing but our Arms and two Jarrs for Water.

I did not care to go out of Sight of the Boat, fearing the coming of Canoes with *Savages* down the River; but the Boy seeing a low Place about a Mile up the Country rambled to it; and by and by I saw him come running towards me, I thought he was pursued by some Savage, or frighted with some wild Beast, and I run forward towards him to help him, but when I came nearer to him, I saw something hanging over his Shoulders which was a Creature that he had shot, like a Hare but different in Colour, and longer Legs, however we were very glad of it, and it was very good Meat; but the great Joy that poor *Xury* came with, was to tell me he had found good Water and seen no wild Mans.

But we found afterwards that we need not take such Pains for Water, for a little higher up the Creek where we were, we found the Water fresh when the Tide was out, which flowed but a little way up; so we filled our Jarrs and feasted on the Hare we had killed, and prepared to go on our Way, having seen no Foot-steps of any humane Creature in that part of the Country.

As I had been one Voyage to this Coast before, I knew very well that the Islands of the *Canaries*,[1] and the *Cape de Verd* Islands[2] also, lay not far off from the Coast. But as I had no Instruments to take an Observation to know what Latitude we were in, and did not exactly know, or at least remember what Latitude they were in; I knew not where to look for them, or when to stand off to Sea towards them; otherwise I might now easily have found some of these Islands. But my hope was, that if I stood along this Coast till I came to that Part where the *English* Traded, I should find some of their Vessels upon their usual Design of Trade, that would relieve and take us in.

By the best of my Calculation, that Place where I now was, must be that Country, which lying between the Emperor of *Morocco's* Dominions and the *Negro's*, lies waste and uninhabited, except by wild Beasts; the *Negroes* having abandon'd it and gone farther South for fear of the *Moors*; and the *Moors* not thinking it worth inhabiting, by reason of its Barrenness; and indeed both forsaking it because of the prodigious Numbers of Tygers, Lyons, Leopards and other furious Creatures which harbour there; so that the *Moors* use it for their Hunting only, where they go like an Army, two or three thousand Men at a time; and indeed for near an hundred Miles together upon this Coast, we saw nothing but a waste uninhabited Country, by Day; and heard nothing but Howlings and Roaring of wild Beasts, by Night.

Once or twice in the Day time, I thought I saw the *Pico* of *Teneriffe*, being the high top of the Mountain *Teneriffe* in the *Canaries*; and had a great mind to venture out in hopes of reaching thither; but having tried twice I was forced in again by contrary Winds, the Sea also going too high for my little Vessel, so I resolved to pursue my first Design and keep along the Shoar.

Several times I was obliged to land for fresh Water, after we had left this Place; and once in particular, being early in the

---

1 An archipelago off the coast of Morocco.
2 A group of islands in the Atlantic, 375 miles west of Senegal.

Morning, we came to an Anchor under a little Point of Land which was pretty high, and the Tide beginning to flow, we lay still to go farther in; *Xury*, whose Eyes were more about him than it seems mine were, calls softly to me, and tells me that we had best go farther off the Shoar; for, says he, look yonder lies a dreadful Monster on the side of that Hillock fast asleep: I look'd where he pointed, and saw a dreadful Monster indeed, for it was a terrible great Lyon that lay on the Side of the Shoar, under the Shade of a Piece of the Hill that hung as it were a little over him. *Xury*, says I, you shall go on Shoar and kill him; *Xury* look'd frighted, and said, *Me kill! he eat me at one Mouth*; one Mouthful he meant; however, I said no more to the Boy, but bad him lye still, and I took our biggest Gun, which was almost Musquet-bore, and loaded it with a good Charge of Powder, and with two Slugs,[1] and laid it down; then I loaded another Gun with two Bullets, and the third, for we had three Pieces, I loaded with five smaller Bullets. I took the best aim I could with the first Piece to have shot him into the Head, but he lay so with his Leg rais'd a little above his Nose, that the Slugs hit his Leg about the Knee, and broke the Bone. He started up growling at first, but finding his Leg broke fell down again, and then got up upon three Legs and gave the most hideous Roar that ever I heard; I was a little suppriz'd that I had not hit him on the Head; however I took up the second Piece immediately, and tho' he began to move off fir'd again, and shot him into the Head, and had the Pleasure to see him drop, and make but little Noise, but lay struggling for Life. Then *Xury* took Heart, and would have me let him go on Shoar: Well, go said I, so the Boy jump'd into the Water, and taking a little Gun in one Hand swam to Shoar with the other Hand, and coming close to the Creature, put the Muzzle of the Piece to his Ear, and shot him into the Head again which dispatch'd[2] him quite.

Shoots lion

This was Game indeed to us, but this was no Food, and I was very sorry to lose three Charges of Powder and Shot upon a Creature that was good for nothing to us. However *Xury* said he would have some of him; so he comes on board, and ask'd me to give him the Hatchet; for what, *Xury*, said I? *Me cut off his Head*, said he. However *Xury* could not cut off his Head, but he cut off a Foot and brought it with him, and it was a monstrous great one.

---

1 Roughly shaped bullets.
2 Killed.

I bethought my self however, that perhaps the Skin of him might one way or other be of some Value to us; and I resolved to take off his Skin if I could. So *Xury* and I went to work with him; but *Xury* was much the better Workman at it, for I knew very ill how to do it. Indeed it took us up both the whole Day, but at last we got off the Hide of him, and spreading it on the top of our Cabbin, the Sun effectually dried it in two Days time, and it afterwards serv'd me to lye upon.

After this Stop we made on to the Southward continually for ten or twelve Days, living very sparing on our Provisions, which began to abate very much, and going no oftner into the Shoar than we were oblig'd to for fresh Water; my Design in this was to make the River *Gambia* or *Sennegall*, that is to say, any where about the *Cape de Verd*, where I was in hopes to meet with some *European* Ship, and if I did not, I knew not what Course I had to take, but to seek out for the *Islands*, or perish there among the *Negroes*. I knew that all the Ships from *Europe*, which sail'd either to the Coast of *Guiney*, or to *Brasil*, or to the *East-Indies*, made this *Cape* or those *Islands*; and in a word, I put the whole of my Fortune upon this single Point, either that I must meet with some Ship, or must perish.

When I had pursued this Resolution about ten Days longer, as I have said, I began to see that the Land was inhabited, and in two or three Places as we sailed by, we saw People stand upon the Shoar to look at us, we could also perceive they were quite Black and Stark-naked. I was once inclin'd to ha' gone on Shoar to them; but *Xury* was my better Councellor, and said to me, *no go, no go*; however I hal'd in nearer the Shoar that I might talk to them, and I found they run along the Shoar by me a good way; I observ'd they had no Weapons in their Hands, except one who had a long slender Stick, which *Xury* said was a Lance, and that they would throw them a great way with good aim; so I kept at a distance, but talk'd with them by Signs as well as I could; and particularly made Signs for some thing to Eat, they beckon'd to me to stop my Boat, and that they would fetch me some Meat; upon this I lower'd the top of my Sail, and lay by, and two of them run up into the Country, and in less than half an Hour came back and brought with them two Pieces of dry Flesh and some Corn, such as is the Produce of their Country, but we neither knew what the one or the other was; however we were willing to accept it, but how to come at it was our next Dispute, for I was not for venturing on Shore to them, and they were as much afraid of us; but they took a safe way for us all, for they brought it to the Shore and laid it down, and went and stood a great way off till we fetch'd it on Board, and then came close to us again.

We made Signs of Thanks to them, for we had nothing to make them amends; but an Opportunity offer'd that very Instant to oblige them wonderfully, for while we were lying by the Shore, came two mighty Creatures one pursuing the other, (as we took it) with great Fury, from the Mountains towards the Sea; whether it was the Male pursuing the Female, or whether they were in Sport or in Rage, we could not tell, any more than we could tell whether it was usual or strange, but I believe it was the latter; because in the first Place, those ravenous Creatures seldom appear but in the Night; and in the second Place, we found the People terribly frighted, especially the Women. The Man that had the Lance or Dart did not fly from them, but the rest did; however as the two Creatures ran directly into the Water, they did not seem to offer to fall upon any of the *Negroes*, but plung'd themselves into the Sea and swam about as if they had come for their Diversion; at last one of them began to come nearer our Boat than at first I expected, but I lay ready for him, for I had loaded my Gun with all possible Expedition, and bad *Xury* load both the other; as soon as he came fairly within my reach, I fir'd, and shot him directly into the Head; immediately he sunk down into the Water, but rose instantly and plung'd up and down as if he was struggling for Life; and so indeed he was, he immediately made to the Shore, but between the Wound which was his mortal Hurt, and the strangling of the Water, he dyed just before he reach'd the Shore.

It is impossible to express the Astonishment of these poor Creatures at the Noise and the Fire of my Gun; some of them were even ready to dye for Fear, and fell down as Dead with the very Terror. But when they saw the Creature dead and sunk in the Water, and that I made Signs to them to come to the Shore; they took Heart and came to the Shore and began to search for the Creature, I found him by his Blood staining the Water, and by the help of a Rope which I slung round him and gave the *Negroes* to hawl, they drag'd him on Shore, and found that it was a most curious Leopard, spotted and fine to an admirable Degree, and the *Negroes* held up their Hands with Admiration to think what it was I had kill'd him with.

The other Creature frighted with the flash of Fire and the Noise of the Gun swam on Shore, and ran up directly to the Mountains from whence they came, nor could I at that Distance know what it was. I found quickly the *Negroes* were for eating the

Flesh of this Creature, so I was willing to have them take it as a Favour from me, which when I made Signs to them that they might take him, they were very thankful for, immediately they fell to work with him, and tho' they had no Knife, yet with a sharpen'd Piece of Wood they took off his Skin as readily, and much more readily than we cou'd have done with a Knife; they offer'd me some of the Flesh, which I declined, making as if I would give it them, but made Signs for the Skin, which they gave me very freely, and brought me a great deal more of their Provision, which tho' I did not understand, yet I accepted; then I made Signs to them for some Water, and held out one of my Jarrs to them, turning it bottom upward, to shew that it was empty, and that I wanted to have it filled. They call'd immediately to some of their Friends, and there came two Women and brought a great Vessel made of Earth, and burnt as I suppose in the Sun; this they set down for me, as before, and I sent *Xury* on Shore with my Jarrs, and filled them all three: The Women were as stark Naked as the Men.

I was now furnished with Roots and Corn, such as it was, and Water, and leaving my friendly *Negroes*, I made forward for about eleven Days more without offering to go near the Shoar, till I saw the Land run out a great Length into the Sea, at about the Distance of four or five Leagues before me, and the Sea being very calm I kept a large offing[1] to make this Point; at length, doubling the Point at about two Leagues from the Land, I saw plainly Land on the other Side to Seaward; then I concluded, as it was most certain indeed, that this was the *Cape de Verd*, and those the *Islands*, call'd from thence *Cape de Verd Islands*. However they were at a great Distance, and I could not well tell what I had best to do, for if I should be taken with a Fresh of Wind I might neither reach one or other.

In this Dilemma, as I was very pensive, I stept into the Cabbin and sat me down, *Xury* having the Helm, when on a suddain the Boy cry'd out, *Master, Master, a Ship with a Sail*, and the foolish Boy was frighted out of his Wits, thinking it must needs be some of his Master's Ships sent to pursue us, when, I knew we were gotten far enough out of their reach. I jump'd out of the Cabbin, and immediately saw not only the Ship, but what she was, (*viz.*) that it was a *Portuguese* Ship, and as I thought was bound to the Coast of *Guinea* for *Negroes*. But when I observ'd the Course she steer'd, I was soon convinc'd they were bound some other way,

---

1 Stayed clear of the land.

and did not design to come any nearer to the Shoar; upon which I stretch'd out to Sea as much as I could, resolving to speak with them if possible.

With all the Sail I could make,[1] I found I should not be able to come in their Way, but that they would be gone by, before I could make any Signal to them; but after I had crowded to the utmost, and began to despair, they it seems saw me by the help of their Perspective-Glasses,[2] and that it was some *European* Boat, which as they supposed must belong to some Ship that was lost, so they shortned Sail to let me come up. I was encouraged with this, and as I had my Patroon's Antient on Board, I made a Waft[3] of it to them for a Signal of Distress, and fir'd a Gun, both which they saw, for they told me they saw the Smoke, tho' they did not hear the Gun; upon these Signals they very kindly brought too, and lay by for me, and in about three Hours time I came up with them.

They ask'd me what I was, in *Portuguese*, and in *Spanish*, and in *French*, but I understood none of them; but at last a *Scots* Sailor who was on board, call'd to me, and I answer'd him, and told him I was an *Englishman*, that I had made my escape out of Slavery from the *Moors* at *Sallee*; then they bad me come on board, and very kindly took me in, and all my Goods. *finds a Portuguese ship*

It was an inexpressible Joy to me, that any one will believe, that I was thus deliver'd, as I esteem'd it, from such a miserable and almost hopeless Condition as I was in, and I immediately offered all I had to the Captain of the Ship, as a Return for my Deliverance; but he generously told me, he would take nothing from me, but that all I had should be deliver'd safe to me when I came to the *Brasils*, for says he, *I have sav'd your Life on no other Terms than I would be glad to be saved my self, and it may one time or other be my Lot to be taken up in the same Condition; besides,* said he, *when I carry you to the* Brasils, *so great a way from your own Country, if I should take from you what you have, you will be starved there, and then I only take away that Life I have given. No, no, Seignor* Inglese, says he, *Mr.* Englishman, *I will carry you thither in Charity, and those things will help you to buy your Subsistance there and your Passage home again.*

As he was Charitable in his Proposal, so he was Just in the Performance to a tittle, for he ordered the Seamen that none should

---

1   The fullest sail possible.
2   Telescopes.
3   Flag used as a signal.

offer to touch any thing I had; then he took every thing into his own Possession, and gave me back an exact Inventory of them, that I might have them, even so much as my three Earthen Jarrs.

As to my Boat it was a very good one, and that he saw, and told me he would buy it of me for the Ship's use, and ask'd me what I would have for it? I told him he had been so generous to me in every thing, that I could not offer to make any Price of the Boat, but left it entirely to him, upon which he told me he would give me a Note of his Hand to pay me 80 Pieces of Eight[1] for it at *Brasil*, and when it came there, if any one offer'd to give more he would make it up; he offer'd me also 60 Pieces of Eight more for my Boy *Xury*, which I was loath to take, not that I was not willing to let the Captain have him, but I was very loath to sell the poor Boy's Liberty, who had assisted me so faithfully in procuring my own. However when I let him know my Reason, he own'd it to be just, and offer'd me this Medium, that he would give the Boy an Obligation to set him free in ten Years, if he turn'd Christian; upon this, and *Xury* saying he was willing to go to him, I let the Captain have him.

We had a very good Voyage to the *Brasils*, and arriv'd in the *Bay de Todos los Santos*, or *All-Saints Bay*, in about Twenty-two Days after. And now I was once more deliver'd from the most miserable of all Conditions of Life, and what to do next with my self I was now to consider.

The generous Treatment the Captain gave me, I can never enough remember; he would take nothing of me for my Passage, gave me twenty Ducats[2] for the Leopard's Skin, and forty for the Lyon's Skin which I had in my Boat, and caused every thing I had in the Ship to be punctually deliver'd me, and what I was willing to sell he bought, such as the Case of Bottles, two of my Guns, and a Piece of the Lump of Bees-wax, for I had made Candles of the rest; in a word, I made about 220 Pieces of Eight of all my Cargo, and with this Stock I went on Shoar in the *Brasils*.

I had not been long here, but being recommended to the House of a good honest Man like himself, who had an *Ingenio* as they call it; that is, a Plantation and a Sugar-House. I lived with him some time, and acquainted my self by that means with the Manner of their planting and making of Sugar; and seeing how well the Planters liv'd, and how they grew rich suddenly, I

---

1 A piece of eight was worth roughly 4 shillings 6 pence. Crusoe thus receives about £18 for the boat and less than £14 for Xury.
2 In 1719, twenty gold ducats would have been worth roughly £10.

resolv'd, if I could get Licence to settle there, I would turn Planter among them, resolving in the mean time to find out some Way to get my Money which I had left in *London* remitted to me. To this Purpose getting a kind of a Letter of Naturalization, I purchased as much Land that was Uncur'd,[1] as my Money would reach, and form'd a Plan for my Plantation and Settlement, and such a one as might be suitable to the Stock which I proposed to my self to receive from *England*.

I had a Neighbour, a *Portugueze* of *Lisbon*, but born of *English* Parents, whose Name was *Wells*, and in much such Circumstances as I was. I call him my Neighbour, because his Plantation lay next to mine, and we went on very sociably together. My Stock was but low as well as his; and we rather planted for Food than any thing else, for about two Years. However, we began to increase, and our Land began to come into Order; so that the third Year we planted some Tobacco, and made each of us a large Piece of Ground ready for planting Canes[2] in the Year to come; but we both wanted Help, and now I found more than before, I had done wrong in parting with my Boy *Xury*.

But alas! for me to do wrong that never did right, was no great Wonder: I had no Remedy but to go on; I was gotten into an Employment quite remote to my Genius, and directly contrary to the Life I delighted in, and for which I forsook my Father's House, and broke thro' all his good Advice; nay, I was coming into the very Middle Station, or upper Degree of low Life, which my Father advised me to before; and which if I resolved to go on with, I might as well ha' staid at Home, and never have fatigu'd my self in the World as I had done; and I used often to say to my self, I could ha' done this as well in *England* among my Friends, as ha' gone 5000 Miles off to do it among Strangers and Salvages[3] in a Wilderness, and at such a Distance, as never to hear from any Part of the World that had the least Knowledge of me.

In this manner I used to look upon my Condition with the utmost Regret. I had no body to converse with but now and then this Neighbour; no Work to be done, but by the Labour of my Hands; and I used to say, I liv'd just like a Man cast away upon some desolate Island, that had no body there but himself. But how just has it been, and how should all Men reflect, that when they compare their present Conditions with others that are

---

1 Not cleared to be cultivated.
2 Sugar cane.
3 Savages.

worse, Heaven may oblige them to make the Exchange, and be convinc'd of their former Felicity by their Experience: I say, how just has it been, that the truly solitary Life I reflected on in an Island of meer Desolation should be my Lot, who had so often unjustly compar'd it with the Life which I then led, in which had I continued, I had in all Probability been exceeding prosperous and rich.

I was in some Degree settled in my Measures for carrying on the Plantation, before my kind Friend the Captain of the Ship that took me up at Sea, went back; for the Ship remained there in providing his Loading, and preparing for his Voyage, near three Months, when telling him what little Stock I had left behind me in *London*, he gave me this friendly and sincere Advice, *Seignior Inglese says he*; for so he always called me, if you will give me Letters, and a Procuration[1] here in Form to me, with Orders to the Person who has your Money in *London*, to send your Effects[2] to *Lisbon*, to such Persons as I shall direct, and in such Goods as are proper for this Country, I will bring you the Produce of them, God willing, at my Return; but since human Affairs are all subject to Changes and Disasters, I would have you give Orders but for One Hundred Pounds *Sterl.*[3] which you say is Half your Stock, and let the Hazard be run for the first; so that if it come safe, you may order the rest the same Way; and if it miscarry, you may have the other Half to have Recourse to for your Supply.

This was so wholesom Advice, and look'd so friendly, that I could not but be convinc'd it was the best Course I could take; so I accordingly prepared Letters to the Gentlewoman with whom I had left my Money, and a Procuration to the *Portuguese* Captain, as he desired.

I wrote the *English* Captain's Widow a full Account of all my Adventures, my Slavery, Escape, and how I had met with the *Portugal* Captain at Sea, the Humanity of his Behaviour, and in what Condition I was now in, with all other necessary Directions for my Supply; and when this honest Captain came to *Lisbon*, he found means by some of the *English* Merchants there, to send over not the Order only, but a full Account of my Story to a Merchant at *London*, who represented it effectually to her; whereupon, she not only delivered the Money, but out of her own

---

1 Authorization to act on Crusoe's behalf.
2 Possessions.
3 Sterling.

Pocket sent the *Portugal* Captain a very handsom Present for his Humanity and Charity to me.

The Merchant in *London* vesting this Hundred Pounds in *English* Goods, such as the Captain had writ for, sent them directly to him at *Lisbon*, and he brought them all safe to me to the *Brasils*, among which, without my Direction (for I was too young in my Business to think of them) he had taken Care to have all Sorts of Tools, Iron-Work, and Utensils necessary for my Plantation, and which were of great Use to me.

When this Cargo arrived, I thought my Fortunes made, for I was surprised with the Joy of it; and my good Steward the Captain had laid out the Five Pounds which my Friend had sent him for a Present for himself, to purchase, and bring me over a Servant under Bond for six Years Service,[1] and would not accept of any Consideration, except a little Tobacco, which I would have him accept, being of my own Produce.

Neither was this all; but my Goods being all *English* Manufactures, such as Cloath, Stuffs, Bays,[2] and things particularly valuable and desirable in the Country, I found means to sell them to a very great Advantage; so that I might say, I had more than four times the Value of my first Cargo, and was now infinitely beyond my poor Neighbour, I mean in the Advancement of my Plantation; for the first thing I did, I bought me a Negro Slave, and an *European* Servant also; I mean another besides that which the Captain brought me from *Lisbon*.

But as abus'd Prosperity is oftentimes made the very Means of our greatest Adversity, so was it with me. I went on the next Year with great Success in my Plantation: I raised fifty great Rolls of Tobacco on my own Ground, more than I had disposed of for Necessaries among my Neighbours; and these fifty Rolls being each of above a 100 *Wt.* were well cur'd and laid by against the Return of the Fleet from *Lisbon*: and now increasing in Business and in Wealth, my Head began to be full of Projects and Undertakings beyond my Reach; such as are indeed often the Ruine of the best Heads in Business.

Had I continued in the Station I was now in, I had room for all the happy things to have yet befallen me, for which my Father so earnestly recommended a quiet retired Life, and of which he

---

1 An indentured servant; in this case, someone who contracted to work for six years in exchange for passage to Brazil.
2 *Baize*: a coarse wool.

had so sensibly describ'd the middle Station of Life to be full of; but other things attended me, and I was still to be the wilful Agent of all my own Miseries; and particularly to encrease my Fault and double the Reflections upon my self, which in my future Sorrows I should have leisure to make; all these Miscarriages were procured by my apparent obstinate adhering to my foolish inclination of wandring abroad and pursuing that Inclination, in contradiction to the clearest Views of doing my self good in a fair and plain pursuit of those Prospects and those measures of Life, which Nature and Providence concurred to present me with, and to make my Duty.

As I had once done thus in my breaking away from my Parents, so I could not be content now, but I must go and leave the happy View I had of being a rich and thriving Man in my new Plantation, only to pursue a rash and immoderate Desire of rising faster than the Nature of the Thing admitted; and thus I cast my self down again into the deepest Gulph of human Misery that ever Man fell into, or perhaps could be consistent with Life and a State of Health in the World.

To come then by the just Degrees, to the Particulars of this Part of my Story; you may suppose, that having now lived almost four Years in the *Brasils*, and beginning to thrive and prosper very well upon my Plantation; I had not only learn'd the Language, but had contracted Acquaintance and Friendship among my Fellow-Planters, as well as among the Merchants at St. *Salvadore*,[1] which was our Port; and that in my Discourses among them, I had frequently given them an Account of my two Voyages to the Coast of *Guinea*, the manner of Trading with the *Negroes* there, and how easy it was to purchase upon the Coast, for Trifles, such as Beads, Toys, Knives, Scissars, Hatchets, bits of Glass, and the like; not only Gold Dust, *Guinea* Grains,[2] Elephants Teeth,[3] &c. but *Negroes* for the Service of the *Brasils*, in great Numbers.

They listened always very attentively to my Discourses on these Heads, but especially to that Part which related to the buying *Negroes*, which was a Trade at that time not only not far

---

1   Salvador da Bahia, the capital of Brazil until 1762, was a major port for the slave trade.

2   West African grains used as spices and medicine.

3   Tusks.

entred into, but as far as it was, had been carried on by the Assiento's,[1] or Permission of the Kings of *Spain* and *Portugal*, and engross'd in the Publick, so that few *Negroes* were brought, and those excessive dear.

It happen'd, being in Company with some Merchants and Planters of my Acquaintance, and talking of those things very earnestly, three of them came to me the next Morning, and told me they had been musing very much upon what I had discoursed with them of, the last Night, and they came to make a secret Proposal to me; and after enjoining me Secrecy, they told me, that they had a mind to fit out a Ship to go to *Guinea*, that they had all Plantations as well as I, and were straiten'd for nothing so much as Servants; that as it was a Trade that could not be carried on, because they could not publickly sell the *Negroes* when they came home, so they desired to make but one Voyage, to bring the *Negroes* on Shoar privately, and divide them among their own Plantations; and in a Word, the Question was, whether I would go their Super-Cargo[2] in the Ship to manage the Trading Part upon the Coast of *Guinea*? And they offer'd me that I should have my equal Share of the *Negroes* without providing any Part of the Stock.

This was a fair Proposal it must be confess'd, had it been made to any one that had not had a Settlement and Plantation of his own to look after, which was in a fair way of coming to be very Considerable, and with a good Stock upon it. But for me that was thus entered and established, and had nothing to do but go on as I had begun for three or four Years more, and to have sent for the other hundred Pound from *England*, and who in that time, and with that little Addition, could scarce ha' fail'd of being worth three or four thousand Pounds Sterling, and that encreasing too; for me to think of such a Voyage, was the most preposterous Thing that ever Man in such Circumstances could be guilty of.

But I that was born to be my own Destroyer, could no more resist the Offer than I could restrain my first rambling Designs, when my Father's good Counsel was lost upon me. In a word, I

---

1 Contracts made by the king of Spain, granting exclusive rights to sell slaves in the Spanish colonies. As part of the Treaty of Utrecht in 1713, an asiento was granted to Great Britain, which assumed most of the slave trade. Crusoe and his neighboring planters are attempting to pursue a private, illegal trade.

2 The officer on a merchant ship who oversees the cargo and commercial transactions.

told them I would go with all my Heart, if they would undertake to look after my Plantation in my Absence, and would dispose of it to such as I should direct if I miscarry'd. This they all engag'd to do, and entred into Writings or Covenants to do so; and I made a formal Will, disposing of my Plantation and Effects, in Case of my Death, making the Captain of the Ship that had sav'd my Life as before, my universal Heir, but obliging him to dispose of my Effects as I had directed in my Will, one half of the Produce being to himself, and the other to be ship'd to *England*.

In short, I took all possible Caution to preserve my Effects, and keep up my Plantation; had I used half as much Prudence to have look'd into my own Intrest, and have made a Judgment of what I ought to have done, and not to have done, I had certainly never gone away from so prosperous an Undertaking, leaving all the probable Views of a thriving Circumstance, and gone upon a Voyage to Sea, attended with all its common Hazards; to say nothing of the Reasons I had to expect particular Misfortunes to my self.

But I was hurried on, and obey'd blindly the Dictates of my Fancy rather than my Reason; and accordingly the Ship being fitted out, and the Cargo furnished, and all things done as by Agreement, by my Partners in the Voyage, I went on Board in an evil Hour, the first of September, 1659, being the same Day eight Year that I went from my Father and Mother at *Hull*, in order to act the Rebel to their Authority, and the Fool to my own Interest.

Our Ship was about 120 Tun Burthen,[1] carried 6 Guns, and 14 Men, besides the Master, his Boy, and my self; we had on board no large Cargo of Goods, except of such Toys as were fit for our Trade with the *Negroes*, such as Beads, bits of Glass, Shells, and odd Trifles, especially little Looking-Glasses, Knives, Scissars, Hatchets, and the like.

The same Day I went on board we set sail, standing away to the Northward upon our own Coast, with Design to stretch over for the *African* Coast, when they came about 10 or 12 Degrees of Northern Latitude, which it seems was the manner of their Course in those Days. We had very good Weather, only excessive hot, all the way upon our own Coast, till we came the Height of *Cape* St. *Augustino*,[2] from whence keeping farther off at Sea we

---

1 Tonnage measures a ship's load capacity (its *burden*), originally figured by its ability to hold wine casks (*tuns*).

2 On the fold-out map that appeared in the fourth edition, St. Augustine is shown as one of the easternmost parts of Brazil. The captain is getting his bearings before heading across the Atlantic.

lost Sight of Land, and steer'd as if we was bound for the Isle *Fernand de Noronha*[1] holding our Course *N.E.* by *N.* and leaving those Isles on the East; in this Course we past the Line in about 12 Days time, and were by our last Observation in 7 Degrees 22 Min. Northern Latitude, when a violent Tournado or Hurricane took us quite out of our Knowledge; it began from the South-East, came about to the North-West, and then settled into the North-East, from whence it blew in such a terrible manner, that for twelve Days together we could do nothing but drive, and scudding away before it, let it carry us whither ever Fate and the Fury of the Winds directed; and during these twelve Days, I need not say, that I expected every Day to be swallowed up, nor indeed did any in the Ship expect to save their Lives.

In this Distress, we had besides the Terror of the Storm, one of our Men dyed of the Calenture, and one Man and the Boy wash'd over board; about the 12th Day the Weather abating a little, the Master made an Observation as well as he could, and found that he was in about 11 Degrees North Latitude, but that he was 22 Degrees of Longitude difference West from *Cape* St. *Augustino*; so that he found he was gotten upon the Coast of *Guiana*, or the North Part of *Brasil*, beyond the River *Amozones*, toward that of the River *Oronoque*, commonly call'd the *Great River*, and began to consult with me what Course he should take, for the Ship was leaky and very much disabled, and he was going directly back to the Coast of *Brasil*.

I was positively against that, and looking over the Charts of the Sea-Coast of *America* with him, we concluded there was no inhabited Country for us to have recourse to, till we came within the Circle of the *Carribbe-Islands*, and therefore resolved to stand away for *Barbadoes*, which by keeping off at Sea, to avoid the Indraft of the Bay or Gulph of *Mexico*, we might easily perform, as we hoped, in about fifteen Days Sail; whereas we could not possibly make our Voyage to the Coast of *Affrica* without some Assistance, both to our Ship and to our selves.

With this Design we chang'd our Course and steer'd away *N. W.* by *W.* in order to reach some of our *English* Islands, where I hoped for Relief; but our Voyage was otherwise determined, for being in the Latitude of 12 Deg. 18 Min. a second Storm came upon us, which carry'd us away with the same Impetuosity Westward, and drove us so out of the very Way of all humane Commerce, that had all our Lives been saved, as to the Sea, we were

---

1   An archipelago roughly 370 miles northeast of St. Augustine.

rather in Danger of being devoured by Savages than ever returning to our own Country.

In this Distress, the Wind still blowing very hard, one of our Men early in the Morning, cry'd out, *Land*; and we had no sooner run out of the Cabbin to look out in hopes of seeing where abouts in the World we were; but the Ship struck upon a Sand, and in a moment her Motion being so stopp'd, the Sea broke over her in such a manner, that we expected we should all have perish'd immediately, and we were immediately driven into our close Quarters to shelter us from the very Foam and Sprye of the Sea.

It is not easy for any one, who has not been in the like Condition, to describe or conceive the Consternation of Men in such Circumstances; we knew nothing where we were, or upon what Land it was we were driven, whether an Island or the Main, whether inhabited or not inhabited; and as the Rage of the Wind was still great, tho' rather less than at first, we could not so much as hope to have the Ship hold many Minutes without breaking in Pieces, unless the Winds by a kind of Miracle should turn immediately about. In a word, we sat looking upon one another, and expecting Death every Moment, and every Man acting accordingly, as preparing for another World, for there was little or nothing more for us to do in this; that which was our present Comfort, and all the Comfort we had, was, that contrary to our Expectation the Ship did not break yet, and that the Master said the Wind began to abate.

Now tho' we thought that the Wind did a little abate, yet the Ship having thus struck upon the Sand, and sticking too fast for us to expect her getting off, we were in a dreadful Condition indeed, and had nothing to do but to think of saving our Lives as well as we could; we had a Boat at our Stern just before the Storm, but she was first stav'd by dashing against the Ship's Rudder, and in the next Place she broke away, and either sunk or was driven off to Sea, so there was no hope from her; we had another Boat on board, but how to get her off into the Sea, was a doubtful thing; however there was no room to debate, for we fancy'd the Ship would break in Pieces every Minute, and some told us she was actually broken already.

In this Distress the Mate of our Vessel lays hold of the Boat, and with the help of the rest of the Men, they got her flung over the Ship's-side, and getting all into her, let go, and committed our selves being Eleven in Number, to God's Mercy, and the wild Sea; for tho' the Storm was abated considerably, yet the Sea went dreadful high upon the Shore, and might well be call'd, *Den wild Zee*,[1] as the *Dutch* call the Sea in a Storm.

And now our Case was very dismal indeed; for we all saw plainly, that the Sea went so high, that the Boat could not live, and that we should be inevitably drowned. As to making Sail, we had none, nor, if we had, could we ha' done any thing with it; so we work'd at the Oar towards the Land, tho' with heavy Hearts, like Men going to Execution; for we all knew, that when the Boat came nearer the Shore, she would be dash'd in a Thousand Pieces by the Breach of the Sea. However, we committed our Souls to God in the most earnest Manner, and the Wind driving us towards the Shore, we hasten'd our Destruction with our own Hands, pulling as well as we could towards Land.

What the Shore was, whether Rock or Sand, whether Steep or Shoal, we knew not; the only Hope that could rationally give us the least Shadow of Expectation, was, if we might happen into some Bay or Gulph, or the Mouth of some River, where by great Chance we might have run our Boat in, or got under the Lee of the Land, and perhaps made smooth Water. But there was nothing of this appeared; but as we made nearer and nearer the Shore, the Land look'd more frightful than the Sea.

After we had row'd, or rather driven about a League and a Half, as we reckon'd it, a raging Wave, Mountain-like, came rowling[2] a-stern of us, and plainly bad us expect the *Coup de Grace*.[3] In a word, it took us with such a Fury, that it overset the Boat at once; and separating us as well from the Boat, as from one another, gave us not time hardly to say, O God! for we were all swallowed up in a Moment.

Nothing can describe the Confusion of Thought which I felt when I sunk into the Water; for tho' I swam very well, yet I could not deliver my self from the Waves so as to draw Breath, till that Wave having driven me, or rather carried me a vast Way on towards the Shore, and having spent it self, went back, and left me upon the Land almost dry, but half-dead with the Water I took in. I had so much Presence of Mind as well as Breath left, that seeing my self nearer the main Land than I expected, I got upon my Feet, and endeavoured to make on towards the Land as fast as I could, before another Wave should return, and take me up again. But I soon found it was impossible to avoid it; for I saw

---

1 The wild sea.
2 Rolling.
3 A finishing blow.

the Sea come after me as high as a great Hill, and as furious as an Enemy which I had no Means or Strength to contend with; my Business was to hold my Breath, and raise my self upon the Water, if I could; and so by swimming to preserve my Breathing, and Pilot my self towards the Shore, if possible; my greatest Concern now being, that the Sea, as it would carry me a great Way towards the Shore when it came on, might not carry me back again with it when it gave back towards the Sea.

The Wave that came upon me again, buried me at once 20 or 30 Foot deep in its own Body; and I could feel my self carried with a mighty Force and Swiftness towards the Shore a very great Way; but I held my Breath, and assisted my self to swim still forward with all my Might. I was ready to burst with holding my Breath, when, as I felt my self rising up, so to my immediate Relief, I found my Head and Hands shoot out above the Surface of the Water; and tho' it was not two Seconds of Time that I could keep my self so, yet it reliev'd me greatly, gave me Breath and new Courage. I was covered again with Water a good while, but not so long but I held it out; and finding the Water had spent it self, and began to return, I strook forward against the Return of the Waves, and felt Ground again with my Feet. I stood still a few Moments to recover Breath, and till the Water went from me, and then took to my Heels, and run with what Strength I had farther towards the Shore. But neither would this deliver me from the Fury of the Sea, which came pouring in after me again, and twice more I was lifted up by the Waves, and carried forwards as before, the Shore being very flat.

The last Time of these two had well near been fatal to me; for the Sea having hurried me along as before, landed me, or rather dash'd me against a Piece of a Rock, and that with such Force, as it left me senseless, and indeed helpless, as to my own Deliverance; for the Blow taking my Side and Breast, beat the Breath as it were quite out of my Body; and had it returned again immediately, I must have been strangled in the Water; but I recover'd a little before the return of the Waves, and seeing I should be cover'd again with the Water, I resolv'd to hold fast by a Piece of the Rock, and so to hold my Breath, if possible, till the Wave went back; now as the Waves were not so high as at first, being nearer Land, I held my Hold till the Wave abated, and then fetch'd another Run, which brought me so near the Shore, that the next Wave, tho' it went over me, yet did not so swallow me up as to carry me away, and the next run I took, I got to the main Land, where, to my great Comfort, I clamber'd up the Clifts of the

Shore, and sat me down upon the Grass, free from Danger, and quite out of the Reach of the Water.

I was now landed, and safe on Shore, and began to look up and thank God that my Life was sav'd in a Case wherein there was some Minutes before scarce any room to hope. I believe it is impossible to express to the Life what the Extasies and Transports of the Soul are, when it is so sav'd, as I may say, out of the very Grave; and I do not wonder now at that Custom, *viz.*:

For sudden Joys, like Griefs, confound at first.[1] *Shipwrecked*

I walk'd about on the Shore, lifting up my Hands, and my whole Being, as I may say, wrapt up in the Contemplation of my Deliverance, making a Thousand Gestures and Motions which I cannot describe, reflecting upon all my Comerades that were drown'd, and that there should not be one Soul sav'd but my self; for, as for them, I never saw them afterwards, or any Sign of them, except three of their Hats, one Cap, and two Shoes that were not Fellows.

I cast my Eyes to the stranded Vessel, when the Breach and Froth of the Sea being so big, I could hardly see it, it lay so far off, and considered, Lord! how was it possible I could get on Shore?

After I had solac'd my Mind with the comfortable Part of my *stranded* Condition, I began to look round me to see what kind of Place I *land* was in, and what was next to be done, and I soon found my Com- *w/* forts abate, and that in a word I had a dreadful Deliverance: For *no* I was wet, had no Clothes to shift me,[2] nor any thing either to eat *stuff* or drink to comfort me, neither did I see any Prospect before me, but that of perishing with Hunger, or being devour'd by wild Beasts; and that which was particularly afflicting to me, was, that I had no Weapon either to hunt and kill any Creature for my Sustenance, or to defend my self against any other Creature that might desire to kill me for theirs: In a Word, I had nothing about me but a Knife, a Tobacco-pipe, and a little Tobacco in a Box, this was all my Provision, and this threw me into terrible Agonies of Mind, that for a while I run about like a Mad-man; Night coming upon me, I began with a heavy Heart to consider what would be

---

1   From "Wild's Humble Thanks for His Majesty's Gracious Declaration for Liberty of Conscience," by Robert Wild (1672) [Sill 1998].
2   To change into.

my Lot if there were any ravenous Beasts in that Country, seeing at Night they always come abroad for their Prey.

All the Remedy that offer'd to my Thoughts at that Time, was, to get up into a thick bushy Tree like a Firr, but thorny, which grew near me, and where I resolv'd to set all Night, and consider the next Day what Death I should dye, for as yet I saw no Prospect of Life; I walk'd about a Furlong[1] from the Shore, to see if I could find any fresh Water to drink, which I did, to my great Joy; and having drank and put a little Tobacco in my Mouth to prevent Hunger, I went to the Tree, and getting up into it, endeavour'd to place my self so, as that if I should sleep I might not fall; and having cut me a short Stick, like a Truncheon,[2] for my Defence, I took up my Lodging, and having been excessively fatigu'd, I fell fast asleep, and slept as comfortably as, I believe, few could have done in my Condition, and found my self the most refresh'd with it, that I think I ever was on such an Occasion.

When I wak'd it was broad Day, the Weather clear, and the Storm abated, so that the Sea did not rage and swell as before: But that which surpris'd me most, was, that the Ship was lifted off in the Night from the Sand where she lay, by the Swelling of the Tyde, and was driven up almost as far as the Rock which I first mention'd, where I had been so bruis' d by the dashing me against it; this being within about a Mile from the Shore where I was, and the Ship seeming to Stand upright Still, I wish'd my self on board, that, at least, I might save some necessary things for my use.

When I came down from my Appartment in the Tree, I look'd about me again, and the first thing I found was the Boat, which lay as the Wind and the Sea had toss'd her up upon the Land, about two Miles on my right Hand, I walk'd as far as I could upon the Shore to have got to her, but found a Neck or Inlet of Water between me and the Boat, which was about half a Mile broad, so I came back for the present, being more intent upon getting at the Ship, where I hop'd to find something for my present Subsistence.

A little after Noon I found the Sea very calm, and the Tyde ebb'd so far out, that I could come within a Quarter of a Mile of the Ship; and here I found a fresh renewing of my Grief, for I saw evidently, that if we had kept on board, we had been all safe, that

---

1 One eighth of a mile.

2 A club.

is to say, we had all got safe on Shore, and I had not been so miserable as to be left entirely destitute of all Comfort and Company, as I now was; this forc'd Tears from my Eyes again, but as there was little Relief in that, I resolv'd, if possible, to get to the Ship, so I pull'd off my Clothes, for the Weather was hot to Extremity, and took the Water, but when I came to the Ship, my Difficulty was still greater to know how to get on board, for as she lay a ground, and high out of the Water, there was nothing within my Reach to lay hold of, I swam round her twice, and the second Time I spy'd a small Piece of a Rope, which I wonder'd I did not see at first, hang down by the Fore-Chains so low, as that with great Difficulty I got hold of it, and by the help of that Rope, got up into the Forecastle[1] of the Ship, here I found that the Ship was bulg'd,[2] and had a great deal of Water in her Hold, but that she lay so on the Side of a Bank of hard Sand, or rather Earth, that her Stern lay lifted up upon the Bank, and her Head low almost to the Water; by this Means all her Quarter[3] was free, and all that was in that Part was dry; for you may be sure my first Work was to search and to see what was spoil'd and what was free; and first I found that all the Ship's Provisions were dry and untouch'd by the Water, and being very well dispos'd to eat, I went to the Bread-room and fill'd my Pockets with Bisket, and eat it as I went about other things, for I had no time to lose; I also found some Rum in the great Cabbin, of which I took a large Dram, and which I had indeed need enough of to spirit me for what was before me: Now I wanted nothing but a Boat to furnish my self with many things which I foresaw would be very necessary to me.

It was in vain to sit still and wish for what was not to be had, and this Extremity rouz'd my Application; we had several spare Yards, and two or three large sparrs of Wood, and a spare Topmast or two in the Ship; I resolv'd to fall to work with these, and I flung as many of them over board as I could manage for their Weight, tying every one with a Rope that they might not drive away; when this was done I went down the Ship's Side, and pulling them to me, I ty'd four of them fast together at both Ends as well as I could, in the Form of a Raft, and laying two or three short Pieces of Plank upon them cross-ways, I found I could walk upon it very well, but that it was not able to bear any great Weight, the Pieces being too light; so I went to work, and with the

---

1 A short raised deck toward the ship's bow.
2 The ship's bilge (the bottom next to the keel) has been broken open.
3 The first part of a ship's upper side toward the stern.

Carpenter's Saw I cut a spare Top-mast into three Lengths, and added them to my Raft, with a great deal of Labour and Pains, but hope of furnishing my self with Necessaries, encourag'd me to go beyond what I should have been able to have done upon another Occasion.

My Raft was now strong enough to bear any reasonable Weight; my next Care was what to load it with, and how to preserve what I laid upon it from the Surf of the Sea; But I was not long considering this, I first laid all the Plank or Boards upon it that I could get, and having consider'd well what I most wanted, I first got three of the Seamens Chests, which I had broken open and empty'd, and lower'd them down upon my Raft; the first of these I fill'd with Provision, *viz.* Bread, Rice, three Dutch Cheeses, five Pieces of dry'd Goat's Flesh, which we liv'd much upon, and a little Remainder of *European* Corn which had been laid by for some Fowls which we brought to Sea with us, but the Fowls were kill'd, there had been some Barly and Wheat together, but, to my great Disappointment, I found afterwards that the Rats had eaten or spoil'd it all; as for Liquors, I found several Cases of Bottles belonging to our Skipper, in which were some Cordial Waters,[1] and in all about five or six Gallons of Rack,[2] these I stow'd by themselves, there being no need to put them into the Chest, nor no room for them. While I was doing this, I found the Tyde began to flow, tho' very calm, and I had the Mortification to see my Coat, Shirt, and Wast-coat which I had left on Shore upon the Sand, swim away; as for my Breeches which were only Linnen and open knee'd, I swam on board in them and my Stockings: However this put me upon rummaging for Clothes, of which I found enough, but took no more than I wanted for present use, for I had other things which my Eye was more upon, as first Tools to work with on Shore, and it was after long searching that I found out the Carpenter's Chest, which was indeed a very useful Prize to me, and much more valuable than a Ship Loading of Gold would have been at that time; I got it down to my Raft, even whole as it was, without losing time to look into it, for I knew in general what it contain'd.

My next Care was for some Ammunition and Arms; there were two very good Fowling-pieces in the great Cabbin, and two Pistols, these I secur'd first, with some Powder-horns, and a small

---

1 Invigorating, stimulating beverages.
2 *Arrack*: spirits distilled from rice and sugar, fermented with coconut juice, or from the fermented sap of the coconut tree.

Bag of Shot, and two old rusty Swords; I knew there were three Barrels of Powder in the Ship, but knew not where our Gunner had stow'd them, but with much search I found them, two of them dry and good, the third had taken Water, those two I got to my Raft, with the Arms, and now I thought my self pretty well freighted, and began to think how I should get to Shore with them, having neither Sail, Oar, or Rudder, and the least Cap full of Wind would have overset all my Navigation.

I had three Encouragements, 1. A smooth calm Sea, 2. The Tide rising and setting in to the Shore, 3. What little Wind there was blew me towards the Land; and thus, having found two or three broken Oars belonging to the Boat, and besides the Tools which were in the Chest, I found two Saws, an Axe, and a Hammer, and with this Cargo I put to Sea: For a Mile, or thereabouts, my Raft went very well, only that I found it drive a little distant from the Place where I had landed before, by which I perceiv'd that there was some Indraft of the Water, and consequently I hop'd to find some Creek or River there, which I might make use of as a Port to get to Land with my Cargo.

As I imagin'd, so it was, there appear'd before me a little opening of the Land, and I found a strong Current of the Tide set into it, so I guided my Raft as well as I could to keep in the Middle of the Stream: But here I had like to have suffer'd[1] a second Ship-wreck, which, if I had, I think verily would have broke my Heart, for knowing nothing of the Coast, my Raft run a-ground at one End of it upon a Shoal, and not being a-ground at the other End, it wanted but a little that all my Cargo had slip'd off towards that End that was a-float, and so fall'n into the Water: I did my utmost by setting my Back against the Chests, to keep them in their Places, but could not thrust off the Raft with all my Strength, neither durst I stir from the Posture I was in, but holding up the Chests with all my Might, stood in that Manner near half an Hour, in which time the rising of the Water brought me a little more upon a Level, and a little after, the Water still rising, my Raft floated again, and I thrust her off with the Oar I had, into the Channel, and then driving up higher, I at length found my self in the Mouth of a little River, with Land on both Sides, and a strong Current or Tide running up, I look'd on both Sides for a proper Place to get to Shore, for I was not willing to be driven too high up the River, hoping in time to see some Ship at Sea, and therefore resolv'd to place my self as near the Coast as I could.

---

1 Endured.

At length I spy'd a little Cove on the right Shore of the Creek, to which with great Pain and Difficulty I guided my Raft, and at last got so near, as that, reaching Ground with my Oar, I could thrust her directly in, but here I had like to have dipt all my Cargo in the Sea again; for that Shore lying pretty steep, that is to say sloping, there was no Place to land, but where one End of my Float, if it run on Shore, would lie so high, and the other sink lower as before, that it would endanger my Cargo again: All that I could do, was to wait 'till the Tide was at the highest, keeping the Raft with my Oar like an Anchor to hold the Side of it fast to the Shore, near a flat Piece of Ground, which I expected the Water would flow over; and so it did: As soon as I found Water enough, for my Raft drew about a Foot of Water, I thrust her on upon that flat Piece of Ground, and there fasten'd or mor'd her by sticking my two broken Oars into the Ground; one on one Side near one End, and one on the other Side near the other End; and thus I lay 'till the Water ebb'd away, and left my Raft and all my Cargoe safe on Shore.

My next Work was to view the Country, and seek a proper Place for my Habitation, and where to stow my Goods to secure them from whatever might happen; where I was I yet knew not, whether on the Continent or on an Island, whether inhabited or not inhabited, whether in Danger of wild Beasts or not: There was a Hill not above a Mile from me, which rose up very steep and high, and which seem'd to over-top some other Hills which lay as in a Ridge from it northward; I took out one of the fowling Pieces, and one of the Pistols, and an Horn of Powder, and thus arm'd I travell'd for Discovery up to the Top of that Hill, where after I had with great Labour and Difficulty got to the Top, I saw my Fate to my great Affliction, (*viz.*) that I was in an Island environ'd every Way with the Sea, no Land to be seen, except some Rocks which lay a great Way off, and two small Islands less than this, which lay about three Leagues to the West.

I found also that the Island I was in was barren, and, as I saw good Reason to believe, un-inhabited, except by wild Beasts, of whom however I saw none, yet I saw Abundance of Fowls, but knew not their Kinds, neither when I kill'd them could I tell what was fit for Food, and what not; at my coming back, I shot at a great Bird which I saw sitting upon a Tree on the Side of a great Wood, I believe it was the first Gun that had been fir'd there since the Creation of the World; I had no sooner fir'd, but from all the Parts of the Wood there arose an innumerable Number of Fowls of many Sorts, making a confus'd Screaming, and crying every one according to his usual Note; but not one of them of any Kind that I knew: As for the Creature I kill'd, I took it to be a Kind of a Hawk, its Colour and Beak resembling it, but had no Talons or Claws more than common, its Flesh was Carrion, and fit for nothing.

Contented with this Discovery, I came back to my Raft, and fell to Work to bring my Cargoe on Shore, which took me up the rest of that Day, and what to do with my self at Night I knew not, nor indeed where to rest; for I was afraid to lie down on the Ground, not knowing but some wild Beast might devour me, tho', as I afterwards found, there was really no Need for those Fears.

However, as well as I could, I barricado'd my self round with the Chests and Boards that I had brought on Shore, and made a Kind of a Hut for that Night's Lodging; as for Food, I yet saw not which Way to supply myself, except that I had seen two or three Creatures like Hares run out of the Wood where I shot the Fowl.

I now began to consider, that I might yet get a great many Things out of the Ship, which would be useful to me, and particularly some of the Rigging, and Sails, and such other Things as might come to Land, and I resolv'd to make another Voyage on Board the Vessel, if possible; and as I knew that the first Storm that blew must necessarily break her all in Pieces, I resolv'd to set all other Things apart, 'till I got every Thing out of the Ship that I could get; then I call'd a Council, that is to say, in my Thoughts, whether I should take back the Raft, but this appear'd impracticable; so I resolv'd to go as before, when the Tide was down, and I did so, only that I stripp'd before I went from my Hut, having nothing on but a Chequer'd Shirt, and a Pair of Linnen Drawers, and a Pair of Pumps on my Feet.

I got on Board the Ship, as before, and prepar'd a second Raft, and having had Experience of the first, I neither made this so unwieldy, nor loaded it so hard, but yet I brought away several Things very useful to me; as first, in the Carpenter's Stores I found two or three Bags full of Nails and Spikes, a great Skrew-Jack,[1] a Dozen or two of Hatchets, and above all, that most useful Thing call'd a Grindstone; all these I secur'd together, with several Things belonging to the Gunner, particularly two or three Iron Crows,[2] and two Barrels of Musquet Bullets, seven Musquets, and another fowling Piece, with some small Quantity of

---

1 A jack used to lift heavy weights.
2 Crowbars.

Powder more; a large Bag full of small Shot, and a great Roll of Sheet Lead:[1] But this last was so heavy, I could not hoise[2] it up to get it over the Ship's Side.

Besides these Things, I took all the Mens Cloths that I could find, and a spare Fore-top-sail, a Hammock, and some Bedding; and with this I loaded my second Raft, and brought them all safe on Shore to my very great Comfort.

I was under some Apprehensions during my Absence from the Land, that at least my Provisions might be devour'd on Shore; but when I came back, I found no Sign of any Visitor, only there sat a Creature like a wild Cat upon one of the Chests, which when I came towards it, ran away a little Distance, and then stood still; she sat very compos'd, and unconcern'd, and look'd full in my Face, as if she had a Mind to be acquainted with me, I presented my Gun at her, but as she did not understand it, she was perfectly unconcern'd at it, nor did she offer to stir away; upon which I toss'd her a Bit of Bisket, tho' by the Way I was not very free of it, for my Store was not great: However, I spar'd her a Bit, I say, and she went to it, smell'd of it, and ate it, and look'd (as pleas'd) for more, but I thank'd her, and could spare no more; so she march'd off.

Having got my second Cargoe on Shore, tho' I was fain[3] to open the Barrels of Powder, and bring them by Parcels, for they were too heavy, being large Casks, I went to work to make me a little Tent with the Sail and some Poles which I cut for that Purpose, and into this Tent I brought every Thing that I knew would spoil, either with Rain or Sun, and I piled all the empty Chests and Casks up in a Circle round the Tent, to fortify it from any sudden Attempt, either from Man or Beast.

When I had done this I block'd up the Door of the Tent with some Boards within, and an empty Chest set up an End without, and spreading one of the Beds upon the Ground, laying my two Pistols just at my Head, and my Gun at Length by me, I went to Bed for the first Time, and slept very quietly all Night, for I was very weary and heavy, for the Night before I had slept little, and had labour'd very hard all Day, as well to fetch all those Things from the Ship, as to get them on Shore.

I had the biggest Maggazin of all Kinds now that ever were laid up, I believe, for one Man, but I was not satisfy'd still; for while

---

1   Crusoe could have used the sheet lead to cast bullets.
2   Hoist.
3   Obliged.

the Ship sat upright in that Posture, I thought I ought to get every Thing out of her that I could; so every Day at low Water I went on Board, and brought away some Thing or other: But particularly the third Time I went, I brought away as much of the Rigging as I could, as also all the small Ropes and Rope-twine I could get, with a Piece of spare Canvass, which was to mend the Sails upon Occasion, the Barrel of wet Gun-powder: In a Word, I brought away all the Sails first and last, only that I was fain to cut them in Pieces, and bring as much at a Time as I could; for they were no more useful to be Sails, but as meer Canvass only.

But that which comforted me more still was, that at last of all, after I had made five or six such Voyages as these, and thought I had nothing more to expect from the Ship that was worth my medling with, I say, after all this, I found a great Hogshead[1] of Bread and three large Runlets[2] of Rum or Spirits, and a Box of Sugar, and a Barrel of fine Flower; this was surprizing to me, because I had given over expecting any more Provisions, except what was spoil'd by the Water: I soon empty'd the Hogshead of that Bread, and wrapt it up Parcel by Parcel in Pieces of the Sails, which I cut out; and in a Word, I got all this safe on Shore also.

The next Day I made another Voyage; and now having plunder'd the Ship of what was portable and fit to hand out, I began with the Cables; and cutting the great Cable into Pieces, such as I could move, I got two Cables and a Hawser[3] on Shore, with all the Iron Work I could get; and having cut down the Spritsail-yard, and the Missen-yard, and every Thing I could to make a large Raft, I loaded it with all those heavy Goods, and came away: But my good Luck began now to leave me; for this Raft was so unwieldy, and so overloaden, that after I was enter'd the little Cove, where I had landed the rest of my Goods, not being able to guide it so handily as I did the other, it overset, and threw me and all my Cargoe into the Water; as for my self it was no great Harm, for I was near the Shore; but as to my Cargoe, it was great Part of it lost, especially the Iron, which I expected would have been of great Use to me: However, when the Tide was out, I got most of the Pieces of Cable ashore, and some of the Iron, tho' with infinite Labour; for I was fain to dip for it into the Water, a Work which fatigu'd me very much: After this I went every Day on Board, and brought away what I could get.

---

1   A large barrel or cask.
2   A cask holding between twelve and eighteen gallons.
3   A heavy rope used to tow or moor a ship.

I had been now thirteen Days on Shore, and had been eleven Times on Board the Ship; in which Time I had brought away all that one Pair of Hands could well be suppos'd capable to bring, tho' I believe verily, had the calm Weather held, I should have brought away the whole Ship Piece by Piece: But preparing the 12th Time to go on Board, I found the Wind begin to rise; however at low Water I went on Board, and tho' I thought I had rumag'd the Cabbin so effectually, as that nothing more could be found, yet I discover'd a Locker with Drawers in it, in one of which I found two or three Razors, and one Pair of large Sizzers, with some ten or a Dozen of good Knives and Forks; in another I found about Thirty six Pounds value in Money, some *European* Coin, some *Brasil*, some Pieces of Eight, some Gold, some Silver.

money of no use

I smil'd to my self at the Sight of this Money, O Drug! Said I aloud, what art thou good for, Thou art not worth to me, no not the taking off of the Ground, one of those Knives is worth all this Heap, I have no Manner of use for thee, e'en remain where thou art, and go to the Bottom as a Creature whose Life is not worth saving. However, upon Second Thoughts, I took it away, and wrapping all this in a Piece of Canvas, I began to think of making another Raft, but while I was preparing this, I found the Sky overcast, and the Wind began to rise, and in a Quarter of an Hour it blew a fresh Gale from the Shore; it presently occur'd to me, that it was in vain to pretend to make a Raft with the Wind off Shore, and that it was my Business to be gone before the Tide of Flood began, otherwise I might not be able to reach the Shore at all: Accordingly I let my self down into the Water, and swam cross the Channel, which lay between the Ship and the Sands, and even that with Difficulty enough, partly with the Weight of the Things I had about me, and partly the Roughness of the Water, for the Wind rose very hastily, and before it was quite high Water, it blew a Storm.[1]

But I was gotten home to my little Tent, where I lay with all my Wealth about me very secure. It blew very hard all that Night,

---

1 Samuel Taylor Coleridge found this passage "worthy of Shakespeare." The 1812 edition he read, however, was punctuated dramatically differently: "I smiled to myself at the sight of this money: 'Oh drug!' said I aloud, 'what art thou good for? ... I have no manner of use for thee; e'en remain where thou art, and go to the bottom, as a creature whose life is not worth saving.' However, upon second thoughts, I took it away; and wrapping all this in a piece of canvas, I began to think of making another raft; ..." [See Rothman].

and in the Morning when I look'd out, behold no more Ship was to be seen; I was a little surpriz'd, but recover'd my self with this satisfactory Reflection, *viz*. That I had lost no time, nor abated no Dilligence to get every thing out of her that could be useful to me, and that indeed there was little left in her that I was able to bring away if I had had more time.

I now gave over any more Thoughts of the Ship, or of any thing out of her, except what might drive on Shore from her Wreck, as indeed divers Pieces of her afterwards did; but those things were of small use to me.

My Thoughts were now wholly employ'd about securing my self against either Savages, if any should appear, or wild Beasts, if any were in the Island; and I had many Thoughts of the Method how to do this, and what kind of Dwelling to make, whether I should make me a Cave in the Earth, or a Tent upon the Earth: And, in short, I resolv'd upon both, the Manner and Discription of which, it may not be improper to give an Account of.

I soon found the Place I was in was not for my Settlement, particularly because it was upon a low moorish[1] Ground near the Sea, and I believ'd would not be wholsome, and more particularly because there was no fresh Water near it, so I resolv'd to find a more healthy and more convenient Spot of Ground.

I consulted several Things in my Situation which I found would be proper for me, 1st. Health, and fresh Water I just now mention'd, 2dly. Shelter from the Heat of the Sun, 3dly. Security from ravenous Creatures, whether Men or Beasts, 4thly. a View to the Sea, that if God sent any Ship in Sight, I might not lose any Advantage for my Deliverance, of which I was not willing to banish all my Expectation yet.

In search of a Place proper for this, I found a little Plain on the Side of a rising Hill, whose Front towards this little Plain, was steep as a House-side, so that nothing could come down upon me from the Top; on the Side of this Rock there was a hollow Place worn a little way in like the Entrance or Door of a Cave, but there was not really any Cave or Way into the Rock at all.

On the Flat of the Green, just before this hollow Place, I resolv'd to pitch my Tent: This Plain was not above an Hundred Yards broad, and about twice as long, and lay like a Green before my Door, and at the End of it descended irregularly every Way down into the Low-grounds by the Sea-side. It was on the *N.N.W.* Side of the Hill, so that I was shelter'd from the Heat

---

1 Resembling a bog or marsh.

building his house

every Day, till it came to a *W.* and by *S.* Sun, or thereabouts, which in those Countries is near the Setting.

Before I set up my Tent, I drew a half Circle before the hollow Place, which took in about Ten Yards in its Semi-diameter from the Rock, and Twenty Yards in its Diameter, from its Beginning and Ending.

In this half Circle I pitch'd two Rows of strong Stakes, driving them into the Ground till they stood very firm like Piles,[1] the biggest End being out of the Ground about Five Foot and a Half, and sharpen'd on the Top: The two Rows did not stand above Six Inches from one another.

Then I took the Pieces of Cable which I had cut in the Ship, and I laid them in Rows one upon another, within the Circle, between these two Rows of Stakes, up to the Top, placing other Stakes in the In-side, leaning against them, about two Foot and a half high, like a Spurr to a Post, and this Fence was so strong, that neither Man or Beast could get into it or over it: This cost me a great deal of Time and Labour, especially to cut the Piles in the Woods, bring them to the Place, and drive them into the Earth.

The Entrance into this Place I made to be not by a Door, but by a short Ladder to go over the Top, which Ladder, when I was in, I lifted over after me, and so I was compleatly fenc'd in, and fortify'd, as I thought, from all the World, and consequently slept secure in the Night, which otherwise I could not have done, tho', as it appear'd afterward, there was no need of all this Caution from the Enemies that I apprehended Danger from.

Into this Fence or Fortress, with infinite Labour, I carry'd all my Riches, all my Provisions, Ammunition and Stores, of which you have the Account above, and I made me a large Tent, which, to preserve me from the Rains that in one Part of the Year are very violent there, I made double, *viz.* One smaller Tent within, and one larger Tent above it, and cover'd the uppermost with a large Tarpaulin which I had sav'd among the Sails.

And now I lay no more for a while in the Bed which I had brought on Shore, but in a Hammock, which was indeed a very good one, and belong'd to the Mate of the Ship.

Into this Tent I brought all my Provisions, and every thing that would spoil by the Wet, and having thus enclos'd all my Goods, I made up the Entrance, which till now I had left open, and so pass'd and re-pass'd, as I said, by a short Ladder.

---

1 Pointed posts often used in a structure's foundation.

When I had done this, I began to work my Way into the Rock, and bringing all the Earth and Stones that I dug down out thro' my Tent, I laid 'em up within my Fence in the Nature of a Terras, that so it rais'd the Ground within about a Foot and a Half; and thus I made me a Cave just behind my Tent, which serv'd me like a Cellar to my House.

It cost me much Labour, and many Days, before all these Things were brought to Perfection, and therefore I must go back to some other Things which took up some of my Thoughts. At the same time it happen'd after I had laid my Scheme for the setting up my Tent and making the Cave, that a Storm of Rain falling from a thick dark Cloud, a sudden Flash of Lightning happen'd, and after that a great Clap of Thunder, as is naturally the Effect of it; I was not so much surpris'd with the Lightning as I was with a Thought which darted into my Mind as swift as the Lightning it self: O my Powder! My very Heart sunk within me, when I thought, that at one Blast all my Powder might be destroy'd, on which, not my Defence only, but the providing me Food, as I thought, entirely depended; I was nothing near so anxious about my own Danger, tho' had the Powder took fire, I had never known who had hurt me.

Such Impression did this make upon me, that after the Storm was over, I laid aside all my Works, my Building, and Fortifying, and apply'd my self to make Bags and Boxes to separate the Powder, and keep it a little and a little in a Parcel, in hope, that whatever might come, it might not all take Fire at once, and to keep it so apart that it should not be possible to make one part fire another: I finish'd this Work in about a Fortnight, and I think my Powder, which in all was about 240 *l.* weight was divided in not less than a Hundred Parcels; as to the Barrel that had been wet, I did not apprehend any Danger from that, so I plac'd it in my new Cave, which in my Fancy I call'd my Kitchin, and the rest I hid up and down in Holes among the Rocks, so that no wet might come to it, marking very carefully where I laid it.

In the Interval of time while this was doing I went out once at least every Day with my Gun, as well to divert my self, as to see if I could kill any thing fit for Food, and as near as I could to acquaint my self with what the Island produc'd. The first time I went out I presently discover'd that there were Goats in the Island, which was a great Satisfaction to me; but then it was attended with this Misfortune to me, *viz.* That they were so shy, so subtile,[1] and so swift of Foot, that it was the difficultest thing

---

1 Cunning.

in the World to come at them: But I was not discourag'd at this, not doubting but I might now and then shoot one, as it soon happen'd, for after I had found their Haunts a little, I laid wait in this Manner for them: I observ'd if they saw me in the Valleys, tho' they were upon the Rocks, they would run away as in a terrible Fright; but if they were feeding in the Valleys, and I was upon the Rocks, they took no Notice of me, from whence I concluded, that by the Position of their Opticks, their Sight was so directed downward, that they did not readily see Objects that were above them; so afterward I took this Method, I always clim'd the Rocks first to get above them, and then had frequently a fair Mark. The first shot I made among these Creatures, I kill'd a She-Goat which had a little Kid by her which she gave Suck to, which griev'd me heartily; but when the Old one fell, the Kid stood stock still by her till I came and took her up, and not only so, but when I carry'd the Old one with me upon my Shoulders, the Kid follow'd me quite to my Enclosure, upon which I laid down the Dam, and took the Kid in my Arms, and carry'd it over my Pale, in hopes to have bred it up tame, but it would not eat, so I was forc'd to kill it and eat it my self; these two supply'd me with Flesh a great while, for I eat sparingly; and sav'd my Provisions (my Bread especially) as much as possibly I could.

Having now fix'd my Habitation, I found it absolutely necessary to provide a Place to make a Fire in, and Fewel to burn; and what I did for that, as also how I enlarg'd my Cave, and what Conveniences I made, I shall give a full Account of in its Place: But I must first give some little Account of my self, and of my Thoughts about Living, which it may well be suppos'd were not a few.

I had a dismal Prospect of my Condition, for as I was not cast away upon that Island without being driven, as is said, by a violent Storm quite out of the Course of our intended Voyage, and a great Way, *viz.* some Hundreds of Leagues out of the ordinary Course of the Trade of Mankind, I had great Reason to consider it as a Determination of Heaven, that in this desolate Place, and in this desolate Manner I should end my Life; the Tears would run plentifully down my Face when I made these Reflections, and sometimes I would expostulate with my self, Why Providence should thus compleatly ruine its Creatures, and render them so absolutely miserable, so without Help abandon'd, so entirely depress'd, that it could hardly be rational to be thankful for such a Life.

But something always return'd swift upon me to check these Thoughts, and to reprove me; and particularly one Day walking with my Gun in my Hand by the Sea-side, I was very pensive upon the Subject of my present Condition, when Reason as it were expostulated with me t'other Way, thus: Well, you are in a desolate Condition 'tis true, but pray remember, Where are the rest of you? Did not you come Eleven of you into the Boat, where are the Ten? Why were not they sav'd and you lost? Why were you singled out? Is it better to be here or there, and then I pointed to the Sea? All Evills are to be consider'd with the Good that is in them, and with what worse attends them. *grateful despite being stranded*

Then it occurr'd to me again, how well I was furnish'd for my Subsistence, and what would have been my Case if it had not happen'd, *Which was an Hundred Thousand to one,* that the Ship floated from the Place where she first struck and was driven so near to the Shore that I had time to get all these Things out of her: What would have been my Case, if I had been to have liv'd in the Condition in which I at first came on Shore, without Necessaries of Life, or Necessaries to supply and procure them? Particularly said I aloud, (tho' to my self) what should I ha' done without a Gun, without Ammunition, without any Tools to make any thing, or to work with, without Clothes, Bedding, a Tent, or any manner of Covering, and that now I had all these to a Sufficient Quantity, and was in a fair way to provide my self in such a manner, as to live without my Gun when my Ammunition was spent; so that I had a tollerable View of subsisting without any Want as long as I liv'd; for I consider'd from the beginning how I would provide for the Accidents that might happen, and for the time that was to come, even not only after my Ammunition should be spent, but even after my Health or Strength should decay.

I confess I had not entertain'd any Notion of my Ammunition being destroy'd at one Blast, I mean my Powder being blown up by Lightning, and this made the Thoughts of it so surprising to me when it lighten'd and thunder'd, as I observ'd just now.

And now being to enter into a melancholy Relation of a Scene of silent Life, such perhaps as was never heard of in the World before, I shall take it from its Beginning, and continue it in its Order. It was, by my Account, the 30th. of *Sept.* when, in the Manner as above said, I first set Foot upon this horrid Island, when the Sun being, to us, in its Autumnal Equinox, was almost just over my Head, for I reckon'd my self, by Observation, to be in the Latitude of 9 Degrees 22 Minutes North of the Line.

After I had been there about Ten or Twelve Days, it came into my Thoughts, that I should lose my Reckoning of Time for want

makes calendar

of[1] Books and Pen and Ink, and should even forget the Sabbath Days from the working Days; but to prevent this I cut it with my Knife upon a large Post, in Capital Letters, and making it into a great Cross I set it up on the Shore where I first landed, viz. *I came on Shore here on the 30th of* Sept. 1659. Upon the Sides of this square Post I cut every Day a Notch with my Knife, and every seventh Notch was as long again as the rest, and every first Day of the Month as long again as that long one, and thus I kept my Kalander, or weekly, monthly, and yearly reckoning of Time.

In the next place we are to observe, that among the many things which I brought out of the Ship in the several Voyages, which, as above mention'd, I made to it, I got several things of less Value, but not all less useful to me, which I omitted setting down before; as in particular, Pens, Ink, and Paper, several Parcels in the Captain's, Mate's, Gunner's, and Carpenter's keeping, three or four Compasses, some Mathematical Instruments, Dials, Perspectives,[2] Charts, and Books of Navigation, all which I huddel'd together, whether I might want them or no; also I found three very good Bibles which came to me in my Cargo from *England*, and which I had pack'd up among my things; some *Portugueze* Books also, and among them two or three Popish[3] Prayer-Books, and several other Books, all which I carefully secur'd. And I must not forget, that we had in the Ship a Dog and two Cats, of whose eminent History I may have occasion to say something in its place; for I carry'd both the Cats with me, and as for the Dog, he jump'd out of the Ship of himself and swam on Shore to me the Day after I went on Shore with my first Cargo, and was a trusty Servant to me many Years; I wanted nothing that he could fetch me, nor any Company that he could make up to me, I only wanted to have him talk to me, but that would not do: As I observ'd before, I found Pen, Ink and Paper, and I husbanded[4] them to the utmost, and I shall shew, that while my Ink lasted, I kept things very exact, but after that was gone I could not, for I could not make any Ink by any Means that I could devise.

dog & 2 cats on island w/ Rob

And this put me in mind that I wanted many things, notwithstanding all that I had amass'd together, and of these, this of Ink was one, as also Spade, Pick-Axe, and Shovel to dig or remove the

---

1 As a result of lacking.
2 Telescopes.
3 Roman Catholic.
4 Rationed, conserved.

Earth, Needles, Pins, and Thread; as for Linnen, I soon learn'd to want that without much Difficulty.

This want[1] of Tools made every Work I did go on heavily, and it was near a whole Year before I had entirely finish'd my little Pale[2] or surrounded Habitation: The Piles or Stakes, which were as heavy as I could well lift, were a long time in cutting and preparing in the Woods, and more by far in bringing home, so that I spent some times two Days in cutting and bringing home one of those Posts, and a third Day in driving it into the Ground; for which Purpose I got a heavy Piece of Wood at first, but at last bethought my self of one of the Iron Crows, which however tho' I found it, yet it made driving those Posts or Piles very laborious and tedious Work.

But what need I ha' been concern'd at the Tediousness of any thing I had to do, seeing I had time enough to do it in, nor had I any other Employment if that had been over, at least, that I could foresee, except the ranging the Island to seek for Food, which I did more or less every Day.

I now began to consider seriously my Condition, and the Circumstance I was reduc'd to, and I drew up the State of my Affairs in Writing, not so much to leave them to any that were to come after me, for I was like to have but few Heirs, as to deliver my Thoughts from daily poring upon them, and afflicting my Mind; and as my Reason began now to master my Despondency, I began to comfort my self as well as I could, and to set the good against the Evil, that I might have something to distinguish my Case from worse, and I stated it very impartially, like Debtor and Creditor, the Comforts I enjoy'd, against the Miseries I suffer'd, Thus,

Evil.	Good.
I am cast upon a horrible desolate Island, void of all hope of Recovery.	*But I am alive, and not drown'd as all my Ship's Company was.*
I am singl'd out and separated, as it were, from all the World to be miserable.	*But I am singl'd out too from all the Ship's Crew to be spar'd from Death; and he that miraculously sav'd me from Death, can deliver me from this Condition.*

---

1 Lack.
2 Enclosure.

I am divided from Mankind, a Solitaire, one banish'd from humane Society.	*But I am not starv'd and perishing on a barren Place, affording no Sustenance.*
I have not Clothes to cover me.	*But I am in a hot Climate, where if I had Clothes I could hardly wear them.*
I am without any Defence or Means to resist any Violence of Man or Beast.	*But I am cast on an Island, where I see no wild Beasts to hurt me, as I saw on the Coast of* Africa: *And what if I had been Shipwreck'd there?*
I have no Soul to speak to, or relieve me.	*But God wonderfully sent the Ship in near enough to the Shore, that I have gotten out so many necessary things as will either supply my Wants, or enable me to supply my self even as long as I live.*

Upon the whole, here was an undoubted Testimony, that there was scarce any Condition in the World so miserable, but there was something *Negative* or something *Positive* to be thankful for in it; and let this stand as a Direction from the Experience of the most miserable of all Conditions in this World, that we may always find in it something to comfort our selves from, and to set in the Description of Good and Evil, on the Credit Side of the Accompt.[1]

Having now brought my Mind a little to relish my Condition, and given over looking out to Sea to see if I could spy a Ship, I say, giving over these things, I began to apply my self to accommodate my way of Living, and to make things as easy to me as I could.

I have already describ'd my Habitation, which was a Tent under the Side of a Rock, surrounded with a strong Pale of Posts and Cables, but I might now rather call it a Wall, for I rais'd a kind of Wall up against it of Turfs,[2] about two Foot thick on the Outside, and after some time, I think it was a Year and Half, I rais'd

---

1 Account.
2 Clods of dirt.

Rafters from it leaning to the Rock, and thatch'd or cover'd it with Bows of Trees, and such things as I could get to keep out the Rain, which I found at some times of the Year very violent.

I have already observ'd how I brought all my Goods into this Pale, and into the Cave which I had made behind me: But I must observe too, that at first this was a confus'd Heap of Goods, which as they lay in no Order, so they took up all my Place, I had no room to turn my self; so I set my self to enlarge my Cave and Works farther into the Earth, for it was a loose sandy Rock, which yielded easily to the Labour I bestow'd on it; and so when I found I was pretty safe as to Beasts of Prey, I work'd side-ways to the Right Hand into the Rock, and then turning to the Right again, work'd quite out and made me a Door to come out, on the Outside of my Pale or Fortification.

This gave me not only Egress and Regress, as it were a back Way to my Tent and to my Storehouse, but gave me room to stow my Goods.

And now I began to apply my self to make such necessary things as I found I most wanted, as particularly a Chair and a Table, for without these I was not able to enjoy the few Comforts I had in the World, I could not write, or eat, or do several things with so much Pleasure without a Table.

So I went to work; and here I must needs observe, that as Reason is the Substance and Original of the Mathematicks, so by stating and squaring every thing by Reason, and by making the most rational Judgment of things, every Man may be in time Master of every mechanick Art. I had never handled a Tool in my Life, and yet in time by Labour, Application, and Contrivance, I found at last that I wanted nothing but I could have made it, especially if I had had Tools; however I made abundance of things, even without Tools, and some with no more Tools than an Adze and a Hatchet, which perhaps were never made that way before, and that with infinite Labour: For Example, If I wanted a Board, I had no other Way but to cut down a Tree, set it on an Edge before me, and hew it flat on either Side with my Axe, till I had brought it to be thin as a Plank, and then dubb[1] it smooth with my Adze. It is true, by this Method I could make but one Board out of a whole Tree, but this I had no Remedy for but Patience, any more than I had for the prodigious deal of Time and Labour which it took me up to make a Plank or Board:

---

1 Smooth.

But my Time or Labour was little worth, and so it was as well employ'd one way as another.

However, I made me a Table and a Chair, as I observ'd above, in the first Place, and this I did out of the short Pieces of Boards that I brought on my Raft from the Ship: But when I had wrought out some Boards, as above, I made large Shelves of the Breadth of a Foot and Half one over another, all along one Side of my Cave, to lay all my Tools, Nails, and Iron-work, and in a Word, to separate every thing at large in their Places, that I might come easily at them; I knock'd Pieces into the Wall of the Rock to hang my Guns and all things that would hang up.

So that had my Cave been to be seen, it look'd like a general Magazine of all Necessary things, and I had every thing so ready at my Hand, that it was a great Pleasure to me to see all my Goods in such Order, and especially to find my Stock of all Necessaries so great.

And now it was when I began to keep a Journal of every Days Employment, for indeed at first I was in too much Hurry, and not only Hurry as to Labour, but in too much Discomposure of Mind, and my Journal would ha' been full of many dull things: For Example, I must have said thus. *Sept.* the 30th. After I got to Shore and had escap'd drowning, instead of being thankful to God for my Deliverance, having first vomited with the great Quantity of salt Water which was gotten into my Stomach, and recovering my self a little, I ran about the Shore, wringing my Hands and beating my Head and Face, exclaiming at my Misery, and crying out, I was undone, undone,[1] till tyr'd and faint I was forc'd to lye down on the Ground to repose, but durst not sleep for fear of being devour'd.

Some Days after this, and after I had been on board the Ship, and got all that I could out of her, yet I could not forbear getting up to the Top of a little Mountain and looking out to Sea in hopes of seeing a Ship, then fancy at a vast Distance I spy'd a Sail, please my self with the Hopes of it, and then after looking steadily till I was almost blind, lose it quite, and sit down and weep like a Child, and thus encrease my Misery by my Folly.

But having gotten over these things in some Measure, and having settled my houshold Stuff[2] and Habitation, made me a Table and a Chair, and all as handsome about me as I could, I

---

1 Ruined.
2 Property, possessions.

began to keep my Journal, of which I shall here give you the Copy (tho' in it will be told all these Particulars over again) as long as it lasted, for having no more Ink I was forc'd to leave it off.

The JOURNAL.

September 30, 1659. I poor miserable *Robinson Crusoe*, being shipwreck'd, during a dreadful Storm, in the offing,[1] came on Shore on this dismal unfortunate[2] Island, which I call'd the *Island of Despair*, all the rest of the Ship's Company being drown'd, and my self almost dead.

All the rest of that Day I spent in afflicting my self at the dismal Circumstances I was brought to, *viz*. I had neither Food, House, Clothes, Weapon, or Place to fly to, and in Despair of any Relief, saw nothing but Death before me, either that I should be devour'd by wild Beasts, murther'd[3] by Savages, or starv'd to Death for Want of Food. At the Approach of Night, I slept in a Tree for fear of wild Creatures, but slept soundly tho' it rain'd all Night.

October 1. In the Morning I saw to my great Surprise the Ship had floated with the high Tide, and was driven on Shore again much nearer the Island, which as it was some Comfort on one hand, for seeing her sit upright, and not broken to Pieces, I hop'd, if the Wind abated, I might get on board, and get some Food and Necessaries out of her for my Relief; so on the other hand, it renew'd my Grief at the Loss of my Comrades, who I imagin'd if we had all staid on board might have sav'd the Ship, or at least that they would not have been all drown'd as they were; and that had the Men been sav'd, we might perhaps have built us a Boat out of the Ruins of the Ship, to have carried us to some other Part of the World. I spent great Part of this Day in perplexing my self on these things; but at length seeing the Ship almost dry, I went upon the Sand as near as I could, and then swam on board; this Day also it continu'd raining, tho' with no Wind at all.

From the 1st of *October*, to the 24th. All these Days entirely spent in many several Voyages to get all I could out of the Ship, which I brought on Shore, every Tide of Flood, upon Rafts.

---

1 Far off shore, in deep water.
2 Characterized by mishaps.
3 Murdered.

Much Rain also in these Days, tho' with some Intervals of fair Weather: But, it seems, this was the rainy Season.

Oct. 20. I overset my Raft, and all the Goods I had got upon it, but being in shoal[1] Water, and the things being chiefly heavy, I recover'd many of them when the Tide was out.

Oct. 25. It rain'd all Night and all Day, with some Gusts of Wind, during which time the Ship broke in Pieces, the Wind blowing a little harder than before, and was no more to be seen, except the Wreck of her, and that only at low Water. I spent this Day in covering and securing the Goods which I had sav'd, that the Rain might not spoil them.

Oct. 26. I walk'd about the Shore almost all Day to find out a place to fix my Habitation, greatly concern'd to secure my self from an Attack in the Night, either from wild Beasts or Men. Towards Night I fix'd upon a proper Place under a Rock, and mark'd out a Semi-Circle for my Encampment, which I resolv'd to strengthen with a Work, Wall, or Fortification made of double Piles, lin'd within with Cables, and without with Turf.

From the 26th. to the 30th. I work'd very hard in carrying all my Goods to my new Habitation, tho' some Part of the time it rain'd exceeding hard.

The 31st. in the Morning I went out into the Island with my Gun to see for some Food, and discover the Country, when I kill'd a She-Goat, and her Kid follow'd me home, which I afterwards kill'd also because it would not feed.

November 1. I set up my Tent under a Rock, and lay there for the first Night, making it as large as I could with Stakes driven in to swing my Hammock upon.

Nov. 2. I set up all my Chests and Boards, and the Pieces of Timber which made my Rafts, and with them form'd a Fence round me, a little within the Place I had mark'd out for my Fortification.

Nov. 3. I went out with my Gun and kill'd two Fowls like Ducks, which were very good Food. In the Afternoon went to work to make me a Table.

Nov. 4. This Morning I began to order my times of Work, of going out with my Gun, time of Sleep, and time of Diversion, *viz.* Every Morning I walk'd out with my Gun for two or three Hours if it did not rain, then employ'd my self to work till about Eleven a-Clock, then eat what I had to live on, and from Twelve to Two I lay down to sleep, the Weather being excessive hot, and then in

---

1 Shallow.

the Evening to work again: The working Part of this Day and of the next were wholly employ'd in making my Table, for I was yet but a very sorry Workman, tho' Time and Necessity made me a compleat natural Mechanick[1] soon after, as I believe it would do any one else.

Nov. 5. This Day went abroad with my Gun and my Dog, and kill'd a wild Cat, her Skin pretty soft, but her Flesh good for nothing: Every Creature I kill'd I took off the Skins and preserv'd them: Coming back by the Sea Shore, I saw many Sorts of Sea Fowls which I did not understand, but was surpris'd and almost frighted with two or three Seals, which, while I was gazing at, not well knowing what they were, got into the Sea and escap'd me for that time.

Nov. 6. After my Morning Walk I went to work with my Table again, and finish'd it, tho' not to my liking; nor was it long before I learn'd to mend it.

Nov. 7. Now it began to be settled fair Weather. The 7th, 8th, 9th, 10th, and Part of the 12th. (for the 11th. was Sunday) I took wholly up to make me a Chair, and with much ado brought it to a tolerable Shape, but never to please me, and even in the making I pull'd it in Pieces several times. *Note,* I soon neglected my keeping Sundays, for omitting my Mark for them on my Post, I forgot which was which.

Nov. 13. This Day it rain'd, which refresh'd me exceedingly, and cool'd the Earth, but it was accompany'd with terrible Thunder and Lightning, which frighted me dreadfully for fear of my Powder; as soon as it was over, I resolv'd to separate my Stock of Powder into as many little Parcels as possible, that it might not be in Danger.

Nov. 14, 15, 16. These three Days I spent in making little square Chests or Boxes, which might hold about a Pound or two Pound, at most, of Powder, and so putting the Powder in, I stow'd it in Places as secure and remote from one another as possible. On one of these three Days I kill'd a large Bird that was good to eat, but I know not what to call it.

Nov. 17. This Day I began to dig behind my Tent into the Rock to make room for my farther Conveniency: *Note,* Two Things I wanted exceedingly for this Work, *viz.* A Pick-axe, a Shovel, and a Wheel-barrow or Basket, so I desisted from my Work, and began to consider how to supply that Want and make me some Tools; as for a Pick-axe, I made use of the Iron Crows, which were proper

---

1 Someone skilled in a manual occupation.

enough, tho' heavy; but the next thing was a Shovel or Spade, this was so absolutely necessary, that indeed I could do nothing effectually without it, but what kind of one to make I knew not.

Nov. 18. The next Day in searching the Woods I found a Tree of that Wood, or like it, which, in the *Brasils* they call the *Iron Tree*, for its exceeding Hardness, of this, with great Labour and almost spoiling my Axe, I cut a Piece, and brought it home too with Difficulty enough, for it was exceeding heavy.

The excessive Hardness of the Wood, and having no other Way, made me a long while upon this Machine,[1] for I work'd it effectually by little and little into the Form of a Shovel or Spade, the Handle exactly shap'd like ours in *England*, only that the broad Part having no Iron shod upon it at Bottom, it would not last me so long, however it serv'd well enough for the uses which I had occasion to put it to; but never was a Shovel, I believe, made after that Fashion, or so long a making.

I was still deficient,[2] for I wanted a Basket or a Wheelbarrow, a Basket I could not make by any Means, having no such things as Twigs that would bend to make Wicker Ware, at least none yet found out; and as to a Wheel-barrow, I fancy'd I could make all but the Wheel, but that I had no Notion of, neither did I know how to go about it; besides I had no possible Way to make the Iron Gudgeons for the Spindle or Axis[3] of the Wheel to run in, so I gave it over, and so for carrying away the Earth which I dug out of the Cave, I made me a Thing like a Hodd, which the Labourers carry Morter in, when they serve the Bricklayers.

This was not so difficult to me as the making the Shovel; and yet this, and the Shovel, and the Attempt which I made in vain, to make a Wheel-Barrow, took me up no less than four Days, I mean always, excepting my Morning Walk with my Gun, which I seldom fail'd, and very seldom fail'd also bringing Home something fit to eat.

Nov. 23. My other Work having now stood still, because of my making these Tools; when they were finish'd, I went on, and working every Day, as my Strength and Time allow'd, I spent eighteen Days entirely in widening and deepening my Cave, that it might hold my Goods commodiously.

Note, During all this Time, I work'd to make this Room or Cave spacious enough to accommodate me as a Warehouse or

---

1 Tool, implement.
2 Missing something.
3 Axle.

Magazin, a Kitchen, a Dining-room, and a Cellar; as for my Lodging, I kept to the Tent, except that some Times in the wet Season of the Year, it rain'd so hard, that I could not keep my self dry, which caused me afterwards to cover all my Place within my Pale with long Poles in the Form of Rafters leaning against the Rock, and load them with Flaggs[1] and large Leaves of Trees like a Thatch.

December 10th, I began now to think my Cave or Vault finished, when on a Sudden, (it seems I had made it too large) a great Quantity of Earth fell down from the Top and one Side, so much, that in short it frighted me, and not without Reason too; for if I had been under it I had never wanted a Grave-Digger: Upon this Disaster I had a great deal of Work to do over again; for I had the loose Earth to carry out; and which was of more Importance, I had the Seiling to prop up, so that I might be sure no more would come down.

Dec. 11. This Day I went to Work with it accordingly, and got two Shores or Posts pitch'd upright to the Top, with two Pieces of Boards a-cross over each Post, this I finish'd the next Day; and setting more Posts up with Boards, in about a Week more I had the Roof secur'd; and the Posts standing in Rows, serv'd me for Partitions to part of my House.

Dec. 17. From this Day to the Twentieth I plac'd Shelves, and knock'd up Nails on the Posts to hang every Thing up that could be hung up, and now I began to be in some Order within Doors.

Dec. 20. Now I carry'd every Thing into the Cave, and began to furnish my House, and set up some Pieces of Boards, like a Dresser,[2] to order my Victuals upon, but Boards began to be very scarce with me; also I made me another Table.

Dec. 24. Much Rain all Night and all Day, no stirring out.

Dec. 25. Rain all Day.

Dec. 26. No Rain, and the Earth much cooler than before, and pleasanter.

Dec. 27. Kill'd a young Goat, and lam'd another so as that I catch'd it, and led it Home in a String; when I had it Home, I bound and splinter'd up its Leg which was broke, *N.B.* I took such Care of it, that it liv'd, and the Leg grew well, and as strong as ever; but by my nursing it so long it grew tame, and fed upon the little Green at my Door, and would not go away: This was the first Time that I entertain'd a Thought of breeding up some tame

---

1 Long bladed leaves from rush-like plants.

2 A kitchen sideboard or table where food was prepared (*dressed*).

Creatures, that I might have Food when my Powder and Shot was all spent.

Dec. 28, 29, 30. Great Heats and no Breeze; so that there was no Stirring abroad, except in the Evening for Food; this Time I spent in putting all my Things in Order within Doors.

January 1. Very hot still, but I went abroad early and late with my Gun, and lay still in the Middle of the Day; this Evening going farther into the Valleys which lay towards the Center of the Island, I found there was plenty of Goats, tho' exceeding shy and hard to come at, however I resolv'd to try if I could not bring my Dog to hunt them down.

Jan. 2. Accordingly, the next Day, I went out with my Dog, and set him upon the Goats; but I was mistaken, for they all fac'd about upon the Dog, and he knew his Danger too well, for he would not come near them.

Jan. 3. I began my Fence or Wall; which being still jealous[1] of my being attack'd by some Body, I resolv'd to make very thick and strong.

N.B. This Wall being describ'd before, I purposely omit what was said in the Journal; it is sufficient to observe, that I was no less Time than from the 3d of January to the 14th of April, working, finishing, and perfecting this Wall, tho' it was no more than about 24 Yards in Length, being a half Circle from one Place in the Rock to another Place about eight Yards from it, the Door of the Cave being in the Center behind it.

All this Time I work'd very hard, the Rains hindering me many Days, nay sometimes Weeks together; but I thought I should never be perfectly secure 'till this Wall was finish'd; and it is scarce credible what inexpressible Labour every Thing was done with, especially the bringing Piles out of the Woods, and driving them into the Ground, for I made them much bigger than I need to have done.

When this Wall was finished, and the Out-side double fenc'd with a Turff-Wall rais'd up close to it, I perswaded my self, that if any People were to come on Shore there, they would not perceive any Thing like a Habitation; and it was very well I did so, as may be observ'd hereafter upon a very remarkable Occasion.

During this Time, I made my Rounds in the Woods for Game every Day when the Rain admitted me, and made frequent Dis-

---

1 Anxious, fearful.

coveries in these Walks of something or other to my Advantage; particularly I found a Kind of wild Pidgeons, who built not as Wood Pidgeons in a Tree, but rather as House Pidgeons, in the Holes of the Rocks; and taking some young ones, I endeavoured to bread them up tame, and did so; but when they grew older they flew all away, which perhaps was at first for Want of feeding them, for I had nothing to give them; however I frequently found their Nests, and got their young ones, which were very good Meat.

And now, in the managing my houshold Affairs, I found my self wanting in many Things, which I thought at first it was impossible for me to make, as indeed as to some of them it was; *for Instance*, I could never make a Cask to be hooped, I had a small Runlet or two, *as I observed before*, but I cou'd never arrive to the Capacity of making one by them, tho' I spent many Weeks about it; I could neither put in the Heads, or joint the Staves[1] so true to one another, as to make them hold Water, so I gave that also over.

In the next Place, I was at a great Loss for Candle; so that as soon as ever it was dark, which was generally by Seven-a-Clock, I was oblig'd to go to Bed: I remembered the Lump of Bees-wax with which I made Candles in my *African* Adventure, but I had none of that now; the only Remedy I had was, that when I had kill'd a Goat, I sav'd the Tallow, and with a little Dish made of Clay, which I bak'd in the Sun, to which I added a Wick of some Oakum,[2] I made me a Lamp; and this gave me Light, tho' not a clear steady Light like a Candle; in the Middle of all my Labours it happen'd, that rumaging my Things, I found a little Bag, which, as I hinted before, had been fill'd with Corn for the feeding of Poultry, not for this Voyage, but before, as I suppose, when the Ship came from *Lisbon*, what little Remainder of Corn had been in the Bag, was all devour'd with the Rats, and I saw nothing in the Bag but Husks and Dust; and being willing to have the Bag for some other Use, I think it was to put Powder in, when I divided it for Fear of the Lightning, or some such Use, I shook the Husks of Corn out of it on one Side of my Fortification under the Rock.

It was a little before the great Rains, just now mention'd, that I threw this Stuff away, taking no Notice of any Thing, and not so

---

1 Thick sticks of wood used to make casks.
2 Hemp fibers picked apart from old ropes, tarred, and used to caulk the seams of ships.

much as remembering that I had thrown any Thing there; when about a Month after, or thereabout, I saw some few Stalks of something green, shooting out of the Ground, which I fancy'd might be some Plant I had not seen, but I was surpriz'd and perfectly astonish'd, when, after a little longer Time, I saw about ten or twelve Ears come out, which were perfect green Barley of the same Kind as our *European*, nay, as our *English* Barley.

It is impossible to express the Astonishment and Confusion of my Thoughts on this Occasion; I had hitherto acted upon no religious Foundation at all, indeed I had very few Notions of Religion in my Head, or had entertain'd any Sense of any Thing that had befallen me, otherwise than as a Chance, or, as we lightly say, what pleases God; without so much as enquiring into the End[1] of Providence in these Things, or his Order in governing Events in the World: But after I saw Barley grow there, in a Climate which I know was not proper for Corn,[2] and especially that I knew not how it came there, it startl'd me strangely, and I began to suggest, that God had miraculously caus'd this Grain to grow without any Help of Seed sown, and that it was so directed purely for my Sustenance, on that wild miserable Place.[3]

This touch'd my Heart a little, and brought Tears out of my Eyes, and I began to bless my self, that such a Prodigy[4] of Nature should happen upon my Account; and this was the more strange to me, because I saw near it still all along by the Side of the Rock, some other straggling Stalks, which prov'd to be Stalks of Ryce, and which I knew, because I had seen it grow in *Africa* when I was ashore there.

I not only thought these the pure Productions of Providence for my Support, but not doubting, but that there was more in the Place, I went all over that Part of the Island, where I had been before, peering in every Corner, and under every Rock, to see for more of it, but I could not find any; at last it occur'd to my Thoughts, that I had shook a Bag of Chickens Meat[5] out in that

---

1 Aim, purpose.
2 Crusoe is referring here and elsewhere to barley, not maize.
3 This scene recalls John 12: 24-25: "Verily, verily, I say unto you, Except a corn of wheat fall into the ground and die, it abideth alone: but if it die, it bringeth forth much fruit. He that loveth his life shall lose it; and he that hateth his life in this world shall keep it unto life eternal" [Damrosch 190].
4 A wondrous occurrence taken as a sign.
5 Feed.

Place, and then the Wonder began to cease; and I must confess, my religious Thankfulness to God's Providence began to abate too upon the Discovering that all this was nothing but what was common; tho' I ought to have been as thankful for so strange and unforseen Providence, as if it had been miraculous; for it was really the Work of Providence as to me, that should order or appoint, that 10 or 12 Grains of Corn should remain unspoil'd, (when the Rats had destroy'd all the rest,) as if it had been dropt from Heaven; as also, that I should throw it out in that particular Place, where it being in the Shade of a high Rock, it sprang up immediately; whereas, if I had thrown it anywhere else, at that Time, it had been burnt up and destroy'd.

I carefully sav'd the Ears of this Corn you may be sure in their Season, which was about the End of *June*; and laying up every Corn, I resolv'd to sow them all again, hoping in Time to have some Quantity sufficient to supply me with Bread; But it was not till the 4th Year that I could allow my self the least Grain of this Corn to eat, and even then but sparingly, as I shall say afterwards in its Order; for I lost all that I sow'd the first Season, by not observing the proper Time; for I sow'd it just before the dry Season, so that it never came up at all, at least, not as it would ha' done: Of which in its Place.

Besides this Barley, there was, as above, 20 or 30 Stalks of Ryce, which I preserv'd with the same Care, and whose Use was of the same Kind or to the same Purpose, (*viz.*) to make me Bread, or rather Food; for I found Ways to cook it up without baking, tho' I did that also after some Time. But to return to my Journal,

I work'd excessive hard these three or four Months to get my Wall done; and the 14th of *April* I closed it up, contriving to go into it, not by a Door, but over the Wall by a Ladder, that there might be no Sign in the Out-side of my Habitation.

April 16. I finish'd the Ladder, so I went up with the Ladder to the Top, and then pull'd it up after me, and let it down in the In-side: This was a compleat Enclosure to me; for within I had Room enough, and nothing could come at me from without, unless it could first mount my Wall.

The very next Day after this Wall was finish'd, I had almost had all my Labour overthrown at once, and my self kill'd, the Case was thus, As I was busy in the Inside of it, behind my Tent, just in the Entrance into my Cave, I was terribly frighted with a most dreadful surprising Thing indeed; for all on a sudden I found the Earth come crumbling down from the Roof of my

Cave, and from the Edge of the Hill over my Head, and two of the Posts I had set up in the Cave crack'd in a frightful Manner; I was heartily scar'd, but thought nothing of what was really the Cause, only thinking that the Top of my Cave was falling in, as some of it had done before; and for Fear I shou'd be bury'd in it, I run foreward to my Ladder, and not thinking my self safe there neither, I got over my Wall for Fear of the Pieces of the Hill which I expected might roll down upon me: I was no sooner stepp'd down upon the firm Ground, but I plainly saw it was a terrible Earthquake, for the Ground I stood on shook three Times at about eight Minutes Distance, with three such Shocks, as would have overturn'd the strongest Building that could be suppos'd to have stood on the Earth, and a great Piece of the Top of a Rock, which stood about half a Mile from me next the Sea, fell down with such a terrible Noise, as I never heard in all my Life, I perceiv'd also, the very Sea was put into violent Motion by it; and I believe the Shocks were stronger under the Water than on the Island.

I was so amaz'd with the Thing it self, having never felt the like, or discours'd with any one that had, that I was like one dead or stupify'd; and the Motion of the Earth made my Stomach sick like one that was toss'd at Sea; but the Noise of the falling of the Rock awak'd me as it were, and rousing me from the stupify'd Condition I was in, fill'd me with Horror, and I thought of nothing then but the Hill falling upon my Tent and all my houshold Goods, and burying all at once; and this sunk my very Soul within me a second Time.

After the third Shock was over, and I felt no more for some Time, I began to take Courage, and yet I had not Heart enough to go over my Wall again, for Fear of being buried alive, but sat still upon the Ground, greatly cast down and disconsolate, not knowing what to do: All this while I had not the least serious religious Thought, nothing but the common, *Lord ha' Mercy upon me*;[1] and when it was over, that went away too.

While I sat thus, I found the Air over-cast, and grow cloudy, as if it would Rain; soon after that the Wind rose by little and little, so that, in less than half an Hour, it blew a most dreadful Hurricane: The Sea was all on a Sudden cover'd over with Foam and Froth, the Shore was cover'd with the Breach of the Water, the Trees were torn up by the Roots, and a terrible Storm it was; and this held about three Hours, and then began to abate, and

---

1 This phrase is frequently repeated in the *Book of Common Prayer*.

in two Hours more it was stark calm,[1] and began to rain very hard.

All this while I sat upon the Ground very much terrify'd and dejected, when on a sudden it came into my thoughts, that these Winds and Rain being the Consequences of the Earthquake, the Earthquake it self was spent and over, and I might venture into my Cave again: With this Thought my Spirits began to revive, and the Rain also helping to perswade me, I went in and sat down in my Tent, but the Rain was so violent, that my Tent was ready to be beaten down with it, and I was forc'd to go into my Cave, tho' very much afraid and uneasy for fear it should fall on my Head.

This violent Rain forc'd me to a new Work, *viz.* To cut a Hole thro' my new Fortification like a Sink to let the Water go out, which would else have drown'd my Cave. After I had been in my Cave some time, and found still no more Shocks of the Earthquake follow, I began to be more compos'd; and now to support my Spirits, which indeed wanted it very much, I went to my little Store and took a small Sup of Rum, which however I did then and always very sparingly, knowing I could have no more when that was gone.

It continu'd raining all that Night, and great Part of the next Day, so that I could not stir abroad, but my Mind being more compos'd, I began to think of what I had best do, concluding that if the Island was subject to these Earthquakes, there would be no living for me in a Cave, but I must consider of building me some little Hut in an open Place which I might surround with a Wall as I had done here, and so make my self secure from wild Beasts or Men; but concluded, if I staid where I was, I should certainly, one time or other, be bury'd alive.

With these Thoughts I resolv'd to remove my Tent from the Place where it stood, which was just under the hanging Precipice of the Hill, and which, if it should be shaken again, would certainly fall upon my Tent: And I spent the two next Days, being the 19th and 20th of *April*, in contriving where and how to remove my Habitation.

The fear of being swallow'd up alive, made me that I never slept in quiet, and yet the Apprehensions of lying abroad without any Fence was almost equal to it; but still when I look'd about and saw how every thing was put in order, how pleasantly conceal'd I was, and how safe from Danger, it made me very loath to remove.

---

1 Absolutely calm.

In the mean time it occur'd to me that it would require a vast deal of time for me to do this, and that I must be contented to run the Venture where I was, till I had form'd a Camp for my self, and had secur'd it so as to remove to it: So with this Resolution I compos'd my self for a time, and resolv'd that I would go to work with all Speed to build me a Wall with Piles and Cables, &c. in a Circle as before, and set my Tent up in it when it was finish'd, but that I would venture to stay where I was till it was finish'd and fit to remove to. This was the 21st.

April 22. The next Morning I began to consider of Means to put this Resolve in Execution, but I was at a great loss about my Tools; I had three large Axes and abundance of Hatchets, (for we carried the Hatchets for Traffick with the *Indians*[1]) but with much chopping and cutting knotty hard Wood, they were all full of Notches and dull, and tho' I had a Grindstone, I could not turn it and grind my Tools too, this cost me as much Thought as a Statesman would have bestow'd upon a grand Point of Politicks, or a Judge upon the Life and Death of a Man. At length I contriv'd a Wheel with a String, to turn it with my Foot, that I might have both my Hands at Liberty: *Note*, I had never seen any such thing in *England*, or at least not to take Notice how it was done, tho' since I have observ'd it is very common there; besides that, my Grindstone was very large and heavy. This Machine cost me a full Weeks Work to bring it to Perfection.

April 28, 29. These two whole Days I took up in grinding my Tools, my Machine for turning my Grindstone performing very well.

April 30. Having perceiv'd my Bread had been low a great while, now I took a Survey of it, and reduc'd my self to one Bisket-cake a Day, which made my Heart very heavy.

May 1. In the Morning looking towards the Sea-side, the Tide being low, I saw something lye on the Shore bigger than ordinary, and it look'd like a Cask, when I came to it, I found a small Barrel, and two or three Pieces of the Wreck of the Ship, which were driven on Shore by the late[2] Hurricane, and looking towards the Wreck itself, I thought it seem'd to lye higher out of the Water than it us'd to do; I examin'd the Barrel which was driven on Shore, and soon found it was a Barrel of Gunpowder, but it had taken Water, and the Powder was cak'd as hard as a Stone, however I roll'd it farther on Shore for the present, and went on

---

1 African natives.
2 Recent.

upon the Sands as near as I could to the Wreck of the Ship to look for more.

When I came down to the Ship I found it strangely remov'd, The Fore-castle which lay before bury'd in Sand, was heav'd up at least Six Foot, and the Stern which was broke to Pieces and parted from the rest by the Force of the Sea soon after I had left rummaging her, was toss'd, as it were, up, and cast on one Side, and the Sand was thrown so high on that Side next her Stern, that whereas there was a great Place of Water before, so that I could not come within a Quarter of a Mile of the Wreck without swimming, I could now walk quite up to her when the Tide was out; I was surpriz'd with this at first, but soon concluded it must be done by the Earthquake, and as by this Violence the Ship was more broken open than formerly, so many Things came daily on Shore, which the Sea had loosen'd, and which the Winds and Water rolled by Degrees to the Land.

This wholly diverted my Thoughts from the Design of removing my Habitation; and I busied my self mightily that Day especially, in searching whether I could make any Way into the Ship, but I found nothing was to be expected of that Kind, for that all the In-side of the Ship was choack'd up with Sand: However, as I had learn'd not to despair of any Thing, I resolv'd to pull every Thing to Pieces that I could of the Ship, concluding, that every Thing I could get from her would be of some Use or other to me.

May 3. I began with my Saw, and cut a Piece of a Beam thro', which I thought held some of the upper Part or Quarter-Deck together, and when I had cut it thro', I clear'd away the Sand as well as I could from the Side which lay highest; but the Tide coming in, I was oblig'd to give over for that Time.

May 4. I went a fishing, but caught not one Fish that I durst eat of, till I was weary of my Sport, when just going to leave off, I caught a young Dolphin. I had made me a long Line of some Rope Yarn, but I had no Hooks, yet I frequently caught Fish enough, as much as I car'd to eat; all which I dry'd in the Sun, and eat them dry.

May 5. Work'd on the Wreck, cut another Beam asunder, and brought three great Fir Planks off from the Decks, which I ty'd together, and made swim on Shore when the Tide of Flood came on.

May 6. Work'd on the Wreck, got several Iron Bolts out of her, and other Pieces of Iron Work, work'd very hard, and came Home very much tyr'd, and had Thoughts of giving it over.[1]

---

1 Giving up, stopping work.

May 7. Went to the Wreck again, but with an Intent not to work, but found the Weight of the Wreck had broke itself down, the Beams being cut, that several Pieces of the Ship seem'd to lie loose, and the In-side of the Hold lay so open, that I could see into it, but almost full of Water and Sand.

May 8. Went to the Wreck, and carry'd an Iron Crow to wrench up the Deck, which lay now quite clear of the Water or Sand; I wrench'd open two Planks, and brought them on Shore also with the Tide: I left the Iron Crow in the Wreck for next Day.

May 9. Went to the Wreck, and with the Crow made Way into the Body of the Wreck, and felt several Casks, and loosen'd them with the Crow, but could not break them up; I felt also the Roll of *English* Lead, and could stir it, but it was too heavy to remove.

May 10, 11, 12, 13, 14. Went every Day to the Wreck, and got a great deal of Pieces of Timber, and Boards, or Plank, and 2 or 300 Weight of Iron.

May 15. I carry'd two Hatchets to try if I could not cut a Piece off of the Roll of Lead, by placing the Edge of one Hatchet, and driving it with the other; but as it lay about a Foot and a half in the Water, I could not make any Blow to drive the Hatchet.

May 16. It had blow'd hard in the Night, and the Wreck appear'd more broken by the Force of the Water; but I stay'd so long in the Woods to get Pidgeons for Food, that the Tide prevented me going to the Wreck that Day.

May 17. I saw some Pieces of the Wreck blown on Shore, at a great Distance, near two Miles off me, but resolv'd to see what they were, and found it was a Piece of the Head, but too heavy for me to bring away.

May 24. Every Day to this Day I work'd on the Wreck, and with hard Labour I loosen'd some Things so much with the Crow, that the first blowing Tide several Casks floated out, and two of the Seamens Chests; but the Wind blowing from the Shore, nothing came to Land that Day, but Pieces of Timber, and a Hogshead which had some *Brazil* Pork in it, but the Salt-water and the Sand had spoil'd it.

I continu'd this Work every Day to the 15th of *June*, except the Time necessary to get Food, which I always appointed, during this Part of my Employment, to be when the Tide was up, that I might be ready when it was ebb'd out, and by this Time I had gotten Timber, and Plank, and Iron-Work enough, to have builded a good Boat, if I had known how; and also, I got at several Times, and in several Pieces, near 100 Weight of the Sheat-Lead.

June 16. Going down to the Sea-side, I found a large Tortoise or Turtle; this was the first I had seen, which it seems was only my Misfortune, not any Defect of the Place, or Scarcity; for had I happen'd to be on the other Side of the Island, I might have had Hundreds of them every Day, as I found afterwards; but perhaps had paid dear enough for them.

June 17. I spent in cooking the Turtle; I found in her three-score Eggs; and her Flesh was to me at that Time the most savoury and pleasant that ever I tasted in my Life, having had no Flesh, but of Goats and Fowls, since I landed in this horrid Place.

June 18. Rain'd all Day, and I stay'd within. I thought at this Time the Rain felt Cold, and I was something chilly, which I knew was not usual in that Latitude.

June 19. Very ill, and shivering, as if the Weather had been cold.

June 20. No Rest all Night, violent Pains in my Head, and feaverish.

June 21. Very ill, frighted almost to Death with the Apprehensions of my sad Condition, to be sick, and no Help: Pray'd to GOD for the first Time since the Storm off of *Hull*, but scarce knew what I said, or why; my Thoughts being all confused.

June 22. A little better, but under dreadful Apprehensions of Sickness.

June 23. Very bad again, cold and shivering, and then a violent Head-ach.

June 24. Much better.

June 25. An Ague[1] very violent; the Fit held me seven Hours, cold Fit and hot, with faint Sweats after it.

June 26. Better; and having no Victuals to eat, took my Gun, but found my self very weak; however I kill'd a She-Goat, and with much Difficulty got it Home, and broil'd some of it, and eat; I wou'd fain[2] have stew'd it, and made some Broath, but had no Pot.

June 27. The Ague again so violent, that I lay a-Bed all Day, and neither eat or drank. I was ready to perish for Thirst, but so weak, I had not Strength to stand up, or to get my self any Water to drink: Pray'd to God again, but was light-headed, and when I was not, I was so ignorant, that I knew not what to say; only I lay and cry'd, *Lord look upon me, Lord pity me, Lord have Mercy upon me*: I suppose I did nothing else for two or three Hours, till the

---

1　Illness characterized by bouts of chills, fever, and sweating.

2　Gladly.

Fit wearing off, I fell asleep, and did not wake till far in the Night; when I wak'd, I found my self much refresh'd, but weak, and exceeding thirsty: However, as I had no Water in my whole Habitation, I was forc'd to lie till Morning, and went to sleep again: In this second Sleep, I had this terrible Dream.

I thought, that I was sitting on the Ground on the Out-side of my Wall, where I sat when the Storm blew after the Earthquake, and that I saw a Man descend from a great black Cloud, in a bright Flame of Fire, and light upon the Ground: He was all over as bright as a Flame, so that I could but just bear to look towards him; his Countenance was most inexpressibly dreadful, impossible for Words to describe; when he stepp'd upon the Ground with his Feet, I thought the Earth trembl'd, just as it had done before in the Earthquake, and all the Air look'd, to my Apprehension, as if it had been fill'd with Flashes of Fire.

He was no sooner landed upon the Earth, but he moved forward towards me, with a long Spear or Weapon in his Hand, to kill me; and when he came to a rising Ground, at some Distance, he spoke to me, or I heard a Voice so terrible, that it is impossible to express the Terror of it; all that I can say, I understood, was this, *Seeing all these Things have not brought thee to Repentance, now thou shalt die*: At which Words, I thought he lifted up the Spear that was in his Hand, to kill me.

No one, that shall ever read this Account, will expect that I should be able to describe the Horrors of my Soul at this terrible Vision, I mean, that even while it was a Dream, I even dreamed of those Horrors; nor is it any more possible to describe the Impression that remain'd upon my Mind when I awak'd and found it was but a Dream.

I had alas! no divine Knowledge;[1] what I had received by the good Instruction of my Father was then worn out by an uninterrupted Series, for 8 Years, of Seafaring Wickedness, and a constant Conversation with nothing but such as were like my self, wicked and prophane to the last Degree: I do not remember that I had in all that Time one Thought that so much as tended either to looking upwards toward God, or inwards towards a Reflection upon my own Ways: But a certain Stupidity[2] of Soul, without Desire of Good, or Conscience of Evil, had entirely overwhelm'd me, and I was all that the most hardned, unthinking, wicked Creature among our common Sailors, can be supposed to be, not

---

1 Knowledge of religious matters.

2 Dulness, inactivity, apathy.

having the least Sense, either of the Fear of God in Danger, or of Thankfulness to God in Deliverances.

In the relating what is already past of my Story, this will be the more easily believ'd, when I shall add, that thro' all the Variety of Miseries that had to this Day befallen me, I never had so much as one Thought of it being the Hand of God, or that it was a just Punishment for my Sin; my rebellious Behaviour against my Father, or my present Sins which were great; or so much as a Punishment for the general Course of my wicked Life. When I was on the desperate Expedition on the desart Shores of *Africa*, I never had so much as one Thought of what would become of me; or one Wish to God to direct me whether[1] I should go, or to keep me from the Danger which apparently surrounded me, as well from voracious Creatures as cruel Savages: But I was meerly thoughtless of a God, or a Providence; acted like a meer Brute from the Principles of Nature, and by the Dictates of common Sense only, and indeed hardly that.

When I was deliver'd and taken up at Sea by the *Portugal* Captain, well us'd, and dealt justly and honourably with, as well as charitably, I had not the least Thankfulness on my Thoughts: When again I was shipwreck'd, ruin'd, and in Danger of drowning on this Island, I was as far from Remorse, or looking on it as a Judgment; I only said to my self often, that I was *an unfortunate Dog*, and born to be always miserable.

It is true, when I got on Shore first here, and found all my Ship's Crew drown'd, and my self spar'd, I was surpriz'd with a Kind of Extasie, and some Transports of Soul, which, had the Grace of God assisted, might have come up to true Thankfulness; but it ended where it begun, in a meer common Flight of Joy, or as I may say, *being glad I was alive*, without the least Reflection upon the distinguishing Goodness of the Hand which had preserv'd me, and had singled me out to be preserv'd, when all the rest were destroy'd; or an Enquiry why Providence had been thus merciful to me; even just the same common Sort of Joy which Seamen generally have after they are got safe ashore from a Shipwreck, which they drown all in the next Bowl of Punch, and forget almost as soon as it is over, and all the rest of my Life was like it.

Even when I was afterwards, on due Consideration, made sensible of my Condition, how I was cast on this dreadful Place, out of the Reach of humane Kind, out of all Hope of Relief, or

---

1 Whither.

Prospect of Redemption, as soon as I saw but a Prospect of living, and that I should not starve and perish for Hunger, all the Sense of my Affliction wore off, and I begun to be very easy, apply'd my self to the Works proper for my Preservation and Supply, and was far enough from being afflicted at my Condition, as a Judgment from Heaven, or as the Hand of God against me; these were Thoughts which very seldom enter'd into my Head.

The growing up of the Corn, as is hinted in my Journal, had at first some little Influence upon me, and began to affect me with Seriousness, as long as I thought it had something miraculous in it; but as soon as ever that Part of the Thought was remov'd, all the Impression which was rais'd from it, wore off also, as I have noted already.

Even the Earthquake, tho' nothing could be more terrible in its Nature, or more immediately directing to the invisible Power which alone directs such Things, yet no sooner was the first Fright over, but the Impression it had made went off also. I had no more Sense of God or his Judgments, much less of the present Affliction of my Circumstances being from his Hand, than if I had been in the most prosperous Condition of Life.

But now when I began to be sick, and a leisurely View of the Miseries of Death came to place itself before me; when my Spirits began to sink under the Burthen of a strong Distemper, and Nature was exhausted with the Violence of the Feaver; Conscience that had slept so long, begun to awake, and I began to reproach my self with my past Life, in which I had so evidently, by uncommon Wickedness, provok'd the Justice of God to lay me under uncommon Strokes, and to deal with me in so vindictive a Manner.

These Reflections oppress'd me for the second or third Day of my Distemper, and in the Violence, as well of the Feaver, as of the dreadful Reproaches of my Conscience, extorted some Words from me, like praying to God, tho' I cannot say they were either a Prayer attended with Desires or with Hopes; it was rather the Voice of meer Fright and Distress; my Thoughts were confus'd, the Convictions great upon my Mind, and the Horror of dying in such a miserable Condition rais'd Vapours[1] into my Head with the meer Apprehensions; and in these Hurries of my Soul, I know not what my Tongue might express: but it was rather Exclamation, such as, Lord! what a miserable Creature am I? If I should

---

1 A nervous disorder supposedly characterized by pent-up exhalations in the body.

be sick, I shall certainly die for Want of Help, and what will become of me! Then the Tears burst out of my Eyes, and I could say no more for a good while.

In this Interval, the good Advice of my Father came to my Mind, and presently his Prediction which I mention'd at the Beginning of this Story, viz. *That if I did take this foolish Step, God would not bless me, and I would have Leisure hereafter to reflect upon having neglected his Counsel, when there might be none to assist in my Recovery.* Now, said I aloud, My dear Father's Words are come to pass: God's Justice has overtaken me, and I have none to help or hear me: I rejected the Voice of Providence, which had mercifully put me in a Posture or Station of Life, wherein I might have been happy and easy; but I would neither see it my self, or learn to know the Blessing of it from my Parents; I left them to mourn over my Folly, and now I am left to mourn under the Consequences of it: I refus'd their Help and Assistance who wou'd have lifted me into the World, and wou'd have made every Thing easy to me, and now I have Difficulties to struggle with, too great for even Nature itself to support, and no Assistance, no Help, no Comfort, no Advice; then I cry'd out, *Lord be my Help, for I am in great Distress.*

This was the first Prayer, if I may call it so, that I had made for many Years: But I return to my Journal.

June 28. Having been somewhat refresh'd with the Sleep I had had, and the Fit being entirely off, I got up; and tho' the Fright and Terror of my Dream was very great, yet I consider'd, that the Fit of the Ague wou'd return again the next Day, and now was my Time to get something to refresh and support my self when I should be ill; and the first Thing I did, I fill'd a large square Case Bottle[1] with Water, and set it upon my Table, in Reach of my Bed; and to take off the chill or aguish Disposition of the Water, I put about a Quarter of a Pint of Rum into it, and mix'd them together; then I got me a Piece of the Goat's Flesh, and broil'd it on the Coals, but could eat very little; I walk'd about, but was very weak, and withal very sad and heavy-hearted in the Sense of my miserable Condition; dreading the Return of my Distemper the next Day; at Night I made my Supper of three of the Turtle's Eggs, which I roasted in the Ashes, and eat, as we call it, in the Shell; and this was the first Bit of Meat I had ever ask'd God's Blessing to, even as I cou'd remember, in my whole Life.

---

1 A square bottle deigned to fit into a case with other bottles.

After I had eaten, I try'd to walk, but found my self so weak, that I cou'd hardly carry the Gun, (for I never went out without that) so I went but a little Way, and sat down upon the Ground, looking out upon the Sea, which was just before me, and very calm and smooth: As I sat here, some such Thoughts as these occurred to me.

What is this Earth and Sea of which I have seen so much, whence is it produc'd, and what am I, and all the other Creatures, wild and tame, humane and brutal, whence are we?

Sure we are all made by some secret Power, who form'd the Earth and Sea, the Air and Sky; and who is that?

Then it follow'd most naturally, It is God that has made it all: Well, but then it came on strangely, if God has made all these Things, He guides and governs them all, and all Things that concern them; for the Power that could make all Things, must certainly have Power to guide and direct them.

If so, nothing can happen in the great Circuit of his Works, either without his Knowledge or Appointment.[1]

And if nothing happens without his Knowledge, he knows that I am here, and am in this dreadful Condition; and if nothing happens without his Appointment, he has appointed all this to befal me.

Nothing occurr'd to my Thought to contradict any of these Conclusions; and therefore it rested upon me with the greater Force, that it must needs be, that God had appointed all this to befal me; that I was brought to this miserable Circumstance by his Direction, he having the sole Power, not of me only, but of every Thing that happen'd in the World. Immediately it follow'd,

Why has God done this to me? What have I done to be thus us'd?

My Conscience presently check'd me in that Enquiry, as if I had blasphem'd, and methought it spoke to me like a Voice; *WRETCH! dost thou ask what thou hast done!* look back upon a dreadful mis-spent Life, and ask thy self *what thou hast not done?* ask, Why is it *that thou wert not long ago destroy'd?* Why *wert thou not drown'd in* Yarmouth Roads? *Kill'd in the Fight when the Ship was taken by* the Sallee Man of War? *Devour'd by the wild Beasts on the* Coast of Africa? Or, *Drown'd HERE, when all the Crew perish'd but thy self?* Dost thou ask, *What have I done?*

I was struck dumb[2] with these Reflections, as one astonish'd,[3]

---

1 Direction, guidance.

2 Mute, unable to speak.

3 Stupefied, stunned.

and had not a Word to say, no not to answer to my self, but rise up pensive and sad, walk'd back to my Retreat, and went up over my Wall, as if I had been going to Bed, but my Thoughts were sadly disturb'd, and I had no Inclination to Sleep; so I sat down in my Chair, and lighted my Lamp, for it began to be dark: Now as the Apprehension of the Return of my Distemper terrify'd me very much, it occurr'd to my Thought, that the *Brasilians* take no Physick but their Tobacco, for almost all Distempers; and I had a Piece of a Roll of Tobacco in one of the Chests, which was quite cur'd, and some also that was green and not quite cur'd.

I went, directed by Heaven no doubt; for in this Chest I found a Cure, both for Soul and Body, I open'd the Chest, and found what I look'd for, *viz.* the Tobacco; and as the few Books, I had sav'd, lay there too, I took out one of the Bibles which I mention'd before, and which to this Time I had not found Leisure, or so much as Inclination to look into; I say, I took it out, and brought both that and the Tobacco with me to the Table.

What Use to make of the Tobacco, I knew not, as to my Distemper, or whether it was good for it or no; but I try'd several Experiments with it, as if I was resolv'd it should hit one Way or other: I first took a Piece of a Leaf, and chew'd it in my Mouth, which indeed at first almost stupify'd my Brain, the Tobacco being green and strong, and that I had not been much us'd to it; then I took some and steeped it an Hour or two in some Rum, and resolv'd to take a Dose of it when I lay down; and lastly, I burnt some upon a Pan of Coals, and held my Nose close over the Smoke of it as long as I could bear it, as well for the Heat as almost for Suffocation.

In the Interval of this Operation, I took up the Bible and began to read, but my Head was too much disturb'd with the Tobacco to bear reading, at least that Time; only having open'd the Book casually, the first Words that occurr'd to me were these, *Call on me in the Day of Trouble, and I will deliver, and thou shalt glorify me.*[1]

The Words were very apt to my Case, and made some Impression upon my Thoughts at the Time of reading them, tho' not so much as they did afterwards; for as for being deliver'd, the Word had no Sound, *as I may say*, to me; the Thing was so remote, so impossible in my Apprehension of Things, that I began to say as the Children of *Israel* did, when they were promis'd Flesh to eat,

---

1 Psalms 50:15.

Can God spread a Table in the Wilderness;[1] so I began to say, Can God himself deliver me from this Place? and as it was not for many Years that any Hope appear'd, this prevail'd very often upon my Thoughts: But however, the Words made a great Impression upon me, and I mused upon them very often. It grew now late, and the Tobacco had, as I said, doz'd[2] my Head so much, that I inclin'd to sleep; so I left my Lamp burning in the Cave, least I should want any Thing in the Night, and went to Bed; but before I lay down, I did what I never had done in all my Life, I kneel'd down and pray'd to God to fulfil the Promise to me, that if I call'd upon him in the Day of Trouble, he would deliver me; after my broken and imperfect Prayer was over, I drunk the Rum in which I had steep'd the Tobacco, which was so strong and rank of the Tobacco, that indeed I could scarce get it down; immediately upon this I went to Bed, I found presently it flew up in my Head violently, but I fell into a sound Sleep, and wak'd no more 'till by the Sun it must necessarily be near Three a-Clock in the Afternoon the next Day; nay, to this Hour, I'm partly of the Opinion, that I slept all the next Day and Night, and 'till almost Three that Day after; for otherwise I knew not how I should lose a Day out of my Reckoning in the Days of the Week, as it appear'd some Years after I had done: for if I had lost it by crossing and re-crossing the Line, I should have lost more than one Day: But certainly I lost a Day in my Accompt, and never knew which Way.

Be that however one Way or th' other, when I awak'd I found my self exceedingly refresh'd, and my Spirits lively and chearful; when I got up, I was stronger than I was the Day before, and my Stomach better, for I was hungry; and in short, I had no Fit the next Day, but continu'd much alter'd for the better; this was the 29th.

The 30th was my well Day of Course, and I went abroad with my Gun, but did not care to travel too far, I kill'd a Sea Fowl or two, something like a brand Goose,[3] and brought them Home, but was not very forward to eat them; so I ate some more of the Turtle's Eggs, which were very good: This Evening I renew'd the Medicine which I had suppos'd did me good the Day before, *viz.* the Tobacco steep'd in Rum, only I did not take so much as

---

1 Psalms 78:19: "Yea, they spake against God; they said, Can God furnish a table in the wilderness?"
2 To make drowsy; but also, to muddle, to confuse.
3 Brant geese are small wild geese that visit the British coasts in the winter.

before, nor did I chew any of the Leaf, or hold my Head over the Smoke; however, I was not so well the next Day, which was the first of *July*, as I hop'd I shou'd have been; for I had a little Spice[1] of the cold Fit, but it was not much.

July 2. I renew'd the Medicine all the three Ways, and doz'd my self with it as at first; and doubled the Quantity which I drank.

3. I miss'd the Fit for good and all, tho' I did not recover my full Strength for some Weeks after; while I was thus gathering Strength, my Thoughts run exceedingly upon this Scripture, *I will deliver thee*, and the Impossibility of my Deliverance lay much upon my Mind in Barr of[2] my ever expecting it: But as I was discouraging my self with such Thoughts, it occurr'd to my Mind, that I pored so much upon my Deliverance from the main Affliction, that I disregarded the Deliverance I had receiv'd; and I was, as it were, made to ask my self such Questions as these, *viz.* Have I not been deliver'd, and wonderfully too, from Sickness? from the most distress'd Condition that could be, and that was so frightful to me, and what Notice I had taken of it: Had I done my Part, *God had deliver'd me, but I had not glorify'd him*; that is to say, I had not own'd and been thankful for that as a Deliverance, and how cou'd I expect greater Deliverance?

This touch'd my Heart very much, and immediately I kneel'd down and gave God Thanks aloud, for my Recovery from my Sickness.

July 4. In the Morning I took the Bible, and beginning at the New Testament, I began seriously to read it, and impos'd upon my self to read a while every Morning and every Night, not tying my self to the Number of Chapters, but as long as my Thoughts shou'd engage me: It was not long after I set seriously to this Work, but I found my Heart more deeply and sincerely affected with the Wickedness of my past Life: The Impression of my Dream reviv'd, and the Words, *All these Things have not brought thee to Repentance*, ran seriously in my Thought: I was earnestly begging of God to give me Repentance, when it happen'd providentially the very Day that reading the Scripture, I came to these Words, *He is exalted a Prince and a Saviour, to give Repentance, and to give Remission*:[3] I threw down the Book, and with my Heart as well as my Hands lifted up to Heaven, in a Kind of Extasy of Joy,

---

1 Trace.
2 As an obstacle to.
3 Acts 5:31: "Him hath God exalted with his right hand to be a Prince and a Saviour, for to give repentance to Israel, and forgiveness of sins."

I cry'd out aloud, *Jesus, thou Son of* David, *Jesus, thou exalted Prince and Saviour, give me Repentance!*

This was the first Time that I could say, in the true Sense of the Words, that I pray'd in all my Life; for now I pray'd with a Sense of my Condition, and with a true Scripture View of Hope founded on the Encouragement of the Word of God; and from this Time, I may say, I began to have Hope that God would hear me.

Now I began to construe the Words mentioned above, *Call on me, and I will deliver you*, in a different Sense from what I had ever done before; for then I had no Notion of any thing being call'd Deliverance, but my being deliver'd from the Captivity I was in; for tho' I was indeed at large in the Place, yet the Island was certainly a Prison to me, and that in the worst Sense in the World; but now I learn'd to take it in another Sense: Now I look'd back upon my past Life with such Horrour, and my Sins appear'd so dreadful, that my Soul sought nothing of God, but Deliverance from the Load of Guilt that bore down all my Comfort: As for my solitary Life it was nothing; I did not so much as pray to be deliver'd from it, or think of it; It was all of no Consideration in Comparison to this: And I add this Part here, to hint to whoever shall read it, that whenever they come to a true Sense of things, they will find Deliverance from Sin a much greater Blessing, than Deliverance from Affliction.

But leaving this Part, I return to my Journal.

My Condition began now to be, tho' not less miserable as to my Way of living, yet much easier to my Mind; and my Thoughts being directed, by a constant reading the Scripture, and praying to God, to things of a higher Nature: I had a great deal of Comfort within, which till now I knew nothing of; also, as my Health and Strength returned, I bestirr'd my self to furnish my self with every thing that I wanted, and make my Way of living as regular as I could.

From the 4th of *July* to the 14th, I was chiefly employ'd in walking about with my Gun in my Hand, a little and a little, at a Time, as a Man that was gathering up his Strength after a Fit of Sickness: For it is hardly to be imagin'd, how low I was, and to what Weakness I was reduc'd. The Application which I made Use of was perfectly new, and perhaps what had never cur'd an Ague before, neither can I recommend it to any one to practise, by this Experiment; and tho' it did carry off the Fit, yet it rather contributed to weakening me; for I had frequent Convulsions in my Nerves and Limbs for some Time.

I learn'd from it also this in particular, that being abroad in the rainy Season was the most pernicious thing to my Health that could be, especially in those Rains which came attended with Storms and Hurricanes of Wind; for as the Rain which came in the dry Season was always most accompany'd with such Storms, so I found that Rain was much more dangerous than the Rain which fell in *September* and *October*.

I had been now in this unhappy Island above 10 Months, all Possibility of Deliverance from this Condition, seem'd to be entirely taken from me; and I firmly believed, that no humane Shape had ever set Foot upon that Place: Having now secur'd my Habitation, as I thought, fully to my Mind, I had a great Desire to make a more perfect Discovery of the Island, and to see what other Productions I might find, which I yet knew nothing of.

It was the 15th of *July* that I began to take a more particular Survey of the Island it self: I went up the Creek first, where, as I hinted, I brought my Rafts on Shore; I found after I came about two Miles up, that the Tide did not flow any higher, and that it was no more than a little Brook of running Water, and very fresh and good; but this being the dry Season, there was hardly any Water in some Parts of it, at least, not enough to run in any Stream, so as it could be perceiv'd.

On the Bank of this Brook I found many pleasant *Savana's*, or Meadows; plain, smooth, and cover'd with Grass; and on the rising Parts of them next to the higher Grounds, where the Water, as it might be supposed, never overflow'd, I found a great deal of Tobacco, green, and growing to a great and very strong Stalk; there were divers other Plants which I had no Notion of, or Understanding about, and might perhaps have Vertues of their own, which I could not find out.

I searched for the *Cassava* Root,[1] which the *Indians* in all that Climate make their Bread of, but I could find none. I saw large Plants of Alloes, but did not then understand them.[2] I saw several Sugar Canes, but wild, and for want of Cultivation, imperfect. I contented my self with these Discoveries for this Time, and came back musing with my self what Course I might take to know the Vertue and Goodness of any of the Fruits or Plants which I should discover; but could bring it to no Conclusion; for in short,

---

1 Cassava leaves are inedible, but the root—boiled, fried, or ground into flour—is a rich source of carbohydrates.
2 Know what to do with them. (Crusoe is ignorant of their medicinal properties.)

I had made so little Observation while I was in the *Brasils*, that I knew little of the Plants in the Field, at least very little that might serve me to any Purpose now in my Distress.

The next Day, the 16th, I went up the same Way again, and after going something farther than I had gone the Day before, I found the Brook, and the *Savana's* began to cease, and the Country became more woody than before; in this Part I found different Fruits, and particularly I found Mellons upon the Ground in great Abundance, and Grapes upon the Trees; the Vines had spread indeed over the Trees, and the Clusters of Grapes were just now in their Prime, very ripe and rich: This was a surprising Discovery, and I was exceeding glad of them; but I was warn'd by my Experience to eat sparingly of them, remembring, that when I was ashore in *Barbary*, the eating of Grapes kill'd several of our *English* Men who were Slaves there, by throwing them into Fluxes[1] and Feavers: But I found an excellent Use for these Grapes, and that was to cure or dry them in the Sun, and keep them as dry'd Grapes or Raisins are kept, which I thought would be, as indeed they were, as wholesom as agreeable to eat, when no Grapes might be to be had.

I spent all that Evening there, and went not back to my Habitation, which by the Way was the first Night, as I might say, I had lain from Home. In the Night I took my first Contrivance, and got up into a Tree, where I slept well, and the next Morning proceeded upon my Discovery, travelling near four Miles, as I might judge by the Length of the Valley, keeping still due North, with a Ridge of Hills on the South and North-side of me.

At the End of this March I came to an Opening, where the Country seem'd to descend to the West, and a little Spring of fresh Water which issued out of the Side of the Hill by me, run the other Way, that is due East; and the Country appear'd so fresh, so green, so flourishing, every thing being in a constant Verdure,[2] or Flourish of *Spring*, that it looked like a planted Garden.

I descended a little on the Side of that delicious[3] Vale, surveying it with a secret Kind of Pleasure, (tho' mixt with my other afflicting Thoughts) to think that this was all my own, that I was

---

1 Dysentery; an illness of the digestive system that causes diarrhea and blood in the feces, often contracted by contaminated water.
2 Greenness.
3 Pleasing, delightful.

King and Lord of all this Country indefeasibly,[1] and had a Right of Possession; and if I could convey it, I might have it in Inheritance, as compleatly as any Lord of a Mannor in *England*. I saw here Abundance of Cocoa Trees, Orange, and Lemmon, and Citron Trees; but all wild, and very few bearing any Fruit, at least not then: However, the green Limes that I gathered, were not only pleasant to eat, but very wholesome; and I mix'd their Juice afterwards with Water, which made it very wholesome, and very cool, and refreshing.

I found now I had Business enough to gather and carry Home; and I resolv'd to lay up a Store, as well of Grapes, as Limes and Lemons, to furnish my self for the wet Season, which I knew was approaching.

In Order to this, I gather'd a great Heap of Grapes in one Place, and a lesser Heap in another Place, and a great Parcel of Limes and Lemons in another Place; and taking a few of each with me, I travell'd homeward, and resolv'd to come again, and bring a Bag or Sack, or what I could make to carry the rest Home.

Accordingly, having spent three Days in this Journey, I came Home; so I must now call my Tent and my Cave: But, before I got thither, the Grapes were spoil'd, the Richness of the Fruits, and the Weight of the Juice having broken them, and bruis'd them, they were good for little or nothing; as to the Limes, they were good, but I could bring but a few.

The next Day, being the 19th, I went back, having made me two small Bags to bring Home my Harvest: But I was surpriz'd, when coming to my Heap of Grapes, which were so rich and fine when I gather'd them, I found them all spread about, trod to Pieces; and dragg'd about, some here, some there, and Abundance eaten and devour'd: By this I concluded, there were some wild Creatures thereabouts, which had done this; but what they were, I knew not.

However, as I found there there was no laying them up on Heaps, and no carrying them away in a Sack, but that one Way they would be destroy'd, and the other Way they would be crush'd with their own Weight, I took another Course; for I gather'd a large Quantity of the Grapes, and hung them up upon the out Branches of the Trees, that they might cure and dry in the Sun; and as for the Limes and Lemons, I carry'd as many back as I could well stand under.

---

1 Unable to be defeated or forfeited.

When I came Home from this Journey, I contemplated with great Pleasure the Fruitfulness of that Valley, and the Pleasantness of the Scituation, the Security from Storms on that Side the Water, and the Wood, and concluded, that I had pitch'd upon a Place to fix my Abode, which was by far the worst Part of the Country. Upon the Whole I began to consider of removing my Habitation; and to look out for a Place equally safe, as where I now was scituate, if possible, in that pleasant fruitful Part of the Island.

This Thought run long in my Head, and I was exceeding fond of it for some Time, the Pleasantness of the Place tempting me; but when I came to a nearer View of it, and to consider that I was now by the Sea-Side, where it was at least possible that something might happen to my Advantage, and by the same ill Fate that brought me hither, might bring some other unhappy Wretches to the same Place; and tho' it was scarce probable that any such Thing should ever happen, yet to enclose my self among the Hills and Woods, in the Center of the Island, was to anticipate my Bondage, and to render such an Affair not only Improbable, but Impossible; and that therefore I ought not by any Means to remove.

However, I was so Enamour'd of this Place, that I spent much of my Time there, for the whole remaining Part of the Month of *July*; and tho' upon second Thoughts I resolv'd as above, not to remove, yet I built me a little kind of a Bower, and surrounded it at a Distance with a strong Fence, being a double Hedge, as high as I could reach, well stak'd, and fill'd between with *Brushwood*; and here I lay very secure, sometimes two or three Nights together, always going over it with a Ladder, as before; so that I fancy'd now I had my Country-House, and my Sea-Coast-House: And this Work took me up to the Beginning of *August*.

I had but newly finish'd my Fence, and began to enjoy my Labour, but the Rains came on, and made me stick close to my first Habitation; for tho' I had made me a Tent like the other, with a Piece of a Sail, and spread it very well; yet I had not the Shelter of a Hill to keep me from Storms, nor a Cave behind me to retreat into, when the Rains were extraordinary.

About the Beginning of *August, as I said*, I had finish'd my Bower, and began to enjoy my self. The third of *August*, I found the Grapes I had hung up were perfectly dry'd, and indeed, were excellent good Raisins of the Sun; so I began to take them down from the Trees, and it was very happy that I did so; for the Rains which follow'd would have spoil'd them, and I had lost the best Part of my Winter Food; for I had above two hundred large Bunches of them. No sooner had I taken them all down, and carry'd most of them Home to my Cave, but it began to rain, and from hence, which was the fourteenth of *August*, it rain'd more or less, every Day, till the Middle of *October*; and sometimes so violently, that I could not stir out of my Cave for several Days.

In this Season I was much surpriz'd with the Increase of my Family; I had been concern'd for the Loss of one of my Cats, who run away from me, or as I thought had been dead, and I heard no more Tale or Tidings of her, till to my Astonishment she came Home about the End of *August*, with three *Kittens*; this was the more strange to me, because tho' I had kill'd a wild Cat, as I call'd it, with my Gun; yet I thought it was a quite differing Kind from our *European* Cats; yet the young Cats were the same Kind of House breed like the old one; and both my Cats being Females, I thought it very strange: But from these three Cats, I afterwards came to be so pester'd with Cats, that I was forc'd to kill them like Vermine, or wild Beasts, and to drive them from my House as much as possible.

From the fourteenth of *August* to the twenty sixth, incessant Rain, so that I could not stir, and was now very careful not to be much wet. In this Confinement I began to be straitned for Food, but venturing out twice, I one Day kill'd a Goat, and the last Day, which was the twenty sixth, found a very large Tortoise, which was a Treat to me, and my Food was regulated thus; I eat a Bunch of Raisins for my Breakfast, a Piece of the Goat's Flesh, or of the Turtle for my Dinner broil'd; for to my great Misfortune, I had no Vessel to boil or stew any Thing; and two or three of the Turtle's Eggs for my Supper.

During this Confinement in my Cover, by the Rain, I work'd daily two or three Hours at enlarging my Cave, and by Degrees work'd it on towards one Side, till I came to the Out-Side of the Hill, and made a Door or Way out, which came beyond my Fence or Wall, and so I came in and out this Way; but I was not perfectly easy at lying so open; for as I had manag'd my self before, I was in a perfect Enclosure, whereas now I thought I lay expos'd, and open for any Thing to come in upon me; and yet I could not perceive that there was any living Thing to fear, the biggest Creature that I had yet seen upon the Island being a Goat.

September the thirtieth, I was now come to the unhappy Anniversary of my Landing. I cast up the Notches on my Post, and found I had been on Shore three hundred and sixty five

Days. I kept this Day as a Solemn Fast, setting it apart to Religious Exercise, prostrating my self on the Ground with the most serious Humiliation, confessing my Sins to God, acknowledging his Righteous Judgments upon me, and praying to him to have Mercy on me, through Jesus Christ; and having not tasted the least Refreshment for twelve Hours, even till the going down of the Sun, I then eat a Bisket Cake, and a Bunch of Grapes, and went to Bed, finishing the Day as I began it.

I had all this Time observ'd no Sabbath-Day; for as at first I had no Sense of Religion upon my Mind, I had after some Time omitted to distinguish the Weeks, by making a longer Notch than ordinary for the Sabbath-Day, and so did not really know what any of the Days were; but now having cast up the Days, as above, I found I had been there a Year; so I divided it into Weeks, and set apart every seventh Day for a Sabbath; though I found at the End of my Account I had lost a Day or two in my Reckoning.

A little after this my Ink began to fail me, and so I contented my self to use it more sparingly, and to write down only the most remarkable Events of my Life, without continuing a daily *Memorandum* of other Things.

The rainy Season, and the dry Season, began now to appear regular to me, and I learn'd to divide them so, as to provide for them accordingly. But I bought all my Experience before I had it;[1] and this I am going to relate, was one of the most discouraging Experiments that I made at all: I have mention'd that I had sav'd the few Ears of Barley and Rice, which I had so surprizingly found spring up, as I thought, of themselves, and believe there was about thirty Stalks of Rice, and about twenty of Barley; and now I thought it a proper Time to sow it after the Rains, the Sun being in its *Southern* Position going from me.

Accordingly I dug up a Piece of Ground as well as I could with my wooden Spade, and dividing it into two Parts, I sow'd my Grain; but as I was sowing, it casually occur'd to my Thoughts, That I would not sow it all at first, because I did not know when was the proper Time for it; so I sow'd about two Thirds of the Seed, leaving about a Handful of each.

It was a great Comfort to me afterwards, that I did so, for not one Grain of that I sow'd this Time came to any Thing; for the dry Months following, the Earth having had no Rain after the Seed was sown, it had no Moisture to assist its Growth, and never

---

1 Crusoe is alluding to the proverb "Bought wit is best." He means that
   he could learn only the hard way, by repeatedly trying and failing.

came up at all, till the wet Season had come again, and then it grew as if it had been but newly sown.

Finding my first Seed did not grow, which I easily imagin'd was by the Drought, I sought for a moister Piece of Ground to make another Trial in, and I dug up a Piece of Ground near my new Bower, and sow'd the rest of my Seed in *February*, a little before the *Vernal Equinox*; and this having the rainy Months of *March* and *April* to water it, sprung up very pleasantly, and yielded a very good Crop; but having Part of the Seed left only, and not daring to sow all that I had, I had but a small Quantity at last, my whole Crop not amounting to above half a Peck[1] of each kind.

But by this Experiment I was made Master of my Business, and knew exactly when the proper Season was to sow; and that I might expect two Seed Times, and two Harvests every Year.

While this Corn was growing, I made a little Discovery which was of use to me afterwards: As soon as the Rains were over, and the Weather began to settle, which was about the Month of *November*, I made a Visit up the Country to my Bower, where though I had not been some Months, yet I found all Things just as I left them. The Circle or double Hedge that I had made, was not only firm and entire; but the Stakes which I had cut out of some Trees that grew thereabouts, were all shot out and grown with long Branches, as much as a Willow-Tree usually shoots the first Year after lopping its Head. I could not tell what Tree to call it, that these Stakes were cut from. I was surpriz'd, and yet very well pleas'd, to see the young Trees grow; and I prun'd them, and led them up to grow as much alike as I could; and it is scarce credible how beautiful a Figure they grew into in three Years; so that though the Hedge made a Circle of about twenty five Yards in Diameter, yet the Trees, for such I might now call them, soon cover'd it; and it was a compleat Shade, sufficient to lodge under all the dry Season.

This made me resolve to cut some more Stakes, and make me a Hedge like this in a Semicircle round my Wall; I mean that of my first Dwelling, which I did; and placing the Trees or Stakes in a double Row, at about eight Yards distance from my first Fence, they grew presently, and were at first a fine Cover to my Habitation, and afterward serv'd for a Defence also, as I shall observe in its Order.

---

1 A quarter of a bushel, about two gallons.

I found now, That the Seasons of the Year might generally be divided, not into *Summer* and *Winter*, as in *Europe*; but into the Rainy Seasons, and the Dry Seasons, which were generally thus,

Half	*February,*	
	March,	Rainy, the *Sun* being then on, or near the
Half	*April,*	Equinox.

Half	*April,*	
	May,	
	June,	Dry, the *Sun* being then to the *North* of
	July,	the Line.
Half	*August,*	

Half	*August,*	
	September,	Rainy, the *Sun* being then come back.
Half	*October,*	

Half	*October,*	
	November,	
	December,	Dry, the *Sun* being then to the *South* of
	January,	the Line.
Half	*February,*	

The Rainy Season sometimes held longer or shorter, as the Winds happen'd to blow; but this was the general Observation I made: After I had found by Experience, the ill Consequence of being abroad in the Rain, I took Care to furnish my self with Provisions before hand, that I might not be oblig'd to go out; and I sat within Doors as much as possible during the wet Months.

This Time I found much Employment, (and very suitable also to the Time) for I found great Occasion of many Things which I had no way to furnish my self with, but by hard Labour and constant Application; particularly, I try'd many Ways to make my self a Basket, but all the Twigs I could get for the Purpose prov'd so brittle, that they would do nothing. It prov'd of excellent Advantage to me now, That when I was a Boy, I used to take great Delight in standing at a *Basket-makers*, in the Town where my Father liv'd, to see them make their *Wicker-ware*; and being as Boys usually are, very officious to help, and a great Observer of the Manner how they work'd those Things, and sometimes lending a Hand, I had by this Means full Knowledge of the Methods of it, that I wanted nothing but the Materials; when it came into my Mind, That the Twigs of that Tree from whence I cut my Stakes that grew, might possibly be as tough as the *Sallows*, and *Willows*, and *Osiers* in *England*, and I resolv'd to try.

Accordingly the next Day, I went to my Country-House, as I call'd it, and cutting some of the smaller Twigs, I found them to my Purpose as much as I could desire; whereupon I came the next Time prepar'd with a Hatchet to cut down a Quantity, which I soon found, for there was great Plenty of them; these I set up to dry within my Circle or Hedge, and when they were fit for Use, I carry'd them to my Cave, and here during the next Season, I employ'd my self in making, *as well as I could*, a great many Baskets, both to carry Earth, or to carry or lay up any Thing as I had occasion; and tho' I did not finish them very handsomly, yet I made them sufficiently serviceable for my Purpose; and thus afterwards I took Care never to be without them; and as my *Wicker-ware* decay'd, I made more, especially, I made strong deep Baskets to place my Corn in, instead of Sacks, when I should come to have any Quantity of it.

Having master'd this Difficulty, and employ'd a World of Time about it, I bestirr'd[1] my self to see if possible how to supply two Wants: I had no Vessels to hold any Thing that was Liquid, except two Runlets which were almost full of Rum, and some Glass-Bottles, some of the common Size, and others which were Case-Bottles square, for the holding of Waters, Spirits, *&c.* I had not so much as a Pot to boil any Thing, except a great Kettle, which I sav'd out of the Ship, and which was too big for such Use as I desir'd it, *viz.* To make Broth, and stew a Bit of Meat by it self. The Second Thing I would fain have had, was a Tobacco-Pipe; but it was impossible to me to make one, however, I found a Contrivance for that too at last.

I employ'd my self in Planting my Second Rows of Stakes or Piles and in this *Wicker* working all the Summer, or dry Season, when another Business took me up more Time than it could be imagin'd I could spare.

I mention'd before, That I had a great Mind to see the whole Island, and that I had travell'd up the Brook, and so on to where I built my Bower, and where I had an Opening quite to the Sea on the other Side of the Island; I now resolv'd to travel quite Cross to the Sea-Shore on that Side; so taking my Gun, a Hatchet, and my Dog, and a larger Quantity of Powder and Shot

---

1 To make active, to exert oneself.

than usual, with two Bisket Cakes, and a great Bunch of Raisins in my Pouch for my Store, I began my Journey; when I had pass'd the Vale where my Bower stood as above, I came within View of the Sea, to the *West*, and it being a very clear Day, I fairly descry'd[1] Land, whether an Island or a Continent, I could not tell; but it lay very high, extending from the *West*, to the *W.S.W.* at a very great Distance; by my Guess it could not be less than Fifteen or Twenty Leagues off.[2]

I could not tell what Part of the World this might be, otherwise than that I know it must be Part of *America*, and as I concluded by all my Observations, must be near the *Spanish* Dominions, and perhaps was all Inhabited by Savages, where if I should have landed, I had been in a worse Condition than I was now; and therefore I acquiesced in the Dispositions of Providence, which I began now to own, and to believe, order'd every Thing for the best; I say, I quieted my Mind with this, and left afflicting my self with Fruitless Wishes of being there.

Besides, after some Pause upon this Affair, I consider'd, that if this Land was the *Spanish* Coast, I should certainly, one Time or other, see some Vessel pass or re-pass one Way or other; but if not, then it was the *Savage* Coast between the *Spanish* Country and *Brasils*, which are indeed the worst of *Savages*; for they are Cannibals, or Men-eaters, and fail not to murther and devour all the humane Bodies that fall into their Hands.[3]

With these Considerations I walk'd very leisurely forward, I found that Side of the Island where I now was, much pleasanter than mine, the open or *Savanna* Fields sweet, adorn'd with Flowers and Grass, and full of very fine Woods. I saw Abundance of Parrots, and fain I would have caught one, if possible to have kept it to be tame, and taught it to speak to me. I did, after some Pains taking, catch a young Parrot, for I knock'd it down with a Stick, and having recover'd it, I brought it home; but it was some Years before I could make him speak: However, at last I taught him to call me by my Name very familiarly: But the Accident that follow'd, tho' it be a Trifle, will be very diverting in its Place.

I was exceedingly diverted with this Journey: I found in the low Grounds Hares, as I thought them to be, and Foxes, but they differ'd greatly from all the other Kinds I had met with; nor could I satisfy my self to eat them, tho' I kill'd several: But I had no

---

1   To catch sight of, to perceive.
2   45 to 60 miles.
3   See Appendix G, "Cannibalism."

Need to be ventrous;[1] for I had no Want of Food, and of that which was very good too; especially these three Sorts, *viz.* Goats, Pidgeons, and Turtle or Tortoise; which, added to my Grapes, *Leaden-hall* Market[2] could not have furnish'd a Table better than I, in Proportion to the Company; and tho' my Case was deplorable enough, yet I had great Cause for Thankfulness, that I was not driven to any Extremities for Food; but rather Plenty, even to Dainties.[3]

I never travell'd in this Journey above two Miles outright in a Day, or thereabouts; but I took so many Turns and Returns, to see what Discoveries I could make, that I came weary enough to the Place where I resolv'd to sit down for all Night; and then I either repos'd my self in a Tree, or surrounded my self with a Row of Stakes set upright in the Ground, either from one Tree to another, or so as no wild Creature could come at me, without waking me.

As soon as I came to the Sea Shore, I was surpriz'd to see that I had taken up my Lot on the worst Side of the Island; for here indeed the Shore was cover'd with innumerable Turtles, whereas on the other Side I had found but three in a Year and half. Here was also an infinite Number of Fowls, of many Kinds, some which I had seen, and some which I had not seen of before, and many of them very good Meat; but such as I knew not the Names of, except those call'd *Penguins*.

I could have shot as many as I pleas'd, but was very sparing of my Powder and Shot; and therefore had more Mind to kill a she Goat, if I could, which I could better feed on; and though there were many Goats here more than on my Side the Island, yet it was with much more Difficulty that I could come near them, the Country being flat and even, and they saw me much sooner than when I was on the Hill.

I confess this Side of the Country was much pleasanter than mine, but yet I had not the least Inclination to remove; for as I was fix'd in my Habitation, it became natural to me, and I seem'd all the while I was here, to be as it were upon a Journey, and from Home: However, I travell'd along the Shore of the Sea, towards the *East*, I suppose about twelve Miles; and then setting up a great Pole upon the Shore for a Mark, I concluded I would go

---

1 Adventurous, willing to run risks.
2 The most popular London food market during Defoe's lifetime. It was significantly rebuilt following the Great Fire of London in 1666.
3 Delicacies, including prepared meats.

Home again; and that the next Journey I took should be on the other Side of the Island, *East* from my Dwelling, and so round till I came to my Post again: Of which in its Place.

I took another Way to come back than that I went, thinking I could easily keep all the Island so much in my View, that I could not miss finding my first Dwelling by viewing the Country; but I found my self mistaken; for being come about two or three Miles, I found my self descended into a very large Valley; but so surrounded with Hills, and those Hills cover'd with Wood, that I could not see which was my Way by any Direction but that of the Sun, nor even then, unless I knew very well the Position of the Sun at that Time of the Day.

It happen'd to my farther Misfortune, That the Weather prov'd hazey for three or four Days, while I was in this Valley; and not being able to see the Sun, I wander'd about very uncomfortably, and at last was oblig'd to find out the Sea Side, look for my Post, and come back the same Way I went; and then by easy Journies I turn'd Homeward, the Weather being exceeding hot, and my Gun, Ammunition, Hatchet, and other Things very heavy.

In this Journey my Dog surpriz'd a young Kid, and seiz'd upon it, and I running in to take hold of it, caught it, and sav'd it alive from the Dog: I had a great Mind to bring it Home if I could; for I had often been musing, Whether it might not be possible to get a Kid or two, and so raise a Breed of tame Goats, which might supply me when my Powder and Shot should be all spent.

I made a Collar to this little Creature, and with a String which I made of some Rope-Yarn, which I always carry'd about me, I led him along, tho' with some Difficulty, till I came to my Bower, and there I enclos'd him, and left him; for I was very impatient to be at Home, from whence I had been absent above a Month.

I cannot express what a Satisfaction it was to me, to come into my old Hutch,[1] and lye down in my Hamock-Bed: This little wandring Journey, without settled Place of Abode, had been so unpleasant to me, that my own House, as I call'd it to my self, was a perfect Settlement to me, compar'd to that; and it rendred every Thing about me so comfortable, that I resolv'd I would never go a great Way from it again, while it should be my Lot to stay on the Island.

I repos'd my self here a Week, to rest and regale my self after my long Journey; during which, most of the Time was taken up in the weighty Affair of making a Cage for my Poll, who began

---

1 A hut, small house.

now to be a meer Domestick,[1] and to be mighty well acquainted with me. Then I began to think of the poor Kid, which I had penn'd in within my little Circle, and resolv'd to go and fetch it Home, or give it some Food; accordingly I went, and found it where I left it; for indeed it could not get out, but almost starv'd for want of Food: I went and cut Bows of Trees, and Branches of such Shrubs as I could find, and threw it over, and having fed it, I ty'd it as I did before, to lead it away; but it was so tame with being hungry, that I had no need to have ty'd it; for it follow'd me like a Dog; and as I continually fed it, the Creature became so loving, so gentle, and so fond, that it became from that Time one of my Domesticks also, and would never leave me afterwards.

The rainy Season of the *Autumnal Equinox* was now come, and I kept the 30th of *Sept.* in the same solemn Manner as before, being the Anniversary of my Landing on the Island, having now been there two Years, and no more Prospect of being deliver'd, than the first Day I came there. I spent the whole Day in humble and thankful Acknowledgments of the many wonderful Mercies which my Solitary Condition was attended with, and without which it might have been infinitely more miserable. I gave humble and hearty Thanks that God had been pleas'd to discover to me, even that it was possible I might be more happy in this Solitary Condition, than I should have been in a Liberty of Society, and in all the Pleasures of the World. That he could fully make up to me, the Deficiencies of my Solitary State, and the want of Humane Society by his Presence, and the Communications of his Grace to my Soul, supporting, comforting, and encouraging me to depend upon his Providence here, and hope for his Eternal Presence hereafter.

It was now that I began sensibly to feel how much more happy this Life I now led was, with all its miserable Circumstances, than the wicked, cursed, abominable Life I led all the past Part of my Days; and now I chang'd both my Sorrows and my Joys; my very Desires alter'd, my Affections chang'd their Gusts,[2] and my Delights were perfectly new, from what they were at my first Coming, or indeed for the two Years past.

Before, as I walk'd about, either on my Hunting, or for viewing the Country; the Anguish of my Soul at my Condition, would break out upon me on a sudden, and my very Heart would die within me, to think of the Woods, the Mountains, the Desarts I

---

1 A domesticated animal, a pet.
2 Tastes, inclinations.

was in; and how I was a Prisoner lock'd up with the Eternal Bars and Bolts of the Ocean, in an uninhabited Wilderness, without Redemption: In the midst of the greatest Composures of my Mind, this would break out upon me like a Storm, and make me wring my Hands, and weep like a Child: Sometimes it would take me in the middle of my Work, and I would immediately sit down and sigh, and look upon the Ground for an Hour or two together; and this was still worse to me; for if I could burst out into Tears, or vent my self by Words, it would go off, and the Grief having exhausted it self would abate.

But now I began to exercise my self with new Thoughts; I daily read the Word of God, and apply'd all the Comforts of it to my present State: One Morning being very sad, I open'd the Bible upon these Words, *I will never, never leave thee, nor forsake thee*;[1] immediately it occurr'd, That these Words were to me, Why else should they be directed in such a Manner, just at the Moment when I was mourning over my Condition, as one forsaken of God and Man? Well then, said I, if God does not forsake me, of what ill Consequence can it be, or what matters it, though the World should all forsake me, seeing on the other Hand, if I had all the World, and should lose the Favour and Blessing of God, there wou'd be no Comparison in the Loss.

From this Moment I began to conclude in my Mind, That it was possible for me to be more happy in this forsaken Solitary Condition, than it was probable I should ever have been in any other Particular State in the World; and with this Thought I was going to give Thanks to God for bringing me to this Place.

I know not what it was, but something shock'd my Mind at that Thought, and I durst not speak the Words: How canst thou be such a Hypocrite, (said I, even audibly) to pretend to be thankful for a Condition, which however thou may'st endeavour to be contented with, thou would'st rather pray heartily to be deliver'd from; so I stopp'd there: But though I could not say, I thank'd God for being there; yet I sincerely gave Thanks to God for opening my Eyes, by whatever afflicting Providences, to see the former Condition of my Life, and to mourn for my Wickedness, and repent. I never open'd the Bible, or shut it, but my very Soul within me, bless'd God for directing my Friend in *England*, without any Order of mine, to pack it up among my Goods; and

---

1 After the death of Moses, God says to Joshua, "There shall not any man be able to stand before thee all the days of thy life: as I was with Moses, so I will be with thee: I will not fail thee, nor forsake thee" (Joshua 1:5).

for assisting me afterwards to save it out of the Wreck of the Ship.

Thus, and in this Disposition of Mind, I began my third Year; and tho' I have not given the Reader the Trouble of so particular Account of my Works this Year as the first; yet in General it may be observ'd, That I was very seldom idle; but having regularly divided my Time, according to the several daily Employments that were before me, such as, *First*, My Duty to God, and the Reading the Scriptures, which I constantly set apart some Time for thrice every Day. *Secondly*, The going Abroad with my Gun for Food, which generally took me up three Hours in every Morning, when it did not Rain. *Thirdly*, The ordering, curing, preserving, and cooking what I had kill'd or catch'd for my Supply; these took up great Part of the Day; also it is to be considered that the middle of the Day when the Sun was in the *Zenith*, the Violence of the Heat was too great to stir out; so that about four Hours in the Evening was all the Time I could be suppos'd to work in; with this Exception, That sometimes I chang'd my Hours of Hunting and Working, and went to work in the Morning, and Abroad with my Gun in the Afternoon.

To this short Time allow'd for Labour, I desire may be added the exceeding Laboriousness of my Work; the many Hours which for want of Tools, want of Help, and want of Skill; every Thing I did, took up out of my Time: For Example, I was full two and forty Days making me a Board for a long Shelf, which I wanted in my Cave; whereas two Sawyers with their Tools, and a Saw-Pit,[1] would have cut six of them out of the same Tree in half a Day.

My Case was this, It was to be a large Tree, which was to be cut down, because my Board was to be a broad one. This Tree I was three Days a cutting down, and two more cutting off the Bows, and reducing it to a Log, or Piece of Timber. With inexpressible hacking and hewing I reduc'd both the Sides of it into Chips, till it begun to be light enough to move; than I turn'd it, and made one Side of it smooth, and flat, as a Board from End to End; then turning that Side downward, cut the other Side, till I brought the Plank to be about three Inches thick, and smooth on both Sides. Any one may judge the Labour of my Hands in such a Piece of Work; but Labour and Patience carry'd me through that and many other Things: I only observe this in Par-

---

1 A hole in the ground, in which one sawyer would stand while another stood above, the two of them cutting the timber with a long two-handed saw.

ticular, to shew, The Reason why so much of my Time went away with so little Work, *viz.* That what might be a little to be done with Help and Tools, was a vast Labour, and requir'd a prodigious Time to do alone, and by hand.

But notwithstanding this, with Patience and Labour I went through many Things; and indeed every Thing that my Circumstances made necessary to me to do, as will appear by what follows.

I was now, in the Months of *November* and *December*, expecting my Crop of Barley and Rice. The Ground I had manur'd or dug up for them was not great; for as I observ'd, my Seed of each was not above the Quantity of half a Peck; for I had lost one whole Crop by sowing in the dry Season; but now my Crop promis'd very well, when on a sudden I found I was in Danger of losing it all again by Enemies of several Sorts, which it was scarce possible to keep from it; as First, The Goats, and wild Creatures which I call'd Hares, who tasting the Sweetness of the Blade, lay in it Night and Day, as soon as it came up, and eat it so close, that it could get no Time to shoot up into Stalk.

This I saw no Remedy for, but by making an Enclosure about it with a Hedge, which I did with a great deal of Toil; and the more, because it requir'd Speed. However, as my Arable Land was but small, suited to my Crop, I got it totally well fenc'd, in about three Weeks Time; and shooting some of the Creatures in the Day Time, I set my Dog to guard it in the Night, tying him up to a Stake at the Gate, where he would stand and bark all Night long; so in a little Time the Enemies forsook the Place, and the Corn grew very strong, and well, and began to ripen apace.

But as the Beasts ruined me before, while my Corn was in the Blade; so the Birds were as likely to ruin me now, when it was in the Ear; for going along by the Place to see how it throve, I saw my little Crop surrounded with Fowls of I know not how many sorts, who stood as it were watching till I should be gone: I immediately let fly among them (for I always had my Gun with me) I had no sooner shot but there rose up a little Cloud of Fowls, which I had not seen at all, from among the Corn it self.

This touch'd me sensibly, for I foresaw, that in a few Days they would devour all my Hopes, that I should be starv'd, and never be able to raise a Crop at all, and what to do I could not tell: However I resolv'd not to loose my Corn, if possible, tho' I should watch it Night and Day. In the first Place, I went among it to see what Damage was already done, and found they had spoil'd a good deal of it, but that as it was yet too Green for them, the Loss was not so great, but that the Remainder was like to be a good Crop if it could be sav'd.

I staid by it to load my Gun, and then coming away I could easily see the Thieves sitting upon all the Trees about me, as if they only waited till I was gone away, and the Event proved it to be so; for as I walk'd off as if I was gone, I was no sooner out of their sight, but they dropt down one by one into the Corn again. I was so provok'd that I could not have Patience to stay till more came on, knowing that every Grain that they eat now, was, *as it might be said*, a Peck-loaf[1] to me in the Consequence; but coming up to the Hedge, I fir'd again, and kill'd three of them. This was what I wish'd for; so I took them up, and serv'd them as we serve notorious Thieves in *England*, (*viz.*) Hang'd them in Chains[2] for a Terror to others; it is impossible to imagine almost, that this should have such an Effect, as it had; for the Fowls wou'd not only not come at the Corn, but in short they forsook all that Part of the Island, and I could never see a Bird near the Place as long as my Scare-Crows hung there.

This I was very glad of, you may be sure, and about the latter end of *December*, which was our second Harvest of the Year, I reap'd my Crop.

I was sadly put to it for a Scythe or a Sicle to cut it down, and all I could do was to make one as well as I could out of one of the Broad Swords or Cutlasses, which I sav'd among the Arms out of the Ship. However, as my first Crop was but small I had no great Difficulty to cut it down; in short, I reap'd it my Way, for I cut nothing off but the Ears, and carry'd it away in a great Basket which I had made, and so rubb'd it out with my Hands; and at the End of all my Harvesting, I found that out of my half Peck of Seed, I had near two Bushels[3] of Rice, and above two Bushels and half of Barley, *that is to say*, by my Guess, for I had no Measure at that time.

However, this was a great Encouragement to me, and I foresaw that in time, it wou'd please God to supply me with Bread: And yet here I was perplex'd again, for I neither knew how to grind or make Meal of my Corn, or indeed how to clean it and part it; nor if made into Meal, how to make Bread of it, and if

---

1 A peck-loaf weighed 17 lb, 6 oz.
2 After an execution, a thief's body—sometimes placed in a kind of chain-mail that would keep its shape as the body decomposed—was suspended in public places as a deterrent.
3 Sixteen gallons.

how to make it, yet I knew not how to bake it; these things being added to my Desire of having a good Quantity for Store, and to secure a constant Supply, I resolv'd not to taste any of this Crop but to preserve it all for Seed against the next Season, and in the mean time to employ all my Study and Hours of Working to accomplish this great Work of Providing my self with Corn and Bread.

It might be truly said, that now I work'd for my Bread; 'tis a little wonderful, and what I believe few People have thought much upon, (*viz.*) the strange multitude of little Things necessary in the Providing, Producing, Curing, Dressing, Making and Finishing this one Article of Bread.

I that was reduced to a meer State of Nature, found this to my daily Discouragement, and was made more and more sensible of it every Hour, even after I had got the first Handful of Seed-Corn, which, as I have said, came up unexpectedly, and indeed to a surprize.

First, I had no Plow to turn up the Earth, no Spade or Shovel to dig it. Well, this I conquer'd, by making a wooden Spade, as I observ'd before; but this did my Work in but a wooden manner, and tho' it cost me a great many Days to make it, yet for want of Iron it not only wore out the sooner, but made my Work the harder, and made it be perform'd much worse.

However this I bore with, and was content to work it out with Patience, and bear with the badness of the Performance. When the Corn was sow'd, I had no Harrow, but was forced to go over it my self and drag a great heavy Bough of a Tree over it, to Scratch it, as it may be call'd, rather than Rake or Harrow it.

When it was growing and grown, I have observ'd already, how many things I wanted, to Fence it, Secure it, Mow or Reap it, Cure and Carry it Home, Thrash, Part it from the Chaff, and Save it. Then I wanted a Mill to Grind it, Sieves to Dress it, Yeast and Salt to make it into Bread, and an Oven to bake it, and yet all these things I did without, as shall be observ'd; and yet the Corn was an inestimable Comfort and Advantage to me too. All this, as I said, made every thing laborious and tedious to me, but that there was no help for; neither was my time so much Loss to me, because as I had divided it, a certain Part of it was every Day appointed to these Works; and as I resolv'd to use none of the Corn for Bread till I had a greater Quantity by me, I had the next six Months to apply my self wholly by Labour and Invention to furnish my self with Utensils proper for the performing all the Operations necessary for the making the Corn (when I had it) fit for my use.

But first, I was to prepare more Land, for I had now Seed enough to sow above an Acre of Ground. Before I did this, I had a Weeks-work at least to make me a Spade, which when it was done was but a sorry one indeed, and very heavy, and requir'd double Labour to work with it; however I went thro' that, and sow'd my Seed in two large flat Pieces of Ground, as near my House as I could find them to my Mind, and fenc'd them in with a good Hedge, the Stakes of which were all cut of that Wood which I had set before, and knew it would grow, so that in one Year's time I knew I should have a Quick[1] or Living-Hedge, that would want but little Repair. This Work was not so little as to take me up less than three Months, because great Part of that time was of the wet Season, when I could not go abroad.

Within Doors, *that is*, when it rained, and I could not go out, I found Employment on the following Occasions; always observing, that all the while I was at work I diverted my self with talking to my Parrot, and teaching him to Speak, and I quickly learn'd[2] him to know his own Name, and at last to speak it out pretty loud POLL,[3] which was the first Word I ever heard spoken in the Island by any Mouth but my own. This therefore was not my Work, but an assistant to my Work, for now, as I said, I had a great Employment upon my Hands, as follows, (*viz.*) I had long study'd by some Means or other, to make my self some Earthen Vessels, which indeed I wanted sorely, but knew not where to come at them: However, considering the Heat of the Climate, I did not doubt but if I could find out any such Clay, I might botch up[4] some such Pot, as might, being dry'd in the Sun, be hard enough, and strong enough to bear handling, and to hold any Thing that was dry, and requir'd to be kept so; and as this was necessary in the preparing Corn, Meal, *&c.* which was the Thing I was upon, I resolv'd to make some as large as I could, and fit only to stand like Jarrs to hold what should be put into them.

It would make the Reader pity me, or rather laugh at me, to tell how many awkward ways I took to raise this Paste, what odd mishapen ugly things I made, how many of them fell in, and how many fell out, the Clay not being stiff enough to bear its own Weight; how many crack'd by the over violent Heat of the Sun, being set out too hastily; and how many fell in pieces with only

---

1 A hedge made of living plants, especially hawthorn.
2 Taught.
3 A conventional name for a parrot.
4 To crudely make.

removing, as well before as after they were dry'd; and in a word, how after having labour'd hard to find the Clay, to dig it, to temper it, to bring it home and work it; I could not make above two large earthern ugly things, I cannot call them Jarrs, in about two Months Labour.

However, as the Sun bak'd these Two, very dry and hard, I lifted them very gently up, and set them down again in two great Wicker-Baskets which I had made on purpose for them, that they might not break, and as between the Pot and the Basket there was a little room to spare, I stuff'd it full of the Rice and Barley Straw, and these two Pots being to stand always dry, I thought would hold my dry Corn, and perhaps the Meal, when the Corn was bruised.

Tho' I miscarried so much in my Design for large Pots, yet I made several smaller things with better Success, such as little round Pots, flat Dishes, Pitchers and Pipkins,[1] and any things my Hand turn'd to, and the Heat of the Sun bak'd them strangely hard.

But all this would not answer my End, which was to get an earthen Pot to hold what was Liquid, and bear the Fire, which none of these could do. It happen'd after some time, making a pretty large Fire for cooking my Meat, when I went to put it out after I had done with it, I found a broken Piece of one of my Earthen-ware Vessels in the Fire, burnt as hard as a Stone, and red as a Tile. I was agreeably suppris'd to see it, and said to my self, that certainly they might be made to burn whole if they would burn broken.

This set me to studying how to order my Fire, so as to make it burn me some Pots. I had no Notion of a Kiln, such as the Potters burn in, or of glazing them with Lead, tho' I had some Lead to do it with; but I plac'd three large Pipkins, and two or three Pots in a Pile one upon another, and plac'd my Fire-wood all round it with a great Heap of Embers under them, I ply'd the Fire with fresh Fuel round the out-side, and upon the top, till I saw the Pots in the inside red hot quite thro', and observ'd that they did not crack at all; when I saw them clear red, I let them stand in that Heat about 5 or 6 Hours, till I found one of them, tho' it did not crack, did melt or run, for the Sand which was mixed with the Clay melted by the violence of the Heat, and would have run into Glass if I had gone on, so I slack'd my Fire gradually till the Pots began to abate of the red Colour, and

---

1   A small, earthen pot or pan.

watching them all Night, that I might not let the Fire abate too fast, in the Morning I had three very good, I will not say handsome Pipkins; and two other Earthen Pots, as hard burnt as cou'd be desir'd; and one of them perfectly glaz'd with the Running of the Sand.

After this Experiment, I need not say that I wanted no sort of Earthen Ware for my Use; but I must needs say, as to the Shapes of them, they were very indifferent, as any one may suppose, when I had no way of making them; but as the Children make Dirt-Pies, or as a Woman would make Pies, that never learn'd to raise Past.

No Joy at a Thing of so mean a Nature was ever equal to mine, when I found I had made an Earthen Pot that would bear the Fire; and I had hardly Patience to stay till they were cold, before I set one upon the Fire again, with some Water in it, to boil me some Meat, which it did admirably well; and with a Piece of a Kid, I made some very good Broth, though I wanted Oatmeal, and several other Ingredients, requisite to make it so good as I would have had it been.

My next Concern was, to get me a Stone Mortar, to stamp or beat some Corn in; for as to the Mill, there was no thought at arriving to that Perfection of Art, with one Pair of Hands. To supply this Want I was at a great Loss; for of all Trades in the World I was as perfectly unqualify'd for a Stone-cutter, as for any whatever; neither had I any Tools to go about it with. I spent many a Day to find out a great Stone big enough to cut hollow, and make fit for a Mortar, and could find none at all; except what was in the solid Rock, and which I had no way to dig or cut out; nor indeed were the Rocks in the Island of Hardness sufficient, but were all of a sandy crumbling Stone, which neither would bear the Weight of a heavy Pestle, or would break the Corn without filling it with Sand; so after a great deal of Time lost in searching for a Stone, I gave it over, and resolv'd to look out for a great Block of hard Wood, which I found indeed much easier; and getting one as big as I had Strength to stir, I rounded it, and form'd it in the Out-side with my Axe and Hatchet, and then with the Help of Fire, and infinite Labour, made a hollow Place in it, as the *Indians* in *Brasil* make their *Canoes*. After this, I made a great heavy Pestle or Beater, of the Wood call'd the Iron-wood, and this I prepar'd and laid by against I had my next Crop of Corn, when I propos'd to my self, to grind, or rather pound my Corn into Meal to make my Bread.

My next Difficulty was to make a Sieve, or Search,[1] to dress my Meal, and to part it from the Bran, and the Husk, without which I did not see it possible I could have any Bread. This was a most difficult Thing, so much as but to think on; for to be sure I had nothing like the necessary Thing to make it; I mean fine thin Canvas, or Stuff,[2] to search the Meal through. And here I was at a full Stop for many Months; nor did I really know what to do; Linnen I had none left, but what was meer Rags; I had Goats Hair, but neither knew I how to weave it, or spin it; and had I known how, here was no Tools to work it with; all the Remedy that I found for this, was, That at last I did remember I had among the Seamens Cloaths which were sav'd out of the Ship, some Neckcloths of Callicoe, or Muslin; and with some Pieces of these, I made three small Sieves, but proper enough for the Work; and thus I made shift for some Years; how I did afterwards, I shall shew in its Place.

The baking Part was the next Thing to be consider'd, and how I should make Bread when I came to have Corn; for first I had no Yeast; as to that Part, as there was no supplying the Want, so I did not concern my self much about it: But for an Oven, I was indeed in great Pain; at length I found out an Experiment for that also, which was this; I made some Earthen Vessels very broad, but not deep; that is to say, about two Foot Diameter, and not above nine Inches deep; these I burnt in the Fire, as I had done the other, and laid them by; and when I wanted to bake, I made a great Fire upon my Hearth, which I had pav'd with some square Tiles of my own making, and burning also; but I should not call them square.

When the Fire-wood was burnt pretty much into Embers, or live Coals, I drew them forward upon this Hearth, so as to cover it all over, and there I let them lye, till the Hearth was very hot, then sweeping away all the Embers, I set down my Loaf, or Loaves, and whelming down[3] the Earthen Pot upon them, drew the Embers all round the Out-side of the Pot, to keep in, and add to the Heat; and thus, as well as in the best Oven in the World, I bak'd my Barley Loaves, and became in little Time a meer Pastry-Cook into the Bargain; for I made my self several Cakes of the Rice, and Puddings; indeed I made no Pies, neither had I any

---

1 Variant spelling for *searce*: a fine sieve.
2 Any woven material, especially wool.
3 Turning upside down.

Thing to put into them, supposing I had, except the Flesh either of Fowls or Goats.

It need not be wondred at, if all these Things took me up most Part of the third Year of my Abode here; for it is to be observ'd, That in the Intervals of these Things, I had my new Harvest and Husbandry to manage; for I reap'd my Corn in its Season, and carry'd it Home as well as I could, and laid it up in the Ear, in my large Baskets, till I had Time to rub it out; for I had no Floor to thrash it on, or Instrument to thrash it with.

And now indeed my Stock of Corn increasing, I really wanted to build my Barns bigger. I wanted a Place to lay it up in; for the Increase of the Corn now yielded me so much, that I had of the Barley about twenty Bushels, and of the Rice as much, or more; insomuch, that now I resolv'd to begin to use it freely; for my Bread had been quite gone a great while; Also I resolved to see what Quantity would be sufficient for me a whole Year, and to sow but once a Year.

Upon the whole, I found that the forty Bushels of Barley and Rice, was much more than I could consume in a Year; so I resolv'd to sow just the same Quantity every Year, that I sow'd the last, in Hopes that such a Quantity would fully provide me with Bread, &c.

All the while these Things were doing, you may be sure my Thoughts run many times upon the Prospect of Land which I had seen from the other Side of the Island, and I was not without secret Wishes that I were on Shore there, fancying the seeing the main Land, and in an inhabited Country, I might find some Way or other to convey my self farther, and perhaps at last find some Means of Escape.

But all this while I made no Allowance for the Dangers of such a Condition, and how I might fall into the Hands of Savages, and perhaps such as I might have Reason to think far worse than the Lions and Tigers of *Africa*. That if I once came into their Power, I should run a Hazard more than a thousand to one of being kill'd, and perhaps of being eaten; for I had heard that the People of the *Carribean* Coast were Canibals, or Man-eaters; and I knew by the Latitude that I could not be far off from that Shore. That suppose they were not Canibals, yet that they might kill me, as many *Europeans* who had fallen into their Hands had been serv'd, even when they had been ten or twenty together; much more I that was but one, and could make little or no Defence: All these Things, I say, which I ought to have consider'd well of, and did cast up in my Thoughts afterwards, yet took up none of my

Apprehensions at first; but my Head run mightily upon the Thought of getting over to the Shore.

Now I wish'd for my Boy *Xury*, and the long Boat, with the Shoulder of Mutton Sail, with which I sail'd above a thousand Miles on the Coast of *Africk*; but this was in vain. Then I thought I would go and look at our Ship's Boat, which, as I have said, was blown up upon the Shore, a great Way in the Storm, when we were first cast away. She lay almost where she did at first, but not quite; and was turn'd by the Force of the Waves and the Winds almost Bottom upward, against a high Ridge of Beachy[1] rough Sand; but no Water about her as before.

If I had had Hands to have refitted her, and to have launch'd her into the Water, the Boat would have done well enough, and I might have gone back into the *Brasils* with her easily enough; but I might have foreseen, That I could no more turn her, and set her upright upon her Bottom, than I could remove the Island: However, I went to the Woods, and cut Levers and Rollers, and brought them to the Boat, resolv'd to try what I could do, suggesting to my self, That if I could but turn her down, I might easily repair the Damage she had receiv'd, and she would be a very good Boat, and I might go to Sea in her very easily.

I spar'd no Pains indeed, in this Piece of fruitless Toil, and spent, I think, three or four Weeks about it; at last finding it impossible to heave it up with my little Strength, I fell to digging away the Sand, to undermine it, and so to make it fall down, setting Pieces of Wood to thrust and guide it right in the Fall.

But when I had done this, I was unable to stir it up again, or to get under it, much less to move it forward, towards the Water; so I was forc'd to give it over; and yet, though I gave over the Hopes of the Boat, my desire to venture over for the Main increased, rather than decreased, as the Means for it seem'd impossible.

This at length put me upon thinking, Whether it was not possible to make my self a *Canoe*, or *Periagua*,[2] such as the Natives of those Climates make, even without Tools, or, as I might say, without Hands, *viz.* of the Trunk of a great Tree. This I not only thought possible, but easy, and pleas'd my self extreamly with the Thoughts of making it, and with my having much more Convenience for it than any of the *Negroes* or *Indians*; but not at all considering the particular Inconveniences which I lay under, more

---

1 Pebbly.
2 A long canoe made from a single hollowed tree trunk.

than the *Indians* did, *viz*. Want of Hands to move it, when it was made, into the Water, a Difficulty much harder for me to surmount, than all the Consequences of Want of Tools could be to them; for what was it to me, That when I had chosen a vast Tree in the Woods, I might with much Trouble cut it down, if after I might be able with my Tools to hew and dub[1] the Out-side into the proper Shape of a Boat, and burn or cut out the In-side to make it hollow, so to make a Boat of it: If after all this, I must leave it just there where I found it, and was not able to launch it into the Water.

One would have thought, I could not have had the least Reflection upon my Mind of my Circumstance, while I was making this Boat; but I should have immediately thought how I should get it into the Sea; but my Thoughts were so intent upon my Voyage over the Sea in it, that I never once consider'd how I should get it off of the Land; and it was really in its own Nature more easy for me to guide it over forty five Miles of Sea, than about forty five Fathom of Land, where it lay, to set it a float in the Water.

I went to work upon this Boat, the most like a Fool, that ever Man did, who had any of his Senses awake. I pleas'd my self with the Design, without determining whether I was ever able to undertake it; not but that the Difficulty of launching my Boat came often into my Head; but I put a stop to my own Enquiries into it, by this foolish Answer which I gave my self, *Let's first make it, I'll warrant I'll find some Way or other to get it along, when 'tis done.*

This was a most preposterous Method; but the Eagerness of my Fancy prevail'd, and to work I went. I fell'd a Cedar Tree: I question much whether *Solomon* ever had such a One for the Building of the Temple at *Jerusalem*.[2] It was five Foot ten Inches Diameter at the lower Part next the Stump, and four Foot eleven Inches Diameter at the End of twenty two Foot, after which it lessen'd for a while, and then parted into Branches: It was not without infinite Labour that I fell'd this Tree: I was twenty Days hacking and hewing at it at the Bottom. I was fourteen more getting the Branches and Limbs, and the vast spreading Head of it cut off, which I hack'd and hew'd through with Axe and Hatchet, and inexpressible Labour: After this, it cost me a Month to shape it, and dub it to a Proportion, and to something like the

---

1 To cut and then work smooth.
2 In 1 Kings 5, Solomon builds an enormous temple of fir and cedar trees from Lebanon.

Bottom of a Boat, that it might swim upright as it ought to do. It cost me near three Months more to clear the In-side, and work it out so, as to make an exact[1] Boat of it: This I did indeed without Fire, by meer Malett and Chissel, and by the dint of hard Labour, till I had brought it to be a very handsome *Periagua*, and big enough to have carry'd six and twenty Men, and consequently big enough to have carry'd me and all my Cargo.

When I had gone through this Work, I was extremely delighted with it. The Boat was really much bigger than I ever saw a *Canoe*, or *Periagua*, that was made of one Tree, in my Life. Many a weary Stroke it had cost, you may be sure; and there remain'd nothing but to get it into the Water; and had I gotten it into the Water, I make no question but I should have began the maddest Voyage, and the most unlikely to be perform'd, that ever was undertaken.

But all my Devices to get it into the Water fail'd me; tho' they cost me infinite Labour too. It lay about one hundred Yards from the Water, and not more: But the first Inconvenience was, it was up Hill towards the Creek; well, to take away this Discouragement, I resolv'd to dig into the Surface of the Earth, and so make a Declivity: This I begun, and it cost me a prodigious deal of Pains; but who grutches[2] Pains, that have their Deliverance in View: But when this was work'd through, and this Difficulty manag'd, it was still much at one; for I could no more stir the *Canoe*, than I could the other Boat.

Then I measur'd the Distance of Ground, and resolv'd to cut a Dock, or Canal, to bring the Water up to the *Canoe*, seeing I could not bring the *Canoe* down to the Water: Well, I began this Work, and when I began to enter into it, and calculate how deep it was to be dug, how broad, how the Stuff to be thrown out, I found, That by the Number of Hands I had, being none but my own, it must have been ten or twelve Years before I should have gone through with it; for the Shore lay high, so that at the upper End, it must have been at least twenty Foot Deep; so at length, tho' with great Reluctancy, I gave this Attempt over also.

This griev'd me heartily, and now I saw, tho' too late, the Folly of beginning a Work before we count the Cost; and before we judge rightly of our own Strength to go through with it.

In the middle of this Work, I finish'd my fourth Year in this Place, and kept my Anniversary with the same Devotion, and with as much Comfort as ever before; for by a constant Study,

---

1 Well-designed, elaborate.
2 Begrudges.

and serious Application of the Word of God, and by the Assistance of his Grace, I gain'd a different Knowledge from what I had before. I entertain'd different Notions of Things. I look'd now upon the World as a Thing remote, which I had nothing to do with, no Expectation from, and indeed no Desires about: In a Word, I had nothing indeed to do with it, nor was ever like to have; so I thought it look'd as we may perhaps look upon it hereafter, *viz.* as a Place I had liv'd in, but was come out of it; and well might I say, as Father *Abraham* to *Dives, Between me and thee is a great Gulph fix'd.*[1]

In the first Place, I was remov'd from all the Wickedness of the World here. I had neither the *Lust of the Flesh, the Lust of the Eye, or the Pride of Life.*[2] I had nothing to covet; for I had all that I was now capable of enjoying: I was Lord of the whole Mannor; or if I pleas'd, I might call my self King, or Emperor over the whole Country which I had Possession of. There were no Rivals. I had no Competitor, none to dispute Sovereignty or Command with me. I might have rais'd Ship Loadings of Corn; but I had no use for it; so I let as little grow as I thought enough for my Occasion. I had Tortoise or Turtles enough; but now and then one, was as much as I could put to any use. I had Timber enough to have built a Fleet of Ships. I had Grapes enough to have made Wine, or to have cur'd into Raisins, to have loaded that Fleet, when they had been built.

But all I could make use of, was, All that was valuable. I had enough to eat, and to supply my Wants, and, what was all the rest to me? If I kill'd more Flesh than I could eat, the Dog must eat it, or the Vermin. If I sow'd more Corn than I could eat, it must be spoil'd. The Trees that I cut down, were lying to rot on the Ground. I could make no more use of them than for Fewel; and that I had no Occasion for, but to dress my Food.

In a Word, The Nature and Experience of Things dictated to me upon just Reflection, That all the good Things of this World, are no farther good to us, than they are for our Use; and that whatever we may heap up indeed to give others, we enjoy just as much as we can use, and no more. The most covetous griping

---

1 Luke 16:19-31. In Jesus's parable, a rich man (given the name *Dives* during the Middle Ages) is in hell, speaking to Abraham and Lazarus who are in heaven.

2 1 John 2:16: "For all that is in the world, the lust of the flesh, and the lust of the eyes, and the pride of life, is not of the Father, but is of the world."

Miser in the World would have been cur'd of the Vice of Covetousness, if he had been in my Case; for I possess'd infinitely more than I knew what to do with. I had no room for Desire, except it was of Things which I had not, and they were but Trifles, though indeed of great Use to me. I had, as I hinted before, a Parcel of Money, as well Gold as Silver, about thirty six Pounds Sterling: Alas! There the nasty sorry useless Stuff lay; I had no manner of Business for it; and I often thought with my self, That I would have given a Handful of it for a Gross of Tobacco-Pipes, or for a Hand-Mill to grind my Corn; nay, I would have given it all for Sixpenny-worth of *Turnip* and *Carrot* Seed out of *England*, or for a Handful of *Pease* and *Beans*, and a Bottle of Ink: *As it was*, I had not the least Advantage by it, or Benefit from it; but there it lay in a Drawer, and grew mouldy with the Damp of the Cave, in the wet Season; and if I had had the Drawer full of Diamonds, it had been the same Case; and they had been of no manner of Value to me, because of no Use.

I had now brought my State of Life to be much easier in it self than it was at first, and much easier to my Mind, as well as to my Body. I frequently sat down to my Meat with Thankfulness, and admir'd the Hand of God's Providence, which had thus spread my Table in the Wilderness.[1] I learn'd to look more upon the bright Side of my Condition, and less upon the dark Side; and to consider what I enjoy'd, rather than what I wanted; and this gave me sometimes such secret Comforts, that I cannot express them; and which I take Notice of here, to put those discontented People in Mind of it, who cannot enjoy comfortably what God has given them; because they see, and covet something that he has not given them: All our Discontents about what we want, appear'd to me, to spring from the Want of Thankfulness for what we have.

Another Reflection was of great Use to me, and doubtless would be so to any one that should fall into such Distress as mine was; and this was, To compare my present Condition with what I at first expected it should be; nay, with what it would certainly have been, if the good Providence of God had not wonderfully order'd the Ship to be cast up nearer to the Shore, where I not only could come at her, but could bring what I got out of her to the Shore, for my Relief and Comfort; without which, I had wanted for Tools to work, Weapons for Defence, or Gun-Powder and Shot for getting my Food.

---

1 See above, p. 126, note 1.

I spent whole Hours, I may say whole Days, in representing to my self in the most lively Colours, how I must have acted, if I had got nothing out of the Ship. How I could not have so much as got any Food, except Fish and Turtles; and that as it was long before I found any of them, I must have perish'd first. That I should have liv'd, if I had not perish'd, like a meer Savage. That if I had kill'd a Goat, or a Fowl, by any Contrivance, I had no way to flea[1] or open them, or part the Flesh from the Skin, and the Bowels, or to cut it up; but must gnaw it with my Teeth, and pull it with my Claws like a Beast.

These Reflections made me very sensible of the Goodness of Providence to me, and very thankful for my present Condition, with all its Hardships and Misfortunes: And this Part also I cannot but recommend to the Reflection of those, who are apt in their Misery to say, *Is any Affliction like mine!* Let them consider, How much worse the Cases of some People are, and their Case might have been, if Providence had thought fit.

I had another Reflection which assisted me also to comfort my Mind with Hopes; and this was, comparing my present Condition with what I had deserv'd, and had therefore Reason to expect from the Hand of Providence. I had liv'd a dreadful Life, perfectly destitute of the Knowledge and Fear of God. I had been well instructed by Father and Mother; neither had they been wanting to me, in their early Endeavours, to infuse a religious Awe of God into my Mind, a Sense of my Duty, and of what the Nature and End of my Being, requir'd of me. But alas! falling early into the Seafaring Life, which of all the Lives is the most destitute of the Fear of God, though his Terrors are always before them; I say, falling early into the Seafaring Life, and into Seafaring Company, all that little Sense of Religion which I had entertain'd, was laugh'd out of me by my Mess-Mates, by a harden'd despising of Dangers; and the Views of Death, which grew habitual to me; by my long Absence from all Manner of Opportunities to converse with any thing but what was like my self, or to hear any thing that was good, or tended towards it.

So void was I of every Thing that was good, or of the least Sense of what I was, or was to be, that in the greatest Deliverances I enjoy'd, such as my Escape from *Sallee*; my being taken up by the *Portuguese* Master of the Ship; my being planted so well in the *Brasils*; my receiving the Cargo from *England*, and the like; I never had once the Word *Thank God*, so much as on my Mind,

---

1 To flay.

or in my Mouth; nor in the greatest Distress, had I so much as a Thought to pray to him, or so much as to say, *Lord have Mercy upon me*; no nor to mention the Name of God, unless it was to swear by, and blaspheme it.

I had terrible Reflections upon my Mind for many Months, as I have already observ'd, on the Account of my wicked and hardned Life past; and when I look'd about me and considered what particular Providences had attended me since my coming into this Place, and how God had dealt bountifully with me; had not only punished me less than my Iniquity had deserv'd, but had so plentifully provided for me; this gave me great hopes that my Repentance was accepted, and that God had yet Mercy in store for me.

With these Reflections I work'd my Mind up, not only to Resignation to the Will of God in the present Disposition of my Circumstances; but even to a sincere Thankfulness for my Condition, and that I who was yet a living Man, ought not to complain, seeing I had not the due Punishment of my Sins; that I enjoy'd so many Mercies which I had no reason to have expected in that Place; that I ought never more to repine at my Condition but to rejoyce, and to give daily Thanks for that daily Bread, which nothing but a Croud of Wonders could have brought. That I ought to consider I had been fed even by Miracle, even as great as that of feeding *Elijah* by Ravens;[1] nay, by a long Series of Miracles, and that I could hardly have nam'd a Place in the unhabitable Part of the World where I could have been cast more to my Advantage: A Place, where as I had no Society, which was my Affliction on one Hand, so I found no ravenous Beast, no furious Wolves or Tygers to threaten my Life, no venomous Creatures or poisonous, which I might feed on to my Hurt, no Savages to murther and devour me.

In a word, as my Life was a Life of Sorrow, one way, so it was a Life of Mercy, another; and I wanted nothing to make it a Life of Comfort, but to be able to make my Sence of God's Goodness

---

1   1 Kings 17:2-6: "And the word of the LORD came unto [Elijah], saying, Get thee hence, and turn thee eastward, and hide thyself by the brook Cherith, that is before Jordan. And it shall be, that thou shalt drink of the brook; and I have commanded the ravens to feed thee there. So he went and did according unto the word of the LORD: for he went and dwelt by the brook Cherith, that is before Jordan. And the ravens brought him bread and flesh in the morning, and bread and flesh in the evening; and he drank of the brook."

to me, and Care over me in this Condition, be my daily Consolation; and after I did make a just Improvement of these things, I went away and was no more sad.

I had now been here so long, that many Things which I brought on Shore for my Help, were either quite gone, or very much wasted and near spent.

My Ink, as I observed, had been gone some time, all but a very little, which I eek'd out with Water a little and a little, till it was so pale it scarce left any Appearance of black upon the Paper: As long as it lasted, I made use of it to minute down the Days of the Month on which any remarkable Thing happen'd to me, and first by casting up Times past: I remember that there was a strange Concurrence of Days, in the various Providences which befel me; and which, if I had been superstitiously inclin'd to observe Days as Fatal or Fortunate, I might have had Reason to have look'd upon with a great deal of Curiosity.

First I had observed, that the same Day that I broke away from my Father and my Friends, and run away to *Hull*, in order to go to Sea; the same Day afterwards I was taken by the Sally Man of War, and made a Slave.

The same Day of the Year that I escaped out of the Wreck of that Ship in *Yarmouth* Rodes, that same Day-Year afterwards I made my escape from *Sallee* in the Boat.

The same Day of the Year I was born on (*viz.*) the 30*th* of *September*, that same Day, I had my Life so miraculously saved 26 Year after, when I was cast on Shore in this Island, so that my wicked Life, and my solitary Life begun both on a Day.

The next Thing to my Ink's being wasted,[1] was that of my Bread, I mean the Bisket which I brought out of the Ship; this I had husbanded to the last degree, allowing my self but one Cake of Bread a Day for above a Year, and yet I was quite without Bread for near a Year before I got any Corn of my own, and great Reason I had to be thankful that I had any at all, the getting it being, as has been already observed, next to miraculous.

My Cloaths began to decay too mightily: As to Linnen, I had had none a good while, except some chequer'd Shirts which I found in the Chests of the other Seamen, and which I carefully preserved, because many times I could bear no other Cloaths on but a Shirt; and it was a very great help to me that I had among all the Men's Cloaths of the Ship almost three dozen of Shirts. There were also several thick Watch Coats of the Seamens, which

---

1 Used up.

were left indeed, but they were too hot to wear; and tho' it is true, that the Weather was so violent hot, that there was no need of Cloaths, yet I could not go quite naked; no, tho' I had been inclin'd to it, which I was not, nor could not abide the thoughts of it, tho' I was all alone.

The Reason why I could not go quite naked, was, I could not bear the heat of the Sun so well when quite naked, as with some Cloaths on; nay, the very Heat frequently blistered my Skin; whereas with a Shirt on, the Air itself made some Motion and whistling under that Shirt was twofold cooler than without it, no more could I ever bring my self to go out in the heat of Sun, without a Cap or a Hat; the heat of the Sun beating with such Violence as it does in that Place, would give me the Head-ach presently, by darting so directly on my Head, without a Cap or Hat on, so that I could not bear it, whereas, if I put on my Hat, it would presently go away.

Upon those Views I began to consider about putting the few Rags I had, which I call'd Cloaths, into some Order; I had worn out all the Wastcoats I had, and my Business was now to try if I could not make Jackets out of the great Watch-Coats which I had by me, and with such other Materials as I had, so I set to Work a Taylering, or rather indeed a Botching, for I made most piteous Work of it. However, I made shift to make two or three new Wast-coats, which I hoped wou'd serve me a great while; as for Breeches or Drawers, I made but a very sorry shift indeed, till afterward.

I have mentioned that I saved the Skins of all the Creatures that I kill'd, I mean four-footed ones, and I had hung them up stretch'd out with Sticks in the Sun, by which means some of them were so dry and hard that they were fit for little, but others it seems were very useful. The first thing I made of these was a great Cap for my Head, with the Hair on the out Side to shoot[1] off the Rain; and this I perform'd so well, that after this I made me a Suit of Cloaths wholly of these Skins, that is to say, a Wast-coat, and Breeches open at Knees, and both loose, for they were rather wanting to keep me cool than to keep me warm. I must not omit to acknowledge that they were wretchedly made; for if I was a bad *Carpenter*, I was a worse *Tayler*. However, they were such as I made very good shift with; and when I was abroad, if it hap-pen'd to rain, the Hair of my Wastcoat and Cap being outermost, I was kept very dry.

---

1 To throw off the rain.

After this I spent a great deal of Time and Pains to make me an Umbrella; I was indeed in great want of one, and had a great Mind to make one; I had seen them made in the *Brasils*, where they are very useful in the great Heats which are there. And I felt the Heats every jot as great here, and greater too, being nearer the Equinox; besides, as I was oblig'd to be much abroad, it was a most useful thing to me, as well for the Rains as the Heats. I took a world of Pains at it, and was a great while before I could make any thing likely to hold; nay, after I thought I had hit the Way, I spoil'd 2 or 3 before I made one to my Mind; but at last I made one that answer'd indifferently well: The main Difficulty I found was to make it to let down. I could make it to spread, but if it did not let down too, and draw in, it was not portable for me any Way but just over my Head, which wou'd not do. However, at last, as I said, I made one to answer, and covered it with Skins, the Hair upwards, so that it cast off the Rains like a Penthouse,[1] and kept off the Sun so effectually, that I could walk out in the hottest of the Weather with greater Advantage than I could before in the coolest, and when I had no need of it, cou'd close it and carry it under my Arm.

Thus I liv'd mighty comfortably, my Mind being entirely composed by resigning to the Will of God, and throwing my self wholly upon the Disposal of his Providence. This made my Life better than sociable, for when I began to regret the want of Conversation, I would ask my self whether thus conversing mutually with my own Thoughts, and, as I hope I may say, with even God himself by Ejaculations,[2] was not better than the utmost Enjoyment of humane Society in the World.

I cannot say that after this, for five Years, any extraordinary thing happened to me, but I liv'd on in the same Course, in the same Posture[3] and Place, just as before; the chief things I was employ'd in, besides my yearly Labour of planting my Barley and Rice, and curing my Raisins, of both which I always kept up just enough to have sufficient Stock of one Year's Provisions beforehand. I say, besides this yearly Labour, and my daily Labour of going out with my Gun, I had one Labour to make me a Canoe, which at last I finished. So that by digging a Canal to it of six Foot wide, and four Foot deep, I brought it into the Creek, almost half a Mile. As for the first, which was so vastly big, as I

---

1 A sloping roof over a door or window, designed to keep away rain.
2 A short verbal outburst or quick prayer.
3 Mental or spiritual condition.

made it without considering before-hand, as I ought to do, how I should be able to launch it; so never being able to bring it to the Water, or bring the Water to it, I was oblig'd to let it lye where it was, as a *Memorandum* to teach me to be wiser next Time: Indeed, the next Time, tho' I could not get a Tree proper for it, and in a Place where I could not get the Water to it, at any less Distance, than as I have said, near half a Mile; yet as I saw it was practicable at last, I never gave it over; and though I was near two Years about it, yet I never grutch'd my Labour, in Hopes of having a Boat to go off to Sea at last.

However, though my little *Periagua* was finish'd; yet the Size of it was not at all answerable to the Design which I had in View, when I made the first; I mean, Of venturing over to the *Terra Firma*, where it was above forty Miles broad; accordingly, the Smallness of my Boat assisted to put an End to that Design, and now I thought no more of it: But as I had a Boat, my next Design was to make a Tour round the Island; for as I had been on the other Side, in one Place, crossing as I have already describ'd it, over the Land; so the Discoveries I made in that little Journey, made me very eager to see other Parts of the Coast; and now I had a Boat, I thought of nothing but sailing round the Island.

For this Purpose, that I might do every Thing with Discretion and Consideration, I fitted up a little Mast to my Boat, and made a Sail to it, out of some of the Pieces of the Ship's Sail, which lay in store; and of which I had a great Stock by me.

Having fitted my Mast and Sail, and try'd the Boat, I found she would sail very well: Then I made little Lockers, or Boxes, at either End of my Boat, to put Provisions, Necessaries and Ammunition, &c. into, to be kept dry, either from Rain, or the Sprye[1] of the Sea; and a little long hollow Place I cut in the In-side of the Boat, where I could lay my Gun, making a Flap to hang down over it to keep it dry.

I fix'd my Umbrella also in a Step at the Stern, like a Mast, to stand over my Head, and keep the Heat of the Sun off of me like an Auning;[2] and thus I every now and then took a little Voyage upon the Sea, but never went far out, nor far from the little Creek; but at last being eager to view the Circumference of my little Kingdom, I resolv'd upon my Tour, and accordingly I vict-uall'd my Ship for the Voyage, putting in two Dozen of my Loaves

---

1 Spray.
2 *Awning*: a sheet of canvas stretched over the boat's deck to keep off the sun.

(Cakes I should rather call them) of Barley Bread, an Earthen Pot full of parch'd Rice, a Food I eat a great deal of, a little Bottle of Rum, half a Goat, and Powder and Shot for killing more, and two large Watch-coats, of those which, as I mention'd before, I had sav'd out of the Seamen's Chests; these I took, one to lye upon, and the other to cover me in the Night.

It was the sixth of *November*, in the sixth Year of my Reign, or my Captivity, which you please, That I set out on this Voyage, and I found it much longer than I expected; for though the Island it self was not very large, yet when I came to the *East* Side of it, I found a great Ledge of Rocks lye out above two Leagues into the Sea, some above Water, some under it; and beyond that, a Shoal of Sand, lying dry half a League more; so that I was oblig'd to go a great Way out to Sea to double the Point.

When first I discover'd them, I was going to give over my Enterprise, and come back again, not knowing how far it might oblige me to go out to Sea; and above all, doubting how I should get back again; so I came to an Anchor; for I had made me a kind of an Anchor with a Piece of a broken Graplin,[1] which I got out of the Ship.

Having secur'd my Boat, I took my Gun, and went on Shore, climbing up upon a Hill, which seem'd to over-look that Point, where I saw the full Extent of it, and resolv'd to venture.

In my viewing the Sea from that Hill where I stood, I perceiv'd a strong, and indeed, a most furious Current, which run to the *East*, and even came close to the Point; and I took the more Notice of it, because I saw there might be some Danger; that when I came into it, I might be carry'd out to Sea by the Strength of it, and not be able to make the Island again; and indeed, had I not gotten first up upon this Hill, I believe it would have been so; for there was the same Current on the other Side the Island, only, that it set off at a farther Distance; and I saw there was a strong Eddy under the Shore; so I had nothing to do but to get in out of the first Current, and I should presently be in an Eddy.

I lay here, however, two Days; because the Wind blowing pretty fresh at *E.S.E.* and that being just contrary to the said Current, made a great Breach[2] of the Sea upon the Point; so that it was not safe for me to keep too close to the Shore for the Breach, nor to go too far off because of the Stream.

---

1 A grappling iron: a tool for grasping hold of something, such as another ship or an object on the bottom of the sea.

2 Breaking waves.

The third Day in the Morning, the Wind having abated over Night, the Sea was calm, and I ventur'd; but I am a warning Piece again, to all rash and ignorant Pilots; for no sooner was I come to the Point, when even I was not my Boat's Length from the Shore, but I found my self in a great Depth of Water, and a Current like the Sluice of a Mill: It carry'd my Boat along with it with such Violence, That all I could do, could not keep her so much as on the Edge of it; but I found it hurry'd me farther and farther out from the Eddy, which was on my left Hand. There was no Wind stirring to help me, and all I could do with my Paddlers signify'd nothing, and now I began to give my self over for lost; for as the Current was on both Sides the Island, I knew in a few Leagues Distance they must joyn again, and then I was irrecoverably gone; nor did I see any Possibility of avoiding it; so that I had no Prospect before me but of Perishing; not by the Sea, for that was calm enough, but of starving for Hunger. I had indeed found a Tortoise on the Shore, as big almost as I could lift, and had toss'd it into the Boat; and I had a great Jar of fresh Water, that is to say, one of my Earthen Pots; but what was all this to being driven into the vast Ocean, where to be sure, there was no Shore, no main Land, or Island, for a thousand Leagues at least.

And now I saw how easy it was for the Providence of God to make the most miserable Condition Mankind could be in *worse*. Now I look'd back upon my desolate solitary Island, as the most pleasant Place in the World, and all the Happiness my Heart could wish for, was to be but there again. I stretch'd out my Hands to it with eager Wishes. O happy Desart, said I, I shall never see thee more. O miserable Creature, said I, whether am I going: Then I reproach'd my self with my unthankful Temper, and how I had repin'd at my solitary Condition; and now what would I give to be on Shore there again. Thus we never see the true State of our Condition, till it is illustrated to us by its Contraries; nor know how to value what we enjoy, but by the want of it. It is scarce possible to imagine the Consternation I was now in, being driven from my beloved Island (for so it appear'd to me now to be) into the wide Ocean, almost two Leagues, and in the utmost Despair of ever recovering it again. However, I work'd hard, till indeed my Strength was almost exhausted, and kept my Boat as much to the *Northward*, that is, towards the Side of the Current which the Eddy lay on, as possibly I could; when about Noon, as the Sun pass'd the Meridian, I thought I felt a little Breeze of Wind in my Face, springing up from the *S.S.E.* This chear'd my Heart a little, and especially when in about half an Hour more, it blew a pretty small gentle Gale. By this Time I was gotten at a frightful Distance from the Island, and had the least Cloud or haizy Weather interven'd, I had been undone another Way too; for I had no Compass on Board, and should never have known how to have steer'd towards the Island, if I had but once lost Sight of it; but the Weather continuing clear, I apply'd my self to get up my Mast again, spread my Sail, standing away to the *North*, as much as possible, to get out of the Current.

Just as I had set my Mast and Sail, and the Boat began to stretch away, I saw even by the Clearness of the Water, some Alteration of the Current was near; for where the Current was so strong, the Water was foul; but perceiving the Water clear, I found the Current abate, and presently I found to the *East*, at about half a Mile, a Breach of the Sea upon some Rocks; these Rocks I found caus'd the Current to part again, and as the main Stress of it ran away more *Southerly*, leaving the Rocks to the *North-East*; so the other return'd by the Repulse of the Rocks, and made a strong Eddy, which run back again to the *North-West*, with a very sharp Stream.

They who know what it is to have a Reprieve brought to them upon the Ladder,[1] or to be rescued from Thieves just a going to murther them, or who have been in such like Extremities, may guess what my present Surprise of Joy was, and how gladly I put my Boat into the Stream of this Eddy, and the Wind also freshning, how gladly I spread my Sail to it, running chearfully before the Wind, and with a strong Tide or Eddy under Foot.

This Eddy carried me about a League in my Way back again directly towards the Island, but about two Leagues more to the Northward than the Current which carried me away at first; so that when I came near the Island, I found my self open to the Northern Shore of it, that is to say, the other End of the Island opposite to that which I went out from.

When I had made something more than a League of Way by the help of this Current or Eddy, I found it was spent and serv'd me no farther. However, I found that being between the two great Currents, (*viz.*) that on the South Side which had hurried me away, and that on the North which lay about a League on the other Side, I say between these two, in the wake of the Island, I found the Water at least still and running no Way, and having still a Breeze of Wind fair for me, I kept on steering directly for the Island, tho' not making such fresh Way as I did before.

---

1 The ladder that a prisoner would climb to the gallows to be hanged.

About four a-Clock in the Evening, being then within about a League of the Island, I found the Point of the Rocks which occasioned this Disaster, stretching out as is describ'd before to the Southward, and casting off the Current more Southwardly, had of Course made another Eddy to the North, and this I found very strong, but not directly setting the Way my Course lay which was due West, but almost full North. However having a fresh Gale, I stretch'd a-cross this Eddy slanting North-west, and in about an Hour came within about a Mile of the Shore, where it being smooth Water, I soon got to Land.

When I was on Shore I fell on my Knees and gave God Thanks for my Deliverance, resolving to lay aside all Thoughts of my Deliverance by my Boat, and refreshing my self with such Things as I had, I brought my Boat close to the Shore in a little Cove that I had spy'd under some Trees, and lay'd me down to sleep, being quite spent with the Labour and Fatigue of the Voyage.

I was now at a great Loss which Way to get Home with my Boat, I had run so much Hazard, and knew too much the Case to think of attempting it by the Way I went out, and what might be at the other Side (I mean the West Side) I knew not, nor had I any Mind to run any more Ventures; so I only resolved in the Morning to make my Way Westward along the Shore and to see if there was no Creek where I might lay up my Frigate in Safety, so as to have her again if I wanted her; in about three Mile or thereabout coasting the Shore, I came to a very good Inlet or Bay about a Mile over, which narrowed till it came to a very little Rivulet or Brook, where I found a very convenient Harbour for my Boat and where she lay as if she had been in a little Dock made on Purpose for her. Here I put in, and having stow'd my Boat very safe, I went on Shore to look about me and see where I was.

I soon found I had but a little past by the Place where I had been before, when I travell'd on Foot to that Shore; so taking nothing out of my Boat, but my Gun and my Umbrella, for it was exceeding hot, I began my March: The Way was comfortable enough after such a Voyage as I had been upon, and I reach'd my old Bower in the Evening, where I found every thing standing as I left it; for I always kept it in good Order, being, as I said before, my Country House.

I got over the Fence, and laid me down in the Shade to rest my Limbs; for I was very weary, and fell asleep: But judge you, if you can, that read my Story, what a Surprize I must be in, when I was wak'd out of my Sleep by a Voice calling me by my Name several times, *Robin, Robin, Robin Crusoe*, poor *Robin Crusoe*, where are you *Robin Crusoe?* Where are you? Where have you been?

I was so dead asleep at first, being fatigu'd with Rowing, or Paddling, as it is call'd, the first Part of the Day, and with walking the latter Part, that I did not wake thoroughly, but dozing between sleeping and waking, thought I dream'd that some Body spoke to me: But as the Voice continu'd to repeat *Robin Crusoe, Robin Crusoe*, at last I began to wake more perfectly, and was at first dreadfully frighted, and started up in the utmost Consternation: But no sooner were my Eyes open, but I saw my *Poll* sitting on the Top of the Hedge; and immediately knew that it was he that spoke to me; for just in such bemoaning Language I had used to talk to him, and teach him; and he had learn'd it so perfectly, that he would sit upon my Finger, and lay his Bill close to my Face, and cry, *Poor* Robin Crusoe, *Where are you? Where have you been? How come you here?* And such things as I had taught him.

However, even though I knew it was the Parrot, and that indeed it could be no Body else, it was a good while before I could compose my self: First, I was amazed how the Creature got thither, and then, how he should just keep about the Place, and no where else: But as I was well satisfied it could be no Body but honest *Poll*, I got it over; and holding out my Hand, and calling him by his Name *Poll*, the sociable Creature came to me, and sat upon my Thumb, as he used to do, and continu'd talking to me, *Poor* Robin Crusoe, and *how did I come here?* and *where had I been?* just as if he had been overjoy'd to see me again; and so I carry'd him Home along with me.

I had now had enough of rambling to Sea for some time, and had enough to do for many Days to sit still, and reflect upon the Danger I had been in: I would have been very glad to have had my Boat again on my Side of the Island; but I knew not how it was practicable to get it about; as to the East Side of the Island, which I had gone round; I knew well enough there was no venturing that Way; my very heart would shrink, and my very Blood run chill but to think of it: And as to the other Side of the Island, I did not know how it might be there; but supposing the Current ran with the same Force against the Shore at the East as it pass'd by it on the other, I might run the same Risk of being driven down the Stream, and carry'd by the Island, as I had been before, of being carry'd away from it; so with these Thoughts I contented my self to be without any Boat, though it had been the Product of so many Months Labour to make it, and of so many more to get it unto the Sea.

In this Government of my Temper, I remain'd near a Year, liv'd a very sedate retir'd Life, as you may well suppose; and my Thoughts being very much composed as to my Condition, and fully comforted in resigning my self to the Dispositions of Providence, I thought I liv'd really very happily in all things, except that of Society.

I improv'd my self in this time in all the mechanick Exercises which my Necessities put me upon applying my self to, and I believe cou'd, upon Occasion, make a very good *Carpenter*, especially considering how few Tools I had.

Besides this, I arriv'd at an unexpected Perfection in my Earthen Ware, and contriv'd well enough to make them with a Wheel, which I found infinitely easier and better; because I made things round and shapable, which before were filthy[1] things indeed to look on. But I think I was never more vain of my own Performance, or more joyful for any thing I found out, than for my being able to make a Tobacco-Pipe. And tho' it was a very ugly clumsy thing, when it was done, and only burnt red like other Earthen Ware, yet as it was hard and firm, and would draw the Smoke, I was exceedingly comforted with it, for I had been always used to smoke, and there were Pipes in the Ship, but I forgot them at first, not knowing that there was Tobacco in the Island; and afterwards, when I search'd the Ship again, I could not come at any Pipes at all.

In my Wicker Ware also I improved much, and made abundance of necessary Baskets, as well as my Invention shew'd me, tho' not very handsome, yet they were such as were very handy and convenient for my laying things up in, or fetching things home in. For Example, if I kill'd a Goat abroad, I could hang it up in a Tree, flea it, and dress it, and cut it in Pieces, and bring it home in a Basket, and the like by a Turtle, I could cut it up, take out the Eggs, and a Piece or two of the Flesh, which was enough for me, and bring them home in a Basket, and leave the rest behind me. Also large deep Baskets were my Receivers for my Corn, which I always rubb'd out as soon as it was dry, and cured, and kept it in great Baskets.

I began now to perceive my Powder abated considerably, and this was a Want which it was impossible for me to supply, and I began seriously to consider what I must do when I should have no more Powder; that is to say, how I should do to kill any Goat.

---

1 Contemptible, despicable.

I had, as is observ'd in the third Year of my being here, kept a young Kid, and bred her up tame, and I was in hope of getting a He-Goat, but I could not by any Means bring it to pass, 'till my Kid grew an old Goat; and I could never find in my Heart to kill her, till she dy'd at last of meer Age.

But being now in the eleventh Year of my Residence, and, as I have said, my Ammunition growing low, I set my self to study some Art to trap and snare the Goats, to see whether I could not catch some of them alive, and particularly I wanted a She-Goat great with young.

To this Purpose I made Snares to hamper them, and I do believe they were more than once taken in them, but my Tackle was not good, for I had no Wire, and I always found them broken, and my Bait devoured.

At length I resolv'd to try a Pit-fall, so I dug several large Pits in the Earth, in Places where I had observ'd the Goats used to feed, and over these Pits I plac'd Hurdles of my own making too, with a great Weight upon them; and several times I put Ears of Barley, and dry Rice, without setting the Trap, and I could easily perceive that the Goats had gone in and eaten up the Corn, for I could see the Mark of their Feet. At length I set three Traps in one Night, and going the next Morning I found them all standing, and yet the Bait eaten and gone: This was very discouraging. However, I alter'd my Trap, and, not to trouble you with Particulars, going one Morning to see my Trap, I found in one of them a large old He-Goat, and in one of the other, three Kids, a Male and two Females.

As to the old one, I knew not what to do with him, he was so fierce I durst not go into the Pit to him; that is to say, to go about to bring him away alive, which was what I wanted. I could have kill'd him, but that was not my Business, nor would it answer my End. So I e'en let him out, and he ran away as if he had been frighted out of his Wits: But I had forgot then what I learn'd afterwards, that Hunger will tame a Lyon. If I had let him stay there three or four Days without Food, and then have carry'd him some Water to drink, and then a little Corn, he would have been as tame as one of the Kids, for they are mighty sagacious tractable Creatures where they are well used.

However, for the present I let him go, knowing no better at that time; then I went to the three Kids, and taking them one by one, I tyed them with Strings together, and with some Difficulty brought them all home.

It was a good while before they wou'd feed, but throwing them some sweet Corn, it tempted them and they began to be tame; and now I found that if I expected to supply my self with Goat-Flesh when I had no Powder or Shot left, breeding some up tame was my only way, when perhaps I might have them about my House like a Flock of Sheep.

But then it presently occurr'd to me, that I must keep the tame from the wild, or else they would always run wild when they grew up, and the only Way for this was to have some enclosed Piece of Ground, well fenc'd either with Hedge or Pale, to keep them in so effectually, that those within might not break out, or those without break in.

This was a great Undertaking for one Pair of Hands, yet as I saw there was an absolute Necessity of doing it, my first Piece of Work was to find out a proper Piece of Ground, *viz.* where there was likely to be Herbage for them to eat, Water for them to drink, and Cover to keep them from the Sun.

Those who understand such Enclosures will think I had very little Contrivance, when I pitch'd upon a Place very proper for all these, being a plain open Piece of Meadow-Land, or *Savanna*, (as our People call it in the Western Collonies,) which had two or three little Drills[1] of fresh Water in it, and at one end was very woody. I say they will smile at my Forecast, when I shall tell them I began my enclosing of this Piece of Ground in such a manner, that my Hedge or Pale must have been at least two Mile about. Nor was the Madness of it so great as to the Compass, for if it was ten Mile about I was like to have time enough to do it in. But I did not consider that my Goats would be as wild in so much Compass as if they had had the whole Island, and I should have so much Room to chace them in, that I should never catch them.

My Hedge was begun and carry'd on, I believe, about fifty Yards, when this Thought occurr'd to me, so I presently stopt short, and for the first beginning I resolv'd to enclose a Piece of about 150 Yards in length, and 100 Yards in breadth, which as it would maintain as many as I should have in any reasonable time, so as my Flock encreased, I could add more Ground to my Enclosure.

This was acting with some Prudence, and I went to work with Courage. I was about three Months hedging in the first Piece, and till I had done it I tether'd the three Kids in the best part of it, and us'd them to feed as near me as possible to make them familiar; and very often I would go and carry them some Ears of

---

1 Small streams.

Barley, or a handful of Rice, and feed them out of my Hand; so that after my Enclosure was finished, and I let them loose, they would follow me up and down, bleating after me for a handful of Corn.

This answer'd my End, and in about a Year and half I had a Flock of about twelve Goats, Kids and all; and in two Years more I had three and forty, besides several that I took and kill'd for my Food. And after that I enclosed five several Pieces of Ground to feed them in, with little Pens to drive them into, to take them as I wanted, and Gates out of one Piece of Ground into another.

But this was not all, for now I not only had Goats Flesh to feed on when I pleas'd, but Milk too, a thing which indeed in my beginning I did not so much as think of, and which, when it came into my Thoughts, was really an agreeable Surprize. For now I set up my Dairy, and had sometimes a Gallon or two of Milk in a Day. And as Nature, who gives Supplies of Food to every Creature, dictates even naturally how to make use of it; so I that had never milk'd a Cow, much less a Goat, or seen Butter or Cheese made, very readily and handily, tho' after a great many Essays and Miscarriages,[1] made me both Butter and Cheese at last, and never wanted it afterwards.

How mercifully can our great Creator treat his Creatures, even in those Conditions in which they seem'd to be overwhelm'd in Destruction. How can he sweeten the bitterest Providences, and give us Cause to praise him for Dungeons and Prisons. What a Table was here spread for me in a Wilderness, where I saw nothing at first but to perish for Hunger.

It would have made a Stoick smile to have seen, me and my little Family sit down to Dinner; there was my Majesty the Prince and Lord of the whole Island; I had the Lives of all my Subjects at my absolute Command. I could hang, draw, give Liberty, and take it away, and no Rebels among all my Subjects.

Then to see how like a King I din'd too all alone, attended by my Servants, *Poll*, as if he had been my Favourite, was the only Person permitted to talk to me. My Dog who was now grown very old and crazy,[2] and had found no Species to multiply his Kind upon, sat always at my Right Hand, and two Cats, one on one Side the Table, and one on the other, expecting now and then a Bit from my Hand, as a Mark of special Favour.

---

1 Attempts and failures.

2 Feeble, ailing.

But these were not the two Cats which I brought on Shore at first, for they were both of them dead, and had been interr'd near my Habitation by my own Hand; but one of them having multiply'd by I know not what Kind of Creature, these were two which I had preserv'd tame, whereas the rest run wild in the Woods, and became indeed troublesom to me at last; for they would often come into my House, and plunder me too, till at last I was obliged to shoot them, and did kill a great many; at length they left me with this Attendance, and in this plentiful Manner I lived; neither could I be said to want any thing but Society, and of that in some time after this, I was like to have too much.

I was something impatient, as I have observ'd, to have the Use of my Boat; though very loath to run any more Hazards; and therefore sometimes I sat contriving Ways to get her about the Island, and at other Times I sat my self down contented enough without her. But I had a strange Uneasiness in my Mind to go down to the Point of the Island, where, as I have said, in my last Ramble, I went up the Hill to see how the Shore lay, and how the Current set, that I might see what I had to do: This Inclination encreas'd upon me every Day, and at length I resolv'd to travel thither by Land, following the Edge of the Shore, I did so: But had any one in *England* been to meet such a Man as I was, it must either have frighted them, or rais'd a great deal of Laughter; and as I frequently stood still to look at my self, I could not but smile at the Notion of my travelling through *Yorkshire* with such an Equipage,[1] and in such a Dress: Be pleas'd to take a Scetch of my Figure as follows,

I had a great high shapeless Cap, made of a Goat's Skin, with a Flap hanging down behind, as well to keep the Sun from me, as to shoot the Rain off from running into my Neck; nothing being so hurtful in these Climates, as the Rain upon the Flesh under the Cloaths.

I had a short Jacket of Goat-Skin, the Skirts coming down to about the middle of my Thighs; and a Pair of open-knee'd Breeches of the same, the Breeches were made of the Skin of an old *He-goat*, whose Hair hung down such a Length on either Side, that like *Pantaloons*[2] it reach'd to the middle of my Legs; Stockings and Shoes I had none, but had made me a Pair of

---

1 Equipment for a journey.
2 Baggy men's trousers extending just below the knee, popular in Restoration England.

some-things, I scarce know what to call them, like Buskins[1] to flap over my Legs, and lace on either Side like Spatter-dashes;[2] but of a most barbarous Shape, as indeed were all the rest of my Cloaths.

I had on a broad Belt of Goats-Skin dry'd, which I drew together with two Thongs of the same, instead of Buckles, and in a kind of a Frog[3] on either Side of this, instead of a Sword and a Dagger, hung a little Saw and a Hatchet, one on one Side, one on the other. I had another Belt not so broad, and fasten'd in the same Manner, which hung over my Shoulder; and at the End of it, under my left Arm, hung two Pouches, both made of Goat's-Skin too; in one of which hung my Powder, in the other my Shot: At my Back I carry'd my Basket, on my Shoulder my Gun, and over my Head a great clumsy ugly Goat-Skin Umbrella, but which, after all, was the most necessary Thing I had about me, next to my Gun: As for my Face, the Colour of it was really not so *Moletta*-like[4] as one might expect from a Man not at all careful of it, and living within nine or ten Degrees of the *Equinox*. My Beard I had once suffer'd to grow till it was about a Quarter of a Yard long; but as I had both Scissars and Razors sufficient, I had cut it pretty short, except what grew on my upper Lip, which I had trimm'd into a large Pair of *Mahometan* Whiskers, such as I had seen worn by some *Turks*, who I saw at *Sallee*; for the *Moors* did not wear such, tho' the *Turks* did; of these Muschatoes or Whiskers, I will not say they were long enough to hang my Hat upon them; but they were of a Length and Shape monstrous enough, and such as in *England* would have pass'd for frightful.

But all this is by the by; for as to my Figure, I had so few to observe me, that it was of no manner of Consequence; so I say no more to that Part. In this kind of Figure I went my new Journey, and was out five or six Days. I travell'd first along the Sea Shore, directly to the Place where I first brought my Boat to an Anchor, to get up upon the Rocks; and having no Boat now to take care of, I went over the Land a nearer Way to the same Height that I was upon before, when looking forward to the Point of the Rocks which lay out, and which I was oblig'd to double with my Boat, as is said above: I was surpriz'd to see the Sea all smooth and

---

1 Laced, thick-soled boots extending half way to the knees.
2 Spats; cloth or leather legging that protects trousers from getting dirty.
3 A leather loop attached to a belt to hold a sword or axe.
4 Archaic form of *mulatto*.

quiet, no Ripling, no Motion, no Current, any more there than in other Places.

I was at a strange Loss to understand this, and resolv'd to spend some Time in the observing it, to see if nothing from the Sets of the Tide had occasion'd it; but I was presently convinc'd how it was, *viz.* That the Tide of Ebb setting from the *West*, and joyning with the Current of Waters from some great River on the Shore, must be the Occasion of this Current; and that according as the Wind blew more forcibly from the *West*, or from the *North*, this Current came nearer, or went farther from the Shore; for waiting thereabouts till Evening, I went up to the Rock again, and then the Tide of Ebb being made, I plainly saw the Current again as before, only, that it run farther off, being near half a League from the Shore; whereas in my Case, it set close upon the Shore, and hurry'd me and my *Canoe* along with it, which at another Time it would not have done.

This Observation convinc'd me, That I had nothing to do but to observe the Ebbing and the Flowing of the Tide, and I might very easily bring my Boat about the Island again: But when I began to think of putting it in Practice, I had such a Terror upon my Spirits at the Remembrance of the Danger I had been in, that I could not think of it again with any Patience; but on the contrary, I took up another Resolution which was more safe, though more laborious; and this was, That I would build, or rather make me another *Periagua* or *Canoe*; and so have one for one Side of the Island, and one for the other.

You are to understand, that now I had, as I may call it, two Plantations in the Island; one my little Fortification or Tent, with the Wall about it under the Rock, with the Cave behind me, which by this Time I had enlarg'd into several Apartments, or Caves, one within another. One of these, which was the dryest, and largest, and had a Door out beyond my Wall or Fortification; that is to say, beyond where my Wall joyn'd to the Rock, was all fill'd up with the large Earthen Pots, of which I have given an Account, and with fourteen or fifteen great Baskets, which would hold five or six Bushels each, where I laid up my Stores of Provision, especially my Corn, some in the Ear cut off short from the Straw, and the other rubb'd out with my Hand.

As for my Wall made, *as before*, with long Stakes or Piles, those Piles grew all like Trees, and were by this Time grown so big, and spread so very much, that there was not the least Appearance to any one's View of any Habitation behind them.

Near this Dwelling of mine, but a little farther within the

Land, and upon lower Ground, lay my two Pieces of Corn-Ground, which I kept duly cultivated and sow'd, and which duly yielded me their Harvest in its Season; and whenever I had occasion for more Corn, I had more Land adjoyning as fit as that.

Besides this, I had my Country Seat, and I had now a tollerable Plantation there also; for first, I had my little Bower, as I call'd it, which I kept in Repair; *that is to say,* I kept the Hedge which circled it in, constantly fitted up to its usual Height, the Ladder standing always in the Inside; I kept the Trees which at first were no more than my Stakes, but were now grown very firm and tall; I kept them always so cut, that they might spread and grow thick and wild, and make the more agreeable Shade, which they did effectually to my Mind. In the Middle of this I had my Tent always standing, being a piece of a Sail spread over Poles set up for that Purpose, and which never wanted any Repair or Renewing; and under this I had made me a Squab[1] or Couch, with the Skins of the Creatures I had kill'd, and with other soft Things, and a Blanket laid on them, such as belong'd to our Sea-Bedding, which I had saved, and a great Watch-Coat to cover me; and here, whenever I had Occasion to be absent from my chief Seat, I took up my Country Habitation.

Adjoyning to this I had my Enclosures for my Cattle, that is to say, my Goats: And as I had taken an inconceivable deal of Pains to fence and enclose this Ground, so I was so uneasy to see it kept entire, lest the Goats should break thro', that I never left off till with infinite Labour I had stuck the Out-side of the Hedge so full of small Stakes, and so near to one another, that it was rather a Pale than a Hedge, and there was scarce Room to put a Hand thro' between them, which afterwards when those Stakes grew, as they all did in the next rainy Season, made the Enclosure strong like a Wall, indeed stronger than any Wall.

This will testify for me that I was not idle, and that I spared no Pains to bring to pass whatever appear'd necessary for my comfortable Support; for I consider'd the keeping up a Breed of tame Creatures thus at my Hand, would be a living Magazine of Flesh, Milk, Butter and Cheese, for me as long as I liv'd in the Place, if it were to be forty Years; and that keeping them in my Reach, depended entirely upon my perfecting my Enclosures to such a Degree, that I might be of keeping them together; which by this Method indeed I so effectually secur'd, that, when these little

---

1 Sofa.

Stakes began to grow, I had planted them so very thick, I was forced to pull some of them up again.

In this Place also I had my Grapes growing, which I principally depended on for my Winter Store of Raisins; and which I never fail'd to preserve very carefully, as the best and most agreeable Dainty of my whole Diet; and indeed they were not agreeable only, but physical,[1] wholesome, nourishing, and refreshing to the last Degree.

As this was also about half Way between my other Habitation, and the Place where I had laid up my Boat, I generally stay'd, and lay here in my Way thither; for I used frequently to visit my Boat, and I kept all Things about or belonging to her in very good Order; sometimes I went out in her to divert my self, but no more hazardous Voyages would I go, nor scarce ever above a Stone's Cast or two from the Shore, I was so apprehensive of being hurry'd out of my Knowledge again by the Currents, or Winds, or any other Accident. But now I come to a new Scene of my Life.

It happen'd one Day about Noon going towards my Boat, I was exceedingly surpriz'd with the Print of a Man's naked Foot on the Shore, which was very plain to be seen in the Sand: I stood like one Thunder-struck, or as if I had seen an Apparition; I listen'd, I look'd round me, I could hear nothing, nor see any Thing, I went up to a rising Ground to look farther, I went up the Shore and down the Shore, but it was all one, I could see no other Impression but that one, I went to it again to see if there were any more, and to observe if it might not be my Fancy; but there was no Room for that, for there was exactly the very Print of a Foot, Toes, Heel, and every Part of a Foot; how it came thither, I knew not, nor could in the least imagine. But after innumerable fluttering Thoughts, like a Man perfectly confus'd and out of my self, I came Home to my Fortification, not feeling, as we say, the Ground I went on, but terrify'd to the last Degree, looking behind me at every two or three Steps, mistaking every Bush and Tree, and fancying every Stump at a Distance to be a Man; nor is it possible to describe how many various Shapes affrighted Imagination represented Things to me in, how many wild Ideas were found every Moment in my Fancy, and what strange unaccountable Whimsies came into my Thoughts by the Way.

When I came to my Castle, for so I think I call'd it ever after this, I fled into it like one pursued; whether I went over by the

---

1 Medicinal, therapeutic.

Ladder as first contriv'd, or went in at the Hole in the Rock, which I call'd a Door, I cannot remember; no, nor could I remember the next Morning, for never frighted Hare fled to Cover, or Fox to Earth, with more Terror of Mind than I to this Retreat.

I slept none that Night; the farther I was from the Occasion of my Fright, the greater my Apprehensions were, which is something contrary to the Nature of such Things, and especially to the usual Practice of all Creatures in Fear: But I was so embarrass'd with my own frightful Ideas of the Thing, that I form'd nothing but dismal Imaginations to my self, even tho' I was now a great way off of it. Sometimes I fancy'd it must be the Devil; and Reason joyn'd in with me upon this Supposition: For how should any other Thing in human Shape come into the Place? Where was the Vessel that brought them? What Marks was there of any other Footsteps? And how was it possible a Man should come there? But then to think that *Satan* should take human Shape upon him in such a Place where there could be no manner of Occasion for it, but to leave the Print of his Foot behind him, and that even for no Purpose too, for he could not be sure I should see it; this was an Amusement[1] the other Way; I consider'd that the Devil might have found out abundance of other Ways to have terrify'd me than this of the single Print of a Foot. That as I liv'd quite on the other Side of the Island, he would never have been so simple[2] to leave a Mark in a Place where 'twas Ten Thousand to one whether I should ever see it or not, and in the Sand too, which the first Surge of the Sea upon a high Wind would have defac'd entirely: All this seem'd inconsistent with the Thing it self, and with all the Notions we usually entertain of the Subtilty of the Devil.

Abundance of such Things as these assisted to argue me out of all Apprehensions of its being the Devil: And I presently concluded then, that it must be some more dangerous Creature, (*viz.*) That it must be some of the Savages of the main Land over-against me, who had wander'd out to Sea in their *Canoes*; and either driven by the Currents, or by contrary Winds had made the Island; and had been on Shore, but were gone away again to Sea, being as loth, perhaps, to have stay'd in this desolate Island, as I would have been to have had them.

While these Reflections were rowling upon my Mind, I was very thankful in my Thoughts, that I was so happy as not to be

---

1 Perplexity.
2 Stupid, foolish.

thereabouts at that Time, or that they did not see my Boat, by which they would have concluded that some Inhabitants had been in the Place, and perhaps have search'd farther for me: Then terrible Thoughts rack'd my Imagination about their having found my Boat, and that there were People here; and that if so, I should certainly have them come again in greater Numbers, and devour me; that if it should happen so that they should not find me, yet they would find my Enclosure, destroy all my Corn, carry away all my Flock of tame Goats, and I should perish at last for meer Want.

Thus my Fear banish'd all my religious Hope; all that former Confidence in God which was founded upon such wonderful Experience as I had had of his Goodness, now vanished, as if he that had fed me by Miracle hitherto, could not preserve by his Power the Provision which he had made for me by his Goodness: I reproach'd my self with my Easiness, that would not sow any more Corn one Year than would just serve me till the next Season, as if no Accident could intervene to prevent my enjoying the Crop that was upon the Ground; and this I thought so just a Reproof, that I resolv'd for the future to have two or three Years Corn beforehand, so that whatever might come, I might not perish for want of Bread.

How strange a Chequer Work[1] of Providence is the Life of Man! and by what secret differing Springs are the Affections hurry'd about as differing Circumstance present! To Day we love what to Morrow we hate; to Day we seek what to Morrow we shun; to Day we desire what to Morrow we fear; nay even tremble at the Apprehensions of; this was exemplify'd in me at this Time in the most lively Manner imaginable; for I whose only Affliction was, that I seem'd banished from human Society, that I was alone, circumscrib'd by the boundless Ocean, cut off from Mankind, and condemn'd to what I call'd silent Life; that I was as one who Heaven thought not worthy to be number'd among the Living, or to appear among the rest of his Creatures; that to have seen one of my own Species, would have seem'd to me a Raising me from Death to Life, and the greatest Blessing that Heaven it self, next to the supreme Blessing of Salvation, could bestow; *I say*, that I should now tremble at the very Apprehensions of seeing a Man, and was ready to sink into the Ground at but the Shadow or silent Appearance of a Man's having set his Foot in the Island.

---

1 Pattern of alternating colors; i.e., life marked by quick contrasts.

Such is the uneven State of human Life: And it afforded me a great many curious Speculations afterwards, when I had a little recover'd my first Surprize; I consider'd that this was the Station of Life the infinitely wise and good Providence of God had determin'd for me, that as I could not foresee what the Ends of Divine Wisdom might be in all this, so I was not to dispute his Sovereignty, who, as I was his Creature, had an undoubted Right by Creation to govern and dispose of me absolutely as he thought fit; and who, as I was a Creature who had offended him, had likewise a judicial Right to condemn me to what Punishment he thought fit; and that it was my Part to submit to bear his Indignation, because I had sinn'd against him.

I then reflected that God, who was not only Righteous but Omnipotent, as he had thought fit thus to punish and afflict me, so he was able to deliver me; that if he did not think fit to do it, 'twas my unquestion'd Duty to resign my self absolutely and entirely to his Will; and on the other Hand, it was my Duty also to hope in him, pray to him, and quietly to attend the Dictates and Directions of his daily Providence.

These Thoughts took me up many Hours, Days; nay, I may say, Weeks and Months; and one particular Effect of my Cogitations on this Occasion, I cannot omit, *viz.* One Morning early, lying in my Bed, and fill'd with Thought about my Danger from the Appearance of Savages, I found it discompos'd me very much, upon which those Words of the Scripture came into my Thoughts, *Call upon me in the Day of Trouble, and I will deliver, and thou shalt glorify me.*[1]

Upon this, rising chearfully out of my Bed, my Heart was not only comforted, but I was guided and encourag'd to pray earnestly to God for Deliverance: When I had done praying, I took up my Bible, and opening it to read, the first Words that presented to me, were, *Wait on the Lord, and be of good Cheer, and he shall strengthen thy Heart; wait, I say, on the Lord:*[2] It is impossible to express the Comfort this gave me. In Answer, I thankfully laid down the Book, and was no more sad, at least, not on that Occasion.

In the middle of these Cogitations, Apprehensions and Reflections, it came into my Thought one Day, that all this might be a meer Chimera of my own; and that this Foot might be the Print of my own Foot, when I came on Shore from my Boat: This

---

1 Psalms 50: 15.
2 Psalms 27: 14.

chear'd me up a little too, and I began to perswade my self it was all a Delusion; that it was nothing else but my own Foot, and why might not I come that way from the Boat, as well as I was going that way to the Boat; again, I consider'd also that I could by no Means tell for certain where I had trod, and where I had not; and that if at last this was only the Print of my own Foot, I had play'd the Part of those Fools, who strive to make stories of Spectres, and Apparitions; and then are frighted at them more than any body.

Now I began to take Courage, and to peep abroad again; for I had not stirr'd out of my Castle for three Days and Nights; so that I began to starve for Provision; for I had little or nothing within Doors, but some Barley Cakes and Water. Then I knew that my Goats wanted to be milk'd too, which usually was my Evening Diversion; and the poor Creatures were in great Pain and Inconvenience for want of it; and indeed, it almost spoil'd some of them, and almost dry'd up their Milk.

Heartning my self therefore with the Belief that this was nothing but the Print of one of my own Feet, and so I might be truly said to start at my own Shadow, I began to go abroad again, and went to my Country House, to milk my Flock; but to see with what Fear I went forward, how often I look'd behind me, how I was ready every now and then to lay down my Basket, and run for my Life, it would have made any one have thought I was haunted with an evil Conscience, or that I had been lately most terribly frighted, and so indeed I had.

However, as I went down thus two or three Days, and having seen nothing, I began to be a little bolder; and to think there was really nothing in it, but my own Imagination: But I cou'd not perswade my self fully of this, till I should go down to the Shore again, and see this Print of a Foot, and measure it by my own, and see if there was any Similitude or Fitness, that I might be assur'd it was my own Foot: But when I came to the Place, *First*, It appear'd evidently to me, that when I laid up my Boat, I could not possibly be on Shore any where there about. *Secondly*, When I came to measure the Mark with my own Foot, I found my Foot not so large by a great deal; both these Things fill'd my Head with new Imaginations, and gave me the Vapours again, to the highest Degree; so that I shook with cold, like one in an Ague: And I went Home again, fill'd with the Belief that some Man or Men had been on Shore there; or in short, that the Island was inhabited, and I might be surpriz'd before I was aware; and what course to take for my Security I knew not.

O what ridiculous Resolution Men take, when possess'd with Fear! It deprives them of the Use of those Means which Reason offers for their Relief. The first Thing I propos'd to my self, was, to throw down my Enclosures, and turn all my tame Cattle wild into the Woods, that the Enemy might not find them; and then frequent the Island in Prospect of the same, or the like Booty: Then to the simple Thing of Digging up my two Corn Fields, that they might not find such a Grain there, and still be prompted to frequent the Island; then to demolish my Bower, and Tent, that they might not see any Vestiges of Habitation, and be prompted to look farther, in order to find out the Persons inhabiting.

These were the Subject of the first Night's Cogitation, after I was come Home again, while the Apprehensions which had so over-run my Mind were fresh upon me, and my Head was full of Vapours, as above: Thus Fear of Danger is ten thousand Times more terrifying than Danger it self, when apparent to the Eyes; and we find the Burthen of Anxiety greater by much, than the Evil which we are anxious about; and which was worse than all this, I had not that Relief in this Trouble from the Resignation I used to practise, that I hop'd to have. I look'd, I thought, like *Saul*, who complain'd not only that the *Philistines* were upon him;[1] but that God had forsaken him; for I did not now take due Ways to compose my Mind, by crying to God in my Distress, and resting upon his Providence, as I had done before, for my Defence and Deliverance; which if I had done, I had, at least, been more cheerfully supported under this new Surprise, and perhaps carry'd through it with more Resolution.

This Confusion of my Thoughts kept me waking all Night; but in the Morning I fell asleep, and having by the Amusement of my Mind, been, as it were, tyr'd, and my Spirits exhausted; I slept very soundly, and wak'd much better compos'd than I had ever been before; and now I began to think sedately; and upon the utmost Debate with my self, I concluded, That this Island, which was so exceeding pleasant, fruitful, and no farther from the main Land than as I had seen, was not so entirely abandon'd as I might imagine: That altho' there were no stated Inhabitants who liv'd on the Spot; yet that there might sometimes come Boats off from the

---

1 In 1 Samuel 28: 15, Saul complains to the spirit of Samuel, "I am sore distressed; for the Philistines make war against me, and God is departed from me, and answereth me no more, neither by prophets, nor by dreams."

Shore, who either with Design, or perhaps never, but when they were driven by cross Winds, might come to this Place.

That I had liv'd here fifteen Years now, and had not met with the least Shadow or Figure of any People yet; and that if at any Time they should be driven here, it was probable they went away again as soon as ever they could, seeing they had never thought fit to fix there upon any Occasion, to this Time.

That the most I cou'd suggest any Danger from, was, from any such casual accidental Landing of straggling People from the Main, who, as it was likely if they were driven hither, were here against their Wills; so they made no stay here, but went off again with all possible Speed, seldom staying one Night on Shore, least they should not have the Help of the Tides, and Day-light back again; and that therefore I had nothing to do but to consider of some safe Retreat, in Case I should see any Savages land upon the Spot.

Now I began sorely to repent, that I had dug my Cave so large, as to bring a Door through again, which Door, as I said, came out beyond where my Fortification joyn'd to the Rock; upon maturely considering this therefore, I resolv'd to draw me a second Fortification, in the same Manner of a Semicircle, at a Distance from my Wall, just where I had planted a double Row of Trees, about twelve Years before, of which I made mention: These Trees having been planted so thick before, they wanted but a few Piles to be driven between them, that they should be thicker, and stronger, and my Wall would be soon finish'd.

So that I had now a double Wall, and my outer Wall was thickned with Pieces of Timber, old Cables, and every Thing I could think of, to make it strong; having in it seven little Holes, about as big as I might put my Arm out at: In the In-side of this, I thickned my Wall to above ten Foot thick, with continual bringing Earth out of my Cave, and laying it at the Foot of the Wall, and walking upon it; and through the seven Holes, I contriv'd to plant the Musquets, of which I took Notice, that I got seven on Shore out of the Ship; these, I say, I planted like my Cannon, and fitted them into Frames that held them like a Carriage, that so I could fire all the seven Guns in two Minutes Time: This Wall I was many a weary Month a finishing, and yet never thought my self safe till it was done.

When this was done, I stuck all the Ground without my Wall, for a great way every way, as full with Stakes or Sticks of the *Osier* like Wood, which I found so apt to grow, as they could well stand; insomuch, that I believe I might set in near twenty thousand of them, leaving a pretty large Space between them and my Wall, that I might have room to see an Enemy, and they might have no shelter from the young Trees, if they attempted to approach my outer Wall.

Thus in two Years Time I had a thick Grove and in five or six Years Time I had a Wood before my Dwelling, growing so monstrous thick and strong, that it was indeed perfectly impassable; and no Men of what kind soever, would ever imagine that there was any Thing beyond it, much less a Habitation: As for the Way which I propos'd to my self to go in and out, for I left no Avenue; it was by setting two Ladders, one to a Part of the Rock which was low, and then broke in, and left room to place another Ladder upon that; so when the two Ladders were taken down, no Man living could come down to me without mischieving himself; and if they had come down, they were still on the Out-side of my outer Wall.

Thus I took all the Measures humane Prudence could suggest for my own Preservation; and it will be seen at length, that they were not altogether without just Reason; though I foresaw nothing at that Time, more than my meer Fear suggested to me.

While this was doing, I was not altogether Careless of my other Affairs; for I had a great Concern upon me, for my little Herd of Goats; they were not only a present Supply to me upon every Occasion, and began to be sufficient to me, without the Expence of Powder and Shot; but also without the Fatigue of Hunting after the wild Ones, and I was loth to lose the Advantage of them, and to have them all to nurse up over again.

To this Purpose, after long Consideration, I could think of but two Ways to preserve them; one was to find another convenient Place to dig a Cave Under-ground, and to drive them into it every Night; and the other was to enclose two or three little Bits of Land, remote from one another and as much conceal'd as I could, where I might keep about half a Dozen young Goats in each Place: So that if any Disaster happen'd to the Flock in general, I might be able to raise them again with little Trouble and Time: And this, tho' it would require a great deal of Time and Labour, I thought was the most rational Design.

Accordingly I spent some Time to find out the most retir'd Parts of the Island; and I pitch'd upon one which was as private indeed as my Heart could wish for; it was a little damp Piece of Ground in the Middle of the hollow and thick Woods, where, as is observ'd, I almost lost my self once before, endeavouring to come back that Way from the Eastern Part of the Island: Here I found a clear Piece of Land near three Acres, so surrounded with Woods, that it was almost an Enclosure by Nature, at least it did not want near so much Labour to make it so, as the other Pieces of Ground I had work'd so hard at.

I immediately went to Work with this Piece of Ground, and in less than a Month's Time, I had so fenc'd it round, that my Flock or Herd, call it which you please, who were not so wild now as at first they might be supposed to be, were well enough secur'd in it. So, without any farther Delay, I removed ten young She-Goats and two He-Goats to this Piece; and when they were there, I continued to perfect the Fence till I had made it as secure as the other, which, however, I did at more Leisure, and it took me up more Time by a great deal.

All this Labour I was at the Expence of, purely from my Apprehensions on the Account of the Print of a Man's Foot which I had seen; for as yet I never saw any human Creature come near the Island, and I had now liv'd two Years under these Uneasinesses, which indeed made my Life much less comfortable than it was before; as may well be imagin'd by any who know what it is to live in the constant Snare of *the Fear of Man*;[1] and this I must observe with Grief too, that the Discomposure of my Mind had too great Impressions also upon the religious Part of my Thoughts, for the Dread and Terror of falling into the Hands of Savages and Canibals, lay so upon my Spirits, that I seldom found my self in a due Temper for Application to my Maker, at least not with the sedate Calmness and Resignation of Soul which I was wont to do; I rather pray'd to God as under great Affliction and Pressure of Mind, surrounded with Danger, and in Expectation every Night of being murther'd and devour'd before Morning; and I must testify from my Experience, that a Temper of Peace, Thankfulness, Love and Affection, is much more the proper Frame for Prayer than that of Terror and Discomposure; and that under the Dread of Mischief impending, a Man is no more fit for a comforting Performance of the Duty of praying to God, than he is for Repentance on a sick Bed: For these Discomposures affect the Mind as the others do the Body; and the Discomposure of the Mind must necessarily be as great a Disability as that of the Body, and much greater, Praying to God being properly an Act of the Mind, not of the Body.

---

1 Proverbs 29: 25: "The fear of man bringeth a snare: but whoso putteth his trust in the LORD shall be safe."

But to go on; After I had thus secur'd one Part of my little living Stock, I went about the whole Island, searching for another private Place, to make such another Deposit; when wandring more to the *West* Point of the Island, than I had ever done yet, and looking out to Sea, I thought I saw a Boat upon the Sea, at a great Distance; I had found a Prospective Glass,[1] or two, in one of the Seamen's Chests, which I sav'd out of our Ship; but I had it not about me, and this was so remote, that I could not tell what to make of it; though I look'd at it till my Eyes were not able to hold to look any longer; whether it was a Boat, or not, I do not know; but as I descended from the Hill, I could see no more of it, so I gave it over; only I resolv'd to go no more out without a Prospective Glass in my Pocket.

When I was come down the Hill, to the End of the Island, where indeed I had never been before, I was presently convinc'd, that the seeing the Print of a Man's Foot, was not such a strange Thing in the Island as I imagin'd; and but that it was a special Providence that I was cast upon the Side of the Island, where the Savages never came: I should easily have known, that nothing was more frequent than for the *Canoes* from the Main, when they happen'd to be a little too far out at Sea, to shoot over to that Side of the Island for Harbour; likewise as they often met, and fought in their *Canoes*, the Victors having taken any Prisoners, would bring them over to this Shore, where according to their dreadful Customs, being all *Canibals*, they would kill and eat them; of which hereafter.

When I was come down the Hill, to the Shore, as I said above, being the *S. W.* Point of the Island, I was perfectly confounded and amaz'd; nor is it possible for me to express the Horror of my Mind, at seeing the Shore spread with Skulls, Hands, Feet, and other Bones of humane Bodies; and particularly I observ'd a Place where there had been a Fire made, and a Circle dug in the Earth, like a Cockpit,[2] where it is suppos'd the Savage Wretches had sat down to their inhumane Feastings upon the Bodies of their Fellow-Creatures. *Cannibalism?*

I was so astonish'd with the Sight of these Things, that I entertain'd no Notions of any Danger to my self from it for a long while; All my Apprehensions were bury'd in the Thoughts of such a Pitch of inhuman, hellish Brutality, and the Horror of the Degeneracy of Humane Nature; which though I had heard of

Bones

---

1 Telescope.
2 A pit dug for cock-fighting.

often, yet I never had so near a View of before; in short, I turn'd away my Face from the horrid Spectacle; my Stomach grew sick, and I was just at the Point of Fainting, when Nature discharg'd the Disorder from my Stomach; and having vomited with an uncommon Violence, I was a little reliev'd; but cou'd not bear to stay in the Place a Moment; so I gat me up the Hill again, with the Speed I cou'd, and walk'd on towards my own Habitation.

When I came a little out of that Part of the Island, I stood still a while as amaz'd; and then recovering my self, I look'd up with the utmost Affection of my Soul, and with a Flood of Tears in my Eyes, gave God Thanks that had cast my first Lot in a Part of the World, where I was distinguish'd from such dreadful Creatures as these; and that though I had esteem'd my present Condition very miserable, had yet given me so many Comforts in it, that I had still more to give Thanks for than to complain of; and this above all, that I had even in this miserable Condition been comforted with the Knowledge of himself, and the Hope of his Blessing, which was a Felicity more than sufficiently equivalent to all the Misery which I had suffer'd, or could suffer.

In this Frame of Thankfulness, I went Home to my Castle, and began to be much easier now, as to the Safety of my Circumstances, than ever I was before; for I observ'd, that these Wretches never came to this Island in search of what they could get; perhaps not seeking, not wanting, or not expecting any Thing here; and having often, no doubt, been up in the cover'd woody Part of it, without finding any Thing to their Purpose. I knew I had been here now almost eighteen Years, and never saw the least Foot-steps of Humane Creature there before; and I might be here eighteen more, as entirely conceal'd as I was now, if I did not discover my self to them, which I had no manner of Occasion to do, it being my only Business to keep my self entirely conceal'd where I was, unless I found a better sort of Creatures than *Canibals* to make my self known to.

Yet I entertain'd such an Abhorrence of the Savage Wretches, that I have been speaking of, and of the wretched inhuman Custom of their devouring and eating one another up, that I continu'd pensive, and sad,[1] and kept close within my own Circle for almost two Years after this: When I say my own Circle, I mean by it, my three Plantations, *viz.* my Castle, my Country Seat, which I call'd my Bower, and my Enclosure in the Woods; nor did I look after this for any other Use than as an Enclosure for my Goats;

---

1 Grave, serious.

for the Aversion which Nature gave me to these hellish Wretches, was such, that I was fearful of seeing them, as of seeing the Devil himself; nor did I so much as go to look after my Boat, in all this Time; but began rather to think of making me another; for I cou'd not think of ever making any more Attempts, to bring the other Boat round the Island to me, least I should meet with some of these Creatures at Sea, in which, if I had happen'd to have fallen into their Hands, I knew what would have been my Lot.

Time however, and the Satisfaction I had, that I was in no Danger of being discover'd by these People, began to wear off my Uneasiness about them; and I began to live just in the same compos'd Manner as before; only with this Difference, that I used more Caution, and kept my Eyes more about me than I did before, least I should happen to be seen by any of them; and particularly, I was more cautious of firing my Gun, least any of them being on the Island, should happen to hear of it; and it was therefore a very good Providence to me, that I had furnish'd my self with a tame Breed of Goats, that I needed not hunt any more about the Woods, or shoot at them; and if I did catch any of them after this, it was by Traps, and Snares, as I had done before; so that for two Years after this, I believe I never fir'd my Gun once off, though I never went out without it; and which was more, as I had sav'd three Pistols out of the Ship, I always carry'd them out with me, or at least two of them, sticking them in my Goat-skin Belt; also I furbish'd up one of the great Cutlashes, that I had out of the Ship, and made me a Belt to put it on also; so that I was now a most formidable Fellow to look at, when I went abroad, if you add to the former Description of my self, the Particular of two Pistols, and a great broad Sword, hanging at my Side in a Belt, but without a Scabbard.

Things going on thus, as I have said, for some Time; I seem'd, excepting these Cautions, to be reduc'd to my former calm, sedate Way of Living, all these Things tended to shewing me more and more how far my Condition was from being miserable, compar'd to some others; nay, to many other Particulars of Life, which it might have pleased God to have made my Lot. It put me upon reflecting, How little repining there would be among Mankind, at any Condition of Life, if People would rather compare their Condition with those that are worse, in order to be thankful, than be always comparing them with those which are better, to assist their Murmurings and Complainings.

As in my present Condition there were not really many Things which I wanted; so indeed I thought that the Frights I had been in about these Savage Wretches, and the Concern I had been in for my own Preservation, had taken off the Edge of my Invention for my own Conveniences; and I had dropp'd a good Design, which I had once bent my Thoughts too much upon; and that was, to try if I could not make some of my Barley into Malt, and then try to brew my self some Beer: This was really a whimsical Thought, and I reprov'd my self often for the Simplicity[1] of it; for I presently saw there would be the want of several Things necessary to the making my Beer, that it would be impossible for me to supply; as First, Casks to preserve it in, which was a Thing, that as I have observ'd already, I cou'd never compass; no, though I spent not many Days, but Weeks, nay, Months in attempting it, but to no purpose. In the next Place, I had no Hops to make it keep, no Yeast to make it work, no Copper or Kettle to make it boil; and yet all these Things, notwithstanding, I verily believe, had not these Things interven'd, I mean the Frights and Terrors I was in about the Savages, I had undertaken it, and perhaps brought it to pass too; for I seldom gave any Thing over without accomplishing it, when I once had it in my Head enough to begin it.

But my Invention now run quite another Way; for Night and Day, I could think of nothing but how I might destroy some of these Monsters in their cruel bloody Entertainment, and if possible, save the Victim they should bring hither to destroy. It would take up a larger Volume than this whole Work is intended to be, to set down all the Contrivances I hatch'd, or rather brooded upon in my Thought, for the destroying these Creatures, or at least frighting them, so as to prevent their coming hither any more; but all was abortive, nothing could be possible to take effect, unless I was to be there to do it my self; and what could one Man do among them, when perhaps there might be twenty or thirty of them together, with their Darts, or their Bows and Arrows, with which they could shoot as true to a Mark, as I could with my Gun?

Sometimes I contriv'd to dig a Hole under the Place where they made their Fire, and put in five or six Pound of Gunpowder, which when they kindled their Fire, would consequently take Fire, and blow up all that was near it; but as in the first Place I should be very loth to wast so much Powder upon them, my Store being now within the Quantity of one Barrel; so neither could I be sure of its going off, at any certain Time; when it might

---

1 Naiveté.

surprise them, and at best, that it would do little more than just blow the Fire about their Ears and fright them, but not sufficient to make them forsake the Place; so I laid it aside, and then propos'd, that I would place my self in Ambush, in some convenient Place, with my three Guns, all double loaded; and in the middle of their bloody Ceremony, let fly at them, when I should be sure to kill or wound perhaps two or three at every shoot; and then falling in upon them with my three Pistols, and my Sword, I made no doubt, but that if there was twenty I should kill them all: This Fancy pleas'd my Thoughts for some Weeks, and I was so full of it, that I often dream'd of it; and sometimes that I was just going to let fly at them in my Sleep.

I went so far with it in my Imagination, that I employ'd my self several Days to find out proper Places to put my self in Ambuscade, as I said, to watch for them; and I went frequently to the Place it self, which was now grown more familiar to me; and especially while my Mind was thus fill'd with Thoughts of Revenge, and of a bloody putting twenty or thirty of them to the Sword, as I may call it; the Horror I had at the Place, and at the Signals of the barbarous Wretches devouring one another, abated my Malice.

Well, at length I found a Place in the Side of the Hill, where I was satisfy'd I might securely wait, till I saw any of their Boats coming, and might then, even before they would be ready to come on Shore, convey my self unseen into Thickets of Trees, in one of which there was a Hollow large enough to conceal me entirely; and where I might sit, and observe all their bloody Doings, and take my full aim at their Heads, when they were so close together, as that it would be next to impossible that I should miss my Shoot, or that I could fail wounding three or four of them at the first Shoot.

In this Place then I resolv'd to fix my Design, and accordingly I prepar'd two Muskets, and my ordinary Fowling Piece. The two Muskets I loaded with a Brace of Slugs each, and four or five smaller Bullets, about the Size of Pistol Bullets; and the Fowling Piece I loaded with near a Handful of Swan-shot, of the largest Size; I also loaded my Pistols with about four Bullets each, and in this Posture, well provided with Ammunition for a second and third Charge, I prepar'd my self for my Expedition.

After I had thus laid the Scheme of my Design, and in my Imagination put it in Practice, I continually made my Tour every Morning up to the Top of the Hill, which was from my Castle, as I call'd it, about three Miles, or more, to see if I cou'd observe any

Boats upon the Sea, coming near the Island, or standing over towards it; but I began to tire of this hard Duty, after I had for two or three Months constantly kept my Watch; but came always back without any Discovery, there having not in all that Time been the least Appearance, not only on, or near the Shore; but not on the whole Ocean, so far as my Eyes or Glasses could reach every Way.

As long as I kept up my daily Tour to the Hill, to look out; so long also I kept up the Vigour of my Design, and my Spirits seem'd to be all the while in a suitable Form, for so outragious an Execution as the killing twenty or thirty naked Savages, for an Offence which I had not at all entred into a Discussion of in my Thoughts, any farther than my Passions were at first fir'd by the Horror I conceiv'd at the unnatural Custom of that People of the Country, who it seems had been suffer'd by Providence in his wise Disposition of the World, to have no other Guide than that of their own abominable and vitiated Passions; and consequently were left, and perhaps had been so for some Ages, to act such horrid Things, and receive such dreadful Customs, as nothing but Nature entirely abandon'd of Heaven, and acted by some hellish Degeneracy, could have run them into: But now, when as I have said, I began to be weary of the fruitless Excursion, which I had made so long, and so far, every Morning in vain, so my Opinion of the Action it self began to alter, and I began with cooler and calmer Thoughts to consider what it was I was going to engage in. What Authority, or Call I had, to pretend to be Judge and Executioner upon these Men as Criminals, whom Heaven had thought fit for so many Ages to suffer unpunish'd, to go on, and to be as it were, the Executioners of his Judgments one upon another. How far these People were Offenders against me, and what Right I had to engage in the Quarrel of that Blood, which they shed promiscuously[1] one upon another. I debated this very often with my self thus; How do I know what God himself judges in this particular Case; it is certain these People either do not commit this as a Crime; it is not against their own Consciences reproving, or their Light reproaching them. They do not know it be an Offence, and then commit it in Defiance of Divine Justice, as we do in almost all the Sins we commit. They think it no more a Crime to kill a Captive taken in War, than we do to kill an Ox; nor to eat humane Flesh, than we do to eat Mutton.

When I had consider'd this a little, it follow'd necessarily, that

---

1 Indiscriminately.

I was certainly in the Wrong in it, that these People were not Murtherers in the Sense that I had before condemn'd them, in my Thoughts; any more than those Christians were Murtherers, who often put to Death the Prisoners taken in Battle; or more frequently, upon many Occasions, put whole Troops of Men to the Sword, without giving Quarter,[1] though they threw down their Arms and submitted.

In the next Place it occurr'd to me, that albeit the Usage they thus gave one another, was thus brutish and inhumane; yet it was really nothing to me: These People had done me no Injury. That if they attempted me, or I saw it necessary for my immediate Preservation to fall upon them, something might be said for it; but that as I was yet out of their Power, and they had really no Knowledge of me, and consequently no Design upon me; and therefore it could not be just for me to fall upon them. That this would justify the Conduct of the *Spaniards* in all their Barbarities practis'd in *America*, and where they destroy'd Millions of these People, who however they were Idolaters and Barbarians, and had several bloody and barbarous Rites in their Customs, such as sacrificing human Bodies to their Idols, were yet, as to the *Spaniards*, very innocent People; and that the rooting them out of the Country, is spoken of with the utmost Abhorrence and Detestation, by even the *Spaniards* themselves, at this Time; and by all other Christian Nations of *Europe*, as a meer Butchery, a bloody and unnatural Piece of Cruelty, unjustifiable either to God or Man; and such, as for which the very Name of a *Spaniard* is reckon'd to be frightful and terrible to all People of Humanity, or of Christian Compassion: As if the Kingdom of *Spain* were particularly Eminent for the Product of a Race of Men, who were without Principles of Tenderness, or the common Bowels of Pity to the Miserable, which is reckon'd to be a Mark of generous Temper in the Mind.[2]

---

1 Showing mercy.
2 The Black Legend, which represented Spanish treatment of Indians as "mere Butchery," was largely Protestant propaganda. The death toll among natives of the New World was horrifying, but mostly due to disease. Originating in the writings of Bartholome de las Casas, who aimed to get the attention of the Spanish crown and prick the conscience of the Spanish church, the Black Legend was promulgated first by Dutch and later by British writers to distinguish themselves from their Catholic colonial rival. In his *General History of Discoveries and Improvements* (1725-26) Defoe cites Las Casas when he claims that forty million Indians were killed during "the great Ravages which the Spaniards made in America, at their first landing among those innocent People" (p. 282).

These Considerations really put me to a Pause, and to a kind of a Full-stop; and I began by little and little to be off of my Design, and to conclude, I had taken wrong Measures in my Resolutions to attack the Savages; that it was not my Business to meddle with them, unless they first attack'd me, and this it was my Business if possible to prevent; but that if I were discover'd, and attack'd, then I knew my Duty.

On the other hand, I argu'd with my self, That this really was the way not to deliver my self, but entirely to ruin and destroy my self; for unless I was sure to kill every one that not only should be on Shore at that Time, but that should ever come on Shore afterwards, if but one of them escap'd, to tell their Country People what had happen'd, they would come over again by Thousands to revenge the Death of their Fellows, and I should only bring upon my self a certain Destruction, which at present I had no manner of occasion for.

Upon the whole I concluded, That neither in Principle or in Policy, I ought one way or other to concern my self in this Affair. That my Business was by all possible Means to conceal my self from them, and not to leave the least Signal to them to guess by, that there were any living Creatures upon the Island; I mean of humane Shape.

Religion joyn'd in with this Prudential,[1] and I was convinc'd now many Ways, that I was perfectly out of my Duty, when I was laying all my bloody Schemes for the Destruction of innocent Creatures, I mean innocent as to me: As to the Crimes they were guilty of towards one another, I had nothing to do with them; they were National, and I ought to leave them to the Justice of God, who is the Governour of Nations, and knows how by National Punishments to make a just Retribution for National Offences; and to bring publick Judgments upon those who offend in a publick Manner, by such Ways as best pleases him.

This appear'd so clear to me now, that nothing was a greater Satisfaction to me, than that I had not been suffer'd to do a Thing which I now saw so much Reason to believe would have been no less a Sin, than that of wilful Murther, if I had committed it; and I gave most humble Thanks on my Knees to God, that had thus deliver'd me from Blood-Guiltiness; beseeching him to grant me the Protection of his Providence, that I might not fall into the Hands of the Barbarians; or that I might not lay my Hands upon

---

1   A precept showing forethought and good sense.

them, unless I had a more clear Call from Heaven to do it, in Defence of my own Life.

In this Disposition I continu'd, for near a Year after this; and so far was I from desiring an Occasion for falling upon these Wretches, that in all that Time, I never once went up the Hill to see whether there were any of them in Sight, or to know whether any of them had been on Shore there, or not, that I might not be tempted to renew any of my Contrivances against them, or be provok'd by any Advantage which might present it self, to fall upon them; only this I did, I went and remov'd my Boat, which I had on the other Side the Island, and carry'd it down to the *East* End of the whole Island, where I ran it into a little Cove which I found under some high Rocks, and where I knew, by Reason of the Currents, the Savages durst not, at least would not come with their Boats, upon any Account whatsoever.

With my Boat I carry'd away every Thing that I had left there belonging to her, though not necessary for the bare going thither, *viz.* A Mast and Sail which I had made for her, and a Thing like an Anchor, but indeed which could not be call'd either Anchor or Grapling; however, it was the best I could make of its kind: All these I remov'd, that there might not be the least Shadow of any Discovery, or any Appearance of any Boat, or of any human Habitation upon the Island.

Besides this, I kept my self, as I said, more retir'd than ever, and seldom went from my Cell, other than upon my constant Employment, *viz.* To milk my She-goats, and manage my little Flock, in the Wood; which as it was quite on the other Part of the Island, was quite out of Danger; for certain it is, that these Savage People who sometimes haunted this Island, never came with any Thoughts of finding any Thing here; and consequently never wandred off from the Coast; and I doubt not, but they might have been several Times on Shore, after my Apprehensions of them had made me cautious as well as before; and indeed, I look'd back with some Horror upon the Thoughts of what my Condition would have been, if I had chop'd upon them,[1] and been discover'd before that, when naked[2] and unarm'd, except with one Gun, and that loaden often only with small Shot, I walk'd every where peeping, and peeping about the Island, to see what I could get; what a Surprise should I have been in, if when I discover'd the Print of a Man's Foot, I had instead of that, seen fifteen or

---

1 To come upon them by chance.
2 Defenseless, vulnerable.

twenty Savages, and found them pursuing me, and by the Swiftness of their Running, no Possibility of my escaping them.

The Thoughts of this sometimes sunk my very Soul within me, and distress'd my Mind so much, that I could not soon recover it, to think what I should have done, and how I not only should not have been able to resist them, but even should not have had Presence of Mind enough to do what I might have done; much less, what now after so much Consideration and Preparation I might be able to do: Indeed, after serious thinking of these Things, I should be very Melancholly, and sometimes it would last a great while; but I resolv'd it at last all into Thankfulness to that Providence, which had deliver'd me from so many unseen Dangers, and had kept me from those Mischiefs which I could no way have been the Agent in delivering my self from; because I had not the least Notion of any such Thing depending,[1] or the least Supposition of it being possible.

This renew'd a Contemplation, which often had come to my Thoughts in former Time, when first I began to see the merciful Dispositions of Heaven, in the Dangers we run through in this Life. How wonderfully we are deliver'd, when we know nothing of it. How when we are in (a *Quandary*, as we call it) a Doubt or Hesitation, whether to go this Way, or that Way, a secret Hint shall direct us this Way, when we intended to go that Way; nay, when Sense, our own Inclination, and perhaps Business has call'd to go the other Way, yet a strange Impression upon the Mind, from we know not what Springs, and by we know not what Power, shall over-rule us to go this Way; and it shall afterwards appear, that had we gone that Way which we should have gone, and even to our Imagination ought to have gone, we should have been ruin'd and lost: Upon these, and many like Reflections, I afterwards made it a certain Rule with me, That whenever I found those secret Hints, or pressings of my Mind, to doing, or not doing any Thing that presented; or to going this Way, or that Way, I never fail'd to obey the secret Dictate; though I knew no other Reason for it, than that such a Pressure, or such a Hint hung upon my Mind: I could give many Examples of the Success of this Conduct in the Course of my Life; but more especially in the latter Part of my inhabiting this unhappy Island; besides many Occasions which it is very likely I might have taken Notice of, if I had seen with the same Eyes then, that I saw with now: But 'tis never too late to be wise; and I cannot but advise all considering

1 Impending.

Men, whose Lives are attended with such extraordinary Incidents as mine, or even though not so extraordinary, not to slight such secret Intimations of Providence, let them come from what invisible Intelligence they will, that I shall not discuss, and perhaps cannot account for; but certainly they are a Proof of the Converse of Spirits, and the secret Communication between those embody'd, and those unembody'd; and such a Proof as can never be withstood: Of which I shall have Occasion to give some very remarkable Instances, in the Remainder of my solitary Residence in this dismal Place.

I believe the Reader of this will not think strange, if I confess that these Anxieties, these constant Dangers I liv'd in, and the Concern that was now upon me, put an End to all Invention, and to all the Contrivances that I had laid for my future Accommodations and Conveniencies. I had the Care of my Safety more now upon my Hands, than that of my Food. I car'd not to drive a Nail, or chop a Stick of Wood now, for fear the Noise I should make should be heard; much less would I fire a Gun, for the same Reason; and above all, I was intollerably uneasy at making any Fire, least the Smoke which is visible at a great Distance in the Day should betray me; and for this Reason I remov'd that Part of my Business which requir'd Fire; such as burning of Pots, and Pipes, *etc.* into my new Apartment in the Woods, where after I had been some time, I found to my unspeakable Consolation, a meer natural Cave in the Earth, which went in a vast way, and where, I dare say, no Savage, had he been at the Mouth of it, would be so hardy as to venture in, nor indeed, would any Man else; but one who like me, wanted nothing so much as a safe Retreat.

The Mouth of this Hollow, was at the Bottom of a great Rock, where by meer accident, (I would say, if I did not see abundant Reason to ascribe all such Things now to Providence) I was cutting down some thick Branches of Trees, to make Charcoal; and before I go on, I must observe the Reason of my making this Charcoal; which was thus:

I was afraid of making a Smoke about my Habitation, as I said before; and yet I could not live there without baking my Bread, cooking my Meat, &c. so I contriv'd to burn some Wood here, as I had seen done in *England*, under Turf, till it became Chark,[1] or dry Coal; and then putting the Fire out, I preserv'd the Coal to carry Home; and perform the other Services which Fire was wanting for at Home without Danger of Smoke.

---

1   Charcoal.

But this is by the by: While I was cutting down some Wood here, I perceiv'd that behind a very thick Branch of low Brushwood, or Underwood, there was a kind of hollow Place; I was curious to look into it, and getting with Difficulty into the Mouth of it, I found it was pretty large; that is to say, sufficient for me to stand upright in it, and perhaps another with me; but I must confess to you, I made more hast[1] out than I did in, when looking farther into the Place, and which was perfectly dark, I saw two broad shining Eyes of some Creature, whether Devil or Man I knew not, which twinkl'd like two Stars, the dim Light from the Cave's Mouth shining directly in and making the Reflection.

However, after some Pause, I recover'd my self, and began to call my self a thousand Fools, and tell my self, that he that was afraid to see the Devil, was not fit to live twenty Years in an Island all alone; and that I durst to believe there was nothing in this Cave that was more frightful than my self; upon this, plucking up my Courage, I took up a great Firebrand, and in I rush'd again, with the Stick flaming in my Hand; I had not gone three Steps in, but I was almost as much frighted as I was before; for I heard a very loud Sigh, like that of a Man in some Pain, and it was follow'd by a broken Noise, *as if* of Words half express'd, and then a deep Sigh again: I stepp'd back, and was indeed struck with such a Surprize, that it put me into a cold Sweat; and if I had had a Hat on my Head, I will not answer for it, that my Hair might not have lifted it off. But still plucking up my Spirits as well as I could, and encouraging my self a little with considering that the Power and Presence of God was every where, and was able to protect me; upon this I stepp'd forward again, and by the Light of the Firebrand, holding it up a little over my Head, I saw lying on the Ground a most monstrous frightful old He-goat, just making his Will, as we say, and gasping for Life, and dying indeed of meer old Age.

I stirr'd him a little to see if I could get him out, and he essay'd to get up, but was not able to raise himself; and I thought with my self, he might even lie there; for if he had frighted me so, he would certainly fright any of the Savages, if any of them should be so hardy as to come in there, while he had any Life in him.

I was now recover'd from my Surprize, and began to look round me, when I found the Cave was but very small, that is to say, it might be about twelve Foot over, but in no manner of Shape, either round or square, no Hands having ever been

---

1 Haste.

employ'd in making it, but those of meer Nature: I observ'd also, that there was a Place at the farther Side of it, that went in farther, but was so low, that it requir'd me to creep upon my Hands and Knees to go into it, and whither I went I knew not; so having no Candle, I gave it over for some Time; but resolv'd to come again the next Day, provided with Candles, and a Tinder-box, which I had made of the Lock of one of the Muskets, with some wild-fire[1] in the Pan.

Accordingly the next Day, I came provided with six large Candles of my own making; for I made very good Candles now of Goat's Tallow; and going into this low Place, I was oblig'd to creep upon all Fours, *as I have said*, almost ten Yards; which by the way, I thought was a Venture bold enough, considering that I knew not how far it might go, nor what was beyond it. When I was got through the Strait, I found the Roof rose higher up, I believe near twenty Foot; but never was such a glorious Sight seen in the Island, I dare say, as it was, to look round the Sides and Roof of this Vault, or Cave; the Walls reflected 100 thousand Lights to me from my two Candles; what it was in Rock, whether Diamonds, or any other precious Stones, or Gold, which I rather suppos'd it to be, I knew not.

The Place I was in, was a most delightful Cavity, or Grotto, of its kind, as could be expected, though perfectly dark; the Floor was dry and level, and had a sort of small loose Gravel upon it, so that there was no nauseous or venemous Creature to be seen, neither was there any damp, or wet, on the Sides or Roof: The only Difficulty in it was the Entrance, which however as it was a Place of Security, and such a Retreat as I wanted, I thought that was a Convenience; so that I was really rejoyc'd at the Discovery, and resolv'd without any Delay, to bring some of those Things which I was most anxious about, to this Place; particularly, I resolv'd to bring hither my Magazine of Powder, and all my spare Arms, *viz*. Two Fowling-Pieces, for I had three in all; and three Muskets, for of them I had eight in all; so I kept at my Castle only five, which stood ready mounted like Pieces of Cannon, on my out-most Fence; and were ready also to take out upon any Expedition.

Upon this Occasion of removing my Ammunition, I took occasion to open the Barrel of Powder which I took up out of the Sea, and which had been wet; and I found that the Water had penetrated about three or four Inches into the Powder, on every Side,

---

1 Mixture of highly inflammable substances, including gunpowder.

which caking and growing hard, had preserv'd the inside like a Kernel in a Shell;[1] so that I had near sixty Pound of very good Powder in the Center of the Cask, and this was an agreeable Discovery to me at that Time; so I carry'd all away thither, never keeping above two or three Pound of Powder with me in my Castle, for fear of a Surprize of any kind: I also carry'd thither all the Lead I had left for Bullets.

I fancy'd my self now like one of the ancient Giants, which are said to live in Caves, and Holes, in the Rocks, where none could come at them; for I perswaded my self while I was here, if five hundred Savages were to hunt me, they could never find me out; or if they did, they would not venture to attack me here.

The old Goat who I found expiring, dy'd in the Mouth of the Cave, the next Day after I made this Discovery; and I found it much easier to dig a great Hole there, and throw him in, and cover him with Earth, than to drag him out; so I interr'd him there, to prevent the Offence to my Nose.

I was now in my twenty third Year of Residence in this Island, and was so naturaliz'd to the Place, and to the Manner of Living, that could I have but enjoy'd the Certainty that no Savages would come to the Place to disturb me, I could have been content to have capitulated for spending the rest of my Time there, even to the last Moment, till I had laid me down and dy'd, like the old Goat in the Cave. I had also arriv'd to some little Diversions and Amusements, which made the Time pass more pleasantly with me a great deal, than it did before; as First, I had taught my Poll, as I noted before, to speak; and he did it so familiarly, and talk'd so articulately and plain, that it was very pleasant to me; and he liv'd with me no less than six and twenty Years: How long he might live afterwards, I know not; though I know they have a Notion in the *Brasils*, that they live a hundred Years; perhaps poor Poll may be alive there still, calling after *Poor Robin Crusoe* to this Day. I wish no *English* Man the ill Luck to come there and hear him; but if he did, he would certainly believe it was the Devil. My Dog was a very pleasant and loving Companion to me, for no less than sixteen Years of my Time, and then dy'd, of meer old Age; as for my Cats, they multiply'd as I have observ'd to that Degree, that I was oblig'd to shoot several of them at first, to keep them from devouring me, and all I had; but at length, when the two old

---

1 Gunpowder is composed primarily of potassium nitrate, which will dissolve in water. If the barrel spent only a small amount of time in the sea, then the gunpowder in the center of the barrel could still be usable.

Ones I brought with me were gone, and after some time continually driving them from me, and letting them have no Provision with me, they all ran wild into the Woods, except two or three Favourites, which I kept tame; and whose Young when they had any, I always drown'd; and these were part of my Family: Besides these, I always kept two or three houshold Kids about me, who I taught to feed out of my Hand; and I had two more Parrots which talk'd pretty well, and would all call *Robin Crusoe*; but none like my first; nor indeed did I take the Pains with any of them that I had done with him. I had also several tame Sea-Fowls, whose Names I know not, who I caught upon the Shore, and cut their Wings; and the little Stakes which I had planted before my Castle Wall being now grown up to a good thick Grove, these Fowls all liv'd among these low Trees, and bred there, which was very agreeable to me; so that as I said above, I began to be very well contented with the Life I led, if it might but have been secur'd from the dread of the Savages.

But it was otherwise directed; and it may not be amiss for all People who shall meet with my Story, to make this just Observation from it, *viz.* How frequently in the Course of our Lives, the Evil which in it self we seek most to shun, and which when we are fallen into it, is the most dreadful to us, is oftentimes the very Means or Door of our Deliverance, by which alone we can be rais'd again from the Affliction we are fallen into. I cou'd give many Examples of this in the Course of my unaccountable Life; but in nothing was it more particularly remarkable, than in the Circumstances of my last Years of solitary Residence in this Island.

It was now the Month of *December*, as I said above, in my twenty third Year; and this being the *Southern* Solstice, for Winter I cannot call it, was the particular Time of my Harvest, and requir'd my being pretty much abroad in the Fields, when going out pretty early in the Morning, even before it was thorow Daylight, I was surpriz'd with seeing a Light of some Fire upon the Shore, at a Distance from me, of about two Mile towards the End of the Island, where I had observ'd some Savages had been as before; but not on the other Side; but to my great Affliction, it was on my Side of the Island.

I was indeed terribly surpriz'd at the Sight, and stepp'd short within my Grove, not daring to go out, least I might be surpriz'd; and yet I had no more Peace within, from the Apprehensions I had, that if these Savages in rambling over the Island, should find my Corn standing, or cut, or any of my Works and Improvements, they would immediately conclude, that there were People in the Place, and would then never give over till they had found me out: In this Extremity I went back directly to my Castle, pull'd up the Ladder after me, and made all Things without look as wild and natural as I could.

Then I prepar'd my self within, putting my self in a Posture of Defence; I loaded all my Cannon, as I call'd them; that is to say, my Muskets, which were mounted upon my new Fortification, and all my Pistols, and resolv'd to defend my self to the last Gasp, not forgetting seriously to commend my self to the Divine Protection, and earnestly to pray to God to deliver me out of the Hands of the Barbarians; and in this Posture I continu'd about two Hours; but began to be mighty impatient for Intelligence abroad, for I had no Spies to send out.

After sitting a while longer, and musing what I should do in this Case, I was not able to bear sitting in Ignorance any longer; so setting up my Ladder to the Side of the Hill, where there was a flat Place, as I observ'd before, and then pulling the Ladder up after me, I set it up again, and mounted to the Top of the Hill; and pulling out my Perspective Glass, which I had taken on Purpose, I laid me down flat on my Belly, on the Ground, and began to look for the Place; I presently found there was no less than nine naked Savages, sitting round a small Fire, they had made, not to warm them; for they had no need of that, the Weather being extreme hot; but as I suppos'd, to dress some of their barbarous Diet, of humane Flesh, which they had brought with them, whether alive or dead I could not know.

They had two *Canoes* with them, which they had haled up upon the Shore; and as it was then Tide of Ebb, they seem'd to me to wait for the Return of the Flood, to go away again; it is not easy to imagine what Confusion this Sight put me into, especially seeing them come on my Side the Island, and so near me too; but when I observ'd their coming must be always with the Current of the Ebb, I began afterwards to be more sedate in my Mind, being satisfy'd that I might go abroad with Safety all the Time of the Tide of Flood, if they were not on Shore before: And having made this Observation, I went abroad about my Harvest Work with the more Composure.

As I expected, so it prov'd; for as soon as the Tide made to the *Westward*, I saw them all take Boat, and row (or paddle as we call it) all away: I should have observ'd, that for an Hour and more before they went off, they went to dancing, and I could easily discern their Postures, and Gestures, by my Glasses: I could not perceive by my nicest Observation, but that they were stark naked, and had not the least covering upon them; but whether they were Men or Women, that I could not distinguish.

As soon as I saw them shipp'd, and gone, I took two Guns upon my Shoulders, and two Pistols at my Girdle, and my great Sword by my Side, without a Scabbard, and with all the Speed I was able to make, I went away to the Hill, where I had discover'd the first Appearance of all; and as soon as I gat thither, which was not less than two Hours; for I could not go apace, being so loaden with Arms as I was; I perceiv'd there had been three *Canoes* more of Savages on that Place; and looking out farther, I saw they were all at Sea together, making over for the Main.

This was a dreadful Sight to me, especially when going down to the Shore, I could see the Marks of Horror, which the dismal Work they had been about had left behind it, *viz.* The Blood, the Bones, and part of the Flesh of humane Bodies, eaten and devour'd by those Wretches, with Merriment and Sport: I was so fill'd with Indignation at the Sight, that I began now to premeditate the Destruction of the next that I saw there, let them be who, or how many soever.

It seem'd evident to me, that the Visits which they thus make to this Island, are not very frequent; for it was above fifteen Months before any more of them came on Shore there again; that is to say, I neither saw them, or any Footsteps, or Signals of them, in all that Time; for as to the rainy Seasons, then they are sure not to come abroad, at least not so far; yet all this while I liv'd uncomfortably, by reason of the constant Apprehensions I was in of their coming upon me by Surprize; from whence I observe, that the Expectation of Evil is more bitter than the Suffering, especially if there is no room to shake off that Expectation, or those Apprehensions.

During all this Time, I was in the murthering Humour;[1] and took up most of my Hours, which should have been better employ'd, in contriving how to circumvent, and fall upon them, the very next Time I should see them; especially if they should be divided, as they were the last Time, into two Parties; nor did I consider at all, that if I kill'd one Party, suppose Ten, or a Dozen, I was still the next Day, or Week, or Month, to kill another, and so another, even *ad infinitum*, till I should be at length no less a Murtherer than they were in being Man-eaters; and perhaps much more so.

---

1 Mood, state of mind.

I spent my Days now in great Perplexity, and Anxiety of Mind, expecting that I should one Day or other fall into the Hands of these merciless Creatures; and if I did at any Time venture abroad, it was not without looking round me with the greatest Care and Caution imaginable; and now I found to my great Comfort, how happy it was that I provided for a tame Flock or Herd of Goats; for I durst not upon any account fire my Gun, especially near that Side of the Island where they usually came, least I should alarm the Savages; and if they had fled from me now, I was sure to have them come back again, with perhaps two or three hundred *Canoes* with them, in a few Days, and then I knew what to expect.

However, I wore out a Year and three Months more, before I ever saw any more of the Savages, and then I found them again, as I shall soon observe. It is true, they might have been there once, or twice; but either they made no stay, or at least I did not hear them; but in the Month of *May*, as near as I could calculate, and in my four and twentieth Year, I had a very strange Encounter with them, of which in its Place.

The Perturbation of my Mind, during this fifteen or sixteen Months Interval, was very great; I slept unquiet, dream'd always frightful Dreams, and often started out of my Sleep in the Night: In the Day great Troubles overwhelm'd my Mind, and in the Night I dream'd often of killing the Savages, and of the Reasons why I might justify the doing of it; but to wave all this for a while; it was in the middle of *May*, on the sixteenth Day I think, as well as my poor wooden Calendar would reckon; for I markt all upon the Post still; I say, it was the sixteenth of *May*, that it blew a very great Storm of Wind, all Day, with a great deal of Lightning, and Thunder, and a very foul Night it was after it; I know not what was the particular Occasion of it; but as I was reading in the Bible, and taken up with very serious Thoughts about my present Condition, I was surpriz'd with a Noise of a Gun as I thought fir'd at Sea.

This was to be sure a Surprize of a quite different Nature from any I had met with before; for the Notions this put into my Thoughts, were quite of another kind. I started up in the greatest hast imaginable, and in a trice[1] clapt my Ladder to the middle Place of the Rock, and pull'd it after me, and mounting it the second Time, got to the Top of the Hill, the very Moment, that a Flash of Fire bid me listen for a second Gun, which accordingly,

---

1 Without delay.

in about half a Minute I heard; and by the sound, knew that it was from that Part of the Sea where I was driven down the Current in my Boat.

I immediately consider'd that this must be some Ship in Distress, and that they had some Comrade, or some other Ship in Company, and fir'd these Guns for Signals of Distress, and to obtain Help: I had this Presence of Mind at that Minute, as to think that though I could not help them, it may be they might help me; so I brought together all the dry Wood I could get at hand, and making a good handsome Pile, I set it on Fire upon the Hill; the Wood was dry, and blaz'd freely; and though the Wind blew very hard, yet it burnt fairly out; that I was certain, if there was any such Thing as a Ship, they must needs see it, and no doubt they did; for as soon as ever my Fire blaz'd up, I heard another Gun, and after that several others, all from the same Quarter; I ply'd my Fire all Night long, till Day broke; and when it was broad Day, and the Air clear'd up, I saw something at a great Distance at Sea, full *East* of the Island, whether a Sail, or a Hull, I could not distinguish, no not with my Glasses,[1] the Distance was so great, and the Weather still something haizy also; at least it was so out at Sea.

I look'd frequently at it all that Day, and soon perceiv'd that it did not move; so I presently concluded, that it was a Ship at an Anchor, and being eager, you may be sure, to be satisfy'd, I took my Gun in my Hand, and run toward the *South* Side of the Island, to the Rocks where I had formerly been carry'd away with the Current, and getting up there, the Weather by this Time being perfectly clear, I could plainly see to my great Sorrow, the Wreck of a Ship cast away in the Night, upon those concealed Rocks which I found, when I was out in my Boat; and which Rocks, as they check'd the Violence of the Stream, and made a kind of Counter-stream, or Eddy, were the Occasion of my recovering from the most desperate hopeless Condition that ever I had been in, in all my Life.

Thus what is one Man's Safety, is another Man's Destruction; for it seems these Men, whoever they were, being out of their Knowledge, and the Rocks being wholly under Water, had been driven upon them in the Night, the Wind blowing hard at *E.* and *E.N.E*: Had they seen the Island, as I must necessarily suppose they did not, they must, as I thought, have endeavour'd to have sav'd themselves on Shore by the Help of their Boat; but their

---

1 Telescopes.

firing of Guns for Help, especially when they saw, as I imagin'd, my Fire, fill'd me with many Thoughts: First, I imagin'd that upon seeing my Light, they might have put themselves into their Boat, and have endeavour'd to make the Shore; but that the Sea going very high, they might have been cast away; other Times I imagin'd, that they might have lost their Boat before, as might be the Case many Ways; as particularly by the Breaking of the Sea upon their Ship, which many Times obliges Men to stave, or take in Pieces their Boat; and sometimes to throw it over-board with their own Hands: Other Times I imagin'd, they had some other Ship, or Ships in Company, who upon the Signals of Distress they had made, had taken them up, and carry'd them off: Other whiles I fancy'd, they were all gone off to Sea in their Boat, and being hurry'd away by the Current that I had been formerly in, were carry'd out into the great Ocean, where there was nothing but Misery and Perishing; and that perhaps they might by this Time think of starving, and of being in a Condition to eat one another.

As all these were but Conjectures at best; so in the Condition I was in, I could do no more than look on upon the Misery of the poor Men, and pity them, which had still this good Effect on my Side, that it gave me more and more Cause to give Thanks to God who had so happily and comfortably provided for me in my desolate Condition; and that of two Ships Companies who were now cast away upon this part of the World, not one Life should be spar'd but mine: I learn'd here again to observe, that it is very rare that the Providence of God casts us into any Condition of Life so low, or any Misery so great, but we may see something or other to be thankful for; and may see others in worse Circumstances than our own.

Such certainly was the Case of these Men, of whom I could not so much as see room to suppose any of them were sav'd; nothing could make it rational, so much as to wish, or expect that they did not all perish there; except the Possibility only of their being taken up by another Ship in Company, and this was but meer Possibility indeed; for I saw not the least Signal or Appearance of any such Thing.

I cannot explain by any possible Energy of Words, what a strange longing or hankering of Desires I felt in my Soul upon this Sight; breaking out sometimes thus; O that there had been but one or two; nay, or but one Soul sav'd out of this Ship, to have escap'd to me, that I might but have had one Companion, one Fellow-Creature to have spoken to me, and to have convers'd with! In all the Time of my solitary Life, I never felt so earnest, so strong a Desire after the Society of my Fellow-Creatures, or so deep a Regret at the want of it.

There are some secret moving Springs in the Affections,[1] which when they are set a going by some Object in view, or be it some Object, though not in view, yet rendred present to the Mind by the Power of Imagination, that Motion carries out the Soul by its Impetuosity to such violent eager embracings of the Object, that the Absence of it is insupportable.

Such were these earnest Wishings, That but one Man had been sav'd! *O that it had been but One!* I believe I repeated the Words, *O that it had been but One!* A thousand Times; and the Desires were so mov'd by it, that when I spoke the Words, my Hands would clinch together, and my Fingers press the Palms of my Hands, that if I had had any soft Thing in my Hand, it wou'd have crusht it involuntarily; and my Teeth in my Head wou'd strike together, and set against one another so strong, that for some time I cou'd not part them again.

Let the Naturalists[2] explain these Things, and the Reason and Manner of them; all I can say to them, is, to describe the Fact, which was even surprising to me when I found it; though I knew not from what it should proceed; it was doubtless the effect of ardent Wishes, and of strong Ideas form'd in my Mind, realizing the Comfort, which the Conversation of one of my Fellow-Christians would have been to me.

But it was not to be; either their Fate or mine, or both, forbid it; for till the last Year of my being on this Island, I never knew whether any were saved out of that Ship or no; and had only the Affliction some Days after, to see the Corps of a drownded Boy come on Shore, at the End of the Island which was next the Ship-wreck: He had on no Cloaths, but a Seaman's Wastcoat, a pair of open knee'd Linnen Drawers, and a blew Linnen Shirt; but nothing to direct me so much as to guess what Nation he was of: He had nothing in his Pocket, but two Pieces of Eight, and a Tobacco Pipe; the last was to me of ten times more value than the first.

It was now calm, and I had a great mind to venture out in my Boat, to this Wreck; not doubting but I might find something on board, that might be useful to me; but that did not altogether

---

1 Strong emotions.
2 Empirical scientists; those who seek natural, rather than supernatural, explanations.

press me so much, as the Possibility that there might be yet some living Creature on board, whose Life I might not only save, but might by saving that Life, comfort my own to the last Degree; and this Thought clung so to my Heart, that I could not be quiet, Night or Day, but I must venture out in my Boat on board this Wreck; and committing the rest to God's Providence, I thought the Impression was so strong upon my Mind, that it could not be resisted, that it must come from some invisible Direction, and that I should be wanting to my self if I did not go.

Under the Power of this Impression, I hasten'd back to my Castle, prepar'd every Thing for my Voyage, took a Quantity of Bread, a great Pot for fresh Water, a Compass to steer by, a Bottle of Rum; for I had still a great deal of that left; a Basket full of Raisins: And thus loading my self with every Thing necessary, I went down to my Boat, got the Water out of her, and got her afloat, loaded all my Cargo in her, and then went Home again for more; my second Cargo was a great Bag full of Rice, the Umbrella to set up over my Head for Shade; another large Pot full of fresh Water, and about two Dozen of my small Loaves, or Barley Cakes, more than before, with a Bottle of Goat's-Milk, and a Cheese; all which, with great Labour and Sweat, I brought to my Boat; and praying to God to direct my Voyage, I put out, and Rowing or Padling the Canoe along the Shore, I came at last to the utmost Point of the Island on that Side, (*viz.*) N.E. And now I was to launch out into the Ocean, and either to venture, or not to venture. I look'd on the rapid Currents which ran constantly on both Sides of the Island, at a Distance, and which were very terrible to me, from the Remembrance of the Hazard I had been in before, and my Heart began to fail me; for I foresaw that if I was driven into either of those Currents, I should be carry'd a vast Way out to Sea, and perhaps out of my Reach, or Sight of the Island again; and that then, as my Boat was but small, if any little Gale of Wind should rise, I should be inevitably lost.

These Thoughts so oppress'd my Mind, that I began to give over my Enterprize, and having haled my Boat into a little Creek on the Shore, I stept out, and sat me down upon a little rising bit of Ground, very pensive and anxious, between Fear and Desire about my Voyage; when as I was musing, I could perceive that the Tide was turn'd, and the Flood come on, upon which my going was for so many Hours impracticable; upon this presently it occurr'd to me, that I should go up to the highest Piece of Ground I could find, and observe, if I could, how the Sets of the Tide, or Currents lay, when the Flood came in, that I might judge whether if I was driven one way out, I might not expect to be driven another way home, with the same Rapidness of the Currents: This Thought was no sooner in my Head, but I cast my Eye upon a little Hill, which sufficiently over-look'd the Sea both ways, and from whence I had a clear view of the Currents, or Sets of the Tide, and which way I was to guide my self in my Return; here I found, that as the Current of the Ebb set out close by the South Point of the Island; so the Current of the Flood set in close by the Shore of the North Side, and that I had nothing to do but to keep to the North of the Island in my Return, and I should do well enough.

Encourag'd with this Observation, I resolv'd the next Morning to set out with the first of the Tide; and reposing my self for the Night in the Canoe, under the great Watch-coat, I mention'd, I launched out: I made first a little out to Sea full North, till I began to feel the Benefit of the Current, which set Eastward, and which carry'd me at a great rate, and yet did not so hurry me as the Southern Side Current had done before, and so as to take from me all Government of the Boat; but having a strong Steerage with my Paddle, I went at a great rate, directly for the Wreck, and in less than two Hours I came up to it.

It was a dismal Sight to look at: The Ship, which by its building was *Spanish*, stuck fast, jaum'd[1] in between two Rocks; all the Stern and Quarter of her was beaten to pieces, with the Sea; and as her Forecastle, which stuck in the Rocks, had run on with great Violence, her Mainmast and Foremast were brought by the Board; that is to say, broken short off; but her Boltsprit[2] was sound, and the Head and Bow appear'd firm; when I came close to her, a Dog appear'd upon her, who seeing me coming, yelp'd, and cry'd; and as soon as I call'd him, jump'd into the Sea, to come to me, and I took him into the Boat; but found him almost dead for Hunger and Thirst: I gave him a Cake of my Bread, and he eat it like a ravenous Wolf, that had been starving a Fortnight in the Snow: I then gave the poor Creature some fresh Water, with which, if I would have let him, he would have burst himself.

After this I went on board; but the first Sight I met with, was two Men drown'd, in the Cook-room, or Forecastle of the Ship, with their Arms fast about one another: I concluded, as is indeed probable, that when the Ship struck, it being in a Storm, the Sea broke so high, and so continually over her, that the Men were not

---

1 Jammed.
2 Bowsprit.

able to bear it, and were strangled with the constant rushing in of the Water, as much as if they had been under Water. Besides the Dog, there was nothing left in the Ship that had Life; nor any Goods that I could see, but what were spoil'd by the Water. There were some Casks of Liquor, whether Wine or Brandy, I knew not, which lay lower in the Hold; and which, the Water being ebb'd out, I could see; but they were too big to meddle with: I saw several Chests, which I believ'd belong'd to some of the Seamen; and I got two of them into the Boat, without examining what was in them.

Had the Stern of the Ship been fix'd, and the Forepart broken off, I am perswaded I might have made a good Voyage; for by what I found in these two Chests, I had room to suppose, the Ship had a great deal of Wealth on board; and if I may guess by the Course she steer'd, she must have been bound from the *Buenos Ayres*, or the *Rio de la Plata*, in the South Part of *America*, beyond the *Brasils*, to the *Havana*, in the Gulph of *Mexico*, and so perhaps to *Spain*: She had no doubt a great Treasure in her; but of no use at that time to any body; and what became of the rest of her People, I then knew not.

I found besides these Chests, a little Cask full of Liquor, of about twenty Gallons, which I got into my Boat, with much Difficulty; there were several Muskets in a Cabin, and a great Powder-horn, with about 4 Pounds of Powder in it; as for the Muskets, I had no occasion for them; so I left them, but took the Powder-horn: I took a Fire Shovel and Tongs, which I wanted extremely; as also two little Brass Kettles, a Copper Pot to make Chocolate, and a Gridiron; and with this Cargo, and the Dog, I came away, the Tide beginning to make home again; and the same Evening, about an Hour within Night, I reach'd the Island again, weary and fatigu'd to the last Degree.

I repos'd that Night in the Boat, and in the Morning I resolved to harbour what I had gotten in my new Cave, not to carry it home to my Castle. After refreshing my self, I got all my Cargo on Shore, and began to examine the Particulars: The Cask of Liquor I found to be a kind of Rum, but not such as we had at the *Brasils*; and in a Word, not at all good; but when I came to open the Chests, I found several Things, of great use to me: For Example, I found in one, a fine Case of Bottles, of an extraordinary kind, and fill'd with Cordial Waters, fine, and very good; the Bottles held about three Pints each, and were tipp'd with Silver: I found two Pots of very good Succades,[1] or Sweetmeats, so

---

1 Candied fruit.

fastned also on top, that the Salt Water had not hurt them; and two more of the same, which the Water had spoil'd: I found some very good Shirts, which were very welcome to me; and about a dozen and half of Linnen white Handkerchiefs, and colour'd Neckcloths; the former were also very welcome, being exceeding refreshing to wipe my Face in a hot Day; besides this, when I came to the Till in the Chest, I found there three great Bags of Pieces of Eight, which held about eleven hundred Pieces in all; and in one of them, wrapt up in a Paper, six Doubloons[1] of Gold, and some small Bars or Wedges of Gold; I suppose they might all weigh near a Pound.

The other Chest I found had some Cloaths in it, but of little Value; but by the Circumstances it must have belong'd to the Gunner's Mate; though there was no Powder in it; but about two Pound of fine glaz'd Powder, in three small Flasks, kept, I suppose, for charging their Fowling-Pieces on occasion: Upon the whole, I got very little by this Voyage, that was of any use to me; for as to the Money, I had no manner of occasion for it: 'Twas to me as the Dirt under my Feet; and I would have given it all for three or four pair of *English* Shoes and Stockings, which were Things I greatly wanted, but had not had on my Feet now for many Years: I had indeed gotten two pair of Shoes now, which I took off of the Feet of the two drown'd Men, who I saw in the Wreck; and I found two pair more in one of the Chests, which were very welcome to me; but they were not like our *English* Shoes, either for Ease, or Service; being rather what we call Pumps, than Shoes: I found in this Seaman's Chest, about fifty Pieces of Eight in Ryals,[2] but no Gold; I suppose this belong'd to a poorer Man than the other, which seem'd to belong to some Officer.

Well, however, I lugg'd this Money home to my Cave, and laid it up, as I had done that before, which I brought from our own Ship; but it was great Pity as I said, that the other Part of this Ship had not come to my Share; for I am satisfy'd I might have loaded my *Canoe* several Times over with Money, which if I had ever escap'd to *England*, would have lain here safe enough, till I might have come again and fetch'd it.

Having now brought all my Things on Shore, and secur'd them, I went back to my Boat, and row'd, or paddled her along the Shore, to her old Harbour, where I laid her up, and made the

---

1 Spanish coin worth thirty-three to thirty-six shillings.
2 *Reals*: small silver coins.

best of my way to my old Habitation, where I found every thing safe and quiet; so I began to repose my self, live after my old fashion, and take care of my Family Affairs; and for a while, I liv'd easy enough; only that I was more vigilant than I us'd to be, look'd out oftner, and did not go abroad so much; and if at any time I did stir with any Freedom, it was always to the *East* Part of the Island, where I was pretty well satisfy'd the Savages never came, and where I could go without so many Precautions, and such a Load of Arms and Ammunition, as I always carry'd with me, if I went the other way.

I liv'd in this Condition near two Years more; but my unlucky[1] Head, that was always to let me know it was born to make my Body miserable, was all this two Years fill'd with Projects and Designs, how, if it were possible, I might get away from this Island; for sometimes I was for making another Voyage to the Wreck, though my Reason told me that there was nothing left there, worth the Hazard of my Voyage: Sometimes for a Ramble one way, sometimes another; and I believe verily, if I had had the Boat that I went from *Sallee* in, I should have ventur'd to Sea, bound any where, I knew not whither.

I have been in all my Circumstances a *Memento*[2] to those who are touch'd with the general Plague of Mankind, whence, for ought I know, one half of their Miseries flow; I mean, that of not being satisfy'd with the Station wherein God and Nature has plac'd them; for not to look back upon my primitive Condition, and the excellent Advice of my Father, the Opposition to which, was, *as I may call it*, my ORIGINAL SIN;[3] my subsequent Mistakes of the same kind had been the Means of my coming into this miserable Condition; for had that Providence, which so happily had seated me at the *Brasils*, as a Planter, bless'd me with confin'd Desires, and I could have been contented to have gone on gradually, I might have been by this Time; *I mean, in the Time of my being in this Island,* one of the most considerable Planters in ·the *Brasils*, nay, I am perswaded, that by the Improvements I had made, in that little Time I liv'd there, and the Encrease I should probably have made, if I had stay'd, I might have been worth an

---

1 Mischievous, causing bad luck.
2 Reminder.
3 Theologically, original sin refers to Adam and Eve's disobedience in the Garden of Eden, when, according to St. Paul, sin first entered the world; but Defoe often used the term as well to describe individuals' predominant faults.

hundred thousand *Moydors*;[1] and what Business had I to leave a settled Fortune, a well stock'd Plantation, improving and encreasing, to turn *Supra-Cargo*[2] to *Guinea*, to fetch Negroes; when Patience and Time would have so encreas'd our Stock at Home, that we could have bought them at our own Door, from those whose Business it was to fetch them; and though it had cost us something more, yet the Difference of that Price was by no Means worth saving, at so great a Hazard.

But as this is ordinarily the Fate of young Heads, so Reflection upon the Folly of it, is as ordinarily the Exercise of more Years, or of the dear bought Experience of Time; and so it was with me now; and yet so deep had the Mistake taken root in my Temper, that I could not satisfy my self in my Station, but was continually poring upon the Means, and Possibility of my Escape from this Place; and that I may with the greater Pleasure to the Reader, bring on the remaining Part of my Story, it may not be improper, to give some Account of my first Conceptions on the Subject of this foolish Scheme, for my Escape; and how, and upon what Foundation I acted.

I am now to be suppos'd retir'd into my Castle, after my late Voyage to the Wreck, my Frigate laid up, and secur'd under Water, as usual, and my Condition restor'd to what it was before: I had more Wealth indeed than I had before, but was not at all the richer; for I had no more use for it, than the *Indians* of *Peru* had, before the *Spaniards* came there.

It was one of the Nights in the rainy Season in *March*, the four and twentieth Year of my first setting Foot in this Island of Solitariness; I was lying in my Bed, or Hammock, awake, very well in Health, had no Pain, no Distemper, no Uneasiness of Body; no, nor any Uneasiness of Mind, more than ordinary; but could by no means close my Eyes; that is, so as to sleep; no, not a Wink all Night long, otherwise than as follows:

It is as impossible, as needless, to set down the innumerable Crowd of Thoughts that whirl'd through that great thorow-fare of the Brain, the Memory, in this Night's Time: I run over the whole History of my Life in Miniature, or by Abridgment,[3] *as I may call it*, to my coming to this Island; and also of the Part of my Life,

---

1   *Moidore*: Portuguese gold coin worth about 27 shillings.
2   Officer in charge of cargo and business transactions.
3   Abridgements of popular books were common in the eighteenth century, including an abridgement of *Robinson Crusoe* that appeared just months after the novel's first edition.

since I came to this Island. In my Reflections upon the State of my Case, since I came on Shore on this Island, I was comparing the happy Posture of my Affairs, in the first Years of my Habitation here, compar'd to the Life of Anxiety, Fear and Care, which I had liv'd ever since I had seen the Print of a Foot in the Sand; not that I did not believe the Savages had frequented the Island even all the while, and might have been several Hundreds of them at Times on Shore there; but I had never known it, and was incapable of any Apprehensions about it; my Satisfaction was perfect, though my Danger was the same; and I was as happy in not knowing my Danger, as if I had never really been expos'd to it: This furnish'd my Thoughts with many very profitable Reflections, and particularly this one, How infinitely Good that Providence is, which has provided in its Government of Mankind, such narrow bounds to his Sight and Knowledge of Things, and though he walks in the midst of so many thousand Dangers, the Sight of which, if discover'd to him, would distract his Mind, and sink his Spirits; he is kept serene, and calm, by having the Events of Things hid from his Eyes, and knowing nothing of the Dangers which surround him.

After these Thoughts had for some Time entertain'd me, I came to reflect seriously upon the real Danger I had been in, for so many Years, in this very Island; and how I had walk'd about in the greatest Security, and with all possible Tranquillity; even when perhaps nothing but a Brow of a Hill, a great Tree, or the casual Approach of Night, had been between me and the worst kind of Destruction, *viz.* That of falling into the Hands of Cannibals, and Savages, who would have seiz'd on me with the same View, as I did of a Goat, or a Turtle; and have thought it no more a Crime to kill and devour me, than I did of a Pidgeon, or a Curlieu: I would unjustly slander my self, if I should say I was not sincerely thankful to my great Preserver, to whose singular Protection I acknowledg'd, with great Humility, that all these unknown Deliverances were due; and without which, I must inevitably have fallen into their merciless Hands.

When these Thoughts were over, my Head was for some time taken up in considering the Nature of these wretched Creatures; I mean, the Savages; and how it came to pass in the World, that the wise Governour of all Things should give up any of his Creatures to such Inhumanity; nay, to something so much below, even Brutality it self, as to devour its own kind; but as this ended in some (at that Time fruitless) Speculations, it occurr'd to me to enquire, what Part of the World these Wretches liv'd in; how far off the Coast was from whence they came; what they ventur'd over so far from home for; what kind of Boats they had; and why I might not order my self, and my Business so, that I might be as able to go over thither, as they were to come to me.

I never so much as troubl'd my self, to consider what I should do with my self, when I came thither; what would become of me, if I fell into the Hands of the Savages; or how I should escape from them, if they attempted[1] me; no, nor so much as how it was possible for me to reach the Coast, and not be attempted by some or other of them, without any Possibility of delivering my self; and if I should not fall into their Hands, what I should do for Provision, or whither I should bend my Course; none of these Thoughts, I say, so much as came in my way; but my Mind was wholly bent upon the Notion of my passing over in my Boat, to the Main Land: I look'd back upon my present Condition, as the most miserable that could possibly be, that I was not able to throw my self into any thing but Death, that could be call'd worse; that if I reached the Shore of the Main, I might perhaps meet with Relief, or I might coast along, as I did on the Shore of *Africk*, till I came to some inhabited Country, and where I might find some Relief; and after all perhaps, I might fall in with some Christian Ship, that might take me in; and if the worse came to the worst, I could but die, which would put an end to all these Miseries at once. Pray note, all this was the fruit of a disturb'd Mind, an impatient Temper, made as it were desperate by the long Continuance of my Troubles, and the Disappointments I had met in the Wreck, I had been on board of; and where I had been so near the obtaining what I so earnestly long'd for, *viz.* Some-body to speak to, and to learn some Knowledge from of the Place where I was, and of the probable Means of my Deliverance; I say, I was agitated wholly by these Thoughts: All my Calm of Mind in my Resignation to Providence, and waiting the Issue of the Dispositions of Heaven, seem'd to be suspended; and I had, as it were, no Power to turn my Thoughts to any thing, but to the Project of a Voyage to the Main, which came upon me with such Force, and such an Impetuosity of Desire, that it was not to be resisted.

When this had agitated my Thoughts for two Hours, or more, with such Violence, that it set my very Blood into a Ferment, and my Pulse beat as high as if I had been in a Feaver, meerly with the extraordinary Fervour of my Mind about it; Nature, as if I

---

1 Tried to attack or capture.

had been fatigued and exhausted with the very Thought of it, threw me into a sound Sleep; one would have thought, I should have dream'd of it: But I did not, nor of any Thing relating to it; but I dream'd, that as I was going out in the Morning as usual from my Castle, I saw upon the Shore, two *Canoes*, and eleven Savages coming to Land, and that they brought with them another Savage, who they were going to kill, in Order to eat him; when on a sudden, the Savage that they were going to kill, jumpt away, and ran for his Life; and I thought in my Sleep, that he came running into my little thick Grove, before my Fortification, to hide himself; and that I seeing him alone, and not perceiving that the other sought him that Way, show'd my self to him, and smiling upon him, encourag'd him; that he kneel'd down to me, seeming to pray me to assist him; upon which I shew'd my Ladder, made him go up, and carry'd him into my Cave, and he became my Servant; and that as soon as I had gotten this Man, I said to my self, now I may certainly venture to the main Land; for this Fellow will serve me as a Pilot, and will tell me what to do, and whether to go for Provisions; and whether not to go for fear of being devoured, what Places to venture into, and what to escape: I wak'd with this Thought, and was under such inexpressible Impressions of Joy, at the Prospect of my Escape in my Dream, that the Disappointments which I felt upon coming to my self, and finding it was no more than a Dream, were equally extravagant the other Way, and threw me into a very great Dejection of Spirit.

Upon this however, I made this Conclusion, that my only Way to go about an Attempt for an Escape, was, if possible, to get a Savage into my Possession; and if possible, it should be one of their Prisoners, who they had condemn'd to be eaten, and should bring thither to kill; but these Thoughts still were attended with this Difficulty, that it was impossible to effect this, without attacking a whole Caravan of them, and killing them all; and this was not only a very desperate Attempt, and might miscarry; but on the other Hand, I had greatly scrupled the Lawfulness of it to me; and my Heart trembled at the thoughts of shedding so much Blood, tho' it was for my Deliverance. I need not repeat the Arguments which occurr'd to me against this, they being the same mention'd before; but tho' I had other Reasons to offer now (*viz.*) that those Men were Enemies to my Life, and would devour me, if they could; that it was Self-preservation in the highest Degree, to deliver my self from this Death of a Life, and was acting in my own Defence, as much as if they were actually assaulting me, and the like. I say, tho' these Things argued for it, yet the Thoughts of shedding Humane Blood for my Deliverance, were very Terrible to me, and such as I could by no Means reconcile my self to, a great while.

However at last, after many secret Disputes with my self, and after great Perplexities about it, for all these Arguments one Way and another struggl'd in my Head a long Time, the eager prevailing Desire of Deliverance at length master'd all the rest; and I resolv'd, if possible, to get one of those Savages into my Hands, cost what it would. My next Thing then was to contrive how to do it, and this indeed was very difficult to resolve on: But as I could pitch upon no probable Means for it, so I resolv'd to put my self upon the Watch, to see them when they came on Shore, and leave the rest to the Event, taking such Measures as the Opportunity should present, let be what would be.

With these Resolutions in my Thoughts, I set my self upon the Scout, as often as possible, and indeed so often till I was heartily tir'd of it, for it was above a Year and Half that I waited, and for great part of that Time went out to the *West* End, and to the *South West* Corner of the Island, almost every Day, to see for Canoes, but none appear'd. This was very discouraging, and began to trouble me much, tho' I cannot say that it did in this Case, as it had done some time before that, (*viz.*) wear off the Edge of my Desire to the Thing. But the longer it seem'd to be delay'd, the more eager I was for it; in a Word, I was not at first so careful to shun the sight of these Savages, and avoid being seen by them, as I was now eager to be upon them.

Besides, I fancied my self able to manage One, nay, Two or Three Savages, if I had them so as to make them entirely Slaves to me, to do whatever I should direct them, and to prevent their being able at any time to do me any Hurt. It was a great while, that I pleas'd my self with this Affair, but nothing still presented; all my Fancies and Schemes came to nothing, for no Savages came near me for a great while.

About a Year and half after I had entertain'd these Notions, and by long musing, had as it were resolved them all into nothing, for want of an Occasion to put them in Execution, I was surpriz'd one Morning early, with seeing no less than five *Canoes* all on Shore together on my side the Island; and the People who belong'd to them all landed, and out of my sight: The Number of them broke all my Measures, for seeing so

many, and knowing that they always came four or six, or sometimes more in a Boat, I could not tell what to think of it, or how
to take my Measures, to attack Twenty or Thirty Men single
handed; so I lay still in my Castle, perplex'd and discomforted:
However I put my self into all the same Postures for an Attack
that I had formerly provided, and was just ready for Action, if
any Thing had presented; having waited a good while, listening
to hear if they made any Noise; at length being very impatient,
I set my Guns at the Foot of my Ladder, and clamber'd up to
the Top of the Hill, by my two Stages as usual; standing so
however that my Head did not appear above the Hill, so that
they could not perceive me by any Means; here I observ'd by
the help of my Perspective Glass, that they were no less than
Thirty in Number, that they had a Fire kindled, that they had
had Meat dress'd. How they had cook'd it, that I knew not,
or what it was; but they were all Dancing in I know not how
many barbarous Gestures and Figures, their own Way, round
the Fire.

slave escapes

While I was thus looking on them, I perceived by my Perspective, two miserable Wretches dragg'd from the Boats, where it
seems they were laid by, and were now brought out for the
Slaughter. I perceived one of them immediately fell, being
knock'd down, I suppose with a Club or Wooden Sword, for that
was their way, and two or three others were at work immediately
cutting him open for their Cookery, while the other Victim was
left standing by himself, till they should be ready for him. In that
very Moment this poor Wretch seeing himself a little at Liberty,
Nature inspir'd him with Hopes of Life, and he started away from
them, and ran with incredible Swiftness along the Sands directly
towards me, I mean towards that part of the Coast, where my
Habitation was.

I was dreadfully frighted, (that I must acknowledge) when I
perceived him to run my Way; and especially, when as I thought
I saw him pursued by the whole Body, and now I expected that
part of my Dream was coming to pass, and that he would certainly take shelter in my Grove; but I could not depend by any
means upon my Dream for the rest of it, (*viz.*) that the other
Savages would not pursue him thither, and find him there.
However I kept my Station, and my Spirits began to recover,
when I found that there was not above three Men that follow'd
him, and still more was I encourag'd, when I found that he out-
strip'd them exceedingly in running, and gain'd Ground of them,

so that if he could but hold it for half an Hour, I saw easily he would fairly get away from them all.

There was between them and my Castle, the Creek which I mention'd often at the first part of my Story, when I landed my Cargoes out of the Ship; and this I saw plainly, he must necessarily swim over, or the poor Wretch would be taken there: But when the Savage escaping came thither, he made nothing of it, tho' the Tide was then up, but plunging in, swam thro' in about Thirty Strokes or thereabouts, landed and ran on with exceeding Strength and Swiftness; when the Three Persons came to the Creek, I found that Two of them could Swim, but the Third cou'd not, and that standing on the other Side, he look'd at the other, but went no further; and soon after went softly back again, which as it happen'd, was very well for him in the main.

I observ'd, that the two who swam, were yet more than twice as long swimming over the Creek, as the Fellow was, that fled from them: It came now very warmly upon my Thoughts, and indeed irresistibly, that now was my Time to get me a Servant, and perhaps a Companion, or Assistant; and that I was call'd plainly by Providence to save this poor Creature's Life; I immediately run down the Ladders with all possible Expedition, fetches my two Guns, for they were both but at the Foot of the Ladders, as I observ'd above; and getting up again, with the same haste, to the Top of the Hill, I cross'd toward the Sea; and having a very short Cut, and all down Hill, clapp'd my self in the way, between the Pursuers, and the Pursu'd; hallowing[1] aloud to him that fled, who looking back, was at first perhaps as much frighted at me, as at them; but I beckon'd with my Hand to him, to come back; and in the mean time, I slowly advanc'd towards the two that follow'd; then rushing at once upon the foremost, I knock'd him down with the Stock of my Piece I was loath to fire, because I would not have the rest hear; though at that distance, it would not have been easily heard, and being out of Sight of the Smoke too, they wou'd not have easily known what to make of it: Having knock'd this Fellow down, the other who pursu'd with him stopp'd, as if he had been frighted; and I advanc'd a-pace towards him; but as I came nearer, I perceiv'd presently, he had a Bow and Arrow, and was fitting it to shoot at me; so I was then necessitated to shoot at him first, which I did, and kill'd him at the first

---

1 To summon with shouts.

Shoot; the poor Savage who fled, but had stopp'd; though he saw both his Enemies fallen, and kill'd, as he thought; yet was so frighted with the Fire, and Noise of my Piece; that he stood Stock still, and neither came forward or went backward, tho' he seem'd rather enclin'd to fly still, than to come on; I hollow'd again to him, and made Signs to come forward, which he easily understood, and came a little way, then stopp'd again, and then a little further, and stopp'd again, and I cou'd then perceive that he stood trembling, as if he had been taken Prisoner, and had just been to be kill'd,[1] as his two Enemies were; I beckon'd him again to come to me, and gave him all the Signs of Encouragement that I could think of, and he came nearer and nearer, kneeling down every Ten or Twelve steps in token of acknowledgement for my saving his Life: I smil'd at him, and look'd pleasantly, and beckon'd to him to come still nearer; at length he came close to me, and then he kneel'd down again, kiss'd the Ground, and laid his Head upon the Ground, and taking me by the Foot, set my Foot upon his Head;[2] this it seems was in token of swearing to be my Slave for ever; I took him up, and made much[3] of him, and encourag'd him all I could. But there was more work to do yet, for I perceived the Savage who I knock'd down, was not kill'd, but stunn'd with the blow, and began to come to himself; so I pointed to him, and showing him the Savage, that he was not dead; upon this he spoke some Words to me, and though I could not understand them, yet I thought they were pleasant to hear, for they were the first sound of a Man's Voice, that I had heard, *my own excepted*, for above Twenty Five Years. But there was no time for such Reflections now, the Savage who was knock'd down recover'd himself so far, as to sit up upon the Ground, and I perceived that my Savage began to be afraid; but when I saw that, I presented my other Piece at the Man, as if I would shoot him, upon this my Savage, *for so I call him now*, made a Motion to me to lend him my Sword, which hung naked in a Belt by my side; so I did: he no sooner had it, but he runs to his Enemy, and at one blow cut off his Head as cleverly,[4] no Executioner in *Germany*, could have done it sooner or better; which I thought very strange, for one who I had Reason to believe never saw a Sword in his Life

---

1 Had been just about to be killed.
2 This scene is one of *Crusoe*'s most frequently illustrated. See Appendix H.
3 To treat with courtesy and affection.
4 *Cleverly*, with a possible pun on *cleaver*.

before, except their own Wooden Swords; however it seems, as I learn'd afterwards, they make their Wooden Swords so sharp, so heavy, and the Wood is so hard, that they will cut off Heads even with them, ay and Arms, and that at one blow too; when he had done this, he comes laughing to me in Sign of Triumph, and brought me the Sword again, and with abundance of Gestures which I did not understand, laid it down with the Head of the Savage, that he had kill'd just before me.

But that which astonish'd him most, was to know how I had kill'd the other Indian so far off, so pointing to him, he made Signs to me to let him go to him, so I bad him go, as well as I could, when he came to him, he stood like one amaz'd, looking at him, turn'd him first on one side, then on t'other, look'd at the Wound the Bullet had made, which it seems was just in his Breast, where it had made a Hole, and no great Quantity of Blood had follow'd, but he had bled inwardly, for he was quite dead; He took up his Bow, and Arrows, and came back, so I turn'd to go away, and beckon'd to him to follow me, making Signs to him, that more might come after them.

gestive communication

Upon this he sign'd to me, that he should bury them with Sand, that they might not be seen by the rest if they follow'd; and so I made Signs again to him to do so; he fell to Work, and in an instant he had scrap'd a Hole in the Sand, with his Hands, big enough to bury the first in, and then dragg'd him into it, and cover'd him, and did so also by the other; I believe he had bury'd them both in a Quarter of an Hour; then calling him away, I carry'd him not to my Castle, but quite away to my Cave, on the farther Part of the Island; so I did not let my Dream come to pass in that Part, *viz.* That he came into my Grove for shelter.

Here I gave him Bread, and a Bunch of Raisins to eat, and a Draught of Water, which I found he was indeed in great Distress for, by his Running; and having refresh'd him, I made Signs for him to go lie down and sleep; pointing to a Place where I had laid a great Parcel of Rice Straw, and a Blanket upon it, which I used to sleep upon my self some times; so the poor Creature laid down, and went to sleep.

He was a comely handsome Fellow, perfectly well made; with straight strong Limbs, not too large; tall and well shap'd, and as I reckon, about twenty six Years of Age. He had a very good Countenance, not a fierce and surly Aspect; but seem'd to have something very manly in his Face, and yet he had all the Sweetness and Softness of an *European* in his Countenance too, especially when he smil'd. His Hair was long and black, not curl'd like

Wool; his Forehead very high, and large, and a great Vivacity and sparkling Sharpness in his Eyes. The Colour of his Skin was not quite black, but very tawny; and yet not of an ugly yellow nauseous tawny, as the *Brasilians*, and *Virginians*, and other Natives of *America* are; but of a bright kind of a dun olive Colour, that had in it something very agreeable; tho' not very easy to describe. His Face was round, and plump; his Nose small, not flat like the Negroes, a very good Mouth, thin Lips, and his fine Teeth well set, and white as Ivory. After he had slumber'd, rather than slept, about half an Hour, he wak'd again, and comes out of the Cave to me; for I had been milking my Goats, which I had in the Enclosure just by: When he espy'd me, he came running to me, laying himself down again upon the Ground, with all the possible Signs of an humble thankful Disposition, making a many antick Gestures to show it: At last he lays his Head flat upon the Ground, close to my Foot, and sets my other Foot upon his Head, as he had done before; and after this, made all the Signs to me of Subjection, Servitude, and Submission imaginable, to let me know, how he would serve me as long as he liv'd; I understood him in many Things, and let him know, I was very well pleas'd with him; in a little Time I began to speak to him, and teach him to speak to me; and first, I made him know his Name should be *Friday*, which was the Day I sav'd his Life; I call'd him so for the Memory of the Time; I likewise taught him to say *Master*, and then let him know, that was to be my Name; I likewise taught him to say, YES, and NO, and to know the Meaning of them; I gave him some Milk, in an earthen Pot, and let him see me Drink it before him, and sop my Bread in it; and I gave him a Cake of Bread, to do the like, which he quickly comply'd with, and made Signs that it was very good for him.

I kept there with him all that Night; but as soon as it was Day, I beckon'd to him to come with me, and let him know, I would give him some Cloaths, at which he seem'd very glad, for he was stark naked: As we went by the Place where he had bury'd the two Men, he pointed exactly to the Place, and shew'd me the Marks that he had made to find them again, making Signs to me, that we should dig them up again, and eat them; at this I appear'd very angry, express'd my Abhorrence of it, made as if I would vomit at the Thoughts of it, and beckon'd with my Hand to him to come away, which he did immediately, with great Submission. I then led him up to the Top of the Hill, to see if his Enemies were gone; and pulling out my Glass, I look'd, and saw plainly the Place where they had been, but no appearance of them, or of their

Canoes; so that it was plain they were gone, and had left their two Comrades behind them, without any search after them.

But I was not content with this Discovery; but having now more Courage, and consequently more Curiosity, I takes my Man *Friday* with me, giving him the Sword in his Hand, with the Bow and Arrows at his Back, which I found he could use very dextrously, making him carry one Gun for me, and I two for my self, and away we march'd to the Place, where these Creatures had been; for I had a Mind now to get some fuller Intelligence of them: When I came to the Place, my very Blood ran chill in my Veins, and my Heart sunk within me, at the Horror of the Spectacle: Indeed it was a dreadful Sight, at least it was so to me; though *Friday* made nothing of it: The Place was cover'd with humane Bones, the Ground dy'd with their Blood, great Pieces of Flesh left here and there, half eaten, mangl'd and scorch'd; and in short, all the Tokens of the triumphant Feast they had been making there, after a Victory over their Enemies: I saw three Skulls, five Hands, and the Bones of three or four Legs and Feet, and abundance of other Parts of the Bodies; and *Friday*, by his Signs, made me understand, that they brought over four Prisoners to feast upon; that three of them were eaten up, and that he, pointing to himself, was the fourth: That there had been a great Battle between them, and their next King, whose Subjects it seems he had been one of; and that they had taken a great Number of Prisoners, all which were carry'd to several Places by those that had taken them in the Fight, in order to feast upon them, as was done here by these Wretches upon those they brought hither.

I caus'd *Friday* to gather all the Skulls, Bones, Flesh, and whatever remain'd, and lay them together on a Heap, and make a great Fire upon it, and burn them all to Ashes: I found *Friday* had still a hankering Stomach after some of the Flesh, and was still a Cannibal in his Nature; but I discover'd[1] so much Abhorrence at the very Thoughts of it, and at the least Appearance of it, that he durst not discover it; for I had by some Means let him know, that I would kill him if he offer'd it.

When we had done this, we came back to our Castle, and there I fell to work for my Man *Friday*; and first of all, I gave him a pair of Linnen Drawers, which I had out of the poor Gunner's Chest I mention'd, and which I found in the Wreck; and which with a little Alteration fitted him very well; then I made him a Jerkin[2] of

---

1 Displayed.

2 A jacket or waistcoat, usually made of leather.

Goat's-skin, as well as my Skill would allow; and I was now grown a tollerable good Taylor; and I gave him a Cap, which I had made of a Hare-skin, very convenient, and fashionable enough; and thus he was cloath'd for the present, tollerably well; and was mighty well pleas'd to see himself almost as well cloath'd as his Master: It is true, he went awkardly in these Things at first; wearing the Drawers was very awkard to him, and the Sleeves of the Wastcoat gall'd his Shoulders, and the inside of his Arms; but a little easing them where he complain'd they hurt him, and using himself to them, at length he took to them very well.

The next Day after I came home to my Hutch with him, I began to consider where I should lodge him, and that I might do well for him, and yet be perfectly easy my self; I made a little Tent for him in the vacant Place between my two Fortifications, in the inside of the last, and in the outside of the first; and as there was a Door, or Entrance there into my Cave, I made a formal fram'd Door Case, and a Door to it of Boards, and set it up in the Passage, a little within the Entrance; and causing the Door to open on the inside, I barr'd it up in the Night, taking in my Ladders too; so that *Friday* could no way come at me in the inside of my innermost Wall, without making so much Noise in getting over, that it must needs waken me; for my first Wall had now a compleat Roof over it of long Poles, covering all my Tent, and leaning up to the side of the Hill, which was again laid cross with smaller Sticks instead of Laths, and then thatch'd over a great Thickness, with the Rice Straw, which was strong like Reeds; and at the Hole or Place which was left to go in or out by the Ladder, I had plac'd a kind of Trap-door, which if it had been attempted on the outside, would not have open'd at all, but would have fallen down, and made a great Noise; and as to Weapons, I took them all in to my Side every Night.

But I needed none of all this Precaution; for never Man had a more faithful, loving, sincere Servant, than *Friday* was to me; without Passions, Sullenness or Designs, perfectly oblig'd and engag'd; his very Affections were ty'd to me, like those of a Child to a Father; and I dare say, he would have sacrific'd his Life for the saving mine, upon any occasion whatsoever; the many Testimonies he gave me of this, put it out of doubt, and soon convinc'd me, that I needed to use no Precautions, as to my Safety on his Account.

This frequently gave me occasion to observe, and that with wonder, that however it had pleas'd God, in his Providence, and in the Government of the Works of his Hands, to take from so great a Part of the World of his Creatures, the best uses to which their Faculties, and the Powers of their Souls are adapted; yet that he has bestow'd upon them the same Powers, the same Reason, the same Affections, the same Sentiments of Kindness and Obligation, the same Passions and Resentments of Wrongs; the same Sense of Gratitude, Sincerity, Fidelity, and all the Capacities of doing Good, and receiving Good, that he has given to us; and that when he pleases to offer to them Occasions of exerting these, they are as ready, nay, more ready to apply them to the right Uses for which they were bestow'd, than we are; and this made me very mellancholly sometimes, in reflecting as the several Occasions presented, how mean a Use we make of all these, even though we have these Powers enlighten'd by the great Lamp of Instruction, the Spirit of God, and by the Knowledge of his Word, added to our Understanding; and why it has pleas'd God to hide the like saving Knowledge from so many Millions of Souls, who if I might judge by this poor Savage, would make a much better use of it than we did.

From hence, I sometimes was led too far to invade the Soveraignty of *Providence*, and as it were arraign the Justice of so arbitrary a Disposition of Things, that should hide that Light from some, and reveal it to others, and yet expect a like Duty from both: But I shut it up, and check'd my Thoughts with this Conclusion, (1st.) That we did not know by what Light and Law these should be Condemn'd; but that as God was necessarily, and by the Nature of his Being, infinitely Holy and Just, so it could not be, but that if these Creatures were all sentenc'd to Absence from himself, it was on account of sinning against that Light which, as the Scripture says, was a Law to themselves,[1] and by such Rules as their Consciences would acknowledge to be just, tho' the Foundation was not discover'd to us: And (2d.) that still as we are all the Clay in the Hand of the Potter, no Vessel could say to him, Why hast thou form'd me thus?[2]

---

1   Romans 2:14: "For when the Gentiles, which have not the law, do by nature the things contained in the law, these, having not the law, are a law unto themselves."

2   Jeremiah 18:6: "Then the word of the LORD came to me, saying, O house of Israel, cannot I do with you as this potter? saith the Lord. Behold, as the clay is in the potter's hand, so are ye in mine hand, O house of Israel." Isaiah 45:9: "Woe unto him that striveth with his Maker! Let the potsherd strive with the potsherds of the earth. Shall the clay say to him that fashioneth it, What makest thou? or thy work, He hath no hands?"

But to return to my New Companion; I was greatly delighted with him, and made it my Business to teach him every Thing, that was proper to make him useful, handy, and helpful; but especially to make him speak, and understand me when I spake, and he was the aptest Schollar that ever was, and particularly was so merry, so constantly diligent, and so pleased, when he cou'd but understand me, or make me understand him, that it was very pleasant to me to talk to him; and now my Life began to be so easy, that I began to say to my self, that could I but have been safe from more Savages, I cared not, if I was never to remove from the place while I lived.

After I had been two or three Days return'd to my Castle, I thought that, in order to bring *Friday* off from his horrid way of feeding, and from the Relish of a Cannibal's Stomach, I ought to let him taste other Flesh; so I took him out with me one Morning to the Woods: I went indeed intending to kill a Kid out of my own Flock, and bring him home and dress it. But as I was going, I saw a She Goat lying down in the Shade, and two young Kids sitting by her, I catch'd hold of *Friday*, hold says I, stand still; and made Signs to him not to stir, immediately I presented my Piece, shot and kill'd one of the Kids. The poor Creature who had at a Distance indeed seen me kill the Savage his Enemy, but did not know, or could imagine how it was done, was sensibly surpriz'd, trembled, and shook, and look'd so amaz'd, that I thought he would have sunk down. He did not see the Kid I shot at, or perceive I had kill'd it, but ripp'd up his Wastcoat to feel if he was not wounded, and as I found, presently thought I was resolv'd to kill him; for he came and kneel'd down to me, and embraceing my Knees, said a great many Things I did not understand; but I could easily see that the meaning was to pray me not to kill him.

I soon found a way to convince him that I would do him no harm, and taking him up by the Hand laugh'd at him, and pointed to the Kid which I had kill'd, beckoned to him to run and fetch it, which he did; and while he was wondering and looking to see how the Creature was kill'd, I loaded my Gun again, and by and by I saw a great Fowl like a Hawk sit upon a Tree within Shot; so to let *Friday* understand a little what I would do, I call'd him to me again, pointed at the Fowl which was indeed a Parrot, tho' I thought it had been a Hawk, I say pointing to the Parrot, and to my Gun, and to the Ground under the Parrot, to let him see I would make it fall, I made him understand that I would shoot and kill that Bird; accordingly I fir'd and bad him look, and immediately he saw the Parrot fall, he stood like one frighted again, notwithstanding all I had said to him; and I found he was the more amaz'd, because he did not see me put any Thing into the Gun; but thought that there must be some wonderful Fund of Death and Destruction in that Thing, able to kill Man, Beast, Bird, or any Thing near, or far off; and the Astonishment this created in him was such, as could not wear off for a long Time; and I believe, if I would have let him, he would have worshipp'd me and my Gun: As for the Gun it self, he would not so much as touch it for several Days after; but would speak to it, and talk to it, as if it had answer'd him, when he was by himself; which, as I afterwards learn'd of him, was to desire it not to kill him.

Well, after his Astonishment was a little over at this, I pointed to him to run and fetch the Bird I had shot, which he did, but stay'd some Time; for the Parrot not being quite dead, was flutter'd away a good way off from the Place where she fell; however, he found her, took her up, and brought her to me; and as I had perceiv'd his Ignorance about the Gun before, I took this Advantage to charge the Gun again, and not let him see me do it, that I might be ready for any other Mark that might present; but nothing more offer'd at that Time; so I brought home the Kid, and the same Evening I took the Skin off, and cut it out as well as I could; and having a Pot for that purpose, I boil'd, or stew'd some of the Flesh, and made some very good Broth; and after I had begun to eat some, I gave some to my Man, who seem'd very glad of it, and lik'd it very well; but that which was strangest to him, was, to see me eat Salt with it; he made a Sign to me, that the Salt was not good to eat, and putting a little into his own Mouth, he seem'd to nauseate it, and would spit and sputter at it, washing his Mouth with fresh Water after it; on the other hand, I took some Meat in my Mouth without Salt, and I pretended to spit and sputter for want of Salt, as fast as he had done at the Salt; but it would not do, he would never care for Salt with his Meat, or in his Broth; at least not a great while, and then but a very little.

Having thus fed him with boil'd Meat and Broth, I was resolv'd to feast him the next Day with roasting a Piece of the Kid; this I did by hanging it before the Fire, in a String, as I had seen many People do in *England*, setting two Poles up, one on each side the Fire, and one cross on the Top, and tying the String to the Cross-stick, letting the Meat turn continually: This *Friday* admir'd very much; but when he came to taste the Flesh, he took so many ways to tell me how well he lik'd it, that I could not but understand him; and at last he told me he would never eat Man's Flesh any more, which I was very glad to hear.

The next Day I set him to work to beating some Corn out, and sifting it in the manner I us'd to do, as I observ'd before, and he soon understood how to do it as well as I, especially after he had seen what the Meaning of it was, and that it was to make Bread of; for after that I let him see me make my Bread, and bake it too, and in a little Time *Friday* was able to do all the Work for me, as well as I could do it my self.

I begun now to consider, that having two Mouths to feed, instead of one, I must provide more Ground for my Harvest, and plant a larger Quantity of Corn, than I us'd to do; so I mark'd out a larger Piece of Land, and began the Fence in the same Manner as before, in which *Friday* not only work'd very willingly, and very hard; but did it very chearfully, and I told him what it was for; that it was for Corn to make more Bread, because he was now with me, and that I might have enough for him, and my self too: He appear'd very sensible of that Part, and let me know, that he thought I had much more Labour upon me on his Account, than I had for my self; and that he would work the harder for me, if I would tell him what to do.

This was the pleasantest Year of all the Life I led in this Place; *Friday* began to talk pretty well, and understand the Names of almost every Thing I had occasion to call for, and of every Place I had to send him to, and talk'd a great deal to me; so that in short I began now to have some Use for my Tongue again, which indeed I had very little occasion for before; that is to say, *about Speech*; besides the Pleasure of talking to him, I had a singular Satisfaction in the Fellow himself; his simple unfeign'd Honesty, appear'd to me more and more every Day, and I began really to love the Creature; and on his Side, I believe he lov'd me more than it was possible for him ever to love any Thing before.

I had a Mind once to try if he had any hankering Inclination to his own Country again, and having learn'd him *English* so well that he could answer me almost any Questions, I ask'd him whether the Nation that he belong'd to never conquer'd in Battle, at which he smil'd; and said; yes, yes, we always fight the better; that is, he meant always get the better in Fight; and so we began the following Discourse: You always fight the better said I, How came you to be taken Prisoner then, *Friday*?

Friday, My Nation beat much, for all that.

Master, How beat; if your Nation beat them, how come you to be taken?

Friday, They more many than my Nation in the Place where me was; they take one, two, three, and me; my Nation over beat them in the yonder Place, where me no was; there my Nation take one, two, great Thousand.

Master, But why did not your Side recover you from the Hands of your Enemies then?

Friday, They run one, two, three, and me, and make go in the *Canoe*; my Nation have no *Canoe* that time.

Master, Well, *Friday*, and What does your Nation do with the Men they take, do they carry them away, and eat them, as these did?

Friday, Yes, my Nation eat Mans too, eat all up.

Master, Where do they carry them?

Friday, Go to other Place where they think.

Master, Do they come hither?

Friday, Yes, yes, they come hither; come other else Place.

Master, Have you been here with them?

Friday, Yes, I been here; [*points to the* N.W. Side of the Island, which it seems was their Side.]

By this I understood, that my Man *Friday* had formerly been among the Savages, who us'd to come on Shore on the farther Part of the Island, on the same Man eating Occasions that he was now brought for; and sometime after, when I took the Courage to carry him to that Side, being the same I formerly mention'd, he presently knew the Place, and told me, he was there once when they eat up twenty Men, two Women, and one Child; he could not tell[1] Twenty in *English*; but he numbred them by laying so many Stones on a Row, and pointing to me to tell them over.

I have told this Passage, because it introduces what follows; that after I had had this Discourse with him, I ask'd him how far it was from our Island to the Shore, and whether the *Canoes* were not often lost; he told me, there was no Danger, no *Canoes* ever lost; but that after a little way out to the Sea, there was a Current, and Wind, always one way in the Morning, the other in the Afternoon.

This I understood to be no more than the Sets of the Tide, as going out, or coming in; but I afterwards understood, it was occasion'd by the great Draft and Reflux of the mighty River *Oroonooko*; in the Mouth, or the Gulph of which River, as I found afterwards, our Island lay; and this Land which I perceiv'd to the *W.* and *N.W.* was the great Island *Trinidad*, on the *North* Point of the Mouth of the River: I ask'd *Friday* a thousand Questions about the Country, the Inhabitants, the Sea, the Coast, and what Nations were near; he

---

1 Count.

told me all he knew with the greatest Openness imaginable; I ask'd him the Names of the several Nations of his Sort of People; but could get no other Name than *Caribs*;[1] from whence I easily understood, that these were the *Caribbees*, which our Maps place on the Part of *America*, which reaches from the Mouth of the River *Oroonooko* to *Guiana*, and onwards to *St. Martha*: He told me that up a great way beyond the Moon, that was, beyond the Setting of the Moon, which must be *W.* from their Country, there dwelt white bearded Men, like me; and pointed to my great Whiskers, which I mention'd before; and that they had kill'd *much Mans*, that was his Word; by all which I understood, he meant the *Spaniards*, whose Cruelties in *America* had been spread over the whole Countries, and was remember'd by all the Nations from Father to Son.

I enquir'd if he could tell me how I might come from this Island, and get among those white Men; he told me, yes, yes, I might go *in two Canoe*; I could not understand what he meant, or make him describe to me what he meant by *two Canoe*, till at last with great Difficulty, I found he meant it must be in a large great Boat, as big as *two Canoes*.

This Part of *Friday*'s Discourse began to relish with me[2] very well, and from this Time I entertain'd some Hopes, that one Time or other, I might find an Opportunity to make my Escape from this Place; and that this poor Savage might be a Means to help me to do it.

During the long Time that *Friday* has now been with me, and that he began to speak to me, and understand me, I was not wanting[3] to lay a Foundation of religious Knowledge in his Mind; particularly I ask'd him one Time who made him? The poor Creature did not understand me at all, but thought I had ask'd him who was his Father; but I took it by another handle, and ask'd him who made the Sea, the Ground we walk'd on, and the Hills, and Woods; he told me it was one old *Benamuckee*,[4] that liv'd beyond all: He could describe nothing of this great Person, but that he was very old; much older he said than the Sea, or the Land; than the Moon, or the Stars: I ask'd him then, if this old Person had made all Things, why did not all Things worship him; he look'd very grave, and with a perfect Look of Innocence, said,

---

1 A group of Amerindians who lived in the Lesser Antilles. The word *cannibal* is derived from the Spanish word for Carib.

2 To please me.

3 Failing.

4 Apparently a name invented by Defoe.

All Things do say O to him: I ask'd him if the People who die in his Country went away any where; he said, yes, they all went to *Bena-muckee*; then I ask'd him whether these they eat up went thither too, he said yes.

From these Things, I began to instruct him in the Knowledge of the true God: I told him that the great Maker of all Things liv'd up there, pointing up towards Heaven: That he governs the World by the same Power and Providence by which he had made it: That he was omnipotent, could do every Thing for us, give every Thing to us, take every Thing from us; and thus by Degrees I open'd his Eyes. He listned with great Attention, and receiv'd with Pleasure the Notion of *Jesus Christ* being sent to redeem us, and of the Manner of making our Prayers to God, and his being able to hear us, even into Heaven; he told me one Day, that if our God could hear us up beyond the Sun, he must needs be a greater God than their *Benamuckee*, who liv'd but a little way off, and yet could not hear, till they went up to the great Mountains where he dwelt, to speak to him; I ask'd him if ever he went thither, to speak to him; he said no, they never went that were young Men; none went thither but the old Men, who he call'd their *Oowocakee*, that is, as I made him explain it to me, their Religious, or Clergy, and that they went to say O, (so he called saying Prayers) and then came back, and told them what *Bena-muckee* said: By this I observ'd, That there is *Priestcraft,*[1] even amongst the most blinded ignorant Pagans in the World; and the Policy of making a secret Religion, in order to preserve the Ven-eration of the People to the Clergy, is not only to be found in the *Roman,*[2] but perhaps among all Religions in the World, even among the most brutish and barbarous Savages.

I endeavour'd to clear up this Fraud, to my Man *Friday*, and told him, that the Pretence of their old Men going up the Moun-tains, to say O to their God *Benamuckee*, was a Cheat, and their bringing Word from thence what he said, was much more so; that if they met with any Answer, or spake with any one there, it must be with an evil Spirit: And then I entred into a long Discourse with him about the Devil, the Original of him, his Rebellion against God, his Enmity to Man, the Reason of it, his setting himself up in the dark Parts of the World to be Worship'd instead of God, and as God; and the many Stratagems he made use of to

---

1 Deceitful actions by priests.
2 Roman Catholic.

delude Mankind to his Ruine; how he had a secret access to our Passions, and to our Affections, to adapt his Snares so to our Inclinations, as to cause us even to be our own Tempters, and to run upon our Destruction by our own Choice.

I found it was not so easie to imprint right Notions in his Mind about the Devil, as it was about the Being of a God. Nature assisted all my Arguments to Evidence to him, even the Necessity of a great first Cause and over-ruling governing Power; a secret directing Providence, and of the Equity, and Justice, of paying Homage to him that made us, and the like. But there appeared nothing of all this in the Notion of an evil Spirit; of his Original, his Being, his Nature, and above all of his Inclination to do Evil, and to draw us in to do so too; and the poor Creature puzzl'd me once in such a manner, by a Question meerly natural and inno- cent, that I scarce knew what to say to him. I had been talking a great deal to him of the Power of God, his Omnipotence, his dreadful Nature[1] to Sin, his being a consuming Fire[2] to the Workers of Iniquity;[3] how, as he had made us all, he could destroy us and all the World in a Moment; and he listen'd with great Seriousness to me all the while.

Teaches bible [handwritten marginal note]

After this, I had been telling him how the Devil was God's Enemy in the Hearts of Men, and used all his Malice and Skill to defeat the good Designs of Providence, and to ruine the Kingdom of Christ in the World; and the like. Well, says *Friday*, but you say, God is so strong, so great, is he not much strong, much might as the Devil? Yes, yes, says I, *Friday*, God is stronger than the Devil, God is above the Devil, and therefore we pray to God to tread him down under our Feet,[4] and enable us to resist his Temptations and quench his fiery Darts.[5] *But,* says he again, *if God much strong, much might as the Devil, why God no kill the Devil, so make him no more do wicked?*

---

1 In later editions, the word *Nature* was changed to *Aversion*. Defoe seems to mean that God's essence is profoundly directed against sin.

2 Deuteronomy 4:24: "For the LORD thy God is a consuming fire, even a jealous God." Hebrews 12:28-29: "[L]et us have grace, whereby we may serve God acceptably with reverence and godly fear: For our God is a consuming fire."

3 A common expression in the Hebrew Bible, especially in the Psalms.

4 Romans 16:20: "And the God of peace shall bruise Satan under your feet shortly."

5 Ephesians 6:16: "Above all, taking the shield of faith, wherewith ye shall be able to quench all the fiery darts of the wicked."

I was strangely surpriz'd at his Question, and after all, tho' I was now an old Man, yet I was but a young Doctor,[1] and ill enough quallified for a Casuist,[2] or a Solver of Difficulties: And at first I could not tell what to say, so I pretended not to hear him, and ask'd him what he said? But he was too earnest for an Answer to forget his Question; so that he repeated it in the very same broken Words, as above. By this time I had recovered my self a little, and I said, *God will at last punish him severely;* he is *reserv'd for the Judgment,*[3] *and is to be cast into the Bottomless-Pit, to dwell with everlasting Fire.*[4] This did not satisfie *Friday*, but he returns upon me, repeating my Words, RESERVE, AT LAST, *me no understand; but, Why not kill the Devil now, not kill great ago?* You may as well ask me, *said I*, Why God does not kill you and I, when we do wicked Things here that offend him? We are preserv'd to repent and be pardon'd: He muses a while at this; *well, well,* says he, mighty affectionately, *that well; so you, I, Devil, all wicked, all preserve, repent, God pardon all.* Here I was run down again by him to the last Degree, and it was a Testimony to me, how the meer Notions of Nature, though they will guide reasonable Creatures to the Knowledge of a God, and of a Worship or Homage due to the supreme Being, of God as the Consequence of our Nature; yet nothing but divine Revelation can form the Knowledge of *Jesus Christ*, and of a Redemption purchas'd for us, of a Mediator of the new Covenant,[5] and of an Intercessor, at the Foot-stool of God's Throne; I say, nothing but a Revelation from Heaven, can form these in the Soul, and that therefore the Gospel of our Lord and Saviour *Jesus Christ*; I mean, the Word of God, and the Spirit of God promis'd for the Guide and Sanctifier of his People, are the absolutely necessary Instructors of the Souls of Men, in the saving Knowledge of God, and the Means of Salvation.

I therefore diverted the present Discourse between me and my Man, rising up hastily, as upon some sudden Occasion of going

---

1 Teacher.

2 Someone who addresses ethical dilemmas by examining the particular circumstances of individual cases.

3 2 Peter 2:4: "For if God spared not the angels that sinned, but cast them down to hell, and delivered them into chains of darkness, to be reserved unto judgment."

4 Revelation 20:2-3: "And he laid hold on the dragon, that old serpent, which is the Devil, and Satan, and bound him a thousand years, And cast him into the bottomless pit."

5 Hebrews 12:24.

out; then sending him for something a good way off, I seriously pray'd to God that he would enable me to instruct savingly this poor Savage, assisting by his Spirit the Heart of the poor ignorant Creature, to receive the Light of the Knowledge of God in *Christ*, reconciling him to himself, and would guide me to speak so to him from the Word of God, as his Conscience might be convinc'd, his Eyes open'd, and his Soul sav'd. When he came again to me, I entred into a long Discourse with him upon the Subject of the Redemption of Man by the Saviour of the World, and of the Doctrine of the Gospel preach'd from Heaven, *viz.* of Repentance towards God, and Faith in our Blessed Lord *Jesus*. I then explain'd to him, as well as I could, why our Blessed Redeemer took not on him the Nature of Angels, but the Seed of *Abraham*,[1] and how for that Reason the fallen Angels had no Share in the Redemption; that he came only to the lost Sheep of the House of *Israel*, and the like.

I had, *God knows*, more Sincerity than Knowledge, in all the Methods I took for this poor Creature's Instruction, and must acknowledge what I believe all that act upon the same Principle will find, That in laying Things open to him, I really inform'd and instructed my self in many Things, that either I did not know, or had not fully consider'd before; but which occurr'd naturally to my Mind, upon my searching into them, for the Information of this poor Savage; and I had more Affection[2] in my Enquiry after Things upon this Occasion, than ever I felt before; so that whether this poor wild Wretch was the better for me, or no, I had great Reason to be thankful that ever he came to me: My Grief set lighter upon me, my Habitation grew comfortable to me beyond Measure; and when I reflected that in this solitary Life which I had been confin'd to, I had not only been moved my self to look up to Heaven, and to seek to the Hand that had brought me there; but was now to be made an Instrument under Providence to save the Life, and *for ought I knew*, the Soul of a poor Savage, and bring him to the true Knowledge of Religion, and of the Christian Doctrine, that he might know Christ Jesus, *to know whom is Life eternal*. I say, when I reflected upon all these Things, a secret Joy run through every Part of my Soul, and I frequently rejoyc'd that ever I was brought to this Place, which I had so often thought the most dreadful of all Afflictions that could possibly have befallen me.

---

1 Hebrews 2:16.

2 Inclination.

In this thankful Frame I continu'd all the Remainder of my Time, and the Conversation which employ'd the Hours between *Friday* and I, was such, as made the three Years which we liv'd there together perfectly and compleatly happy, *if any such Thing as compleat Happiness can be form'd in a sublunary*[1] *State.* The Savage was now a good Christian, a much better than I; though I have reason to hope, and bless God for it, that we were equally penitent, and comforted restor'd Penitents; we had here the Word of God to read, and no farther off from his Spirit to instruct, than if we had been in *England.*

I always apply'd my self in Reading the Scripture, to let him know, as well as I could, the Meaning of what I read; and he again, by his serious Enquiries, and Questionings, made me, *as I said before,* a much better Scholar in the Scripture Knowledge, than I should ever have been by my own private meer Reading. Another thing I cannot refrain from observing here also from Experience, in this retir'd Part of my Life, *viz.* How infinite and inexpressible a Blessing it is, that the Knowledge of God, and of the Doctrine of Salvation by *Christ Jesus,* is so plainly laid down in the Word of God; so easy to be receiv'd and understood: That as the bare reading the Scripture made me capable of understanding enough of my Duty, to carry me directly on to the great Work of sincere Repentance for my Sins, and laying hold of a Saviour for Life and Salvation, to a stated Reformation in Practice, and Obedience to all God's Commands, and this without any Teacher or Instructer; I mean, humane; so the same plain Instruction sufficiently serv'd to the enlightning this Savage Creature, and bringing him to be such a Christian, as I have known few equal to him in my Life.

As to all the Disputes, Wranglings, Strife and Contention, which has happen'd in the World about Religion, whether Niceties in Doctrines, or Schemes of Church Government, they were all perfectly useless to us; as for ought I can yet see, they have been to all the rest of the World: We had the *sure Guide* to Heaven, *viz.* The Word of God; and we had, *blessed be God,* comfortable Views of the Spirit of God teaching and instructing us by his Word, *leading us into all Truth,*[2] and making us both willing and obedient to the Instruction of his Word, and I cannot see the least Use that the greatest Knowledge of the disputed Points in Religion which have made such Confusions in the World would have

---

1 Earthly (literally, *beneath the moon*).
2 John 16:13.

been to us, if we could have obtain'd it; but I must go on with the Historical Part of Things, and take every Part in its order.

After *Friday* and I became more intimately acquainted, and that he could understand almost all I said to him, and speak fluently, though in broken *English* to me; I acquainted him with my own Story, or at least so much of it as related to my coming into the Place, how I had liv'd there, and how long. I let him into the Mystery, for such it was to him, of Gunpowder, and Bullet, and taught him how to shoot: I gave him a Knife, which he was wonderfully delighted with, and I made him a Belt, with a Frog hanging to it, such as in *England* we wear Hangers[1] in; and in the Frog, instead of a Hanger, I gave him a Hatchet, which was not only as good a Weapon in some Cases, but much more useful upon other Occasions.

I describ'd to him the Country of *Europe*, and particularly *England*, which I came from; how we liv'd, how we worshipp'd God, how we behav'd to one another; and how we traded in Ships to all Parts of the World: I gave him an Account of the Wreck which I had been on board of, and shew'd him as near as I could, the Place where she lay; but she was all beaten in Pieces before, and gone.

I shew'd him the Ruins of our Boat, which we lost when we escap'd, and which I could not stir with my whole Strength then; but was now fallen almost all to Pieces: Upon seeing this Boat, *Friday* stood musing a great while, and said nothing; I ask'd him what it was he study'd upon, at last says he, *me see such Boat like come to Place at my Nation.*

I did not understand him a good while; but at last, when I had examin'd farther into it, I understood by him, that a Boat, such as that had been, came on Shore upon the Country where he liv'd; that is, as he explain'd it, was driven thither by Stress of Weather: I presently imagin'd, that some *European* Ship must have been cast away upon their Coast, and the Boat might get loose, and drive a Shore; but was so dull, that I never once thought of Men making escape from a Wreck thither, much less whence they might come; so I only enquir'd after a Description of the Boat.

Friday describ'd the Boat to me well enough; but brought me better to understand him, when he added with some Warmth, *we save the white Mans from drown*: Then I presently ask'd him, if there was any *white Mans*, as he call'd them, in the Boat; *yes*, he

---

1 Short sword.

said, *the Boat full white Mans*: I ask'd him how many; he told upon his Fingers seventeen: I ask'd him then what become of them; he told me, *they live, they dwell at my Nation.*

This put new Thoughts into my Head; for I presently imagin'd, that these might be the Men belonging to the Ship, that was cast away in Sight of *my Island*, as I now call it; and who after the Ship was struck on the Rock, and they saw her inevitably lost, had sav'd themselves in their Boat, and were landed upon that wild Shore among the Savages.

Upon this, I enquir'd of him more critically, What was become of them? He assur'd me they lived still there; that they had been there about four Years; that the Savages let them alone, and gave them Victuals to live. I ask'd him, How it came to pass they did not kill them and eat them? He said, *No, they make Brother with them*; that is, as I understood him, a Truce: And then he added, *They no eat Mans but when make the War fight*; that is to say, they never eat any Men but such as come to fight with them, and are taken in Battle.

It was after this some considerable Time, that being upon the Top of the Hill, at the *East* Side of the Island, from whence as I have said, I had in a clear Day discover'd the Main,[1] or Continent of *America*; *Friday*, the Weather being very serene, looks very earnestly towards the Main Land, and in a kind of Surprise, falls a jumping and dancing, and calls out to me, for I was at some Distance from him: I ask'd him, What was the Matter? *O joy!* Says he, *O glad! There see my Country, there my Nation!*

I observ'd an extraordinary Sense of Pleasure appear'd in his Face, and his Eyes sparkled, and his Countenance discover'd a strange Eagerness, as if he had a Mind to be in his own Country again; and this Observation of mine, put a great many Thoughts into me, which made me at first not so easy about my new Man *Friday* as I was before; and I made no doubt, but that if *Friday* could get back to his own Nation again, he would not only forget all his Religion, but all his Obligation to me; and would be forward enough to give his Countrymen an Account of me, and come back perhaps with a hundred or two of them, and make a Feast upon me, at which he might be as merry as he us'd to be with those of his Enemies, when they were taken in War.

But I wrong'd the poor honest Creature very much, for which I was very sorry afterwards. However as my Jealousy[2] encreased,

---

1 Mainland.

2 Apprehension, mistrust.

and held me some Weeks, I was a little more circumspect, and not so familiar and kind to him as before; in which I was certainly in the Wrong too, the honest grateful Creature having no thought about it, but what consisted[1] with the best Principles, both as a religious Christian, and as a grateful Friend, as appeared afterwards to my full Satisfaction.

While my Jealousy of him lasted, you may be sure I was every Day pumping him to see if he would discover any of the new Thoughts, which I suspected were in him; but I found every thing he said was so Honest, and so Innocent, that I could find nothing to nourish my Suspicion; and in spight of all my Uneasiness he made me at last entirely his own again, nor did he in the least perceive that I was Uneasie, and therefore I could not suspect him of Deceit.

One Day walking up the same Hill, but the Weather being haizy at Sea, so that we could not see the Continent, I call'd to him, and said, *Friday*, do not you wish your self in your own Country, your own Nation? Yes, he said, *he be much O glad to be at his own Nation.* What would you do there said I, would you turn Wild again, eat Mens Flesh again, and be a Savage as you were before. He lookt full of Concern, and shaking his Head said; *No no,* Friday *tell them to live Good*, tell them *to pray God*, tell them *to eat Corn bread, Cattle-flesh, Milk, no eat Man again*: Why then said I to him, *They will kill you.* He look'd grave at that, and then said, *No, they no kill me, they willing love learn*: He meant by this, they would be willing to learn. He added, they learn'd much of the Bearded-Mans that come in the Boat. Then I ask'd him if he would go back to them? He smil'd at that, and told me he could not swim so far. I told him I would make a *Canoe* for him. He told me, *he would go, if I would go with him.* I go! says I, why they will Eat me if I come there? No, no, says he, *me make they no Eat you; me make they much Love you*: He meant he would tell them how I had kill'd his Enemies, and sav'd his Life, and so he would make them love me; then he told me as well as he could, how kind they were to seventeen White-men, or Bearded-men, as he call'd them, who came on Shore there in Distress.

From this time I confess I had a Mind to venture over, and see if I could possibly joyn with these Bearded-men, who I made no doubt were *Spaniards* or *Portuguese*; not doubting but if I could we might find some Method to Escape from thence, being upon

---

1 Was consistent.

the Continent, and a good Company together; better than I could from an Island 40 Miles off the Shore, and alone without Help. So after some Days I took *Friday* to work again, by way of Discourse, and told him I would give him a Boat to go back to his own Nation; and accordingly I carry'd him to my Frigate which lay on the other Side of the Island, and having clear'd it of Water, for I always kept it sunk in the Water; I brought it out, shewed it him, and we both went into it.

I found he was a most dextrous Fellow at managing it, would make it go almost as swift and fast again as I could; so when he was in, I said to him, Well now, *Friday*, shall we go to your Nation? He look'd very dull[1] at my saying so, which it seems was, because he thought the Boat too small to go so far. I told him then I had a bigger; so the next Day I went to the Place where the first Boat lay which I had made, but which I could not get into Water: He said that was big enough; but then as I had taken no Care of it, and it had lain two or three and twenty Years there, the Sun had split and dry'd it, that it was in a manner rotten. *Friday* told me such a Boat would do very well, and would carry *much enough Vittle,*[2] *Drink, Bread,* that was his Way of Talking.

Upon the whole, I was by this Time so fix'd upon my Design of going over with him to the Continent, that I told him we would go and make one as big as that, and he should go home in it. He answer'd not one Word, but look'd very grave and sad: I ask'd him what was the matter with him? He ask'd me again thus; *Why, you angry mad with* Friday, *what me done?* I ask'd him what he meant; I told him I was not angry with him at all. *No angry! No angry!* says he, repeating the Words several Times, *Why send* Friday *home away to my Nation?* Why, (says I) *Friday*, did you not say you wish'd you were there? *Yes, yes*, says he, *wish be both there, no wish* Friday *there, no Master there*. In a Word, he would not think of going there without me; *I go there!* Friday, (says I) *what shall I do there?* He turn'd very quick upon me at this: *You do great deal much good*, says he, *you teach wild Mans be good sober tame Mans; you tell them know God, pray God, and live new Life. Alas!* Friday, (says I) *thou knowest not what thou sayest, I am but an ignorant Man my self. Yes, yes*, says he, *you teachee me Good, you teachee them Good. No, no*, Friday, (says I) *you shall go without me, leave me here to live*

---

1 Sad, gloomy, cheerless.
2 Victuals.

by my self, as I did before. He look'd confus'd again at that Word, and running to one of the Hatchets which he used to wear, he takes it up hastily, comes and gives it me, *What must I do with this?* says I to him. *You take, kill* Friday; (says he.) *What must I kill you for?* said I again. He returns very quick, *What you send* Friday *away for? take, kill* Friday, *no send* Friday *away.* This he spoke so earnestly, that I saw Tears stand in his Eyes: In a Word, I so plainly discover'd the utmost Affection in him to me, and a firm Resolution in him, that I told him then, and often after, that I would never send him away from me, if he was willing to stay with me.

Upon the whole, as I found by all his Discourse a settled Affection to me, and that nothing should part him from me, so I found all the Foundation of his Desire to go to his own Country, was laid in his ardent Affection to the People, and his Hopes of my doing them good; a Thing which as I had no Notion of my self, so I had not the least Thought or Intention, or Desire of undertaking it. But still I found a strong Inclination to my attempting an Escape as above, founded on the Supposition gather'd from the Discourse, (*viz.*) That there were seventeen bearded Men there; and therefore, without any more Delay, I went to Work with *Friday* to find out a great Tree proper to fell, and make a large Periagua or Canoe to undertake the Voyage. There were Trees enough in the Island to have built a little Fleet, not of Periagua's and Canoes, but even of good large Vessels. But the main Thing I look'd at, was to get one so near the Water that we might launch it when it was made, to avoid the Mistake I committed at first.

At last, *Friday* pitch'd upon a Tree, for I found he knew much better than I what kind of Wood was fittest for it, nor can I tell to this Day what Wood to call the Tree we cut down, except that it was very like the Tree we call *Fustic*, or between that and the *Nicaragua* Wood, for it was much of the same Colour and Smell. *Friday* was for burning the Hollow or Cavity of this Tree out to make it for a Boat. But I shew'd him how rather to cut it out with Tools, which, after I had shew'd him how to use, he did very handily, and in about a Month's hard Labour, we finished it, and made it very handsome, especially when with our Axes, which I shew'd him how to handle, we cut and hew'd the out-side into the true Shape of a Boat; after this, however, it cost us near a Fortnight's Time to get her along as it were Inch by Inch upon great Rowlers into the Water. But when she was in, she would have carry'd twenty Men with great Ease.

When she was in the Water, and tho' she was so big it amazed me to see with what Dexterity and how swift my Man *Friday* would manage her, turn her, and paddle her along; so I ask'd him if he would, and if we might venture over in her; *Yes*, he said, *he venture over in her very well, tho' great blow Wind.* However, I had a farther Design that he knew nothing of, and that was to make a Mast and Sail and to fit her with an Anchor and Cable: As to a Mast, that was easy enough to get; so I pitch'd upon a strait young Cedar-Tree, which I found near the Place, and which there was great Plenty of in the Island, and I set *Friday* to Work to cut it down, and gave him Directions how to shape and order it. But as to the Sail, that was my particular Care; I knew I had old Sails, or rather Pieces of old Sails enough; but as I had had them now six and twenty Years by me, and had not been very careful to preserve them, not imagining that I should ever have this kind of Use for them, I did not doubt but they were all rotten, and indeed most of them were so; however, I found two Pieces which appear'd pretty good, and with these I went to Work, and with a great deal of Pains, and awkward tedious stitching (you may be sure) for Want of Needles, I at length made a three Corner'd ugly Thing, like what we call in *England*, a Shoulder of Mutton Sail, to go with a Boom at bottom, and a little short Sprit at the Top, such as usually our Ship's Long-Boats sail with, and such as I best knew how to manage; because it was such a one as I had to the Boat, in which I made my Escape from *Barbary*, as related in the first Part of my Story.

I was near two Months performing this last Work, *viz.* rigging and fitting my Mast and Sails; for I finish'd them very compleat, making a small Stay,[1] and a Sail, or Foresail to it, to assist, if we should turn to Windward; and which was more than all, I fix'd a Rudder to the Stern of her, to steer with; and though I was but a bungling Shipwright, yet as I knew the Usefulness, and even Necessity of such a Thing, I apply'd my self with so much Pains to do it, that at last I brought it to pass; though considering the many dull Contrivances I had for it that fail'd, I think it cost me almost as much Labour as making the Boat.

After all this was done too, I had my Man *Friday* to teach as to what belong'd to the Navigation of my Boat; for though he

---

1 A strong rope that supports the mast, and from which the sail is hoisted.

knew very well how to paddle a *Canoe*, he knew nothing what belong'd to a Sail, and a Rudder; and was the most amaz'd, when he saw me work the Boat too and again[1] in the Sea by the Rudder, and how the Sail gyb'd,[2] and fill'd this way, or that way, as the Course we sail'd chang'd; I say, when he saw this, he stood like one, astonish'd, and amaz'd: However, with a little Use, I made all these Things familiar to him; and he became an expert Sailor, except that as to the Compass, I could make him understand very little of that. On the other hand, as there was very little cloudy Weather, and seldom or never any Fogs in those Parts, there was the less occasion for a Compass, seeing the Stars were always to be seen by Night, and the Shore by Day, except in the rainy Seasons, and then no body car'd to stir abroad, either by Land or Sea.

I was now entred on the seven and twentieth Year of my Captivity in this Place; though the three last Years that I had this Creature with me, ought rather to be left out of the Account, my Habitation being quite of another kind than in all the rest of the Time. I kept the Anniversary of my Landing here with the same Thankfulness to God for his Mercies, as at first; and if I had such Cause of Acknowledgment at first, I had much more so now, having such additional Testimonies of the Care of Providence over me, and the great Hopes I had of being effectually, and speedily deliver'd; for I had an invincible Impression upon my Thoughts, that my Deliverance was at hand, and that I should not be another Year in this Place: However, I went on with my Husbandry, digging, planting, fencing, as usual; I gather'd and cur'd my Grapes, and did every necessary Thing as before.

The rainy Season was in the mean Time upon me, when I kept more within Doors than at other Times; so I had stow'd our new Vessel as secure as we could, bringing her up into the Creek, where as I said, in the Beginning I landed my Rafts from the Ship, and haling her up to the Shore, at high Water mark, I made my Man *Friday* dig a little Dock, just big enough to hold her, and just deep enough to give her Water enough to fleet in; and then when the Tide was out, we made a strong Dam cross the End of it, to keep the Water out; and so she lay dry, as to the Tide from the Sea; and to keep the Rain off, we laid a great many Boughs of Trees, so thick, that she was as well thatch'd as a House; and

---

1 To and fro.

2 *Jibed*: swung from one side of the boat to the other.

thus we waited for the Month of *November* and *December,* in which I design'd to make my Adventure.

When the settled Season began to come in, as the thought of my Design return'd with the fair Weather, I was preparing daily for the Voyage; and the first Thing I did, was to lay by a certain Quantity of Provisions, being the Stores for our Voyage; and intended in a Week or a Fortnight's Time, to open the Dock, and launch out our Boat. I was busy one Morning upon some Thing of this kind, when I call'd to *Friday,* and bid him go to the Sea Shore, and see if he could find a Turtle, or Tortoise, a Thing which we generally got once a Week, for the Sake of the Eggs, as well as the Flesh: *Friday* had not been long gone, when he came running back, and flew over my outer Wall, or Fence, like one that felt not the Ground, or the Steps he set his Feet on; and before I had time to speak to him, he cries out to me, *O Master! O Master! O Sorrow! O bad!* What's the Matter, *Friday,* says I; *O yonder, there,* says he, *one, two, three Canoe! one, two, three!* By his way of speaking, I concluded there were six; but on enquiry, I found it was but three: Well, *Friday,* says I, do not be frighted; so I heartned him up as well as I could: However, I saw the poor Fellow was most terribly scar'd; for nothing ran in his Head but that they were come to look for him, and would cut him in Pieces, and eat him; and the poor Fellow trembled so, that I scarce knew what to do with him: I comforted him as well as I could, and told him I was in as much Danger as he, and that they would eat me as well as him; *but,* says I, *Friday, we must resolve to fight them; Can you fight,* Friday? *Me shoot,* says he, *but there come many great Number.* No matter for that, said I again, our Guns will fright them that we do not kill; so I ask'd him, Whether if I resolv'd to defend him, he would defend me, and stand by me, and do just as I bid him? He said, *Me die, when you bid die, Master;* so I went and fetch'd a good Dram of Rum, and gave him; for I had been so good a Husband of my Rum, that I had a great deal left: When he had drank it, I made him take the two Fowling-Pieces, which we always carry'd, and load them with large Swan-Shot, as big as small Pistol Bullets; then I took four Muskets, and loaded them with two Slugs, and five small Bullets each; and my two Pistols I loaded with a Brace[1] of Bullets each; I hung my great Sword as usual, naked by my Side, and gave *Friday* his Hatchet.

When I had thus prepar'd my self, I took my Perspective-Glass, and went up to the Side of the Hill, to see what I could dis-

---

1 Pair.

cover; and I found quickly, by my Glass, that there were one and twenty Savages, three Prisoners, and, three *Canoes*; and that their whole Business seem'd to be the triumphant Banquet upon these three humane Bodies, (a barbarous Feast indeed) but nothing more than as I had observ'd was usual with them.

I observ'd also, that they were landed not where they had done, when *Friday* made his Escape; but nearer to my Creek, where the Shore was low, and where a thick Wood came close almost down to the Sea: This, with the Abhorrence of the inhumane Errand these Wretches came about, fill'd me with such Indignation, that I came down again to *Friday*, and told him, I was resolv'd to go down to them, and kill them all; and ask'd him, If he would stand by me? He was now gotten over his Fright, and his Spirits being a little rais'd, with the Dram I had given him, he was very chearful, and told me, as before, *he would die, when I bid die.*

In this Fit of Fury, I took first and divided the Arms which I had charg'd, as before, between us; I gave *Friday* one Pistol to stick in his Girdle, and three Guns upon his Shoulder; and I took one Pistol, and the other three my self; and in this Posture we march'd out: I took a small Bottle of Rum in my Pocket, and gave *Friday* a large Bag, with more Powder and Bullet; and as to Orders, I charg'd him to keep close behind me, and not to stir, or shoot, or do any Thing, till I bid him; and in the mean Time, not to speak a Word: In this Posture I fetch'd a Compass[1] to my Right-Hand, of near a Mile, as well to get over the Creek, as to get into the Wood; so that I might come within shoot of them, before I should be discover'd, which I had seen by my Glass, it was easy to do.

While I was making this March, my former Thoughts return-ing, I began to abate my Resolution; I do not mean, that I enter-tain'd any Fear of their Number; for as they were naked, unarm'd Wretches, 'tis certain I was superior to them; nay, though I had been alone; but it occurr'd to my Thoughts, What Call? What Occasion? much less, What Necessity I was in to go and dip my Hands in Blood, to attack People, who had neither done, or intended me any Wrong? Who as to me were innocent, and whose barbarous Customs were their own Disaster, being in them a Token[2] indeed of God's having left them, with the other Nations of that Part of the World, to such Stupidity,[3] and to such inhu-

---

1 Made a circle.

2 Sign.

3 Indifference, inability to feel emotion.

mane Courses; but did not call me to take upon me to be a Judge of their Actions, much less an Executioner of his Justice; that whenever he thought fit, he would take the Cause into his own Hands, and by national Vengeance punish them as a People, for national Crimes; but that in the mean time, it was none of my Business; that it was true, *Friday* might justify it, because he was a declar'd Enemy, and in a State of War with those very particular People; and it was lawful for him to attack them; but I could not say the same with respect to me: These Things were so warmly press'd upon my Thoughts, all the way as I went, that I resolv'd I would only go and place my self near them, that I might observe their barbarous Feast, and that I would act then as God should direct; but that unless something offer'd that was more a Call to me than yet I knew of, I would not meddle with them.

With this Resolution I enter'd the Wood, and with all possible Waryness and Silence, *Friday* following close at my Heels, I march'd till I came to the Skirt of the Wood, on the Side which was next to them; only that one Corner of the Wood lay between me and them; here I call'd softly to *Friday*, and shewing him a great Tree, which was just at the Corner of the Wood, I bad him go to the Tree, and bring me Word if he could see there plainly what they were doing; he did so, and came immediately back to me, and told me they might be plainly view'd there; that they were all about their Fire, eating the Flesh of one of their Prisoners; and that another lay bound upon the Sand, a little from them, which he said they would kill next, and which fir'd all the very Soul within me; he told me it was not one of their Nation; but one of the bearded Men, who he had told me of, that came to their Country in the Boat: I was fill'd with Horror at the very naming the white-bearded Man, and going to the Tree, I saw plainly by my Glass, a white Man who lay upon the Beach of the Sea, with his Hands and his Feet ty'd, with Flags, or Things like Rushes; and that he was an *European*, and had Cloaths on.

There was another Tree, and a little Thicket beyond it, about fifty Yards nearer to them than the Place where I was, which by going a little way about, I saw I might come at undiscover'd, and that then I should be within half Shot of them; so I with-held my Passion, though I was indeed enrag'd to the highest Degree, and going back about twenty Paces, I got behind some Bushes, which held all the way, till I came to the other Tree; and then I came to a little rising Ground, which gave me a full View of them, at the Distance of about eighty Yards.

I had now not a Moment to loose; for nineteen of the dreadful Wretches sat upon the Ground, all close huddled together, and had just sent the other two to butcher the poor *Christian*, and bring him perhaps Limb by Limb to their Fire, and they were stoop'd down to untie the Bands, at his Feet; I turn'd to *Friday*, now *Friday*, said I, do as I bid thee; *Friday* said he would; then *Friday*, says I, do exactly as you see me do, 'fail in nothing; so I set down one of the Muskets, and the Fowling-Piece, upon the Ground, and *Friday* did the like by his; and with the other Musket, I took my aim at the Savages, bidding him do the like; then asking him, If he was ready? He said, yes, then fire at them, said I; and the same Moment I fir'd also.

Friday took his Aim so much better than I, that on the Side that he shot, he kill'd two of them, and wounded three more; and on my Side, I kill'd one, and wounded two: They were, you may be sure, in a dreadful Consternation; and all of them, who were not hurt, jump'd up upon their Feet, but did not immediately know which way to run, or which way to look; for they knew not from whence their Destruction came: *Friday* kept his Eyes close upon me, that as I had bid him, he might observe what I did; so as soon as the first Shot was made, I threw down the Piece, and took up the Fowling-Piece, and *Friday* did the like; he see me cock, and present, he did the same again; Are you ready? *Friday*, said I; yes, says he; let fly then, says I, in the Name of God, and with that I fir'd again among the amaz'd[1] Wretches, and so did *Friday*; and as our Pieces were now loaden with what I call'd Swan-Shot, or small Pistol Bullets, we found only two drop; but so many were wounded, that they run about yelling, and skreaming, like mad Creatures, all bloody, and miserably wounded, most of them; whereof three more fell quickly after, though not quite dead.

Now *Friday*, says I, laying down the discharg'd Pieces, and taking up the Musket, which was yet loaden; follow me, says I, which he did, with a great deal of Courage; upon which I rush'd out of the Wood, and shew'd my self, and *Friday* close at my Foot; as soon as I perceiv'd they saw me, I shouted as loud as I could, and bad *Friday* do so too; and running as fast as I could, *which by the way, was not very fast, being loaden with Arms as I was*, I made directly towards the poor Victim, who was, as I said, lying upon the Beach, or Shore, between the Place where they sat, and the Sea; the two Butchers who were just going to work with him, had left him, at the Suprize of our first Fire, and fled in a terrible

---

1   Terror-stricken; also, bewildered.

Fright, to the Sea Side, and had jump'd into a *Canoe*, and three more of the rest made the same way; I turn'd to *Friday*, and bid him step forwards, and fire at them; he understood me immediately, and running about forty Yards, to be near them, he shot at them, and I thought he had kill'd them all; for I see them all fall of a Heap into the Boat; though I saw two of them up again quickly: However, he kill'd two of them, and wounded the third; so that he lay down in the Bottom of the Boat, as if he had been dead.

While my Man *Friday* fir'd at them, I pull'd out my Knife, and cut the Flags that bound the poor Victim, and loosing his Hands, and Feet, I lifted him up, and ask'd him in the *Portuguese* Tongue, What he was? He answer'd in Latin,[1] *Christianus*; but was so weak, and faint, that he could scarce stand, or speak; I took my Bottle out of my Pocket, and gave it him, making Signs that he should drink, which he did; and I gave him a Piece of Bread, which he eat; then I ask'd him, What Countryman he was? And he said, *Espagniole*; and being a little recover'd, let me know by all the Signs he could possibly make, how much he was in my Debt for his Deliverance; *Seignior*, said I, with as much *Spanish* as I could make up, we will talk afterwards; but we must fight now; if you have any Strength left, take this Pistol, and Sword, and lay about you; he took them very thankfully, and no sooner had he the Arms in his Hands, but as if they had put new Vigour into him, he flew upon his Murtherers, like a Fury, and had cut two of them in Pieces, in an instant; for the Truth is, as the whole was a Surprize to them; so the poor Creatures were so much frighted with the Noise of our Pieces, that they fell down for meer Amazement, and Fear; and had no more Power to attempt their own Escape, than their Flesh had to resist our Shot; and that was the Case of those Five that *Friday* shot at in the Boat; for as three of them fell with the Hurt they receiv'd; so the other two fell with the Fright.

I kept my Piece in my Hand still, without firing, being willing to keep my Charge ready; because I had given the *Spaniard* my Pistol, and Sword; so I call'd to *Friday*, and bad him run up to the Tree, from whence we first fir'd, and fetch the Arms which lay there, that had been discharg'd, which he did with great Swiftness; and then giving him my Musket, I sat down my self to load all the rest again, and bad them come to me when they wanted:

---

1   The Spaniard presumably knows the Latin word *Christianus* from the
    Catholic liturgy.

While I was loading these Pieces, there happen'd a fierce Engagement between the *Spaniard*, and one of the Savages, who made at
him with one of their great wooden Swords, the same Weapon
that was to have kill'd him before, if I had not prevented it: The
Spaniard, who was as bold, and as brave as could be imagin'd,
though weak, had fought this *Indian* a good while, and had cut
him two great Wounds on his Head; but the Savage being a stout
lusty Fellow, closing in with him, had thrown him down (being
faint) and was wringing my Sword out of his Hand, when the
Spaniard, tho' undermost, wisely quitting the Sword, drew the
Pistol from his Girdle, shot the Savage through the Body, and
kill'd him upon the Spot; before I, who was running to help him,
could come near him.

Friday being now left to his Liberty, pursu'd the flying
Wretches with no Weapon in his Hand, but his Hatchet; and with
that he dispatch'd those three, who, as I said before, were
wounded at first and fallen, and all the rest he could come up
with, and the *Spaniard* coming to me for a Gun, I gave him one
of the Fowling-Pieces, with which he pursu'd two of the Savages,
and wounded them both; but as he was not able to run, they both
got from him into the Wood, where *Friday* pursu'd them, and
kill'd one of them; but the other was too nimble for him, and
though he was wounded, yet had plunged himself into the Sea,
and swam with all his might off to those two who were left in the
Canoe, which three in the *Canoe*, with one wounded, who we
know not whether he dy'd or no, were all that escap'd our Hands
of one and twenty: The Account of the Rest is as follows;

3 Kill'd at our first Shot from the Tree.
2 Kill'd at the next Shot.
2 Kill'd by *Friday* in the Boat.
2 Kill'd by *Ditto*, of those at first wounded.
1 Kill'd by *Ditto*, in the Wood.
3 Kill'd by the *Spaniard*.
4 Kill'd, being found dropp'd here and there of their Wounds,
or kill'd by *Friday* in his Chase of them.
4 Escap'd in the Boat, whereof one wounded if not dead.

———

21 In all.

———

Those that were in the *Canoe*, work'd hard to get out of Gun-
Shot; and though *Friday* made two or three Shot at them, I did

not find that he hit any of them: *Friday* would fain have had me took one of their *Canoes*, and pursu'd them; and indeed I was very anxious about their Escape, least carrying the News home to their People, they should come back perhaps with two or three hundred of their *Canoes*, and devour us by meer Multitude; so I consented to pursue them by Sea, and running to one of their *Canoes*, I jump'd in, and bad *Friday* follow me; but when I was in the *Canoe*, I was surpriz'd to find another poor Creature lye there alive, bound Hand and Foot, as the *Spaniard* was, for the Slaughter, and almost dead with Fear, not knowing what the Matter was; for he had not been able to look up over the Side of the Boat, he was ty'd so hard, Neck and Heels, and had been ty'd so long, that he had really but little Life in him.

I immediately cut the twisted Flags, or Rushes, which they had bound him with, and would have helped him up; but he could not stand, or speak, but groan'd most piteously, believing it seems still that he was only unbound in order to be kill'd.

When *Friday* came to him, I bad him speak to him, and tell him of his Deliverance, and pulling out my Bottle, made him give the poor Wretch a Dram, which, with the News of his being deliver'd, reviv'd him, and he sat up in the Boat; but when *Friday* came to hear him speak, and look in his Face, it would have mov'd any one to Tears, to have seen how *Friday* kiss'd him, embrac'd him, hugg'd him, cry'd, laugh'd, hollow'd, jump'd about, danc'd, sung, then cry'd again, wrung his Hands, beat his own Face, and Head, and then sung, and jump'd about again, like a distracted[1] Creature: It was a good while before I could make him speak to me, or tell me what was the Matter; but when he came a little to himself, he told me, that it was his Father.

It is not easy for me to express how it mov'd me to see what Extasy and filial Affection had work'd in this poor *Savage*, at the Sight of his Father, and of his being deliver'd from Death; nor indeed can I describe half the Extravagancies of his Affection after this; for he went into the Boat and out of the Boat a great many times: When he went in to him, he would sit down by him, open his Breast, and hold his Father's Head close to his Bosom, half an Hour together, to nourish it; then he took his Arms and Ankles, which were numb'd and stiff with the Binding, and chaffed and rubbed them with his Hands; and I perceiving what the Case was, gave him some Rum out of my Bottle, to rub them with, which did them a great deal of Good.

---

1   Crazed, out of one's mind.

This Action put an End to our Pursuit of the Canoe, with the other *Savages*, who were now gotten almost out of Sight; and it was happy for us that we did not; for it blew so hard within two Hours after, and before they could be gotten a Quarter of their Way, and continued blowing so hard all Night, and that from the *North-west*, which was against them, that I could not suppose their Boat could live, or that they ever reach'd to their own Coast.

But to return to *Friday*, he was so busy about his Father, that I could not find in my Heart to take him off for some time: But after I thought he could leave him a little, I call'd him to me, and he came jumping and laughing, and pleas'd to the highest Extream; then I ask'd him, If he had given his Father any Bread? He shook his Head, and said, *None: Ugly Dog eat all up self*; so I gave him a Cake of Bread out of a little Pouch I carry'd on Purpose; I also gave him a Dram for himself, but he would not taste it, but carry'd it to his Father: I had in my Pocket also two or three Bunches of my Raisins, so I gave him a Handful of them for his Father. He had no sooner given his Father these Raisins, but I saw him come out of the Boat, and run away, as if he had been bewitch'd, he run at such a Rate; for he was the swiftest Fellow of his Foot that ever I saw; I say, he run at such a Rate, that he was out of Sight, as it were, in an instant; and though I call'd, and hollow'd too, after him, it was all one, away he went, and in a Quarter of an Hour, I saw him come back again, though not so fast as he went; and as he came nearer, I found his Pace was slacker, because he had something in his Hand.

When he came up to me, I found he had been quite Home for an Earthen Jugg or Pot to bring his Father some fresh Water, and that he had got two more Cakes, or Loaves of Bread: The Bread he gave me, but the Water he carry'd to his Father: However, as I was very thirsty too, I took a little Sup of it. This Water reviv'd his Father more than all the Rum or Spirits I had given him; for he was just fainting with Thirst.

When his Father had drank, I call'd to him to know if there was any Water left; he said, yes; and I bad him give it to the poor *Spaniard*, who was in as much Want of it as his Father; and I sent one of the Cakes, that *Friday* brought, to the *Spaniard* too, who was indeed very weak, and was reposing himself upon a green Place under the Shade of a Tree; and whose Limbs were also very stiff, and very much swell'd with the rude Bandage he had been ty'd with. When I saw that upon *Friday's* coming to him with the Water, he sat up and drank, and took the Bread, and began to eat, I went to him, and gave him a Handful of Raisins; he look'd up in my Face with all the Tokens of Gratitude and Thankfulness, that could appear in any Countenance; but was so weak, notwithstanding he had so exerted himself in the Fight, that he could not stand up upon his Feet; he try'd to do it two or three times, but was really not able, his Ankles were so swell'd and so painful to him; so I bad him sit still, and caused *Friday* to rub his Ankles, and bathe them with Rum, as he had done his Father's.

I observ'd the poor affectionate Creature every two Minutes, or perhaps less, all the while he was here, turn'd his Head about, to see if his Father was in the same Place, and Posture, as he left him sitting; and at last he found he was not to be seen; at which he started up, and without speaking a Word, flew with that Swiftness to him, that one could scarce perceive his Feet to touch the Ground, as he went: But when he came, he only found he had laid himself down to ease his Limbs; so *Friday* came back to me presently, and I then spoke to the *Spaniard* to let *Friday* help him up if he could, and lead him to the Boat, and then he should carry him to our Dwelling, where I would take Care of him: But *Friday*, a lusty strong Fellow, took the *Spaniard* quite up upon his Back, and carry'd him away to the Boat, and set him down softly upon the Side or Gunnel of the Canoe, with his Feet in the inside of it, and then lifted him quite in, and set him close to his Father, and presently stepping out again, launched the Boat off, and paddled it along the Shore faster than I could walk, tho' the Wind blew pretty hard too; so he brought them both safe into our Creek; and leaving them in the Boat, runs away to fetch the other Canoe. As he pass'd me, I spoke to him, and ask'd him, whither he went, he told me, *Go fetch more Boat*; so away he went like the Wind; for sure never Man or Horse run like him, and he had the other Canoe in the Creek, almost as soon as I got to it by Land; so he wafted[1] me over, and then went to help our new Guests out of the Boat, which he did; but they were neither of them able to walk; so that poor *Friday* knew not what to do.

To remedy this, I went to Work in my Thought, and calling to *Friday* to bid them sit down on the Bank while he came to me, I soon made a Kind of Hand-Barrow to lay them on, and *Friday* and I carry'd them up both together upon it between us: But when we got them to the outside of our Wall or Fortification, we were at a worse Loss than before; for it was impossible to get them over; and I was resolv'd not to break it down: So I set to Work again; and *Friday* and I, in about 2 Hours time, made a

---

1 Waved.

very handsom Tent, cover'd with old Sails, and above that with Boughs of Trees, being in the Space without our outward Fence, and between that and the Grove of young Wood which I had planted: And here we made them two Beds of such things as I had (*viz.*) of good Rice-Straw, with Blankets laid upon it to lye on, and another to cover them on each Bed.

My Island was now peopled, and I thought my self very rich in Subjects; and it was a merry Reflection which I frequently made, How like a King I look'd. First of all, the whole Country was my own meer Property; so that I had an undoubted Right of Dominion. *2dly*, My People were perfectly subjected: I was absolute Lord and Law-giver; they all owed their Lives to me, and were ready to lay down their Lives, *if there had been Occasion of it*, for me. It was remarkable too, we had but three Subjects, and they were of three different Religions. My Man *Friday* was a Protestant, his Father was a *Pagan* and a *Cannibal*, and the *Spaniard* was a Papist:[1] However, I allow'd Liberty of Conscience throughout my Dominions: But this is by the Way.

As soon as I had secur'd my two weak rescued Prisoners, and given them Shelter, and a Place to rest them upon, I began to think of making some Provision for them: And the first thing I did, I order'd *Friday* to take a yearling Goat, betwixt a Kid and a Goat, out of my particular Flock, to be kill'd, when I cut off the hinder Quarter, and chopping it into small Pieces, I set *Friday* to Work to boiling and stewing, and made them a very good Dish, I assure you, of Flesh and Broth, having put some Barley and Rice also into the Broth; and as I cook'd it without Doors, for I made no Fire within my inner Wall, so I carry'd it all into the new Tent; and having set a Table there for them, I sat down and eat my own Dinner also with them, and, as well as I could, chear'd them and encourag'd them; *Friday* being my Interpreter, especially to his Father, and indeed to the *Spaniard* too; for the *Spaniard* spoke the Language of the *Savages* pretty well.

After we had dined, or rather supped, I order'd *Friday* to take one of the Canoes, and go and fetch our Muskets and other Fire-Arms, which for Want of time we had left upon the Place of Battle, and the next Day I order'd him to go and bury the dead Bodies of the Savages, which lay open to the Sun, and would presently be offensive; and I also order'd him to bury the horrid Remains of their barbarous Feast, which I knew were pretty much, and which I could not think of doing my self; nay, I could

---

1 Roman Catholic.

not bear to see them, if I went that Way: All which he punctually performed, and defaced[1] the very Appearance of the *Savages* being there; so that when I went again, I could scarce know where it was, otherwise than by the Corner of the Wood pointing to the Place.

I then began to enter into a little Conversation with my two new Subjects; and first I set *Friday* to enquire of his Father, what he thought of the Escape of the *Savages* in that Canoe, and whether we might expect a Return of them with a Power too great for us to resist: His first Opinion was, that the Savages in the Boat never could live out the Storm which blew that Night they went off, but must of Necessity be drowned or driven *South* to those other Shores where they were as sure to be devoured as they were to be drowned if they were cast away; but as to what they would do if they came safe on Shore, he said he knew not; but it was his Opinion that they were so dreadfully frighted with the Manner of their being attack'd, the Noise and the Fire, that he believed they would tell their People, they were all kill'd by Thunder and Lightning, not by the Hand of Man, and that the two which appear'd, *(viz.) Friday* and me, were two Heavenly Spirits or Furies, come down to destroy them, and not Men with Weapons: This he said he knew, because he heard them all cry out so in their Language to one another, for it was impossible to them to conceive that a Man could dart Fire, and speak Thunder, and kill at a Distance without lifting up the Hand, as was done now: And this old Savage was in the right; for, as I understood since by other Hands, the Savages never attempted to go over to the Island afterwards; they were so terrified with the Accounts given by those four Men, (for it seems they did escape the Sea) that they believ'd whoever went to that enchanted Island would be destroy'd with Fire from the Gods.

This however I knew not, and therefore was under continual Apprehensions for a good while, and kept always upon my Guard, me and all my Army; for as we were now four of us, I would have ventur'd upon a hundred of them fairly in the open Field at any Time.

In a little Time, however, no more Canoes appearing, the Fear of their Coming wore off, and I began to take my former Thoughts of a Voyage to the Main into Consideration, being likewise assur'd by *Friday's* Father, that I might depend upon good Usage from their Nation on his Account, if I would go.

---

1 Effaced, got rid of.

But my Thoughts were a little suspended, when I had a serious Discourse with the *Spaniard*, and when I understood that there were sixteen more of his Countrymen and *Portuguese*, who having been cast away, and made their Escape to that Side, liv'd there at Peace indeed with the Savages, but were very sore put to it for Necessaries, and indeed for Life: I ask'd him all the Particulars of their Voyage, and found they were a *Spanish* Ship bound from the *Rio de la Plata* to the *Havana*, being directed to leave their Loading there, which was chiefly Hides and Silver, and to bring back what *European* Goods they could meet with there; that they had five *Portuguese* Seamen on Board, who they took out of another Wreck; that five of their own Men were drowned when the first Ship was lost, and that these escaped thro' infinite Dangers and Hazards, and arriv'd almost starv'd on the *Cannibal* Coast, where they expected to have been devour'd every Moment.

He told me, they had some Arms with them, but they were perfectly useless, for that they had neither Powder or Ball, the Washing of the Sea having spoil'd all their Powder but a little, which they used at their first Landing to provide themselves some Food.

I ask'd him what he thought would become of them there, and if they had form'd no Design of making any Escape? He said, They had many Consultations about it, but that having neither Vessel, or Tools to build one, or Provisions of any kind, their Councils always ended in Tears and Despair.

I ask'd him how he thought they would receive a Proposal from me, which might tend towards an Escape? And whether, if they were all here, it might not be done? I told him with Freedom, I fear'd mostly their Treachery and ill Usage of me, if I put my Life in their Hands; for that Gratitude was no inherent Virtue in the Nature of Man; nor did Men always square their Dealings by the Obligations they had receiv'd, so much as they did by the Advantages they expected. I told him it would be very hard, that I should be the Instrument of their Deliverance, and that they should afterwards make me their Prisoner in *New Spain*,[1] where an *English* Man was certain to be made a Sacrifice, what Necessity, or what Accident soever, brought him thither: And that I had rather be deliver'd up to the *Savages*, and be devour'd alive, than fall into the merciless Claws of the Priests,

---

1 Spanish colonies in the Americas.

and be carry'd into the *Inquisition*.[1] I added, That otherwise I was perswaded, if they were all here, we might, with so many Hands, build a Bark[2] large enough to carry us all away, either to the *Brasils* South-ward, or to the Islands or *Spanish* Coast North-ward: But that if in Requital they should, when I had put Weapons into their Hands, carry me by Force among their own People, I might be ill used for my Kindness to them, and make my Case worse than it was before.

He answer'd with a great deal of Candor and Ingenuity, That their Condition was so miserable, and they were so sensible of it, that he believed they would abhor the Thought of using any Man unkindly that should contribute to their Deliverance; and that, if I pleased, he would go to them with the old Man, and discourse with them about it, and return again, and bring me their Answer: That he would make Conditions with them upon their solemn Oath, That they should be absolutely under my Leading, as their Com-mander and Captain; and that they should swear upon the Holy Sacraments and the Gospel, to be true to me, and to go to such Christian Country, as that I should agree to, and no other; and to be directed wholly and absolutely by my Orders, 'till they were landed safely in such Country, as I intended; and that he would bring a Contract from them under their Hands for that Purpose.

Then he told me, he would first swear to me himself, That he would never stir from me as long as he liv'd, 'till I gave him Orders; and that he would take my Side to the last Drop of his Blood, if there should happen the least Breach of Faith among his Country-men.

He told me, they were all of them very civil honest Men, and they were under the greatest Distress imaginable, having neither Weapons or Cloaths, nor any Food, but at the Mercy and Dis-cretion of the *Savages*; out of all Hopes of ever returning to their own Country; and that he was sure, if I would undertake their Relief, they would live and die by me.

Upon these Assurances, I resolv'd to venture to relieve them, if possible, and to send the old *Savage* and this *Spaniard* over to them to treat: But when we had gotten all things in a Readiness to go, the *Spaniard* himself started an Objection, which had so

---

1 Crusoe's fears are probably misplaced. The Spanish Church determined early in the sixteenth century that the Inquisition would not be applied to natives, and it was never rigorously applied in the New World. See p. 191, note 2.

2 A small ship.

much Prudence in it on one hand, and so much Sincerity on the other hand, that I could not but be very well satisfy'd in it; and by his Advice, put off the Deliverance of his Comerades, for at least half a Year. The Case was thus:

He had been with us now about a Month; during which time, I had let him see in what Manner I had provided, with the Assistance of Providence, for my Support; and he saw evidently what Stock of Corn and Rice I had laid up; which as it was more than sufficient for my self, so it was not sufficient, at least without good Husbandry, for my Family; now it was encreas'd to Number four: But much less would it be sufficient, if his Country-men, who were, as he said, fourteen[1] still alive, should come over. And least of all should it be sufficient to victual our Vessel, if we should build one, for a Voyage to any of the Christian Colonies of *America*. So he told me, he thought it would be more advisable, to let him and the two other, dig and cultivate some more Land, as much as I could spare Seed to sow; and that we should wait another Harvest, that we might have a Supply of Corn for his Country-men when they should come; for Want might be a Temptation to them to disagree, or not to think themselves delivered, otherwise than out of one Difficulty into another. You know, says he, the Children of *Israel*, though they rejoyc'd at first for their being deliver'd out of *Egypt*, yet rebell'd even against God himself that deliver'd them, when they came to want Bread in the Wilderness.[2]

His Caution was so seasonable,[3] and his Advice so good, that I could not but be very well pleased with his Proposal, as well as I was satisfy'd with his Fidelity. So we fell to digging all four of us, as well as the Wooden Tools we were furnish'd with permitted; and in about a Month's time, by the End of which it was Seed time, we had gotten as much Land cur'd[4] and trim'd up, as we sowed 22 Bushels of Barley on, and 16 Jarrs of Rice, which was in short all the Seed we had to spare; nor indeed did we leave our selves Barley sufficient for our own Food, for the six Months that

---

1 Elsewhere, Crusoe refers to sixteen Spaniards.

2 Exodus 16: 3: "And the children of Israel said unto [Moses and Aaron], Would to God we had died by the hand of the LORD in the land of Egypt, when we sat by the flesh pots, and when we did eat bread to the full; for ye have brought us forth into this wilderness, to kill this whole assembly with hunger."

3 Timely.

4 Cleared.

we had to expect our Crop, that is to say, reckoning from the time we set our Seed aside for sowing; for it is not to be supposed it is six Months in the Ground in the Country.

Having now Society enough, and our Number being sufficient to put us out of Fear of the *Savages*, if they had come, unless their Number had been very great, we went freely all over the Island, where-ever we found Occasion; and as here we had our Escape or Deliverance upon our Thoughts, it was impossible, *at least for me*, to have the Means of it out of mine; to this Purpose, I mark'd out several Trees which I thought fit for our Work, and I set *Friday* and his Father to cutting them down; and then I caused the *Spaniard*, to whom I imparted my Thought on that Affair, to oversee and direct their Work. I shewed them with what indefatigable Pains I had hewed a large Tree into single Planks, and I caused them to do the like, till they had made about a Dozen large Planks of good Oak, near 2 Foot broad, 35 Foot long, and from 2 Inches to 4 Inches thick: What prodigious Labour it took up, any one may imagine.

At the same time I contriv'd to encrease my little Flock of tame Goats as much as I could; and to this Purpose, I made *Friday* and the *Spaniard* go out one Day, and my self with *Friday* the next Day; for we took our Turns: And by this Means we got above 20 young Kids to breed up with the rest; for when-ever we shot the Dam, we saved the Kids, and added them to our Flock: But above all, the Season for curing the Grapes coming on, I caused such a prodigious Quantity to be hung up in the Sun, that I believe, had we been at *Alicant*,[1] where the Raisins of the Sun are cur'd, we could have fill'd 60 or 80 Barrels; and these with our Bread was a great Part of our Food, and very good living too, I assure you; for it is an exceeding nourishing Food.

It was now Harvest, and our Crop in good Order; it was not the most plentiful Encrease I had seen in the Island, but however it was enough to answer our End; for from our 22 Bushels of Barley, we brought in and thrashed out above 220 Bushels; and the like in Proportion of the Rice, which was Store enough for our Food to the next Harvest, tho' all the 16 *Spaniards* had been on Shore with me; or if we had been ready for a Voyage, it would very plentifully have victualled our Ship, to have carry'd us to any Part of the World, that is to say, of *America*.

When we had thus hous'd and secur'd our Magazine of Corn, we fell to Work to make more Wicker Work, (*viz.*) great Baskets

---

1 Mediterranean port in Spain.

in which we kept it; and the *Spaniard* was very handy and dexterous at this Part, and often blam'd me that I did not make some things, for Defence, of this Kind of Work; but I saw no Need of it.

And now having a full Supply of Food for all the Guests I expected, I gave the *Spaniard* Leave to go over to the *Main*, to see what he could do with those he had left behind him there. I gave him a strict Charge in Writing, Not to bring any Man with him, who would not first swear in the Presence of himself and of the old *Savage*, That he would no way injure, fight with, or attack the Person he should find in the Island, who was so kind to send for them in order to their Deliverance; but that they would stand by and defend him against all such Attempts, and wherever they went, would be entirely under and subjected to his Commands; and that this should be put in Writing, and signed with their Hands: How we were to have this done, when I knew they had neither Pen or Ink; that indeed was a Question which we never asked.

Under these Instructions, the *Spaniard*, and the old *Savage* the Father of *Friday*, went away in one of the Canoes, which they might be said to come in, or rather were brought in, when they came as Prisoners to be devour'd by the *Savages*.

I gave each of them a Musket with a Firelock on it, and about eight Charges of Powder and Ball, charging them to be very good Husbands of both, and not to use either of them but upon urgent Occasion.

This was a chearful Work, being the first Measures used by me in View of my Deliverance for now 27 Years and some Days. I gave them Provisions of Bread, and of dry'd Grapes, sufficient for themselves for many Days, and sufficient for all their Countrymen for about eight Days time; and wishing them a good Voyage, I see them go, agreeing with them about a Signal they should hang out at their Return, by which I should know them again, when they came back, at a Distance, before they came on Shore.

They went away with a fair Gale on the Day that the Moon was at Full by my Account, in the Month of *October*. But as for an exact Reckoning of Days, after I had once lost it, I could never recover it again; nor had I kept even the Number of Years so punctually, as to be sure that I was right, tho' as it prov'd, when I afterwards examin'd my Account, I found I had kept a true Reckoning of Years.

It was no less than eight Days I had waited for them, when a

Strange and unforeseen Accident interveen'd, of which the like has not perhaps been heard of in History: I was fast asleep in my Hutch one Morning, when my Man *Friday* came running in to me, and call'd aloud, Master, Master, they are come, they are come.

I jump'd up, and regardless of Danger, I went out, as soon as I could get my Cloaths on, thro' my little Grove, which by the Way was by this time grown to be a very thick Wood; I say, regardless of Danger, I went without my Arms, which was not my Custom to do: But I was surpriz'd, when turning my Eyes to the Sea, I presently saw a Boat at about a League and half's Distance, standing in for the Shore, with a *Shoulder of Mutton Sail*, as they call it; and the Wind blowing pretty fair to bring them in; also I observ'd presently, that they did not come from that Side which the Shore lay on, but from the Southermost End of the Island: Upon this I call'd *Friday* in, and bid him lie close, for these were not the People we look'd for, and that we might not know yet whether they were Friends or Enemies.

In the next Place, I went in to fetch my Perspective Glass, to see what I could make of them; and having taken the Ladder out, I climb'd up to the Top of the Hill, as I used to do when I was apprehensive of any thing, and to take my View the plainer without being discover'd.

I had scarce set my Foot on the Hill, when my Eye plainly discover'd a Ship lying at an Anchor, at about two Leagues and an half's Distance from me South-south-east, but not above a League and an half from the Shore. By my Observation it appear'd plainly to be an *English* Ship, and the Boat appear'd to be an *English* Long-Boat.

I cannot express the Confusion I was in, tho' the Joy of seeing a Ship, and one who I had Reason to believe was Mann'd by my own Country-men, and consequently Friends, was such as I cannot describe; but yet I had some secret Doubts hung about me, I cannot tell from whence they came, bidding me keep upon my Guard. In the first Place, it occurr'd to me to consider what Business an *English* Ship could have in that Part of the World, since it was not the Way to or from any Part of the World, where the *English* had any Traffick; and I knew there had been no Storms to drive them in there, as in Distress; and that if they were *English* really, it was most probable that they were here upon no good Design; and that I had better continue as I was, than fall into the Hands of Thieves and Murtherers.

Let no Man despise[1] the secret Hints and Notices of Danger, which sometimes are given him, when he may think there is no Possibility of its being real. That such Hints and Notices are given us, I believe few that have made any Observations of things, can deny; that they are certain Discoveries[2] of an invisible World, and a Converse of Spirits, we cannot doubt; and if the Tendency of them seems to be to warn us of Danger, why should we not suppose they are from some friendly Agent, whether supreme, or inferior, and subordinate, is not the Question; and that they are given for our Good?

The present Question abundantly confirms me in the Justice of this Reasoning; for had I not been made cautious by this secret Admonition, come it from whence it will, I had been undone inevitably, and in a far worse Condition than before, as you will see presently.

I had not kept my self long in this Posture, but I saw the Boat draw near the Shore, as if they look'd for a Creek to thrust in at for the Convenience of Landing; however, as they did not come quite far enough, they did not see the little Inlet where I formerly landed my Rafts; but run their Boat on Shore upon the Beach, at about half a Mile from me, which was very happy for me; for otherwise they would have landed just as I may say at my Door, and would soon have beaten me out of my Castle, and perhaps have plunder'd me of all I had.

When they were on Shore, I was fully satisfy'd that they were *English* Men; at least, most of them; one or two I thought were *Dutch*; but it did not prove so: There were in all eleven Men, whereof three of them I found were unarm'd, and as I thought, bound; and when the first four or five of them were jump'd on Shore, they took those three out of the Boat as Prisoners: One of the three I could perceive using the most passionate Gestures of Entreaty, Affliction and Despair, even to a kind of Extravagance; the other two I could perceive lifted up their Hands sometimes, and appear'd concern'd indeed, but not to such a Degree as the first.

I was perfectly confounded at the Sight, and knew not what the Meaning of it should be. *Friday* call'd out to me in *English*, as well as he could, *O* Master! *You see* English *Mans eat Prisoner as well as* Savage *Mans.* Why, says I, *Friday, Do you think they are a going to eat them then? Yes,* says Friday, *They will eat them: No, no,*

---

1 Disdain, look down on.
2 Disclosures.

says I, Friday, *I am afraid they will murther them indeed, but you may be sure they will not eat them.*

All this while I had no thought of what the Matter really was; but Stood trembling with the Horror of the Sight, expecting every Moment when the three Prisoners should be kill'd; nay, once I saw one of the Villains lift up his Arm with a great Cutlash,[1] as the Seamen call it, or Sword, to strike one of the poor Men; and I expected to see him fall every Moment, at which all the Blood in my Body seem'd to run chill in my Veins.

I wish'd heartily now for my *Spaniard*, and the *Savage* that was gone with him; or that I had any way to have come undiscover'd within shot of them, that I might have rescu'd the three Men; for I saw no Fire Arms they had among them; but it fell out to my Mind another way.

After I had observ'd the outragious Usage of the three Men, by the insolent Seamen, I observ'd the Fellows run scattering about the Land, as if they wanted to see the Country: I observ'd that the three other Men had Liberty to go also where they pleas'd; but they sat down all three upon the Ground, very pensive, and look'd like Men in Despair.

This put me in Mind of the first Time when I came on Shore, and began to look about me; How I gave my self over for lost: How wildly I look'd round me: What dreadful Apprehensions I had: And how I lodg'd in the Tree all Night for fear of being devour'd by wild Beasts.

As I knew nothing that Night of the Supply I was to receive by the providential Driving of the Ship nearer the Land, by the Storms and Tide, by which I have since been so long nourish'd and supported; so these three poor desolate Men knew nothing how certain of Deliverance and Supply they were, how near it was to them, and how effectually and really they were in a Condition of Safety, at the same Time that they thought themselves lost, and their Case desperate.

So little do we see before us in the World, and so much reason have we to depend chearfully upon the great Maker of the World, that he does not leave his Creatures so absolutely destitute, but that in the worst Circumstances they have always something to be thankful for, and sometimes are nearer their Deliverance than they imagine; nay, are even brought to their Deliverance by the Means by which they seem to be brought to their Destruction.

---

1 Cutlass.

It was just at the Top of High-Water when these People came on Shore, and while partly they stood parlying with the Prisoners they brought, and partly while they rambled about to see what kind of a Place they were in; they had carelessly staid till the Tide was spent, and the Water was ebb'd considerably away, leaving their Boat a-ground.

They had left two Men in the Boat, who as I found afterwards, having drank a little too much Brandy, fell a-sleep; however, one of them waking sooner than the other, and finding the Boat too fast a-ground for him to stir it, hollow'd for the rest who were straggling about, upon which they all soon came to the Boat; but it was past all their Strength to launch her, the Boat being very heavy, and the Shore on that Side being a soft ousy[1] Sand, almost like a Quick-Sand.

In this Condition, like true Seamen who are perhaps the least of all Mankind given to fore-thought, they gave it over, and away they stroll'd about the Country again; and I heard one of them say aloud to another, calling them off from the Boat, *Why let her alone*, Jack, *can't ye, she will float next Tide*; by which I was fully confirm'd in the main Enquiry, of what Countrymen they were.

All this while I kept my self very close, not once daring to stir out of my Castle, any farther than to my Place of Observation, near the Top of the Hill; and very glad I was, to think how well it was fortify'd: I knew it was no less than ten Hours before the Boat could be on float again, and by that Time it would be dark, and I might be at more Liberty to see their Motions, and to hear their Discourse, if they had any.

In the mean Time, I fitted my self up for a Battle, as before; though with more Caution, knowing I had to do with another kind of Enemy than I had at first: I order'd *Friday* also, who I had made an excellent Marks-Man with his Gun, to load himself with Arms: I took my self two Fowling-Pieces, and I gave him three Muskets; my Figure indeed was very fierce; I had my formidable Goat-Skin Coat on, with the great Cap I have mention'd, a naked Sword by my Side, two Pistols in my Belt, and a Gun upon each Shoulder.

It was my Design, as I said above, not to have made any Attempt till it was Dark: But about Two a Clock, being the Heat of the Day, I found that in short they were all gone straggling into the Woods, and as I thought were laid down to Sleep. The three poor distressed Men, too Anxious for their Condition to get any

1 Oozy.

Sleep, were however set down under the Shelter of a great Tree, at about a quarter of a Mile from me, and as I thought out of sight of any of the rest.

Upon this I resolv'd to discover my self to them, and learn something of their Condition: Immediately I march'd in the Figure as above, my Man *Friday* at a good Distance behind me, as formidable for his Arms as I, but not making quite so staring a *Spectre-like* Figure as I did.

I came as near them undiscover'd as I could, and then before any of them saw me, I call'd aloud to them in *Spanish, What are ye Gentlemen?*

They started up at the Noise, but were ten times more confounded when they saw me, and the uncouth Figure that I made. They made no Answer at all, but I thought I perceiv'd them just going to fly from me, when I spoke to them in *English*, Gentlemen, said I, do not be surpriz'd at me; perhaps you may have a Friend near you when you did not expect it. He must be sent directly from Heaven then, *said one of them very gravely to me, and pulling off his Hat at the same time to me*, for our Condition is past the Help of Man. All Help is from Heaven, *Sir, said I*. But can you put a Stranger in the way how to help you, for you seem to me to be in some great Distress? I saw you when you landed, and when you seem'd to make Applications to the Brutes that came with you, I saw one of them lift up his Sword to kill you.

The poor Man with Tears running down his Face, and trembling, looking like one astonish'd, return'd, *Am I talking to God, or Man! Is it a real Man, or an Angel!* Be in no fear about that, Sir, *said I*, if God had sent an Angel to relieve you, he would have come better Cloath'd, and Arm'd after another manner than you see me in; pray lay aside your Fears, I am a Man, an *English-man*, and dispos'd to assist you, you see; I have one Servant only; we have Arms and Ammunition; tell us freely, Can we serve you?— —What is your Case?

Our Case, said he, Sir, is too long to tell you, while our Murtherers are so near; but in short, Sir, I was Commander of that Ship, my Men have Mutinied against me; they have been hardly prevail'd on not to Murther me, and at last have set me on Shore in this desolate Place, with these two Men with me; one my Mate, the other a Passenger, where we expected to Perish, believing the Place to be uninhabited, and know not yet what to think of it.

Where are those Brutes, your Enemies, said I, do you know where they are gone? *There they lye*, Sir, said he, pointing to a

Thicket of Trees; *my Heart trembles, for fear they have seen us, and heard you speak, if they have, they will certainly Murther us all.*

Have they any Fire-Arms, *said I*, He answered they had only two Pieces, and one which they left in the Boat. Well then, said I, leave the rest to me; I see they are all asleep, it is an easie thing to kill them all; but shall we rather take them Prisoners? He told me there were two desperate Villains among them, that it was scarce safe to shew any Mercy to; but if they were secur'd, he believ'd all the rest would return to their Duty. I ask'd him, which they were? He told me he could not at that distance describe them; but he would obey my Orders in any thing I would direct. Well, says I, let us retreat out of their View or Hearing, least they awake, and we will resolve[1] further; so they willingly went back with me, till the Woods cover'd us from them.

Look you, Sir, said I, if I venture upon your Deliverance, are you willing to make two Conditions with me; he anticipated my Proposals, by telling me, that both he and the Ship, if recover'd, should be wholly Directed and Commanded by me in every thing; and if the Ship was not recover'd, he would live and dye with me in what Part of the World soever I would send him; and the two other Men said the same.

Well, says I, *my Conditions are but two.* 1. That while you stay on this Island with me, you will not pretend to any Authority here; and if I put Arms into your Hands, you will upon all Occasions give them up to me, and do no Prejudice[2] to me or mine, upon this Island, and in the mean time be govern'd by my Orders.

2. That if the Ship is, or may be recover'd, you will carry me and my Man to *England* Passage free.

He gave me all the Assurances that the Invention and Faith of Man could devise, that he would comply with these most reasonable Demands, and besides would owe his Life to me, and acknowledge it upon all Occasions as long as he liv'd.

Well then, *said I*, here are three Muskets for you, with Powder and Ball; tell me next what you think is proper to be done. He shew'd all the Testimony of his Gratitude that he was able; but offer'd to be wholly guided by me. I told him I thought it was hard venturing any thing; but the best Method I could think of was to fire upon them at once, as they lay; and if any was not kill'd at the first Volley, and offered to submit, we might save them, and so put it wholly upon God's Providence to direct the Shot.

---

1 Consult.
2 Harm.

He said very modestly, that he was loath to kill them, if he could help it, but that those two were incorrigible Villains, and had been the Authors of all the Mutiny in the Ship, and if they escaped, we should be undone still; for they would go on Board, and bring the whole Ship's Company, and destroy us all. *Well then*, says I, *Necessity* legitimates my Advice; for it is the only Way to save our Lives. However, seeing him still cautious of shedding Blood, I told him they should go themselves, and manage as they found convenient.

In the Middle of this Discourse, we heard some of them awake, and soon after, we saw two of them on their Feet, I ask'd him, if either of them were of the Men who he had said were the Heads of the Mutiny? He said, *No*: Well then, said I, you may let them escape, and Providence seems to have wakned them on Purpose to save themselves. Now, says I, if the rest escape you, *it is your Fault.*

Animated with this, he took the Musket, I had given him, in his Hand, and a Pistol in his Belt, and his two Comerades with him, with each Man a Piece in his Hand, The two Men who were with him, going first, made some Noise, at which one of the Seamen who was awake, turn'd about, and seeing them coming, cry'd out to the rest; but it was too late then; for the Moment he cry'd out, they fir'd; *I mean the two Men*, the Captain wisely reserving his own Piece: They had so well aim'd their Shot at the Men they knew, that one of them was kill'd on the Spot, and the other very much wounded; but not being dead, he started up upon his Feet, and call'd eagerly for help to the other; but the Captain stepping to him, told him, 'twas too late to cry for help, he should call upon God to forgive his Villany, and with that Word knock'd him down with the Stock of his Musket, so that he never spoke more: There were three more in the Company, and one of them was also slightly wounded: By this Time I was come, and when they saw their Danger, and that it was in vain to resist, they begg'd for Mercy: The Captain told them, he would spare their Lives, if they would give him any Assurance of their Abhorrence of the Treachery they had been guilty of, and would swear to be faithful to him in recovering the Ship, and afterwards in carrying her back to *Jamaica*, from whence they came: They gave him all the Protestations of their Sincerity that could be desir'd, and he was willing to believe them, and spare their Lives, which I was not against, only that I oblig'd him to keep them bound Hand and Foot while they were upon the Island.

While this was doing, I sent *Friday* with the Captain's Mate to the Boat, with Orders to secure her, and bring away the Oars, and Sail, which they did; and by and by, three Straggling Men that were (happily for them) parted from the rest, came back upon hearing the Guns fir'd, and seeing their Captain, who before was their Prisoner, now their Conqueror, they submitted to be bound also; and so our Victory was compleat.

It now remain'd, that the Captain and I should enquire into one another's Circumstances: I began first, and told him my whole History, which he heard with an Attention even to Amazement; and particularly, at the wonderful Manner of my being furnish'd with Provisions and Ammunition; and indeed, as my Story is a whole Collection of Wonders, it affected him deeply; but when he reflected from thence upon himself, and how I seem'd to have been preserv'd there, on purpose to save his Life, the Tears ran down his Face, and he could not speak a Word more.

After this Communication was at an End, I carry'd him and his two Men into my Apartment, leading them in, just where I came out, *viz.* At the Top of the House, where I refresh'd them with such Provisions as I had, and shew'd them all the Contrivances I had made, during my long, long, inhabiting that Place.

All I shew'd them, all I said to them, was perfectly amazing; but above all, the Captain admir'd my Fortification, and how perfectly I had conceal'd my Retreat with a Grove of Trees, which having been now planted near twenty Years, and the Trees growing much faster than in *England*, was become a little Wood, and so thick, that it was unpassable in any Part of it, but at that one Side, where I had reserv'd my little winding Passage into it: I told him, this was my Castle, and my Residence; but that I had a Seat in the Country, as most Princes have, whither I could retreat upon Occasion, and I would shew him that too another Time; but at present, our Business was to consider how to recover the Ship: He agreed with me as to that; but told me, he was perfectly at a Loss what Measures to take; for that there were still six and twenty Hands on board, who having entred into a cursed Conspiracy, by which they had all forfeited their Lives to the Law, would be harden'd in it now by Desperation; and would carry it on, knowing that if they were reduc'd, they should be brought to the Gallows, as soon as they came to *England*, or to any of the *English* Colonies; and that therefore there would be no attacking them, with so small a Number as we were.

I mus'd for some Time upon what he had said, and found it was a very rational Conclusion; and that therefore something was to be resolv'd on very speedily, as well to draw the Men on board into some Snare for their Surprize, as to prevent their Landing upon us, and destroying us; upon this it presently occurr'd to me, that in a little while the Ship's Crew wondring what was become of their Comrades, and of the Boat, would certainly come on Shore in their other Boat, to see for them, and that then perhaps they might come arm'd, and be too strong for us; this he allow'd was rational.

Upon this, I told him the first Thing we had to do, was to stave[1] the Boat, which lay upon the Beach, so that they might not carry her off; and taking every Thing out of her, leave her so far useless as not to be fit to swim; accordingly we went on board, took the Arms which were left on board, out of her, and whatever else we found there, which was a Bottle of Brandy, and another of Rum, a few Bisket Cakes, a Horn of Powder, and a great Lump of Sugar, in a Piece of Canvas; the Sugar was five or six Pounds, all which was very welcome to me, especially the Brandy, and Sugar, of which I had had none left for many Years.

When we had carry'd all these Things on Shore (the Oars, Mast, Sail, and Rudder of the Boat, were carry'd away before, as above) we knock'd a great Hole in her Bottom, that if they had come strong enough to master us, yet they could not carry off the Boat.

Indeed, it was not much in my Thoughts, that we could be able to recover the Ship; but my View was that if they went away without the Boat, I did not much question to make her fit again, to carry us away to the *Leeward* Islands,[2] and call upon our Friends, the *Spaniards*, in my Way, for I had them still in my Thoughts.

While we were thus preparing our Designs, and had first, by main[3] Strength heav'd the Boat up upon the Beach, so high that the Tide would not fleet her off at High-Water-Mark; and besides, had broke a Hole in her Bottom, too big to be quickly stopp'd, and were sat down musing what we should do; we heard the Ship fire a Gun, and saw her make a Waft with her Antient, as a Signal for the Boat to come on board; but no Boat stirr'd; and they fir'd several Times, making other Signals for the Boat.

At last, when all their Signals and Firings prov'd fruitless, and they found the Boat did not stir, we saw them by the Help of my

---

1 To make a hole in.
2 The northern islands of the Lesser Antilles.
3 Sheer, fully exerted.

Glasses, hoist another Boat out, and row towards the Shore; and we found as they approach'd, that there was no less than ten Men in her, and that they had Fire-Arms with them.

As the Ship lay almost two Leagues from the Shore, we had a full View of them as they came, and a plain Sight of the Men even of their Faces, because the Tide having set them a little to the *East* of the other Boat, they row'd up under Shore, to come to the same Place, where the other had landed, and where the Boat lay.

By this Means, I say, we had a full View of them, and the Captain knew the Persons and Characters of all the Men in the Boat, of whom he said, that there were three very honest Fellows, who he was sure were led into this Conspiracy by the rest, being over-power'd and frighted.

But that as for the Boatswain, who it seems was the chief Officer among them, and all the rest, they were as outragious as any of the Ship's Crew, and were no doubt made desperate in their new Enterprize, and terribly apprehensive he was, that they would be too powerful for us.

I smil'd at him, and told him, that Men in our Circumstances were past the Operation of Fear: That seeing almost every Condition that could be, was better than that which we were suppos'd to be in, we ought to expect that the Consequence, whether Death or Life, would be sure to be a Deliverance: I ask'd him, What he thought of the Circumstances of my Life? And, Whether a Deliverance were not worth venturing for? And where, Sir, said I, is your Belief of my being preserv'd here on purpose to save your Life, which elevated you a little while ago? For my Part, said I, there seems to be but one Thing amiss in all the Prospect of it; *What's that?* Says he; why, said I, 'Tis, that as you say, there are three or four honest Fellows among them, which should be spar'd; had they been all of the wicked Part of the Crew, I should have thought God's Providence had singled them out to deliver them into your Hands; for depend upon it, every Man of them that comes a-shore are our own, and shall die, or live, as they behave to us.

As I spoke this with a rais'd Voice and chearful Countenance, I found it greatly encourag'd him; so we set vigorously to our Business: We had upon the first Appearance of the Boat's coming from the Ship, consider'd of separating our Prisoners, and had indeed secur'd them effectually.

Two of them, of whom the Captain was less assur'd than ordinary, I sent with *Friday*, and one of the three (deliver'd Men) to my Cave, where they were remote enough, and out of Danger of being heard or discover'd, or of finding their way out of the Woods, if they could have deliver'd themselves: Here they left them bound, but gave them Provisions, and promis'd them if they continu'd there quietly, to give them their Liberty in a Day or two; but that if they attempted their Escape, they should be put to Death without Mercy: They promis'd faithfully to bear their Confinement with Patience, and were very thankful that they had such good Usage, as to have Provisions, and a Light left them; for *Friday* gave them Candles (such as we made our selves) for their Comfort; and they did not know but that he stood Sentinel over them at the Entrance.

The other Prisoners had better Usage; two of them were kept pinion'd indeed, because the Captain was not free to trust them; but the other two were taken into my Service upon their Captain's Recommendation, and upon their solemnly engaging to live and die with us; so with them and the three honest Men, we were seven Men, well arm'd; and I made no doubt we shou'd be able to deal well enough with the Ten that were a coming, considering that the Captain had said, there were three or four honest Men among them also.

As soon as they got to the Place where their other Boat lay, they run their Boat in to the Beach, and came all on Shore, haling the Boat up after them, which I was glad to see; for I was afraid they would rather have left the Boat at an Anchor, some Distance from the Shore, with some Hands in her, to guard her; and so we should not be able to seize the Boat.

Being on Shore, the first Thing they did, they ran all to their other Boat, and it was easy to see that they were under a great Surprize, to find her stripp'd as above, of all that was in her, and a great hole in her Bottom.

After they had mus'd a while upon this, they set up two or three great Shouts, hollowing with all their might, to try if they could make their Companions hear; but all was to no purpose: Then they came all close in a Ring, and fir'd a Volley of their small Arms, which indeed we heard, and the Ecchos made the Woods ring; but it was all one,[1] those in the Cave we were sure could not hear, and those in our keeping, though they heard it well enough, yet durst give no Answer to them.

They were so astonish'd at the Surprize of this, that as they told us afterwards, they resolv'd to go all on board again to their Ship, and let them know, that the Men were all murther'd, and

---

1 All the same; it didn't matter.

the Long-Boat stav'd; accordingly they immediately launch'd their Boat again, and gat all of them on board.

The Captain was terribly amaz'd, and even confounded at this, believing they would go on board the Ship again, and set Sail, giving their Comrades for lost, and so he should still lose the Ship, which he was in Hopes we should have recover'd; but he was quickly as much frighted the other way.

They had not been long put off with the Boat, but we perceiv'd them all coming on Shore again; but with this new Measure in their Conduct, which it seems they consulted together upon, *viz.* To leave three Men in the Boat, and the rest to go on Shore, and go up into the Country to look for their Fellows.

This was a great Disappointment to us; for now we were at a Loss what to do; for our seizing those seven Men on Shore would be no Advantage to us, if we let the Boat escape; because they would then row away to the Ship, and then the rest of them would be sure to weigh[1] and set Sail, and so our recovering the Ship would be lost.

However, we had no Remedy, but to wait and see what the Issue of Things might present; the seven Men came on Shore, and the three who remain'd in the Boat, put her off to a good Distance from the Shore, and came to an Anchor to wait for them; so that it was impossible for us to come at them in the Boat.

Those that came on Shore, kept close together, marching towards the Top of the little Hill, under which my Habitation lay; and we could see them plainly, though they could not perceive us: We could have been very glad they would have come nearer to us, so that we might have fir'd at them, or that they would have gone farther off, that we might have come abroad.

But when they were come to the Brow of the Hill, where they could see a great way into the Valleys and Woods, which lay towards the *North-East* Part, and where the Island lay lowest, they shouted, and hollow'd, till they were weary; and not caring it seems to venture far from the Shore, nor far from one another, they sat down together under a Tree, to consider of it: Had they thought fit to have gone to sleep there, as the other Party of them had done, they had done the Jobb for us; but they were too full of Apprehensions of Danger, to venture to go to sleep, though they could not tell what the Danger was they had to fear neither.

The Captain made a very just Proposal to me, upon this Consultation of theirs, *viz.* That perhaps they would all fire a Volley

---

1 To weigh anchor.

again, to endeavour to make their Fellows hear, and that we should all Sally[1] upon them, just at the Juncture when their Pieces were all discharg'd, and they would certainly yield, and we should have them without Bloodshed: I lik'd the Proposal, provided it was done while we were near enough to come up to them, before they could load their Pieces again.

But this Event did not happen, and we lay still a long Time, very irresolute what Course to take; at length I told them, there would be nothing to be done in my Opinion till Night, and then if they did not return to the Boat, perhaps we might find a way to get between them, and the Shore, and so might use some Stratagem with them in the Boat, to get them on Shore.

We waited a great while, though very impatient for their removing; and were very uneasy, when after long Consultations, we saw them start all up, and march down toward the Sea: It seems they had such dreadful Apprehensions upon them, of the Danger of the Place, that they resolv'd to go on board the Ship again, give their Companions over for lost, and so go on with their intended Voyage with the Ship.

As soon as I perceiv'd them go towards the Shore, I imagin'd it to be as it really was, That they had given over their Search, and were for going back again; and the Captain, as soon as I told him my Thoughts, was ready to sink at the Apprehensions of it; but I presently thought of a Stratagem to fetch them back again, and which answer'd my End to a Tittle.

I order'd *Friday*, and the Captain's Mate, to go over the little Creek *Westward*, towards the Place were the *Savages* came on Shore, when *Friday* was rescu'd; and as soon as came to a little rising Ground, at about half a Mile Distance, I bad them hollow, as loud as they could, and wait till they found the Seamen heard them; that as soon as ever they heard the Seamen answer them, they should return it again, and then keeping out of Sight, take a round, always answering when the other hollow'd, to draw them as far into the Island, and among the Woods, as possible, and then wheel about again to me, by such ways as I directed them.

They were just going into the Boat, when *Friday* and the Mate hollow'd, and they presently heard them, and answering, run along the Shore *Westward*, towards the Voice they heard, where they were presently stopp'd by the Creek, where the Water being up, they could not get over, and call'd for the Boat to come up, and set them over, as indeed I expected.

---

1 Suddenly spring out of hiding and attack.

When they had set themselves over, I observ'd, that the Boat being gone up a good way into the Creek, and as it were, in a Harbour within the Land, they took one of the three Men out of her to go along with them, and left only two in the Boat, having fastned her to the Stump of a little Tree on the Shore.

This was what I wish'd for, and immediately leaving *Friday* and the Captain's Mate to their Business, I took the rest with me, and crossing the Creek out of their Sight, we surpriz'd the two Men before they were aware; one of them lying on Shore, and the other being in the Boat; the Fellow on Shore, was between sleeping and waking, and going to start up, the Captain who was foremost, ran in upon him, and knock'd him down, and then call'd out to him in the Boat, to yield, or he was a dead Man.

There needed very few Arguments to perswade a single Man to yield, when he saw five Men upon him, and his Comrade knock'd down; besides, this was it seems one of the three who were not so hearty in the Mutiny as the rest of the Crew, and therefore was easily perswaded, not only to yield, but afterwards to joyn very sincere with us.

In the mean time, *Friday* and the Captain's Mate so well manag'd their Business with the rest, that they drew them by hollowing and answering, from one Hill to another, and from one Wood to another, till they not only heartily tyr'd them, but left them, where they were very sure they could not reach back to the Boat, before it was dark; and indeed they were heartily tyr'd themselves also by the Time they came back to us.

We had nothing now to do, but to watch for them, in the Dark, and to fall upon them, so as to make sure work with them.

It was several Hours after *Friday* came back to me, before they came back to their Boat; and we could hear the foremost of them long before they came quite up, calling to those behind to come along, and could also hear them answer and complain, how lame and tyr'd they were, and not able to come any faster, which was very welcome News to us.

At length they came up to the Boat; but 'tis impossible to express their Confusion, when they found the Boat fast a-Ground in the Creek, the Tide ebb'd out, and their two Men gone: We could hear them call to one another in a most lamentable Manner, telling one another, they were gotten into an inchanted Island; that either there were Inhabitants in it, and they should all be murther'd, or else there were Devils and Spirits in it, and they should be all carry'd away, and devour'd.

They hallow'd again, and call'd their two Comerades by their

Names, a great many times, but no Answer. After some time, we could see them, by the little Light there was, run about wringing their Hands like Men in Despair; and that sometimes they would go and sit down in the Boat to rest themselves, then come ashore again, and walk about again, and so over the same thing again.

My Men would fain have me given them Leave to fall upon them at once in the Dark; but I was willing to take them at some Advantage, so to spare them, and kill as few of them as I could; and especially I was unwilling to hazard the killing any of our own Men, knowing the other were very well armed. I resolved to wait to see if they did not separate; and therefore to make sure of them, I drew my Ambuscade nearer, and order'd *Friday* and the Captain, to creep upon their Hands and Feet as close to the Ground as they could, that they might not be discover'd, and get as near them as they could possibly, before they offered to fire.

They had not been long in that Posture, but that the Boatswain, who was the principal Ringleader of the Mutiny, and had now shewn himself the most dejected and dispirited of all the rest, came walking towards them with two more of their Crew; the Captain was so eager, as having this principal Rogue so much in his Power, that he could hardly have Patience to let him come so near, as to be sure of him; for they only heard his Tongue before: But when they came nearer, the Captain and *Friday* starting up on their Feet, let fly at them.

The Boatswain was kill'd upon the Spot, the next Man was shot into the Body, and fell just by him, tho' he did not die 'till an Hour or two after; and the third run for it.

At the Noise of the Fire, I immediately advanc'd with my whole Army, which was now 8 Men, *viz.* my self *Generalissimo,*[1] *Friday* my Lieutenant-General, the Captain and his two Men, and the three Prisoners of War, who we had trusted with Arms.

We came upon them indeed in the Dark, so that they could not see our Number; and I made the Man we had left in the Boat, who was now one of us, call to them by Name, to try if I could bring them to a Parley, and so might perhaps reduce them to Terms, which fell out just as we desir'd: for indeed it was easy to think, as their Condition then was, they would be very willing to capitulate; so he calls out as loud as he could, to one of them, *Tom Smith, Tom Smith; Tom Smith* answered immediately, *Who's that, Robinson?* for it seems he knew his Voice: T'other answered, *Ay,*

---

1 The chief commander of a combined force.

ay; for God's Sake, Tom Smith, *throw down your Arms, and yield,* or, *you are all dead Men this Moment.*

Who must we yield to? where are they? (says *Smith* again;) *Here they are,* says he, here's our Captain, and fifty Men with him, have been hunting you this two Hours; the Boatswain is kill'd, *Will Frye* is wounded, and I am a Prisoner; and if you do not yield, you are all lost.

Will they give us Quarter then, (says *Tom Smith*) and we will yield? *I'll go and ask, if you promise to yield,* says *Robinson;* so he ask'd the Captain, and the Captain then calls himself out, You *Smith,* you know my Voice, if you lay down your Arms immediately, and submit, you shall have your Lives all but *Will. Atkins.*

Upon this, *Will Atkins* cry'd out, *For God's Sake, Captain, give me Quarter, what have I done? They have been all as bad as I,* which by the Way was not true neither; for it seems this *Will. Atkins* was the first Man that laid hold of the Captain, when they first mutiny'd, and used him barbarously, in tying his Hands, and giving him injurious Language. However, the Captain told him he must lay down his Arms at Discretion, and trust to the Governour's Mercy, by which he meant me; for they all call'd me Governour.

In a Word, they all laid down their Arms, and begg'd their Lives; and I sent the Man that had parley'd with them, and two more, who bound them all; and then my great Army of 50 Men, which particularly with those three, were all but eight, came up and seiz'd upon them all, and upon their Boat, only that I kept my self and one more out of Sight, for Reasons of State.

Our next Work was to repair the Boat, and think of seizing the Ship; and as for the Captain, now he had Leisure to parley with them: He expostulated with them upon the Villany of their Practices with him, and at length upon the farther Wickedness of their Design, and how certainly it must bring them to Misery and Distress in the End, and perhaps to the Gallows.

They all appear'd very penitent, and begg'd hard for their Lives; as for that, he told them, they were none of his Prisoners, but the Commander of the Island; that they thought they had set him on Shore in a barren uninhabited Island, but it had pleased God so to direct them, that the Island was inhabited, and that the Governour was an *English* Man; that he might hang them all there, if he pleased; but as he had given them all Quarter, he supposed he would send them to *England* to be dealt with there, as Justice requir'd, except *Atkins,* who he was commanded by the Governour to advise to prepare for Death; for that he would be hang'd in the Morning.

Though this was all a Fiction of his own, yet it had its desired Effect; *Atkins* fell upon his Knees to beg the Captain to interceed with the Governour for his Life; and all the rest beg'd of him for God's Sake, that they might not be sent to *England*.

It now occurr'd to me, that the time of our Deliverance was come, and that it would be a most easy thing to bring these Fellows in, to be hearty in getting Possession of the Ship; so I retir'd in the Dark from them, that they might not see what Kind of a Governour they had, and call'd the Captain to me; when I call'd, as at a good Distance, one of the Men was order'd to speak again, and say to the Captain, *Captain, the Commander calls for you*; and presently the Captain reply'd, *Tell his Excellency, I am just a coming*: This more perfectly amused[1] them; and they all believed that the Commander was just by with his fifty Men.

Upon the Captain's coming to me, I told him my Project for seizing the Ship, which he lik'd of wonderfully well, and resolv'd to put it in Execution the next Morning.

But in Order to execute it with more Art, and secure of Success, I told him, we must divide the Prisoners, and that he should go and take *Atkins* and two more of the worst of them, and send them pinion'd to the Cave where the others lay: This was committed to *Friday* and the two Men who came on Shore with the Captain.

They convey'd them to the Cave, as to a Prison; and it was indeed a dismal Place, especially to Men in their Condition.

The other I order'd to my *Bower*, as I call'd it, of which I have given a full Description; and as it was fenc'd in, and they pinion'd, the Place was secure enough, considering they were upon their Behaviour.

To these in the Morning I sent the Captain, who was to enter into a Parley with them, in a Word to try them, and tell me, whether he thought they might be trusted or no, to go on Board and surprize the Ship. He talk'd to them of the Injury done him, of the Condition they were brought to; and that though the Governour had given them Quarter for their Lives, as to the present Action, yet that if they were sent to *England*, they would all be hang'd in Chains, to be sure; but that if they would join in so just an Attempt, as to recover the Ship, he would have the Governour's Engagement for their Pardon.

Any one may guess how readily such a Proposal would be accepted by Men in their Condition; they fell down on their

---

1 Deceived.

Knees to the Captain, and promised with the deepest Impreca-
tions, that they would be faithful to him to the last Drop, and that
they should owe their Lives to him, and would go with him all
over the World, that they would own him for a Father to them as
long as they liv'd.

Well, says the Captain, I must go and tell the Governour what
you say, and see what I can do to bring him to consent to it: So
he brought me an Account of the Temper he found them in; and
that he verily believ'd they would be faithful.

However, that we might be very secure, I told him he should
go back again, and choose out five of them, and tell them, they
might see that he did not want Men, that he would take out those
five to be his Assistants, and that the Governour would keep the
other two, and the three that were sent Prisoners to the Castle,
(*my Cave*) as Hostages, for the Fidelity of those five; and that if
they prov'd unfaithful in the Execution, the five Hostages should
be hang'd in Chains alive upon the Shore.

This look'd severe, and convinc'd them that the Governour
was in Earnest; however they had no Way left them, but to accept
it; and it was now the Business of the Prisoners, as much as of the
Captain, to perswade the other five to do their Duty.

Our Strength was now thus ordered for the Expedition: 1. The
Captain, his Mate, and Passenger. 2. Then the two Prisoners of
the first Gang, to whom having their Characters from the
Captain, I had given their Liberty, and trusted them with Arms.
3. The other two who I had kept till now, in my Bower, pinion'd;
but upon the Captain's Motion, had now releas'd. 4. These five
releas'd at last: So that they were twelve in all, besides five we kept
Prisoners in the Cave, for Hostages.

I ask'd the Captain, if he was willing to venture with these
Hands on Board the Ship; for as for me and my Man *Friday*, I
did not think it was proper for us to stir, having seven Men left
behind; and it was Employment enough for us to keep them
assunder, and supply them with Victuals.

As to the five in the Cave, I resolv'd to keep them fast, but
Friday went in twice a Day to them, to supply them with Necessaries; and I made the other two carry Provisions to a certain Distance, where *Friday* was to take it.

When I shew'd my self to the two Hostages, it was with the
Captain, who told them, I was the Person the Governour had
order'd to look after them, and that it was the Governour's Pleasure they should not stir any where, but by my Direction; that if
they did, they should be fetch'd into the Castle, and be lay'd in

Irons; so that as we never suffered them to see me as Governour, so I now appear'd as another Person, and spoke of the Governour, the Garrison, the Castle, and the like, upon all Occasions.

The Captain now had no Difficulty before him, but to furnish his two Boats, Stop the Breach of one, and Man them. He made his Passenger Captain of one, with four other Men; and himself, and his Mate, and five more, went in the other: And they contriv'd their Business very well; for they came up to the Ship about Midnight: As soon as they came within Call of the Ship, he made *Robinson* hale them, and tell them they had brought off the Men and the Boat, but that it was a long time before they had found them, and the like; holding them in a Chat 'till they came to the Ship's Side; when the Captain and the Mate entring first with their Arms, immediately knock'd down the second Mate and Carpenter, with the But-end of their Muskets, being very faithfully seconded by their Men, they secur'd all the rest that were upon the Main and Quarter Decks, and began to fasten the Hatches to keep them down who were below, when the other Boat and their Men entring at the fore Chains, secur'd the Fore-Castle of the Ship, and the Scuttle[1] which went down into the Cook Room, making three Men they found there, Prisoners.

When this was done, and all safe upon Deck, the Captain order'd the Mate with three Men to break into the Round-House[2] where the new Rebel Captain lay, and having taken the Alarm, was gotten up, and with two Men and a Boy had gotten Fire Arms in their Hands, and when the Mate with a Crow split open the Door, the new Captain and his Men fir'd boldly among them, and wounded the Mate with a Musket Ball, which broke his Arm, and wounded two more of the Men but kill'd no Body.

The Mate calling for Help, rush'd however into the Round-House, wounded as he was, and with his Pistol shot the new Captain thro' the Head, the Bullet entring at his Mouth, and came out again behind one of his Ears; so that he never spoke a Word; upon which the rest yielded, and the Ship was taken effectually, without any more Lives lost.

As soon as the Ship was thus secur'd, the Captain order'd seven Guns to be fir'd, which was the Signal agreed upon with me, to give me Notice of his Success, which you may be sure I was very glad to hear, having sat watching upon the Shore for it till near two of the Clock in the Morning.

---

1 A small hole cut in the deck of the ship, a hatchway.
2 A cabin on the quarterdeck, its roof formed by the poop deck.

Having thus heard the Signal plainly, I laid me down; and it having been a Day of great Fatigue to me, I slept very sound, 'till I was something surpriz'd with the Noise of a Gun; and presently starting up, I heard a Man call me by the Name of Governour, Governour, and presently I knew the Captain's Voice, when climbing up to the Top of the Hill, there he stood, and pointing to the Ship, he embrac'd me in his Arms, *My dear Friend and Deliverer*, says he, *there's your Ship, for she is all yours, and so are we and all that belong to her.* I cast my Eyes to the Ship, and there she rode within little more than half a Mile of the Shore; for they had weighed her Anchor as soon as they were Masters of her; and the Weather being fair, had brought her to an Anchor just against the Mouth of the little Creek; and the Tide being up, the Captain had brought the Pinnace in near the Place where I at first landed my Rafts, and so landed just at my Door.

I was at first ready to sink down with the Surprize. For I saw my Deliverance indeed visibly put into my Hands, all things easy, and a large Ship just ready to carry me away whither I pleased to go. At first, for some time, I was not able to answer him one Word; but as he had taken me in his Arms, I held fast by him, or I should have fallen to the Ground.

He perceived the Surprize, and immediately pulls a Bottle out of his Pocket, and gave me a Dram of Cordial,[1] which he had brought on Purpose for me; after I had drank it, I sat down upon the Ground; and though it brought me to my self, yet it was a good while before I could speak a Word to him.

All this while the poor Man was in as great an Extasy as I, only not under any Surprize, as I was; and he said a thousand kind tender things to me, to compose me and bring me to my self; but such was the Flood of Joy in my Breast, that it put all my Spirits into Confusion, at last it broke out into Tears, and in a little while after, I recovered my Speech.

Then I took my Turn, and embrac'd him as my Deliverer; and we rejoyc'd together. I told him, I look upon him as a Man sent from Heaven to deliver me, and that the whole Transaction seemed to be a Chain of Wonders; that such things as these were the Testimonies we had of a secret Hand of Providence governing the World, and an Evidence, that the Eyes of an infinite Power could search into the remotest Corner of the World, and send Help to the Miserable whenever he pleased.

I forgot not to lift up my Heart in Thankfulness to Heaven,

---

1 A stimulating medicinal drink.

and what Heart could forbear to bless him, who had not only in a miraculous Manner provided for one in such a Wilderness, and in such a desolate Condition, but from whom every Deliverance must always be acknowledged to proceed.

When we had talk'd a while, the Captain told me, he had brought me some little Refreshment, such as the Ship afforded, and such as the Wretches that had been so long his Master had not plunder'd him of: Upon this he call'd aloud to the Boat, and bid his Men bring the things ashore that were for the Governour; and indeed it was a Present, as if I had been one not that was to be carry'd away along with them, but as if I had been to dwell upon the Island still, and they were to go without me.

First he had brought me a Case of Bottles full of excellent Cordial Waters, six large Bottles of *Madera* Wine; the Bottles held two Quarts a-piece; two Pound of excellent good Tobacco, twelve good Pieces of the Ship's Beef, and six Pieces of Pork, with a Bag of Pease, and about a hundred Weight of Bisket.

He brought me also a Box of Sugar, a Box of Flower,[1] a Bag full of Lemons, and two Bottles of Lime-Juice, and Abundance of other things: But besides these, and what was a thousand times more useful to me, he brought me six clean new Shirts, six very good Neckcloaths, two Pair of Gloves, one Pair of Shoes, a Hat, and one Pair of Stockings, and a very good Suit of Cloaths of his own, which had been worn but very little: In a Word, he cloathed me from Head to Foot.

It was a very kind and agreeable Present, as any one may imagine to one in my Circumstances: But never was any thing in the World of that Kind so unpleasant, awkard, and uneasy, as it was to me to wear such Cloaths at their first putting on.

After these Ceremonies past, and after all his good things were brought into my little Apartment, we began to consult what was to be done with the Prisoners we had; for it was worth considering, whether we might venture to take them away with us or no, especially two of them, who we knew to be incorrigible and refractory to the last Degree; and the Captain said, he knew they were such Rogues, that there was no obliging them, and if he did carry them away, it must be in Irons, as Malefactors to be delivered over to Justice at the first *English* Colony he could come at; and I found that the Captain himself was very anxious about it.

Upon this, I told him, that if he desir'd it, I durst undertake to bring the two Men he spoke of, to make it their own Request that

---

1 Flour.

he should leave them upon the Island: *I should be very glad of that*, says the Captain, *with all my Heart*.

Well, says I, I will send for them up, and talk with them for you; so I caused *Friday* and the two Hostages, for they were now discharg'd, their Comrades having perform'd their Promise; I say, I caused them to go to the Cave, and bring up the five Men pinion'd, as they were, to the Bower, and keep them there 'till I came.

After some time, I came thither dress'd in my new Habit, and now I was call'd Governour again; being all met, and the Captain with me, I caused the Men to be brought before me, and I told them, I had had a full Account of their villanous Behaviour to the Captain, and how they had run away with the Ship, and were preparing to commit farther Robberies, but that Providence had ensnar'd them in their own Ways, and that they were fallen into the Pit which they had digged for others.

I let them know, that by my Direction the Ship had been seiz'd, that she lay now in the Road; and they might see by and by, that their new Captain had receiv'd the Reward of his Villany; for that they might see him hanging at the Yard-Arm.[1]

That as to them, I wanted to know what they had to say, why I should not execute them as Pirates taken in the Fact,[2] as by my Commission they could not doubt I had Authority to do.

One of them answer'd in the Name of the rest, That they had nothing to say but this, That when they were taken, the Captain promis'd them their Lives, and they humbly implor'd my Mercy; But I told them, I knew not what Mercy to shew them; for as for my self, I had resolv'd to quit the Island with all my Men, and had taken Passage with the Captain to go for *England*: And as for the Captain, he could not carry them to *England*, other than as Prisoners in Irons to be try'd for Mutiny, and running away with the Ship; the Consequence of which, they must needs know, would be the Gallows; so that I could not tell which was best for them, unless they had a Mind to take their Fate in the Island; if they desir'd, that I did not care, as I had Liberty to leave it, I had some Inclination to give them their Lives, if they thought they could shift on Shore.

They seem'd very thankful for it, said they would much rather venture to stay there, than to be carry'd to *England* to be hang'd; so I left it on that Issue.

---

1 The end of the yard, where the ship's signal was usually flown.
2 In the act.

However, the Captain seem'd to make some Difficulty of it, as if he durst not leave them there: Upon this I seem'd a little angry with the Captain, and told him, That they were my Prisoners, not his; and that seeing I had offered them so much Favour, I would be as good as my Word; and that if he did not think fit to consent to it, I would set them at Liberty, as I found them; and if he did not like it, he might take them again if he could catch them.

Upon this they appear'd very thankful, and I accordingly set them at Liberty, and bad them retire into the Woods to the Place whence they came, and I would leave them some Fire Arms, some Ammunition, and some Directions how they should live very well, if they thought fit.

Upon this I prepar'd to go on Board the Ship, but told the Captain, that I would stay that Night to prepare my things, and desir'd him to go on Board in the mean time, and keep all right in the Ship, and send the Boat on Shore the next Day for me; ordering him in the mean time to cause the new Captain who was kill'd, to be hang'd at the Yard-Arm that these Men might see him.

When the Captain was gone, I sent for the Men up to me to my Apartment, and entred seriously into Discourse with them of their Circumstances, I told them, I thought they had made a right Choice; that if the Captain carry'd them away, they would certainly be hang'd. I shewed them the new Captain, hanging at the Yard-Arm of the Ship, and told them they had nothing less to expect.

When they had all declar'd their Willingness to stay, I then told them, I would let them into the Story of my living there, and put them into the Way of making it easy to them: Accordingly I gave them the whole History of the Place, and of my coming to it; shew'd them my Fortifications, the Way I made my Bread, planted my Corn, cured my Grapes; and in a Word, all that was necessary to make them easy: I told them the Story also of the sixteen *Spaniards* that were to be expected; for whom I left a Letter, and made them promise to treat them in common with themselves.

I left them my Fire Arms, *viz.* Five Muskets, three Fowling Pieces, and three Swords. I had above a Barrel and half of Powder left; for after the first Year or two, I used but little, and wasted none. I gave them a Description of the Way I manag'd the Goats, and Directions to milk and fatten them, and to make both Butter and Cheese.

In a Word, I gave them every Part of my own Story; and I told them, I would prevail with the Captain to leave them two Barrels of Gun-Powder more, and some Garden-Seeds, which I told them I would have been very glad of; also I gave them the Bag of Pease which the Captain had brought me to eat, and bad them be sure to sow and encrease them.

Having done all this, I left them the next Day, and went on Board the Ship: We prepared immediately to sail, but did not weigh that Night: The next Morning early, two of the five Men came swimming to the Ship's Side, and making a most lamentable Complaint of the other three, begged to be taken into the Ship, for God's Sake, for they should be murthered, and begg'd the Captain to take them on Board, tho' he hang'd them immediately.

Upon this the Captain pretended to have no Power without me; But after some Difficulty, and after their solemn Promises off Amendment, they were taken on Board, and were some time after soundly whipp'd and pickl'd;[1] after which, they prov'd very honest and quiet Fellows.

Some time after this, the Boat was order'd on Shore, the Tide being up, with the things promised to the Men, to which the Captain at my Intercession caused their Chests and Cloaths to be added, which they took, and were very thankful for; I also encourag'd them, by telling them, that if it lay in my Way to send any Vessel to take them in, I would not forget them.

When I took leave of this Island, I carry'd on board for Reliques,[2] the great Goat's-Skin-Cap I had made, my Umbrella, and my Parrot; also I forgot not to take the Money I formerly mention'd, which had lain by me so long useless, that it was grown rusty, or tarnish'd, and could hardly pass for Silver, till it had been a little rubb'd, and handled; as also the Money I found in the Wreck of the *Spanish* Ship.

And thus I left the Island, the Nineteenth of *December*, as I found by the Ship's Account, in the Year 1686, after I had been upon it eight and twenty Years, two Months, and 19 Days;[3] being deliver'd from this second Captivity, the same Day of the Month,

---

1 Rubbing salt or vinegar into a wound increased the punishment; it also helped the wound to heal.

2 Souvenirs, mementos.

3 Crusoe's math is askew here. He lands on 30 September 1659 and departs on 19 December 1686, so the actual length of his stay is 27 years, 2 ½ months.

that I first made my Escape in the *Barco-Longo*,[1] from among the *Moors* of *Sallee*.

In this Vessel, after a long Voyage, I arriv'd in *England*, the Eleventh of *June*, in the Year 1687, having been thirty and five Years absent.

When I came to *England*, I was as perfect a Stranger to all the World, as if I had never been known there. My Benefactor and faithful Steward, who I had left in Trust with my Money, was alive; but had had great Misfortunes in the World; was become a Widow the second Time, and very low in the World: I made her easy as to what she ow'd me, assuring her, I would give her no Trouble; but on the contrary, in Gratitude to her former Care and Faithfulness to me, I reliev'd her as my little Stock would afford, which at that Time would indeed allow me to do but little for her; but I assur'd her, I would never forget her former Kindness to me; nor did I forget her, when I had sufficient to help her, as shall be observ'd in its Place.

I went down afterwards into *Yorkshire*; but my Father was dead, and my Mother, and all the Family extinct, except that I found two Sisters, and two of the Children of one of my Brothers; and as I had been long ago given over for dead, there had been no Provision made for me; so that in a Word, I found nothing to relieve, or assist me; and that little Money I had, would not do much for me, as to settling in the World.

I met with one Piece of Gratitude indeed, which I did not expect; and this was, That the Master of the Ship, who I had so happily deliver'd, and by the same Means sav'd the Ship and Cargo, having given a very handsome Account to the Owners, of the Manner how I had sav'd the Lives of the Men, and the Ship, they invited me to meet them, and some other Merchants concern'd, and altogether made me a very handsome Compliment upon the Subject, and a Present of almost two hundred Pounds Sterling.

But after making several Reflections upon the Circumstances of my Life, and how little way this would go towards settling me in the World, I resolv'd to go to *Lisbon*, and see if I might not come by some Information of the State of my Plantation in the *Brasils*, and of what was become of my Partner, who I had reason to suppose had some Years now given me over for dead.

With this View I took Shipping for *Lisbon*, where I arriv'd in *April* following; my Man *Friday* accompanying me very honestly

---

1 Literally *long barge*; a Spanish fishing boat reaching up to 70 feet in length.

in all these Ramblings, and proving a most faithful Servant upon all Occasions.

When I came to *Lisbon*, I found out by Enquiry, and to my particular Satisfaction, my old Friend the Captain of the Ship, who first took me up at Sea, off of the Shore of *Africk*: He was now grown old, and had left off the Sea, having put his Son, who was far from a young Man, into his Ship; and who still used the *Brasil* Trade. The old Man did not know me, and indeed, I hardly knew him; but I soon brought him to my Remembrance, and as soon brought my self to his Remembrance, when I told him who I was.

After some passionate Expressions of the old Acquaintance, I enquir'd, you may be sure, after my Plantation and my Partner: The old Man told me he had not been in the *Brasils* for about nine Years; but that he could assure me, that when he came away, my Partner was living, but the Trustees, who I had join'd with him to take Cognizance of my Part, were both dead; that however, he believ'd that I would have a very good Account of the Improvement of the Plantation; for that upon the general Belief of my being cast away, and drown'd, my Trustees had given in the Account of the Produce of my Part of the Plantation, to the Procurator Fiscal,[1] who had appropriated it, in Case I never came to claim it; one Third to the King, and two Thirds to the Monastery of St. *Augustine*, to be expended for the Benefit of the Poor, and for the Conversion of the *Indians* to the Catholick Faith; but that if I appear'd, or any one for me, to claim the Inheritance, it should be restor'd; only that the Improvement, or Annual Production, being distributed to charitable Uses, could not be restor'd; but he assur'd me, that the Steward of the King's Revenue (from Lands) and the Proviedore, or Steward of the Monastery, had taken great Care all along, that the Incumbent, that is to say my Partner, gave every Year a faithful Account of the Produce, of which they receiv'd duly my Moiety.

I ask'd him if he knew to what height of Improvement he had brought the Plantation? And, Whether he thought it might be worth looking after? Or, Whether on my going thither, I should meet with no Obstruction to my Possessing my just Right in the Moiety?[2]

---

1 In Scottish law, the officer who is appointed by the court to act as the executor of an estate when someone has died or disappeared.

2 Share.

He told me, he could not tell exactly, to what Degree the Plantation was improv'd; but this he knew, that my Partner was grown exceeding Rich upon the enjoying but one half of it; and that to the best of his Remembrance, he had heard, that the King's Third of my Part, which was it seems granted away to some other Monastery, or Religious House, amounted to above two hundred Moidores a Year; that as to my being restor'd to a quiet Possession of it, there was no question to be made of that, my Partner being alive to witness my Title, and my Name being also enrolled in the Register of the Country; also he told me, That the Survivors of my two Trustees, were very fair honest People, and very Wealthy; and he believ'd I would not only have their Assistance for putting me in Possession, but would find a very considerable Sum of Money in their Hands, for my Account; being the Produce of the Farm while their Fathers held the Trust, and before it was given up as above, which as he remember'd, was for about twelve Years.

I shew'd my self a little concern'd, and uneasy at this Account, and enquir'd of the old Captain, How it came to pass, that the Trustees should thus dispose my Effects, when he knew that I had made my Will, and had made him, the *Portuguese* Captain, my universal Heir, &c.

He told me, that was true; but that as there was no Proof of my being dead, he could not act as Executor, until some certain Account should come of my Death, and that besides, he was not willing to intermeddle with a thing so remote; that it was true he had registred my Will, and put in his Claim; and could he have given any Account of my being dead or alive, he would have acted by Procuration, and taken Possession of the *Ingenio*, so they call'd the Sugar-House, and had given his Son, who was now at the *Brasils*, Order to do it.

But, says the old Man, I have one Piece of News to tell you, which perhaps may not be so acceptable to you as the rest, and that is, That believing you were lost, and all the World believing so also, your Partner and Trustees did offer to accompt to me in your Name, for six or eight of the first Years of Profits, which I receiv'd; but there being at that time, says he, great Disbursements for encreasing the Works, building an *Ingenio*, and buying Slaves, it did not amount to near so much as afterwards it produced: However, says the old Man, I shall give you a true Account of what I have received in all, and how I have disposed of it.

After a few Days farther Conference with this ancient Friend, he brought me an Account of the six first Years Income of my Plantation, sign'd by my Partner and the Merchants Trustees, being always deliver'd in Goods, *viz.* Tobacco in Roll, and Sugar in Chests, besides Rum, Molossus, &c. which is the Consequence of a Sugar Work; and I found by this Account, that every Year the Income considerably encreased; but as above, the Disbursement being large, the Sum at first was small: However, the old Man let me see, that he was Debtor to me 470 Moidores of Gold, besides 60 Chests of Sugar, and 15 double Rolls of Tobacco which were lost in his Ship; he having been Ship-wreck'd coming Home to *Lisbon* about 11 Years after my leaving the Place.

The good Man then began to complain of his Misfortunes, and how he had been obliged to make Use of my Money to recover his Losses, and buy him a Share in a new Ship: However, my old Friend, says he, you shall not want a Supply in your Necessity; and as soon as my Son returns, you shall be fully satisfy'd.

Upon this, he pulls out an old Pouch, and gives me 160 *Portugal* Moidores in Gold; and giving me the Writing of his Title to the Ship, which his Son was gone to the *Brasils* in, of which he was a Quarter Part Owner, and his Son another, he puts them both into my Hands for Security of the rest.

I was too much mov'd with the Honesty and Kindness of the poor Man, to be able to bear this; and remembring what he had done for me, how he had taken me up at Sea, and how generously he had used me on all Occasions, and particularly, how sincere a Friend he was now to me, I could hardly refrain Weeping at what he said to me: Therefore, first I asked him, if his Circumstances admitted him to spare so much Money at that time, and if it would not straiten him?[1] He told me, he could not say but it might straiten him a little; but however it was my Money, and I might want it more than he.

Every thing the good Man said was full of Affection, and I could hardly refrain from Tears while he spoke: In short, I took 100 of the Moidores, and call'd for a Pen and Ink to give him a Receipt for them; then I returned him the rest, and told him, If ever I had Possession of the Plantation, I would return the other to him also, as indeed I afterwards did; and that as to the Bill of Sale of his Part in his Son's Ship, I would not take it by any Means; but that if I wanted the Money, I found he was honest

---

1 Leave him short of money.

enough to pay me; and if I did not, but came to receive what he gave me reason to expect, I would never have a Penny more from him.

When this was pass'd, the old Man began to ask me, If he should put me into a Method to make my Claim to my Plantation? I told him, I thought to go over to it my self: He said, I might do so if I pleas'd; but that if I did not, there were Ways enough to secure my Right, and immediately to appropriate the Profits to my Use; and as there were Ships in the River of *Lisbon*,[1] just ready to go away to *Brasil*, he made me enter my Name in a Publick Register, with his Affidavit, affirming upon Oath that I was alive, and that I was the same Person who took up the Land for the Planting the said Plantation at first.

This being regularly attested by a Notary, and a Procuration affix'd, he directed me to send it with a Letter of his Writing, to a Merchant of his Acquaintance at the Place, and then propos'd my staying with him till an Account came of the Return.

Never any Thing was more honourable, than the Proceedings upon this Procuration; for in less than seven Months, I receiv'd a large Packet from the Survivors of my Trustees the Merchants, for whose Account I went to Sea, in which were the following particular Letters and Papers enclos'd.

First, There was the Account Current of the Produce of my Farm, or Plantation, from the Year when their Fathers had ballanc'd with my old *Portugal* Captain, being for six Years; the Ballance appear'd to be 1174 Moidores in my Favour.

Secondly, There was the Account of four Years more while they kept the Effects in their Hands, before the Government claim'd the Administration, as being the Effects of a Person not to be found, which they call'd *Civil Death;* and the Ballance of this, the Value of the Plantation encreasing, amounted to [38,892][2] Cruisadoes, which made 3241 Moidores.

Thirdly, There was the Prior of the *Augustin*'s Account, who had receiv'd the Profits for above fourteen Years; but not being to account for what was dispos'd to the Hospital, very honestly declar'd he had 872 Moidores not distributed, which he acknowledged to my Account, as to the King's Part, that refunded nothing.

---

1   The Tagus River.
2   In all the 1719 editions, this number was left blank, and the precise number would depend on the value of the cruzados. The figure of 38,892 cruzados was calculated by W.P. Trent and has been used in most editions for the past century.

There was a Letter of my Partner's, congratulating me very affectionately upon my being alive, giving me an Account how the Estate was improv'd, and what it produced a Year, with a Particular of the Number of Squares or Acres that it contained; how planted, how many Slaves there were upon it, and making two and twenty Crosses for Blessings, told me he had said so many *Ave Marias* to thank the Blessed Virgin that I was alive; inviting me very passionately to come over and take Possession of my own; and in the mean time to give him Orders to whom he should deliver my Effects, if I did not come my self; concluding with a hearty Tender of his Friendship, and that of his Family, and sent me, as a Present, seven fine Leopard's Skins, which he had it seems received from *Africa*, by some other Ship which he had sent thither, and who it seems had made a better Voyage than I: He sent me also five Chests of excellent Sweet-meats, and an hundred Pieces of Gold uncoin'd, not quite so large as Moidores.

By the same Fleet, my two Merchant Trustees shipp'd me 1200 Chests of Sugar, 800 Rolls of Tobacco, and the rest of the whole Accompt in Gold.

I might well say, now indeed, That the latter End of *Job* was better than the Beginning.[1] It is impossible to express here the Flutterings of my very Heart, when I look'd over these Letters, and especially when I found all my Wealth about me; for as the *Brasil* Ships come all in Fleets, the same Ships which brought my Letters, brought my Goods; and the Effects were safe in the River before the Letters came to my Hand. In a Word, I turned pale, and grew sick; and had not the old Man run and fetch'd me a Cordial, I believe the sudden Surprize of Joy had overset Nature, and I had dy'd upon the Spot.

Nay after that, I continu'd very ill, and was so some Hours, 'till a Physician being sent for, and something of the real Cause of my Illness being known, he order'd me to be let Blood; after which, I had Relief, and grew well: But I verily believe, if it had not been eas'd by a Vent[2] given in that Manner, to the Spirits, I should have dy'd.

---

1 Job 42:12-17: "So the Lord blessed the latter end of Job more than his beginning: for he had fourteen thousand sheep, and six thousand camels, and a thousand yoke of oxen, and a thousand she asses. He had also seven sons and three daughters.... After this lived Job an hundred and forty years, and saw his sons, and his sons' sons, even four generations. So Job died, being old and full of days."

2 An opening cut to let out blood.

I was now Master, all on a Sudden, of above 5000 *l. Sterling* in Money, and had an Estate, as I might well call it, in the *Brasils*, of above a thousand Pounds a Year, as sure as an Estate of Lands in *England*: And in a Word, I was in a Condition which I scarce knew how to understand, or how to compose my self, for the Enjoyment of it.

The first thing I did, was to recompense my original Benefactor, my good old Captain, who had been first charitable to me in my Distress, kind to me in my Beginning, and honest to me at the End: I shew'd him all that was sent me, I told him, that next to the Providence of Heaven, which disposes all things, it was owing to him; and that it now lay on me to reward him, which I would do a hundred fold: So I first return'd to him the hundred Moidores I had receiv'd of him, then I sent for a Notary, and caused him to draw up a general Release or Discharge for the 470 Moidores, which he had acknowledg'd he ow'd me in the fullest and firmest Manner possible; after which, I caused a Procuration to be drawn, impowering him to be my Receiver of the annual Profits of my Plantation, and appointing my Partner to accompt to him, and make the Returns by the usual Fleets to him in my Name; and a Clause in the End, being a Grant of 100 Moidores a Year to him, during his Life, out of the Effects, and 50 Moidores a Year to his Son after him, for his Life: And thus I requited[1] my old Man.

I was now to consider which Way to steer my Course next, and what to do with the Estate that Providence had thus put into my Hands; and indeed I had more Care upon my Head now, than I had in my silent State of Life in the Island, where I wanted nothing but what I had, and had nothing but what I wanted: Whereas I had now a great Charge upon me, and my Business was how to secure it. I had ne'er a Cave now to hide my Money in, or a Place where it might lye without Lock or Key, 'till it grew mouldy and tarnish'd before any Body would meddle with it: On the contrary, I knew not where to put it, or who to trust with it. My old Patron, the Captain, indeed was honest, and that was the only Refuge I had.

In the next Place, my Interest in the *Brasils* seem'd to summon me thither, but now I could not tell, how to think of going thither, 'till I had settled my Affairs, and left my Effects in some safe Hands behind me. At first I thought of my old Friend the Widow, who I knew was honest, and would be just to me; but then she

---

1 Repaid.

was in Years, and but poor, and for ought I knew, might be in Debt; so that in a Word, I had no Way but to go back to *England* my self, and take my Effects with me.

It was some Months however before I resolved upon this; and therefore, as I had rewarded the old Captain fully, and to his Satisfaction, who had been my former Benefactor, so I began to think of my poor Widow, whose Husband had been my first Benefactor, and she, while it was in her Power, my faithful Steward and Instructor. So the first thing I did, I got a Merchant in *Lisbon* to write to his Correspondent in *London*, not only to pay a Bill, but to go find her out, and carry her in Money, an hundred Pounds from me, and to talk with her, and comfort her in her Poverty, by telling her she should, if I liv'd, have a further Supply: At the same time I sent my two Sisters in the Country, each of them an Hundred Pounds, they being, though not in Want, yet not in very good Circumstances; one having been marry'd, and left a Widow; and the other having a Husband not so kind to her as he should be.

But among all my Relations, or Acquaintances, I could not yet pitch upon one, to whom I durst commit the Gross of my Stock, that I might go away to the *Brasils*, and leave things safe behind me; and this greatly perplex'd me.

I had once a Mind to have gone to the *Brasils*, and have settled my self there; for I was, as it were, naturaliz'd to the Place; but I had some little Scruple in my Mind about Religion, which insensibly drew me back, of which I shall say more presently. However, it was not Religion that kept me from going there for the present; and as I had made no Scruple of being openly of the Religion of the Country,[1] all the while I was among them, so neither did I yet; only that now and then having of late thought more of it, (than formerly) when I began to think of living and dying among them, I began to regret my having profess'd my self a Papist, and thought it might not be the best Religion to die with.

But, as I have said, this was not the main thing that kept me from going to the *Brasils*, but that really I did not know with whom to leave my Effects behind me; so I resolv'd at last to go to *England* with it, where, if I arrived, I concluded I should make some Acquaintance, or find some Relations that would be faithful to me; and according I prepar'd to go for *England* with all my Wealth.

---

1 Worshipping as a Catholic.

In order to prepare things for my going Home, I first, the *Brasil* Fleet being just going away, resolved to give Answers suitable to the just and faithful Account of things I had from thence; and first to the Prior of St. *Augustine* I wrote a Letter full of Thanks for their just Dealings, and the Offer of the 872 Moidores, which was indisposed of, which I desir'd might be given 500 to the Monastery, and 372 to the Poor, as the Prior should direct, desiring the good *Padres* Prayers for me, and the like.

I wrote next a Letter of Thanks to my two Trustees, with all the Acknowledgment that so much Justice and Honesty call'd for; as for sending them any Present, they were far above having any Occasion of it.

Lastly, I wrote to my Partner, acknowledging his Industry in the Improving the Plantation, and his Integrity in encreasing the Stock of the Works, giving him Instructions for his future Government of my Part, according to the Powers I had left with my old Patron, to whom I desir'd him to send whatever became due to me, 'till he should hear from me more particularly; assuring him that it was my Intention, not only to come to him, but to settle my self there for the Remainder of my Life: To this I added a very handsom Present of some *Italian* Silks for his Wife, and two Daughters, for such the Captain's Son inform'd me he had; with two Pieces of fine *English* broad Cloath, the best I could get in *Lisbon*, five Pieces of black Bays, and some *Flanders* Lace of a good Value.

Having thus settled my Affairs, sold my Cargoe, and turn'd all my Effects into good Bills of Exchange, my next Difficulty was, which Way to go to *England*: I had been accustom'd enough to the Sea, and yet I had a strange Aversion to going to *England* by Sea at that time; and though I could give no Reason for it, yet the Difficulty encreas'd upon me so much, that though I had once shipp'd my Baggage, in order to go, yet I alter'd my Mind, and that not once, but two or three times.

It is true, I had been very unfortunate by Sea, and this might be some of the Reason: But let no Man slight the strong Impulses of his own Thoughts in Cases of such Moment: Two of the Ships which I had singl'd out to go in, I mean, more particularly singl'd out than any other, that is to say, so as in one of them to put my things on Board, and in the other to have agreed with the Captain; I say, two of these Ships miscarry'd, *viz.* One was taken by the *Algerines*,[1] and the other was cast away on the *Start* near

---

1 Algerian pirates.

Torbay,[1] and all the People drown'd except three; so that in either of those Vessels I had been made miserable; and in which most, it was hard to say.

Having been thus harass'd in my Thoughts, my old Pilot, to whom I communicated every thing, press'd me earnestly not to go by Sea, but either to go by Land to the *Groyne*,[2] and cross over the Bay of *Biscay* to *Rochell*, from whence it was but an easy and safe Journey by Land to *Paris*, and so to *Calais* and *Dover*; or to go up to *Madrid*, and so all the Way by Land thro' *France*.

In a Word, I was so prepossess'd against my going by Sea at all, except from *Calais* to *Dover*, that I resolv'd to travel all the Way by Land; which as I was not in Haste, and did not value the Charge, was by much the pleasanter Way; and to make it more so, my old Captain brought an *English* Gentleman, the Son of a Merchant in *Lisbon*, who was willing to travel with me: After which, we pick'd up two more *English* Merchants also, and two young *Portuguese* Gentlemen, the last going to *Paris* only; so that we were in all six of us, and five Servants; the two Merchants and the two *Portuguese*, contenting themselves with one Servant, between two, to save the Charge; and as for me, I got an *English* Sailor to travel with me as a Servant, besides my Man *Friday*, who was too much a Stranger to be capable of supplying the Place of a Servant on the Road.

In this Manner I set out from *Lisbon*; and our Company being all very well mounted and armed, we made a little Troop, whereof they did me the Honour to call me Captain, as well because I was the oldest Man, as because I had two Servants, and indeed was the Original of the whole Journey.

As I have troubled you with none of my Sea-Journals, so I shall trouble you now with none of my Land-Journal: But some Adventures that happen'd to us in this tedious and difficult Journey, I must not omit.

When we came to *Madrid*, we being all of us Strangers to *Spain*, were willing to stay some time to see the Court of *Spain*, and to see what was worth observing; but it being the latter Part of the Summer, we hasten'd away, and set out from *Madrid* about the Middle of *October*. But when we came to the Edge of *Navarre*,[3] we were alarm'd at several Towns on the Way, with an

---

1 Start Point, a promontory in Devonshire, was the site of numerous shipwrecks.
2 An archaic variation of *A Coruña*, an important port town in Galicia in north-west Spain.
3 At the time, under French rule.

Account, that so much Snow was fallen on the *French* Side of the Mountains, that several Travellers were obliged to come back to *Pampeluna*,[1] after having attempted, at an extream Hazard, to pass on.

When we came to *Pampeluna* it self, we found it so indeed; and to me that had been always used to a hot Climate, and indeed to Countries where we could scarce bear any Cloaths on, the Cold was insufferable; nor indeed was it more painful than it was surprising, to come but ten Days before out of the old Castile where the Weather was not only warm but very hot, and immediately to feel a Wind from the *Pyrenean* Mountains, so very keen, so severely cold, as to be intollerable, and to endanger benumbing and perishing of our Fingers and Toes.

Poor *Friday* was really frighted when he saw the Mountains all cover'd with Snow, and felt cold Weather, which he had never seen or felt before in his Life.

To mend the Matter, when we came to *Pampeluna*, it continued snowing with so much Violence, and so long, that the People said, Winter was come before its time, and the Roads which were difficult before, were now quite impassable: For in a Word, the Snow lay in some Places too thick for us to travel; and being not hard frozen, as is the Case in Northern Countries: There was no going without being in Danger of being bury'd alive every Step. We stay'd no less than twenty Days at *Pampeluna*; when (seeing the Winter coming on, and no Likelihood of its being better; for it was the severest Winter all over *Europe* that had been known in the Memory of Man) I propos'd that we should all go away to *Fonterabia*,[2] and there take Shipping for *Bourdeaux*, which was a very little Voyage.

But while we were considering this, there came in four *French* Gentlemen, who having been stopp'd on the *French* Side of the Passes, as we were on the *Spanish*, had found out a Guide, who traversing the Country near the Head of *Languedoc*, had brought them over the Mountains by such Ways, that they were not much incommoded with the Snow; and where they met with Snow in any Quantity, they said it was frozen hard enough to bear them and their Horses.

We sent for this Guide, who told us, he would undertake to carry us the same Way with no Hazard from the Snow, provided we were armed sufficiently to protect our selves from wild Beasts;

---

1 Pamplona, the capital of Navarre.
2 Fuentarrabia, a Spanish port on the Bay of Biscay.

for he said, upon these great Snows, it was frequent for some Wolves to show themselves at the Foot of the Mountains, being made ravenous for Want of Food, the Ground being covered with Snow: We told him, we were well enough prepar'd for such Creatures as they were, if he would ensure us from a Kind of two-legged Wolves, which we were told, we were in most Danger from, especially on the *French* Side of the Mountains.

He satisfy'd us there was no Danger of that kind in the Way that we were to go; so we readily agreed to follow him, as did also twelve other Gentlemen, with their Servants, some *French*, some *Spanish*; who, as I said, had attempted to go, and were oblig'd to come back again.

Accordingly, we all set out from *Pampeluna*, with our Guide, on the fifteenth of *November*; and indeed, I was surpriz'd, when instead of going forward, he came directly back with us, on the same Road that we came from *Madrid*, above twenty Miles; when being pass'd two Rivers, and come into the plain Country, we found our selves in a warm Climate again, where the Country was pleasant, and no Snow to be seen; but on a sudden, turning to his left, he approach'd the Mountains another Way; and though it is true, the Hills and Precipices look'd dreadful, yet he made so many Tours, such Meanders, and led us by such winding Ways, that we were insensibly pass'd the Height of the Mountains, without being much incumbred with the Snow; and all on a sudden, he shew'd us the pleasant fruitful Provinces of *Languedoc* and *Gascoign*, all green and flourishing; tho' indeed it was at a great Distance, and we had some rough Way to pass yet.

We were a little uneasy however, when we found it snow'd one whole Day, and a Night, so fast, that we could not travel; but he bid us be easy, we should soon be past it all: We found indeed, that we began to descend every Day, and to come more *North* than before; and so depending upon our Guide, we went on.

It was about two Hours before Night, when our Guide being something before us, and not just in Sight, out rushed three monstrous Wolves, and after them a Bear, out of a hollow Way, adjoyning to a thick Wood; two of the Wolves flew upon the Guide, and had he been half a Mile before us, he had been devour'd indeed, before we could have help'd him: One of them fastned upon his Horse, and the other attack'd the Man with that Violence, that he had not Time, or not Presence of Mind enough to draw his Pistol, but hollow'd and cry'd out to us most lustily; my Man *Friday* being next me, I bid him ride up, and see what was the Matter; as soon as *Friday* came in Sight of the Man, he hollow'd as loud as t'other, *O Master! O Master!* But like a bold Fellow, rode directly up to the poor Man, and with his Pistol shot the Wolf that attack'd him into the Head.

It was happy for the poor Man, that it was my Man *Friday*; for he having been us'd to that kind of Creature in his Country, had no Fear upon him; but went close up to him, and shot him as above; whereas any of us, would have fir'd at a farther Distance, and have perhaps either miss'd the Wolf, or endanger'd shooting the Man.

But it was enough to have terrify'd a bolder Man than I, and indeed it alarm'd all our Company, when with the Noise of *Friday's* Pistol, we heard on both Sides the dismallest Howling of Wolves, and the Noise redoubled by the Eccho of the Mountains, that it was to us as if there had been a prodigious Multitude of them; and perhaps indeed there was not such a Few, as that we had no cause of Apprehensions.

However, as *Friday* had kill'd this Wolf, the other that had fastned upon the Horse, left him immediately, and fled; having happily fastned upon his Head, where the Bosses of the Bridle had stuck in his Teeth; so that he had not done him much Hurt: The Man indeed was most Hurt; for the raging Creature had bit him twice, once on the Arm, and the other Time a little above his Knee; and he was just as it were tumbling down by the Disorder of his Horse, when *Friday* came up and shot the Wolf.

It is easy to suppose, that at the Noise of *Friday's* Pistol, we all mended our Pace, and rid up as fast as the Way (which was very difficult) would give us leave, to see what was the Matter; as soon as we came clear of the Trees, which blinded us before, we saw clearly what had been the Case, and how *Friday* had disengag'd the poor Guide; though we did not presently discern what kind of Creature it was he had kill'd.

But never was a Fight manag'd so hardily, and in such a sur- prizing Manner, as that which follow'd between *Friday* and the Bear, which gave us all (though at first we were surpriz'd and afraid for him) the greatest Diversion imaginable: As the Bear is a heavy, clumsey Creature, and does not gallop as the Wolf does, who is swift, and light; so he has two particular Qualities, which generally are the Rule of his Actions; First, As to Men, who are not his proper Prey; I say, not his proper Prey; because tho' I cannot say what excessive Hunger might do, which was now their Case, the Ground being all cover'd with Snow; but as to Men, he does not usually attempt them, unless they first attack him: On the contrary, if you meet him in the Woods, if you don't meddle with him, he won't meddle with you; but then you must take Care to be very Civil to him, and give him the Road; for he is a very nice[1] Gentleman, he won't go a Step out of his Way for a Prince; nay, if you are really afraid, your best way is to look another Way, and keep going on; for sometimes if you stop, and stand still, and look steadily at him, he takes it for an Affront; but if you throw or toss any Thing at him, and it hits him, though it were but a bit of a Stick, as big as your Finger, he takes it for an Affront, and sets all his other Business aside to pursue his Revenge; for he will have Satisfaction in Point of Honour; that is his first Quality: The next is, That if he be once affronted, he will never leave you, Night or Day, till he has his Revenge; but follows at a good round rate, till he overtakes you.

My Man *Friday* had deliver'd our Guide, and when we came up to him, he was helping him off from his Horse; for the Man was both hurt and frighted, and indeed, the last more than the first; when on the sudden, we spy'd the Bear come out of the Wood, and a vast monstrous One it was, the biggest by far that ever I saw: We were all a little surpriz'd, when we saw him; but when *Friday* saw him, it was easy to see Joy and Courage in the Fellow's Countenance; *O! O! O!* Says *Friday*, three Times, pointing to him; O Master! *You give me te Leave! Me shakee te Hand with him: Me make you good laugh.*

I was surpriz'd to see the Fellow so pleas'd; *You Fool you*, says I, *he will eat you up: Eatee me up! Eatee me up! Says Friday, twice over again; Me eatee him up: Me make you good laugh: You all stay here, me show you good laugh*; so down he sits, and gets his Boots off in a Moment, and put on a Pair of Pumps (as we call the flat Shoes they wear) and which he had in his Pocket, gives my other Servant his Horse, and with his Gun away he flew swift like the Wind.

The Bear was walking softly on, and offer'd to meddle with no Body, till *Friday* coming pretty near, calls to him, as if the Bear could understand him; *Hark ye, hark ye*, says *Friday, me speakee wit you*: We follow'd at a Distance; for now being come down on the *Gascoign* side of the Mountains, we were entred a vast great Forest, where the Country was plain, and pretty open, though many Trees in it scatter'd here and there.

Friday, who had as we say, the Heels of the Bear, came up with him quickly, and takes up a great Stone, and throws at him, and hit him just on the Head; but did him no more harm, than if he

---

1 Difficult to please, fastidious.

had thrown it against a Wall; but it answer'd *Friday's* End; for the Rogue was so void of Fear, that he did it purely to make the Bear follow him, and show us some Laugh as he call'd it.

As soon as the Bear felt the Stone, and saw him, he turns about, and comes after him, taking Devilish long Strides, and shuffling along at a strange Rate, so as would have put a Horse to a midling Gallop; away runs *Friday*, and takes his Course, as if he run towards us for Help; so we all resolv'd to fire at once upon the Bear, and deliver my Man; though I was angry at him heartily, for bringing the Bear back upon us, when he was going about his own Business another Way; and especially I was angry that he had turn'd the Bear upon us, and then run away; and I call'd out, *You Dog*, said I, *is this your making us laugh? Come away, and take your Horse, that we may shoot the Creature*; he hears me, and crys out, *No shoot, no shoot, stand still, you get much Laugh*. And as the nimble Creature run two Foot for the Beast's one, he turn'd on a sudden, on one side of us, and seeing a great Oak-Tree, fit for his Purpose, he beckon'd to us to follow, and doubling his Pace, he gets nimbly up the Tree, laying his Gun down upon the Ground, at about five or six Yards from the Bottom of the Tree.

The Bear soon came to the Tree, and we follow'd at a Distance; the first Thing he did, he stopp'd at the Gun, smelt to it, but let it lye, and up he scrambles into the Tree, climbing like a Cat, though so monstrously heavy: I was amaz'd at the Folly, as I thought it, of my Man, and could not for my Life see any Thing to laugh at yet, till seeing the Bear get up the Tree, we all rod nearer to him.

When we came to the Tree, there was *Friday* got out to the small End of a large Limb of the Tree, and the Bear got about half way to him; as soon as the Bear got out to that part where the Limb of the Tree was weaker, *Ha*, says he to us, *now you see me teachee the Bear dance*; so he falls a jumping and shaking the Bough, at which the Bear began to totter, but stood still, and begun to look behind him, to see how he should get back; then indeed we did laugh heartily: But *Friday* had not done with him by a great deal; when he sees him stand still, he calls out to him again, as if he had suppos'd the Bear could speak *English*; *What you no come farther, pray you come farther*; so he left jumping and shaking the Trees; and the Bear, just as if he had understood what he said, did come a little further, then he fell a jumping again, and the Bear stopp'd again.

We thought now was a good time to knock him on the Head, and I call'd to *Friday* to stand still, and we would shoot the Bear;

but he cry'd out earnestly, *O pray! O pray! No shoot, me shoot, by and then*; he would have said, *By and by*: However, to shorten the Story, *Friday* danc'd so much, and the Bear Stood so ticklish, that we had laughing enough indeed, but still could not imagine what the Fellow would do; for first we thought he depended upon shaking the Bear off; and we found the Bear was too cunning for that too; for he would not go out far enough to be thrown down, but clings fast with his great broad Claws and Feet, so that we could not imagine what would be the End of it, and where the Jest would be at last.

But *Friday* put us out of doubt quickly; for seeing the Bear cling fast to the Bough, and that he would not be perswaded to come any farther; *Well, well*, says *Friday, you no come farther, me go, me go; you no come to me, me go come to you*; and upon this, he goes out to the smallest End of the Bough, where it would bend with his Weight, and gently lets himself down by it, sliding down the Bough, till he came near enough to jump down on his Feet, and away he run to his Gun, takes it up, and stands still.

Well, said I to him, *Friday*, What will you do now? Why don't you shoot him? *No shoot*, says *Friday, no yet, me shoot now, me no kill; me stay, give you one more laugh*; and indeed so he did, as you will see presently; for when the Bear see his Enemy gone, he comes back from the Bough where he stood; but did it mighty leisurely, looking behind him every Step, and coming backward till he got into the Body of the Tree; then with the same hinder End foremost, he came down the Tree, grasping it with his Claws, and moving one Foot at a Time, very leisurely; at this Juncture, and just before he could set his hind Feet upon the Ground, *Friday* stept up close to him, clapt the Muzzle of his Piece into his Ear, and shot him dead as a Stone.

Then the Rogue turn'd about, to see if we did not laugh, and when he saw we were pleas'd by our Looks, he falls a laughing himself very loud; *so we kill Bear in my Country*, says *Friday*; so you kill them, says I, Why you have no Guns: *No*, says he, *no Gun, but shoot, great much long Arrow*.

This was indeed a good Diversion to us; but we were still in a wild Place, and our Guide very much hurt, and what to do we hardly knew; the Howling of Wolves run much in my Head; and indeed, except the Noise I once heard on the Shore of *Africa*, of which I have said something already, I never heard any thing that filled me with so much Horrour.

These things, and the Approach of Night, called us off, or else, as *Friday* would have had us, we should certainly have taken the

Skin of this monstrous Creature off, which was worth saving; but we had three Leagues to go, and our Guide hasten'd us, so we left him, and went forward on our Journey.

The Ground was still cover'd with Snow, tho' not so deep and dangerous as on the Mountains, and the ravenous Creatures, as we heard afterwards, were come down into the Forest and plain Country, press'd by Hunger to seek for Food; and had done a great deal of Mischief in the Villages, where they surpriz'd the Country People, kill'd a great many of their Sheep and Horses, and some People too.

We had one dangerous Place to pass, which our Guide told us, if there were any more Wolves in the Country, we should find them there; and this was in a small Plain, surrounded with Woods on every Side, and a long narrow Defile[1] or Lane, which we were to pass to get through the Wood, and then we should come to the Village where we were to lodge.

It was within half an Hour of Sun-set when we entred the first Wood; and a little after Sun-set, when we came into the Plain. We met with nothing in the first Wood, except, that in a little Plain within the Wood, which was not above two Furlongs over, we saw five great Wolves cross the Road, full Speed one after another, as if they had been in Chase of some Prey, and had it in View, they took no Notice of us, and were gone, and out of our Sight in a few Moments.

Upon this our Guide, who by the Way was a wretched faint-hearted Fellow, bid us keep in a ready Posture; for he believed there were more Wolves a coming.

We kept our Arms ready, and our Eyes about us, but we saw no more Wolves, 'till we came thro' that Wood, which was near half a League, and entred the Plain; as soon as we came into the Plain, we had Occasion enough to look about us: The first Object we met with, was a dead Horse; that is to say, a poor Horse which the Wolves had kill'd, and at least a Dozen of them at Work; we could not say eating of him, but picking of his Bones rather; for they had eaten up all the Flesh before.

We did not think fit to disturb them at their Feast, neither did they take much Notice of us: *Friday* would have let fly at them, but I would not suffer him by any Means; for I found we were like to have more Business upon our Hands than we were aware of. We were not gone half over the Plain, but we began to hear the Wolves howl in the Wood on our Left, in a frightful Manner, and

---

1 A narrow passage through which troops can pass only in file.

presently after we saw about a hundred coming on directly towards us, all in a Body, and most of them in a Line, as regularly as an Army drawn up by experienc'd Officers. I scarce knew in what Manner to receive them; but found to draw our selves in a close Line was the only Way: so we form'd in a Moment: But that we might not have too much Interval, I order'd, that only every other Man should fire, and that the others who had not fir'd should stand ready to give them a second Volley immediately, if they continued to advance upon us, and that then those who had fir'd at first, should not pretend[1] to load their Fusees again, but stand ready with every one a Pistol; for we were all arm'd with a Fusee, and a Pair of Pistols each Man; so we were by this Method able to fire six Volleys, half of us at a Time; however, at present we had no Necessity; for upon firing the first Volley, the Enemy made a full Stop, being terrify'd as well with the Noise, as with the Fire; four of them being shot into the Head, dropp'd, several others were wounded, and went bleeding off, as we could see by the Snow: I found they stopp'd, but did not immediately retreat; whereupon remembring that I had been told, that the fiercest Creatures were terrify'd at the Voice of a Man, I caus'd all our Company to hollow as loud as we could; and I found the Notion not altogether mistaken; for upon our Shout, they began to retire, and turn about; then I order'd a second Volley to be fir'd, in their Rear, which put them to the Gallop, and away they went to the Woods.

This gave us leisure to charge our Pieces again, and that we might loose no Time, we kept going; but we had but little more than loaded our Fusees, and put our selves into a Readiness, when we heard a terrible Noise in the same Wood, on our Left, only that it was farther onward the same Way we were to go.

The Night was coming on, and the Light began to be dusky, which made it worse on our Side; but the Noise encreasing, we could easily perceive that it was the Howling and Yelling of those hellish Creatures; and on a sudden, we perceiv'd 2 or 3 Troops of Wolves, one on our Left, one behind us, and one on our Front; so that we seem'd to be surrounded with 'em; however, as they did not fall upon us, we kept our Way forward, as fast as we could make our Horses go, which the Way being very rough, was only a good large Trot; and in this Manner we came in View of the Entrance of a Wood, through which we were to pass, at the farther Side of the Plain; but we were greatly surpriz'd, when coming

---

1 Presume, attempt.

nearer the Lane, or Pass, we saw a confus'd Number of Wolves standing just at the Entrance.

On a sudden, at another opening of the Wood, we heard the Noise of a Gun; and looking that Way, out rush'd a Horse, with a Saddle, and a Bridle on him, flying like the Wind, and sixteen or seventeen Wolves after him, full Speed; indeed, the Horse had the Heels of them; but as we suppos'd that he could not hold it at that rate, we doubted not but they would get up with him at last, and no question but they did.

But here we had a most horrible Sight; for riding up to the Entrance where the Horse came out, we found the Carcass of another Horse, and of two Men, devour'd by the ravenous Creatures, and one of the Men was no doubt the same who we heard fir'd the Gun; for there lay a Gun just by him, fir'd off; but as to the Man, his Head, and the upper Part of his Body was eaten up.

This fill'd us with Horror, and we knew not what Course to take, but the Creatures resolv'd us[1] soon; for they gather'd about us presently, in hopes of Prey; and I verily believe there were three hundred of them: It happen'd very much to our Advantage, that at the Entrance into the Wood, but a little Way from it, there lay some large Timber Trees, which had been cut down the Summer before, and I suppose lay there for Carriage; I drew my little Troop in among those Trees, and placing our selves in a Line, behind one long Tree, I advis'd them all to light, and keeping that Tree before us, for a Breast Work, to stand in a Triangle, or three Fronts, enclosing our Horses in the Center.

We did so, and it was well we did; for never was a more furious Charge than the Creatures made upon us in the Place; they came on us with a growling kind of a Noise (and mounted the Piece of Timber, which as I said, was our Breast Work) as if they were only rushing upon their Prey; and this Fury of theirs, it seems, was principally occasion'd by their seeing our Horses behind us, which was the Prey they aim'd at: I order'd our Men to fire as before, every other Man; and they took their Aim so sure, that indeed they kill'd several of the Wolves at the first Volley; but there was a Necessity to keep a continual Firing; for they came on like Devils, those behind pushing on those before.

When we had fir'd our second Volley of our Fusees, we thought they stopp'd a little, and I hop'd they would have gone off; but it was but a Moment; for others came forward again; so we fir'd two Volleys of our Pistols, and I believe in these four

---

1 Made up our minds for us.

Firings, we had kill'd seventeen or eighteen of them, and lam'd twice as many; yet they came on again.

I was loath to spend our last Shot too hastily; so I call'd my Servant, not my Man *Friday*, for he was better employ'd; for with the greatest Dexterity imaginable, he had charg'd my Fusee, and his own, while we were engag'd; but as I said, I call'd my other Man, and giving him a Horn of Powder, I bad him lay a Train, all along the Piece of Timber, and let it be a large Train; he did so, and had but just Time to get away, when the Wolves came up to it, and some were got up upon it; when I snapping an uncharg'd Pistol, close to the Powder, set it on fire; those that were upon the Timber were scorcht with it, and six or seven of them fell, or rather jump'd in among us, with the Force and Fright of the Fire; we dispatch'd these in an Instant, and the rest were so frighted with the Light, which the Night, for it was now very near Dark, made more terrible, that they drew back a little.

Upon which I order'd our last Pistol to be fir'd off in one Volley, and after that we gave a Shout; upon this, the Wolves turn'd Tail, and we sally'd immediately upon near twenty lame Ones, who we found struggling on the Ground, and fell a cutting them with our Swords, which answer'd our Expectation; for the Crying and Howling they made, was better understood by their Fellows, so that they all fled and left us.

We had, first and last, kill'd about three Score of them; and had it been Day-Light, we had kill'd many more: The Field of Battle being thus clear'd, we made forward again; for we had still near a League to go. We heard the ravenous Creatures houl and yell in the Woods as we went, several Times; and sometimes we fancy'd we saw some of them, but the Snow dazling our Eyes, we were not certain; so in about an Hour more, we came to the Town, where we were to lodge, which we found in a terrible Fright, and all in Arms; for it seems, that the Night before, the Wolves and some Bears had broke into the Village in the Night, and put them in a terrible Fright, and they were oblig'd to keep Guard Night and Day, but especially in the Night, to preserve their Cattle, and indeed their People.

The next Morning our Guide was so ill, and his Limbs swell'd with the rankling[1] of his two Wounds, that he could go no farther; so we were oblig'd to take a new Guide there, and go to *Tholouse*, where we found a warm Climate, a fruitful pleasant Country, and no Snow, no Wolves, or any Thing like them; but when we told

---

1 Festering.

our Story at *Tholouse*, they told us it was nothing but what was ordinary in the great Forest at the Foot of the Mountains, especially when the Snow lay on the Ground: But they enquir'd much what kind of a Guide we had gotten, that would venture to bring us that Way in such a severe Season; and told us, it was very much we were not all devour'd. When we told them how we plac'd our selves, and the Horses in the Middle, they blam'd us exceedingly, and told us it was fifty to one but we had been all destroy'd; for it was the Sight of the Horses which made the Wolves so furious, seeing their Prey; and that at other Times they are really afraid of a Gun; but the being excessive Hungry, and raging on that Account, the Eagerness to come at the Horses had made them sensless of Danger; and that if we had not by the continu'd Fire, and at last by the Stratagem of the Train of Powder, master'd them, it had been great Odds but that we had been torn to Pieces; whereas had we been content to have sat still on Horseback, and fir'd as Horsemen, they would not have taken the Horses for so much their own, when Men were on their Backs, as otherwise; and withal they told us, that at last, if we had stood altogether, and left our Horses, they would have been so eager to have devour'd them, that we might have come off safe, especially having our Fire Arms in our Hands, and being so many in Number.

For my Part, I was never so sensible of Danger in my Life; for seeing above three hundred Devils come roaring and open mouth'd to devour us, and having nothing to shelter us, or retreat to, I gave my self over for lost; and as it was, I believe, I shall never care to cross those Mountains again; I think I would much rather go a thousand Leagues by Sea, though I were sure to meet with a Storm once a Week.

I have nothing uncommon to take Notice of, in my Passage through *France*; nothing but what other Travellers have given an Account of, with much more Advantage than I can. I travell'd from *Tholouse* to *Paris*, and without any considerable Stay, came to *Callais*, and landed safe at *Dover*, the fourteenth of *January*, after having had a severely cold Season to travel in.

I was now come to the Center of my Travels, and had in a little Time all my new discover'd Estate safe about me, the Bills of Exchange which I brought with me having been very currently paid.

My principal Guide, and Privy Councellor, was my good antient Widow, who in Gratitude for the Money I had sent her, thought no Pains too much, or Care too great, to employ for me;

and I trusted her so entirely with every Thing, that I was perfectly easy as to the Security of my Effects; and indeed, I was very happy from my Beginning, and now to the End, in the unspotted Integrity of this good Gentlewoman.

And now I began to think of leaving my Effects with this Woman, and setting out for *Lisbon*, and so to the *Brasils*; but now another Scruple came in my Way, and that was Religion; for as I had entertain'd some Doubts about the *Roman* Religion, even while I was abroad, especially in my State of Solitude; so I knew there was no going to the *Brasils* for me, much less going to settle there, unless I resolv'd to embrace the *Roman* Catholick Religion, without any Reserve; unless on the other hand, I resolv'd to be a Sacrifice to my Principles, be a Martyr for Religion, and die in the Inquisition; so I resolv'd to stay at Home, and if I could find Means for it, to dispose of my Plantation.

To this Purpose I wrote to my old Friend at *Lisbon*, who in Return gave me Notice, that he could easily dispose of it there: But that if I thought fit to give him Leave to offer it in my Name to the two Merchants, the Survivors of my Trustees, who liv'd in the *Brasils*, who must fully understand the Value of it, who liv'd just upon the Spot, and who I knew were very rich; so that he believ'd they would be fond of buying it; he did not doubt, but I should make 4 or 5000 Pieces of Eight, the more of it.

Accordingly I agreed, gave him Order to offer it to them, and he did so; and in about 8 Months more, the Ship being then return'd, he sent me Account, that they had accepted the Offer, and had remitted 33000 Pieces of Eight, to a Correspondent of theirs at *Lisbon*, to pay for it.

In Return, I sign'd the Instrument of Sale in the Form which they sent from *Lisbon*, and sent it to my old Man, who sent me Bills of Exchange for 328000 Pieces of Eight to me, for the Estate; reserving the Payment of 100 Moidores a Year to him, the old Man, during his Life, and 50 Moidores afterwards to his Son for his Life, which I had promised them, which the Plantation was to make good as a Rent-Charge. And thus I have given the first Part of a Life of Fortune and Adventure, a Life of Providences Checquer-Work, and of a Variety which the World will seldom be able to show the like of: Beginning foolishly, but closing much more happily than any Part of it ever gave me Leave so much as to hope for.

Any one would think, that in this State of complicated good Fortune, I was past running any more Hazards; and so indeed I had been, if other Circumstances had concurr'd, but I was inur'd[1] to a wandring Life, had no Family, not many Relations, nor however rich had I contracted much Acquaintance; and though I had sold my Estate in the *Brasils*, yet I could not keep the Country out of my Head, and had a great Mind to be upon the Wing again, especially I could not resist the strong Inclination I had to see my Island, and to know if the poor *Spaniards* were in Being there, and how the Rogues I left there had used them.

My true Friend, the Widow, earnestly diswaded me from it, and so far prevail'd with me, that for almost seven Years she prevented my running Abroad; during which time, I took my two Nephews, the Children of one of my Brothers into my Care: The eldest having something of his own, I bred up as a Gentleman, and gave him a Settlement of some Addition to his Estate, after my Decease; the other I put out to a Captain of a Ship; and after five Years, finding him a sensible bold enterprising young Fellow, I put him into a good Ship, and sent him to Sea: And this young Fellow afterwards drew me in, as old as I was, to farther Adventures my self.

In the mean time, I in Part settled my self here; for first of all I marry'd, and that not either to my Disadvantage or Dissatisfaction, and had three Children, two Sons and one Daughter: But my Wife dying, and my Nephew coming Home with good Success from a Voyage to *Spain*, my Inclination to go Abroad, and his Importunity prevailed and engag'd me to go in his Ship, as a private Trader to the *East Indies*: This was in the Year 1694.

In this Voyage I visited my new Collony in the Island, saw my Successors the *Spaniards*, had the whole Story of their Lives, and of the Villains I left there; how at first they insulted the poor *Spaniards*, how they afterwards agreed, disagreed, united, separated, and how at last the *Spaniards* were oblig'd to use Violence with them, how they were subjected to the *Spaniards*, how honestly the *Spaniards* used them; a History, if it were entred into, as full of Variety and wonderful Accidents, as my own Part, particularly also as to their Battles with the *Carribeans*, who landed several times upon the Island, and as to the Improvement they made upon the Island it self, and how five of them made an Attempt upon the main Land, and brought away eleven Men and five Women Prisoners, by which, at my coming, I found about twenty young Children on the Island.

Here I stay'd about 20 Days, left them Supplies of all necessary things, and particularly of Arms, Powder, Shot, Cloaths,

---

1 Accustomed, habituated.

Tools, and two Workmen, which I brought from *England* with me, *viz.* a Carpenter and a Smith.

Besides this, I shar'd the Island into Parts with 'em, reserv'd to my self the Property of the whole, but gave them such Parts respectively as they agreed on; and having settled all things with them, and engaged them not to leave the Place, I left them there.

From thence I touch'd at the *Brasils*, from whence I sent a Bark, which I bought there, with more People to the Island, and in it, besides other Supplies, I sent seven Women, being such as I found proper for Service, or for Wives to such as would take them: As to the *English* Men, I promis'd them to send them some Women from *England*, with a good Cargoe of Necessaries, if they would apply themselves to Planting, which I afterwards perform'd. And the Fellows prov'd very honest and diligent after they were master'd, and had their Properties set apart for them. I sent them also from the *Brasils* five Cows, three of them being big with Calf, some Sheep, and some Hogs, which, when I came again, were considerably encreas'd.

But all these things, with an Account how 300 *Caribbees* came and invaded them, and ruin'd their Plantations, and how they fought with that whole Number twice, and were at first defeated, and three of them kill'd; but at last a Storm destroying their Enemies Cannoes, they famish'd or destroy'd almost all the rest, and renew'd and recover'd the Possession of their Plantation, and still liv'd upon the Island.

All these things, with some very surprizing Incidents in some new Adventures of my own, for ten Years more, I may perhaps give a farther Account of hereafter.

FINIS.

Appendix A

Daniel Defoe, Preface and Publisher's Introduction to Serious Reflections During the Life and Surprising Adventures of Robinson Crusoe: With his Vision of the Angelick World *(1720)*

[Throughout the eighteenth and nineteenth centuries, *The Life and Strange Surprizing Adventures of Robinson Crusoe* was usually paired with its sequel, *The Farther Adventures of Robinson Crusoe*. The third volume, *Serious Reflections During the Life and Surprising Adventures of Robinson Crusoe*, by contrast, has never found a wide audience and has been reprinted much less frequently. Still, two parts of it have inflected our reading of the first volume: this preface, in which Defoe responds to Charles Gildon's charge that Crusoe is his creator's "true Allegorick Image" (see Appendix B), and the first section, "Of Solitude," which is printed in Appendix D4.]

Robinson Crusoe's PREFACE.

As the Design of every Thing is said to be first in the Intention, and last in the Execution; so I come now to acknowledge to my Reader, That the present Work is not merely the Product of the two first Volumes, but the two first Volumes may rather be called the Product of this: The Fable is always made for the Moral, not the Moral for the Fable.[1]

I have heard, that the envious and ill-disposed Part of the World have rais'd some Objections against the two first Volumes, on Pretence, *for want of a better Reason*; That (*as they say*) the Story is feign'd, that the Names are borrow'd, and that it is all a Romance; that there never were any such Man or Place, or Circumstances in any Man's Life; that it is all form'd and embellish'd by Invention to impose upon the World.

I *Robinson Crusoe* being at this Time in perfect and sound Mind and Memory, Thanks be to God therefore; do hereby declare, their Objection is an Invention scandalous in Design, and false in Fact; and do affirm, that the Story, though Allegorical, is also Historical; and that it

---

1   Unlike the first two volumes, which recount Crusoe's adventures (the fable), this third volume presents Crusoe's reflections (the moral).

is the beautiful Representation of a Life of unexampled Misfortunes, and of a Variety not to be met with in the World, sincerely adapted to, and intended for the common Good of Mankind, and designed at first, *as it is now farther apply'd*, to the most serious Uses possible.

Farther, that there is a Man alive,[1] and well known too, the Actions of whose Life are the just Subject of these Volumes, and to whom all or most Part of the Story most directly alludes, this may be depended upon for Truth, and to this I set my Name.

The famous History of *Don Quixot*, a Work which thousands read with Pleasure, to one that knows the Meaning of it, was an emblematic History of, and a just Satyr upon the Duke *de Medina Sidonia*;[2] a Person very remarkable at that Time in *Spain:* To those who knew the Original, the Figures were lively and easily discovered themselves, as they are also here, and the Images were just; and therefore, when a malicious, but foolish Writer,[3] in the abundance of his Gall,[4] spoke of the *Quixotism* of *R. Crusoe*, as he called it, he shewed evidently, that he knew nothing of what he said; and perhaps will be a little startled, when I shall tell him that what he meant for a Satyr, was the greatest of Panegyrics.

Without letting the Reader into a nearer Explication of the Matter, I proceed to let him know, that the happy Deductions I have employ'd myself to make from all the Circumstances of my Story, will abundantly make him amends for his not having the Emblem explained by the Original; and that when in my Observations and Reflections of any Kind in this Volume, I mention my Solitudes and Retirements, and allude to the Circumstances of the former Story, all those Parts of the Story are real Facts in my History, whatever borrow'd Lights they may be represented by: Thus the Fright and Fancies which succeeded the Story of the Print of a Man's Foot, and Surprise of the old Goat, and the Thing rolling on my Bed, and my jumping out in a Fright, are all Histories and real Stories; as are likewise the Dream of being taken by Messengers, being arrested by Officers, the Manner of being driven on Shore by the Surge of the Sea, the Ship on Fire, the Description of starving; the Story of my Man *Friday*, and many more most material

---

1   Defoe himself.

2   Miguel de Cervantes's novel *Don Quixote* (1604, 1615) was hugely popular in eighteenth-century England. There is little evidence that Cervantes intended to satirize the Duke of Sidonia.

3   Thomas Cox, who published a pirated edition of *Crusoe* in 1719, was sued by Defoe's publisher, William Taylor. In a letter defending himself, Cox refers to Defoe as "the author of Crusoe's Don Quixotism" (*The Flying Post*, 29 October 1719).

4   Bitterness (once believed to arise from the gall bladder).

Passages observ'd here, and on which any religious Reflections are made, are all historical and true in Fact: It is most real, that I had a Parrot, and taught it to call me by my Name, such a Servant a Savage, and afterwards a Christian, and that his Name was called *Friday*, and that he was ravish'd[1] from me by force, and died in the Hands that took him, which I represent by being killed; this is all literally true, and should I enter into Discoveries, many alive can testify them: His other Conduct and Assistance to me also have just References in all their Parts to the Helps I had from that faithful Savage, in my real Solitudes and Disasters.

The Story of the Bear in the Tree, and the Fight with the Wolves in the Snow, is likewise Matter of real History; and, in a Word, the Adventures of *Robinson Crusoe* are one whole Scheme of a real Life of eight and twenty Years, spent in the most wandring desolate and afflicting Circumstances that ever Man went through, and in which I have lived so long in a Life of Wonders in continu'd Storms, fought with the worst kind of Savages and Man-eaters, by unaccountable surprising Incidents, fed by Miracles greater than that of Ravens, suffered all Manner of Violences and Oppressions, injurious Reproaches, contempt of Men, Attacks of Devils, Corrections from Heaven, and Oppositions on Earth; have had innumerable Ups and Downs in Matters of Fortune, been in Slavery worse than *Turkish*, escaped by an exquisite Management, as that in the story of *Xury*, and the boat at *Sallee*, been taken up at sea in Distress, rais'd again and depress'd again, and that oftener perhaps in one Man's Life than ever was known before; Shipwreck'd often, tho' more by Land than by Sea: In a Word, there's not a Circumstance in the imaginary Story but has its just Allusion to a real Story, and chimes Part for Part, and Step for Step with the inimitable Life of *Robinson Crusoe*.

In like Manner, when in these Reflections, I speak of the Times and Circumstances of particular Actions done, or Incidents which happened in my Solitude and Island-Life, an impartial Reader will be so just to take it as it is; *viz.* that it is spoken or intended of that Part of the real Story which the Island-Life is a just Allusion to; and in this the Story is not only illustrated, but the real Part I think most justly approv'd: *For Example*, in the latter Part of this Work called the Vision, I begin thus, *When I was in my Island Kingdom, I had abundance of strange Notions of my seeing Apparitions,* &c. all these Reflections are just History of a State of forc'd Confinement, which in my real History is represented by a confin'd Retreat in an Island; and 'tis as reasonable to represent one kind of Imprisonment by another, as it is to represent

---

1   Seized, taken away.

any Thing that really exists by that which exists not. The Story of my Fright with something on my Bed, was Word for Word a History of what happened, and indeed all those Things received very little Alteration, except what necessarily attends removing the Scene from one Place to another.

My Observations upon Solitude are the same, and I think I need say no more, than that the same Remark is to be made upon all the References made here, to the Transactions of the former Volumes, and the Reader is desired to allow for it as he goes on.

Besides all this, here is the just and only good End of all Parable or Allegorick History brought to pass, *viz.* for moral and religious Improvement. Here is invincible Patience recommended under the worst of Misery; indefatigable Application and undaunted Resolution under the greatest and most discouraging Circumstances; I say, these are recommended, as the only Way to work through those Miseries, and their Success appears sufficient to support the most dead-hearted Creature in the World.

Had the common Way of Writing a Mans private History been taken, and I had given you the Conduct or Life of a Man you knew, and whose Misfortunes and Infirmities, perhaps you had sometimes unjustly triumph'd over; all I could have said would have yielded no Diversion, and perhaps scarce have obtained a Reading, or at best no Attention; the Teacher, *like a greater,* having no Honour in his own Country.[1] Facts that are form'd to touch the Mind, must be done a great Way off, and by somebody never heard of: Even the Miracles of the Blessed Saviour of the World suffered Scorn and Contempt, when it was reflected, that they were done by the Carpenter's Son; one whose Family and Original they had a mean Opinion of, and whose Brothers and Sisters were ordinary People like themselves.

There even yet remains a Question, whether the Instruction of these Things will take place, when you are supposing the Scene, which is placed so far off, had its Original so near Home.

But I am far from being anxious about that, seeing I am well assur'd, that if the Obstinacy of our Age should shut their Ears against the just Reflections made in this Volume, upon the Transactions taken Notice of in the former, there will come an Age, when the Minds of Men shall be more flexible, when the Prejudices of their Fathers shall have no Place, and when the Rules of Vertue and Religion justly recommended, shall be more gratefully accepted than they may be now, that our Children may rise up in Judgment against their fathers, and

---

1 Mark 6:4: "But Jesus said unto them, A prophet is not without honour, but in his own country, and among his own kin, and in his own house."

one Generation be edified by the same Teaching, which another Generation had despised.

ROB. CRUSOE.

The Publisher's INTRODUCTION.

The publishing this extraordinary Volume will appear to be no Presumption, when it shall be remembred, with what unexpected Good *and Evil* Will the former Volumes have been accepted in the World.

If the Foundation has been so well laid, the Structure cannot but be expected to bear a Proportion; and while the Parable has been so diverting, the Moral must certainly be equally agreeable.

The success the two former Parts have met with, has been known by the Envy it has brought upon the Editor, express'd in a thousand hard Words from the Men of Trade; the Effect of that Regret which they entertain'd, at their having no Share in it: And I must do the Author the Justice to say, that not a Dog has wag'd his Tongue at the Work itself, nor has a Word been said to lessen the Value of it, but which has been the visible Effect of that Envy at the good Fortune of the Bookseller.

The Riddle is now expounded, and the intelligent Reader may see clearly the End and Design of the whole Work; that it is calculated for, and dedicated to the Improvement and Instruction of Mankind in the Ways of Vertue and Piety, by representing the various Circumstances to which Mankind is exposed; and encouraging such as fall into ordinary or extraordinary Casualties of Life, how to work thro' Difficulties, with unwearied Diligence and Application, and look up to Providence for Success.

The Observations and Reflections, that take up this Volume, crown the work; if the Doctrine has been accepted, the Application must of Necessity please; and the Author shews now, that he has learn'd sufficient Experience, how to make other Men wise and himself happy.

The Moral of the Fable, *as the Author calls it,* is most instructing; and those who challeng'd him most maliciously, with not making his Pen useful, will have Leisure to reflect, that they pass'd their Censure too soon; and, like *Solomon*'s Fool, *judged of the Matter before they heard it.*[1]

Those whose Avarice prevailing over their Honesty, had invaded

---

1 *Solomon's fool* is a generic term for the embodiment of foolishness in Proverbs and Ecclesiastes. Proverbs 18: 13: "He that answereth a matter before he heareth it, it is folly and shame unto him."

the Property of this Book by a corrupt Abridgment,[1] have both fail'd in their Hope, and been ashamed of the Fact; shifting off the Guilt as well as they could, *tho' weakly*, from one to another: The Principal Pyrate is gone to his Place, and we say no more of him, *De mortuis nil nisi bonum*;[2] 'tis Satisfaction enough, that the Attempt has prov'd abortive, as the Baseness of the Design might give them Reason to expect it would.

---

1 The 1719 duodecimo abridgment by Cox. In order to "make it Circulate thro' all Hands," Cox claimed in the preface, "we have Abridg'd it, and not only made the Book more portable, but lower'd its Price to the Circumstances of most People."
2 An abbreviated form of *de mortuis nil nisi bonum dicendum est*: "Say nothing but good things about the dead."

Appendix B

From Charles Gildon, The Life and Strange Surprizing Adventures of Mr. D—— De F—, of London, Hosier,[1] Who Has liv'd above fifty Years by himself, in the Kingdoms of North[2] and South Britain. The various Shapes he has appear'd in, and the Discoveries he has made for the Benefit of his Country. In a DIALOGUE between Him, Robinson Crusoe, and his Man Friday. With REMARKS Serious and Comical upon the Life of CRUSOE *(1719)*

[With the possible exception of Alexander Pope, no early eighteenth-century writer was the brunt of as many printed attacks as Daniel Defoe. But while most of those attacks targeted Defoe's political works, the most famous of them was directed toward *Robinson Crusoe*. Defoe's adversary this time was Charles Gildon (c. 1665-1724), a playwright, pamphleteer, biographer, essayist, and general hack writer, who saw in *Crusoe* an opportunity for quick sales. The pamphlet, which appeared just after *The Farther Adventures of Robinson Crusoe*, is divided into four parts: the preface, the dialogue between Defoe and his characters, an open letter in which Gildon exposes narrative inconsistencies in the novel, and a postscript that addresses *The Farther Adventures*. In the dialogue, Gildon insists that Crusoe is the "the true Allegorick Image" of Defoe; rather than arguing otherwise, Defoe adopted this notion in the Preface to the *Serious Reflections*.]

The PREFACE.

IF *ever the Story of any private Man's Adventures in the World were worth making publick, and were acceptable when publish'd, the Editor of this Account thinks this will be so.*

The Wonders of this Man's Life exceed all that (he thinks) is to be found Extant; the Life of one Man being scarce capable of greater Variety.

---

1 Someone who sells socks and stockings. Gildon's implication that the Defoe was a shopkeeper is misleading: Defoe was a wholesaler but never a retailer in hose.
2 Scotland, where Defoe traveled extensively in 1706-07, reporting to Harley and writing in support of Union.

The Story is told with greater Modesty than perhaps some Men may think necessary to the Subject, the Hero of our Dialogue not being very conspicuous for that Virtue, a more than common Assurance carrying him thro' all those various Shapes and Changes which he has pass'd without the least Blush.[1] The Fabulous Proteus[2] *of the Ancient Mythologist was but a very faint Type of our Hero, whose Changes are much more numerous, and he far more difficult to be constrain'd to his own Shape. If his Works should happen to live to the next Age, there would in all probability be a greater Strife among the several Parties, whose he really was, than among the seven* Graecian *Cities, to which of them* Homer *belong'd: The* Dissenters *first would claim him as theirs, the* Whigs *in general as theirs, the* Tories *as theirs, the* Non-jurors *as theirs, the* Papists *as theirs, the* Atheists *as theirs, and so on to what Sub-divisions there may be among us; so that it cannot be expected that I should give you in this short Dialogue his Picture at length; no, I only pretend to present you with him in Miniature, in Twenty Fours, and not in Folio.[3] But of all these Things, with some very surprizing Incidents in some new Adventures of his own for the rest of his Life, I may perhaps give a farther Account hereafter.*

A Dialogue betwixt D—— F—e, ROBINSON CRUSOE,
and his Man FRIDAY.

SCENE, *A great Field betwixt* Newington-Green *and* Newington *Town, at one a Clock in a Moon-light Morning.*[4]

Enter D—— F— with two Pocket Pistols.

D—l. A Fine pleasurable Morning, I believe about one a Clock; and, I suppose, all the Lazy Kidnapping Rogues are by this Time got drunk with *Geneva*[5] or Malt-Spirits to Bed, and I may pass Home without any farther Terror. However, I am pretty well arm'd to keep off their unsanctified Paws from my Shoulder——

---

1 Defoe's contemporaries often noted his willingness to change political loyalties, most notably when the Tories came to power in 1710.
2 In Homer's *Odyssey*, a sea-god able to change shape at will.
3 The size of an eighteenth-century book depended on the size of the printed sheet and the number of times it was folded. "Twenty fours" were small books whose sheets were each folded and cut to create twenty four pages, whereas "folios" used sheets folded just once to create two large pages.
4 Morton's Academy, where Defoe was educated, was located in Newington Green. During the composition of *Robinson Crusoe*, he was living in Newington Towne, or Stoke Newington.
5 Gin.

Bless my Eye-sight, what's this I see! I was secure too soon here, the *Philistines* are come upon me; this is the Effect of my not obeying the *Secret Hint*[1] I had not to come Home this Night. But, however, here they shall have a couple of Bullets in their Bellies—— ha! two of them, great tall Gigantick Rogues, with strange High-crown'd Caps, and Flaps hanging upon their Shoulders, and two Muskets a-piece, one with a Cutlass, and the other with a Hatchet; e—g-d I'll e'en run back again to the Green.   *[Turns and runs.*

Oh, plague upon that swift leg'd Dog, he's got before me; I must now stand upon my Guard, for he turns upon me and presents his Musket———— Gentlemen, what would you have? would you murder me? take what I have, and save my Life.

Cru. Why, Father *D—n*, dost thou not know thy own Children? art thou so frighted at Devils of thy own raising? I am thy *Robinson Crusoe*, and that, my Man *Friday*.

D—l. Ah! poor Crusoe, how came you hither? what do you do here?

Cru. Ho, ho, do you know me now? You are like the Devil in *Milton*, that could not tell the Offspring of his own Brain, *Sin* and *Death*, till *Madam Sin* discover'd to him who they were.[2] Yes, it is *Crusoe* and his Man *Friday*, who are come to punish thee now, for making us such Scoundrels in thy Writing: Come *Friday*, make ready, but don't shoot till I give the Word.

Fri. No shoot Master, no shoot; me will show you how we use Scribblers in my Country.

Cru. In your Country *Friday*, why, you have no Scribblers there?

Fri. No Matter that Master, we have as many Scribblers as Bears in my Country; and me will make Laugh, me will make *D—l* dance upon a Tree like *Bruin*. Oh! me will make much Laugh, and then me will shoot.

D—l. Why, ye airy Fantoms, are you not my Creatures? mayn't I make of you what I please?

Cru. Why, yes, you may make of us what you please; but when you raise Beings contradictory to common Sense, and destructive of Religion and Morality; they will rise up against you in *Foro Conscientiae*;[3] that *Latin* I learn'd in my *Free-School* and *House Education*.[4]

---

1 See Crusoe's explanation of "secret hints" on p. 194.

2 In John Milton's *Paradise Lost*, Satan meets two creatures on his way through the Gates of Hell. The first, with the torso of a woman and the lower body of a snake, is Sin, his daughter who sprang from his own brain. The second, dark and formless, is Death, the offspring of Satan and Sin.

3 Latin legal term: "Before the tribunal of conscience." Defoe's adversaries often mocked his lack of a classical education.

4 Crusoe remarks that he received "a competent Share of Learning, as far as House-Education, and a Country Free-School generally goes" (p. 47).

D—l. Hum, hum ——— well, and what are your Complaints of me?

Cru. Why, that you have made me a strange whimsical, inconsistent Being, in three Weeks losing all the Religion of a Pious Education; and when you bring me again to a Sense of the Want of Religion, you make me quit that upon every Whimsy; you make me extravagantly Zealous, and as extravagantly Remiss; you make me an Enemy to all *English* Sailors, and a Panegyrist upon all other Sailors that come in your way: Thus, all the *English* Seamen laugh'd me out of Religion, but the *Spanish* and *Portuguese* Sailors were honest religious Fellows; you make me a Protestant in *London*, and a Papist in *Brasil*; and then again, a Protestant in my own Island, and when I get thence, the only Thing that deters me from returning to *Brasil*, is meerly, because I did not like to die a Papist; for you say, *that* Popery *may be a good Religion to live in, but not to die in*; as if that Religion could be good to live in, which was not good to die in; for, Father *D—l*, whatever you may think, no Man is sure of living one Minute. But tho' you keep me thus by Force a Sort of Protestant, yet, you all along make me very fond of Popish Priests and the Popish Religion; nor can I forgive you the making me such a Whimsical Dog, to ramble over three Parts of the World after I was sixty five. Therefore, I say, *Friday*, prepare to shoot.

Fri. No shoot yet Master, me have something to say, he much Injure me too.

D—l. Injure you too, how the Devil have I injur'd you?

Fri. Have injure me, to make me such Blockhead, so much contradiction, as to be able to speak *English tolerably well* in a Month or two, and not to speak it better in twelve Years after; to make me go out to be kill'd by the Savages, only to be a Spokesman to them, tho' I did not know, whether they understood one Word of my Language; for you must know, Father D—n, that almost ev'ry Nation of us *Indians* speak a different Language. Now Master shall me shoot?

Cru. No *Friday*, not yet, for here will be several more of his Children with Complaints against him; here will be the *French Priest, Will Atkins*, the Priest in *China*, his Nephews Ship's Crew, and———

D—l. Hold, hold, dear Son *Crusoe*, hold, let me satisfy you first before any more come upon me. You are my Hero, I have made you, out of nothing, fam'd from *Tuttle-Street* to *Limehouse-hole*;[1] there is not an old Woman that can go to the Price of it, but buys thy Life and Adventures, and leaves it as a Legacy, with the *Pilgrims Progress*, the *Practice of Piety*, and *God's Revenge against Murther*,[2] to her Posterity.

---

1 Tothill Street, near to Westminster Abbey, and Limehouse Hole, downriver, were both run-down parts of London.

2 John Bunyan's *The Pilgrim's Progress* (1678); Lewis Bayly's *The Practice of Piety, directing a Christian how to walk that he may please God* (1611); John

Cru. Your Hero! your Mob Hero! your *Pyecorner* Hero![1] on a foot with *Guy* of *Warwick, Bevis* of *Southampton,* and the *London Prentice!*[2] for *M—w—r*[3] has put me in that Rank, and drawn me much better; therefore, Sir, I say....

D—l. Dear Son *Crusoe,* be not in a Passion, hear me out.

Cru. Well, Sir, I will hear you out for once.

D—l. Then know, my dear Child, that you are a greater Favorite to me than you imagine; you are the true Allegorick Image of thy tender Father *D—l;*[4] I drew thee from the Consideration of my own Mind; I have been all my Life that Rambling, Inconsistent Creature, which I have made thee.

I set out under the Banner of *Kidderminster,*[5] and was long a noisy, if not zealous Champion for that Cause; and tho' I had not that *Free-school* and *House Learning* which I have given you, yet being endow'd with a wonderful Loquaciousness and a pretty handsome Assurance, being out of my Time, I talk'd myself into a pretty large Credit, by which I might, perhaps, have thriv'd in my Way very well, but, like you at *Brasil,* my Head run upon Whimsies, and I quitted a Certainty for new Adventures: First, I set up for Scribbling of Verses, and dabbling in other Sort of Authorizing, both Religious and Prophane. I have no Call to tell you, whether this Itch of Scribbling, or some other Project of *Lime Kilns* or the like, oblig'd me to quit a certain Court near the *Royal-Exchange,* and to play at Hide and Seek;[6] but this did not much trouble me, for it put me on a Sort of diving more agreeable to my Inclinations, forcing me to ramble from Place to Place Incognito; and, indeed, I thought myself something like the great Monarchs of the East, for I took care to be more seldom seen by my Acquaintance, than they by their Subjects. My old Walk from my Court to the Change[7] was too short for my rambling Spirit, it look'd like a Seaman's Walk

---

Reynolds' *The Triumphs of God's Revenge against Murther, expressed in 30 tragical histories* (1622). All three were best-selling Puritan works.

1 A disreputable part of London near Smithfield Market.

2 All heroes of English romances that were retold frequently in inexpensive ballads and chapbooks throughout the seventeenth and eighteenth centuries.

3 An unidentified printer or engraver.

4 Defoe responds to this charge of allegory in the Preface to the *Serious Reflections* (Appendix A).

5 Kidderminster, in the county of Worcestershire, was famous as a Puritan stronghold; Richard Baxter had been the Presbyterian minister there from 1641 to 1660.

6 Hiding from the bailiffs who might arrest him for debt.

7 The Royal Exchange: the center of business and shopping in London.

betwixt Decks; and for that, and some other Reasons which shall be nameless, I pursu'd the Course which I told you.

Well, all my Projects failing, I e'en took up with the Vocation of an Author, which tho' it promis'd but little in the common Way, I took care to make it more Beneficial to me; the principal Method of doing that, was to appear Zealous for some Party, and in the Party I was soon determin'd by my Education, and scribbled on in a violent Manner; till, by making myself a constant Pensioner to all the Rich and Zealous of my Party, I pickt up a good handsome Penny, with little Expence to myself of Time or Labour; for any Thing that is boldly Writ, will go down with either Party; but at last, by a plaguy Irony, I got myself into the damnable *Nutcrackers*;[1] however, that but encreas'd my Market, and brought my Pension in, at least, five fold. I writ on, till some of the wise heads of the contrary Party thought me worth retaining in their Service; and, I confess, their Bribes were very powerful. I manag'd Matters so well a great while, that both Sides kept me in Pay; but that would not do, my old Friends found that I had in reality forsaken them, and that I trim'd my Boat so ill, that they plainly saw to which Side it inclin'd; and, therefore, a certain Captain not far from *Thames Street*, who had been my Steward or Collector in chief, comes to me, and like the Witch of *Endor*, cried, *God has left thee*, Saul;[2] that is, the Money would be no more given me by the Party, who had every one discover'd that I was enter'd into another Cause. I did all I could to satisfy him and answer his Objections, but all to no purpose, *Buenos Nocoius*[3] was the Word, good Night *Nicholas*, they would no longer be bubbled; so I set out entirely for St. *Germans*[4] or any other Port to which my Proprietors should direct me; but here again, like you, my Son *Crusoe*, in burning the Idol in *Tartary*,[5] I went a little too far, and by another Irony, instead of the *Nutcrackers*, I had brought myself to the *Tripos* at *Paddington*,[6] but that my good Friend[7] that set me to work got me a Pardon, and so, safe was the Word; and I have never forsaken

---

1   The pillory. Defoe was sentenced to stand three days in the pillory after being found guilty for libel for his 1702 satire *The Shortest Way with the Dissenters*.
2   In Samuel 1:28, these words are spoken to Saul by the ghost of Samuel, not by the Witch of Endor.
3   *Buenas Noches*: good night (Spanish).
4   James II, the Pretender, held his court at Saint-Germain. Gildon's suggestion here that Defoe had Jacobite tendencies is unfounded.
5   In the *Farther Adventures*, Crusoe burns a wooden idol, provoking a narrowly averted attack by 10,000 Mogul Tartars.
6   To the gallows of Tyburn. A tripos is a three-legged stool upon which one would stand before being hanged.
7   Robert Harley.

him for that good Office—and his Money, my dear Son *Crusoe*, for it is that which always sets me to Work; and which ever Side the most Money is to be got, that Side is sure of *D—l*. 'Tis true, I made a pretty good penny among the Whigs, tho' nothing to what I have since done among the Tories: Let me see, let me see, I think, I made by Subscription for my *Jure Divino*[1] about some five hundred Pounds, and yet I writ it in about three Weeks or a Month, six or seven hundred Verses a Day coming constantly out of this Prolifick Head; as for the Sense and Poetry of them, e'en let my Subscribers look to that; they had a *Book*, and a *Book* in *Folio*, and I had their Money, and so all Parties were contented. But what's this to the Tory Writers, where for a Translation one shall get you three or four thousand Pounds subscrib'd; and for an Original, seven or eight Thousand; the Tories therefore for my Money; not that I value the Tories more than I do the Whigs; but nothing for the Whigs will sell, and every Thing for the Tories does. You seem to take it amiss, that I made you speak against the *English* Seamen, but that was only according to my own Nature, for I always hated the *English*, and took a Pleasure in depreciating and villifying of them, witness my *True Born Englishman*,[2] and my changing my Name to make it sound like *French*; for my Father's Name was plain *F—e*, but I have adorn'd it with a *de*, so that I am now, Mr. *D— —l De F—e*.[3] Next, you seem concern'd that I make you so favourable to Popery, and to ramble at such an Age about the World: First, you must known, that by speaking favourably of Popery, I lay up a Friend in a Corner, and make all of that Religion favourable to me and what I write; and should the Fox Hunters prevail, that Religion must be the Mode; if it never does, I at least pass for a Moderate Man both with the Papists and Protestant Fox Hunters; and to give them the better Idea of me, and the surer Hopes of having me a Convert, I have written against my old Teachers in the Shape and Form of a *Quaker*, as in a Pamphlet to *T.B. a Dealer in many Words*; and in the same Form I have attack'd the B—of B—,[4] one who is equally hated by them. To tell you the Truth, Son *Crusoe*, tho' I am now pass'd sixty five, I am just setting out for a Ramble thro' all Religions, and therefore liquor my Boots first with *Holy Water* and the Sacred Unctions of Popery; and next, I don't know but I may step to *Mahometism*, and take a Trip with

---

1 Defoe began his long satiric poem *Jure Divino* while he was in prison in 1703. It was issued by subscription in 1706.
2 An immensely popular poem (1701) designed to undermine notions of English purity and lend support to William of Orange.
3 Defoe, born Daniel Foe, added the *De* to his name in 1695.
4 Benjamin Hoadly, the Bishop of Bangor, whom Defoe lightly mocked in his pamphlet *A Declaration of Truth to Benjamin Hoadly* (1717).

Tom. Coryat[1] to the *Great Moguls* Country, from thence, perhaps, I may turn down to *Siam* and *China*, and make a sort of a Breakfast upon the *Multitheism* of those Countries

Cru. Multitheism, why Father *D—n*, why not *Polytheism?* why do you chuse rather to coin a Word compounded of *Greek* and *Latin*, whereas the other is in common Use?

D—l. Common; I hate all that's common, even to common Sense— but no Interruptions Son *Crusoe*, no Interruptions; from thence I may take a Jaunt to the *Greek* Church, in a sort of Whimsical *Caravan*, over the Desarts which I made you pass, if by the way I don't happen to catch a Tartar,[2] that is, take a Leap into the Dark. By this Ramble thro' all Religions, I shall be thoroughly qualified for whatever Side may come uppermost, whether the *Spanish* Inquisition, the Janesaries of *Mecca*, or any other Propagators of particular Religions; for betwixt you and I, Son *Crusoe*, I care not who Reigns, whether the *Czar* of *Muscovy*, or the Emperor of *Monomotopa*. I defy them to set up any Religion, to oppose which I will be at the Pain of so much as a Fleabite. And now you have my Picture, Son *Crusoe*, as well as my Justification in my Draught of yours; I would not have you therefore complain any more of the Contradiction of your Character, since that is of a Piece with the whole Design of my Book. I made you set out as undutiful and disobedient to your Parents; and to make your Example deter all others, I make you Fortunate in all your Adventures, even in the most unlucky, and give you at last a plentiful Fortune and a safe Retreat, Punishments so terrible, that sure the Fear of them must deter all others from Disobedience to Parents, and venturing to Sea: And now, as for you *Friday*, I did not make you speak broken *English* to represent you as a Blockhead, incapable of learning to speak it better, but meerly for the Variety of Stile, to intermix some broken *English* to make my Lie go down the more glibly with the Vulgar[3] Reader; and in this, I use you no worse than I do the *Bible* itself, which I quote for the very same End only.

Cru. Enough, Enough, Father *D—n*, you have confest enough, and now prepare for your Punishment, for here come all the rest of our Number which we expected; come *Friday*, pull out the Books, you have both Volumes, have you not *Friday*?

Fri. Yes Master, and me will make him swallow his own Vomit.

Cru. Here, Gentlemen, every one hold a Limb of him.

---

1 An English traveler (c. 1577–1617) whose letters from the Indian subcontinent were reprinted frequently in the seventeenth and eighteenth centuries.
2 To catch hold of an opponent who turns out to be overpowering.
3 Common.

D—l. Oh, oh, Mercy! Mercy!

Fri. Swallow, swallow, Father *D—n,* your Writings be good for the Heartburn, swallow, Father *D—n* —— so me have cram'd down one Volume, must he have the other now Master?

Cru. Yes, yes, *Friday,* or else the Dose will not be compleat, and so perhaps mayn't work and pass thro' him kindly.

Fri. Come, Father *D—n,* t'other Pill, or I think I may call it Bolus[1] for the bigness of it, it is good for your Health; come, if you will make such large Compositions, you must take them for your Pains.

D—l. Oh, oh, oh, oh.

Cru. Now, Gentlemen, each Man take his Part of the Blanket and toss him immoderately; for you must know, Gentlemen, that this is a sort of Physick, which never works well without a violent Motion.

[They toss him lustily, he crying out all the while.]

Cru. Hold, Gentlemen, I think our Business is done; for by the unsavoury Stench which assaults my Nostrils, I find the Dose is past thro' him, and so good Morrow, Father *D—n. Past three a Clock and a Moon light Morning.*   *[They all vanish.]*

D—l *solus.*[2]

Bless me! what Company have I been in? or rather, what Dream have I had? for certainly 'tis nothing but a Dream; and yet I find by the Effects in my Breeches, that I was most damnably frighted with this Dream; nay, more than ever I was in my Life; even more, than when we had News that King *William* design'd to take into *Flanders* the *Royal Regiment.*[3] But this is a fresh Proof of my Observation in the second Volume of my *Crusoe,* that *there's no greater Evidence of an invisible World, than that Connexion betwixt second Causes,* (as that in my Trowsers) *and those Ideas* we *have in our Minds.*

The End of the Dialogue.

---

1 A large pill, often associated with quack remedies.
2 Alone.
3 If William had taken the Royal Regiment to Flanders in 1691-92, Jacobite forces could have invaded England.

Appendix C: Castaway Narratives

[When Defoe wrote *Robinson Crusoe*, there were already scores of castaway narratives in print, from fictional island tales such as Henry Neville's *The Isle of Pines* (1668) and Ibn Ṭufayl's *Hai Ebn Yokdhan* (translated 1708) to journalistic accounts of actual castaways, the most famous being the Scotsman Alexander Selkirk. Once published, *Robinson Crusoe* breathed new life into the genre. Almost immediately, Crusoe-like shipwreck stories (so-called Robinsonades) proliferated, beginning with *The Adventures, and Surprising Deliverances of James Dubourdieu, and his Wife* (1719) and soon including Penelope Aubin's *The Strange Adventures of the Count* de Vinevil *and his Family. ... And of Madamoiselle Ardelisa, his Daughter's being shipwreck'd on the Uninhabited Island Delos* (1721) and Peter Longueville's *The Hermit: or, The Unparalleled Sufferings and Surprising Adventures of Mr. Philip Quarll, Englishman* (1727). Also continuing to appear were accounts of "authentick" castaways such as the Dutchman Leendert Hasenbosch.]

1. **From Ibn Ṭufayl, *The Improvement of Human Reason, Exhibited in the Life of Hai Ebn Yokdhan: Written in Arabick above 500 Years ago*, by *Abu Jaafar Ebn Tophail. In which it is demonstrated, By what Methods one may, by the meer Light of Nature, attain the Knowledg of things Natural and Supernatural; more particularly the Knowledg of God, and the Affairs of another Life* (1708)[1]**

... [W]hen she [the deer] grew Old and Feeble, he us'd to lead her where there was the best Food, and pluck the best Fruits for her, and give them to eat.

---

1 Written by Ibn Ṭufayl (c. 1105-85) in the early twelfth century, this philosophical tale reflourished in the late seventeenth and eighteenth centuries when it was translated, once into Latin and three times into English. Either born out of clay or abandoned as an infant—the narrative recognizes both possibilities—Hai Ebn Yokdhan (now generally transliterated *Hayy ibn Yaqzân*) is suckled by a deer, learns by watching the animals, and eventually develops an understanding of God. Through he lacks language for most of his life, he nonetheless develops nuanced Aristotelian categories for astronomy, botany, anatomy, and theology. In the first of these excerpts, Hai Ebn Yokdhan dissects the body of the deer who raised him. In the second, he interacts with Asal, a castaway whose knowledge of the Qur'an confirms his religious discoveries.

§ 16. Notwithstanding this she grew lean and weak, and continu'd a while in a languishing Condition, till at last she Dyed, and then all her Motions and Actions ceas'd. When the Boy perceiv'd her in this Condition, he was ready to dye for Grief. He call'd her with the same voice which she us'd to answer to, and made what Noise he could, but there was no Motion, no Alteration. Then he began to peep into her Eyes and Ears, but could perceive no visible defect in either; in like manner he examin'd all the Parts of her Body, and found nothing amiss, but every thing as it should be. He had a vehement desire to find, if possible, that part were[1] the defect was, that he might remove it, and she return to her former State, of Life and Vigour. But he was altogether at a loss, how to compass[2] his design, nor could he possibly bring it about.

... § 19. Having, by this way of reasoning, assur'd himself that the disaffected Part lay in the Breast; he was resolv'd to make a search, in order to find it out, that whatsoever the Impediment was, he might remove it if possible; but then again, he was afraid on the other side, lest his Undertaking should be worse than the Disease, and prove prejudicial.[3] He began to consider next, whether or no he had ever remembred any Beasts, or other Animals, which he had seen in that condition, recover again, and return to the same State which they were in before: but he could call to Mind no such Instance; from whence he concluded, that if she was let alone there would be no hopes at all, but if he should be so fortunate as to find that Part, and find the Impediment, there might be some hope. Upon this he resolv'd to open her Breast and make enquiry; in order to which he provides himself with sharp Flints, and Splinters of dry Cane almost like Knives, with which he made an incision between the Ribs, and cutting through the Flesh, came to the *Diaphragma*; which he finding very Tough and not easily broken, assur'd himself, that such a Covering must needs belong to that organ which he lookt for, and that if he could once get through that, he should find it. He met with some difficulty in his Work, because his Instruments were none of the best, but he had none but such as were made either of Flint or Cane.

... § 21. Therefore he first Attacks the *Pericardium*, which, after a long tryal and a great deal of pains, he made shift[4] to tear; and when he had laid the Heart bare, and perceiv'd that it was solid on every side, he began to examin it, to see if he could find any hurt in it; but

---

1 Where.
2 Accomplish.
3 Harmful.
4 Managed.

finding none, he squeez'd it with his Hands, and perceiv'd that it was hollow. He began than to think that what he look'd for, might possibly be contain'd in that Cavity. When he came to open it, he found in it two Cavities, one on the right side, the other on the left. That on the right side was full of clotted Blood, that on the left quite empty. "Then (says he,) without all doubt, one of those two Cavities must needs be the Receptacle of what I look for; as for that on this side there's nothing in it but congealed Blood, which was not so, be sure, till the whole body was in that condition in which it now is" (for he had observ'd that all Blood congeals when it flows from the Body, and that this Blood did not differ in the least from any other,) "and therefore what I look for, cannot by any means, be such a matter as this; for that which I mean, is something which is peculiar to this place, which I find I could not subsist without, so much as the Twinkling of an Eye. And this is that which I look'd for at first. For as for this Blood, how often have I lost a great deal of it in my Skirmishes with the Wild Beasts, and yet it never did me any considerable harm, nor rendred me incapable of performing any Action of Life, and therefore what I look for is not in this Cavity. Now as for the Cavity on the left side, I find 'tis altogether empty, and I have no reason in the World to think that it was made in vain, because I find every part appointed for such and such particular Functions. How then can this Ventricle of the Heart, which I see is of so excellent a Frame, serve for no use at all? I cannot think but that the same thing which I am in search of, once dwelt here, but has now deserted his Habitation and left it empty, and that the Absence of that thing, has occasion'd this Privation of Sense and Cessation of Motion, which happen'd to the Body." Now when he perceiv'd that the Being which had inhabited there before had left its house before it fell to Ruine, and forsaken it when as yet it continu'd whole and entire, he concluded that it was highly probable that it would never return to it any more, after its being so cut and mangled.

§ 22. Upon this the whole Body seemed to him a very inconsiderable thing, and worth nothing in respect of that Being, he believed once inhabited, and now had left it. Therefore he applied himself wholly to the consideration of that Being. *What it was?* and *how it subsisted? what joyn'd it to the body? Whether it went, and by what passage, when it left the Body? What was the Cause of its Departure, whether it were forc'd to leave its Mansion, or left the Body of its own accord? and in case it went away Voluntarily, what it was that rendred the Body so disagreeable to it, as to make it forsake it?* And whilst his Mind was perplext with such variety of Thoughts, he laid aside all concern for the Carcass, and threw it away; for now he perceiv'd that his Mother, which had Nurs'd him so Tenderly and had Suckled him, was that *something* which was departed: and from it proceeded all those Actions by which she shew'd her Care of him, and Affection to him, and not from this inactive Body; but that the Body was to it only as an Instrument or Tool, like his Cudgel which he had made for himself, with which he used to Fight with the Wild Beasts. So that now, all his regard to the Body was remov'd, and transferr'd to that by which the Body is govern'd, and by whose Power it moves. Nor had he any other desire but to make enquiry after that.

... § 84. But he found that his own Being was not excluded his Thoughts, no not at such times when he was most deeply immers'd in the Contemplation of the *first, true, necessarily self-existent Being*. Which concern'd him very much, for he knew that even this was a Mixture in this simple Vision, and the Admission of an extraneous Object in that Contemplation. Upon which he endeavour'd to disappear from himself, and be wholly taken up in the Vision of that *true Being*; till at last he attain'd it; and then both the Heavens and the Earth, and whatsoever is between them, and all Spiritual Forms, and Corporeal Faculties; and all those Powers which are separate from Matter, and are those Beings which know the *necessarily self-existent Being*, all disappear'd and vanish'd, and were as if they had never been, and amongst these his own Being disappear'd too, and there remain'd nothing but this ONE, TRUE Perpetually Self-existent Being, who spoke thus in that Saying of his (which is not a Notion superadded to his Essence) *To whom now belongs the Kingdom? To this One, Almighty God*. Which Words of his *Hai Ebn Yokdhan* understood, and heard his Voice: nor was his being unacquainted with Words, and not being able to speak, any Hindrance at all to the understanding him. Wherefore he deeply immers'd himself into this State, and witness'd that which neither Eye hath seen, nor Ear heard; nor hath it ever enter'd into the Heart of Man to conceive.

§ 90. After he was wholly immers'd in the Speculation of these things, and perfectly abstracted from all other Objects, and in the nearest Approach;[1] he saw in the highest Sphere, beyond which there is no *Body*, a Being free from Matter, which was not the Being of that ONE, TRUE ONE, nor the Sphere itself, nor yet any thing different from them both; but was like the Image of the Sun which appears in a well-polish'd Looking-glass, which is neither the Sun nor the Looking-glass, and yet not distinct from them. And he saw in the Essence of that separate Sphere, such Perfection, Splendor and Beauty, as is too great to be express'd by any Tongue, and too subtil to be cloath'd in Words; and he perceiv'd that it was in the utmost Perfection of Delight and Joy, Exultation and Gladness, by reason of its beholding that TRUE Essence, whose Glory be exalted.

---

1 The Author means, *the nearest Approach to God*. [Translator's note]

... § 109. Then *Asâl* began to enquire of him concerning his way of Living, and from whence he came into that Island? And *Hai Ebn Yokdhan* told him, that he knew nothing of his own Original, nor any Father or Mother that he had, but only that *Roe* which brought him up. Then he describ'd to him his manner of Living, from first to last, and by what de grees he advanc'd in Knowledge, till he attain'd the *Union with God*. When *Asâl* heard him give an Account of those Truths, and those Essences which are separate from the Sensible World, and which have the Knowledge of that TRUE ONE, (whose Name be prais'd); and heard him give an account of the Essence of that TRUE ONE, and describe, as far as was possible, what he witness'd (when he had attain'd to that Union) of the Joys of those who are near united to God, and the Torments of those who are separated from him. He made no doubt but that all those things which are contain'd in the Law of God [i.e., the *Alcoran*] concerning his Command, his Angels, Books and Messengers, the Day of Judgment, Paradise and Hell, were Resemblances of what *Hai Ebn Yokdhan* had seen; and the Eyes of his Understanding were open'd, and he found that the *Original* and the *Copy* did exactly agree together. And the ways of Mystical Interpretation became easie to him, and there appear'd nothing difficult to him in those Precepts which he had receiv'd, but all was clear; nor any thing shut up, but all was open; nor any thing profound, but all was plain. By this means his intellectual Faculty grew strong and vigorous, and he look'd upon *Hai Ebn Yokdhan* with Admiration and Respect, and assur'd himself that he was one of the Saints of God, *which have no Fear upon them, neither shall they suffer Pain.*[1] Upon which he address'd himself to wait upon him, and imitate him, and to follow his Direction in the Performance of such Works as he had occasion to make use of; namely, those legal ones which he had formerly learn'd from his own Sect.

2. Accounts of Alexander Selkirk

[In 1704, following an argument with First Lieutenant Thomas Stradling about the seaworthiness of their ship, Alexander Selkirk requested that he be left behind on Juan Fernandez Island. (His fears were justified: the *Cinque Ports* later broke apart and foundered, killing most of the crew.) Four years later, he was rescued by Captain Woodes Rogers and returned to England. The first published account of Selkirk was written by Edward Cooke, who had served as the second captain on the boat that rescued Selkirk; it was soon followed by the

---

1 ·This phrase occurs repeatedly in the Qur'an, Surah 2.

narrative of Rogers himself in 1712, and then by Richard Steele's essay in 1713. Though it is possible that Defoe met Selkirk, there is no evidence of a meeting.]

(a) From Woodes Rogers, *A Cruising Voyage round the World: first to the South-Sea, thence to the East-Indies, and homewards by the Cape of Good Hope* (1712)[1]

Immediately our Pinnace return'd from the Shore, and brought abundance of Craw-fish, with a Man clothed in Goat-Skins, who look'd wilder than the first Owners of them. He had been on the Island four Years and four Months, being left there by Capt. *Stradling* in the *Cinque-Ports*; his Name was *Alexander Selkirk*, a *Scotch* Man who had been Master of the *Cinque-Ports*, a Ship that came here last with Capt. *Dampier*, who told me that this was the best Man in her; so I immediately agreed with him to be a Mate on board our Ship. 'Twas he that made the Fire last night when he saw our Ships, which he judged to be *English*. During his stay here, he saw several Ships pass by, but only two came in to anchor. As he went to view them, he found 'em to be *Spaniards*, and retir'd from 'em; upon which they shot at him. Had they been *French*, he would have submitted; but chose to risque his dying alone on the Island, rather than fall into the hands of the *Spaniards* in these parts, because he apprehended they would murder him, or make a Slave of him in the Mines, for he feared they would spare no Stranger that might be capable of discovering the *South-Sea*.[2] The *Spaniards* had landed, before he knew what they were, and they came so near him that he had much ado to escape; for they not only shot at him, but pursu'd him into the Woods, where he climbed to the top of a Tree, at the foot of which they made water, and killed several Goats just by, but went off again without discovering him. He told us that he was born at *Largo* in the County of *Fife* in *Scotland*, and was bred a Sailor from his Youth. The reason of his being left here was a Difference betwixt him and his Captain; which, together with the Ship's being leaky,[3] made him willing rather to stay here, than go along with him at first; and when he was at last willing, the Captain would not receive him. He had been in the Island before to wood and water, when two of the Ships Company were left upon it for six Months till the Ship return'd, being chas'd thence by two *French South-Sea* Ships.

1 The text is taken from the second edition, corrected (1718).
2 The Pacific.
3 The *Cinque Ports'* oak timbers were infested with shipworms, mollusks that bore into submerged wood.

He had with him his Clothes and Bedding, with a Firelock, some Powder, Bullets, and Tobacco, a Hatchet, a Knife, a Kettle, a Bible, some practical Pieces, and his Mathematical Instruments and Books. He diverted and provided for himself as well as he could; but for the first eight Months had much ado to bear up against Melancholy and the Terror of being left alone in such a desolate Place. He built two Hutts with Piemento Trees, cover'd them with long Grass, and lin'd them with the Skins of Goats, which he killed with his Gun as he wanted, so long as his Powder lasted, which was but a pound; and that being near spent, he got fire by rubbing two Sticks of Piemento Wood together upon his Knee. In the lesser Hutt, at some Distance from the other, he dress'd his Victuals; and in the larger he slept, and employ'd himself in reading, singing Psalms, and praying; so that he said he was a better Christian while in this Solitude than ever he was before, or than, he was afraid, he should ever be again. At first he never eat any thing till Hunger constrain'd him, partly for grief, and partly for want of Bread and Salt; nor did he go to Bed till he could watch no longer: the Piemento Wood, which burnt very clear, served him both for Firing and Candle, and refresh'd him with its fragrant Smell.

He might have had Fish enough, but could not eat 'em for want of Salt, because they occasion'd a Looseness;[1] except Craw-fish, which are there as large as our Lobsters, and very good: These he sometimes boil'd, and at other times broil'd, as he did his Goats Flesh, of which he made very good Broth, for they are not so rank as ours: he kept an Account of 500 that he killed while there, and caught as many more, which he marked on the Ear and let go. When his Powder fail'd, he took them by speed of foot; for his way of living and continual Exercise of walking and running, clear'd him of all gross Humours, so that he ran with wonderful Swiftness thro the Wood and up the Rocks and Hills, as we perceiv'd when we employ'd him to catch Goats for us. We had a Bull-Dog, which we sent with several of our nimblest Runners, to help him in catching Goats; but he distanc'd and tir'd both the Dog and the Men, catch'd the Goats, and brought 'em to us on his back. He told us that his Agility in pursuing a Goat had once like to have cost him his Life; he pursu'd it with so much Eagerness, that he catch'd hold of it on the brink of a Precipice, of which he was not aware, the Bushes having hid it from him; so that he fell with the Goat down the said Precipice a great height, and was so stun'd and bruis'd with the Fall, that he narrowly escap'd with his Life, and when he came to his Senses, found the Goat dead under him. He lay there

---

1 Diarrhea.

about 24 hours, and was scarce able to crawl to his Hutt which was about a mile distant, or to stir abroad again in ten days.

He came at last to relish his Meat well enough without Salt or Bread, and in the Season had plenty of good Turnips, which had been sow'd there by Capt. *Dampier*'s Men, and have now overspread some Acres of Ground. He had enough of good Cabbage from the Cabbage-Trees, and season'd his Meat with the Fruit of the Piemento Trees,[1] which is the same as the *Jamaica* Pepper, and smells deliciously. He found there also a black Pepper called *Malagita*, which was very good to expel Wind, and against griping of the Guts.[2]

He soon wore out all his Shoes and Clothes by running thro the Woods; and at last being forc'd to shift without them, his Feet became so hard, that he run every where without Annoyance: and it was some time before he could wear Shoes after we found him; for not being used to any so long, his Feet swell'd when he came first to wear them again.

After he had conquer'd his Melancholy, he diverted himself sometimes by cutting his Name on the Trees, and the Time of his being left, and Continuance there. He was at first much pester'd with Cats and Rats, that had bred in great numbers from some of each Species which had got ashore from Ships that put in there to wood and water. The Rats gnaw'd his Feet and Clothes while asleep, which obliged him to cherish the Cats with his Goats-flesh; by which many of them became so tame, that they would lie about him in hundreds, and soon deliver'd him from the Rats. He likewise tam'd some Kids, and to divert himself would now and then sing and dance with them and his Cats: so that by the Care of Providence and Vigour of his Youth, being now about 30 Years old, he came at last to conquer all the Inconveniences of his Solitude, and to be very easy. When his Clothes wore out, he made himself a Coat and a Cap of Goat-Skins, which he stitch'd together with little Thongs of the same, that he cut with his Knife. He had no other Needle but a Nail; and when his Knife was wore to the back, he made others as well as he could of some Iron Hoops that were left ashore, which he beat thin and ground upon Stones. Having some Linen Cloth by him, he sow'd himself Shirts with a Nail, and stitch'd 'em with the Worsted of his old Stockings, which he pulled out on purpose. He had his last Shirt on when we found him in the Island.

At his first coming on board us, he had so much forgot his Language for want of Use, that we could scarce understand him, for he seem'd to speak his words by halves. We offered him a Dram, but he

---

1 Allspice.
2 Dysentery.

would not touch it, having drank nothing but Water since his being there, and 'twas some time before he could relish our Victuals.

He could give us an account of no other Product of the Island than what we have mentioned, except small black Plums, which are very good, but hard to come at, the Trees which bear 'em growing on high Mountains and Rocks. Piemento Trees are plenty here, and we saw some of 60 foot high, and about two yards thick; and Cotton Trees higher, and near four fathom round in the Stock.[1]

The Climate is so good, that the Trees and Grass are verdant all the Year. The Winter lasts no longer than *June* and *July*, and is not then severe, there being only a small Frost, and a little Hail, but sometimes great Rains. The Heat of the Summer is equally moderate, and there's not much Thunder or tempestuous Weather of any sort. He saw no venomous or savage Creature on the Island, nor any other sort of Beast but Goats, *&c.* as above-mention'd; the first of which had been put ashore here on purpose for a Breed by *Juan Fernando* a *Spaniard*, who settled there with some Families for a time, till the Continent of *Chili* began to submit to the *Spaniards*; which being more profitable, tempted them to quit this Island, which is capable of maintaining a good number of People, and of being made so strong that they could not be easily dislodg'd.

Ringrose[2] in his Account of Capt. *Sharp*'s Voyage and other Buccaneers, mentions one who had escap'd ashore here out of a Ship which was cast away with all the rest of the Company, and says he liv'd five years alone before he had the opportunity of another Ship to carry him off. Capt. *Dampier* talks of a *Moskito Indian* that belong'd to Capt. *Watlin*,[3] who being a hunting in the Woods when the Captain left the Island, liv'd here three years alone, and shifted much in the same manner as Mr. *Selkirk* did, till Capt. *Dampier* came hither in 1684 and carry'd him off. The first that went ashore was one of his Countrymen, and they saluted one another first by prostrating themselves by turns on the ground, and then embracing. But whatever there is in these Stories, this of Mr. *Selkirk* I know to be true; and his Behaviour afterwards gives me reason to believe the Account he gave me how he spent his time, and bore up under such an Affliction, in which nothing but

---

1 Twenty-four feet around the trunk.

2 Basil Ringrose, a buccaneer who accompanied Captain Bartholomew Sharp on raids on the Pacific coast of South America. His journal was published as a second volume of the *History of the Buccaneers* (1685).

3 John Watling (d. 1681) briefly took command from Sharp on Juan Fernandez. When the buccaneers spotted Spanish warships and hastily sailed away from the island, a Mosquito Indian named Will was left behind. Watling was killed a month later during an attack on the Spanish settlement of Arica, Chile.

the Divine Providence could have supported any Man. By this one may see that Solitude and Retirement from the World is not such an insufferable State of Life as most Men imagine, especially when People are fairly called or thrown into it unavoidably, as this Man was; who in all probability must otherwise have perished in the Seas, the Ship which left him being cast away not long after, and few of the Company escaped. We may perceive by this Story the Truth of the Maxim, That Necessity is the Mother of Invention, since he found means to supply his Wants in a very natural manner, so as to maintain his Life, tho not so conveniently, yet as effectually as we are able to do with the help of all our Arts and Society. It may likewise instruct us, how much a plain and temperate way of living conduces to the Health of the Body and the Vigour of the Mind, both which we are apt to destroy by Excess and Plenty, especially of strong Liquor, and the Variety as well as the Nature of our Meat and Drink: for this Man, when he came to our ordinary Method of Diet and Life, tho he was sober[1] enough, lost much of his Strength and Agility. But I must quit these Reflections, which are more proper for a Philosopher and Divine than a Mariner, and return to my own Subject.

(b) Richard Steele, *The Englishman*, no. 26 (1-3 December 1713)[2]

UNDER the Title of this Paper, I do not think it foreign to my Design, to speak of a Man born in Her Majesty's Dominions, and relate an Adventure in his Life so uncommon, that it's doubtful whether the like has happen'd to any of human Race. The Person I speak of is *Alexander Selkirk*, whose Name is familiar to Men of Curiosity, from the Fame of his having lived four Years and four Months alone in the Island of *Juan Fernandez*. I had the pleasure frequently to converse with the Man soon after his Arrival in *England*, in the Year 1711. It was matter of great Curiosity to hear him, as he is a Man of good Sense, give an Account of the different Revolutions in his own Mind in that long Solitude. When we consider how painful Absence from Company for the Space of but one Evening, is to the generality of Mankind, we may have a sense how painful this necessary and constant Solitude was to a Man bred a Sailor, and ever accustomed to enjoy and suffer, eat, drink, and sleep, and perform all Offices of Life, in Fellowship and

---

1 Moderate in food and drink.
2 Richard Steele (1672-1729): essayist, dramatist, briefly Member of Parliament, and cofounder with Joseph Addison of the periodicals *The Tattler* and *The Spectator*. The text is taken from *The Englishman: Being the Sequel of the Guardian* (1714).

Company. He was put ashore from a leaky Vessel, with the Captain[1] of which he had had an irreconcilable difference; and he chose rather to take his Fate in this place, than in a crazy[2] Vessel, under a disagreeable Commander. His Portion were a Sea Chest, his wearing Cloaths and Bedding, a Firelock, a Pound of Gun-powder, a large quantity of Bullets, a Flint and Steel, a few Pounds of Tobacco, an Hatchet, a Knife, a Kettle, a Bible, and other Books of Devotion, together with Pieces that concerned Navigation, and his Mathematical Instruments. Resentment against his Officer, who had ill used him, made him look forward on this Change of Life, as the more eligible one, till the Instant in which he saw the Vessel put off; at which moment, his Heart yearned within him, and melted at the parting with his Comrades and all Human Society at once. He had in Provisions for the Sustenance of Life but the quantity of two Meals, the Island abounding only with wild Goats, Cats and Rats. He judged it most probable that he should find more immediate and easy Relief by finding Shell-fish on the Shore, than seeking Game with his Gun. He accordingly found great quantities of Turtles, whose Flesh is extreamly delicious, and of which he frequently ate very plentifully on his first Arrival, till it grew disagreeable to his Stomach, except in Jellies. The Necessities of Hunger and Thirst, were his greatest Diversions from the Reflections on his lonely Condition. When those Appetites were satisfied, the Desire of Society was as strong a Call upon him, and he appeared to himself least necessitous when he wanted every thing; for the Supports of his Body were easily attained, but the eager Longings for seeing again the Face of Man during the Interval of craving bodily Appetites, were hardly supportable. He grew dejected, languid, and melancholy, scarce able to refrain from doing himself Violence, till by Degrees, by the Force of Reason and frequent reading of the Scriptures, and turning his Thoughts upon the Study of Navigation, after the Space of eighteen Months, he grew thoroughly reconciled to his Condition. When he had made this Conquest, the Vigour of his Health, Disengagement from the World, a constant, chearful, serene Sky, and a temperate Air, made his Life one continual Feast, and his Being much more joyful than it had before been irksome. He now taking Delight in every thing, made the Hutt in which he lay, by Ornaments which he cut down from a spacious Wood, on the side of which it was situated, the most delicious Bower, fann'd with continual Breezes, and gentle Aspirations[3] of Wind, that made his Repose after the Chase equal to the most sensual Pleasures.

---

1 Thomas Stradling.
2 Unsound, full of cracks.
3 Breath, puff.

I forgot to observe, that during the Time of his Dissatisfaction, Monsters of the Deep, which frequently lay on the Shore, added to the Terrors of his Solitude; the dreadful Howlings and Voices seemed too terrible to be made for human Ears; but upon the Recovery of his Temper, he could with Pleasure not only hear their Voices, but approach the Monsters themselves with great Intrepidity. He speaks of Sea-Lions, whose Jaws and Tails were capable of seizing or breaking the Limbs of a Man, if he approached them: But at that Time his Spirits and Life were so high, and he could act so regularly and unconcerned, that merely from being unruffled in himself, he killed them with the greatest Ease imaginable; For observing, that though their Jaws and Tails were so terrible, yet the Animals being mighty slow in working themselves round, he had nothing to do but place himself exactly opposite to their Middle, and as close to them as possible, he dispatched them with his Hatchet at Will.

THE Precautions which he took against Want, in case of Sickness, was to lame Kids when very young, so as that they might recover their Health, but never be capable of Speed. These he had in great Numbers about his Hutt; and when he was himself in full Vigour, he could take at full Speed the swiftest Goat running up a Promontory, and never failed of catching them but on a Descent.

HIS Habitation was extreamly pester'd with Rats, which gnaw'd his Cloaths and Feet when sleeping. To defend himself against them he fed and tamed Numbers of young Kitlings,[1] who lay about his Bed, and preserved him from the Enemy. When his Cloaths were quite worn out, he dried and tacked together the Skins of Goats, with which he cloathed himself, and was enured to pass through Woods, Bushes, and Brambles with as much Carelessness and Precipitance as any other Animal. It happened once to him, that running on the Summit of a Hill, he made a Stretch to seize a Goat, with which under him, he fell down a Precipice, and lay helpless for the Space of three Days, the Length of which Time he Measured by the Moon's Growth since his last Observation. This manner of Life grew so exquisitely pleasant, that he never had a Moment heavy upon his Hands; his Nights were untroubled, and his Days joyous, from the Practice of Temperance and Exercise. It was his Manner to use stated Hours and Places for Exercises of Devotion, which he performed aloud, in order to keep up the Faculties of Speech, and to utter himself with greater Energy.

WHEN I first saw him, I thought, if I had not been let into his Character and Story, I could have discerned that he had been much separated from Company, from his Aspect and Gesture; there was a

---

1 Kittens.

strong but chearful Seriousness in his Look, and a certain Disregard to the ordinary things about him, as if he had been sunk in Thought. When the Ship which brought him off the Island came in, he received them with the greatest Indifference, with relation to the Prospect of going off with them, but with great Satisfaction in an Opportunity to refresh and help them. The Man frequently bewailed his Return to the World, which could not, he said, with all its Enjoyments, restore him to the Tranquility of his Solitude. Though I had frequently conversed with him, after a few months Absence he met me in the Street, and though he spoke to me, I could not recollect that I had seen him; familiar Converse in this Town had taken off the Loneliness of his Aspect, and quite altered the Air of his Face.

THIS plain Man's Story is a memorable Example, that he is happiest who confines his Want to natural Necessities; and he that goes further in his Desires, increases his Want in Proportion to his Acquisitions; or, to use his own Expression, *I am now worth 800 Pounds, but shall never be so happy, as when I was not worth a Farthing.*[1]

3. **From Penelope Aubin, *The Strange Adventures of the Count de Vinevil and his Family. Being an Account of what happen'd to them whilst they resided at Constantinople. And of Madamoiselle Ardelisa, his Daughter's being shipwreck'd on the Uninhabited Island Delos, in her Return to France, with Violetta a Venetian Lady, the Captain of the Ship, a Priest, and five Sailors. The Manner of their living there, and strange Deliverance by the Arrival of a Ship commanded by Violetta's Father. Ardelisa's Entertainment at Venice, and safe Return to France* (1721)[2]**

Chap. XIII.
They had now sailed six Days, when the seventh Night it grew dark and tempestuous; the Wind chang'd, and about Midnight a Storm arose so dreadful, the Pilot could no longer steer the Ship; so that she

---

1 A quarter of a penny.
2 Penelope Aubin (1685-1731): novelist, poet, and dramatist. In her preface to *The Strange Adventures of the Count de Vinevil,* her first novel, Aubin writes, "As for the truth of what this Narrative contains, since Robinson Cruso has been so well received, which is more improbable, I know no Reason why this should be thought a Fiction. I hope the World has not grown so abandoned to Vice, as to believe there is no such Ladies to be found, as would prefer Death to Infamy; or a Man that for Remorse of Conscience would quit a plentiful Fortune, retire, and choose to die in a dismal Cell." This work was one of the first Robinsonades to appear.

drove they knew not whither. At break of day they found themselves amongst the *Aegean Isles*; the Ship had lost all her Masts, they had but thirteen hands aboard, when the Carpenter going down into the Hold, came back with a Face that express'd the Terrors of his Mind; he cry'd, "Hoist out the Boats quickly, there is five Foot Water in the Hold." At these words a Death-like Paleness spread o'er every Face; the Captain, Ladies, Priest, *Nannetta*, *Joseph*, and five Sailors enter'd the first Boat, taking with them their Gold, Jewels, some Trunks of Clothes, Biscuit, a Vessel of Wine, and some Quilts, Bedding, and Salt-Meat, what they could possibly put in without endangering the Boat's sinking; and then they made away for the Island which was nearest, on which they landed safely; but had the Misfortune to see the other Boat sink, which the greedy Sailors had too deeply loaded. The Ship floated a little while, and then disappear'd, being swallow'd up by the merciless Waves. And now, being on Shore, they were desirous to know where they were; which they soon discover'd to be on the Island *Delos*, which lies in the *Archipelago*, the largest of the *Cyclades*, once famous for the Temple of *Apollo*,[1] but now entirely abandon'd by the *Turks*, and desolate of all Inhabitants. Here they must remain, till some Discovery could be made of a better Place to remove to, which they propos'd to do by means of their Boat; in which, next to Providence, they plac'd all their Hopes. They hasted to bring all ashore, the Tempest continuing, and drew the Boat on land. And now Necessity taught them what to do in a Place, where there was neither House nor Market. Going up a little way from the Shore, they found two or three ruinous Huts, which they enter'd as joyfully as if they had been Palaces. In one of these the two Ladies went, with *Nannetta*, the Captain ordering a Quilt and some Coverlids,[2] the best they had sav'd, to be put into it; as likewise *Ardelisa*'s Trunk, in which was the Clothes and Treasure belonging to the Ladies. Into another Hut the Priest, *Joseph*, and he enter'd; there he plac'd the Wine, Biscuit, and Meat, knowing he must now husband[3] that, lest they should want before they could be supply'd with more.

And now having order'd all things the best that was possible in so unhappy a Place and Circumstance, the Captain and Priest went to the Ladies, whom they found much dejected, and out of order. They said all they could to comfort them, desiring them to eat something; *Joseph* brought them Meat and Wine, and the Sailors gather'd Leaves and Sticks, and made Fires in the Huts, being handy, and us'd to

---

1 According to Greek mythology, Delos was the birthplace of the twins Apollo and Artemis.

2 Variation of *coverlet*: a quilt.

3 Conserve, economize.

shift.[1] The Captain order'd them also some Meat and Wine, which they eat as chearfully as if nothing had happen'd. And now the good Father, seeing the Ladies sad, address'd himself thus to *Ardelisa*: "Madam, ever since I have had the Honour to know you, I have observ'd something so Noble and Christian in all your Deportment, that I believ'd you incapable of Fear or Ingratitude to God, who this day has given you a signal Deliverance from Death. It is not many hours ago since we expected to be swallow'd up in the Deep, and thought Death stared us in the Face; but now the Divine Power has brought us to firm Land, and to a Place where, if we are alone, and have no Inhabitants to comfort or relieve us, we have no Enemies to fear, no inhuman *Turks* to murder or enslave us; we may here sleep in Security. And as for Food, Providence, that provides for the wild Beasts and Birds, will doubtless provide for us; in us, who have had such uncommon and extraordinary Proofs of his Favour, it would be an unpardonable Sin to distrust him now. Summon up then your Faith and Reason to aid you, and be not cast down." These words seem'd as Cordials to them all; they eat thankfully what was set before them, and the Captain, Priest, and Boy returning to their Hut, the Sailors to theirs, they slept as sweetly as if they had lain in Palaces on Beds of Down.

Chap. XIV.
The next Morning, the Sky being clear'd up, and the Winds ceas'd, the chearful Sun began to shine; the Captain, Priest, and Sailors walk'd out of their Huts, to view the Shore and Country: they saw many Sea-Birds upon it, and Plenty of Ruins, with some Goats and Swine, which they suppos'd cast there by some Shipwreck; but so wild, that they fled away as soon as any body came in sight of them. At last the Captain thought it best to send three of the Sailors out in the Boat, to discover if any Place could be found near that more convenient to remove to, or buy Provisions at, till some Christian Ship arriv'd to take them in; which, it was probable, would not be long, because this Island affords Plenty of good Water, and is safe for Christians to air Goods on, or mend their Vessels. The Boat was accordingly got out, and the Sailors enter'd it, the Captain charging them not to venture far from that Island; but they were either taken, or drown'd, for they never return'd again with the Boat. For some days they liv'd on what Provisions they had brought with them, and the two Sailors and *Joseph* walking daily up and down the Island, which is many miles in Circumference, gather'd up Plenty of Eggs, which the Sea-Fowl laid there, and now and

---

1 To share.

then some small Fishes, which they catch'd in some little Brooks, which are in the Island.

But now the Biscuit was spent, and Bread wanting, they began to despair of the Boat's Return, which they had every day expected till now. The Ladies, unus'd to such Hardships, fell both sick. The good Father search'd every where for Herbs medicinal to relieve them; but, alas! so many things were wanting, that they were ineffectual. How could Cordials and Restoratives be had, when neither Wine or Spirits could be made? The Captain, whose Concern for *Violetta* equall'd the Passion he had for her, deny'd himself what was requisite to support his own Life, for fear of her wanting; whilst the poor Ladies, whom Sickness and Want had render'd unable to walk, were watch'd by *Nannetta*, who was almost as feeble as they. The Priest, Captain, and Sailors did nothing but wander about in search of Food: they had brought two Musquets, and some Powder ashore with them; but that being spent, the Guns were useless. They now contriv'd Pitfalls and Snares, which they made with Twigs plucked from small Trees and Bushes, which were very plenty by the Seaside; and with these they had pretty good Success, catching Sea-Fowls, and sometimes Rabbits. These they brought home, dress'd, and divided, giving first to the Ladies: But, alas! what could this do but to sustain the Lives of eight Persons; Water was all they had to drink.

One Evening the Boy catch'd a young Goat, and, unable to carry it, ty'd a String about its Neck, and let it home. The Dam,[1] with another Twin-Kid, follow'd, hearing it bleat. This young Goat being brought to the Hut belonging to the Captain, and ty'd there, drew the other two to follow her in, and so they were taken. One of the young ones they immediately kill'd, and feasted upon; the Dam they preserv'd for her Milk, and the other Kid as a Treasure, when they could get no other Food. With the Milk of this Goat the Ladies Lives were in a manner wholly preserv'd, the Boy feeding her and the Kid with what he could get of Greens, of which there was no want. And now they all grew so weak for want of Food, that they were scarce able to much as to seek for it; Silence seem'd almost to reign amongst them, every one being unwilling to speak his Despair to his Friend; their hollow Eyes were continually directed to the Sea, from whence they only hoped Relief; nothing but the Arrival of some Christian Ship could save them from perishing.

The Priest, on this Occasion, show'd himself more than Man; he encourag'd every body else, and seem'd chearful himself: and tho he eat less than they, yet seem'd always satisfy'd; tho his meager Face and

---

1 Mother.

Leanness show'd his Decay, yet his Tongue utter'd no Complaint: "Come, my Children, *says he*, Mortality is subject to Misfortunes, the way to Heaven is difficult, but the End glorious; there we shall want nothing: The Almighty's Ears are always open to our Complaints; trust him, in his own time he will deliver us, or take us to eternal Rest." With these, and such like Discourses, he comforted them daily.

Chap. XV.

One Night, as they were retir'd to Rest, (for indeed sleep they could not, or at least but little, want of Food having made them almost Strangers to those sweet Slumbers, which are produc'd by good Meat, or wholesome Nourishment) they heard a mighty Storm, the Winds blew, as if nature were Convulsions, and the Elements at strife; then Guns went off, by which they guess'd some Ship was near, and in Distress. So soon as the Day-break, the Boy and Sailors ventur'd out to see what they could discover; and there saw the dismal Remains of a Shipwreck upon the Shore, by the Carcases of several drowned Men, huge Coffers[1] floated on the Waters, and some lay upon the Shore. The Seamen and Boy got what they were able, and found some Casks of Salt-Beef, Biscuit, Rum, and Bails of *India* Goods, which show'd it was some *East-India* Ship that was lost; they hoped to find some of the Sailors, but none were sav'd alive on that Place: by those that lay dead, they guess'd them *Venetians*.

By this time Father *Francis* and the Captain came to them, and gave them their Assistance; and now getting home to their Huts what they had got, a new Life seem'd to appear in them. Thus the Ruin of others procur'd their Preservation, as is frequent in this World; and one of the Vessels of Rum being broach'd, and each taking a Dram, with a Biscuit, they resolv'd to return to work, and search all the Shore, the Sea now ebbing, to see if they could get more, especially Food, for Treasure was to them useless. That Gold, that causes so much Mischief in the World, for which Men sell their Souls, and change their Faiths, was here less valuable than a Crust of Bread. They succeeded so well, that in five hours they had five Barrels of Beef and Pork, seven of Biscuit, three of Rum, one of Brandy, five of Wine, and many rich Goods and Chests of Clothes. Thus Providence, to preserve them, caus'd the Winds and Seas to bring them Food and Raiment.[2] They likewise gather'd up many Pieces of the ship, Planks, Ropes, broken Masts, Sail-Cloth, &c. and now they began to think of making a Habitation for all the Family to dwell together, and nothing but a Boat was wanting to make them happy. They in a few days accomplish'd their

---

1 Chests.
2 Clothing.

Design of a House; for they made a large Tent, with the Sail-Cloth on Poles, with Partitions, so that it reach'd from one Hut to the other. Here the Ladies could be brought, and seated, to take a little Air, and to eat: They had likewise saved some Barrels of Powder and Shot, which was of great use to them; for the Men soon got strength enough to walk again about the Island, and shot Wild-Hogs and Fowl frequently. Thus they lived for two Months.

Chap. XVI

One Evening *Joseph* return'd from Shooting, and told them, "at the farther end of the Island he saw a Ship lie at an Anchor, at some distance from a Creek, into which he saw a Boat put. The Men came ashore, and about six of them left the Boat, and walk'd up the Land towards a Brook, as he suppos'd, for Water; and on the Ship's Stern he could discern a Red Cross, and thence concluded they were Christians." This News made them long for the next morning, when the Captain, Priest, and Boy set out by Day-break, and went to the Place, which they reach'd in three hours time, so much had Hope strengthen'd them; and there found the Shore full of Seamen, and a Tent set up, in which they suppos'd the Captain and Passengers were. The Priest went up to the first man he found near enough to speak to, and ask'd him, "Whence they were?" The Man answer'd, "From *Venice*." "What is your Captain's name," *said the Father;* "Don *Manuel, answer'd the Sea-man,* and the Ship is a Man of War call'd the *St. Mark*." "Now, Friend, *said the Priest,* where are you bound?" "Home, Sir, *he reply'd*." "Pray bring me and my Friend to the Captain, *said the Priest;* we are Christians cast on this Island, and beg to speak to him." "Speak and welcome, Gentlemen, *said the Man,* my Captain's a noble *Venetian,* and will treat you generously; a worthier man ne'er sail'd the Seas."

They follow'd him to the Tent, and were receiv'd with such Humanity as surpriz'd them; but discoursing the Captain, to whom they related part of their Misfortunes, they discover'd it was *Violetta's* Father they were talking with. Then the *French* Captain, looking on the good Father, said to the Captain, "Sir, did you not lose a Daughter in the last dreadful War with the *Turks?* a Lady the most lovely of all her Sex, call'd *Violetta*." "Yes, *answer'd Don* Manuel, I did; but why do you mention that?" "She's here, my Lord, *said he,* and in my Care."

Then the good Father and he related all the manner of her Escape: what Joy and Satisfaction this News was to Don *Manuel,* the Mind can much better conceive, than words express; they din'd with him, and, after a noble Treat, he agreed to go along with them, ordering the Ship to be brought round. In walking with them, he told them, "That as he was at Sea with his Ship, with three other Men of War in Company, going to meet some *Venetian* Merchant-Ships, that they expected from the *East-Indies*, which they were order'd to convoy home; the Storm happen'd, which had shipwreck'd one of those Ships, as he was since inform'd. This Tempest parted the Men of War, and drove him out to Sea, so that he was in great want of fresh Water; for which reason he put in here."

They entertain'd him with *Ardelisa's* whole History, and so they pass'd the time, till they reach'd their Tarpaulin Palace; into which being enter'd, they found the two Ladies: But when *Violetta* saw herself embrac'd by her Father, Joy so overcame her, that she fainted in his Arms; and, recovering, was congratulated by the whole Company. And now the Ladies and Servants seem'd so reviv'd, that all Sorrow was forgotten; Supper was brought in, and nothing spar'd of the Provisions that yet remain'd, which before they us'd to divide with care, for fear of wanting. As they were at Supper, the first Lieutenant of the Ship was brought in, to inform Don *Manuel*, that the Ship was come to an Anchor near that Place. Soon after him came several young Gentlemen to compliment their Commander, on account of *Violetta*: this Company past some hours very agreeably, admiring the strange Accidents that had befallen them, and particularly their meeting in this Place. Don *Manuel*, and those belonging to him, return'd to the Ship; and next morning, returning to Shore, pass'd the Day with his Daughter and Friends, bringing rich Wines and Sweetmeats to regale them. The Seamen hasted to water the Ship, and to get all things on board belonging to *Ardelisa*, and her Family, which they perform'd in five days; and then the Ladies, *Nannetta*, *Joseph*, and the two Sailors went aboard the *Venetian* Ship, leaving the desolate Island, and their Huts, with many things which they thought not worth taking away, which might nevertheless be of great use to any others, who should have the same Occasion for them. *Ardelisa* desir'd the Goat and Kid might be brought aboard, which she loved much, because its Milk had preserv'd hers and *Violetta's* Life; and therefore she resolv'd to carry it to *France* with her: So it was brought in the Boat, being grown so tame, it would follow *Joseph* like a Dog.

They set Sail for *Venice* the 2d of *February*, 1715/6, having lived on the Island from the 29th of *August* to that time, which was five Months and four Days; and they arriv'd safe at *Venice* in fourteen Days, where the Ladies were conducted to Don *Manuel's* House, accompany'd by the *French* Captain, the Priest, and their Servants; and there Donna *Catherina* receiv'd her Daughter with the greatest Transports imaginable, weeping for Joy, the young Lady doing the same; a sight so moving, it touch'd all the Company. Here *Ardelisa* and the rest were entertain'd magnificently, and not only invited, but even constrain'd, to continue till a *French* Ship arriv'd to carry them to *France*.

4. From Leendert Hasenbosch, *An Authentick Relation of the Many Hardships and Sufferings of a Dutch Sailor, Who was put on Shore on the uninhabited Isle of Ascension, by Order of the Commadore of a Squadron of Dutch Ships. With a Remarkable Account of his Converse with Apparitions and Evil Spirits, during his Residence on the Island. And a particular Diary of his Transactions from the Fifth of May to the Fourteenth of October, on which Day he perished in a miserable Condition. Taken from the Original Journal found in his Tent by some Sailors, who landed from on Board the Compton, Captain Morson Commander, in January 1725/6 (1728)*[1]

To the Reader. *As the following Journal carries all possible Marks of Truth and Sincerity in it; so we have thought fit to publish it exactly as it was wrote, by the miserable Wretch, who is the Subject of it, without adding any borrowed Descriptions of Places, Coasts, &c. which is too frequently done in Pieces of this Nature, in order to increase their bulk.*

The detestable Crime for which the Dutch *Commadore thought fit to abandon and leave this Sailor on a desert Island, is pretty plainly pointed out, p.* 15.[2] *of the Journal. The Miseries and Hardships he lingered under for more than five Months, were so unusually terrible, that the bare Reading his Account of 'em must make the hardest Heart melt with Compassion. Tormented with excessive Thirst; in want of almost every Thing necessary to defend him from the Inclemency of Weather; left to the severe Upbraidings and Reflections of a guilty Conscience; harass'd by the blasphemous Conversations of evil Spirits, haunted by Apparitions, even tumbled up and down in his Tent by Demons; and at the same time not one Person upon the Island from whom to seek Consolation or Advice: These are such Calamities as no Mortal could ever long support himself under. But at the same time the*

---

1 On 5 May 1725, the Dutchman Leendert Hasenbosch was marooned on Ascension Island for crimes of sodomy. For the next five months, until his death, he kept a journal, which was subsequently found by the English captain William Mawson, translated, and published anonymously in English in 1728. (The Dutchman was first identified by name by Michael Koolbergen, *Een Hollandse Robinson Crusoe* [Leiden: Menken & Kasander, 2002].) Several years later, probably in 1730, another pamphlet appeared, also purporting to be a translation of the Dutchman's journal. But whereas the first pamphlet, *An Authentic Relation*, stresses the veracity of the account, this second pamphlet, *The Just Vengeance of Heaven Exemplify'd*, is a moralizing work that uses the journal as an occasion for anti-gay rhetoric. Several excerpts from that work are included in the footnotes.

2 In this edition, p. 347.

Frontispiece to *The Just Vengeance of Heaven* (1730?). By permission of
The Huntington Library, San Marino, California.

fatal Catastrophe of this Man recommends to us, the preserving that Wall of Brass (as the Poet calls it) which will be a Comfort to us under all Misfortunes, viz. a Conscience free from Guilt.

————Hic Murus Aheneus esto,
Nil conscire sibi, nulla pallescere culpa.[1]

N.B. The Original Manuscript from whence this Journal was printed, may be seen at the Publishers.

A COPY of a JOURNAL, &c.

Saturday, May 5.

By Order of the Commodore and Captains of the *Dutch* Fleet, I was set on Shore on the Island of *Ascension*,[2] which gave me a great deal of Dissatisfaction, but I hope Almighty God will be my Protection. They put on Shore with me a Cask of Water, two Buckets, and an old Frying-Pan, &c. I made my Tent on the Beach near a Rock, wherein I put some of my Clothes.

May the 6th, I went upon the Hills to see if I could discover any Thing on the other side of the Island that was more commodious for my Living, and to see if there were any Thing green; but to my great Sorrow found nothing at all worth mentioning. I sincerely wished that some Accident wou'd befall me, to finish these my miserable Days. In the Evening I walked to my Tent again, but cou'd not very well find the way. I walked very melancholly along the Strand,[3] praying to God Almighty to put a Period to my Days or help me off this desolate Island. I went back again to my Tent, and secured it the best I could with Stones and a Tarpaulin from the Weather. About Four, or five a Clock, I kill'd three Birds called *Boobys*;[4] I skinned and salted them,

---

1 Horace, Epistle 1, I. 60: "Be this the bronze wall: to be aware of no guilt, to turn pale from no blame."
2 A British territory just south of the equator in the Atlantic. In 1725, Ascension was a frequent stopping point for ships returning from the East Indies after they had passed the Cape of Good Hope. It appears on the fold-out map of Crusoe's travels.
3 Shore.
4 According to William Funnell, who sailed with William Dampier, "The Booby is much about the bigness of a Duck; some are quite White, some Grey; They have Feet like a Duck, being a Water foul; They feed mostly upon Flying-fish, which they catch Flying. I have made many a Meal of this sort of Birds, but it was for want of other victuals; They taste very Fishy; and if you do not salt them very well before you eat them, they will make you sick; They are so silly, that when they are weary of flying, they will, if you hold out your Hand, come and sit upon it: From thence I conjecture that they are called *Boobies*" (*A Voyage Round the World* [1707]: 10).

and put them into the Sun to dry, being the first Thing I killed upon the Island. The same Night I caught two more, which I served as before.

The 7th Ditto in the Morning I went to my Water-Cask, it being half a League from my Tent. I first put a Peg in, but lost much Water by that; so got him upon his head, and took the head out with a great deal of trouble. I made a white Flag, which I put upon my Piece, having nothing else, and set it upon a Hill near the Sea. I had no Powder nor Shot, which render'd my Gun useless. That Night I put more Stones about my Tent.

The 8th Ditto in the Morning, I took my Flag again, and set it upon a Hill on the other side of the Island. In the way I found a *Turtle*, and killed him with the Butt-end of my Musket; and so went back again to my Tent, and sat me down very weary.

I trust in God Almighty, that he will deliver me some time or other by some Ship that may touch here. This Night I moved my Tent on the other side of the Rock, being afraid that it wou'd fall on my Head, and by that means endanger my Life: I wou'd by no means be accessory to my own Death, still hoping that God will preserve me to see better Days. On the whole Island I can't find a better Place than where I now am, and that I must be contented in my Condition. I thank God I am now in good Health. In the Evening I killed some more *Boobys*, which I served as the former, and in the Morning did the same.

The 9th Ditto in the Morning I went to look for the *Turtle* which I kill'd yesterday: I carried my Hatchet, and cut him upon the Back, for he was so big that I could not turn him. I cut off some of the Flesh from the Fore-Finn, and brought it to my Tent, and put it in Salt, and dry'd it in the Sun. I began again to make a Bulwark of Stones round my Tent and secured it from the Weather with my Tarpaulin.

The 10th Ditto in the Morning, I took four or five Onions, a few Peas and Calavances,[1] and went to the *South* side of the Island, to see if I cou'd find a proper Place to set them. I looked carefully on the Strand, to see if I cou'd discover the Tracts of any Beasts, or Water, or anything else that might be servicable; but found nothing but a little Purslain[2] on the other side of the Island, which I eat for Refreshment, being very dry, and cou'd find no Water, and but a little of it in my Sack; walking back, eat what I had before reserved. When I was half way back, found some more Greans, but knew not whether they were good to eat.

---

1 Beans.
2 A succulent weed sometimes used in salads.

The 11th Ditto in the Morning, went into the Country again, and found some Roots, the Skin somewhat resembling Potatoes, but cou'd not think they were good to eat. I made a diligent search for a greater Discovery, but found nothing else. I sate me down very disconsolate almost dead with Thirst, and afterwards went to my Tent. On the other side of the Island there is a sandy Bay by the biggest Hill. This Evening boil'd a little Rice, being the first time I was somewhat out of order.

The 12th Ditto in the Morning, boiled a little more Rice, of which I eat some. After I had pray'd, I went again to the Country to see if I could discover any Ships, but to my great Sorrow saw none: so went back again to my Tent, and then walked along the Beach, and found nothing but some Shells of Fish. I kept constantly walking about the Island, that being all my Hopes; then went to my Tent, and read till I was weary, and afterwards mended my Clothes. This Afternoon put the Onions, Peas and Calavances in the Ground just by my Tent, to see if they wou'd produce any more; for as it was, I cou'd not afford Water to boil them.

The 13th Ditto in the Morning, went to see if I could find any Sea-Fowls, but found none. At my walking back, I found a small *Turtle* just by my Tent: I took some of its Eggs and Flesh, and boiled with my Rice for my Dinner, and buried the rest in the Sand, that it might not infect me; its Eggs I buried in the Sand likewise. Afterwards I found some Nests of Fowls Eggs, of which I boiled in the Evening, and 'twas very good Diet. I melted some of the *Turtles* Fat to make Oil, and in the Night burnt of it, having nothing for a Lamp but a Saucer.

The 14th Ditto in the Morning, after I had pray'd, I took my usual walk, but found nothing new; so I return'd again to my Tent, and sat down and mended my Banyan-Coat,[1] and writ my Journal. [...]

The 22d Ditto, after Breakfast went to the other Side of the Island, to see if I cou'd discover any thing; but went back as I came. At Four in the Afternoon took my line, and fish'd on the Rock for three or four Hours, but to no Purpose. I then took a melancholly Walk to my Flag; but much to my Concern could descry nothing. At my return to my Tent, much to my surprize, I found it all of a smoak. After a serious Consideration, I thought that I had left my Tinder-Box a-fire on my Quilt; but the Smoke smothered me so much, that I could not enter before I had brought a Bucket of Water and quenched it. I return God Almighty my hearty Thanks that all my Things were not burnt: I have lost nothing by it but a Banyan Shirt, a corner of my Quilt, and my Bible singed. I intreat God Almighty to give me the Patience of holy *Job*, to bear with my Sufferings.

---

1 Loose jacket originally from India.

The 23d Ditto, all this Day was remaking what was burnt yesterday.[1] [...]

The 29th, Nothing remarkable. The 30th, As before. The 31st, was forced to feed on the Provision which I had before salted.

From the 1st of *June* to the 4th Ditto, it would be needless to write how often my Eyes are cast on the Sea to look for Shipping, and every little Atom in the Sky I take for a Sail; then look till my Eyes dazzle, and immediately the Object disappears. When I was put on Shore, the Captain told me it was the time of Year for Shipping to pass this way; which makes me look out the more diligently.

June the 5th, 6th and 7th, I never neglected taking my usual Walks; but to no Purpose.

The 8th, My Water was so much reduced, that I had but two Quarts left, and that so thick as obliged me to strain it through a Handkerchief. I then too late began to dig, and after I had dug seven Foot deep, found no moisture: the Place where I began, was in the middle of the Island. I then came back again to my Tent and began a new Well just by my Tent, but to no Purpose, having digg'd a Fathom deep. It is impossible to express my Concern, first in not seeing any Ships to convey me off the Island, and then in finding no Sustenance on it.

The 9th, Found nothing; past away the Day in Meditations on a future State.

The 10th, With the very last of my Water boil'd some Rice; having but very little Hopes in any thing but perishing, I commended my Soul to Almighty God entreating him that he will have mercy on it, but not caring to give over all Hopes while I cou'd yet walk, I went to the other side of the Island to see for some Water: having heard talk that there was a Well of Water on it, I walked up and down the Hills, thinking not to leave any place secret from me. After four Hours tedious walking, began to grow very thirsty, and the heat of the Sun withal made my Life a greater Burthen than I was well able to bear; but was resolved to proceed as long as I cou'd stand. Walking among the Rocks, God of his great Bounty led me to a Place where some Water run out of a hollow place in the Rock: it's impossible to express my great Joy and Satisfaction in finding of it, and thought I should have

---

1 From *The Just Vengeance of Heaven*: "The 23d I spent the whole Day in admiring the infinite Goodness of Almighty God, who had so miraculously preserved the small Remainder of my worldly treasure; and sometimes tortured myself with the melancholy Reflection of the inexpressible Punishments my crimes deserved, well knowing the Wages of Sin was inevitable Death, and that my crime was of the blackest Dye; nor could I possibly form an idea in my Mind of a Punishment that could make the least Atonement for so great an Offence."

drank till I burst. I sate me down for some time by it, then drank again and walked home to my Tent, having no Vessel to carry any along with me.

The 11th Ditto, In the Morning, after I had return'd God Almighty my hearty Thanks, I took my Tea Kettle with some Rice in it and some Wood along with me to the place where the Water was, and there boil'd and eat it.

The 12th Ditto, I boil'd some rice to break my Fast, and afterwards with much trouble carried two Buckets of Water to my Tent. I often think I am possess'd with Things that I really want; but when I come to search, find it only a Shadow. My Shoes being worn out, the Rocks cut my Feet to pieces; and I am often afraid of tumbling, and by that means endanger the breaking my Buckets, which I can't be without.

The 13th, I went to look out for Wood, but found none but a little Weeds somewhat like *Birch*; brought it to my Tent, and boil'd some Rice with it for my Dinner. Afterwards went and look'd out for Shipping, but to no purpose: it makes me very melancholly to think that I have no Hopes of getting off this unhappy[1] Island.

The 14th Ditto, took my Tea Kettle with some Rice, and went into the Country where the Water was. Afterwards returned again to my Tent, and mended my Clothes, and past away the rest of the Day in reading.

The 15th Ditto, all the Day employ'd in getting of Sea-Fowls Eggs and *Birch*.

The 16th Ditto, to no Purpose looked out for Ships; and in the Night was surpriz'd by a Noise round my Tent, of Cursing and Swearing, and the most blasphemous Conversations that I ever heard. My Concern was so great, that I thought I should have died with the Fright. I did nothing but offer up my Prayers to the Almighty to protect me in this miserable Circumstance: but my Fright rendered me in a very bad Condition of Praying, I trembling to that Degree, that I could not compose my Thoughts; and any body wou'd have believed that the Devil had moved his Quarters, and was coming to keep Hell on *Ascension*. I was certain that there was no human Creature on the Island, but my self, having not seen the Foot-steps of any Man but my own; and so much libidinous Talk was impossible to be express'd by any body but Devils: And to my greater Surprize was certain that I was very well acquainted with one of the Voices, it bearing an Affinity of an intimate Acquaintance of mine; and I really thought that I was sometimes touched by an invisible Spirit. I made my Application to the Father, Son, and Holy Ghost for forgiveness of

---

1 Characterized by misfortune.

my Sins, and that they would protect me from these evil Spirits. It was Three a Clock in the Morning before they ceased tormenting me, and then being very weary, I fell to sleep. In the Morning I awoke about Seven a-clock, and return'd God Almighty my hearty and sincere Thanks for his last Night's Protection of me, but still heard some Shrieks near my Tent, but cou'd see nothing. I took my Prayer-book, and read the Prayers proper for a Man in my Condition, and at the same Time heard a Voice, crying, *Bouger*.[1] I can't afford Paper enough to set down every particular of this unhappy Day.

The 17th Ditto, I fetch'd home two Buckets of Water, and dreaded Night's coming on, and interceeded with God Almighty that I might not be troubled again with those evil Spirits; and I hope God Almighty heard my Prayers, for I was not perplex'd with them this Night. Before I came upon this miserable Island, I was of the *Protestant* Religion, and used to laugh at the *Romans* when they talked to me of Apparitions: but to my great Sorrow now find smarting Reasons to the contrary, and shall henceforth embrace their Opinions. This Day an Apparition appear'd to me in the similitude of a Man, whom I perfectly knew; he conversed with me like a Human Creature, and touched me so sensibly of the Sins of my past Life (of which I have a sincere and hearty Repentance) and was such a terrible Shock to me, that I wish'd it would kill me.

The 18th Ditto, After my Devotions went to look out, and carried my Hatchet with me. On the Strand, the other side of the Island, I found a Tree, which I believe Providence had cast a-shore for me. I cut it in two Pieces, the whole being too big for me to carry. I put one half on my Shoulders, and when I was half way home, set it down and rested myself on it. During which time, the Apparition appear'd to me again: his Name I am afraid to utter, fearing the Event. He haunts me so often, that I begin to grow accustomed to him. After I had rested my self, I carried it home, and then went back and fetch'd the other half.[2]

The 19th Ditto, In the Morning went to my Colours to see if I could discover any Ships. Last Night nor this Day I have not seen any thing, and I trust in God I shall be no more troubled with them.

The 20th *June*, This Night, contrary to my expectation, was so prodigiously perplex'd with Spirits, and tumbled up and down in my

---

1 Sodomite.

2 From *The Just Vengeance of Heaven*: "On the 18th, after my Devotions, I went to look out as usual, and took my hatchet with me, but finding myself disappointed, made all possible Haste to the other part of the island, where to my great satisfaction I found a Tree, which I believe Providence had thrown on shore in some measure to alleviate my present Misery: I divided it with my

Tent to that degree, that in the Morning my Flesh was like a Mummy; and the Person that I was formerly acquainted with, spoke to me several times this Night: but I can't think he wou'd do me any harm, for when he was in this World, we were as great as two own Brothers. He was a Soldier at *Batavia*.[1] It is impossible for a Man to survive so many Misfortunes, I not being able to keep a Light; but the Saucer that contains it is jumbled about and broke: and, if God of his Infinite Goodness does not help me, I must inevitably perish. I hope this my Punishment in this World may suffice for my most heinous Crime of making Use of my Fellow-Creature to satisfy my Lust, whom the Almighty Creator had ordain'd another Sex for. I only desire to live to make an atonement for my Sins, which I believe my Comrade is damned for. I spent all Day in Meditations and Prayers, and eat nothing. My Strength decays, and my Life is become a great Burthen to me.

The 21st Ditto, in the Morning, I lifted up my Hands to Heaven, and offer'd up my Prayers, and then went to my Flag; and in the way looked for Provisions to assuage my raging Hunger, but found none, so was forced to be satisfied with salted Fowls. [...]

The 29th, I could not sleep all Night, being so dry, and my Head grows dizzy, that I thought I should have run mad. I went again and searched in all the Pits, but found them dry; the deepest of them, I dug seven Foot deeper, but at last found no moisture.

The 30th, I pray'd very earnestly most part of the Day, and then laid down in my Tent, and wish'd that it would rain, or that I should die before I rose. In the Afternoon got out of my Tent, but was so weak that I could not walk. I was forced to take some of the Eggs of the

---

hatchet, the whole being more than was capable of carrying at once: I took part of it on my Shoulder, and having carried it half way to my Tent, laid it down, and rested myself thereon. Alas! how wretched is that Man whose Bestial Pleasures have render'd him odious to the rest of his Fellow-Creatures, and turned him loose on a barren island, *Nebuchadnessar* like, to herd and graze with Beasts, till loathsome to himself and spurn'd by Man, he prays to end his wretched Days! His guilty Conscience checks him, his Crimes stare him full in the Face, and his misspent Life calls aloud for Vengeance from on High. Such was the Case of me unhappy Wretch, which proves the Justice of All-gracious Heaven; and whilst I was resting my wearied Limbs, and seriously reflecting with myself, the Apparition again appeared to me, which gave me the Horror inexpressible; his Name, I am unwilling to mention, not knowing what the Consequence may be; he haunted me for so long, that he began to be familiar with me: After I had rested some time I carried my Burthen to the Tent, and returned to fetch the other part."

1   Now Jakarta, Indonesia.

Turtle that I kill'd two days past, not finding one now, and eat of them. The Flesh stunk, but the Eggs did not: my Head was swell'd, and so dizzy, that I knew not what I did. But I was in such agony with Thirst, that it's impossible for any body to express it. I could not see any *Turtles*, so caught five *Boobys*, and drank the Blood of them.

August the 31*st*, I was walking, or, more properly speaking, crawling on the Sand, for I could not walk three Steps together. I saw a living *Turtle*. I was not able to carry my Bucket, but cut off his Head with my Razor, and lay all along and sucked his Blood as it run out; and afterwards got my Hand into him, and got out the Bladder, which I carry'd home with me, and put the Water out into my Kettle. Afterwards I took my Hatchet, and went to cut him up, to get its Eggs; and in cutting the Shell broke the Helve[1] of it. This was still an Addition to my Misfortunes, but I got some of its Eggs, and carried them home, and fry'd them, and afterwards drank some boil'd Piss mixed with Tea; which, tho' it was so very nauseous, revived me much. I made a Virtue of Necessity, and in my deplorable Condition thought it good.

September the 1*st*, I kill'd another *Turtle*, but never was any poor Creature so mangled, having broke my Hatchet, and raking among his Entrails, broke the Gall; which made the Blood so bitter, that after I had boil'd it, I could hardly drink it, but was forced to get it down. I thought of nothing but the other World, and soon brought up again what I had before drank; and was so extreme dry, that I drank a quart of Salt Water, but could not contain it. I was so very ill after it, that I expected immediate death, and prepared my self in the best manner I could for it; and I hope the Lord will have mercy on my Soul. After it was dark, I saw a *Turtle* crawling towards my Tent, which I kill'd, and drank about two Quarts of his Blood; all the rest that I could catch I reserved, and then endeavour'd to go to Sleep.

The 3d, All the Day was employed in fixing a Helve to my Hatchet. I was somewhat better than yesterday, and lived upon the *Turtle* that I kill'd last Night.

The 4th Ditto, Drank the last of the Blood, which was well settled, and a little sour. The 5th, 6th, 7th and 8th, I lived upon *Turtles* Blood and Eggs; but my Strength decays so, that it will be impossible I should live long. I resign my self wholly to Providence, being hardly able to kill a *Turtle*. The 9th, 10th and 11th, I am so much decay'd, that I am a perfect Skeleton, and can't write the Particulars, my Hand shakes so. The 12th, 13th, 14th, 15th, 16th and 17th, Lived as before. I'm in a declining Condition. The 18th, 19th, 20th, 21st, 22d, 23d, 24th, 25th, 26th, 27th, 28th, 29th, 30th. *October* the 1st, 2d, 3d, 4th, 5th and 6th, All as before.

---

1 Handle.

The 7th Ditto, My Wood's all gone, so that I am forced to eat raw Flesh and salted Fowls. I can't live long, and I hope the Lord will have Mercy on my Soul. The 8th, Drank my own Urine, and eat raw Flesh. The 9th, 10th, 11th, 12th, 13th and 14th of *October*, All as before.[1]

---

1   From *The Just Vengeance of Heaven*: "*September* the 1st I killed another Turtle; but having broke my Hatchet I crushed it to Pieces and raking among the Entrails broke the Gaul, which made the Blood very bitter, but was forced to drink it, or should instantly have died. My Thoughts were bent upon another World, and the ardent Desire to meet approaching Death, both cherished and tortured my departing Soul; drank a Quart of Salt Water, and expecting nothing but an immediate Dissolution; I prostrate, begging to taste the bitter Cup, till oppressed and harassed out with Care afforded some interrupted Slumbers. On the 3d I awoke and finding myself something better, employ'd my time in fitting a Helve to my Hatchet and Eat some of the turtle, which I had killed the Night before. From the 5th to the 8th I lived upon Turtles Blood and Eggs, from the 8th to the 14th I linger'd on with no other Food to subsist me. I am become a moving Skeleton, my Strength is intirely decayed, I cannot write much longer: I sincerely repent of the sins I committed and pray, henceforth, no Man may ever merit the Misery which I have undergone. For the Sake of which, leaving this Narrative behind me to deter Mankind from following such Diabolical Inventions. I now resign my Soul to him that gave it, hoping for Mercy in —"

Appendix D: Explorations of Solitude

[Crusoe's solitude is psychologically unrealistic: as Defoe knew, castaways who spent extended time alone (like prisoners placed in unbroken solitary confinement) frequently lost control of their mental faculties. Alexander Selkirk was rumored to have danced with the goats and to have lost his ability to speak. But as a mythical topos, Crusoe's solitude has made him an important figure of autonomy and individualism. In 1719, solitude could take various forms. When voluntary, it could provide the space for idealized Horatian retirement from a busy world; when involuntary or misused, it could lead to madness and solipsism. Insofar as Crusoe reimagines his forced confinement as a potentially productive part of the human condition, he prefigures the Romantic solitude of the late eighteenth century.]

1. From Richard Baxter,[1] "Of Conversing with God in Solitude," *The Divine Life: In Three Treatises* (1664)

You must not causelessly withdraw from humane society into *Solitude*. A weariness of converse with men, is oft conjunct with a weariness of our duty: and a retiring voluntarily into solitude, when God doth not call or drive us thither, is oft but a retiring from the place and work which God hath appointed us: And consequently a retiring rather from God, than to God.

... I shall now come to the *Affirmative*, and tell you for all this, that [*If God call us into Solitude, or men forsake us, we may rejoyce in this, that we are not alone, but the Father is with us.*] *Fear not such Solitude*, but be ready to improve it, if you be cast upon it. If God be your God, reconciled to you in Christ, and his Spirit be in you, you are provided for Solitude, and need not fear if all the world should cast you off. If you be banished, imprisoned, or left alone, it is but a Relaxation from your greatest labours; which though you may not cast off your selves, you may lawfully be sensible of your ease, if God take off your burden. It is but a cessation from your sharpest conflicts, and removal from a multitude of great temptations. And though you may not cowardly retreat or shift your selves from the fight and danger, yet if God will dispense with you, and let you live in greater peace and safety, you have no cause to murmur at his

---

1 Richard Baxter (1615-91): Dissenting minister and theologian.

dealing.... In your Solitude with God, you shall not hear the lyes and malicious revilings of the ungodly against the generation of the just: nor the subtile cheating words of Hereticks, who being themselves deceived, would deceive others of their faith, and corrupt their lives. You shall not there be distracted with the noise and clamours of contending uncharitable professors of Religion, endeavoring to make odious first the opinions, and then the persons of one another: one saying, Here is the Church, and another, There is the Church: one saying, This is the true Church Government, and another saying, Nay, but that is it: One saying, God will be worshipped thus, and another, Not so, but thus or thus: You shall not there be drawn to side with one against another, nor to joyn with any faction, or be guilty of divisions: You shall not be troubled with the oaths and blasphemies of the wicked, nor with the imprudent miscarriages of the weak; with the persecutions of enemies, or the falling out of friends: You shall not see the cruelty of proud oppressors, that set up lyes by armed violence, and care not what they say or do, nor how much other men are injured or suffer, so that themselves may tyrannize, and their wills and words may rule the world, when they do so unhappily rule themselves. In your Solitude with God, you shall not see the prosperity of the wicked to move you to envy, nor the adversity of the just to be your grief: You shall see no worldly pomp and splendor to befool you; nor adorned beauty to entice you, nor wasting calamities to afflict you: You shall not hear the laughter of fools, nor the sick mans groans, nor the wronged mans complaints, nor the poor mans murmurings, nor the proud mans boastings, nor the angry mans abusive ragings. As you lose the help of your gracious friends, so you are freed from the fruits of their peevishness and passions; of their differing opinions and wayes and tempers; of their inequality, unsuitableness, and contrariety of minds or interests; of their levity and unconstancy, and the powerful temptations of their friendship, to draw you to the errors or other sins which they are tainted with themselves. In a word, you are there half delivered from the VANITY and VEXATION of the world; and were it not that you are yet undelivered from *your selves*, and that you take distempered corrupted hearts with you, O what a felicity would your solitude be! But, alas, we cannot overrun our own diseases, we must carry with us the remnants of our corrupted nature; our deadness, and dulness, our selfishness and earthly minds, our impatience and discontents, and worst of all, our lamentable weakness of faith and love and heavenly mindedness, and our strangeness to God, and backwardness to the matters of eternal life.

2. From Mary, Lady Chudleigh,[1] "Of Solitude," *Essays Upon Several Subjects in Prose and Verse* (1710)

[...] From what I've said, it seems evident, that we were not created wholly for our selves, but design'd to be serviceable to each other, to do Good to all within the Circle of our Acquaintance, and some way or other render ourselves useful to those we converse with; for which reason *Solitude* ought never to be our Choice, an active Life including in it much greater Perfection: But if it is our Fortune to live retir'd, to be shut up in a Corner of the World, and deny'd the Pleasures of Conversation, I mean those Delights which naturally result from rational and instructive Discourses, we ought to endeavour to become good Company to our selves, ought to consider, that if we husband[2] our Time well, improve our Abilities, lay in a rich Stock of Knowledge, and by our Diligence and Industry, make a happy Progress in the necessary, as well as the pleasant Parts of Learning, we shall be always agreeably employ'd, and perfectly easie, without calling in auxiliary Aids, be chearful alone, and very entertaining to our selves, without being obliged for any part of our Satisfaction to those Diversions, of which the generality of Mankind are fond.

What can afford a higher, a more masculine Pleasure, a purer, a more transporting Delight, than to retire into our selves, and there curiously and attentively inspect the various Operations of our Souls, compare Idea's, consult our Reason, and view all the Beauties of our Intellect, the inimitable Stroaks of Divine Wisdom, which are visible in our Faculties, and those Participations of infinite Power, which are discoverable in our Wills?

Without us there is nothing but what will be a fit Subject for our Contemplation, and prove a constant and delectable Entertainment. If we look on our Bodies, the Fineness of their Composure, the admirable Symmetry and exact Proportion of their Parts, that Majesty which appears in the Face, that Vivacity which sparkles in the Eye, together with that noble and commanding Air which accompanies every Motion, will afford ample Matter for Meditation: If we extend our View to the sensitive and vegetative Kingdoms,[3] make a strict Scrutiny into the Individuals of each respective Kind, consider their Forms, their Properties, their Uses, and their peculiar Virtues; and if to these we add the inanimate part of the Creation, and observe Nature as she's there luxuriantly exhibiting her Skill in numberless Productions, we shall find abundant Matter for Thought to work

---

1 Mary, Lady Chudleigh (1656-1710): author of a long dialogue poem, *The Ladies Defence*, and two collections of poetry and essays.

2 Manage.

3 Animals and plants.

upon; but if we widen our Prospect, and look beyond the narrow Confines of this Globe, we shall be pleasingly confounded with a charming Variety of Objects, be lost in a delightful Maze, shall stray from one Wonder to another, and always find something new, something great, something surprizingly admirable, and every way worthy of that infinite, that incomprehensible Wisdom, to whom they owe their Original.

Thus may we delightfully, as well as advantageously, employ our selves in our Studies, in our Gardens, and in the silent lonely Retirement of a shady Grove. [...]

But none can be thus happy in *Solitude*, unless they have an inward Purity of Mind, their Desires contracted, and their Passions absolutely under the Government of their Reason. Learning without Virtue will not, cannot bestow Felicity: Where there is an internal Disturbance, a Tumult of Thought, a Consciousness of Guilt, and an Anxiousness of Soul, there can be no easie Reflections, no satisfying Pleasures; no, there must be Innocency, Calmness, and a true Understanding of the Value of Things, before the Soul can take a Complacency in herself. To render a private Life truly easie, there must be Piety, as well as humane Knowledge, uncorrupted Morals, as well as an Insight into Nature, a Regardlessness of Wealth, at least no eager Solicitude for it, a being wean'd from the World, from its Vanity, its Applause, its Censure, its Pomp, all that it has of inticing or disturbing, all that it can give, or take away; for without an absolute Independence on all things here, we cannot properly be said to enjoy our selves; and without we do so, we cannot be happy alone.

3. From Anne Kingsmill Finch, Countess of Winchilsea,[1] "The Petition for an Absolute Retreat," *Miscellany Poems on Several Occasions* (1713)

Inscribed to the Right Hon[ble] *CATHARINE* Countess of *THANET*, mention'd in the Poem under the Name of *ARMINDA*.[2]
Give me O indulgent Fate!
Give me yet, before I Dye,
A sweet, but absolute Retreat,
'Mongst Paths so lost, and Trees so high,
That the World may ne'er invade,
Through such Windings and such Shade,
My unshaken Liberty.

---

1 Anne Kingsmill Finch, Countess of Winchilsea (1661-1720). Following several years as maid of honor to Mary of Modena in the court of Charles II, Finch married and moved to an estate near the south coast of England, where she wrote most of her poems in "the solitude and security of the country."
2 Catharine Cavendish, Countess of Thanet, a close friend of Anne Finch.

No Intruders thither come!
Who visit, but to be from home;
None who their vain Moments pass,
Only studious of their Glass,[1]
News, that charm to listning Ears;
That false Alarm to Hopes and Fears;
That common Theme for every Fop,
From the Statesman to the Shop,
In those Coverts[2] ne'er be spread,
Of who's Deceas'd, or who's to Wed,
Be no Tidings thither brought,
But Silent, as a Midnight Thought,
Where the World may ne'er invade,
Be those Windings, and that Shade:
    Courteous Fate! afford me there
A *Table* spread without my Care,
With what the neighb'ring Fields impart,
Whose Cleanliness be all it's Art,
When, of old, the Calf was drest,
(Tho' to make an Angel's Feast)
In the plain, unstudied Sauce
Nor *Treufle*, nor *Morillia*[3] was;
Nor cou'd the mighty Patriarch's Board
One far-fetch'd *Ortolane*[4] afford.
Courteous Fate, then give me there
Only plain, and wholesome Fare.
Fruits indeed (wou'd Heaven bestow)
All, that did in *Eden* grow,
All, but the *Forbidden Tree*,[5]
Wou'd be coveted by me;
Grapes, with Juice so crouded up,
As breaking thro' the native Cup;
Figs (yet growing) candy'd o'er,
By the Sun's attracting Pow'r;
Cherries, with the downy Peach,
All within my easie Reach;
Whilst creeping near the humble Ground,
Shou'd the Strawberry be found

---

1 Mirror.
2 Secluded places.
3 Truffle and morel, used in sauces.
4 A small songbird, eaten as a delicacy.
5 In Genesis, the tree of the knowledge of good and evil.

Springing wheresoe'er I stray'd,
Thro' those Windings and that Shade. [...]
　　Give me there (since Heaven has shown
It was not Good to be alone)
A Partner suited to my Mind,
Solitary, pleas'd and kind;
Who, partially, may something see
Preferr'd to all the World in me;
Slighting, by my humble Side,
Fame and Splendor, Wealth and Pride.
When but Two[1] the Earth possest,
'Twas their happiest Days, and best;
They by Bus'ness, nor by Wars,
They by no Domestick Cares,
From each other e'er were drawn,
But in some Grove, or flow'ry Lawn,
Spent the swiftly flying Time,
Spent their own, and Nature's Prime,
In Love; that only Passion given
To perfect Man, whilst Friends with Heaven.
Rage, and Jealousie, and Hate,
Transports of his fallen State,
(When by *Satan*'s Wiles betray'd)
Fly those Windings, and that Shade!

　　Thus from Crouds, and Noise remov'd,
Let each Moment be improv'd;
Every Object still produce,
Thoughts of Pleasure, and of Use:
When some River slides away,
To encrease the boundless Sea;
Think we then, how Time do's haste,
To grow Eternity at last,
By the Willows, on the Banks,
Gather'd into social Ranks,
Playing with the gentle Winds,
Strait the Boughs, and smooth the Rinds,[2]
Moist each Fibre, and each Top,
Wearing a luxurious Crop,
Let the time of Youth be shown,
The time alas! too soon outgrown; [...]

1　Adam and Eve.
2　Bark.

Friendship still has been design'd,
The Support of Human-kind;
The safe Delight, the useful Bliss,
The next World's Happiness, and this.
Give then, O indulgent Fate!
Give a Friend in that Retreat
(Tho' withdrawn from all the rest)
Still a Clue, to reach my Breast.
Let a Friend be still convey'd
Thro' those Windings, and that Shade! [...]
Give me then, in that Retreat,
Give me, O indulgent Fate!
For all Pleasures left behind,
Contemplations of the Mind.
Let the Fair, the Gay, the Vain
Courtship and Applause obtain;
Let th' Ambitious rule the Earth;
Let the giddy Fool have Mirth;
Give the Epicure his Dish,
Ev'ry one their sev'ral Wish;
Whilst my Transports I employ
On that more extensive Joy,
When all Heaven shall be survey'd
From those Windings and that Shade.

4. From Daniel Defoe, "Of Solitude," *Serious Reflections During the Life and Surprising Adventures of Robinson Crusoe* (1720)

INTRODUCTION

I Must have made very little Use of my solitary and wandring Years, if, after such a Scene of Wonders, as my Life may be justly call'd, I had nothing to say, and had made no Observations which might be useful and instructing, as well as pleasant and diverting to those that are to come after me.

CHAP. I.
Of Solitude

How uncapable to make us happy, and
How unqualify'd to a Christian Life.

I have frequently look'd back, you may be sure, and that with different Thoughts, upon the Notions of a long tedious Life of Solitude, which I have represented to the World, and of which you must have formed some Ideas from the Life of a Man in an Island. Sometimes I have wonder'd how it could be supported, especially for the first Years, when the Change was violent and impos'd, and Nature unacquainted with any thing like it. Sometimes I have as much wonder'd, why it should be any Grievance or Affliction; seeing upon the whole View of the Stage of Life which we act upon in this World, it seems to me, that Life in general is, or ought to be, but one universal Act of Solitude: But I find it is natural to judge of Happiness, by its suiting or not suiting our own Inclinations. Every Thing revolves in our Minds by innumerable circular Motions, all centring in our selves. We judge of Prosperity, and of Affliction, Joy and Sorrow, Poverty, Riches, and all the various Scenes of Life: I say, we judge of them by our selves: Thither we bring them Home, as Meats touch the Palat, by which we try them; the gay Part of the World, or the heavy Part; it is all one, they only call it pleasant or unpleasant, as they suit our Taste.

The World, I say, is nothing to us, but as it is more or less to our Relish: All Reflection is carry'd Home, and our Dear-self is, in one Respect, the End of Living. Hence Man may be properly said to be *alone* in the Midst of the Crowds and Hurry of Men and Business: All the Reflections which he makes, are to himself; all that is pleasant, he embraces for himself; all that is irksome and grievous, is tasted but by his own Palat.

What are the Sorrows of other Men to us? And what their Joy? Something we may be touch'd indeed with, by the Power of Sympathy, and a secret Turn of the Affections; but all the solid Reflection is directed to our selves. Our Meditations are all Solitude in Perfection; our Passions are all exercised in Retirement; we love, we hate, we covet, we enjoy, all in Privacy and Solitude: All that we communicate of those Things to any other, is but for their Assistance in the Pursuit of our Desires; the End is at Home; the Enjoyment, the Contemplation, is all Solitude and Retirement; 'tis for our selves we enjoy, and for our selves we suffer.

What, then, is the Silence of Life? And, How is it afflicting, while a Man has the Voice of his Soul to speak to God, and to himself? That Man can never want Conversation, who is Company for himself; and he that cannot converse profitably with himself, is not fit for any Conversation at all; and yet there are many good Reasons why a Life of Solitude, as Solitude is now understood by the Age, is not at all suited to the Life of a Christian, or of a wise Man. Without enquiring therefore into the Advantages of Solitude, and how it is to be managed, I desire to be heard concerning what Solitude really is; for I must confess, I have different Notions about it, far from those which are generally understood in the World, and far from all those Notions upon which those People in the primitive Times, and since that also, acted, who separated themselves into Desarts and unfrequented Places, or confin'd themselves to Cells, Monasteries, and the like, retir'd, as they call it, from the World; All which, I think, have nothing of the Thing I call Solitude in them, nor do they answer any of the true Ends of Solitude, much less those Ends which are pretended to be sought after, by those who have talk'd most of those Retreats from the World.

As for Confinement in an Island, if the Scene was plac'd there for this very End, it were not at all amiss. I must acknowledge, there was Confinement from the Enjoyments of the World, and Restraint from human Society: *But all that was no Solitude*; indeed no Part of it was so, except that which, as in my Story, I apply'd to the Contemplation of sublime Things, and that was but a very little, as my Readers well know, compar'd to what a Length of Years my forced Retreat lasted.

It is evident then, that as I see nothing but what is far from being retir'd, in the forced Retreat of an Island, the Thoughts being in no Composure suitable to a retired Condition, no not for a great While; so I can affirm, that I enjoy much more Solitude in the Middle of the greatest Collection of Mankind in the World, I mean, at *London*, while I am writing this, than ever I could say I enjoy'd in eight and twenty Years Confinement to a desolate Island. [...]

Christians may without doubt come to enjoy all the desirable Advantages of Solitude, by a strict Retirement, and exact Government of their Thoughts, without any of these Formalities, Rigours, and apparent Mortifications, which I think I justly call a Rape upon human Nature, and consequently without the Breach of Christian Duties, which they necessarily carry with them, such as rejecting Christian Communion, Sacraments, Ordinances, and the like.

There is no need of a Wilderness to wander among wild Beasts, no necessity of a Cell on the top of a Mountain, or a desolate Island in the Sea; if the Mind be confin'd, if the Soul be truly Master of it self, all is safe; for it is certainly and effectually Master of the Body, and what signify Retreats, especially a forc'd Retreat as mine was? The anxiety of my Circumstances there, I can assure you, was such for a Time, as were very suitable[1] to heavenly Meditations, and even when that was got over, the frequent Alarms from the Savages, put the Soul sometimes to such Extremities of Fear and Horrour, that all manner of Temper was lost, and I was no more fit for religious Exercises, than a sick Man is fit for Labour. [...]

Solitude therefore, as I understand by it, a Retreat from human Society, on a religious or philosophical Account, is a meer Cheat; it

---

1 Possibly a printer's error for *un*suitable.

neither can answer the End it proposes, or qualify us for the Duties of Religion, which we are commanded to perform; and is therefore both irreligious in it self, and inconsistent with a Christian Life many Ways. Let the Man that would reap the Advantage of Solitude, and that understands the Meaning of the Word, learn to retire into himself: Serious Meditation is the Essence of Solitude; all the Retreats into Woods and Desarts are short of this; and though a Man that is perfectly Master of this Retirement, may be a little in Danger of Quietism,[1] that is to say, of an Affectation of Reservedness; yet it may be a Slander upon him in the main, and he may make himself amends upon the World, by the blessed Calm of his Soul, which they perhaps who appear more chearful may have little of. [...]

[I]f Meditation could not be practis'd beneficially, and to all the Intents and Purposes for which it was ordain'd a Duty, without flying from the Face of human Society, the Life of Man would be very unhappy.

But doubtless the Contrary is evident, and all the Parts of a compleat Solitude are to be as effectually enjoy'd, if we please, and sufficient Grace assisting, even in the most populous Cities, among the Hurries of Conversation, and Gallantry of a Court, or the Noise and Business of a Camp, as in the Desarts of *Arabia* and *Lybia*, or in the desolate Life of an uninhabited Island.

5. Alexander Pope, "Ode on Solitude," *Poems on Several Occasions* (1717)[2]

Happy the man, whose wish and care
A few paternal acres bound,
Content to breathe his native air,
    In his own ground.

Whose heards with milk, whose fields with bread,
Whose flocks supply him with attire,
Whose trees in summer yield him shade,
    In winter fire.

---

1 A philosophical system that emphasizes passive contemplation over active engagement.
2 In his 1729 poem *The Dunciad*, Alexander Pope (1688-1744) satirically described the pillory where "Earless on high, stood unabash'd Defoe." But Pope also commented to his friend Joseph Spence, "The first part of *Robinson Crusoe*, good. Defoe wrote many things, and none bad, though none excellent. There's something good in all he has writ" (Rogers, *Defoe: The Critical Heritage*, pp. 39-40). Pope claimed to have written the first version of this poem when he was only twelve years old; he continued to revise it throughout his life.

Blest! who can unconcern'dly find
Hours, days, and years slide soft away,
In health of body, peace of mind,
Quiet by day,

Sound sleep by night; study and ease
Together mix'd; sweet recreation,
And innocence, which most does please,
With meditation.

Thus let me live, unseen, unknown;
Thus unlamented let me dye;
Steal from the world, and not a stone
Tell where I lye.

6. From Edmund Burke,[1] "Society and Solitude," *A Philosophical Enquiry into the Origin of our Ideas of the Sublime and Beautiful* (1757)

The second branch of the social passions, is that which administers to *society in general*. With regard to this, I observe, that society, merely as society, without any particular heightenings, gives us no positive pleasure in the enjoyment; but absolute and entire *solitude*, that is, the total and perpetual exclusion from all society, is as great a positive pain as can almost be conceived. Therefore in the balance between the pleasure of general *society*, and the pain of absolute solitude, *pain* is the predominant idea. But the pleasure of any particular social enjoyment outweighs very considerably the uneasiness caused by the want of that particular enjoyment; so that the strongest sensations relative to the habitudes of *particular society* are sensations of pleasure. Good company, lively conversation, and the endearments of friendship, fill the mind with great pleasure; a temporary solitude, on the other hand, is itself agreeable. This may perhaps prove that we are creatures designed for contemplation as well as action; since solitude as well as society has its pleasures; as from the former observation we may discern, that an entire life of solitude contradicts the purposes of our being, since death itself is scarcely an idea of more terror.

---

1 Edmund Burke (1729-97): Anglo-Irish statesman, philosopher, and political theorist.

7. From Jean-Jacques Rousseau,[1] *Emilius and Sophia: or, a New System of Education*, tr. William Kenrick (1762)

I hate books; they only teach people to talk about what they don't understand. It is said that Hermes engraved the elements of the sciences on columns, to secure his discoveries from being lost, in the time of a general deluge. Had he imprinted them on the minds of men, they had been better preserved by tradition. The organs of the memory, duly prepared, are the monuments on which human science would be most indelibly engraven.

Is there no expedient to be thought of, to collect the various instructions, scattered up and down in so many voluminous tomes? to unite them under one general head, which may be easy to comprehend, interesting to pursue, and which may serve as a *stimulus*, even to children of this age? If one could but conceive a situation, in which all the natural wants of man would be displayed, in a manner adapted to the understanding of a child, and wherein the means of satisfying those wants are gradually discovered with the same ease and simplicity, it would be in a just and lively description of such a state, that we should first exercise his imagination.

I see the imagination of the philosopher already take fire. Impetuous genius! give yourself no trouble; such a situation is already discovered; it is already described, and I may say, without any impeachment to your talents, much better than you could describe it yourself; at least with much more exactness, and simplicity. Since we must have books, there is already one which, in my opinion, affords a complete treatise on natural education. This book shall be the first Emilius[2] shall read: In this, indeed, will, for a long time, consist his whole library, and it will always hold a distinguished place among others. It will afford us the text, to which all our conversations on the objects of natural science, will serve only as a comment. It will serve as our guide during our progress to a state of reason; and will even afterwards give us constant pleasure unless our taste be totally vitiated. You ask impatiently, what is the title of this wonderful book? Is it Aristotle, Pliny, or Buffon?[3] No. It is Robinson Crusoe.

---

1 Jean-Jacques Rousseau (1712-78): Enlightenment novelist, philosopher, composer, and autobiographer.

2 Latinized name for Emile, Rousseau's imagined student.

3 Aristotle (384 BCE–322 BCE): Greek philosopher whose corpus includes works about poetry, natural history, ethics, biology, metaphysics, logic, and rhetoric. Pliny the Elder (23 BCE-79 CE): Roman commander, natural philosopher, and author of *Naturalis Historia*. Georges-Louis Leclerc, Comte de Buffon (1707-88): French naturalist and author of the encyclopedic *Histoire Naturelle*.

Robinson Crusoe, cast ashore on a desolate island, destitute of human assistance, and of mechanical implements, providing, nevertheless, for his subsistence, for self-preservation, and even procuring for himself a kind of competency. In these circumstances, I say, there cannot be an object more interesting to persons of every age; and there are a thousand ways to render it agreeable to children. Such a situation, I confess, is very different from that of man in a state of society. Very probably it will never be that of Emilius; but it is from such a state he ought to learn to estimate[1] others. The most certain method for him to raise himself above vulgar prejudices and to form his judgment on the actual relations of things, is to take on himself the character of such a solitary adventurer, and to judge of every thing about him, as a man in such circumstances would, by its real utility. This romance beginning with his shipwreck on the island, and ending with the arrival of the vessel that brought him away, would, if cleared of its rubbish, afford Emilius, during the period we are now treating of, at once both instruction and amusement. I would have him indeed personate the hero of the tale, and be entirely taken up with his castle, his goats and his plantations; he should make himself minutely acquainted, not from books but circumstances, with every thing requisite for a man in such a situation. He should affect even his dress, wear a coat of skins, a great hat, a large hanger, in short, he should be entirely equipt in his grotesque manner, even with his umbrello, though he would have no occasion for it. I would have him when at a loss about the measures necessary to be taken for his provision or security, upon this or the other occasion, examine the conduct of his hero; he should see if he omitted nothing, or if any thing better could be substituted in the room of what was actually done; and, on the discovery of any mistake in Robinson, should amend it in a similar case himself: for I doubt not but he will form a project of going to make a like settlement. Not unlike to this were those ancient castles in Spain, in that happy age when the height of human felicity consisted in the enjoyment of liberty and the necessaries of life.

What opportunities of instruction would such an amusement afford an able preceptor, who should project it only with a view to that end! The pupil, eager to furnish a magazine[2] for his island, would be more ready to learn than his tutor to teach him. He would be solicitous to know every thing that is useful, and nothing else: You would in such a case have no more occasion to direct; but only to restrain him. Let us hasten, therefore, to establish him in this imaginary isle, since to this he confines his present happiness; for the time will now soon come, in

---

1 To judge, to form an opinion of.
2 Storehouse.

which, if he is desirous of life, it is not to live alone, and in which even a man *Friday*, the want of whom does not now affect him, would not be long satisfactory.

The practice of simple manual arts, to the exercise of which the abilities of the individual are equal, leads to the invention of the arts of industry, the exercise of which requires the concurrence of many. The former may be practised by hermits, and savages; but the latter can be exercised only in a state of society, and render that state necessary. While man is subject only to the calls of physical necessity, he is capable of satisfying them himself: but, by the introduction of superfluous wants, the joint concern and distribution of labour becomes indispensible: for though a man by his own labour, when alone, procures only subsistence for an individual, yet an hundred men working in concert, will easily procure, in the same time, subsistence for double the number. As soon, therefore, as one part of mankind take upon themselves to live idle, it becomes necessary that the concurrent labour of numbers should supply the place of those who live without work.

Your greatest care should be to keep from your pupil the notions of those social relations, which he is not in a capacity to comprehend; but when the connection of his ideas oblige you to speak of the mutual dependance of mankind, instead of presenting him at first the moral side of the question, divert his attention as much as possible to industry and the mechanic arts, which render men useful to one another. In going about with him to the work-shops of various artisans, never let him see any thing performed without lending a hand to the work, nor come out of the shop without perfectly understanding the reason of what he observes there. To this end, you should work yourself, and in every thing set him an example. To make him a master, be you in every thing the apprentice; and reflect that he will learn more by one hour of manual labour, than he will retain from a whole day's verbal instructions.

The different arts are entitled to various proportions of public esteem, and that in an inverse ratio to their real use. This esteem is directly as their inutility, and so it politically ought to be. The most useful arts are those which are the worst paid for or least rewarded; because the number of workmen is proportioned to the wants of the whole society, and the labour the poor must purchase must necessarily be at a low price. On the contrary, those important artisans, who, by way of distinction, are termed artists, and are employed only in the service of the rich and idle, set an arbitrary price on their workmanship; and as the excellence of their baubles is mere matter of opinion, their high price constitutes great part of their merit, and they are esteemed in proportion to what they cost. The value thus set upon them is not on account of any use they are of to the rich, but because they are too costly to be purchased by the poor. *Nolo habere bona nisi quibus populus invederit.*[1]

What will become of your pupils, if you permit them to adopt this ridiculous prejudice, if you encourage it yourself, or see them, for example, enter, with more respect the shop of a jeweller than that of a locksmith? What a judgment will they form of the real merit of the arts and the intrinsic value of things, when they see whim and caprice universally opposed to real utility, and find the more a thing costs the less it is worth? If ever such ideas as these take root in their minds, you may as well give up at once the remaining part of their education; they will, in spite of all you can do, be educated like the rest of the world, and you will have taken, for fourteen years past, all your trouble for nothing.

Emilius will see things in a very different light, while he is employed in furnishing his island. Robinson Crusoe would have set a greater value on the stock in trade of a petty ironmonger, than on that of the most magnificent and best-furnished toy-shop in Europe. The first had appeared to him a respectable personage, while the owner of the latter had been despised as frivolous and contemptible.

8. William Cowper,[2] "Verses Supposed to be Written by Alexander Selkirk, During his Solitary Abode in the Island of Juan Fernandez," *Poems by William Cowper* (1782)

1.

I am monarch of all I survey,
 My right there is none to dispute,
From the center all round to the sea,
 I am lord of the fowl and the brute.
Oh, solitude! where are the charms
 That sages have seen in thy face?
Better dwell in the midst of alarms,
 Than reign in this horrible place.

2.

I am out of humanity's reach,
 I must finish my journey alone,
Never hear the sweet music of speech,
 I start at the sound of my own.

---

1 Petronius, *Satyricon*: "I want only those good things that the people envy."
2 William Cowper (1731-1800): Evangelical English poet and hymnodist.

The beasts that roam over the plain,
　　My form with indifference see,
They are so unacquainted with man,
　　Their tameness is shocking to me.

3.

Society, friendship, and love,
　　Divinely bestow'd upon man,
Oh had I the wings of a dove,
　　How soon wou'd I taste you again!
My sorrows I then might assuage
　　In the ways of religion and truth,
Might learn from the wisdom of age,
　　And be cheer'd by the sallies of youth.

4.

Religion! what treasure untold
　　Resides in that heav'nly word!
More precious than silver and gold,
　　Or all that this earth can afford.
But the sound of the church going bell
　　These vallies and rocks never heard,
Ne'er sigh'd at the sound of a knell,
　　Or smil'd when a sabbath appear'd.

5.

Ye winds that have made me your sport,
　　Convey to this desolate shore
Some cordial endearing report
　　Of a land I shall visit no more.
My friends do they now and then send
　　A wish or a thought after me?
O tell me I yet have a friend,
　　Though a friend I am never to see.

6.

How fleet is a glance of the mind!
　　Compar'd with the speed of its flight,
The tempest itself lags behind,
　　And the swift winged arrows of light.
When I think of my own native land
　　In a moment I seem to be there;
But, alas! recollection at hand
　　Soon hurries me back to despair.

7.

But the sea fowl is gone to her nest,
   The beast is laid down in his lair,
Ev'n here is a season of rest,
   And I to my cabbin repair.
There is mercy in ev'ry place;
   And mercy, encouraging thought!
Gives even affliction a grace,
   And reconciles man to his lot.

9. Charlotte Smith,[1] Sonnet XLIV, "Written in the Church-yard at Middleton in Sussex," *Elegiac Sonnets*, 5th ed. (1789)

Press'd by the Moon, mute arbitress of tides,
   While the loud equinox its power combines,
   The sea no more its swelling surge confines,
But o'er the shrinking land sublimely rides.
The wild blast, rising from the Western cave,
   Drives the huge billows from their heaving bed;
   Tears from their grassy tombs the village dead,[2]
And breaks the silent sabbath of the grave!
With shells and sea-weed mingled, on the shore
   Lo! their bones whiten in the frequent wave;
   But vain to them the winds and waters rave;
They hear the warring elements no more:
While I am doom'd—by life's long storm opprest,
To gaze with envy on their gloomy rest.

---

1 Charlotte Smith (1749-1806): English Romantic poet and novelist, whose
   Elegiac Sonnets (1784) helped to revitalize the sonnet form.

2 "Middleton is a village on the margin of the sea, in Sussex, containing only
   two or three houses. There were formerly several acres of ground between its
   small church and the sea, which now, by its continual encroachments,
   approaches within a few feet of this half-ruined and humble edifice. The wall,
   which once surrounded the church-yard, is entirely swept away, many of the
   graves broken up, and the remains of bodies interred washed into the sea;
   whence human bones are found among the sand and shingles on the shore."
   [Smith's note]

10. From Samuel Taylor Coleridge, "The Rime of the Ancyent Marinere," *Lyrical Ballads* (1798)

Part IV.[1]

"I fear thee, ancyent Marinere!
   I fear thy skinny hand;
And thou art long and lank and brown
   As is the ribb'd Sea-sand.

"I fear thee and thy glittering eye
   And thy skinny hand so brown—"
Fear not, fear not, thou wedding guest!
   This body dropt not down.

Alone, alone, all all alone
   Alone on the wide wide Sea;
And Christ would take no pity on
   My soul in agony.

The many men so beautiful
   And they all dead did lie!
And a million million slimy things
   Liv'd on—and so did I.

---

1   Samuel Taylor Coleridge (1772-1834): English Romantic poet, philosopher, and literary critic. Coleridge deeply admired *Crusoe*, which he claimed to have read before age six. In the margins of his heavily annotated copy, he wrote, "The writer who makes me sympathise with his presentations with the *whole* of my being, is more estimable than the writer who calls forth and appeals to but a part of my being—my sense of the ludicrous, for instance; and again, he who makes me forget my *specific* class, character, and circumstances, raises me into the universal man. Now this is De Foe's excellence. You become a man while you read" (Rogers, *Defoe: The Critical Heritage*, p. 81). Like *Crusoe*, *The Ancient Mariner* explores transgression, repentance, and the possibility of redemption. In the three parts that precede this section, the Mariner has forced a wedding guest to listen to the tale of his Antarctic voyage: after he shot an albatross that followed his ship, the wind stopped blowing, and the crew blamed him and hung the albatross around his neck. A ghostly ship appeared, manned by Death and Night-mare Life-in-Death, who played dice for the crew's souls. The first six lines of this excerpt are spoken by the wedding guest; the rest is spoken by the Mariner. The text of the poem is taken from the first printed edition of *Lyrical Ballads*.

I look'd upon the rotting Sea,
    And drew my eyes away;
I look'd upon the eldritch deck,
    And there the dead men lay.

I look'd to Heaven, and try'd to pray;
    But or ever a prayer had gusht,
A wicked whisper came and made
    My heart as dry as dust.

I clos'd my lids and kept them close,
    Till the balls like pulses beat;
For the sky and the sea, and the sea and the sky
Lay like a load on my weary eye,
    And the dead were at my feet.

The cold sweat melted from their limbs,
    Ne rot, ne reek did they;
The look with which they look'd on me,
    Had never pass'd away.

An orphan's curse would drag to Hell
    A spirit from on high:
But O! more horrible than that
    Is the curse in a dead man's eye!
Seven days, seven nights I saw that curse,
    And yet I could not die.

The moving Moon went up the sky
    And no where did abide:
Softly she was going up
    And a star or two beside—

Her beams bemock'd the sultry main
    Like morning frosts yspread;
But where the ship's huge shadow lay,
The charmed water burnt alway
    A still and awful red.

Beyond the shadow of the ship
    I watch'd the water-snakes:
They mov'd in tracks of shining white;
And when they rear'd, the elfish light
    Fell off in hoary flakes.

Within the shadow of the ship
  I watch'd their rich attire:
Blue, glossy green, and velvet black
They coil'd and swam; and every track
  Was a flash of golden fire.

O happy living things! no tongue
  Their beauty might declare:
A spring of love gusht from my heart,
  And I bless'd them unaware!
Sure my kind saint took pity on me,
  And I bless'd them unaware.

The self-same moment I could pray;
  And from my neck so free
The Albatross fell off, and sank
  Like lead into the sea.

11. William Wordsworth,[1] "Nutting," *Lyrical Ballads* (1800)

——————It seems a day
(I speak of one from many singled out)
One of those heavenly days that cannot die;
When, in the eagerness of boyish hope,
I left our cottage-threshold, sallying forth
With a huge wallet o'er my shoulders slung,
A nutting-crook in hand; and turned my steps
Tow'rd some far-distant wood, a Figure quaint,
Tricked out in proud disguise of cast-off weeds
Which for that service had been husbanded,
By exhortation of my frugal Dame—
Motley accoutrement, of power to smile
At thorns, and brakes, and brambles,—and, in truth,
More ragged than need was! O'er pathless rocks,
Through beds of matted fern, and tangled thickets,

---

1 William Wordsworth (1770-1850), the English Romantic poet, rarely mentions Defoe, but he reportedly observed that "the chief interest of [Robinson Crusoe] arose from the extraordinary energy and resource of the hero under his difficult circumstances from their being so far beyond what it was natural to expect or what would have been exhibited by the average man, and that similarly the high pleasure derives from his successes and good fortunes arose from the peculiar source of these uncommon merits of his character" (Rogers, *Defoe: The Critical Heritage*, p. 115).

Forcing my way, I came to one dear nook
Unvisited, where not a broken bough
Drooped with its withered leaves, ungracious sign
Of devastation; but the hazels rose
Tall and erect, with tempting clusters hung,
A virgin scene!—A little while I stood,
Breathing with such suppression of the heart
As joy delights in; and, with wise restraint
Voluptuous, fearless of a rival, eyed
The banquet;—or beneath the trees I sate
Among the flowers, and with the flowers I played;
A temper known to those, who, after long
And weary expectation, have been blest
With sudden happiness beyond all hope.
Perhaps it was a bower beneath whose leaves
The violets of five seasons re-appear
And fade, unseen by any human eye;
Where fairy water-breaks do murmur on
For ever; and I saw the sparkling foam,
And—with my cheek on one of those green stones
That, fleeced with moss, under the shady trees,
Lay round me, scattered like a flock of sheep—
I heard the murmur, and the murmuring sound,
In that sweet mood when pleasure loves to pay
Tribute to ease; and, of its joy secure,
The heart luxuriates with indifferent things,
Wasting its kindliness on stocks and stones,
And on the vacant air. Then up I rose,
And dragged to earth both branch and bough, with crash
And merciless ravage: and the shady nook
Of hazels, and the green and mossy bower,
Deformed and sullied, patiently gave up
Their quiet being: and, unless I now
Confound my present feelings with the past;
Ere from the mutilated bower I turned
Exulting, rich beyond the wealth of kings,
I felt a sense of pain when I beheld
The silent trees, and saw the intruding sky.—
Then, dearest Maiden, move along these shades
In gentleness of heart; with gentle hand
Touch—for there is a spirit in the woods.

12. William Cowper, "The Castaway," *The Life and Letters of William Cowper* (1803)[1]

Obscurest night involv'd the sky,
  The Atlantic billows roar'd,
When such a destin'd wretch as I,
  Wash'd headlong from on board,
Of friends, of hope, of all bereft,
His floating home forever left.

No braver chief could Albion[2] boast
  Than he[3] with whom he went,
  Nor ever ship left Albion's coast,
  With warmer wishes sent.
He lov'd them both, but both in vain,
Nor him beheld, nor her again.

Not long beneath the whelming brine,
  Expert to swim, he lay;
Nor soon he felt his strength decline,
  Or courage die away;
But wag'd with death a lasting strife,
Supported by despair of life.

---

1 Cowper based his poem on a passage from George Anson's *Voyage Round the World* (1748): "We were attacked by another storm still more furious than the former; for it proved a perfect hurricane, and reduced us to the necessity of lying to under our bare poles. As our ship kept the wind better than any of the rest, we were obliged, in the afternoon, to wear ship, in order to join the squadron to the leeward, which otherwise we should have been in danger of losing in the night: And as we dared not venture any sail abroad, we were obliged to make use of an expedient, which answered our purpose: this was putting the helm a weather, and manning the fore-shrouds: But though this method proved successful for the end intended, yet in the execution of it, one of our ablest seamen was canted over-board; we perceived that and notwithstanding the prodigious agitation of the waves, he swam very strong, and it was with the utmost concern that we found ourselves incapable of assisting him; indeed we were the more grieved at his unhappy fate, as we lost sight of him struggling with the waves, and conceived from the manner in which he swam, that he might continue sensible for a considerable time longer, of the horror attending his irretrievable situation."
2 Great Britain.
3 Anson.

He shouted: nor his friends had fail'd
  To check the vessel's course,
But so the furious blast prevail'd,
  That, pitiless perforce,
They left their outcast mate behind,
And scudded still before the wind.

Some succour yet they could afford;
  And, as such storms allow,
The cask, the coop, the floated cord,
  Delayed not to bestow.
But he (they knew) nor ship, nor shore,
Whate'er they gave, should visit more.

Nor, cruel as it seem'd, could he
  Their haste himself condemn,
Aware that flight, in such a sea,
  Alone could rescue them;
Yet bitter felt it still to die
Deserted, and his friends so nigh.

He long survives, who lives an hour
  In ocean, self-upheld;
And so long he, with unspent pow'r,
  His destiny repell'd;
And ever, as the minutes flew,
Entreated help, or cried, "Adieu!"

At length, his transient respite past,
  His comrades, who before
Had heard his voice in ev'ry blast,
  Could catch the sound no more.
For then, by toil subdued, he drank
The stifling wave, and then he sank.

No poet wept him: but the page
  Of narrative sincere,
That tells his name, his worth, his age,
  Is wet with Anson's tear.
And tears by bards or heroes shed
Alike immortalize the dead.

I therefore purpose not, or dream,
  Descanting on his fate,
To give the melancholy theme
  A more enduring date;
But misery still delights to trace
Its semblance in another's case.

No voice divine the storm allay'd,[1]
  No light propitious shone,
When, snatch'd from all effectual aid,
  We perish'd, each alone;
But I beneath a rougher sea,
And whelm'd in deeper gulfs than he.

---

1 Matthew 8: 23-26: "And when he was entered into a ship, his disciples followed him. And, behold, there arose a great tempest in the sea, insomuch that
  the ship was covered with the waves: but he was asleep. And his disciples
  came to him, and awoke him, saying, Lord, save us: we perish. And he saith
  unto them, Why are ye fearful, O ye of little faith? Then he arose, and rebuked
  the winds and the sea; and there was a great calm."

Appendix E: Economic Contexts

[In the final issue of *The Review* in 1713, Defoe commented that trade was the "Whore I really doated upon, and design'd to have taken up with," so it is not surprising that even a novel set mostly on a deserted island should reflect his economic thinking. Arguably, *Crusoe* reveals the ways that an isolated individual allocates resources, calculates profit and loss, and ascertains value. Of the following four excerpts, only the passage from Locke was known to Defoe; the others illuminate Defoe's treatment of economic specialization, commodity value, the dignity of labor, and the relationship between economics and Puritanism.]

1. From John Locke,[1] "Of Property," *Two Treatises on Government* (1698)

27. Though the Earth, and all inferior Creatures be common to all Men, yet every Man has a *Property* in his own *Person*. This no Body has any Right to but himself. The *Labour* of his Body, and the *Work* of his Hands, we may say, are properly his. Whatsoever then he removes out of the State that Nature hath provided, and left it in, he hath mixed his *Labour* with, and joyned to it something that is his own, and thereby makes it his *Property*. It being by him removed from the common state Nature placed it in, hath by this *labour* something annexed to it, that excludes the common right of other Men. For this *Labour* being the unquestionable Property of the Labourer, no man but he can have a right to what that is once joyned to, at least where there is enough, and as good left in common for others.

28. He that is nourished by the Acorns he pickt up under an Oak, or the Apples he gathered from the Trees in the Wood, has certainly appropriated them to himself. No Body can deny but the nourishment is his. I ask then, When did they begin to be his? When he digested? Or when he eat? Or when he boiled? Or when he brought them home? Or when he pickt them up? And 'tis plain, if the first gathering made them not his, nothing else could. That *labour* put a distinction between them and common. That added something to them more than Nature, the common Mother of all, had done; and so they became his private right. And will any one say he had no right to those Acorns or Apples he thus appropriated, because he had not the consent of all Mankind

---

1 John Locke (1632-1704): English empiricist, philosopher, and political theorist.

to make them his? Was it a Robbery thus to assume to himself what belonged to all in Common? If such a consent as that was necessary, Man had starved, notwithstanding the Plenty God had given him. We see in *Commons*, which remain so by Compact, that 'tis the taking any part of what is common, and removing it out of the state Nature leaves it in, which *begins the Property*; without which the Common is of no use. And the taking of this or that part, does not depend on the express consent of all the Commoners. Thus the Grass my Horse has bit; the Turfs my Servant has cut; and the Ore I have digg'd in any place where I have a right to them in common with others, become my *Property*, without the assignation or consent of any body. The *labour* that was mine, removing them out of that common state they were in, hath *fixed* my *Property* in them.

29. By making an explicit consent of every Commoner, necessary to any ones appropriating to himself any part of what is given in common, Children or Servants could not cut the Meat which their Father or Master had provided for them in common, without assigning to every one his peculiar part. Though the Water running in the Fountain be every ones, yet who can doubt, but that in the Pitcher is his only who drew it out? His *labour* hath taken it out of the hands of Nature, where it was common, and belong'd equally to all her Children, and *hath* thereby *appropriated* it to himself.

30. Thus this Law of reason makes the Deer, that *Indian's* who hath killed it; 'tis allowed to be his goods who hath bestowed his labour upon it, though before, it was the common right of every one. And amongst those who are counted the Civiliz'd part of Mankind, who have made and multiplied positive Laws to determine Property, this original Law of Nature for the *beginning of Property*, in what was before common, still takes place; and by vertue thereof, what Fish any one catches in the Ocean, that great and still remaining Common of Mankind; or what Ambergriese[1] any one takes up here, is *by* the *Labour* that removes it out of that common state Nature left it in, *made* his *Property* who takes that pains about it. And even amongst us the Hare that any one is Hunting, is thought his who pursues her during the Chase. For being a Beast that is still looked upon as common, and no Man's private Possession; whoever has imploy'd so much *labour* about any of that kind, as to find and pursue her, has thereby removed her from the state of Nature, wherein she was common, and hath *begun a Property*.

31. It will perhaps be objected to this, That if gathering the Acorns, or other Fruits of the Earth, *&c.* makes a right to them, then any one

---

1   A valuable waxy substance produced in the intestines of sperm whales and collected in tropical seas to be used in perfumes.

may *ingross* as much as he will. To which I Answer, Not so. The same Law of Nature, that does by this means give us Property, does also *bound* that *Property* too. *God has given us all things richly,* 1 Tim. vi. 17. is the Voice of Reason confirmed by Inspiration.[1] But how far has he given it us? *To enjoy.* As much as any one can make use of to any advantage of life before it spoils; so much he may by his labour fix a Property in. Whatever is beyond this, is more than his share, and belongs to others. Nothing was made by God for Man to spoil or destroy. And thus considering the plenty of natural Provisions there was a long time in the World, and the few spenders, and to how small a part of that provision the industry of one Man could extend it self, and ingross it to the prejudice of others; especially keeping within the *bounds,* set by reason of what might serve for his *use;* there could be then little room for Quarrels or Contentions about Property so establish'd.

32. But the *chief matter of Property* being now not the Fruits of the Earth, and the Beasts that subsist on it, but the *Earth it self;* as that which takes in and carries with it all the rest: I think it is plain, that *Property* in that too is acquired as the former. *As much Land* as a Man Tills, Plants, Improves, Cultivates, and can use the Product of, so much is his *Property.* He by his Labour does, as it were, inclose it from the Common. Nor will it invalidate his right to say, Every body else has an equal Title to it; and therefore he cannot appropriate, he cannot inclose, without the Consent of all his Fellow-Commoners, all Mankind. God, when he gave the World in common to all Mankind, commanded Man also to labour, and the penury of his Condition required it of him. God and his Reason commanded him to subdue the Earth, *i.e.,* improve it for the benefit of Life, and therein lay out something upon it that was his own, his labour. He that in Obedience to this Command of God, subdued, tilled and sowed any part of it, thereby annexed to it something that was his *Property,* which another had no Title to, nor could without injury take from him. [...]

40. Nor is it so strange, as perhaps before consideration it may appear, that the *Property of labour* should be able to over-ballance the Community of Land. For 'tis *Labour* indeed that *puts the difference of value* on every thing; and let any one consider, what the difference is between an Acre of Land planted with Tobacco, or Sugar, sown with Wheat or Barley; and an Acre of the same Land lying in common, without any Husbandry upon it, and he will find, that the improvement of *labour makes* the far greater part of *the value.* I think it will be

---

1 1 Timothy 6: 17: "Charge them that are rich in this world, that they be not highminded, nor trust in uncertain riches, but in the living God, who giveth us richly all things to enjoy."

but a very modest Computation to say, that of the *Products* of the Earth useful to the Life of man 9/10 are the *effects of labour:* nay, if we will rightly estimate things as they come to our use, and cast up the several Expenses about them, what in them is purely owing to *Nature*, and what to *labour*, we shall find, that in most of them 99/100 are wholly to be put on the account of *labour*.

41. There cannot be a clearer demonstration of any thing, than several Nations of the *Americans* are of this, who are rich in Land, and poor in all the Comforts of Life; whom Nature having furnished as liberally as any other people, with the materials of Plenty, *i.e.*, a fruitful Soil, apt to produce in abundance, what might serve for food, rayment,[1] and delight; yet for want of improving it by labour, have not one hundredth part of the Conveniencies we enjoy: And a King of a large fruitful Territory there feeds, lodges, and is clad worse than a day Labourer in *England*.

42. To make this a little clearer, let us but trace some of the ordinary provisions of Life, through their several progresses, before they come to our use, and see how much they receive of their *value from Humane Industry*. Bread, Wine and Cloth, are things of daily use, and great plenty, yet notwithstanding, Acorns, Water, and Leaves, or Skins, must be our Bread, Drink and Clothing, did not *labour* furnish us with these more useful Commodities. For whatever *Bread* is more worth than Acorns, *Wine* than Water, and *Cloth* or *Silk* than Leaves, Skins, or Moss, that is wholly *owing to labour* and industry. The one of these being the Food and Rayment which unassisted Nature furnishes us with; the other provisions which our industry and pains prepare for us, which how much they exceed the other in value, when any one hath computed, he will then see, how much *labour makes the far greatest part of the value* of things, we enjoy in this World: And the ground which produces the materials, is scarce to be reckon'd in, as any, or at most, but a very small, part of it; So little, that even amongst us, Land that is left wholly to Nature, that hath no improvement of Pasturage, Tillage, or Planting, is called, as indeed it is, *wast*; and we shall find the benefit of it amount to little more than nothing. This shews, how much numbers of men are to be preferd to largenesse of dominions, and that the increase of lands and the right imploying of them is the great art of government. And that Prince who shall be so wise and godlike as by established laws of liberty to secure protection and incouragement to the honest industry of Mankind against the oppression of power and narrownesse of Party will quickly be too hard for his neighbours. But this bye the bye. To return to the argument in hand.

---

1 Clothing.

43. An Acre of Land that bears here Twenty Bushels of Wheat, and another in *America*, which, with the same Husbandry, would do the like, are without doubt, of the same natural, intrinsick Value. But yet the Benefit Mankind receives from the one, in a Year, is worth 5 *l.* and from the other possibly not worth a Penny, if all the Profit an *Indian* received from it were to be valued, and sold here; at least, I may truly say, not 1/1000. 'Tis *Labour* then which *puts the greatest part of Value upon Land,* without which it would scarcely be worth any thing: 'tis to that we owe the greatest part of all its useful Products; for all that the Straw, Bran, Bread, of that Acre of Wheat, is more worth than the Product of an Acre of as good Land, which lies wast, is all the Effect of Labour. For 'tis not barely the Plough-man's Pains, the Reaper's and Thresher's Toil, and the Bakers Sweat, is to be counted into the *Bread* we eat; the Labour of those who broke the Oxen, who digged and wrought the Iron and Stones, who felled and framed the Timber imployed about the Plough, Mill, Oven, or any other Utensils, which are a vast Number, requisite to this Corn, from its being seed to be sown to its being made Bread, must all be *charged on* the account of *Labour,* and received as an effect of that; Nature and the Earth furnished only the almost worthless Materials, as in themselves. 'Twould be a strange *Catalogue of things, that Industry provided and made use of, about every Loaf of Bread,* before it came to our use, if we could trace them; Iron, Wood, Leather, Bark, Timber, Stone, Bricks, Coals, Lime, Cloth, Dying-Drugs, Pitch, Tar, Masts, Ropes, and all the Materials made use of in the Ship, that brought any of the Commodities made use of by any of the Workmen, to any part of the Work, all which, 'twould be almost impossible, at least too long, to reckon up. [...]

48. And as different degrees of Industry were apt to give Men Possessions in different Proportions, so this *Invention of Money* gave them the opportunity to continue to enlarge them. For supposing an Island, separated from all possible Commerce with the rest of the World, wherein there were but a hundred Families, but there were Sheep, Horses and Cows, with other useful Animals, wholsome Fruits, and Land enough for Corn for a hundred thousand times as many, but nothing in the Island, either because of its Commonness, or Perishableness, fit to supply the place of *Money*: What reason could any one have there to enlarge his Possessions beyond the use of his Family, and a plentiful supply to its Consumption, either in what their own Industry produced, or they could barter for like perishable, useful Commodities, with others? Where there is not something both lasting and scarce, and so valuable to be hoarded up, there Men will not be apt to enlarge their *Possessions of Land,* were it never so rich,

never so free for them to take. For I ask, What would a Man value Ten Thousand, or an Hundred Thousand Acres of excellent *Land*, ready cultivated, and well stocked too with Cattle, in the middle of the inland Parts of *America*, where he had no hopes of Commerce with other Parts of the World, to draw *Money* to him by the Sale of the Product? It would not be worth the inclosing, and we should see him give up again to the wild Common of Nature, whatever was more than would supply the Conveniencies of Life to be had there for him and his Family.

49. Thus in the beginning all the World was *America*, and more so than that is now; for no such thing as *Money* was any where known. Find out something that hath the *Use and Value of Money* amongst his Neighbours, you shall see the same Man will begin presently to *enlarge* his *Possessions*.

50. But since Gold and Silver, being little useful to the Life of Man in proportion to Food, Rayment, and Carriage, has its *value* only from the consent of Men, whereof Labour yet makes, in great part, *the measure*, it is plain, that Men have agreed to disproportionate and unequal Possession of the Earth, they having by a tacit and voluntary consent found out a way, how a man may fairly possess more land than he himself can use the product of, by receiving in exchange for the overplus, Gold and Silver, which may be hoarded up without injury to any one, these metalls not spoileing or decaying in the hands of the possessor. This partage[1] of things, in an inequality of private possessions, men have made practicable out of the bounds of Societie, and without compact, only by putting a value on gold and silver and tacitly agreeing in the use of Money. For in Governments the Laws regulate the right of property, and the possession of land is determined by positive constitutions.

51. And thus, I think, it is very easie to conceive without any difficulty, *how Labour could at first begin a title of Property* in the common things of Nature, and how the spending it upon our uses bounded it. So that there could then be no reason of quarrelling about Title, nor any doubt about the largeness of Possession it gave. Right and conveniency went together; for as a Man had a Right to all he could imploy his Labour upon, so he had no temptation to labour for more than he could make use of. This left no room for Controversie about the Title, nor for Incroachment on the Right of others; what Portion a Man carved to himself, was easily seen; and it was useless as well as dishonest to carve himself too much, or take more than he needed.

---

1 Division into parts.

2. From Adam Smith,[1] *An Inquiry into the Nature and Causes of the Wealth of Nations* (1776)

From Book I, Ch. 1, "Of the Division of Labour"

Observe the accommodation of the most common artificer or day-labourer in a civilized and thriving country, and you will perceive that the number of people of whose industry a part, though but a small part, has been employed in procuring him this accommodation exceeds all computation. The woollen coat, for example, which covers the day-labourer, as coarse and rough as it may appear, is the produce of the joint labour of a great multitude of workmen. The shepherd, the sorter of the wool, the wool-comber or carder, the dyer, the scribbler, the spinner, the weaver, the fuller, the dresser, with many others, must all join their different arts in order to complete even this homely production. How many merchants and carriers, besides, must have been employed in transporting the materials from some of those workmen to others who often live in a very distant part of the country! how much commerce and navigation in particular, how many ship-builders, sailors, sail-makers, rope-makers, must have been employed in order to bring together the different drugs made use of by the dyer, which often come from the remotest corners of the world! What a variety of labour too is necessary in order to produce the tools of the meanest of those workmen! To say nothing of such complicated machines as the ship of the sailor, the mill of the fuller, or even the loom of the weaver, let us consider only what a variety of labour is requisite in order to form that very simple machine, the shears with which the shepherd clips the wool. The miner, the builder of the furnace for smelting the ore, the feller of the timber, the burner of the charcoal to be made use of in the smelting-house, the brick-maker, the brick-layer, the workmen who attend the furnace, the mill-wright, the forger, the smith, must all of them join their different arts in order to produce them. Were we to examine, in the same manner, all the different parts of his dress and household furniture, the coarse linen shirt which he wears next his skin, the shoes which cover his feet, the bed which he lies on, and all the different parts which compose it, the kitchen grate at which he prepares his victuals, the coals which he makes use of for that purpose, dug from the bowels of the earth, and brought to him perhaps by a long sea and a long land carriage, all the other utensils of his kitchen, all the furniture of his table, the knives and forks, the earthen or pewter plates upon which he serves up and

---

1 Adam Smith (1723-90): Scottish political economist and moral philosopher.

divides his victuals, the different hands employed in preparing his bread and his beer, the glass window which lets in the heat and the light, and keeps out the wind and the rain, with all the knowledge and art requisite for preparing that beautiful and happy invention, without which these northern parts of the world could scarce have afforded a very comfortable habitation, together with the tools of all the different workmen employed in producing those different conveniencies; if we examine, I say, all these things, and consider what a variety of labour is employed about each of them, we shall be sensible that without the assistance and co-operation of many thousands, the very meanest person in a civilized country could not be provided, even according to what we very falsely imagine the easy and simple manner in which he is commonly accommodated. Compared, indeed, with the more extravagant luxury of the great, his accommodation must no doubt appear extremely simple and easy; and yet it may be true, perhaps, that the accommodation of an European prince does not always so much exceed that of an industrious and frugal peasant, as the accommodation of the latter exceeds that of many an African king, the absolute master of the lives and liberties of ten thousand naked savages.

From Book I, Ch. 3, "That the Division of Labour is Limited by the Extent of the Market"

[...] There are some sorts of industry, even of the lowest kind, which can be carried on no where but in a great town. A porter, for example, can find employment and subsistence in no other place. A village is by much too narrow a sphere for him; even an ordinary market town is scarce large enough to afford him constant occupation. In the lone houses and very small villages which are scattered about in so desert a country as the Highlands of Scotland, every farmer must be butcher, baker and brewer for his own family. In such situations we can scarce expect to find even a smith, a carpenter, or a mason, within less than twenty miles of another of the same trade. The scattered families that live at eight or ten miles distance from the nearest of them, must learn to perform themselves a great number of little pieces of work, for which, in more populous countries, they would call in the assistance of those workmen. Country workmen are almost every where obliged to apply themselves to all the different branches of industry that have so much affinity to one another as to be employed about the same sort of materials. A country carpenter deals in every sort of work that is made of wood: a country smith in every sort of work that is made of iron. The former is not only a carpenter, but a joiner, a cabinet maker, and even a carver in wood, as well as a wheelwright, a ploughwright, a cart and waggon maker. The employments of the latter are still more various. It is impossible there should be such a trade as even that of a nailer in the remote and inland parts of the Highlands of Scotland. Such a workman at the rate of a thousand nails a day, and three hundred working days in the year, will make three hundred thousand nails in the year. But in such a situation it would be impossible to dispose of one thousand, that is, of one day's work in the year.

3. From Karl Marx,[1] *Capital: A Critique of Political Economy* (1867)[2]

A commodity appears, at first sight, a very trivial thing, and easily understood. Its analysis shows that it is, in reality, a very queer thing, abounding in metaphysical subtleties and theological niceties. So far as it is a value in use, there is nothing mysterious about it, whether we consider it from the point of view that by its properties it is capable of satisfying human wants, or from the point that those properties are the product of human labour. It is as clear as noon-day, that man, by his industry, changes the forms of the materials furnished by Nature, in such a way as to make them useful to him. The form of wood, for instance, is altered, by making a table out of it. Yet, for all that, the table continues to be that common, every-day thing, wood. But, so soon as it steps forth as a commodity, it is changed into something transcendent. It not only stands with its feet on the ground, but, in relation to all other commodities, it stands on its head, and evolves out of its wooden brain grotesque ideas, far more wonderful than "table-turning" ever was. [...]

Since Robinson Crusoe's experiences are a favourite theme with political economists, let us take a look at him on his island. Moderate though he be, yet some few wants he has to satisfy, and must therefore do a little useful work of various sorts, such as making tools and furniture, taming goats, fishing and hunting. Of his prayers and the like we take no account, since they are a source of pleasure to him, and he looks upon them as so much recreation. In spite of the variety of his work, he knows that his labour, whatever its form, is but the activity of one and the same Robinson, and consequently, that it consists of nothing but different modes of human labour. Necessity itself compels him to apportion his time accurately between his different kinds of

---

1 Karl Marx (1818-83): German philosopher, political economist, historian, and political theorist.
2 *Das Kapital*, translated by Samuel Moore and Edward Aveling (1887, reprinted 1921). From Chapter 1 ("The Two Factors of a Commodity: Use-Value and Value"), Section 4 ("The Fetishism of Commodities and the Secret thereof").

work. Whether one kind occupies a greater space in his general activity than another, depends on the difficulties, greater or less as the case may be, to be overcome in attaining the useful effect aimed at. This our friend Robinson soon learns by experience, and having rescued a watch, ledger, and pen and ink from the wreck, commences, like a true-born Briton, to keep a set of books. His stock-book contains a list of the objects of utility that belong to him, of the operations necessary for their production; and lastly, of the labour time that definite quantities of those objects have, on an average, cost him. All the relations between Robinson and the objects that form this wealth of his own creation, are here so simple and clear as to be intelligible without exertion, even to Mr. Sedley Taylor.[1] And yet those relations contain all that is essential to the determination of value.

Let us now transport ourselves from Robinson's island bathed in light to the European middle ages shrouded in darkness. Here, instead of the independent man, we find everyone dependent, serfs and lords, vassals and suzerains, laymen and clergy. Personal dependence here characterises the social relations of production just as much as it does the other spheres of life organised on the basis of that production. But for the very reason that personal dependence forms the ground-work of society, there is no necessity for labour and its products to assume a fantastic form different from their reality. They take the shape, in the transactions of society, of services in kind and payments in kind. Here the particular and natural form of labour, and not, as in a society based on production of commodities, its general abstract form is the immediate social form of labour. Compulsory labour is just as properly measured by time, as commodity-producing labour; but every serf knows that what he expends in the service of his lord, is a definite quantity of his own personal labour power. The tithe to be rendered to the priest is more matter of fact than his blessing. No matter, then, what we may think of the parts played by the different classes of people themselves in this society, the social relations between individuals in the performance of their labour, appear at all events as their own mutual personal relations, and are not disguised under the shape of social relations between the products of labour.

For an example of labour in common or directly associated labour, we have no occasion to go back to that spontaneously developed form which we find on the threshold of the history of all civilised races. We have one close at hand in the patriarchal industries of a peasant family, that produces corn, cattle, yarn, linen, and clothing for home use. These different articles are, as regards the family, so many prod-

---

1 Economist and Cambridge don, 1834-1920.

ucts of its labour, but as between themselves, they are not commodities. The different kinds of labour, such as tillage, cattle tending, spinning, weaving and making clothes, which result in the various products, are in themselves, and such as they are, direct social functions, because functions of the family, which, just as much as a society based on the production of commodities, possesses a spontaneously developed system of division of labour. The distribution of the work within the family, and the regulation of the labour time of the several members, depend as well upon differences of age and sex as upon natural conditions varying with the seasons. The labour power of each individual, by its very nature, operates in this case merely as a definite portion of the whole labour power of the family, and therefore, the measure of the expenditure of individual labour power by its duration, appears here by its very nature as a social character of their labour.

Let us now picture to ourselves, by way of change, a community of free individuals, carrying on their work with the means of production in common, in which the labour power of all the different individuals is consciously applied as the combined labour power of the community. All the characteristics of Robinson's labour are here repeated, but with this difference, that they are social, instead of individual. Everything produced by him was exclusively the result of his own personal labour, and therefore simply an object of use for himself. The total product of our community is a social product. One portion serves as fresh means of production and remains social. But another portion is consumed by the members as means of subsistence. A distribution of this portion amongst them is consequently necessary. The mode of this distribution will vary with the productive organisation of the community, and the degree of historical development attained by the producers. We will assume, but merely for the sake of a parallel with the production of commodities, that the share of each individual producer in the means of subsistence is determined by his labour time. Labour time would, in that case, play a double part. Its apportionment in accordance with a definite social plan maintains the proper proportion between the different kinds of work to be done and the various wants of the community. On the other hand, it also serves as a measure of the portion of the common labour borne by each individual, and of his share in the part of the total product destined for individual consumption. The social relations of the individual producers, with regard both to their labour and to its products, are in this case perfectly simple and intelligible, and that with regard not only to production but also to distribution.

4. From Max Weber,[1] *The Protestant Ethic and the Spirit of Capitalism* (1920-21)[2]

The phenomenon of the division of labour and occupations in society had, among others, been interpreted by Thomas Aquinas, to whom we may most conveniently refer, as a direct consequence of the divine scheme of things. But the places assigned to each man in this cosmos follow *ex causis naturalibus*[3] and are fortuitous (contingent in the Scholastic terminology). The differentiation of men into the classes and occupations established through historical development became for Luther, as we have seen, a direct result of the divine will. The perseverance of the individual in the place and within the limits which God had assigned to him was a religious duty. This was the more certainly the consequence since the relations of Lutheranism to the world were in general uncertain from the beginning and remained so. Ethical principles for the reform of the world could not be found in Luther's realm of ideas; in fact it never quite freed itself from Pauline indifference. Hence the world had to be accepted as it was, and this alone could be made a religious duty.

But in the Puritan view, the providential character of the play of private economic interests takes on a somewhat different emphasis. True to the Puritan tendency to pragmatic interpretation, the providential purpose of the division of labour is to be known by its fruits. On this point Baxter[4] expresses himself in terms which more than once directly recall Adam Smith's well-known apotheosis of the division of labour. The specialization of occupations leads, since it makes the development of skill possible, to a quantitative and qualitative improvement in production, and thus serves the common good, which is identical with the good of the greatest possible number. So far, the motivation is purely utilitarian, and is closely related to the customary view-point of much of the secular literature of the time.

But the characteristic Puritan element appears when Baxter sets at the head of his discussion the statement that "outside of a well-marked calling the accomplishments of a man are only casual and irregular, and he spends more time in idleness than at work," and when he con-

---

1 Max Weber (1864-1920): German sociologist of religion and political economist. Weber's *Protestant Ethic and the Spirit of Capitalism*, from which this excerpt is taken, suggests the inseparability of Crusoe's economic and religious impulses.

2 Translated by Talcott Parsons (1930).

3 From natural causes.

4 Richard Baxter. See Appendix D1.

cludes it as follows: "and he [the specialized worker] will carry out his work in order while another remains in constant confusion, and his business knows neither time nor place ... therefore is a certain calling the best for everyone." Irregular work, which the ordinary labourer is often forced to accept, is often unavoidable, but always an unwelcome state of transition. A man without a calling thus lacks the systematic, methodical character which is, as we have seen, demanded by worldly asceticism.

The Quaker ethic also holds that a man's life in his calling is an exercise in ascetic virtue, a proof of his state of grace through his conscientiousness, which is expressed in the care and method with which lie pursues his calling. What God demands is not labour in itself, but rational labour in a calling. In the Puritan concept of the calling the emphasis is always placed on this methodical character of worldly asceticism, not, as with Luther, on the acceptance of the lot which God has irretrievably assigned to man.

Hence the question whether anyone may combine several callings is answered in the affirmative, if it is useful for the common good or one's own, and not injurious to anyone, and if it does not lead to unfaithfulness in one of the callings. Even a change of calling is by no means regarded as objectionable, if it is not thoughtless and is made for the purpose of pursuing a calling more pleasing to God, which means, on general principles, one more useful.

It is true that the usefulness of a calling, and thus its favour in the sight of God, is measured primarily in moral terms, and thus in terms of the importance of the goods produced in it for the community. But a further, and, above all, in practice the most important, criterion is found in private profitableness. For if that God, whose hand the Puritan sees in all the occurrences of life, shows one of His elect a chance of profit, he must do it with a purpose. Hence the faithful Christian must follow the call by taking advantage of the opportunity. "If God show you a way in which you may lawfully get more than in another way (without wrong to your soul or to any other), if you refuse this, and choose the less gainful way, you cross one of the ends of your calling, and you refuse to be God's steward, and to accept His gifts and use them for Him when He requireth it: you may labour to be rich for God, though not for the flesh and sin."

Wealth is thus bad ethically only in so far as it is a temptation to idleness and sinful enjoyment of life, and its acquisition is bad only when it is with the purpose of later living merrily and without care. But as a performance of duty in a calling it is not only morally permissible, but actually enjoined. The parable of the servant who was rejected because he did not increase the talent which was entrusted to him seemed to say so directly.[1] To wish to be poor was, it was often argued, the same as wishing to be unhealthy; it is objectionable as a glorification of works and derogatory to the glory of God. Especially begging, on the part of one able to work, is not only the sin of slothfulness, but a violation of the duty of brotherly love according to the Apostle's own word.

The emphasis on the ascetic importance of a fixed calling provided an ethical justification of the modern specialized division of labour. In a similar way the providential interpretation of profit-making justified the activities of the business man. The superior indulgence of the *seigneur* and the parvenu ostentation of the *nouveau riche* are equally detestable to asceticism. But, on the other hand, it has the highest ethical appreciation of the sober, middle-class, self-made man. "God blesseth His trade" is a stock remark about those good men who had successfully followed the divine hints. The whole power of the God of the Old Testament, who rewards His people for their obedience in this life, necessarily exercised a similar influence on the Puritan who, following Baxter's advice, compared his own state of grace with that of the heroes of the Bible, and in the process interpreted the statements of the Scriptures as the articles of a book of statutes.

---

1   Matthew 25: 14-30.

Appendix F: Defoe on Slavery and the African Trade

[Prior to the abolitionist movement of the mid-eighteenth century, English opposition to slavery was relatively uncommon (Quaker opposition being a notable exception). Defoe has sometimes been credited with opposing the cruel treatment of slaves, as he does in his poetic satire *A Reformation of Manners*, but more frequently he staunchly defended the slave trade, which he viewed as an integral part of colonial expansion. A shareholder in the Royal African Company and frequent advocate of increased trade between Africa and the colonies, Defoe addresses slavery primarily in economic terms.]

1. From *Reformation of Manners, A Satyr* (1702)

Satyr, the Arts and Mysteries forbear,
Too black for thee to write, or us to hear:
No Man, but he that is as vile as they,
Can all the Tricks and Cheats of Trade survey.
     [...] Some fit out Ships, and double Fraights ensure,
And burn the Ships to make the Voyage secure:
Promiscuous Plunders thro' the World commit,
And *with the Money* buy their safe Retreat.
     Others seek out to *Africk*'s Torid Zone,[1]
And search the burning Shores of *Serralone*;[2]
There in unsufferable Heats *they fry*,
And run vast Risques to see the Gold, *and die*:
The harmless Natives basely they trepan,[3]
And barter Baubles for the *Souls of Men*:
The Wretches they to Christian Climes bring o'er,
To serve worse Heathens than they did before.
The Cruelties they suffer there are such,
Amboyna's[4] nothing, they've out-done the *Dutch*:

---

1 The tropics.
2 Sierra Leone.
3 To cheat, to ensnare.
4 The Amboyna massacre (1623) refers to the torture and execution of British traders by the Dutch on Ambon Island in Indonesia. The massacre is the subject of John Dryden's play *Amboyna, or the Cruelties of the Dutch to the English Merchants* (1673).

Cortez, Pizarro, Guzman, Penaloe,[1]
Who drank the Blood of Gold and *Mexico*,
Who thirteen Millions of Souls destroy'd,
And left one third of God's Creation void;
By Birth for Natures Butchery design'd,
Compar'd to these[2] are merciful and kind;
Death cou'd *their* cruellest Designs fulfil,
Blood quench't *their* Thirst, and it suffic'd to kill:
But these the tender *Coup de Grace* deny,
And make Men beg in vain for leave to die;
To more than *Spanish* Cruelty inclin'd,
Torment the Body and debauch'd the Mind;
The lingring Life of Slavery preserve,
And vilely teach them both to sin and serve.
In vain they talk to them of Shades below,
They fear no Hell, *but where such Christians go*;
Of *Jesus Christ* they very often hear,
Often as his Blaspheming Servants swear,
They hear and wonder what strange Gods they be,
Can bear with Patience such Indignity.
They look for Famines, Plagues, Disease, and Death,
Blasts from above, and Earthquakes from beneath:
But when they see regardless Heaven looks on,
They curse our Gods, or think that we have none.
Thus Thousands to Religion are brought o'er,
And made worse Devils than they were before.

2. From *An Essay upon the Trade to Africa, In Order to Set the Merits of that Cause in a True Light and Bring the Disputes between the African Company and the Separate Traders into a narrower Compass* (1711)[3]

The Original of the Company is known, and needs take up none of our Time, only it may a little concern the present Dispute, to make this one

---

1 Hernán Cortés (1485-1547), conqueror of Aztec Empire in Mexico; Francisco Pizarro (c. 1478-1541), conqueror of Inca Empire in Peru; Nuño de Guzmán (c. 1490-1544), conqueror of Western Mexico; Diego Dionisio de Penalosa (1624-87), governor and captain general of New Mexico. For an explanation of the Black Legend that vilified Spain, see p. 191, note 2.
2 Compared to slave traders.
3 In 1672, the Royal African Company, of which Defoe was a later shareholder, was granted a 1,000 year monopoly on the slave trade to the West Indies; but in 1698, so-called "separate traders" or interlopers were allowed to trade as well. The issue before Parliament in 1711-12 was whether or not to end a 10% duty that separate traders had been required to pay to the Company.

Remark, *viz.* That they came in by Purchase, a Just, Lawful, and Honourable Way; the Circumstances of the former Company declining, and they being in no Condition to carry on the Trade; and the Trade itself appearing then in its Infancy, to be a most Profitable, Useful, and absolutely necessary Branch of our Commerce; for these Reasons, the Government concern'd itself, as no doubt all wise Governments will, that so great an Advantage should not be lost to the Nation.

[...] If any Persons yet remain'd doubtful of the Necessity and Advantage of this Trade, or of the Magnitude it rose to under the Protection of the several Princes aforesaid, it might not be amiss to enlarge here, by telling them, What in the Space of Twenty Years, or thereabout, they Exported in *English* Manufactures; How many Negroes, they sent to the *English* Colonies in the *West Indies*; and how many Thousand Ounces of Gold they brought into *England*, beside the Export of Foreign Goods by Debentures,[1] and the Import of many Thousand Pounds *Sterl.* in Wax, Elephants Teeth, Drugs and valuable Commodities, the Growth of the Country there, and necessary to ours here.

We might tell you how, had this Trade been neglected and left languishing, as it has been since, under the Depredations of Interlopers and Separate Traders, the Hazards of the War, and Losses at Sea; had they been worried, and kept in constant Alarm by the Attacks and Barking of their Rivals in the Trade, not a third Part of the Poor had been employ'd, whom their Trade kept Alive; not a third Part of the Negroes had been carryed to *America*, tho' at double Price; and not a Tenth Part of the Gold had been brought in to help our declining Cash to circulate, in a Time when long War had stopt the Channels of Bullion from *Mexico* and *Peru*.

But these Things need not to be enlarg'd on, they come within every Man's Reach; and the most ignorant in the Trade know them.

3. From *A Review of the State of the British Nation*[2]

Thursday, August 23, 1711

I have heard indeed of Slaves that would not go Free when they might; The Divine Institution of God in *Hebrew* Law, put a Mark upon such as these, *viz.* That *their Ears should be bored thorow to the Posts of the*

---

1 IOUs.
2 Defoe's *Review* was printed from 1704 to 1713, first twice, then later three times a week. Though the initial focus was on the war with France, Defoe broadened it to cover many of his interests, including politics, domestic and foreign trade, and family relationships.

Door; and might all our Friends here, that are for giving up to the Arbitrary Will of a Tyrant, *have their Ears bored thorow*, I think we should find few of them stand to the Operation; for what was the Consequence? The Man was a Servant from that Day as long as he lived, and so indeed they that love Bondage should be.

I have heard of a Planter in *Barbadoes*, that being fill'd with Compassion for the Miseries of his poor *Negro* Slaves, and having a strong Regret upon his Mind at Oppressing Human Nature and his Fellow Creatures, call'd all the *Negroes* of his Plantation together, who were bought with his Money, and cost him several Hundred Pounds, and told them that they were all made by the same Power, That they had all Souls of equal and estimable Value; that they were all, by Nature, alike Free with him and others; That they had a Right to Liberty as well as he, and that he could not bear to oppress his Fellow Creatures in such a manner, and that therefore he was resolv'd to do them Justice, and make them all Free, and so had them go whither they pleas'd.

The poor Wretches were at first overjoy'd at their Liberty, but having no View of the Advantages of it, no Tast of the Pleasure of it, and not knowing what to do, they went about to get Employ for Wages; when they had earn'd it, they knew not what to do with the Money—
—They were quite out of their Element, and away they went to their Old Master, and desired him to take them again, and set them to Work.

Liberty is a Jewel, which like the Diamond, lies rough in the Earth, it is of no Value but to them that understand it, and know what to do with it. Liberty to a Man that understands it not, is like a Ship full of Gold and Silver, but no Provisions in it; the Seamen would be starv'd: The Value of Liberty is in the Use of it; he that knows not how to use it, has no Tast for it, no Relish of it, and 'tis of no Value to him, he cannot live upon it.

Thursday, May 22, 1712

A Word or two now, *good People*, upon Trade: I had thought to have adjourn'd my Observations upon Trade, till I began a New Volume of this Work, or till I enter upon a new kind of *Review*, which I have Projected, upon the new Regulation of the Press; but the Case will not admit a delay, Things must be spoken to in their Season, or they had as good be let quite alone. [...]

I take Trade to be to the State, as the *Negroes* in *Barbadoes* are to the Planters there; the *Negroes* are indeed Slaves, and our good People use them like Slaves, or rather like Dogs, *but that by the Way*: He that keeps them in Subjection, Whips, and Corrects them in order, to make them grind and labour, *does Right*, for out of their Labour he gains his Wealth: But he that in his Passion and Cruelty, Maims, Lames, and Kills them, *is a Fool*, for they are his Estate, his Stock, his Wealth, and his Prosperity.

4. From *The History and Remarkable Life of the Truly Honourable Col. Jacque, Commonly call'd Col. Jack* (1722)[1]

Master. ... [A]s I have said, nothing can be more agreeable to me, nothing has so much robb'd me of the Comfort of all my Fortunes, as the Cruelty used in my Name, on the Bodies of those poor Slaves.

Jack. It is certainly wrong, Sir; it is not only wrong, as it is barbarous and cruel; but it is wrong too, as it is the worst way of Managing, and of having your Business done.

Master. It is my Aversion, it fills my very Soul, with Horror; I believe, if I should come by, while they were using those Cruelties on the poor Creatures, I should either sink down at the Sight of it, or fly into a Rage, and kill the Fellow that did it; tho' it is done too, by my own Authority.

Jack. But, Sir, I dare say, I shall convince you also that it is wrong, in Respect of Interest; and that your Business shall be better discharg'd, and your Plantations better order'd, and more Work done by the *Negroes*, who shall be engaged by Mercy and Lenity, than by those, who are driven, and dragg'd by the Whips, and the Chains of a merciless Tormentor.

Master. I think the Nature of the Thing speaks it self, doubtless it should be so, and I have often thought it would be so, and a thousand Times wish'd it might be so; but all my *English* People pretend otherwise, and that it is impossible to bring the *Negroes* to any Sence of Kindness, and Consequently not to any Obedience of Love.

Jack. It may be true, Sir, that there may be found here and there a *Negro* of a senceless, stupid, sordid Disposition; perfectly Untractable, undocible, and incapable of due Impressions; especially incapable of the Generosity of Principle which I am speaking of; you know very well, Sir, there are such among Christians, as well as among *Negroes*, whence else came the *English* Proverb; *that if you save a Thief from the*

---

1 In Defoe's 1722 novel, Colonel Jack finds himself the overseer of a Virginia plantation whose owner expects him to whip the slaves into submission. Jack decides instead to "imprint Principles of Gratitude on their Minds, to tell them what Kindness is shewn them, and what they are Indebted for it, and what they might Gain in the End by it." In the following dialogue, he justifies his actions.

Gallows, he shall be the first to Cut your Throat. But, Sir, if such a Refractory, undocible Fellow comes in our way, he must be dealt with, first, by the smooth ways, to Try him; then by the Violent way to Break his Temper, as they Break a Horse; and if nothing will do, such a Wretch should be Sold off, and others Bought in his Room; for the Peace of the Plantation should not be broken for one Devilish temper'd Fellow; and if this was done, I doubt not, you should have all your Plantation carried on, and your Work done, and not a *Negro* or a Servant upon it, but what would not only Work for you, but even Die for you, if there was an Occasion for it.

5. From *A Plan of the English Commerce* (1728)[1]

What great Improvements might be made in Trade, on the north Coast of *Africa* I have shewn I think past Contradiction; the only Objection, *Which as the Case stands, I think is no Objection at all*, is, that it must be made by Conquest, a Thing attended with Difficulty, Hazard, Expense, and a Possibility of Miscarriage.

However easy it is to remove all the Objections of that Kind, it is not my business here, nor have I Room for it; but I mention them here to illustrate and set off the happy Circumstance of another Proposal of Improvement on the same Continent; I mean this of *Guinea*.

Here are no Conquests to be made, no Enemies to fight with, at least none worth naming; and yet here is a visible, an apparent, an undisputed Improvement to be made, of which this only is to be said, That 'tis rather wonderful, that it has never yet been attempted, and gone about with Vigour and Resolution, than doubtful whether it would succeed, if it were undertaken.

The Climate on the West Coast of *Africa*, at least within the Bounds mention'd, is sufficiently known, being from the Latitude of about 13 Deg. to that of 5 Deg. North of the Line: The Soil is good in most Places, very fruitful, well water'd, notwithstanding the Heat of the Climate, with abundance of small Rivers, and in some Places with very great ones.

The Commerce to this Country is carried on, if a Kind of Stagnation of Business, or a going backward thro' innumerable Discouragements may be call'd a carrying it on, by the *English* having Possession of the Coast, and having made Settlements in proper Places, with Forts and Castles, and other Strengths for defending those Settle-

---

1 From Chapter III, "Being a Proposal for the Improvement and Encrease of Commerce upon the Western Coast of *Africa*, the Coast of *Guinea*, from *Sierra Leon*, vulgarly called *Seraloon*, to the Coast and Gulph of *Benin*."

ments, as well against their Christian Neighbours by Sea, as their Savage Neighbours on Land.

The Trade carried on here, whether by the *English*, or other European Nations, consists in but three capital Articles, viz. *Slaves, Teeth*,[1] and *Gold*; a very gainful and advantageous Commerce, especially as it was once carried on, when these were all purchas'd at low Rates from the Savages; and even those low Rates paid in Trifles, and Toys, such as Knives and Sissars, Kettles and Clouts, Glass Beads, and Cowries, Things of the smallest Value, and as we may say next to nothing; but even this Part of the Trade is abated in its Goodness, since by the Strife and Envy among the Traders, we have had the Folly to instruct the Savages in the Value of their own Goods, and inform them of the Cheapness of our own; endeavouring to supplant one another, by underselling and overbidding, by which we have taught the Negroes to supplant both, by holding up the Price of their own Productions, and running down the Rates of what we carry them for Sale.

Thus the gainful Commerce once superior to all the Trades in the World, which carried out the meanest of all Exportations, and brought home the richest, is sinking dayly into a Kind of Rubbish as to Trade; and we are sometimes said to buy even the Gold too dear.

But all this while here is not the least Use made of the Land; the fruitful Soil lies waste, a vast extended Country, pleasant Vallies, the Banks of charming Rivers, spacious Plains, capable of Improvement and Cultivation, to infinite Advantage, lie waste and untouch'd, overrun with Shrubage and useless Trees; as a Forrest trod under Foot with wild Creatures; and the yet wilder Negroes, who just plant their Maize, and a few Roots and Herbs, like as we do for our Garden-stuff, and all the rest is left naked, and thrown up to the Wilderness. [...]

Add to this [the conduciveness of the climate to trading coffee beans and sugar cane] the particular Advantages which offer themselves to the Planter, in such an Attempt as this, on the Coast of *Africa*, which he has not, nor can have, in any of those Parts where the Sugar is now planted, especially by the *English*. For Example,

1. The Easiness of procuring Negroe Slaves, which would here cost from 30 s. to 50 s. or at most 3 l. *per* Head; whereas they are at this Time in *Barbadoes* and *Jamaica*, worth from 25 l. to 30 l. a Head; at the *Brasils* from 30 l. to 40 l. and to the Spaniards in the Provinces of *Guaxaca*,[2] *Guatimala*, &c. 50 to 60 l. *Sterling per* Head.

N.B. The Difficulty of keeping the Negroes from running away, is not so great as some imagine, since as they are brought from distant Provinces, tho' it be upon the same Continent, they know nothing of

---

1   Tusks.

2   Oaxaca, Mexico.

their own Country; nor do they understand the Language of the next Negroes, any more than they do *English;* and if they should fly to these neighbouring Negroes, they would but make Slaves of them again, and sell them to the Ships; so that the Slaves would not be apt to fly, and if they did, the Loss would not be near so great as in *Jamaica,* &c. [...]

I cannot quit the Improvements which might be made on the Coast of *Africa,* without mentioning a great Correspondence carried on among the several Nations in the northern Part of that Country, which *even as it is now* causes a great Commerce over Land, taking Notice withal how wonderfully it might be improv'd: This Trade is said to be carried on by the Negroe Natives, upon the great River *Nigris* or *Niger;* or as our Seamen corruptly call it, the River *Gambia,* in Conjunction with the Natives of several Nations, upon the same River, East from the Shore; and by all these together corresponding with the Moors on the north Coast of *Africa,* at *Fez,* at *Morocco,* at *Mesquiness,* and other Cities, where they now carry on a Commerce, by vast Annual Caravans. They tell us, that it is already a very great Trade; but how would our Proposal not only encrease this Trade it self, but quite change and alter the very people themselves, while the North Part of the Country, (being Christians,) the Savage Part would be soon civiliz'd, and become so too, and the People learn to live to be cloth'd, and to be furnish'd with many Things from *Europe,* which they now want; and by Consequence would with their Manners change the very Nature of their Commerce, and fall in upon the Consumption of the European Manufactures.

It would be needless to lay out Schemes of Commerce among the Inhabitants of the Nations within those southern Lands; Numbers of European People being but once settled on the Sea Coast, would soon spread the Commerce into the inland Nations, and employ and enrich the Inhabitants, by instructing them in the Arts of living, as well as of Trade; and this brings me to a View of one of the greatest Scenes of Improvement in the World, which is in short this, (*viz.*)

That there needs little more than to instruct and inure the barbarous Nations in all our Colonies, Factories, &c. in the Arts of Living; clothing with Decency, not shameless and naked; feeding with Humanity, and not in a Manner brutal; dwelling in Towns and Cities, with Oeconomy and civil Government, and not like Savages. [...]

What then have the People of *England* more to do, but to encrease the Colonies of their own Nation in all the remote Parts, where it is proper and practicable, and to civilize and instruct the Savages and Natives of those Countries, wherever they plant, so as to bring them by the softest and gentlest Methods to fall into the Customs and Usage of their own Country, and incorporate among our People as one Nation.

I say nothing of christianizing the Savages, 'tis remote from my present Purpose; and I doubt much more remote from our practice, at least in most Places; but I speak of an Incorporation of Customs and Usages, as may in Time bring them to live like Christians, whether they may turn Christians or no.

To bring this Home to the Coast and Country of *Africa*, of which I was but just now speaking; let them calculate the Improvements proposed in Business, in Planting, Fishing, Shipping, and all the necessary Employments that would attend a public improv'd Colony; and let them tell me, if the Consequence would not be a Consumption of Manufacture, among a People where there was none before, and in a Place where we had no Commerce to carry on before. [...]

[T]here is a vast ocean of Improvement in View upon the *African* Coast, (tho' the single planting of Sugar was omitted) and as there are as well on this Side of the Country, as on the Eastern Shores, of which I come next to speak, vastly populous Nations, nay Empires, where there are Millions of People yet to trade with, who were never traded with before the prevailing on these Nations to civilize and govern themselves, according as inform'd Nature would soon direct them, would necessarily introduce Trade, consume Manufacture, employ Shipping, employ Hands, and in Time establish such a Commerce, as would be more than equal to any one foreign Exportation we have yet to boast of.

Appendix G: Cannibalism

[Before the 16th century, people who ate other people were known as *anthropophagi*, Greek for *man-eater*. Only following Columbus's 1492 voyage did Europeans begin to use the word *cannibal*, which they derived from the ethnic name of the Caribs who lived in the Lesser Antilles. Though the prevalence of cannibalism was, and is, highly debatable—just compare the excerpts in this Appendix from William Dampier and Charles de Rochefort—cannibalism proved to be a malleable trope in European writing, and Defoe was just one of many writers who featured cannibals in their representations of New World encounters.]

1. From Michel de Montaigne,[1] "Of Cannibals," *Essays of Michael Seigneur de Montaigne*, tr. Charles Cotton (1685-86)

... They have continual War with the Nations that live further within the main Land, beyond their Mountains, to which they go Naked, and without other Arms, than their Bows, and Wooden-Swords, fashion'd at one end like the head of a Javelin. The Obstinacy of their Battels is wonderful, and never end without great effusion of Blood: For as to running away, they know not what it is. Every one for a Trophy brings home the Head of an Enemy he has kill'd, which he fixes over the Door of his House. After having a long time treated the Prisoners very well, and given them all the Regalia's they can think of, he to whom the Prisoner belongs, invites a great Assembly of his Kindred and Friends, who being come, he ties a Rope to one of the Arms of the Prisoner, of which, at a distance, out of his reach, he holds the one end himself, and gives to the Friend he loves best, the other Arm to hold after the same manner; which being done, they two in the presence of all the Assembly, dispatch him with their Swords. After that, they Roast him, Eat him amongst them, and send some Chops to their absent Friends, which nevertheless they do not do, as some think, for Nourishment, as the *Scythians*,[2] anciently did, but as a Representation

---

1 Michel de Montaigne (1533-92): French essayist. In this essay, Montaigne describes the cannibals of Brazil as recounted to him by "a man in my House, that liv'd ten or twelve Years in the new World." The excerpt is taken from the 1711 edition of Cotton's translation.
2 According to Pliny the Elder's *Natural History*, some Scythians "drink out of human skulls and use the scalps with the hair on as napkins hung round their necks."

of an extream Revenge; as will appear by this, That having observ'd the *Portugals*, who were in League with their Enemies, to inflict another sort of Death upon any of them they took Prisoners: Which was, to set them up to the Girdle[1] in the Earth, to shoot at the remaining part till it was stuck full of Arrows, and then to hang them: They that thought those People of the other World, (as those who had sown the knowledge of a great many Vices amongst their Neighbours, and who were much greater Masters in all sorts of Mischief than they,) did not exercise this sort of Revenge without Mystery, and that it must needs be more painful than theirs; and so began to leave their old way, and to follow this. I am not sorry that we should here take notice of the Barbarous Horror of so Cruel an Action, but that seeing so clearly into their Faults, we should be so blind to our own: For I conceive, there is more Barbarity in eating a Man alive, than when he is dead; in tearing a Body Limb from Limb, by Racks and Torments, that is yet in perfect Sense,[2] in roasting it by degrees, causing it to be bit and worried[3] by Dogs and Swine, (as we have not only read, but lately seen; not amongst inveterate and mortal Enemies, but Neighbours, and fellow Citizens, and which is worse, under colour of Piety and Religion,) than to Roast, and Eat him after he is Dead. [...]

But to return to my Story, these Prisoners are so far from discovering[4] the least Weakness, for all the Terrors can be represented to them, that, on the contrary, during the two or three Months, that they are kept, they always appear with a chearful Countenance; importune their Masters to make hast to bring them to the Test, Defie, Rail at them, and Reproach them with Cowardize, and the number of Battels they have lost against those of their Country. I have a Song made by one of these Prisoners, wherein he bids them *come all, and Dine upon him, and welcome, for they shall withal eat their own Fathers, and Grandfathers, whose Flesh has serv'd to feed and nourish him. Those Muscles,* says he, *this Flesh, and these Veins, are your own: Poor silly Souls as you are, you little think that the Substance of your Ancestors Limbs is here yet: but mind as you eat, and you will find in it the Tast of your own Flesh:* In which Song there is to be observ'd, an Invention[5] that does nothing relish of the *Barbarian.* Those that paint these People dying after this manner, represent the Prisoner spitting in the faces of his Executioners, and making at them a wry Mouth. And 'tis most certain, that to the very last gasp, they never cease to be Brave and Defie them both in Word

---

1 Up to the waist.
2 Conscious, able to feel.
3 Mistreated, mangled.
4 Revealing.
5 Inventiveness.

and Gesture. In plain truth, these Men are very Savage in comparison of us, and of necessity, they must either be absolutely so, or else we are Savager: for there is a vast difference betwixt their Manners, and ours.

2. From Charles de Rochefort,[1] *The History of the Caribby-Islands*, tr. John Davies (1666)

We are now going to dip our Pen in Blood, and to draw a Picture which must raise horrour in the beholder; in this there must appear nothing but Inhumanity, Barbarism, and Rage; We shall find rational Creatures cruelly devouring those of the same *Species* with them, and filling themselves with their Flesh and Blood, after they had cast off Humane Nature, and put on that of the most bloody and furious Beasts: A thing which the Pagans themselves, in the midst of their darkness, heretofore thought so full of execration, that they imagin'd the Sun withdrew himself, because he would not shew his light at such Repasts.

When the *Cannibals,* or *Anthropophagi,* that is, *Eaters of Men* (for here it is that we are properly to call them by that Name, which is common to them with that of the *Caribbians*); when I say they bring home Prisoner of War from among the *Arouagues*,[2] he belongs of right to him who either seiz'd on him in the Fight, or took him running away; so that being come into his Island, he keeps him in his house; and that he may not get away in the night, he ties him in an *Amac*,[3] which he hangs up almost at the roof of his dwelling; and after he has kept him fasting four or five days, he produces him upon some day of solemn debauch, to serve for a publick Victim to the immortal hatred of his Country-men towards that Nation.

If there be any of their Enemies dead upon the place, they there eat them ere they leave it: They design for slavery only the young Maids and Women taken in the War: They do not eat the Children of their She-prisoners, much less the Children they have by them themselves: They have heretofore tasted of all the Nations that frequented them, and affirm, That the *French* are the most delicate, and the *Spaniards* of hardest digestion; but now they do not feed on any Christians at all.

They abstain also from several cruelties which they were wont to use before they kill'd their Enemies; for whereas at present they think it enough to dispatch them at a blow or two with the Club, and after-

---

1 Charles de Rochefort: seventeenth-century French Protestant missionary.
2 Rivals of the Caribs, the Arawaks were the first indigenous group encountered by Columbus in the Bahamas.
3 Hammock.

wards cut them into pieces, and having broyl'd them, to devour them; they heretofore put them to several torments, before they gave them the mortal blow: We shall not think it besides our purpose to set down in this place some of the inhumanities which they exercis'd upon these sad occasions, as they themselves have given an account thereof to those have had the curiosity to inform themselves from their own mouths.

The Prisoner of War who had been so unfortunate as to fall into their hands, and was not ignorant that he was design'd to receive the most cruel treatment which rage could suggest, arm'd himself with constancy, and, to express how generous a people the *Arouagues* were, march'd very chearfully to the place of execution, not being either bound or drag'd thereto, and presented himself with a smiling and steady countenance in the midst of the Assembly, which he knew desir'd nothing so much as his death.

As soon as he perceiv'd those people who express'd so great joy at the approach of him, who was to be the mess[1] of their abominable Entertainment, not expecting their discourses and their bitter abuses, he prevented them in these termes; "I know well enough upon what account you have brought me to this place; I doubt not but you are desirous to fill your selves with my blood, and that you are impatient to exercise your teeth upon my body; but you have not so much reason to triumph to see me in this condition, nor I much to be troubled thereat: My Country-men have put your Predecessors to greater miseries than you are now able to invent against me; and I have done my part with them in mangling, massacring, and devouring your people, your friends, and your fathers; besides that I have Relations who will not fail to revenge my quarrel with advantage upon you and upon your Children, for the most inhumane treatment you intend against me: What torments soever the most ingenious cruelty can dictate to you for the taking away of my life, is nothing in comparison of those which my generous Nation prepares for you in exchange: therefore delay not the utmost of your cruelty any longer, and assure your selves I both slight and laugh at it." Somwhat of this nature is that brave and bloody Bravado which may be read of a *Brasilian* Prisoner, ready to be devour'd by his Enemies;[2] "Come on boldly, *said he to them*, and feast your selves upon me; for at the same time you will feed on your Fathers and Grandfathers, who serv'd for nourishment to my Body: These Muscles, this Flesh, and these Veins are yours, blind Fools as

---

1 Meal.

2 In a marginal note, Rochefort refers to Montaigne's essay "Of Cannibals," above.

you are; you do not observe, that the substance of the Members of your Ancestors are yet to be seen in them; taste them well, and you will find the taste of your own Flesh." But let us return to our *Arouagues*.

His soul was not only in his lips, but shew'd it self also in the effects which follow'd that Bravado; for after the Company had a while endur'd his menaces and arrogant defiances without touching him, one among them came and burnt his sides with a flaming brand; another cut good deep pieces out of him, and would have made them bigger, had it not been for the bones, in several parts of the body: Then they cast into his smarting wounds that sharp kind of Spice which the *Caribbians* call *Pyman*:[1] Others diverted themselves in shooting Arrows at the poor Patient; and every one took a pleasure in tormenting him; but he suffer'd with the same countenance, and expressed not the least sentiment of pain: After they had made sport thus a long time with the poor wretch, at last growing weary of insulting, and outbrav'd by his constancy, which seem'd still the same, one of them came and at one blow dispatch'd him with his Club. This is the Treatment which the *Caribbians* made heretofore to their Prisoners of War; but now they think it enough to put them to a speedy death, as we have already represented.

As soon as this unfortunate person is thus laid dead upon the place, the young men take the body, and having wash'd it cut it in pieces, and then boyl some part, and broil some upon wooden Frames, made for that purpose, like Gridirons: When this detestable Dish is ready, and season'd according to their palates, they divide it into so many parts as there are persons present, and joyfully devour it, thinking that the World cannot afford any other repast equally delicious: The Women lick the very sticks on which the fat of the *Arouague* dropp'd; which proceeds not so much from the deliciousness they find in that kind of sustenance, and that fat, as from the excessive pleasure they conceive in being reveng'd in that manner of their chiefest Enemies.

But as they would be extreamly troubled that the enraged hatred they bear the *Arouagues* should ever end, so do they make it their main endeavour to foment and heighten it: thence it comes, that while this poor Carcass is a dressing, they carefully gather and save all the fat that comes from it; not to put into Medicines, as Chirurgeons[2] sometimes do; or to make wildfire of it, to set their Enemies houses on fire, as the *Tartars* do; but they gather together that fat to be afterwards distributed among the chiefest of them, who carefully keep it in little Gourds, to pour some few drops thereof into their Sauces at their

---

1 A hot pepper.
2 Surgeons.

solemn Entertainments, so to perpetuate, as much as lies in their power, the motive of their Revenge.

I must needs acknowledge, the Sun would have more reason to withdraw himself from these Barbarians, than to be present at such detestable Solemnities; but it would be requisite that he withdrew himself at the same time from most of the Countries of *America*, nay from some parts of *Africk* and *Asia*, where the like and worse cruelties are daily exercis'd.

3. From William Dampier,[1] "Of the Reports about Cannibals," *A New Voyage Round the World*, vol. 1 (1703)

As for the common Opinion of *Anthropophogi*, or Man-eaters, I did never meet with any such People: All Nations or Families in the World, that I have seen or heard of, having some sort of Food to live on, either Fruit, Grain, Pulse,[2] or Roots, which grown naturally, or else planted by them; if not Fish and Land-Animals besides; (yea, even the People of *New-Holland*, had Fish amidst all their Penury) and would scarce kill a Man purposely to eat him. I know not what barbarous Customs may formerly have been in the World; and to Sacrifice their Enemies to their Gods, is a thing hath been much talked of, with relation to the Savages of *America*. I am a Stranger to that also, if it be, or have been customary in any Nation there; and yet, if they Sacrifice their Enemies it is not necessary they should Eat them too. After all, I will not be peremptory in the Negative, but I speak as to the compass of my own Knowledge, and know some of these Cannibal Stories to be false, and many of them have been disproved since I first went to the *West-Indies*. At that time how Barbarous were the poor *Florida Indians* accounted, which now we find to be Civil enough? what strange Stories have we heard of the *Indians*, whose Islands were called the Isles of *Cannibals*? Yet we find that they do Trade very civilly with the *French* and *Spaniards*; and have done so with us. I do own that they have formerly endeavored to destroy our Plantations at *Barbadoes*, and have since hindred us from settling the Island *Santa Loca*, by destroying two or three Colonies successively of those that were settled there; and even the Island *Tabago* has been often annoyed and ravaged by them, when settled by the Dutch, and still lies wast (though a delicate Fruitful Island) as being too near the *Caribbees* on the Continent, who visit it every Year. But this was to preserve their own right, by endeavouring

---

1 William Dampier (1651-1715): English captain, buccanneer, and author. Dampier led the South Seas expedition in which Alexander Selkirk was marooned on Juan Fernandez Island (see Appendix C2).

2 The seeds of pod-bearing plants, such as peas, beans, and lentils.

to keep out any that would settle themselves on those Islands, where they had planted themselves; yet even these People would not hurt a single Person, as I have been told by some that have been Prisoners among them. I could instance also in the *Indians* of *Bocca Toro*, and *Boca Drago*, and many other Places where they do live, as the *Spaniards* call it, Wild and Savage; yet there they have withdrawn their Friendship again. As for these *Nicobar* People, I found them Affable enough, and therefore I did not fear them; but I did not much care whether I had gotten any more Company or no.

4. From Daniel Defoe, *Serious Reflections During the Life and Surprising Adventures of Robinson Crusoe* (1720)

From these I went among the Negroes of *Africa*; many of them I saw without any the least Notion of a Deity among them, much less any Form of Worship; but I had not any Occasion to converse with them on Shore, other than I have done since by Accident, but went away to the *Brazils*: Here I found the Natives, and that even before the *Portuguese* came among them, and since also, had Abundance of Religion, *such as it was*: But it was all so bloody, so cruel; consisting of Murders, human Sacrifices, Witchcrafts, Sorceries, and Conjurings, that I could not so much as call them honest Pagans, as I do the Negroes.

As for the Cannibals, as I have observ'd in the Discourse of them, on Account of their Landing on my Island, I can say but very little of them: As for their eating human Flesh, I take it to be a Kind of martial Rage, rather than a civil Practice, for 'tis evident, they eat no human Creatures, but such as are taken Prisoners in their Battles; and as I have observ'd in giving the Account of those things, they do not Esteem it Murder, no nor so much as unlawful. I must confess, saving its being a Practice in itself unnatural, especially to us, I say, saving that Part, I see little Difference between that and our Way, which in the War is frequent in Heat of Action, *viz.*, refusing Quarter; for as to the Difference between Eating and Killing those that offer to yield, it matters not much. And this I observed at the same Time, that in their other Conduct those Savages were as human, as mild, and gentle, as most I have met with in the World, and as easily civiliz'd.

Appendix H: Illustrations of Friday's Rescue

[The first edition of *Robinson Crusoe* included a single illustration: the famous image of Crusoe, clad in goat skins, a rifle over each shoulder, a ship tossing about in the background (p. 2). Soon, though, editions included numerous illustrations, especially of two iconic episodes, Crusoe's discovery of the footprint and his first encounter with Friday. The changing representations of both Crusoe—protective, imperial, industrious, divine, quotidian—and of Friday—enslaved, noble, rustic, romanticized, feminized—suggest how interpretations of the novel have changed over time. The most extensive exploration of the illustrations is David Blewett's *The Illustration of* Robinson Crusoe, *1719-1920* (Gerrards Cross: Colin Smythe, 1995).]

1. Anonymous (1720)

Le Sauvage apres sa delivrance se prosterne aux pieds de Robinson.

By permission of the William Andrews Clark Memorial Library.

2. Anonymous (1722)

R. Crusoe rescues his Man Friday and Kills his Pursuers. *Vol. I. Page* 238

By permission of The Huntington Library, San Marino, California.

3. Clément Pierre Marillier (1787)

Il prend un de mes pieds et le pose sur sa tête, pour me faire comprendre sans doute qu'il ne jurait fidélité.

By permission of The Huntington Library, San Marino, California.

4. Charles Ansell (1790)

ROBINSON CRUSOE
Rescuing & Protecting Friday.

By permission of The Huntington Library, San Marino, California.

5. Thomas Stothard (1790)

By permission of the William Andrews Clark Memorial Library.

6. George Cruikshank (1831)

G. Cruikshank, pinx.ᵗ　　　　　　　　　　　Augᵗ Fox. sculp.ᵗ

Frontispiece

Vol. 1. page 289.

Published by John Major, 50. Fleet Street, July 1, 1831.

By permission of The Huntington Library, San Marino, California.

7. J.J. Grandville (1840)

Il se rapprocha de plus en plus, s'agenouillant tous les dix pas en signe de respect.

By permission of the William Andrews Clark Memorial Library.

8. Phiz (Hablot Knight Browne) (1846)

Robinson Crusoe rescues Friday.

By permission of the William Andrews Clark Memorial Library.

9. Jules Fesquet (1877)

By permission of the British Library Board.

10. Otis Turner (1913)

Otis Turner (director, *Robinson Crusoe*, 1913). Robert Z. Leonard as Crusoe; Edward Alexander as Friday. Courtesy of the Academy of Motion Picture Arts and Sciences.

Select Bibliography

Biographies

Backscheider, Paula R. *Daniel Defoe: His Life*. Baltimore: Johns
  Hopkins UP, 1989.
Furbank, P.N., and W.R. Owens. *A Political Biography of Daniel Defoe*.
  London: Pickering and Chatto, 1998.
Lee, William. *Daniel Defoe: His Life, and Recently Discovered Writings*.
  London, 1869.
Moore, John Robert. *Daniel Defoe: Citizen of the Modern World*.
  Chicago: U of Chicago P, 1958.
Novak, Maximillian E. *Daniel Defoe: Master of Fictions*. Oxford:
  Oxford UP, 2001.
Richetti, John J. *The Life of Daniel Defoe: A Critical Biography*.
  Oxford: Wiley-Blackwell, 2005.
Sutherland, James. *Daniel Defoe*. Philadelphia: J. B. Lippincott, 1938.

General Studies

Alkon, Paul K. *Defoe and Fictional Time*. Athens: U of Georgia P,
  1979.
Aravamudan, Srinivas. *Tropicopolitans: Colonialism and Agency, 1688-
  1804*. Durham: Duke UP, 1999.
Backscheider, Paula R. *A Being More Intense: A Study of the Prose
  Works of Bunyan, Swift, and Defoe*. New York: AMS P, 1984.
——. *Daniel Defoe: Ambition and Innovation*. Lexington: UP of Ken-
  tucky, 1986.
Bell, Ian A. *Defoe's Fiction*. Totowa, NJ: Barnes and Noble Books,
  1985.
Bender, John B. *Imagining the Penitentiary: Fiction and the Architecture
  of Mind in Eighteenth-Century England*. Chicago: U of Chicago P,
  1987.
Birdsall, Virginia Ogden. *Defoe's Perpetual Seekers: A Study of the
  Major Fiction*. Lewisburg, PA: Bucknell UP, 1985.
Blewett, David. *Defoe's Art of Fiction—Robinson Crusoe, Moll Flanders,
  Colonel Jack and Roxana*. Toronto: U of Toronto P, 1979.
Boardman, Michael M. *Defoe and the Uses of Narrative*. New
  Brunswick, NJ: Rutgers UP, 1983.
Brown, Homer O. "The Displaced Self in the Novels of Daniel
  Defoe." *ELH* 38.4 (1971): 562-90.

Carnochan, W.B. *Confinement and Flight: An Essay on English Literature of the Eighteenth Century*. Berkeley: U of California P, 1977.

Curtis, Laura Ann. *The Elusive Daniel Defoe*. London: Vision, 1984.

Damrosch, Leopold. *God's Plot and Man's Stories: Studies in the Fictional Imagination from Milton to Fielding*. Chicago: U of Chicago P,
1985.

David, Dierdre, John Richetti, and Michael Seidel, eds. *The Columbia
History of the British Novel*. New York: Columbia UP, 1994.

Davis, Lennard J. *Factual Fictions: The Origins of the English Novel*.
New York: Columbia UP, 1983.

Downie, J.A. "Defoe, Imperialism, and the Travel Books Reconsid-
ered." *Yearbook of English Studies* 13 (1983): 66-83.

Eagleton, Terry. *The English Novel: An Introduction*. Malden, MA:
Blackwell Pub, 2005.

Faller, Lincoln B. *Crime and Defoe: A New Kind of Writing*. Cambridge: Cambridge UP, 1993.

Flynn, Carol Houlihan. *The Body in Swift and Defoe*. Cambridge:
Cambridge UP, 1990.

Furbank, P.N., and W.R. Owens. *The Canonisation of Daniel Defoe*.
New Haven: Yale UP, 1988.

——. *A Critical Bibliography of Daniel Defoe*. London: Pickering and
Chatto, 1998.

Hammond, Brean, and Shaun Regan. *Making the Novel: Fiction and
Society in Britain, 1660-1789*. Basingstoke: Palgrave Macmillan,
2006.

Hulme, Peter. *Colonial Encounters: Europe and the Native Caribbean,
1492-1797*. London: Routledge, 1992.

Hunter, J. Paul. *Before Novels: The Cultural Contexts of Eighteenth-
Century English Fiction*. New York: Norton, 1990.

Lestringant, Frank. *Cannibals: The Discovery and Representation of the
Cannibal from Columbus to Jules Verne*. Berkeley: U of California P,
1997.

Lund, Roger, ed. *Critical Essays on Daniel Defoe*. New York: G.K.
Hall, 1997.

Mayer, Robert. *History and the Early English Novel: Matters of Fact
from Bacon to Defoe*. Cambridge: Cambridge UP, 1997.

——. *Eighteenth-Century Fiction on Screen*. Cambridge: Cambridge
UP, 2002.

McKeon, Michael. *The Origins of the English Novel, 1600-1740*. Baltimore: Johns Hopkins UP, 1987.

Merrett, Robert James. *Daniel Defoe's Moral and Rhetorical Ideas*. Victoria, BC: U of Victoria, 1980.

Novak, Maximillian E. *Defoe and the Nature of Man*. London: Oxford
UP, 1963.

———. "Defoe's Theory of Fiction." *Studies in Philology* 61 (1964): 650-68.

———. *Economics and the Fiction of Daniel Defoe*. Berkeley: U of California P, 1962.

———. *Realism, Myth, and History in Defoe's Fiction*. Lincoln: U of Nebraska P, 1983.

Parrinder, Patrick. *Nation and Novel: The English Novel from its Origins to the Present Day*. Oxford: Oxford UP, 2006.

Richetti, John. *Daniel Defoe*. Boston: Twayne Publishers, 1987.

———. *Defoe's Narratives: Situations and Structures*. Oxford: Clarendon P, 1975.

———. *The English Novel in History, 1700-1780*. London: Routledge, 1999.

———. *Popular Fiction Before Richardson: Narrative Patterns, 1700-1739*. Oxford: Clarendon P, 1992.

Rogers, Pat. *Defoe: the Critical Heritage*. Boston: Routledge and Kegan Paul, 1972.

Schonhorn, Manuel. *Defoe's Politics: Parliament, Power, Kingship, and Robinson Crusoe*. Cambridge: Cambridge UP, 1991.

Seidel, Michael. *Exile and the Narrative Imagination*. New Haven: Yale UP, 1986.

Sherman, Sandra. *Finance and Fictionality in the Early Eighteenth Century: Accounting for Defoe*. Cambridge: Cambridge UP, 2005.

Shinagel, Michael. *Daniel Defoe and Middle-Class Gentility*. Cambridge: Harvard UP, 1968.

Sill, Geoffrey M. *Defoe and the Idea of Fiction, 1713-1719*. Newark: U of Delaware P, 1983.

———. *The Cure of the Passions and the Origins of the English Novel*. New York: Cambridge UP, 2001.

Sim, Stuart. *Negotiations with Paradox: Narrative Practice and Narrative Form in Bunyan and Defoe*. Savage, MD: Barnes and Noble Books, 1990.

Spearman, Diana. *The Novel and Society*. New York: Barnes and Noble, 1966.

Starr, George A. *Defoe and Casuistry*. Princeton: Princeton UP, 1971.

———. *Defoe and Spiritual Autobiography*. Princeton: Princeton UP, 1965.

Sutherland, James Runcieman. *Daniel Defoe; a Critical Study*. Cambridge: Harvard UP, 1971.

Tillyard, E.M.W. *The Epic Strain in the English Novel*. Fair Lawn, NJ: Essential Books, 1958.

Trotter, David. *Circulation: Defoe, Dickens, and the Economies of the Novel*. New York: St. Martin's P, 1988.

Van Ghent, Dorothy Bendon. *The English Novel, Form and Function.* New York: Rinehart, 1953.

Vickers, Ilse. *Defoe and the New Sciences.* Cambridge: Cambridge UP, 2006.

Watt, Ian P. *Myths of Modern Individualism: Faust, Don Quixote, Don Juan, Robinson Crusoe.* Cambridge: Cambridge UP, 1996.

——. *The Rise of the Novel: Studies in Defoe, Richardson, and Fielding.* Berkeley: U of California P, 1957.

Weaver-Hightower, Rebecca. *Empire Islands: Castaways, Cannibals, and Fantasies of Conquest.* Minneapolis: U of Minnesota P, 2007.

Wheeler, Roxann. *The Complexion of Race: Categories of Difference in Eighteenth-Century British Culture.* Philadelphia: U of Pennsylvania P, 2000.

Zimmerman, Everett. *Defoe and the Novel.* Berkeley: U of California P, 1975.

Studies on *Robinson Crusoe*

Armstrong, Dianne. "The Myth of Cronus: Cannibal and Sign in *Robinson Crusoe*." *Eighteenth-Century Fiction* 4.3 (1992): 207-20.

Ayers, Robert. "*Robinson Crusoe*: Allusive Allegorick History." *PMLA* 82 (1967): 399-407.

Barchas, Janine. "Crusoe's Struggles with Sexuality." *Eighteenth-Century Novel* 5 (2006): 93-116.

Beesemyer, Irene B. "Crusoe the *Isolato*: Daniel Defoe Wrestles with Solitude." *1650-1850: Ideas, Aesthetics, and Inquiries in the Early Modern Era* 10 (2004): 79-102.

Bell, Ian A. "King Crusoe: Locke's Political Theory in *Robinson Crusoe*." *English Studies* 69.1 (1988): 27-36.

Blackburn, Timothy C. "Friday's Religion: Its Nature and Importance in *Robinson Crusoe*." *Eighteenth-Century Studies* 18.3 (1985): 360-82.

Blewett, David. *The Illustration of Robinson Crusoe, 1719-1920.* Gerrards Cross: Colin Smythe, 1995.

——. "The Retirement Myth in *Robinson Crusoe*: A Reconsideration." *Studies in the Literary Imagination* 15 (1982): 37-50.

Bloom, Harold, ed. *Daniel Defoe's Robinson Crusoe.* New York: Chelsea House, 1988.

Butler, Mary E. "The Effect of the Narrator's Rhetorical Uncertainty on the Fiction of *Robinson Crusoe*." *Studies in the Novel* 15.2 (1983): 77-90.

Ellis, Frank H., ed. *Twentieth Century Interpretations of Robinson Crusoe; a Collection of Critical Essays.* Englewood Cliffs, NJ: Prentice-Hall, 1969.

Faller, Lincoln. "Captain Misson's Failed Utopia, Crusoe's Failed Colony: Race and Identity in New, Not Quite Imaginable Worlds." *Eighteenth Century: Theory and Interpretation* 43.1 (2002): 1-17.

Fisher, Carl, and Maximillian E. Novak. *Approaches to Teaching Defoe's Robinson Crusoe*. New York: Modern Language Association of America, 2005.

Flint, Christopher. "Orphaning the Family: The Role of Kinship in *Robinson Crusoe*." *ELH* 55.2 (1988): 381-419.

Gautier, Gary. "Slavery and the Fashioning of Race in *Oroonoko*, *Robinson Crusoe*, and Equiano's *Life*." *Eighteenth Century: Theory and Interpretation* 42.2 (2001): 161-79.

Hopes, Jeffrey. "Real and Imaginary Stories: *Robinson Crusoe* and the *Serious Reflections*." *Eighteenth-Century Fiction* 8.3 (1996): 313-28.

Hudson, Nicholas. "'Why God No Kill the Devil?' The Diabolical Disruption of Order in *Robinson Crusoe*." *Review of English Studies* 39 (1988): 494-501.

Hunter, J. Paul. *The Reluctant Pilgrim: Defoe's Emblematic Method and Quest for Form in Robinson Crusoe*. Baltimore: Johns Hopkins UP, 1966.

Keane, Patrick J. "Slavery and the Slave Trade: Crusoe as Defoe's Representative." *Critical Essays on Daniel Defoe*. Ed. Roger Lund. New York: G.K. Hall, 1997. 97-120.

——. *Coleridge's Submerged Politics: The Ancient Mariner and Robinson Crusoe*. Columbia: U of Missouri P, 1994.

Knox-Shaw, Peter. "Defoe and the Politics of Representing the African Interior." *Modern Language Review* 96.4 (2001).

Loar, Christopher F. "How to Say Things with Guns: Military Technology and the Politics of *Robinson Crusoe*." *Eighteenth-Century Fiction* 19.1-2 (2006): 1-20.

Maddox, James H. "Interpreter Crusoe." *ELH* 51.1 (1984): 33-52.

Marzec, Robert P. "Enclosures, Colonization, and the Robinson Crusoe Syndrome: A Genealogy of Land in a Global Context." *boundary 2*: 29.2 (2002): 129-56.

McFarlane, Cameron. "Reading Crusoe Reading Providence." *English Studies in Canada* 21.3 (1995): 257-67.

Neill, Anna. "Crusoe's Farther Adventures: Discovery, Trade, and the Law of Nations." *Eighteenth Century: Theory and Interpretation* 38.3 (1997): 213-30.

Novak, Maximillian E. "Crusoe the King and the Political Evolution of His Island." *SEL* 2.3 (1962): 337-50.

——. "Edenic Desires: Robinson Crusoe, the Robinsonade, and Utopias." *Historical Boundaries, Narrative forms: Essays on British Literature in the Long Eighteenth Century in Honor of Everett Zim-*

merman. Ed. Lorna Clymer and Robert Mayer. Newark: U of Delaware P, 2007. 19-36.

——. "Imaginary Islands and Real Beasts: The Imaginative Genesis of *Robinson Crusoe.*" *Tennessee Studies in Literature* 19 (1974): 57-78.

——. "'Looking with Wonder upon the Sea': Defoe's Maritime Fictions, *Robinson Crusoe,* and 'the Curious Age We Live In.'" *Sustaining Literature: Essays on Literature, History, and Culture, 1500-1800.* Ed. Greg Clingham. Lewisburg: Bucknell UP, 2007. 171-94.

——. "Robinson Crusoe's Fear and the Search for Natural Man." *Modern Philology* 58.4 (1961): 238-45.

Pastor, Antonio. *The Idea of Robinson Crusoe.* Watford: The Gongora P, 1930.

Paulin, Tom. *Crusoe's Secret: The Aesthetics of Dissent.* London: Faber and Faber, 2005.

Rogers, Pat. "Crusoe's Home." *Essays in Criticism: A Quarterly Journal of Literary Criticism* 24 (1974): 375-90.

——. *Robinson Crusoe.* London: G. Allen and Unwin, 1979.

Rogers, Shef. "Crusoe among the Maori: Translation and Colonial Acculturation in Victorian New Zealand." *Book History* 1 (1998): 182-95.

Rothman, Irving N. "Coleridge on the Semi-colon in *Robinson Crusoe*: Problems in Editing Defoe." *Studies in the Novel* 27.3 (1995), 320-40.

Secord, Arthur Wellesley. *Studies in the Narrative Method of Defoe.* New York: Russell and Russell, 1963.

Seidel, Michael. "Crusoe in Exile." *PMLA* 96 (1981): 363-74.

——. *Robinson Crusoe: Island Myths and the Novel.* Boston: Twayne, 1991.

Sill, Geoffrey M. "Crusoe in the Cave: Defoe and the Semiotics of Desire." *Eighteenth-Century Fiction* 6.3 (1994): 215-32.

——. "The Source of Robinson Crusoe's 'Sudden Joys.'" *Notes and Queries* 45.1 (1998): 67-68.

Sim, Stuart. "Interrogating an Ideology: Defoe's *Robinson Crusoe.*" *British Journal for Eighteenth-Century Studies* 10.2 (1987): 163-73.

Spaas, Lieve, and Brian Stimpson, eds. *Robinson Crusoe: Myths and Metamorphoses.* London: Macmillan P, 1996.

Svilpis, Janis. "Bourgeois Solitude in *Robinson Crusoe.*" *English Studies in Canada* 22.1 (1996): 35-43.

Watt, Ian P. "*Robinson Crusoe* as Myth." *Essays in Criticism* 1 (1951): 95-119.

Wheeler, Roxann. "'My Savage,' 'My Man': Racial Multiplicity in *Robinson Crusoe.*" *ELH* 62.4 (1995): 821-61.

From the Publisher

A name never says it all, but the word "Broadview" expresses a good deal of the philosophy behind our company. We are open to a broad range of academic approaches and political viewpoints. We pay attention to the broad impact book publishing and book printing has in the wider world; for some years now we have used 100% recycled paper for most titles. Our publishing program is internationally oriented and broad-ranging. Our individual titles often appeal to a broad readership too; many are of interest as much to general readers as to academics and students.

Founded in 1985, Broadview remains a fully independent company owned by its shareholders—not an imprint or subsidiary of a larger multinational.

For the most accurate information on our books (including information on pricing, editions, and formats) please visit our website at www.broadviewpress.com. Our print books and ebooks are also available for sale on our site.

broadview press
www.broadviewpress.com

This book is made of paper from well-managed FSC® - certified
forests, recycled materials, and other controlled sources.